DAWN POWELL AT HER BEST

DAWN POWELL

AT HER BEST

EDITED WITH AN INTRODUCTION BY TIM PAGE

STEERFORTH PRESS
SOUTH ROYALTON, VERMONT

Library of Congress Cataloging-in-Publication Data
Powell, Dawn.
Dawn Powell at her best: including the novels Turn, magic wheel and
Dance night & selected stories / with an introduction by Tim Page. —1st ed.
p.   cm.
ISBN 1–883642–16–7
1. City and town life—New York (N.Y.)—Fiction. 2. City and town life—
Ohio—Fiction. 3. Working class—Ohio—Fiction. I. Title.
PS3531.0936A6   1994
813'.54—dc20   94-30416

Manufactured in the United States of America

First Edition

CONTENTS

INTRODUCTION

A FEW YEARS AGO, impelled by an old Edmund Wilson essay and the rapt enthusiasm of some friends, I began to hunt down the novels of Dawn Powell. I called my favorite used-book stores from Portland to Portland, Oregon to Maine, and came up with nothing. Finally I found a few Powells, in carefully preserved dust jackets, on prominent display in a New York shop, but the prices were dismaying. Determined to justify the expense as an investment, I put on my most sternly bibliophilic voice and harrumphed: "I *assume* these are first editions."

The proprietor looked up from her adding machine, a friendly, bemused smile on her face. "Did Dawn Powell *have* any second editions?"

She does now. Since 1989, five of Powell's novels have been reissued in paperback. Gore Vidal, James Wolcott, and Michael Feingold, among others, have written lengthy appreciations; Vidal called her America's best comic novelist. And with this volume her work is between hard covers for the first time in 30 years.

It is the purest, most triumphant kind of literary rehabilitation, neither orchestrated by publishers and press agents, nor hatched by English professors with an agenda to serve. Instead, the Powell revival has its origins in nothing more complicated than the shared delight of her devotees, passing on volume after dusty volume to one another with evangelical fervor.

Throughout her career, Powell was compared to Dorothy Parker (as if there could be only one witty woman in New York at a given time!).

Powell resented the comparison and, indeed, it does her a disservice. We remember Parker for a handful of one-liners, short stories and rather rudimentary verse, most of it dating from the early part of her career. Powell, on the other hand, during forty years of intensive, disciplined work, produced not only aphorisms and sketches but page after page, book after book, of impeccably constructed fiction, melding merriment with insight.

"True wit should break a wise man's heart," Powell once said. "It should strike at the exact point of weakness and it should scar. It should rest on a pillar of truth and not on a gelatin base, and the truth is not so shameful that it cannot be recorded." And, similarly: "My novels are based on the fantastic designs made by real human beings earnestly laboring to maladjust themselves to fate. My characters are not slaves to an author's propaganda. I give them their heads. They furnish their own nooses." For all of Powell's philosophical pessimism—about which more later—few authors provide such steady, unalloyed *pleasure* for their readers.

Still, this sort of revival is decidedly out of the ordinary; in American literature one must go back to the great posthumous discovery of Nathanael West in the 1950s to find a parallel. After all, Powell has been dead for more than a quarter century and most of her books (none of which had an initial printing of more than 5,000 copies) disappeared before she did. Her compatriots are long since retired and the New York City (or, specifically, the Greenwich Village) she loved has changed forever. Moreover, Powell was not a natural candidate for adoption by the idealistic feminists; as Edmund Wilson noted, "the women who appear in her stories are likely to be as sordid and absurd as the men."

And yet it is possible to make too much of the "sordid" and the "absurd" in Powell's work. There is absurdity aplenty (along with most other human qualities) in her books, but she rejects the easy, sweeping nihilism of many 20th-century writers. On the contrary, she may be described as a worldly, determinedly clear-sighted, deeply skeptical romantic—but a romantic all the same. Love and joy, however transitory they may prove, both *exist* (Powell has seen them plain) and are well worth fighting for, at virtually any cost this side of self-delusion. Underneath the relentless good humor of her New York novels, Powell took life very seriously indeed—a prerequisite, or so it seems to me, for the creation of lasting art.

We are as yet at the beginning of Powell scholarship; her papers have been inaccessible since shortly after her death. Through the efforts of family and friends, the situation has been remedied, but too recently for much new information to be absorbed into this introduction. This is what we know now; it is to be hoped that we will know much more in the not-so-distant future.

Dawn Powell was born in Mt. Gilead—then, as now, the seat of Morrow County, Ohio—on November 28, 1897, the second of three daughters. (The tiny, clapboard houses in which she grew up still stand, a few hundred feet from the town square.) Her father, Roy Powell, was a rakish, improvident salesman, on the road much of the time. Her mother, Hattie Sherman Powell, died a few days after Dawn turned six. Even more than most authors, Powell mined her own experience for material; asked to provide an autobiographical statement for a reference book in 1942, she replied in the third person:

> "Since the father traveled, the three small daughters were dispatched from one relative to another, from a year of farm life with this or that aunt, to village life, life in small-town boarding houses, life with very prim strict relatives, to rougher life in the middle of little factory-towns . . . About 1909, Mr. Powell made a second marriage and moved to his wife's farm near Cleveland, where the three children were very unhappy and it was from here that Dawn Powell ran away with thirty cents she had earned by berry-picking. There were two reasons for her runaway—one, she had won a scholarship to high school but there was no school there for her to attend; and, two, the new stepmother had burned up all the stories she had been writing, a form of discipline that the ego could not endure, even at twelve."

Eventually, Powell arrived at the home of a maternal aunt, Orpha May Sherman Steinbrueck, in Shelby, Ohio. Powell spent her early teen years living directly opposite the Shelby Junction train station—then an important transfer point for the New York Central, Baltimore & Ohio, and Pennsylvania railroads, now demolished—and the cries of locomotives, promising escape to a better life, are a recurring motif throughout her work. (*Angels on Toast* and *A Time To Be Born* both begin on trains; *My*

Home Is Far Away ends on one; *Dance Night* concludes with Morry's decision to board for an unspecified city and "What Are You Doing In My Dreams?," perhaps the last important piece Powell wrote—and the final selection in this volume—includes a memoir of an overnight train ride from New York to Ohio.)

In Shelby, Powell edited her high school newspaper and the yearbook while publishing her first professional writing in the local *Daily Globe*. Determined to educate herself, she was accepted into Lake Erie College in Painesville, Ohio, as part of the class of 1918. According to her roommate Eleanor Farnham, Powell heard about the college and wrote to the president, Vivian Small, with a plea that went something along the lines of "I'd like to come to your school and will do anything to work my way through, from scrubbing back stairs to understudying your job."

At Lake Erie College, Powell earned her keep as an elevator operator while editing both the college magazine and an anonymous, dissenting newspaper called "The Sheet." Appropriately enough, the diminutive, high-spirited Powell also played Puck in a drama club presentation of *A Midsummer's Night Dream*. "I was sorry for any Lake Erie students who were not there at the time of Dawn Powell," Farnham recalled in an oral history deposition (later summarized in Margaret Geissman Gross's *Dancing On The Table: A History of Lake Erie College*). "Dawn turned everything upside down . . . [She] stimulated me to question, which is part of going to school."

After graduation, Powell moved to New York where she put in three weeks of war work with the U. S. Naval Reserve before the Armistice and where she would live the rest of her life. In 1920, she married Joseph R. Gousha (goo-SHAY), an advertising executive from Pittsburgh who had himself worked on a newspaper as a music critic. And, on August 22, 1921, Joseph R. Gousha, Jr.—the great joy and the great tragedy of Dawn Powell's life—was born in New York's St. Luke's Hospital.

Most earlier accounts of the younger Gousha—always known as Jojo—have described him as "retarded." This is an oversimplification; a more accurate description would probably be some mixture of cerebral palsy and schizophrenia, compounded by a disastrous birth. "I didn't know till two days afterward that they didn't think the baby was going to live," Powell wrote to her sisters from the hospital on September 3, 1921. "I had a terrible time and it was just as hard on the baby. He is awfully husky but being born was a tough business for him and just before he came out his heart went bad. . . I didn't dilate at all. Poor little lamb had a clot on his brain that caused a sort of convulsive paralysis besides several bad bruises from the forceps. Joe didn't tell me but the doctors let it leak out to me by saying that it looked as if the baby had a chance after all . . ."

Jojo needed close medical supervision from the start. He spent much of his life in hospitals and was confined more or less permanently well before his mother died. And yet I can attest to his extraordinary memory for dates and places; even now, in his 70s, he can recount every address at which he lived with his family and the exact years he was there. Michelle Borsack, his social worker, has described Jojo's animated, by-heart piano renditions of favorite carols every Christmas. "He is really very intelligent and just *different* from other people," Dawn Powell once told Matthew Josephson; this seems a fair assessment.

"She was small and somewhat plump," Josephson wrote of Powell in a memoir published by the *Southern Review* in 1973, "with black hair and brown eyes set off by skin of unusual pallor, and had finely shaped hands. In a word, she was no classical beauty, and not chic in dress, and yet she had great attraction for women friends as well as men. Her expression was at once puckish and alert, her eyes never stopped moving, dancing. She drank copiously for the joy of living, but seldom appeared overborne by drink even in the small morning hours."

By the mid-20s Powell had begun to contribute feature stories to New York magazines and newspapers. "I hated the people I had to interview," she later said. "I always felt like beginning, 'Well, what have *you* got to say for yourself?' I felt we were like a couple of strange dogs circling around each other wondering where to bite first."

Her first novel, *Whither*, was published in 1925 by the Boston firm of Small, Maynard and almost immediately disavowed by its author. It is not so bad as Powell made out: the main flaw, to this taste, is the assumption, fairly common among young writers, that enthusiasm can be put across to a reader through the overuse of exclamation points and intensifying adjectives. Whatever its failings, *Whither* remains of interest for Powell's picture of New York life in the 20s; it would be more than a decade before she again took on the city in one of her novels.

In the meantime, Powell began the remarkable series that has come to be known as her Ohio cycle with *She Walks in Beauty* (1928), an altogether more assured and concentrated creation than *Whither. Dance Night* (1930) is the first of the Ohio books to be reissued; as late as 1957, with 14 novels behind her, Powell told the *New York Herald Tribune* it was her favorite work. All of the Ohio novels—the others are *The Bride's House* (1929), *The Tenth Moon* (1932), *The Story of a Country Boy* (1934) and, after a ten year hiatus, *My Home Is Far Away* (1944)—are strong and somber; they present a very different, infinitely more vulnerable and haunted Dawn Powell than do the New York books.

Still, although Ohio was the setting for most of her early books, Powell was a convinced, passionate New Yorker from the start. In a vibrant letter she wrote in 1931 to her favorite cousin, Jack F. Sherman (who was himself growing up in the Shelby home of the perpetually generous and nurturing "Auntie May" Steinbrueck and to whom *My Home Is Far Away* would be dedicated) she enumerated some of the reasons:

"New York City [is] the only place where people with nothing behind them but their wits can be and do everything . . . Every place else but New York, you have to hide all your low beginnings and pretend everybody in the family is white and can read and write and play the harp. What I mean, friend, is that you can be yourself here and it's the only place where being genuine will absolutely get you anywhere you want. If it suits you—as it does me—to live in the toughest quarter of downtown, semi-slums, because the houses are old and quaint and have little courts in back and pushcarts and hurdy-gurdies go by your window with fruit and vegetables and straw hats and geraniums—well, that doesn't prevent you from being asked to Park Avenue penthouses or anyplace. The very *best* people think to be able to do as you damn please, not caring what anyone thinks, is the mark of aristocracy. . . ."

It would be reductive to suggest that a novelist so versatile as Powell had only one principal "subject"; still, she is especially fond of small-town boys and girls who have come to the Big City to prove their worth—and, not-so-incidentally, to have a grand old time in the barrooms and bedrooms along the way. Powell would never affect the blasé ennui of the seen-it-all New Yorker; throughout her life she called herself a "permanent visitor" and jubilantly celebrated the multiplicity and sheer sensory overload of her adopted Manhattan.

By 1936, she had begun her New York cycle—an altogether brighter, faster, funnier group of books than the Ohio novels—with the marvelous *Turn, Magic Wheel.* The Ohio books are mostly about people yearning to escape from gritty small towns; in the New York novels, the escape is accomplished but the memories remain and influence whatever cosmopolitan present a Powell character has set up for herself.

The best single line about Powell—and particularly the Powell of the New York novels—belongs to Vidal: "She saw life with a bright Petronian neutrality, and every host at life's feast was a potential Trimalchio to be sent up." From *Turn, Magic Wheel* through *The Golden Spur* (1962), her last book, Powell played the satirist, eternally wise, eternally mocking and yet, somehow, eternally empathetic ("What fools these mortals be!"). There are only two exceptions: the last of the Ohio novels, *My Home Is Far Away,* which is lyrical, longing, and as close as Powell ever came to pure autobiography; and a curious venture into romantic fiction, *A Cage for Lovers* (1957), complete with Parisian setting, that Powell later claimed was ruined in the editing process.

Powell's own romantic life was unconventional. By the mid-30s, she had established a long-running affair with a dapper, Colorado-born magazine editor named Coburn ("Coby") Gilman. Josephson again: "During more than 30 years Dawn and Gilman ate and drank together or laughed and quarreled together and even—like some long married couples—regularly trumped each other. When the Depression came Gilman lost his good jobs and lived from hand to mouth, dignified as always in his hand-me-down clothes. There was no possibility thereafter of Dawn Powell divorcing Gousha and marrying Gilman, as some had expected, because of the heavy expenses for their son which she and Gousha loyally shared. She and her nearly invisible husband lived toward 1940 in a duplex apartment at East Ninth Street and University Place, with Gousha using the upper floor and its separate entrance, while Dawn received her own friends and Gilman on the lower floor. This arrangement of the *ménage à trois* was continued during long years; when the two men sometimes met they addressed each other with formal politeness, 'just like two old clubmates,' one of Dawn's women friends remarked."

And yet, by most accounts, Powell really *loved* both men; she saw Gousha through the loss of his prestigious job, debilitating alcoholism, eviction from the duplex on Ninth Street, and a long battle with cancer that ended in 1962; Gilman remained devoted to Powell until her own death from cancer, three years later. Her early book, *The Bride's House* is a daring plea for sexual tolerance that either prefigured or may have been built upon Powell's own situation: "A woman needed two lovers," a character states, "one to comfort her for the torment the other caused her."

Powell's circle included Josephson, Vidal, Wilson, and his daughter Rosalind Baker Wilson, John Dos Passos, John Howard Lawson, John LaTouche, Malcolm Cowley, Ernest Hemingway, Lloyd Frankenberg and Loren MacIver, Gerald and Sara Murphy, J. B. Priestley, Djuna Barnes, Charles Norman, and Margaret DeSilver, among many others. She seemed to have had a genius for putting people at ease; even the famously shy Malcolm Lowry, on an otherwise nightmarish New York visit to promote *Under the Volcano*, took to Powell immediately and the two corresponded for some time afterward. Late in life, she grew close to two young women, the novelist Hannah Green and Jacqueline Miller Rice, who became her executor.

Dawn Powell died on November 14, 1965—during the week of the first great New York blackout, a coincidence she might have appreciated. Edmund Wilson paid sad tribute in his diary, ultimately published as *The Sixties*: "She was so courageous and never complained. When she came to T'ville [Talcottville, New York, the site of Wilson's family home] two summers ago, when Rosalind and I were there, she would turn quite yellow and have to lie down, but then always come to at dinnertime to have some drinks and do her best to be amusing . . . She was really an old-fashioned American woman not far from the pioneering civilization: strong-willed, stoical, plainspoken, not to be imposed upon . . . She was really closer to me than any other of my friends of my own generation— she was 67 when she died—because she was the only one that I saw and corresponded with steadily, and I have felt that some part of my own life was gone."

The neglect of Powell during her own lifetime has been overstated: most of her books were favorably reviewed and some of them received a good deal of attention (*The Wicked Pavilion,* for example, was given pride of place on the front page of the *New York Herald Tribune* Sunday book review for Sept. 12, 1954). But she made it into few of the literary histories—one looks in vain for her name in the pages of Alfred Kazin, Carl Van Doren, Bernard Smith, Granville Hicks, Ludwig Lewisohn and other contemporary chroniclers of the period. (It is a little surprising that

H. L. Mencken, with his iconoclasm, earthy sense of humor, and acknowledged fondness for Midwestern writers, never became a booster, but he stopped reviewing new fiction at about the same time Powell began to publish.) In common with many unpretentious creators who set out with no apologies to entertain, Powell seems to have been more often "enjoyed" than "appreciated."

Beyond the old Art vs. Entertainment dichotomy (the validity of which I question; any work of art that doesn't entertain us on *some* level won't hold our interest for very long) I think Powell's reputation also suffered from her determined resistance to any form of Utopianism. She was bound to displease social conservatives with characters who drank a lot, slept around, behaved foolishly and without discernible moral purpose, yet still did rather well for themselves, with no promise of impending damnation. For critics on the left, one suspects that Powell's satire wasn't angry enough. She never suggested that some pie-in-the-sky revolution might redeem us all; she drew her millionaires with as much affection and acerbity as she drew her workers, and found them equally foolish and transparent. Her characters are rarely admirable but they are usually eminently likable, in their own deluded and floundering ways. Within the last few decades we have grown justly suspicious of theoretical absolutes; Powell's enlightened skepticism will impress many latter-day readers as endearingly devoid of piety and cant.

The title and contents of this volume have been carefully chosen. It does not purport to offer *all* of Dawn Powell at her best: any such book would have to include several of the Ohio novels and two of the New York novels that have already been reissued, *A Time To Be Born* (1942)—which Powell, against overwhelming evidence, always insisted was *not* about Clare Boothe Luce—and *The Locusts Have No King* (1948). (I find her last New York books, *The Wicked Pavillion* and *The Golden Spur,* for all of their charm, somewhat diffuse—collections of wonderful comic/nostalgic "bits" rather than fully realized novels.)

An artist is not always a reliable judge of his or her own work but the high value Powell placed on *Dance Night* and *Turn, Magic Wheel* (which she once called "very likely my best, simplest, most original book") is well-merited. *Dance Night* will come as a shock to readers who know only the New York novels and may be numbered among the masterpieces of American realism, from the bleak opening panorama of a gloomy factory town on the edge of a summer evening through the blunt, brutal execution of what is virtually the only scene of mortal violence in all of Powell's writing. Special attention should be paid to the care Powell expends upon her minor characters: simple, kindly Mrs. Pepper, in particular, will not easily be forgotten.

Dance Night, conceived and largely written in the last years of the 20s boom, was published in the fall of 1930, just as the enormity of the Great Depression was beginning to sink in; created on the cusp of two vastly different periods of American history, it belongs to both of them. While it has been compared to the proletarian novels of the 1930s, it has none of their didacticism. Powell is telling a tale, not giving a lecture, and she knows the working-class town too well to romanticize it. *Dance Night* is a study in frustration and misunderstanding, crossed signals and fumbled gestures, and the narrative plays itself out with a sense of tragic inevitability.

Powell's "Lamptown" is clearly Shelby, home of the Shelby Electric Company—where some of the first electric incandescent lightbulbs were manufactured—and of the Ohio Steel Tube Company. "Clover Heights," the fine residential section of Lamptown that Morry dreams of developing, was modeled on Shelby's Grand Boulevard, long the area's most prestigious address. 121 North Broadway, where Powell grew up, was in a very different neighborhood, down the street from "Irish Town" ("Shantyville" in *Dance Night*) where railroad men and factory girls comingled in a hard-living, roisterous squalor.

The great villains in Powell's fiction—indeed, the only characters she seems constitutionally incapable of forgiving—are the ones based on real people, particularly her father and stepmother. Her stepmother, Sabra Powell, while still alive, was eviscerated in *My Home Is Far Away;* Roy Powell, who had died in 1926, is the model for not only Harry Willard in *My Home Is Far Away* but also to some degree (in what is admittedly a violently distorted caricature) for Charles Abbott in *Dance Night,* the traveling man who, on his rare visits home, concocts lurid fantasies of his wife Elsinore's supposed infidelities. (As Elsinore herself puts it, "No one but a person who has been guilty himself could read guilt in others so well.") Significantly, *Dance Night* is dedicated to Powell's younger sister, Phyllis, from whom she was separated much of her childhood, and whom she must have dreamed of "rescuing" from Sabra Powell in the same manner the character Jen dreams of rescuing her own sister Lil from the orphanage.

Lamptown is a narrow world; its radius extends to Marion, Akron, Lorain, Norwalk, Mansfield, Dayton, and fabled Cleveland, then the sixth largest city in the United States. Pittsburgh and Detroit are distant lands; New York seems the end of the universe. Yet outside life filters in; postcards of Lillian Russell, picture shows with Clara Kimball Young; unconfirmed rumors of the latest big-city fashions. Powell quotes from popular songs without condescension and with a sure appreciation of their potency ("Some of These Days" would also recur throughout Jean-Paul Sartre's first novel, *Nausea,* published three years after *Dance Night*). Throughout the book there is an overwhelming sense of constriction, whether in the corsets sold in Mrs. Abbott's shop or in the martial counting of the dance master (ONE-two or ONE-two-three or ONE-two-three-four). Sex is omnipresent but inevitably furtive and disturbed, with the wrong partners, at the wrong times. Jen and Morry want to escape but the small town undertow is no myth and nothing ever works out. When Jen steels herself and flees, she follows a circuitous route that leads her inevitably back to . . . Lamptown.

Those of us who remember childhood as something less than an idyllic experience will recognize Jen's fury: "Rage swept over her at being young, young and little, as if some evil fairy had put that spell on her. Why must you be locked up in this dreadful cage of childhood for twenty or a hundred years? Nothing in life was possible unless you were old and rich, until then you were only small and futile before your tormentors, desperately waiting for the release that only years could bring."

And yet the vision of escape sustains Powell's characters through the greasy, bug-ridden summers and numbing, desolate winters: "Trains whirred through the air, their whistles shrieking a red line through the sky behind them, they landed on Jen's bed without weight, vanished and other trains, pop-eyed, roared toward her. Trains slid noiselessly across her eyelids, long transcontinental trains with diners, club cars, observation cars. The people on these trains leaned out of their windows and held out their hands to Jen. 'California, Hawaii, Denver, Quebec, Miami,' they chanted, 'oh you dear child, New Orleans, Chicago, Boston, Rocky Mountains, New York City'. . . ."

It is recognizably the same author who leads us through the streets of New York at the beginning of *Turn, Magic Wheel*—there is no mistaking the economy of means, the ability to project a world in the meanderings of one individual—but everything else is transformed. Whereas *Dance Night* was a dingy portrait of a tiny boomtown in the last years of the 1920s, *Turn, Magic Wheel* is a dizzying, hilarious sendup of Manhattan literary life in the midst of the Depression. It also addresses, however airily, a dilemma facing any writer who would use friends for inspiration— namely, when does artistic license cross the line into personal betrayal?

In this case, the answer is on page four of a new novel called "The Hunter's Wife" by the central character, Dennis Orphen. Orphen has taken the love life of one of his mistresses—Mrs. Andrew Callingham, *nee* Effie Thorne, whose famous husband deserted her some years hence—and constructed a *roman à clef* around it: "Past youth the sweet creature lies about her age, not through ordinary female coquetry but in the way men lie, men who having failed to do the great deed by the given hour, ease their desperate fear of failure by cheating with the calendar. Fifteen years and he has not come back to me, she says, perhaps never, then, and this cannot be borne so she swears she is only thirty-nine, this year the miracle must happen, he will come back, the hunter will return and see the wise gentle wife she has become in his long absence. . . ."

Orphen, who will reappear in later New York novels, is both a supreme egoist and something of a rotter. Yet he is also the character to whom Powell obviously feels the closest and she provides him with his defense in her very first paragraph: "That was the demon behind his every deed, the reason for his kindness to beggars, organ-grinders, old ladies and little children, his urgent need to know what they were knowing, see, hear, feel what they were sensing, for a brief moment to *be* them. It was the motivating vice of his career, the whole horrid reason for his writing, and some day he warned himself he must pay for this barter in souls." One suspects that this is in part Powell talking about herself: her letters and diaries often make fun of just those people who were the dearest to her.

By the time *Turn, Magic Wheel* is over we know everything about this ambitious young writer—his vanities, his fantasies, his fears ("the growing conviction that his genius was no more wondrous than an old file") and his flashes of self-reproach ("How clever I was, how damnably clever, Dennis thought, furious with his own demon now that made him see so savagely into people's bones and guts that he could not give up his nice analysis even if it broke a heart, he could not see less or say less.") We have also been introduced to a staggering array of New York grotesques—Belle Glaenzer, a "monument to Hollandaise in the black velvet chair," rivals anything in Evelyn Waugh—and two touching heroines, both of whom have loved Andrew Callingham and come to an understanding that helps one of them die in peace and the other to renew herself.

Anybody who has made a study of the book world of the 1930s will derive some extra-narrative pleasure from the stray darts Powell wings at critic Lewis Gannett and at popular writers and blurb-makers such as Hugh Walpole and Louis Bromfield (the last of whom was briefly a classmate of Powell's in Mansfield, Ohio). But one need not be a literary scholar to enjoy Powell's exposure of the conformity that, then as now, rules the decisions made by the sultans of American entertainment. As I write, my local movie-house is showing four films, every one of them a numbered follow-up to some previous hit. Powell makes it clear that this sort of herdmind is not a new phenomenon in her waspish portrayal of the rising book executive Johnson: "Already he was reputed to be one of the most brilliant of the younger publishers. He had discovered more young proletarian writers than MacTweed could shake a stick at. He was so brilliant he could tell in advance that in the years 1934–35 and –36 a book would be hailed as exquisitely well written if it began: 'The boxcar swung out of the yards. Pip rolled over in the straw. He scratched himself where the straw itched him.' " But fashions change and the "brilliant" publisher eventually gets his comeuppance: "The type of literature he represented, the type religiously encouraged by Johnson heretofore was imperceptibly retreating before the avalanche of Old South novels . . . No novel was acceptable or publishable unless it registered a dreamy, high class nostalgia for the Old South; and such sagas were springing up by the hundreds." (It should be noted that *Turn, Magic Wheel* predated the publication of *Gone With The Wind* by several months.)

Turn, Magic Wheel takes its opening epigram from the 3rd Century B.C. bucolic poet Theocritus and is dedicated in its turn to Powell's friend, a nightclub entertainer named Dwight Fiske—an appropriately jumbled pedigree for a dazzling book. If there is another novel that manages simultaneously to be so funny and so sad, so riotous and so realistic, so acute and yet so accepting in the portrayal of flawed humankind, I have not yet found it.

Powell wrote occasional short stories throughout her career, published in *The New Yorker, Mademoiselle, Harper's Bazaar* and *Story,* among other magazines. In 1952, she culled a selection of eighteen of them for publication as *Sunday, Monday and Always.* She seems to have found the medium somewhat confining—with the exceptions of *A Cage For Lovers* and the play *Jig-Saw, Sunday, Monday and Always,* despite its twenty-year gestation, is the shortest of her books—but the best of her stories are typically bright and satisfying.

They need no introduction, no explication; they sparkle, flash, and are gone. Malcolm Cowley, in a spectacularly wrong-headed review for the *New York Post* that can, unfortunately, stand for much of Powell's early criticism, objected to her "comically foreshortened figures, monsters and gargoyles. It is an interesting museum," he continued, "worth the price of admission in laughs but still there might be more relief from these creeps, drips, jerks, phonies, fussbudgets, finaglers and fuddy-duddies." John Nerber, in *The New York Times* (which itself plays an important role in "Here Today, Gone Tomorrow") came closer to the truth: "It is impossible to reduce these stories to plots, to apt descriptions. Her method, simply put, is to catch a human being in so typical and unguarded a moment that his whole life is revealed in its entirety . . . It is one of Miss Powell's triumphs that somehow, unobtrusively, the warmth of her pity comes through."

"Such A Pretty Day" is probably the most famous of the stories; originally published in 1939, it was reprinted in the first anthology of short fiction from *The New Yorker.* "The Glads" has a shock ending right out of some hybrid of O. Henry and Ambrose Bierce, while "The Roof" is about as close as Powell would ever come to the urban alienation that became a hallmark of New York City fiction in the 1950s and 1960s—an era when Powell's beloved Village became almost as famous for its muggings as it had been for its parties.

Rounding out this volume is a short, poignant, autobiographical sketch, "What Are You Doing In My Dreams?", that may serve as a pocket summary of Powell's art. All the familiar elements are here—life and death; Ohio and New York; the awkward, hungry country girl and the city sophisticate; romantic yearning and realist self-deprecation—brought together one last time at the close of a half-century of meditation.

One hopes that more of Powell's work will become generally available over the next few years (*The Bride's House, The Tenth Moon, The Story of a Country Boy* and *My Home Is Far Away* especially deserve reissue). And there is a wealth of unpublished material—diaries, letters, book reviews and playful, spontaneous drawings—among the Powell papers.

One of Samuel Johnson's acquaintances made an effort to become a philosopher but gave it up, because, he said, "cheerfulness was always breaking in." Powell, a merciless observer of the human condition who never pretended she was any nobler than the rest of her besotted, scattered, doomed characters—dear and valuable in spite of themselves—would have understood.

Her novels are both period pieces and absolutely up-to-date. Although her favorite bars have long been shuttered or (worse yet, perhaps) rehabbed and renovated, gone "upscale" for a new generation, the mix of poets, privileged and poseurs that flocked to Powell's "Rubberleg Square" may still be found in Manhattan nightclubs, in the receiving room after a concert, at any publication party, Broadway first night or gallery opening. The details of Bohemian life—fashions, neighborhoods (there are few "struggling artists" left in the golden garrets of Greenwich Village), mating dances—may have changed; the spirit has not. And somewhere an eager, frustrated youngster, trapped and misunderstood in a town that does not comprehend ambition, is listening to trains roar through the night—automobiles and airplanes, too—and dreaming of cities far away.

Tim Page

DANCE NIGHT

FOR MY SISTER PHYLLIS

WHAT MORRY HEARD ABOVE THE LAMPTOWN NIGHT NOISES was a woman's high voice rocking on mandolin notes far far away. This was like no music Morry had ever known, it was a song someone else remembered, perhaps his mother, when he was only a sensation in her blood, a slight quickening when she met Charles Abbott, a mere wish for love racing through her veins.

The song bewildered Morry reading Jules Verne by gaslight, it unspiralled somewhere high above the Bon Ton Hat Shop, above Bauer's Chop House, over the Casino, and over Bill Delaney's Saloon and Billiard Parlor. It came from none of these places but from other worlds and then faded into a factory whistle, a fire engine bell, and a Salvation Army chorus down on Market Street.

Morry leaned far out the window and looked above and below, but there was no woman in the sky nor any sign of a miracle for blocks around. Girls from the Works in light dresses wandered, giggling, up and down the street waiting for the Casino Dance Hall above Bauer's to open, farm couples stood transfixed before Robbin's Jewelry Store window, the door of Delaney's Saloon swung open, shut, open, shut, releasing then withdrawing the laughter and the gaudy music of a pianola. Everything was as it was on any other Thursday night in Lamptown.

Nevertheless to Morry this had become a strange night and he could read no more. He thrust "Twenty Thousand Leagues Under the Sea" into his washstand drawer, turned down the gas, picked up a pack of cigarettes, thrust them in his hip pocket, and went downstairs. In the dark narrow hallway he ran into Nettie Farrell, assistant in the Bon Ton, her arms encircling a tower of hat boxes. Morry, absorbed in his new and curious quest, had no desire to meet anyone from his mother's shop and he hung back. But Nettie deliberately left the workroom door open and there was his mother, her pale cold face bent over a basket of cotton pansies, a blue-shaded lamp burning intently above her.

"You've been smoking!" Nettie whispered accusingly. "I'm going to tell your mother. And now you're going over to Bill's place! You are—you know you are!"

"I wasn't!" Morry denied everything sullenly.

"Hanging around poolrooms! You ought to be ashamed!"

A bell tinkled in the front of the shop and Nettie, hat boxes tipping perilously eastward, backed into the workroom without another word, only her black eyes blinking reproachfully at him.

Morry hurried out the side door into the little stone court where half a dozen Market Street shops ended in kitchen stoops, and half a dozen lights from these dwellings back and above shops united in a feeble illumination of a cistern, old garbage cans, a broken-down doll-buggy, and a pile of shipping boxes.

Where was the song now, Morry wondered, and vaguely he blamed Nettie Farrell and the Bon Ton for having lost it. A freight train rumbled past a few yards from the court, its smoke spread over the Lamptown moon, and then he heard above its roar a girl's voice calling. Though certainly no girl in all Lamptown could be calling Morry Abbott, he was always expecting it, and he tiptoed hastily across rubbish-strewn cinders toward the voice. A flight of steps went up the side of the saloon to where Bill Delaney lived with his mother, and here Morry stopped short for at the very top of these steps huddled a dark figure.

Morry hesitated.

"Did you call me?" he asked uncertainly.

"Yes," said the girl and since Bill had neither sister, wife, nor daughter, Morry could not for the life of him imagine who it was. "I was lonesome. Come on up."

Morry was embarrassed.

"I—I can't." He felt scornful of a girl who would talk to him without even being able to see who he was. If it had been daylight or even dusk a strange girl speaking to him would have meant that in spite of Nettie Farrell's repeated taunts, he was good-looking, his black eyes, his broad shoulders, oh something about him was appealing. But it was clear that to the girl at the top of the stairs he might be just anyone.

"Come on," she urged. "I've got to talk to somebody, haven't I?"

The saloon back door opened and the bartender stood there against a sudden brilliant background of glasses, polished brass, and a rainbow of bottles. Morry ducked up the stairs, and the girl moved over for him to sit down. He could see now that she was a stranger in Lamptown, a queer pointed-faced girl, whose hair, black and tangled, hung to her shoulders. He would see if she was pretty when the next engine flashed its headlight down the tracks.

"There's a dance tonight, isn't there?" she demanded of him. In the darkness they eagerly tried to study each other's face, but all Morry could find in hers was a wildness that made him feel oddly older and more responsible.

"Even if I'm not old enough to go," she pursued, "why won't Bill let me go and watch? You ask him."

This terrified Morry. He didn't want to be teased by the factory girls at the dance, and he certainly didn't want to be ragged by the train men in Bill's saloon. Facing their good-natured challenges on his own account was torture enough, but to take on the added burden of a girl . . .

"We don't want to go to any dance," he said. "It's no fun watching. Look, who are you?"

"I'm adopted now," she explained triumphantly. "The Delaneys took me from the Home. This is where we live and I have a room of my own."

"Well." Morry didn't know why you were glad over being adopted but he supposed you ought to be congratulated. "Do you like it here?"

"I like the trains going by," she said. "I like it in my sleep when I hear them whistle way off. And I like it in my sleep when I hear the piano going downstairs and the men laughing. But I don't like to make beds. I can't make the sheets stay under."

Morry lit a cigarette.

"Let me see if I can smoke," she took the one he had lit, made a few masterful draws on it and then gave it back. "Oh well," she coughed, "I guess I can learn."

"What's your name?" he asked her. He liked sitting there beside her but he was a little afraid of her. He must remember, he thought, to hang on to her skirt if she should take it into her head to jump down stairs.

"Jen St. Clair. Maybe I'm Delaney now, but Bill and his mother say they don't care what I call myself." She casually fished in his pocket and drew out a pack of gum, unwrapped it and carefully stuck the wrappings back into his pocket. "But I'm going back to the Home sometime—when I get money."

"Why?" he wanted to know.

"To get Lil. She's my sister and she's still there."

An engine shrieked down the tracks, then a window flew up in the court, a woman thrust her head out and called, "Billy! Oh, Bill--ee!"

"'You'll come back for me, won't you, Jen,' is what Lil said to me," Jen went on. "I said I would."

The saloon back door opened again and a quiet scuffling noise was heard—the engine's searchlight briefly revealed Bill in white apron, wrestling with a heavy but feebly organized man in shirtsleeves.

"There!" muttered Bill. "There, damn you. . . . Oh, Shorty! Give us a hand here."

Bill always handled the toughs but Shorty, the barkeep, had to pick them up afterward and start them home. Morry explained all this to Jen. She seemed pleased to hear of her benefactor's power. She stood up.

"Come in the house," she invited. "I want to show you something."

"But Bill's old lady wouldn't like it." It was Morry's experience that you weren't wanted in people's houses any more than they were wanted in yours.

"Asleep," Jen tersely nodded toward the old woman's bedroom. "Come on, I want to show you this."

She softly opened the screen door and Morry gingerly followed her into the dark vestibule. The rooms smelled of laundry and doughnuts. He caught her hand held out to guide him. It was the parlor, he knew, by the damp, musty air. Jen stood up on a chair and lit the gas light over the mantelpiece. With the flare of light Morry could see that although her hair and brows were black her eyes were sky-blue, he saw the patch of new calico on her faded blue dress. But she did not look at him again. It no longer mattered what he looked like since they were already established as friends. She took some little thing from the mantel and held it out to him in the palm of her hand.

"Look."

It was a tiny gold chair, barely an inch high, an armchair with delicate filagree for its cane back and seat. Morry took it and examined it, gave it back to her. Jen let it lay in her palm a moment, then with a sigh put it back on the mantel.

"It's so little. . . . I wish I could keep it in my room," she said. "But I suppose it's all right here. I can come in and look at it every once in a while. She got it at the World's Fair in St. Louis."

"I've got to go," Morry decided, watching the door uneasily.

Jen looked stricken.

"No, you can't—you mustn't go yet. Wait."

She tiptoed hurriedly into the next room and came back with a pair of shining tan shoes.

"I've got new shoes with high heels. See? I wanted pumps, black patent leather, but Bill got me these. Look!" She reached down her blouse and drew out a locket on the end of a thin gold chain. "Asafetida. Smell."

Morry smelled. It was asafetida. But he still had to go. He was already out the door. Jen turned down the gas and ran after him.

"There's duck in the ice box," she said. "We could eat it."

Morry only pulled his cap down with more finality. He was amazed at an adopted girl's boldness in entering parlors, and offering delicacies that were undoubtedly reserved by Bill Delaney for his own midnight supper.

"Well, I guess I'm off," he said brusquely.

Jen hung on to the railing and swung her foot back and forth. She wasn't over thirteen or fourteen, he thought.

"I've got folks somewhere," she informed him rather aloofly now, as if she sensed criticism of her lack of background. "They've got papers at the Home. There's a Mrs. St. Clair somewhere and that's my mother—Lil's and mine."

Morry said nothing, but he was impressed. An unknown mother—a Mrs. St. Clair somewhere who might be a millionaire or an actress.

The window on the court flew open again.

"Billy! Oh Bill--ee!"

And this must have reminded Nettie Farrell to tell something for the next moment Morry heard his mother on their back stoop.

"Morry! Where are you?"

"You're Morry," Jen whispered, and he nodded. Why not Billy, then he wondered. . . . He did not answer and his mother never called twice. He heard her go indoors and close the door.

"Listen!" Jen seized his wrist. From across the street in front of the building came the sound of a drum, presently joined by a piano. Then a man's voice, rich, resonant—on Thursday nights you heard this voice above all other sounds for a block away; it belonged to Harry Fischer, the dancing teacher.

"ONE and two, and ONE and two and ONE and two and—"

"Can't we go and watch?" Jen appealed again.

Morry shook his head. He started down the steps. She said nothing, just swung her foot back and forth, but when halfway down he turned to look back he was startled at the desolation in her face, as if this parting was forever, and as if he, Morry Abbott, meant everything in the world to her.

"What is it?" he wanted to know.

Jen twisted her hands.

"Nothing. Only people last such a little while with me. There's no way to keep them, I guess. Everybody goes away—that's why I've got to go back for Lil because I know how terrible it is to be left always—never see people again."

"I'll see you tomorrow," he promised hurriedly. "I live over the Bon Ton. Probably we'll always be seeing each other."

Jen shook her head. Morry hesitated a moment, then went slowly down the stairs.

"ONE and two and ONE and two and ONE and two—"

The dancing lesson lasted from eight to nine and then the counting stopped and the Ball began. Morry wanted to tell all this to Jen but it was better not to go back once you had said you were going. He looked up. She sat hugging her knees, leaning against the railing.

"Well—goodnight."

She didn't answer. Embarrassed, Morry stumbled over ashcans and cinders to his own stone-paved courtyard. He wanted to look back again but he did not dare. He went down the little alley and slipped in the side door. The workroom door was open and his mother was in there arranging her hair before a handmirror with deep concentration. He wondered if she was going to the dance. Behind her he saw Nettie Farrell's trim plump figure. She was rummaging through a large pasteboard box of ribbons. Morry went upstairs before she saw him.

The gaslight in Morry's room went up and shadows were chased up the low sloping ceiling. Jules Verne emerged from the washstand drawer. Morry, in bed, smoked as he read and squashed his cigarette stubs in to a cracked yellow soapdish. The short little dimity curtains at his infinitesimal windows quivered steadily with a busy breeze. Below, on Market Street, a group of factory girls gathered about two trainmen just come from Bill's place, and were convulsed by their masculine wit. The Salvation Army moved up a block; its aim was to reach the Casino and save at least a few of those headed for that modest hell. Tambourines clinked.

Morry jammed a third pillow at the back of his head, absently flicked ashes over the quilt, and turned page after page until words again took living shapes and allowed him to enter the book.

He had forgotten the unknown lady singing in the sky.

"Come to me my melancholy baby," sang Nettie, "Huddle up and don't be blue. So you're going to the dance again, Mrs. Abbott."

Elsinore lowered her eyes over the hat for Dode O'Connell. The factory girls always liked flamboyant trimming and she thoughtfully added a green ribbon to the flowers pinned on the straw brim. This was what Charles Abbott would facetiously refer to as a Vegetable Blue Plate.

"There's plenty of time," she answered Nettie. "I don't want to be there first, besides the lesson is still on."

"Huddle up and don't be blue," hummed Nettie. She watched the street door waiting for customers. She was eighteen, she had been in the shop a year and the importance of her work continued to overwhelm her. Other girls in Lamptown worked in the factory or the telephone office, but God had chosen to favor her with this amazingly attractive niche in the Bon Ton Hat Shop. This must be because she was superior, a cut above the factory type, she was on lodge programs, for instance at the Lady Maccabees' meeting she sometimes sang, "When the dawn flames in the sky—I love you."

"Mr. Abbott ought to be in from the road soon," Nettie said. "What does he think of your going to the dances? I guess he's glad you have a little pleasure, maybe."

"He doesn't mind. He knows I work hard and don't get out much. I don't think Charlie minds." It had never occurred to Elsinore, for ten years self-and-home-supporting, that Mr. Abbott's opinion deserved little attention. She accepted his husbandly domination without demanding any of its practical benefits. If Charles, home for a week from a three months' Southern tour, objected to a gown of hers or a new arrangement of furniture, things were quietly changed to his taste. In Elsinore's scheme a husband was always a husband.

Nettie sat down on a work stool and examined her fingernails. She was a plump, sleek little girl, black hair parted in the middle and drawn back to a loose knot on her neck, her face a neat oval with full satisfied lips. Men followed Nettie on the street but Nettie's chin went up more haughtily, her hips swung more insolently from side to side because Nettie was better than factory girls or telephone operators, she did not speak to strange men, she wanted to get on. Some day she would have a shop of her own. Mrs. Abbott said she was a good worker.

"I don't care about dancing," she observed to Mrs. Abbott. "That's why I never took lessons."

Elsinore held a straw frame out at arm's length.

"I never cared at your age," she said. "It was only this winter I learned."

The echo of the maestro's voice could be heard again—One two three—ONE two three—One—and Elsinore colored ever so faintly. It was easier to wait from one Thursday to the next than from eight o'clock until nine, she thought. She always hoped—yet perhaps not quite hoped, for she was a quiet contained woman, that this night—or next week, then—Mr. Fischer would select her as partner. This had happened once, just last winter in fact, when she had stayed over from the lesson to the regular dance; Fischer had been demonstrating a new dance and he turned to her, "Mrs. Abbott knows these steps from the class lesson tonight. May I ask you to come forward, Mrs. Abbott?"

Usually shy, Elsinore had known no hesitation in going straight across the dance floor to him, aware of her own limitations as a dancer she yet was certain that with him all things were possible. If from a raft in mid ocean this man had called to her, "Now, Mrs. Abbott, just swim out to me," she would have swum to him without hesitation, safe in her enchantment. A few bars of music, two to the left, two to the right, swing, swing, dip . . . "All right, Mr. Sanderson"—then to the musician.

That was all. It might happen again. Always someone was chosen casually like that for a brief demonstration and even if it didn't happen again, there was that one time to remember.

"The girls are beginning to go up," said Nettie.

Elsinore's fingers trembled arranging the trimmings in their labeled boxes but she said nothing. Nettie drew out a nail buff and polished her nails intently. Her hands were plump, white, and tapering. Nettie greased them and wore silk gloves over them at night.

"Bill Delaney's adopted a girl from the orphanage for his mother to take care of," said Nettie. "Imagine."

"That's no home for a girl," said Elsinore, "over a saloon."

Nettie tossed the buff into her drawer and looked toward the front door. Still no customers.

Fay's coming for her hat tonight," she said, remembering. "She wants it for the Telephone Company's picnic. . . . She said people thought the girl might belong to Bill—you know men are that way, and Bill used to run around a lot."

"Maybe," said Elsinore but she didn't care. In three minutes more she would go over to the Casino. In three minutes. "Did Morry come in?"

Nettie shrugged.

"How do I know, Mrs. Abbott? Morry never pays any attention to what anybody says. He hangs around poolrooms, he smokes, he sits up late reading and smoking. You ought to get his father to talk to him."

Elsinore's straight eyebrows drew together.

"I must, Nettie, that's quite true. He's just at that age."

"Seventeen-year-old hanging around Bill Delaney's!" said Nettie. Talking about Morry Nettie's face always got red, her eyes flashed, every reminder of this boy's existence subtly offended her.

Two more minutes and Elsinore could stand up and say, "Well, Nettie, I'll leave the shop to you. Shut it up as soon as Fay gets her hat and put the key under the stoop."

Now she said, "He's lonely, Nettie, he goes to Bill's for the company. But it's not a good place for a boy."

She heard a step upstairs and called Morry's name. A sleepy bored voice responded.

"At least he's in," said Nettie.

One more minute. The piano from across the street pounded out the rhythm Fischer had announced—ONE and two and three and FOUR— Come to me my melancholy baby, huddle up and don't be blue. . . .

"Oh it's g-r-e-a-t to be f-r-e-e," sang the Salvation Army, "from the chains of s-i-n that bondage me. . . ."

"Well, Nettie, I'll leave the shop to you," said Elsinore, standing up at last. "Shut it up as soon as Fay gets her hat—and put the key under the stoop."

She did things, rubbed a chamois over her face, patted her hair, adjusted her dress, but these motions were curiously automatic for already she was swimming across oceans to a raft where Harry Fischer stood beating his hands to a dance rhythm—"one and two and three and four—"

"Here's Fay now," said Nettie, but Elsinore was gone. Elsinore gone, Morry asleep upstairs—it instantly became Nettie's shop and Nettie bloomed. She chatted patronizingly with Fay's young man while Fay tried on the hat.

"Smile my honey dear," sang Fay softly into the mirror for the hat was becoming, "while I kiss away each tear—"

Behind her back her young man grasped Nettie's arm. He slid his hand along her biceps and pressed a knuckle into her armpit.

"That's the vein to tap when you embalm people," he said, for he was going to be an undertaker.

Two floors above Bauer's Chop House fifty pairs of feet went slip a-slip a-slip to a drum's beating. Sometimes a piano melody crept through the drum's reverberation, sometimes the voice of Fischer emerged with a one-and-two and a one-and-two, and when this rhythm stopped suddenly there was a clap-clap-clap of hands, a silence and in this silence the clock sitting on the top of Bauer's cash register marked off the hush into ones and twos and ones and twos and ones and twos.

Behind the counter Hermann Bauer, fat, immobile, leaned on his elbows and looked out of the window without stirring for thirty-nine minutes when a lady got off the Interurban and came in to order a fried egg sandwich. Behind the other counter Mrs. Hulda Bauer, fat, immobile, sat on a high stool and crocheted an ugly but innocent device for a counterpane. Parades of girls from the Works went by and tramped up the stairs behind the restaurant to the Casino. Every Thursday night for six years Hermann had turned from the counter to say to his wife, "Hulda, look how these girls dress! Every cent on their backs. Gott! Silk, satins, and the perfume! I can smell it in here!"

"That will all change when they marry," Hulda answered always, but now Hermann remained silent so that Hulda need not look up from her crocheting. Why shouldn't the factory girls dress well—they made high wages, living was cheap, and nine hundred girls in a town needed to step fast to compete for the stray men. They went down the street giggling and nudging each other, in pink velvets, accordion pleats, lavender and orange satins, their hair peroxided or natural but always elaborately curled, their faces heavily powdered. In front of Bauer's they dallied, waiting for the saloon door across the street to swing open. From behind that door you could hear men's laughter, the pianola, and sometimes a hearty curse, with so much private fun it was amazing that the men should ever come out for a mere dance. But at nine o'clock when the lesson music changed to Dance Number One, a two-step, the saloon door swung open and the men came out—the firemen, brakemen, factory workers—all dressed up to the nines. The girls tossed their heads and hurried up the steps ahead.

"Hello, Jim," a girl leaning out the Casino window upstairs called down to one of the men.

The Bauers had taken in all this play for years but never once had it inspired them to go upstairs to watch as some older people did. It was the duty of one of them to wait for after the dance couples would come in to this place for coffee and sandwiches.

In the kitchen Grace Terris, the waitress, having finished helping the cook with the dishes, hurried upstairs to frizz her hair. She was a thin blonde with a pale face and glasses. She was very neat—her hair and her waist ribbons must always be just so, her outside garments spotless and starched, even though out of sheer love of its texture she sometimes wore a silk chemise three weeks.

Grace brushed past Mrs. Bauer half a dozen times in quest of pins in the cash drawer, a pocketbook left under a serving table, a powder puff hidden under the counter. No matter how busy the place might be on Thursday nights, neither Hermann nor Hulda would ever ask Grace to stay and help. Thursday was her night off—nothing could ever alter that. She couldn't dance but she liked to go somewhere even if she just sat and watched. Presently in a nimbus of azalea perfume, a rose-colored scarf wound around her head as a badge of evening dress, her dark green silk bristling with anticipation, Grace swept through the restaurant and out the front door.

Dance Number Two, a Waltz. At the dark railroad station just beyond Bill Delaney's saloon Number Eleven drew in and a dozen more men from Birchfield, Galion, and Ashland dropped off, and girls leaning out the Casino window hurried to the dressing room to powder again. Hermann Bauer nodded to a group passing the window. Upstairs the feet went slip a-slip a-slip to a waltz, on the stool opposite him Hulda crocheted a daisy over a waltz foundation.

The Salvation Army stood in front of Hermann's, they fixed their eyes on his motionless face while they sang shrilly and mechanically to the dreary jangle of a tambourine. Bill Delaney's place was silent, a little light gleamed in the attic above the Bon Ton Hat Shop, the Bon Ton itself was dark. Now the life of Lamptown had concentrated two floors above Bauer's Chop House.

Dance Number Three, a Robber's Two-step.

In front of Bauer's a long low roadster stopped. Hunt Russell's. Hunt, by some freak of inheritance, certainly due to no fault of his languid self, owned the Works, owned Lamptown, you might say. Now his tall lean person swung out of the car, followed by the equally lean figure of Dode O'Connell, the factory forewoman—a proud hard face she had beneath masses of red hair. She was Hunt Russell's woman. No matter whom she had belonged to before, now she was Hunt's. They went up the steps to the Casino. Dance Number Four.

Quietly Hulda Bauer laid down her crocheting, nodded to her husband, and waddled up to bed. It had been quite an outing for her.

"Tonight I am going to demonstrate to you," said Mr. Fischer, "the dance I created for the United Dancing Masters of the World last summer at our convention in Atlantic City. This dance, ladies and gentlemen, is now taking New York by storm. It is called the Duck Slide. If you please, Mr. Sanderson."

One and two and a three and dip. One and a two and a three and turn. One and a two and a dip and turn and two-step right and two-step left— thank you, Mr. Sanderson.

Elsinore Abbott usually danced first with Mr. Klein the gas man. He was too old for the factory girls and besides he admired a woman who had spunk enough to run a business, always looked trim, always a lady. In the midst of the factory girls' gay colors her dark blue taffeta and black satin pumps seemed wistfully chic, her pale clear-cut face beneath the heavy brown hair gave no hint of naïve pleasure in the dance, her cool gray eyes revealed no vulgar excitement over crowds and music. Over Klein's honest shoulder she watched Fischer, immaculate in evening dress, demonstrating the next movement of the next dance. Fischer had broader shoulders than any man in the room. It was curious that his great muscular body should yield so exquisitely to a dance for it belonged to mighty masculine deeds. He had thick sleek black hair, hard black eyes, a strong-boned heavy face. In a bathing suit at Atlantic City the muscles of his back must have shown powerful and rippling, muscles must have bulged from his shoulders, arms, and legs, his throat must have looked thick and strong like an animal's, like a prize-fighter's. Elsinore followed Mr. Klein's painstaking lead through the second movement.

"In a little while we will pass him standing there," she thought. "In a little while . . . there's no hurry."

When they passed she did not look at him.

In the center of the floor Hunt Russell and Dode O'Connell, cheek to cheek, danced beautifully, silently, as couples do who are certain of other contacts. Hunt Russell, worth a quarter of a million, with a background of Boston Russells and Carolina Blairs, owner of Lamptown, preferred a factory forewoman to a woman of quality, chose Harry Fischer, small-town dancing master as his boon companion, lounged in Bill Delaney's saloon, a billiard cue in one hand, instead of in country clubs, drove his expensive cars down dingy Lamptown streets instead of on foreign boulevards. There were men who would not dare be like that, but no one slapped Hunt on the back, few women dared solicit too frankly the inquiry of his cold amused eyes. And because for two years she had been Hunt's woman Dode O'Connell's head was always high, her proud red mouth flaunted the exclusiveness of her kisses.

After Mr. Klein there were the uncertain young men who had gone to last winter's dancing class with Elsinore, who knew that her own lack of skill would make her less critical of their mistakes. They would learn with her, thought Elsinore without resentment, but after they became expert they would choose younger women as their partners. One of these men, in a waltz, brushed her past Fischer. He stood in a corner talking in a low voice to Hunt while Dode whirled by with one of the train dispatchers.

"You'll have to wait till about one," Fischer said looking at his watch. "Then I'm good for all night. But what about Red?"

"I'll fix that," Hunt tossed a cigarette in a palm bucket. He was not over thirty but his temples were already gray.

Fischer laughed.

"Better look out—she'd kill you for less than that. . . ." and then he clapped his hands. "All right, people . . . one moment, Mr. Sanderson. I want to announce the date of the tango contest to be held in Akron two weeks from tomorrow night. The rules for the contestants, ladies and gentlemen, are as follows . . ."

He stood almost at Elsinore's elbow, no more conscious of her than of the palm on the other side of him. Elsinore did not mind. She wanted nothing from him, after all, only the rare privilege of being allowed to think about him, as she had thought of him for over a year. Nights after the Bon Ton was closed she had lain in bed wondering where Fischer was now. In Birchfield Mondays, Columbus Tuesdays, Delaware Wednesdays, Marion Fridays. Tonight I am going to demonstrate to you, ladies and gentlemen, the Duck Slide. . . . She saw the young girls of Marion, Birchfield, Delaware looking at him, and saw him selecting this or that eighteen year old for an exhibition dance. With these petal-cheeked young girls surrounding him, why should he remember that once he had singled out Elsinore Abbott for a schottische demonstration? Yet she had been eighteen once as these girls would one day be thirty-six. And he was even older than that. But why should he remember her—why indeed should he trouble her mind, Elsinore sometimes wondered, his ways, his manner, littered her memory as confusingly as a man's clothes in a woman's bedroom. She tried to recall what she had thought of before she saw him, but it was as difficult as trying to decide what she wanted of him now that she did think of him. She was married to Charles. He was married to someone in Columbus. What else could there be?

In the doorway of the Casino two new men appeared, and Elsinore, thinking of her husband at the very moment, saw him invoked before her eyes. The natty checked suit, the flawless necktie, the perfect fedora, the cigar—it was indeed Charles Abbott. His roving blue eyes had found her at once, and quietly she left her partner and went up to him.

"I didn't expect you for another three weeks, Charles," she said following him into the hall.

"No?" Charles looked at her with faintly mocking suspicion. "Since when have you been going to factory girl dances?"

Elsinore flushed.

"You knew I had taken it up," she said in a low voice. "I told you I was taking the course last winter. I go out very little, Charles. You know that. This—I like."

Charles watched the dancers with a fixed smile, tapping his cigar against the railing by the door. He nodded to a dancer now and then whom he knew either as a patron of his wife's shop or as a fellow patron of Bill Delaney's place.

Elsinore's partner looked at her questioningly and she shook her head in the negative.

"Close the shop, do you, to come over here?" inquired Charles with seeming affability.

"I never neglect the shop, Charles, you ought to know that," said Elsinore. The color had not left her face. She turned to him abruptly. "Let's go now. Things are almost over. We can talk."

"No hurry," Charles said. He waved his cigar nonchalantly to Hunt Russell. Elsinore went to the dressing room for her coat. She passed Fischer again, standing with arms folded beside the palms. He bowed to her, his face a smooth ruddy mask of courtesy.

"Goodnight, Mrs. Abbott," he said.

Elsinore lowered her head.

"All right, Mr. Sanderson, the next dance will be a Circle Two-step. A Circle Two-step, ladies and gentlemen."

"Come sweetheart mine,
Don't sit and pine,
Tell me of the cares that make you oh so blue—"

Hunt Russell leaned against the exit door and sang the words softly. Charles followed Elsinore with the suggestion of a swagger, an air of being made to leave a gay occasion against his will. Elsinore did not look back. The music, the laughter, had ceased to be once she turned her back upon them. Abruptly she locked away her thoughts of Fischer for these were precious matters not to be dwelt upon with strangers like Charles nearby.

"The good old Bon Ton," Charles observed lightly as Elsinore fitted her key into the lock of the shop door. Elsinore did not answer.

Long afterward Morry was awakened by the dance music stopping. He heard voices in the street and stumbled sleepily to the window. The Casino windows were dark—only one light burned in Bauer's Chop House. Before the restaurant Hunt Russell's car stood, and beside it were Hunt and Dode O'Connell facing each other.

"You cur," Dode was saying in a cold hard voice, "You dirty double-crossing cur."

Morry yawned and went back to bed.

Trains whirred through the air, their whistles shrieking a red line through the sky behind them, they landed on Jen's bed without weight, vanished, and other trains, pop-eyed, roared toward her. Trains slid noiselessly across her eyelids, long transcontinental trains with diners, clubcars, observation cars. The people on these trains leaned out of their windows and held out their hands to Jen.

"California, Hawaii, Denver, Quebec, Miami," they chanted, "oh you dear child, New Orleans, Chicago, Boston, Rocky Mountains, New York City."

Then two dark porters made a London bridge and caught her, they said, "Which would you rather have, a diamond palace or a solid gold piano?"

Old Mrs. Delaney finally put on her carpet slippers and opened Jen's door.

"Well, what's the matter with you now?" she wanted to know. "Waking folks up this hour with your yelling?"

She was irritable, for Bill had been hiding in a closet ever since he came upstairs. He'd been drinking too much and after the big Akron wreck when he'd been the faulty engineer he had spells when every engine chugging by sent him sobbing to some hiding place. There was nothing you could do with him but sometimes his mother, her withered old face grim and dark, her gnarled hands clenched, sat waiting all night for him to quit moaning and come to his senses again.

"No—no, I've changed my mind," Jen cried. "Not the piano—the other—the diamond palace."

"That'll be about enough out of you tonight," said Mrs. Delaney. Jen opened her eyes and blinked at the old woman in the feeble dawn light.

"There won't be any diamonds for you, young lady," grumbled Mrs. Delaney. She pulled the cover over Jen, jerked a pillow into place. "Diamond palace my eye."

"All right," murmured Jen as her foster parent slipped out of the room, "I'll take the gold piano."

"Aren't you afraid of the old woman?" Morry Abbott asked one night when they sat out on the steps above the saloon.

Jen shook her head.

"I'm not afraid of her," she said. "That's just the way old women are. I'm not afraid of anybody. I feel sorry for them, coming to me someday begging me to forgive 'em because they didn't realize I was going to turn out so rich and famous."

"You kid yourself a lot, don't you?" Morry said curiously. He heard voices in the saloon backroom of older boys about town and he instinctively drew up his cap down over his eyes. His own place at seventeen was in the saloon downstairs, instead of hanging around kids like Jen. He was old enough to be getting over that queer sickness the saloon smell gave to him, about time he stopped coughing over whiskey, listening frankly awestricken to tales of amorous adventures. He would go down in a little while for the only way to learn anything was to get used to it.

"What did the Delaneys take you out of the Home for?" he wanted to know.

Jen looked at him suspiciously and then brushed back a lock of black hair, stuck it behind her ear.

"What's the matter with me—why shouldn't they pick me?" she demanded.

Morry blushed, at her attack.

"Well, people usually adopt those little yellow-haired blue-eyed dolls—you know—you're all right only—"

"The hell they do," said Jen and Morry was conscious of the same sick feeling the saloon smell gave to him. "They always pick somebody that looks like a good worker. Once in a while some woman that's had her pet cat run over picks out one of those pretty ones. There aren't many of them."

"You don't have to say hell," said Morry. It annoyed him that words which stuck in his own throat should flow so easily from a young girl's lips.

Jen wriggled and sucked her thumb sulkily.

"Well, anyway Lil's like that—she looks like a little wax doll," she went on. "Everybody that visits the Home always wants to hold her . . . but nobody's adopted her. I told the matron not to let anybody because I'm the one to take care of Lil. She's so little—she can't stand it without me. I've got to look after her. Gee!"

She suddenly brushed her sleeve over her eyes. Morry was fired with an aim in life.

"You leave Lil to me," he said. "What about me adopting her myself?"

Jen seized his arm. She was radiant.

"Will you—Morry—will you do that?"

And then Morry remembered the truths that his father mockingly and Nettie Farrell bitterly had so often flung at him. Worthless, overgrown cub, no good to anybody, in everybody's way. If he was going to amount to anything in the world, why was he hanging around talking big instead of hunting a job, why didn't he study one of those correspondence courses at night instead of reading romantic trash till way after midnight? Fellows no older than he was were making money out selling or working in garages or factories and if they could do it he supposed he could stand it. But here Morry shuddered. He couldn't see himself in overalls, he dared not picture himself an agonized applicant for an office job. Somehow he always saw himself a sort of Hunt Russell, a success without callouses and without the embarrassment of however honest sweat. But even Morry could see that this wasn't the way a young man ought to enter the struggle—gasping at the very start. He was miserable remembering the dooms forecast for him by Nettie and his father. Still—Jen St. Clair didn't know all these things about him. On the contrary she seemed to think he could manage anything he promised to do.

"We'll take care of Lil all right," he repeated with slightly less emphasis this time.

"That's fixed, I guess," sighed Jen. "I'll write Lil and tell her. I didn't want to write until I could promise something."

"Does the old woman make you work?" Morry asked, relieved to have the subject of Lil's rescue safely out of the way. "I mean if that's what they got you for—"

Jen looked over her shoulder to make sure Mrs. Delaney was out of earshot.

"I guess they made a mistake," she whispered. "I look bright but I can't seem to pick up anything. The covers stay in little bumps when I make the beds."

She looked gloomy.

"The bottoms of the dishes get egg all over as fast as they're washed," she went on, "even when we haven't had eggs, they do that, no matter how hard I scrub. And when I made popovers yesterday they didn't come out popovers at all. Sort of like pancakes . . . You'd think popovers would be easy, wouldn't you, Morry?"

Jen sunk her chin in her hands.

"It makes it pretty hard for the old woman," she said regretfully. "It was Bill's idea adopting somebody and now they've picked me they've got to keep me."

Morry got up. He thought he might as well go down and get the saloon over with. Jen's black brows contracted. Tomorrow or the next day she would see him again and yet it was a lamp going out each time he went away. She wished for some marvellous surprise to detain him with—a diamond palace or a solid gold piano. "Wait," she would cry and he would come back. She would open the door. "Look," and there would be the palace, its towers glittering, a sapphire light glowing in each window. And so he would have to take off his hat and stay.

Jen didn't answer when he said goodbye. She stood with one hand on the wall and the other on the railing and scuffed the toe of her shoe on the top step.

"Wait," she said when he was halfway down, but when he turned expectantly, she said lifelessly, "Oh nothing."

Diamonds, my eye!

"One beer," Morry said standing at the bar with Hogan, fireman on Number Eleven, and a couple of brakemen from the short line.

The boys of Morry's age usually played pool in the front room and only occasionally joined the older men in the barroom, but now the front room was empty and so Morry went back to the bar. Here Bill Delaney, short, blonde, serious, stood leaning over the back of a chair at one of the card tables talking to three men from the freight yards.

"You've got no kick," he was saying. "You pull down your hundred and fifty smackers every month, you're all right. I'm tellin' you you fellows got it pretty goddam soft."

"You tell all that to the pope," Hogan advised over his shoulder.

"Your dad was here yesterday, Morry," Shorty said wiping up the counter. "Some sport, Charlie Abbott, let me tell you. Some sport even for a traveling man."

"Yeah?" said Morry, whose one aim in life was to keep out of his father's way, or at least out of range of his father's ironic eye.

"You goin' sellin' on the road like your dad?" Shorty asked.

"No," Morry said and then explained, "I'm sort of looking around."

"How about brakin'?" said the brown young man in blue overalls on the other side of Hogan. "You get good pay."

"Don't do no railroadin', buddy," Hogan advised. "We're a tough old bunch, listen to me. You've got to know how to handle your liquor and your women."

"Leave that to Charlie Abbott's boy all right," chuckled Shorty.

"Jesus, when Buck here and me had that seven-hour run out of Pittsburgh—" Hogan drained his glass, banged it on the counter, raised one finger significantly to Shorty.

"Seems to me I get more on the local," Buck said. "Girls in these little towns around here ain't so damned aristocratic."

"He ain't goin' railroadin'," Shorty dismissed the whole business. "He looks all right but he's just a kid. How's the game there, Skin?"

"These fellas don't want to play poker they want to crab about life," Bill Delaney shrugged and came back to the bar. "Enough guys come in here hollerin' for jobs you ought to be glad you're workin'."

"That's a lot of baloney from Father Tooey," growled one of the three shuffling the cards again. "You damn micks let him run this whole town."

"Leave Father Tooey out of it, see," Bill retorted. He poured himself a seltzer. "You fellas make me tired always sore about somethin', always crabbin'. You don't have to work, you know. You could get a room in the poorhouse."

"Aw, a guy wants to see something ahead of him, Bill, that's all," the youngest of the three men cut the pack, the oldest silently dealt a round. "Hell, we don't want to be stuck in this god-forsaken dump all our lives at the same stinkin' little jobs."

"Have another?" Bill asked Morry but Morry shook his head.

Hogan leaned back, his elbows on the bar.

"I would rather have been a French peasant and wear wooden shoes. I would rather have lived in a hut with a vine growing over the door and the grapes growing purple in the kisses of the autumn sun," he said in a sing-song voice, his eyes closed. "I would rather have been that poor peasant with my loving wife by my side with my children on my knees, I would rather have been that man and gone down to the tongueless silence of the dreamless dust than to have been that imperial impersonation of force and murder known as Napoleon the Great."

He looked at Morry with bright blue eyes.

"That's old Bob Ingersoll, the greatest man that ever lived, bar none. Have a drink."

But Morry dropped two dimes on the counter and with a quick nod to the others, went out the front door. Even two beers made him feel dizzy. He almost collided with his father coming in, hat jauntily at an angle, cigar in his mouth.

"Well, well, so you've made the club," Charles Abbott said, his eyes mockingly on his son's red face. "Isn't that splendid! Isn't that just splendid! . . . Go on home, there, and see if there isn't something else you can do to worry your mother."

"I'm going," said Morry.

He dodged the Bon Ton's front door where Nettie stood and went in the alley entrance.

"I would rather have been a French peasant and gone down to the tongueless silence of the dreamless dust," he mused going upstairs. "That's Bob Ingersoll, the greatest man who ever lived, bar none."

Elsinore knew that Charles Abbott was a weak, blustering man, but after the day he first kissed her these matters receded, a curtain dropped definitely between her and his faults. She had worked in a millinery shop when he was a candy salesman from a Chicago wholesale dealer, she had gone on working until now the shop was hers, and he still traveled. Every three or four months he was home for a fortnight. He was a spendthrift, a gambler, a sport, people said, but on the other hand, as Nettie Farrell frequently pointed out to gossips, he was a jealous husband and that always proved something.

When he was home Morry went out early in the morning and hung closely to his room at night for his father held him in complete scorn. Charles slept all morning, drank whiskey quietly and steadily all afternoon, and aware of being drunk, stood silent around the Bon Ton showroom, his hat on the side of his head, always smoking a cigar. He flicked ashes over the workroom table, left his cigar stubs on the showcases, but Elsinore said no word of reproach. Sometimes he dropped into Bill Delaney's for a card game but he drank mostly at home. In Elsinore's plain little bedroom he lay evenings reading the Columbus newspapers, dropping his cigar ashes over the white bedspread, hanging his heavy suits over her slight woman's things, keeping his whiskey bottle on the dressing table between her lilac water and her talcum.

In the cities of Charles Abbott's world there were painted little blonde girls who kept his picture on their dressers, there were women who made engagements with him for three months ahead, and all these were gay party women with whom a man liked to be seen. But even now, nineteen years married, there was still for him something curiously chic in Elsinore's manner and dress, something haunting in her white cold face, her isolation made her desirable.

When she closed the shop and came up to bed the night after the dance, and for many nights after that, Morry in the next room was kept awake by their low voices.

"See here, there's something in this dance business, Elsinore. . . . Some guy there you go to meet."

Elsinore's voice then, cool and tired.

"Don't be silly, Charles, you know there's no one else."

"That's all right, you're not taking up this dance idea all of a sudden for no reason at all. It's some man. Somebody's got you running at last."

"You know how I am, Charles," Elsinore would say wearily.

"I do know—cold as hell, but I always knew if you ever snapped out of it there wouldn't be any limit for you. . . . I know you. . . . Who is the fellow, anyway? Come on, now, let's hear it."

Elsinore would turn out the lights, go to the window in her white nightdress to draw up the shades, stand for a moment to look at the pale far-off moon. She got into bed quietly.

"I tell you, Elsinore. I don't like this business of you starting to run around," Charles's voice in the dark, bereft of his mocking eyes, his jaunty cigar, was weak and querulous. "It's not like you. It means something and I don't like it. I've got to find out, damn it."

Elsinore drew the sheets over her. A freight train rumbling by hushed him for a little while. And then—

"Who is it, Elsinore—come on. Is it Russell? Is it one of those railroad bastards? . . . Elsinore, for the love of Christ. . . ."

"Go to sleep, Charles. . . . I've told you there never was anyone else."

Grumbling still he fell asleep and she put her arm across her eyes.

Where was Fischer tonight—what young girl's light body was bent to his in a dance, what town was rocking to his one and two and one and two?

When you stepped out of the back door into the alley at night you stomped your feet to scare away the rats. For a moment you heard them rushing over the rotten boards of back porches, scuttling over the ash cans, over the cistern bucket, and into weeds. And then you could proceed in safety to the pump or to the storehouse shed where old frames were packed away in trunks, where from a shelf there leered antique window heads with hay-colored pompadours drooping over one eye, or with black bangs madly frizzed and stiff enough to balance any hat three inches above the head.

Nettie came back from this shed with a stack of wire frames on one arm, a flashlight in the other hand.

Morry, about to go out, ducked back in the hall.

"Going to the saloon, I suppose," said Nettie, a little out of breath. "Going over there and drink, you're just a good-for-nothing, Morry Abbott, you ought to be ashamed."

"Well, what are you going to do about it?" Morry retorted sulkily. "What do you want me to do, stick around here and trim hats?"

"Better than hanging around saloon trash and girls out of foundling homes," Nettie flashed back in a low tense voice. "Better than sitting up nights reading books by atheists."

"What were you doing in my room?" Morry demanded, amazed and angry.

Nettie tossed her head defiantly.

"I have a right to go where I please, Morry Abbott, in this house. If you're reading things you're ashamed of I'd advise you to hide them, before your father sees them. I've heard about that Ingersoll man. . . . The idea!"

Morry opened the workroom door for her, angry at his own inability to be devastatingly rude to her. His mother saw him.

"Don't go out, Morry," she said quietly. "Your father's over at Delaney's and he wouldn't want to see you there."

"All right," said Morry.

He heard Jen's voice—"Hoo-oo!" softly calling from outside. He would go upstairs and wait awhile, then go over for a minute to sit on the steps. In the hatshop he heard the voice of Mrs. Pepper, the corsetiere, and in some alarm he hurried upstairs. But was even his room safe from feminine intrusion, he wondered bitterly, since Nettie's admission of having snooped around? Very likely the next time Mrs. Pepper arrived in town she would use his room for fitting. If only he didn't mind the smell of saloons so much, he thought, he would spend his days and nights all in that safely male retreat.

"Just something to confine the hips, that's all," he heard Mrs. Pepper say, "but darling, if you don't mind my saying so—you really do need that—"

And then Morry hurriedly banged his door shut, while downstairs the female figure came into its own. Every fortnight Mrs. Pepper called in Lamptown and with her headquarters at the Bon Ton fitted the factory girls and shop-keepers' wives who could afford it with marvellous devices in pink and orchid satin-covered steel. She was a short, laughing, fat little woman, with a delicate charm and effect of feminine frailty conveyed by a tinkling laugh, tiny plump hands, jewelled, fluttering in perpetual astonishment to her heavy brassiered bosom.

"Oooh—why Mrs. Abbott!" she would gurgle breathlessly, "Why—why!" and then her tinkling silver little laugh.

A woman's figure was to her a serious matter, and her blue eyes would widen thoughtfully over any dilemma of too big hips, flat chest, or protruding stomach.

"I had a lady—Mrs. Forest in Canton—you know A. Z. Forest, the lawyer, and she was big here the way you are and then thin right through here the same as you. You know Mrs. Forest, don't you, Nettie? Nettie remembers her. She came here for a hat once. I gave her the Nympholette Number 43 and everyone says, 'Why, Mrs. Forest, why you look so *stunning!*'"

Mrs. Pepper made everyone lie down to be fitted for that was the only way she could get their real lines. For this purpose Elsinore had a screened couch in the alcove between salesroom and workroom.

"Now just relax," Mrs. Pepper would say. "Put down 38, Nettie. And 46 for the hips."

Mrs. Pepper sometimes went to the Casino but only to watch for she had never learned dancing. It was only because Mr. Fischer was such an old friend—they had the same territory, the same towns to cover.

When Mrs. Pepper's round baby face was bent over her orderbooks Elsinore sometimes stole a look at her. Fischer never talked to Mrs. Pepper, except in the formal way he did to every lady in his hall. Yet someone said once they were seen together in the back seat of Hunt Russell's automobile long after midnight, and that those foursomes with Hunt and Dode occurred other times. Was this the woman, then, that Fischer cared for—or had once cared for? Elsinore wondered again and again about it, for Mrs. Pepper with her lace-frilled daintily powdered throat, her little white hands, her tiny silken ankles swelling to heavy thighs, her delicate sacheted underthings, had the air of being desired by men. Yet Mrs. Pepper was a lady, ridiculously refined.

Once Elsinore, driven by her wonder, deliberately mentioned Fischer's name to her but Mrs. Pepper's childish blue eyes never blinked.

"Mr. Fischer is such a gentleman, isn't he," she said. "He must be a lovely husband. Mrs. Fischer is a lucky woman, I'm sure."

"He must see a great many pretty women in his work," Elsinore, faintly coloring at her own tenacity, went on, "A dancing teacher like that."

"And he is so handsome," sighed Mrs. Pepper. "Such a strong man, too, don't you think? Such a big strong man."

And that was all Elsinore could get out of her.

The Bon Ton was in a state of all day excitement when Mrs. Pepper was there. It must keep open until after eleven to accommodate the working girls. Their outer garments hung over customer's chairs while they tried on samples, and Nettie, with both hats and corsets on her mind, fussed about like a hen with chicks. Charles lounged in Elsinore's room upstairs or in the poolroom and ate at Bauer's.

Elsinore alone remained serene as she would if her business suddenly included all of Ohio and two thousand Netties fussed about in the workrooms.

Morry kept upstairs this evening for a little while until a confusion of feminine voices below assured him that he would not be noticed. Then he tiptoed downstairs. The workroom door was open and lying on the table, a pillow under her head, was a girl naked except for a gauze undershirt. Nettie, frowning, was measuring her waist with a tape, which meant that Mrs. Pepper was so besieged with customers that the hat business had been temporarily pushed aside. Morry tried to tiptoe past but the girl sat up and squealed.

"Oh, Nettie—there's a man!" She clutched, rather futilely, a cluster of velvet roses and held them before her protectively. She was Grace Terris, the Bauers' waitress. Before Nettie could answer Morry shot out the back door, quite pale, his ears burning furiously.

The people around her grave were satisfied with their hides because of course they were used to them now, though Jen, in this dream, wondered how they could feel so content when the skins complete were passed out by the public bath house with no regard for individual expression.

These dream people held their handkerchiefs before their unknown faces and wept; their black taffeta dresses and their black swallow-tail coats and their black cotton gloves holding tall black hats almost hid the white wreaths, and the moth-ball smell of their clothes covered the sweet sick smell of funeral flowers. Mrs. Hulda Bauer in vast black dabbed a crocheted medallion at her eyes, but the other people, Jen knew, were hired funeral people who came with the rented coaches.

Morry Abbott, wandering past the cemetery, came in and saw the name done in red carnations on a white rose wreath "Jennia St. Clair." But he did not cry.

More people in black arrived with faces for funerals handed out to them at the gate, all Lamptown and all the Children's Home came, and their shoulders shook silently, rhythmically beside the grave, but Morry Abbott only looked on, smoking a cigarette, no more than half interested as he always was. Presently, although the singing was about to begin, he pulled his cap down over his eyes and went away.

"Come back, come back," Jen called to him faintly, but even in dreams she could not keep him from leaving, there was nothing she could do alive or dead to make him stay beside her. There was nothing you could do about Morry Abbott. So Jen threw away the graveyard scene and if he wouldn't care, then he wouldn't care.

But sitting on the stairs with him the next evening, Jen remembered her dream and that he wouldn't cry at her funeral, and was very snappish with him. She thought, resentfully, "Some day I'll make him have feelings, I will."

Old Mrs. Delaney was in. She came out and saw them sitting on the stoop, she stood in the doorway, bent and old and fierce, looking at them.

"You'd better get in here, young woman," she said. "Get your socks darned and your towels mended or you'll get what's coming to you."

"When I get ready," Jen answered serenely, and Morry, who was afraid to talk back to even Nettie, cringed. The old woman didn't mind Jen's back-talk, she muttered something and went back in the house.

"I'm going to get out of this town," Morry said somberly. "A young fella hasn't got a chance except to go on the railroad or out selling like my dad, or go in the Works, and stick all his life. I'm thinking about doing things, getting somewhere."

"Working?"

"Sure, working. 'The hand that holds Aladdin's lamp must be the hand of toil'—that's Robert Green Ingersoll," said Morry. "He was a great man. I got the book."

"Going to do something in Lamptown?" Jen asked, worshipping.

"Not a chance. I'm going somewhere where there's something doing," bragged Morry. "This town's run by a bunch of micks from Shantyville."

"I guess they're better than rich loafers like Hunt Russell," Jen retorted. "The micks work, but what'd Hunt ever do for his money?"

"Hunt's all right," said Morry. "He's a gentleman and that's enough. He could be a barkeep or a fireman but he'd always be Mr. Russell. I'm going to be like that."

Jen dug her chin in her hands.

"Well, what about Aladdin's lamp and the hand of toil? Why don't he do something with his money? Why couldn't he get Lil out of the Home, he could without bothering. I hate him and people like him."

"Will you hush up, you young ones?" Mrs. Delaney's voice complained from inside. "People hear you for miles around with your big talk."

Jen stood up when the door banged shut again and held her finger to her lips.

"Let's go somewhere," she whispered.

They tiptoed down the stairs and then across the tracks to the dark factory road.

"His house cost about a million dollars, Bill said," Jen said. "It's got real marble for steps and it's got solid crystal doorknobs. But *he* never earned it. Hunt Russell never really earned a nickel, and it's not fair."

Hunt Russell's house was no such palace, Morry knew, but he wouldn't have cared if it was. He wanted Hunt to have things and to be a king because in his own mind he, Morry Abbott, was Hunt. Now that he and Jen seemed to be on the way to the Lamptown showplace, Morry was as anxious for Jen's awed admiration as if the estate was his own. He took Jen's hand and they ran part of the way down the silent dark road.

By day Hunt's home was to the passerby a mile of high iron fence backed by a thick hedge and broken by an arched stone gateway through which one glimpsed a leafy winding drive. At the end of the drive was a huge old brick house spreading out in white-pillared porches and glass-roofed sun parlors. A flagstone terrace sloped into rosebushes and flowerbeds and overgrown grass. An iron deer lifted its antlered head in perpetual fright in the middle of the great shaded lawn, and near the driveway a pair of stone Cupids gazed into a cracked stone fountain bowl and saw that their noses were broken off.

By night the place was a dozen black acres of complete stillness for Hunt lived here now all alone with the caretaker's family. It was far beyond the factory houses, past block after block of empty lots, past an abandoned pickle works and the charred foundations of an old farm.

Jen and Morry clung to the iron fence and peered into the darkness.

"Gee, that's a big house," said Jen and then added indignantly, "Why it's bigger than the Home! He's got no business living there as if he was a king. He's got no right."

"Sh!" Morry squirmed uncomfortably at her resentment because if she belonged to Lamptown's laboring class, he, for his part, was with the aristocrats. He looked on luxury without envy but breathed deep with pride in it.

"You got to give Hunt credit for staying in Lamptown, at least," he argued. "He could have been a big bug in Chicago or New York if he wanted."

Jen, climbing up higher on the iron grilling, was not impressed.

"Well, why doesn't he go there, then," she wanted to know, "instead of hanging around this town aggravating people that have to work for their money. . . . Come on, I'm going on up to the house."

"No—he might see us," Morry protested, but Jen was over the fence and he had to follow. They crept up across the thick grass until they were right by the house. It was dark but for a light in the kitchen and another light in an upstairs room. Jen picked up a pebble and tossed it lightly against the house, and then she and Morry stood looking at each other, paralyzed, for the stone crashed right through one of the dark French windows.

"Gee!"

A light flashed on in the room and before they could move Hunt stepped quietly out of the window. He was in white flannels and Morry could never forget him standing on the porch looking at them, not saying a word, just tapping his pipe on the porch railing. Then—

"Well," he said looking from one to the other, "Are you just out breaking windows or are you up to some other damage, too?"

Morry's tongue would not move. Jen nudged him and then it angered her that anyone should have the power to frighten Morry—Morry, of all people.

"Aw, you can buy more windows," she answered defiantly.

Hunt lit a match and peered down at her.

"You're not big enough to talk that way, young lady. I might take it in my head to spank you."

"Try and do it!" urged Jen. "I'm not sorry I smashed your window. Go buy stained glass next time, why don't you?"

Hunt whistled. Morry, who had been sick at Jen's outburst, now found himself angry at Hunt for lighting a match again to coolly examine Jen. His gray eyes traveled from her black hair to her checked gingham dress and then to her flashing blue eyes.

"Come on, Jen," Morry's voice came back, hard and cold. "We'll fix up the window, Hunt. It was just an accident."

"I don't know about that. I'm not so sure it was an accident," Hunt said slowly. "What were you doing here, anyway, you two?"

Morry was amazed to find words again in his mouth—smooth, convincing words.

"I was coming in to ask you about a job at the Works, and we—we were walking by and I thought I'd come in."

Hunt gave a short laugh.

"A business call, I see. Not social. I thought when the window crashed it was just a friend. . . . All right, Abbott, I believe you. Come down to the factory next week if you want a job—don't go around crashing my windows. And you—young lady—"

"Don't worry about me," Jen snapped, "I'd like to break every window of your rotten old house."

Again Morry was furious at Hunt's roar of laughter—it was laughter he wanted to carry Jen away from. He seized Jen's arm to leave but Jen twisted around to shake her fist at Hunt.

"I'll do it, too," she threatened and Hunt laughed again. He said something—it sounded like an invitation to call again, but Morry did not hear. They heard the sound of a woman's voice and when they looked back from the gateway they could see two figures in the lighted doorway, one of them a woman with red hair.

"You—you workin' for him!" stormed Jen, "I won't stand for it. You're worth ten of him, but you'll have to run errands for him. It's no fair, I tell you."

"It's the way things are," Morry said, "You don't need to start crying about it."

But Jen would cry anyway. They stood outside the big iron gate, Morry sullen and uncomfortable, while Jen cried against his unwilling arm.

"It's no fair, that's what I'm crying about," she insisted. "He lives there like a king—he owns the town, he owns you now, too. He's got everything, all we get is little bits he doesn't want. I'm glad we broke his old window, that's what I am.

Jen hung on to his arm, fuming, all the way home, but Morry wasn't conscious of her. He felt sick and afraid but a little excited, too. For now he had a job. His 'future' had begun and it was no gay golden door swinging open, either, but a heavy iron factory door with a time clock beside it. For a second he was scared, wondering what came after that.

"Ten dollars a week—fancy!" Charles Abbott smiled charmingly at his son and pushed aside his plate as tactful reminder of the fabulous dinners to which he was accustomed elsewhere. "Next it will be twelve dollars and by the time you're fifty, my boy, you'll be earning sixteen or eighteen dollars a week. Elsinore, I congratulate you on your son."

"That's all right," said Elsinore absently.

When they did not snatch their meals at Bauer's Chop House, they ate in a corner of the workroom. A gas plate and sink were behind a curtain and usually it was Nettie who fixed the meal—canned beans, soup, and sandwiches, with one of Mrs. Bauer's pies for dessert. Then Nettie pulled out the ironing board and with this as a dining table the meal became a sort of family picnic. Eating together in this way was so intimate that Morry always had to fight against the tenderness he suddenly felt for his family, as if they were like some other family. He wanted to tell about his job, to tell everything that happened from eight in the morning till six at night, what the foreman said, what Hunt Russell said. . . . But you couldn't say these things before your father or Nettie, you had to act as if the whole business was of no consequence to you. If you talked to your mother she listened patiently but never lifted her eyes from her plate, or if she did, made some abstracted reply. It was very hard and Morry ate fast to get out the quicker. After all, when you stopped to think of it, it was sissy for a young man to be eating on an ironing board in a millinery shop.

"I'm surprised he can earn ten dollars," said Nettie. "I'm surprised he could get a job at all, Mr. Abbott, I really am."

Charles broke a sardine sandwich carefully and disdainfully so that, Morry thought, each sardine must apologize for not being an anchovy or a shrimp.

"Oh you're perfectly right, Nettie, Morry isn't the factory type. More of the artist, don't you think? . . . Ten dollars a week. See that you give eight of it to your mother, young man."

"I'm sure he'll give what he can, Charles, stop nagging him," Elsinore said impatiently. She did not see fit to remind Charles that eight dollars a week was more than she had ever had from him and that this solicitude for her, was as a matter of fact exquisitely ironic.

"He ought to give every cent and let Mrs. Abbott give him money when he asks," said Nettie.

Charles nodded approval of this suggestion and Nettie shot a complacent glance in Morry's direction.

"See here," said Charles, "since you're grown up enough to work why don't you take care of your mother—a great lummox like you sitting up there reading all winter while your poor mother has to go out to dances alone. You ought to be ashamed."

"Charles—I—" began Elsinore.

Charles waved her aside.

"It won't hurt him to take you to and from places when I'm away," he went on virtuously. "I don't like you coming home alone at midnight from the Casino dances."

"But—Mr. Abbott—just across the street!" Nettie was incredulous at such beautiful concern. Elsinore kept her eyes on her plate.

"All very well but my wife can't come three steps alone like some common woman. I won't have it. No sir. I never liked to see a woman alone at night. Morry, that won't hurt you, understand, you're to see your mother to and from these dances."

Morry suppressed a groan.

"I can't dance."

"It's time you learned," said Charles sternly. "Seventeen years old and not able to take a woman to a dance!"

"He might as well learn, I suppose," Elsinore said, weary of the wrangling. "He really ought to know how to dance."

The horror of exposing his deficiencies in grace made Morry choke with misery. It was enough getting up early every morning, trying to be as good as hundreds of inferior factory people, wasn't it, without letting himself be the joke of the factory girls and boys at Lamptown public dances. . . .

"Unless, of course, you'd rather go alone, dear," Charles added gently to his wife, his eyes on her face. "If you'd like to have your fun privately of course—"

"Morry will come with me, I'm sure," Elsinore answered evenly.

Morry, dejected, nodded his head.

"Oh, sure," he murmured.

Suddenly Nettie got up and flounced over to the sink, and banged her plate and cup into the dishpan.

"Why shouldn't I take lessons, then—I ought to learn dancing as much as Morry ought," she snapped. "But I suppose I'm to take care of your old shop while Mrs. Abbott and Morry are over at the Casino having a good time."

Elsinore looked up in amazement.

"I thought you liked the shop, Nettie."

"Oh, I like the shop all right," Nettie sulkily answered. "But Morry needn't act so smart with his ten dollars a week and dancing class. I'm sure I could go to Mr. Fischer myself and he'd be glad to give me special private lessons."

"No! That's too ridiculous, Nettie!" Elsinore's voice was harsh.

Something hot surged in her veins, a swift desire to slap Nettie's young impudent mouth for speaking a sacred name so lightly—the thought of Nettie smirking through a dancing lesson alone with Fischer angered her.

"Don't worry, I wouldn't go near the Casino," retorted Nettie. She washed her dishes under the faucet, rattling them against each other. "I don't go out with those factory girls, thank you."

The consciousness of having earned two weeks' salary emboldened Morry.

"What about the factory girls? What's so different about them?" he challenged. "They're as good as you are."

Nettie stared at him with horrified eyes.

"Oh you would say that, Morry Abbott—you would! You'd even go out with them, I suppose—that's just your level. Delaney's back room and factory girls!"

Morry's courage, under his father's contemptuous amusement, faded. He choked down the last of a sandwich and made a dive for the door.

"Don't forget you're taking your mother out next Thursday night," called out his father commandingly, as he slid out.

"I think he's just too terrible, Mrs. Abbott!" declared Nettie. "He's getting coarse, that's what he is."

She helped Elsinore fold up the ironing board while Charles, leaning against the sink, lit a cigarette.

"What do you think of having him as a bodyguard from now on, Else?" he asked, tossing the lighted match into the sink. He did not dare look at her.

"A good idea, Charles," said Elsinore gravely. "Very good, I think."

"Morry's going to be a swell dancer, you know," said Grace Terris, beaming at Morry through her glasses. "Mr. Fischer said he had rhythm. This young man has rhythm, he said the other night."

Jen and Mrs. Bauer both looked at Morry critically to see if this odd quality showed, but apparently it only came out on Thursday nights for he looked just as he always looked. Mrs. Bauer resumed her crocheting and Grace and Jen went on polishing silver.

Jen did not really have to help in the Bauers' kitchen, nor for that matter did Morry have to lounge there late at night this way, but Mrs. Bauer liked to have Jen around and somehow Morry drifted in there too, particularly now that the cold weather made Delaney's stairs unappealing.

"I don't care for a dancing man," pronounced Mrs. Bauer. She twisted her chair to get a view through the dining room of Hermann at the cash register. "Dancing men don't make good husbands."

Grace giggled and looked coyly at Morry. Jen laid down a knife and cleaning rag and stared at her indignantly, then at Morry. Morry was smoking calmly. He didn't even know when someone was flirting with him, Jen thought with disgust.

"Hermann is such a good husband," went on Mrs. Bauer. "I've never had a care. When we were first married it was the same. What, doing the supper dishes when you're so tired, he'd say! No, no, Hulda, he'd say, I won't have you worn out like that. You wait and do them in the morning, he'd say."

Morry yawned. Jen and Grace scoured knives silently and diligently. Grace stole a beguiling glance now and then at Morry, and Jen, puzzled, stared from one to the other.

"I'll never forget one day he called me stupid," Hulda's fat moonface became ruddy with sentiment, her fingers dawdled with the crochet hook, "I was hurt—you know how a young bride is—and then lo and behold! That afternoon a wagon came to the door with a present from Hermann to make it up to me. Two bushels of the finest peaches you ever laid your eyes on. As big as your head, Jen."

"But what could you do with two bushels of peaches?" Jen inquired.

"Can them, dear. Hermann always loved preserved peaches. I put cloves in them and English walnuts. I was up till long after midnight putting them up." Mrs. Bauer smiled wistfully at the glimpse through the doorway of Hermann's bald head. "He was a good husband. Always. If he had to go away on a trip he always said, 'Enjoy yourself, Hulda. Let things go. You can do them all when I get back.' That's your good husband, let me tell you, girls."

"I'm not going to marry anyone in the restaurant business," said Grace. "Believe me."

"I guess you'll marry a railroad man," prophesied Jen. "They're always around."

"Don't pick a dancing man, girls, they're no good," warned Mrs. Bauer. "You never find them in a nice business of their own later on in life."

"I don't see why all a man's for is to be a good husband," Morry objected, "Is that all he's made for?"

"Yes," answered Mrs. Bauer placidly, "that's all."

"Morry dances too well, then," Grace giggled. Not even Cleopatra could have had Grace's complacent assurance of mastery over men. Jen glared at her jealously, and Morry squirmed, uncertain of the cause of the curious tension. "You know the class gets to stay over to the regular dance next week, Morry. Won't it be exciting?"

Morry thought of all the older girls sitting in a row waiting to be asked to dance, and he thought of his own inability to control their motions or to synchronize his own with theirs. He mumbled an evasive agreement with Grace's enthusiasm.

"You and I will have to stick to each other," laughed Grace.

At this point Jen got abruptly to her feet. She wasn't going to be left out of things—she'd get out of her own accord.

"Where you goin', Jen?" Mrs. Bauer demanded in surprise. "I thought you was going to help Grace finish."

"Oh, let her boyfriend help her," Jen retorted haughtily. "I'm going home."

Morry was embarrassed and reached for his cap.

"You're not going home now, are you Morry?" Grace's pale blue eyes conveyed a coquettish challenge but Morry didn't want to understand it. He couldn't help thinking of Grace's thin white thighs as she lay on the table being fitted for a corset by Mrs. Pepper. He grew red at the mere memory.

"Gotta get up early," he explained and started to follow Jen out.

"See you Thursday night at the dance," Grace called.

"Sure," said Morry and reached the door just as Jen let it bang good and hard in his face. Grace laughed shrilly as Morry pulled the door open again.

"A temper, that Jen," said Mrs. Bauer, and counted four stitches under her breath.

"One, two, three, FOUR, one, two, three, FOUR, one, two, three, FOUR," chanted Mr. Fischer, walking backwards, and the line of thirty wooden figures advanced toward him, one, two, three, steps, then kicked out a stiff left foot on the fourth count.

"Right foot first, one, two three—hold it please. Miss Barry is out of step. One, two, three—now, ladies and gentlemen, we'll try it with music. Mr. Sanderson, please."

> "Will someone kindly tell me
> Will someone answer why
> To me it is a riddle
> And will be till I die—"

In a long even row they followed Mr. Fischer across the floor.

"Dance with the lady on your left!" roared Mr. Fischer.

Stiff country boys placed arms around factory girls' hard little bodies, damp hand clutched damp hand, iron foot matched iron foot, and each dancer kept count under his breath. Mr. Fischer clapped his hands and the music stopped.

"The class is getting on magnificently," he said, "I'm sure you will have no trouble at the regular dance tonight. All you need is confidence. I want each and every one of you to dance every dance on the program. Now we'll try it again. Mr. Sanderson, please."

So Mr. Sanderson's thick hands came down on the keys again and young men danced with the ladies on their left. Morry placed a rigid arm around Grace with a one two three kick, and a one two three kick. He thought if he could lose Grace somewhere he might learn but if you danced you had to have a partner as a lawful handicap. No matter how beautifully you waltzed, you'd never have a chance to waltz alone because it wasn't done.

Grace paid no attention to the commands. She tipped her head to one side and smiled perpetually. When she lost count she said, "Oh, I'm just terrible." Then Mr. Fischer would correct her posture.

"Not quite so close, Miss Terris—the arm should not go all the way round the young man's neck."

Solemnly then the fifteen couples stepped around the room behind Fischer, and since they were afraid to lose step by turning around on the corners, the dance became nothing more than a march with odd little jerks on the fourth count.

"Fine!" said Mr. Fischer and clapped his hands twice. "The class for this evening is now over. You will please remain for the regular Ball."

And then the rope at the door was let down and the line of people waiting outside were allowed to present their tickets and enter. The drummer arrived and experimented with his instrument, gravely aided by Mr. Sanderson. Crowds of giggling girls, with chiffon scarfs over their curled hair, hurried from the door to the dressing room, and their vivid perfumes mixed intoxicatingly in the air. Mr. Fischer stood by the ticket man at the door, shaking hands with this or that one, greeting everyone with formal politeness, while his black eyes shot appraisingly from time to time toward the cash-box. Then he tweaked the ends of his white bow tie and whirled around toward the dance floor.

"Dance Number One!" he shouted above the excited chattering. "Dance Number One!"

The music began again and men slid from the doorway to the women's dressing room across the floor to select their partners as they emerged. Morry Abbott stood beside the solitary palm-tree, first on one foot and then the other. His breath came fast and he had to struggle with a feeling that he, too, could sway and whirl with marvellous ease. This assured feeling must be checked, he thought, before he impulsively invited someone to dance and then woke to his inadequacy with a load of responsibility in his arms. So he went into the smoking room and sat down by one of the brakemen he'd seen in Bill Delaney's often. The young man, dressed up in a much too blue suit and a green tie, was looking through a magazine of photographs. On the paper cover was painted a cream-white blonde in a very decollete spangled silver dress. The man rapped the picture with his pipe and looked up at Morry.

"There she is," he said proudly. "That's her. Lillian Russell. A looker, eh?"

Morry squinted at it judicially.

"All right," he granted. But she was beautiful as no woman could ever be, at least, he thought, no woman in Lamptown. Underneath was printed, "America's Most Beautiful Actress."

"You bet she's all right," insisted his friend. "I'd marry her like a shot, I would."

He picked up the magazine and stuffed it into his pocket.

"Like to cut these out to paste up in my room," he explained, as he started out. "So long."

Through the door Morry could see Grace dancing with one of the engineers who ate at Bauer's, and he was amazed that she seemed no different in action than the other girls on the floor. He had rather expected everyone to stop dancing and point the finger of shame at her. Since they didn't seem to notice her errors, he felt encouraged to go out on the floor again, and when the music stopped he boldly asked Grace for the next.

"Isn't it swell, Morry?" gurgled Grace. "I'm having a lot of fun, aren't you?"

Now that the dance had started it was all easy, easier than the lesson, for in this crowd your feet were not observed. Then in his arms Grace changed curiously. She was not the Bauers' waitress at all, a thin blonde with glasses, but a stranger, a stranger who belonged mysteriously to dancehalls and to music and perfume.

"Like Lillian Russell," Morry thought and if he just kept looking at Grace's curious blue eyes it almost seemed that she had on a silver dress. When the dance was over Grace kept her hand on his arm, but Morry thought, "I wouldn't dare ask her for another dance just yet."

He went back to the smoking room to wait the proper length of time for he did not dare ask any other girl. The boys his age who hung around Bill Delaney's saloon did not dance, they stood in a little group outside the hall door smoking and sometimes jeering at friends inside. Before this night Morry thought he would have died at their ragging, but when they called teasingly to him two or three times he was not afraid to answer back with certain pride. After all he was the one on the inside.

Elsinore was there. Morry caught a glimpse of her slender black-gowned figure without knowing who she was for a few seconds, and then he wondered at the flare of pride he had in her. He tried to puzzle out just why she stood out among the others. Was it because the factory girls were all powdered and painted and wore loud colors, was it because she was his mother, or was it that she looked startlingly out of place without a background of hats and trimmings? She looked over her partner's shoulder from across the room and smiled faintly at her son. Suddenly Morry wanted to do something wonderful for his mother, something to make her glad of him; but what could one do?

"It's almost over, Morry," Grace said, standing beside him. "We ought not to miss this one."

Morry obediently started dancing with her. She pressed against him with a sigh.

"You seem a lot older somehow than some of the railroad fellas," she said. "I don't know why, but you do. More like somebody that's been around, know what I mean?"

Morry wished she wouldn't talk. It made him lose count and it made the picture of the woman in the silver dress fade further away. Couples were dancing very close and very quietly now. Grace kept her head demurely on his shoulder. He wasn't quite sure what was expected of him but knew something was.

"Do you want to stay for the other dance?" he found himself asking her. "It's the Home Waltz."

Grace looked at him thoughtfully.

"We could go now," she said. "If we go down the backstairs no one will notice us. My room is right at the back—just above the kitchen."

They danced around again. Morry's head was swimming. He saw his mother, he saw Hunt with Dode and Mr. Fischer, and he wondered if they knew about this spinning in the head, a sort of premonition of disaster, yet you couldn't exactly call it disaster.

"You go first—I'll follow," he whispered, and Grace dropped out of his arms with a sweet smile. Presently he saw her, with her wrap over her arm, going out and he got his hat and followed, after a few minutes. He went along the dirty outside hallway to the back where a staircase went down to the Bauers' rooms on the second floor. Morry fumbled his way down the pitch-dark stairs. On the second floor there was another dark old hallway with a gas jet dimly flickering in the far end. No one was in sight, but Morry's heart stopped at the creaking of the old floor beneath his feet. He passed dark doors with tin numbers tacked on—'27'—'29'—'31'—and the sweat came out on his forehead wondering what would happen if one of these doors should suddenly open. It wasn't likely though, for a lodger didn't come to Bauer's more than four or five times a year....

At the end of the hall water leaked slowly from the ceiling above and made a dirty puddle beneath the gas jet. Morry wanted to drop the whole business and run. He thought with a shock of horror that he was to have taken his mother home, that indeed had been the sole purpose of his dancing lessons. . . . It was too late now—or was it? . . . Then he saw Grace motioning to him from the farthest doorway. She held her finger to her lips warningly. Oh, yes, it was too late now....

Morry, with sinking heart, tiptoed toward her. She reached out a thin bare arm and pulled him coquettishly in, and the door swung swiftly shut behind him.

Old Mrs. Delaney stood inside the Bon Ton's workroom door. She had on her black bonnet and black mitts and a market basket on her arm. It was barely breakfast time, and Nettie had only a moment before unlocked the shop door. Elsinore was washing the coffee cups at the sink.

"What is it?" she wanted to know in some surprise.

"I want to tell you this much, Mrs. Abbott," said the old woman. "It's got to stop or I speak to your husband. That's all I came to say."

Nettie sat down quickly to her sewing so that she would have an excuse to hear all. Elsinore stood looking at her caller, puzzled and alarmed.

"But what is it? What are you talking about? Is it about Morry?"

"Who else would it be about?" snapped the old woman. "It's about that boy of yours all right. Things have got to stop, that's what I'm telling you."

Nettie tried to keep on sewing casually but she had to look up every now and then, first to the old woman and then to the hall doorway, because she had heard Morry's footsteps outside. He was out there now listening, she thought, listening and afraid to pass the door lest he be called in.

"But Morry's a good boy," Elsinore protested. "I can't see what he's done to worry you, Mrs. Delaney."

"He's going on eighteen, ain't he?" retorted Mrs. Delaney. "Old enough to be getting girls in trouble. I speak out that way, Mrs. Abbott, because an adopted girl's a big responsibility. I'm telling you he's got to stay away from my Jen."

Nettie sewed furiously and kept an eye furtively on Elsinore. But Elsinore just stood there looking quietly at the old woman. Mrs. Delaney sat down on one of the work stools.

"I don't mean to worry you, Mrs. Abbott—I don't mean you're not a lady," she muttered in a gruff attempt at apology. "Only when you've taken a girl from the Home and she's got old ideas and an older boy keeps hanging around her—well, she's got bad blood in her, that Jen. . . . You can't trust bad blood, you know."

"Morry has never cared about girls," Elsinore said. "He'd never dream of bothering your Jen."

Mrs. Delaney's gnarled fingers tightened over the market basket.

"I'm telling you he does, Mrs. Abbott," she said somberly. "He carries on with the Bauers' waitress—Hulda Bauer told me that. And don't I hear him and Jen out on the steps night after night whispering and talking? Don't I hear her out there cryin' and snifflin' when he don't show up? That's what I'm telling you."

"Oh! Oh!" came from Nettie Farrell's mouth, and Elsinore looked at her, rather surprised.

"That's bad when girls cry over someone," Nettie said hurriedly. "I'm sure Morry isn't as good as you think because you're his mother and you don't see anything. Things right under your nose, too. But he's always going over to that saloon—I could tell you that much—and when you ask men in there about him they say they haven't seen him. He goes upstairs to see that girl, that's all."

"That's right," confirmed Mrs. Delaney.

"But what harm is there in it?" Elsinore argued gently. "A child like that—barely fourteen—"

"Pooh!" sniffed Nettie. "That kind learn young."

"She's got old ideas," insisted Mrs. Delaney. "Old ideas and wild blood in her and outside of that I trust no young girl. They're all alike, crazy to get into trouble, always stuck on the boys. I've had 'em go wrong with me before and I won't have it this time."

"But Morry's so safe," Elsinore said incredulously.

"I don't trust him neither," the old woman flashed back. "What's his father, I ask? A hard drinker and a fast man. I don't mind coming out with truths once in a while when it's necessary. That boy's old enough to know what he's about and you've got to keep him away from my Jen. Hear me?"

Elsinore could only nod weakly. Mrs. Delaney got up, panting a little. She drew her black shawl over her humped old back, jerked her bonnet down over her ears.

"I said I'd come and I did," she grumbled. "I said I'd put a stop to it and I did. I won't have any more girls in my house going wrong. Won't have it."

She went out the door banging it angrily behind her. Nettie held her needle transfixed in the air and her mouth wide open. Elsinore stood still and thoughtful for a moment, then sat down and picked up a ribbon she was to shir. Suddenly Nettie threw her sewing down and her shears.

"That boy!" she exclaimed. "You can see it's all true—he's running after that girl just because she's wild and now he's working in the factory and dancing he thinks he can do whatever he pleases. What are you going to say to him, Mrs. Abbott? Or will you tell his father?"

"Oh no, I wouldn't ever tell Charles," Elsinore murmured. "And after all, Nettie, Mrs. Delaney's so old she gets funny ideas. Morry isn't a bad boy at all."

"But he's grown up, nearly, and you can't tell what he'd do if girls started getting after him," Nettie rushed on. "He thinks he's so smart, not paying attention to them. He just acts that way to show off. Then he goes and picks some little foundling over a saloon! He would!"

Elsinore went to the drawer for a cluster of satin ribbons. There was a creaking of boards in the hall outside. Nettie jerked her head significantly.

"I knew he was out there!" she whispered. "He heard every word! He was afraid to let on he was out there."

The cloud on Elsinore's horizon lifted with dazzling speed.

"He really heard, do you think?"

Nettie nodded impatiently.

"Of course he did. Shall I go call him in for you to talk to?"

"Not now, Nettie," Elsinore said and Nettie's face fell.

Her full red lips pursed into a sullen line. Mrs. Abbott was afraid to talk about things to Morry, it was silly how shy she was with her own son that way. She'd rather let him run wild than speak up to him. It angered Nettie. She got up and walked determinedly to the hall door. She opened it swiftly and was in time to see Morry sliding out on tiptoe, his dark face burning red. Nettie whirled back.

"He did hear! He stood there listening!" she was triumphant. "Serve him right, too. And now's the time for the whistle to blow and he's late to work besides. Oh, you must talk to him, Mrs. Abbott."

"If he heard us, then he knows all there is for me to say," Elsinore said tranquilly. "I needn't go into it any further."

She never even looked up to say this. Nettie stabbed her needle into her straw braid and muttered something quite savage under her breath.

Lamptown hummed from dawn to dusk with that mysterious humming of the Works, the monotonous switching of engines and coupling of cars at the Yard. The freight cars rumbled back and forth across the heart of town. They slid out past the factory windows and brakemen swinging lanterns on top the cars would shout to whatever girls they saw working at the windows. Later, in the factory washroom one girl might whisper to another, "Kelly's in the Yard today. Said be sure and be at Fischer's Thursday night."

"Who was firing?" the other would ask, mindful of a beau of her own.

"Fritz was in the cab but I couldn't see who was firing. Looked like that Swede of Ella's used to be on Number 10."

The humming of this town was jagged from time to time by the shriek of an engine whistle or the bellow of a factory siren or the clang-clang of a red street car on its way from one village to the next. The car jangled through the town flapping doors open and shut, admitting and discharging old ladies on their way to a D.A.R. picnic in Norwalk, section workers or linesmen in overalls, giggling girls on their way to the Street Carnival in Chicago Junction. As if hunting for something very important the car rattled past the long row of Lamptown's factory boarding houses, past the Lots, then on into long stretches of low, level hay fields where farm girls pitched hay, stopping to wave their huge straw hats at the gay world passing by in a street car.

There was gray train smoke over the town most days, it smelled of travel, of transcontinental trains about to flash by, of important things about to happen. The train smell sounded the 'A' for Lamptown and then a treble chord of frying hamburger and onions and boiling coffee was struck by Hermann Bauer's kitchen, with a sostenuto of stale beer from Delaney's back door. These were all busy smells and seemed a 6 to 6 smell, a working town's smell, to be exchanged at the last factory whistle for the festival night odors of popcorn, Spearmint chewing gum, barber-shop pomades, and the faint smell of far-off damp cloverfields. Mornings the cloverfields retreated when the first Columbus local roared through the town. Bauer's coffee pot boiled over again, and the factory's night watchmen filed into Delaney's for their morning beer.

It was always the last minute when Morry left his house for work and on this morning he had been trapped into eavesdropping on Mrs. Delaney and his mother. If he only could have gotten out of the house before she said those dreadful things. He slipped out of the alleyway, his hands jammed into his pockets, his cap slouched over his eyes, and he burned with shame thinking of what the old lady had said to his mother. He'd never look at Jen again without remembering—never! Of course it wasn't Jen's fault but he was angry with her, too. She was the one who called him to come over, wasn't she? He only went because the kid was lonesome, never saw anybody else hardly, didn't seem to make friends in school. Now he was afraid of her. Next time she called he wouldn't hear her.

Along Market Street the shopkeepers were out lowering their awnings, shouting their morning greetings across the street to each other, or peering from behind their show windows at rival window displays. Old Tom, Lamptown's street cleaner, sat on the curbstone in front of the Saloon in dirty white painter's overalls, broom in hand, and held a sort of welcoming reception for all passersby.

"Morning, Mr. Robinson. Morning, Miss Burnet. Howdy, Morry, how's your old lady? Late today, ain't you? I just see the last of the girls going in."

Morry crossed the street before he remembered Grace, and there she was in the Bauers' window smiling at him significantly. Morry jerked his head into a sort of nod of greeting and went on. He was ashamed of his winter's affair with Grace. In the saloon the trainmen talked about her. "God's gift to the Big Four," they called her. Morry hated her. She always acted as if he was hers, always beaming at him when he went by and lifting her eyebrows so knowingly. He was eighteen now. He wasn't going to work in the factory all his life, was he, and run with waitresses. . . . Maybe he'd better get a job on the train. You saw cities that way and in the right one you could drop off and start doing things. But do what? Something, this much he knew, that would make his mother very proud of him, because now he felt overwhelmingly grateful to her. He knew she wouldn't say a word to him about Mrs. Delaney's visit and about Jen—as far back as he could remember she had never said anything to reproach him. She could easily have called him after the old woman left and scolded him, but how could they ever have looked at each other saying such intimate things? . . .

He knew. He'd get out of this town, that's what he'd do. He'd study— but what did you study? Fellows went to college but that cost money and nobody in Lamptown went to college, except a guy now and then who went to Case Engineering School in Cleveland. Fellows in Lamptown went into the Works or into their fathers' stores or on the railroad. If they got on the railroad, they stuck there. It was like the Navy, they said, you had a hard time working into a regular job after you got out. . . . All right then, he'd stick to the factory. He'd work until he owned the Factory, that's what he'd do. He'd work—hell, he hated to work. He hated plugging away at lamps and accessories. He wasn't adept like the girls and he felt perpetually ill at ease around them. They worked faster than he did and made more money, and they kidded him.

Morry could remember when he was only six he was so overgrown that the little girls were afraid of him. "He's so big!" they sobbed into the teacher's lap. "We don't want him to play in our games." Now even when the girls in the packing room smiled invitingly to him, he was sure they were making fun of him; he didn't know where to hide when they whispered, "Morry Abbott's a swell-looker now, ain't he? Look at them shoulders!"

He would always feel like the unwanted stranger with these factory girls. He wasn't like them—he wasn't like the fellows in the saloon, either. He'd be a big somebody some day, a big gun—but Morry didn't see himself grubbing away, getting there a little at a time. He saw himself already arrived, a Hunt Russell, a somebody who got there without plugging. Got where, though? . . . Morry saw himself on the decks of great liners, sitting on balconies in tropical cities, always at ease, always secure from Netties and fathers and Graces. He was the master of this fabulous orange grove, he was the manager of this beautiful actress, he was the owner of this estate on the Hudson, stocked with books, thousands of them, and pictures, and liquor, too, French wines and things that weren't so hard to drink as Delaney's Scotch. He'd—but here he was at the factory, twenty minutes late to punch the time-clock.

"Docked again," jeered the office boy in a jubilant whisper. Morry sidled through Door 6 to his table in the packing room. His foreman came toward him scowling.

"With men out of work all over this country," he began sternly, "it seems a damn shame, Abbott, that a fellow with the luck to have a job can't get to it on time. Now, I'll tell you what's coming to you if this keeps up. . . ."

But really Lamptown was no place for a boy, Mrs. Pepper said.

Take Mansfield or Norwalk or Elyria—pretty little towns they were, every one of them, with nice homes on pleasant boulevards and lovely girls for a young man to marry. But Lamptown! All railroad tracks and factory warehouses and for a park nothing but the factory woods or the acres of Lots which were nothing but clover fields with big signs every few yards—

"LOTS $40 an acre and up
See HUNT RUSSELL—"

Rows of gray frame factory boarding houses on dusty roads in the east and to the west the narrow noisy Market Street—choose your home between these two sections.

"Really, Mrs. Abbott, actually you know," gravely said Mrs. Pepper, "it's not the place at all for a young man. Don't you know anyone in Columbus or Cleveland who would board him there—some place where he would have opportunities?"

"If Morry went to the city he'd get a swelled head and never be anything," declared Nettie crossly. "I don't see what's the matter with Lamptown, if he's any good he can get on here. The trouble with Morry is he thinks he's too good for everybody here. He's too good for the girls, he stays upstairs and reads novels instead of acting like a regular fellow."

"I'd hate to have him go away," Elsinore murmured. "I wouldn't know what to do without Morry."

Nettie looked to Mrs. Pepper for sympathy.

"As if he ever talked to anyone or as if he was any company to you," she said sarcastically. "Why, Mrs. Abbott, you know you hardly ever talk to each other."

Elsinore put her hand to her forehead and smoothed it thoughtfully.

"I know, but you see that's just it. We don't need to talk to each other. We never have needed to talk to each other."

Mrs. Pepper tried to assume an understanding expression.

"I know," she sighed, "Indeed I know."

She went to the mirror and daintily replaced a straying lock of hair behind her ear. Nettie watched her with critical eyes.

"Pretty dress," she said.

Mrs. Pepper was pleased.

"I got it in Akron," she explained. She patted her hips and turned around to view the skin-tight perfection of the back. "Cute, isn't it?"

Nettie examined it and urged Elsinore to admire its lines. It was a tight silk dress bursting into irrepressible ruffles at the hem and at the wrist,

and yoked with tiny lace ruffling deep on her bosom so that a garnet sunburst was coquettishly lost there. A circlet of tiny pearls followed a seductive line around her fat creamy throat and was matched by a pearl and
opal ring on her fat little finger.

"I wonder," mused Mrs. Pepper leaning further toward the mirror,
twisting her head a little to one side, "if perhaps my neck is a little too
plump for pearls."

Over her pearls and the sunburst her dove-like little hands hovered
ceaselessly. She sat down again and the wide silk bows on her tiny kid
slippers flopped down like the ears of a sleepy dachshund. Sometimes
when she was crossing the freight Yard a young fireman would stick his
head out of the cab and yell, "Hello Fatty!" This would make Mrs.
Pepper tighten her little red mouth to keep from smiling for after all
there was something flatteringly endearing in the term 'Fatty.' But when
she kept her lips so sternly from smiling three dimples popped out in her
cheeks and the next bold fireman was likely to call out, "Hi there,
Dimples." So Mrs. Pepper, after many such experiences had decided that
men were always teases and there was no use being cross with them.

"Lamptown does make the young men rough, you know that," Mrs.
Pepper pursued, now doing her nails carefully while Nettie stood in the
doorway looking up and down Market Street for possible customers. "If
you traveled from town to town the way I do you'd know. People say this
is the toughest town on the Big Four."

"It doesn't have as many bad houses as other towns," Nettie said without turning around.

"Well, you see, there are all those factory girls," delicately innuendoed
Mrs. Pepper with a blush. "Not that some of them aren't lovely girls, understand, and they do take the best care of their figures. Only last week I
took orders from the girls for upwards of sixty dollars worth of corsets."

"This shop couldn't do without the girls," Elsinore reminded her.
"We've got no kick, Mrs. Pepper, you and I."

"I know—I'm saying the girls give me my living," Mrs. Pepper hurried to explain, "but I only mean it's not a good town for a boy. I don't see
how you ever raised him to be so decent in such a rough place."

"I did my best," said Elsinore and then she thought of Morry.

She thought of Morry consciously so seldom that she came to the subject with almost a shock. Morry—grown up! Morry—old enough to go
away just as she'd gotten used to having a baby around the shop. Because

even as a baby he'd been a stranger—oh yes, part of her in some curious way that made his presence always welcome, but nonetheless he was a stranger. She wondered if other mothers were perpetually astonished at their maternity and secretly a little skeptical of the miracle, more willing to believe in the cabbage patch or stork legend than in their own biological responsibility. She had moved over for Morry as you would move over for someone on a street car, certain that the intimacy is only for a few minutes, but now it was eighteen years and she thought why, Morry was hers, hers more than anything in the world was.

"Don't I know you did your best with that child?" exclaimed Mrs. Pepper. "She had a lonely time of it too, Nettie, let me tell you—Mrs. Abbott had no easy time."

Elsinore stared at Mrs. Pepper's shoe ribbon flapping on the floor, and for a second she ached for that lost baby with startling pain. The young man Morry they spoke of was hers only because he too could remember the baby. Upstairs in the front bedroom he had been born—with Charles away of course. Charles only came home twice a year then, but Elsinore never complained. Husbands were like that, and Morry and his mother understood.

Whenever Charles did come home Elsinore and the baby moved into the little room, now Morry's, because crying inspired Charles to frenzies of temper. Elsinore's calm protection of the baby annoyed Charles even more than the crying. Both Morry and his mother were relieved when Charles picked up his sample cases and went away. Once Morry, aged two, had gotten into the sample cases and found them full of candies. Usually just before he came home a printed business postcard arrived with the red-lettered tidings—

"The Candy Man will visit you on—"

Then the date was written in by Charles and after digesting this warning Elsinore let the baby have the postcard with its cartooned Candy Man. Charles beat the child after that invasion of his wares so that ever afterward the arrival of the Candy Man's card sent Morry under the bed or downstairs hiding in one of the hat drawers. Indeed Elsinore suspected that it was the beginning of his learning to read.

Elsinore, thinking of all this now, forgot to sew and the black ribbon in her lap that was to be a turban, unrolled on the floor.

"Do you remember when I used to keep Morry in his baby carriage all day in front of the shop?" she asked Mrs. Pepper.

Mrs. Pepper sighed.

"Oh dear yes. . . . He was such a big baby and you were so small to be taking care of him. . . . I only had one model to sell then, the Diana Girdle. Gracious, what a long time ago. Let's see—he was three or four when I started working . . . hm. . . . I was twenty. Just twenty. Imagine that."

"Think of it, you and Mrs. Abbott were making your own living then just the way I am now," Nettie said, coming back to the counter and leaning her elbows on it, "and you didn't think anything much of it, but all the same Mrs. Abbott thinks it would be too bad for Morry to get out on his own. And he's eighteen. Older than his mother was when she started this shop."

"I need a man here with me," Elsinore said, irritated. "There's no use your talking about it, Nettie, I need Morry. You don't understand these things at all."

"Some factory girl will marry him and that'll be the end of him," grumbled Nettie.

Mrs. Pepper, as always, strove to soothe everyone by switching their interest.

"There are so many of the girls, you can't blame them for going after the younger men," she said. "Nine hundred girls, all young and lively there at the Works with no men's factory around to give them beaux. Why Mr. Fischer tells me half the time they have to dance with each other at the Casino because there aren't enough men."

"There's never enough men. . . . A girl's got no chance in this town," Nettie complained. "There's twenty-five of us for every man. Every time a new man comes to town it's like dividing a mouse up for a hundred cats. If I was a boy in this town I'd almost be afraid to grow up, I would."

"No chance for a girl to marry," Elsinore said, as if marrying were still to her mind the ideal state for any woman.

"Sometimes the girls go away and marry," Mrs. Pepper said brightly. "Dode O'Connell told me they write their addresses on the crates that are shipped out from the factory and they get answers back sometimes from all over the world. That little Tucker girl they say went all the way to Australia to marry a man she'd never seen. He'd gotten her address from the shipment and they started writing each other."

"Yes, they'd all go to Australia at that factory if they got the same chance," said Nettie gloomily. "Those girls do anything to get a man. They hang around the high school freshmen even. They're wild for men.

I've seen 'em calling up to Morry's window sometimes after he's gone upstairs, telling him to come out and take a walk."

Elsinore was puzzled and startled too. This was so new to her, considering her son as a potential husband for someone.

"But he doesn't go out," she said.

Nettie laughed sardonically.

"Oh no, only if she's real pretty and then maybe he goes out. Or if he's on his way to go over and see that Delaney kid, that Jen."

Elsinore stared at Nettie.

"But he doesn't go over there any more, Nettie, I'm quite sure."

"They sit on the top stairs still plenty of times," Nettie blurted out indignantly. "That's what they do. And if he isn't with her then he's in the saloon or probably with some little tart from the factory. That's the way Morry Abbott is and that's the way he's always going to be."

"But you said a little while ago that he thought he was too good for the Lamptown girls," protested Elsinore.

"Too good for good girls!" Nettie flared up. "That's what I meant."

Her nose quite red Nettie whirled into the back room and for several minutes Elsinore and Mrs. Pepper heard her banging drawers shut and whistling shrilly to indicate how well under control was her temper.

"How funny Nettie acts about things," Elsinore commented.

She bent frowning over her work once more and the little chamber of her mind marked "Morry—Private Thoughts"—swung slowly shut again. Mrs. Pepper picked up her orangestick again and coaxed an elegant half-moon on her rosy thumbnail.

Mrs. Pepper thought the crying doll was simply sweet, but Nettie detested it because ever since Charles Abbott had sent it, the factory girls were constantly running into the shop to listen to it.

"Wind it up for Ethel, now," they would beg, and Nettie, with a scowl of resignation would take the doll out of the show window, reach under its red satin ruffles and wind it up again. A thin little tinkle of doll music wailed faintly through the shop, while the girls listened in rapt silence.

"This is a hat shop, not a doll store," she complained to Elsinore.

"Charles says in the city the best hat shops always have a doll in the window," said Elsinore. "He wouldn't like it if he came home and didn't see it there. After all he sent it for that purpose."

"Well, you don't have to wind it, but I do," muttered Nettie, not really meaning her employer to hear her mutiny, but always unable to keep her annoyance to herself.

Elsinore was used to Charles sending strange presents. He sent seaweed picture frames from Florida, enormous bottles of perfume from New York, knowing she never cared for scents; once he sent her a pair of chameleons which alarmed her so that Mrs. Pepper with many delighted squeals took them away. He never sent her money or any practical thing. Usually if Charles fancied an article he bought three, one for the blonde girl in Chicago, one for Elsinore, and one for the last hotel telephone operator he had entertained. If Elsinore suspected this she never said so. She kept his gifts carefully wrapped up, as a rule, and wrote him polite little letters of thanks.

"The doll must have cost twenty dollars," declared Mrs. Pepper. "What a thoughtful husband, Mrs. Abbott. You are lucky! And letters almost every day Nettie says. Did he always write you every day?"

"Oh no," said Elsinore, "only lately."

Charles's letters . . .

"I suppose you think I don't know what you're doing while I'm gone. You think because I'm away you can get away with anything you like. Else, old girl, you'd better get that out of your head. I know you too well, and I can tell when things aren't right. Answer me this—why did you get two new silk dresses last fall if it wasn't to show some man? What made you start in powdering your face when you never used to do more than brush it off with a chamois? Think that over, Else, and you'll realize your husband's not so dumb as you think. . . ."

Then a few days later from another town . . .

"Well, while I'm lying here in this rotten little hotel with the grippe, I suppose you're having your good time, going to your dances and dancing with this guy whoever he is! I guess you didn't notice me watching you when you dressed for the dance last time I was home. I pretended to be reading the paper but out of the corner of my eye I saw you put perfume on your hair, the way a chorus girl does when she's got a date. You did up your hair and looked at yourself in the mirror and then took it all down again and did it over. I said to you, why did you do that, and you said, oh it makes me look so old the other way.

"Yes, I went to the Casino and I stood out in the smoking room watching you as I guess you knew because you were too smart for me and knew better than to give yourself away that night. If you've fallen for one of those train men you're a damn fool, Else, and I'll lick the man if I ever see him, I swear I will."

Elsinore wrote her usual brief letter in reply, ignoring all of Charles's suspicions, but this made him write even more insistently. Sometimes she opened a letter, came to an accusing paragraph, and tore up the letter, not angrily, but quite coolly, because what she read might stay in her mind, so she had to protect herself from all disturbing thoughts.

"You said in your letter two weeks ago you were either going to Cleveland or Columbus for some velvets in a few days. Then yesterday in your letter you never said anything about the trip. It's easy to see that you made that trip all right and just don't want to tell about it. It wasn't on any millinery business either but to meet someone. I can just see you going to some hotel there thinking your husband is far away up in Minnesota and won't know what you're up to, but I got enough brains to read women and I can read between the lines, don't forget it."

If Elsinore herself could read between the lines she would have seen the erasure marks on the crying doll package when it arrived. She might have detected another woman's address written in pencil and then rubbed out and she would have concluded that the crying doll had been originally purchased for someone else, someone with a taste for such novelties. And then inexplicably Charles had decided that his wife should have it, instead. She might, too, have thought from his letters, "No one but a person who has been guilty himself could read guilt in others so well."

But Elsinore would not allow such thoughts to become important. If she permitted Charles's slowly developing jealousy to worry her, then it might creep in her mind when she was dreaming of really vital things, of Fischer, for instance. There had never been a moment that Charles existed in her imagination. Charles—well Charles *was.* He was not real. His letters—his jealousy—these things *were,* and things that *were* could not enter Elsinore's mind except it gave her pleasure. She wondered if Fischer himself were as real as her thoughts of him.

When she sat fashioning a hat silently, there was no room in her for fretting over an absent husband's suspicion; there was room only to listen to the mechanical rhythm of Mr. Sanderson's piano thumping, there was room only to see Fischer at the Casino, or in the Palace, in Marion, or Akron, or Cleveland, demonstrating a pirouette with his shining patent-leather feet. . . . She had no time to wonder over Charles's wanderings, for she was wondering what fresh-cheeked young girl was at this minute being selected as Fischer's partner. Did this fortunate one have blue eyes and yellow hair? Unconsciously Elsinore discarded the red ribbon for the hat under her hand and selected a blue strip more suitable to this blonde image. Did the new love have a baby face or did she have, in spite of her youth and fairness, a strong handsome nose like Nettie's with the same full lips . . . with this new image Elsinore tore the blue strip off of the frame and from the deep drawer beside her drew out a wider model, more becoming to long noses. With thoughtful eyes she tried the blue velvet strip across the front and underneath the brim.

Nettie watched this changing design, bewildered.

"Will you please tell me, Mrs. Abbott, why you threw away the poke for that big milan?"

Elsinore's reply left her assistant completely baffled.

"Because a girl with a nose like that shouldn't wear a poke. You know that well enough, Nettie."

"Like what? What are you talking about?" asked Nettie, still staring, and Elsinore, conscious of Nettie's scrutiny, turned her head away ever so slightly, as if Nettie might read there a whole catalogue of hat designs for Fischer's probable women.

"I was thinking of something else, Nettie," she said. "I was thinking that next week we must make an entire new outfit for the crying doll— something in rose-colored velvet, I think. . . . And remind me to write Charles and thank him."

She wished Nettie wouldn't ask things—she wished people wouldn't always intrude.

Charles came home late in the summer. He was thinner and without a new line in his face or a single new gray hair he managed to seem ten years older. He walked into the Bon Ton one Saturday afternoon with no greeting but a "Pretty as ever I see, Nettie" for Nettie, an ironic "Well,

Mrs. Abbott" for Elsinore and then seeing Morry in the workroom eating a sandwich he scowled.

"Still hanging around your mother's skirts, I see."

Morry never answered. If he lived to be eighty his father's mockery would still make him curl up with hopeless shame and mortification. A mere glance from his father would always be enough to remind him that he was a huge clumsy fellow—with no more business in a house, least of all a woman's millinery store—than some prize steer. He was taller than his father by at least six inches, but this could only give him a feeling of inferiority. With his father home there was less than ever a place for him here. While Charles took his bags upstairs, Morry quietly dove out the back alley. Where would he go? He didn't think Delaney's was safe because it was a hang-out of his father's. Bauer's Chop House had been out of the question for some time, because Morry shuddered at the mere sight of Grace now. She was apt to say whenever she saw him, "When am I going to see you again, Morry? What's the matter—are you afraid of me?"

Morry stood out in the alleyway, lighting a cigarette, looking up and down the street. He wondered if old Mrs. Delaney was in—if it was safe to run up Jen's stairs. But he didn't really want to see Jen. He was vaguely annoyed with her now. The kid was always tagging after him and the old woman glared at him like some old witch every time he had the bad luck to run into her. The only thing—and this Morry would scarcely admit even to himself—was that nobody believed so firmly in Morry's importance as Jen did. She thought he was somebody. Away from her he remembered the old lady's warning, Nettie's taunts, and the factory girls' kidding. But with Jen he fell under the sweet spell of her worship, her reverent, adoring eyes, her perfect conviction that he was incredibly superior to anyone in the world. While Morry stood in the alley weighing these matters he heard Nettie's voice inside answering some inquiry of his father's.

"No, he's gone out, Mr. Abbott. He's probably up on the Delaney's backstairs with that girl of theirs. He always is there."

This decided him. He threw away his cigarette quickly and hurried through the courtyard to the saloon backdoor.

"Kid Abbott!" roared Hogan as Morry sauntered up to the bar. "Don't he look like a prizefighter though? Say, wait till he gets mad once! Look at the chest on him, will you, Delaney? Got that delivering bonnets for his

ma. Look at them shoulders. Say, there's muscle for you. Kid, you're all
right. Understand? You're OK and I like you. Delaney, another beer for
the Lamptown heavyweight."

"What about the factory laying off men, Abbott, anything in it?" Bill
leaned across the bar toward Morry but Morry, as usual, had heard none
of the inside rumors.

Three men sitting at a card table started grumbling.

"Yeah, Russell would lay off the men before he would the women.
That redhead of his would see to that. . . ."

"I seen in the Dispatch that Lamptown Works was cutting out the accessories. Next the Works will go," Hogan said. "You fellows will be out
in less than six months, the factory will be closed up unless the girls keep
it open for their own private business, eh, Bill?"

"Russell's all right, he's got enough dough," one of the men at the table
said. "If the Works gets shaky he can put money back into it. I ain't worried so long as my thirty-two fifty comes in every payday."

"Yeah, and what if Russell ain't all right," Hogan argued, his nose now
a bright pink. "Who's going to pick up the pieces of this town, then? As I
see it the whole damned town goes round to Russell's tune and if he stops
the town stops. What's he ever done but inherit the money that lets things
skid along on their own wheels while he sits there on his twaloo or runs
around with cookies."

"Say, Hogan, you don't know it all, just because you live in Bucyrus
and shook hands once with Bishop Brown. What the hell do you know
about Lamptown? You run down the tracks here once or twice on a
three-wheeler and you think you saw everything. Who's you, squintin'
into beer steins and spoutin' Colonel R. G. Ingersoll?" The overalled mechanic from the Works spat toward the cuspidor and missed. "Let me tell
you this guy Hunt Russell's got brains, he don't have to break his back
learning things. He's got the brains of this town as well as the kale."

Hogan went over to the table and planted both hands on it. A couple of
chips rolled under the table and were stopped by a big rubber boot.

"All right, he's got brains, has he? Listen, if he had brains, do you
think he'd let his town—the town his old man made—be the state honey-
dump? Do you think he'd sit up there on his pink plush carpets eating
his little bonbons while the town around him stood rotting? He's the
guy here with the power and he's got the money. Why, if he had any
brains he'd wipe out your Market Street there and build a row of office

buildings down to Extension Avenue, he'd tear out that street of old boarding houses and build a big swell hotel, he'd get himself made mayor and throw out all these Irish politicians from Shantyville, he'd have all the sayso and by Judas he'd say something, he'd build chateaux on his lots, yonder, chateaux with gardens around them. He'd make this little mud-hole the gardenspot of Ohio, he'd make playgrounds for his employees. But does he do it? Hell, no."

The cardplayers were impressed, and Hogan leaned back and folded his arms across his blue shirt.

"Why, boys, you don't know things, that's all. You haven't read, you haven't seen. You let one guy run your whole town, a guy that don't give a hoot in hell for any of you."

"How are you going to do anything else?" Morry asked, excited as he always was, by Hogan's fantasies.

"You fellows ought to get your own hooks into that factory so you won't be wiped out when Russell lays down for his beauty nap, and the business blows up. . . . Oh, I don't say Shantyville will be wiped out—you'll always have your little flower-bed, the priests will take care of that all right."

"What'll it be, Morry?" Bill picked up Morry's glass and Morry dropped another dime on the counter by way of answer. What about a Lamptown such as Hogan described? What about avenues of green sur-rounded "chateaux"? Shutting his eyes, Morry could see them now, rows of houses, all different, this one all gables and low-spreading, white, and the next one rough-stone like a little castle. He saw the picture post cards of these places stuck up on Bauer's cigar counter instead of the perpetual three-for-a-nickel—"The Yards, Lamptown," "The Works, Lamptown," "Bauer's Chop House, Lamptown." He saw one picture very clearly, a mansion looking like the State Capitol vaguely, and beneath the tinted photograph these printed words, "Home of Morris Abbott, Lamptown, Ohio."

Suddenly he thought he had lived over stores long enough, he wanted some place to stretch his long limbs, some place where he belonged, where he wasn't always ducking to keep out of peoples' way. Gardens, chateaux—Morry saw them laid out like spangled Christmas cards—vividly colored invitations to a fairy-tale world. He felt homesick for spacious houses set in spreading lawns fringed with great calm shade trees—he was homesick for things he had never known, for families he had only read about, he missed people—old friends that had lived only in the novels he had read. Homesick . . . for a Lamptown that Hogan had just created out of six beers. He wanted to do something fabulous, something incredible, that would bring this Lamptown nearer to reality. He'd do all those things Hogan thought Hunt Russell ought to do. . . . But then Hunt had the money, that's what mattered, what did he, Morry, have but two suits and forty dollars in the savings bank?

"Say, if I had Russell's bank account I'd tear up this damned town and go right back to where old man Russell started with it. I'd make it all over again, I would," Hogan leaned one elbow on the bar and became impressively oratorical again. "Why in no time at all I'd have this town a god-damned Utopia, I would. I'd have an opera-house where the Paradise Picture Palace is now, I'd have a business college where kids could learn how to make a living, I'm damned if I wouldn't."

"Say—say Hogan, how would you go about building those chateaux for instance?" Morry edged up closer to the oracle. "How's a fellow going to learn how to plan and build like that? I don't mean like those Extension Avenue frame houses but—well, you know, different houses like you see in the magazines."

"Thing for you to do is to get a job with a contractor," Bill Delaney told him. "Get in with Hogan's wife's old man. He's a builder, if that's the trade you want to learn."

The mechanic at the table scraped his chair around to face Hogan.

"Yeah, Hogan, that's what you'd do with money, is it? What'd you do with the two thousand your wife got from her old lady? Bought stock in a Mexican opal mine, that's what you did, Big Noise. An opal mine—Christ!"

Hogan wiped his mouth on his sleeve and patted his stomach fondly.

"Well, boys, I'm off. The old horse waits without."

"Hey, Hogan, what about it? How about that there opal mine?" yelled Delaney, and the others roared with laughter as Hogan vanished, grinning, through the swinging doors.

Four Italian section hands strayed in and began dropping nickels in the pianola. An air from "Il Trovatore" rattled out. The darkest, hairiest of the four leaped beside the piano to bellow the words, gesturing ardently to the painting of a fat nymph surrounded by dazzled doves. Morry dropped into one of the big chairs that lined the barroom walls. A copy of the Cincinnati Enquirer was in the next seat and he picked it up.

"Cut out the opery," yelled Delaney good-naturedly.

"Come on, Spaghett, give us Down Among the Sheltering Palms."

"So that was opera," mused Morry enviously. If you were a wop working on the railroad you knew a lot of things like that. What doors did you open to find out these things, where were these doors anyway? Restlessly Morry started reading. A familiar cough at his side startled him. There in the seat next to him was his father, his gray fedora pulled over one eye, a cigar held between two fingers, a faint smile on his lips.

"This is a surprise," said Charles, "and a pleasure. Stand up! Or no, you needn't. I can see already that you're built for big things . . . moving pianos, say, or pitching hay."

"Great kidder, your dad," Bill Delaney, wiping off the table, said. "How's Frisco, Charlie?"

Morry didn't feel that he disliked his father—he only wanted to keep away from him. He didn't remember ever having thought of his father one way or the other. His only thought had been to keep out of reach, and therefore free from this scalding sense of shame that a look from his father could bring to him.

It was after supper time and the Saturday night crowd had begun to filter in . . . a few farmers, but mostly factory men or loafers from Shantyville whose wives did Lamptown's washing. Charles motioned Morry to come to a corner table with him, and trying not to show his reluctance, Morry followed. Charles ordered a highball and Morry was about to take a beer, when Charles called Shorty, Bill's helper, back.

"Two highballs, Shorty," he said. "No beer drinkers in this family."

"Now, isn't this a picture," he chuckled sardonically. "Father and son on a happy holiday."

He tipped his glass expertly into his mouth, set it down, and studied Morry's less finished drinking.

"And now you're a man, what about it?" he said. "Do you plan to spend the rest of your life in a little tank town or is it possible you have ambitions?"

"I was just thinking about planning houses," Morry blurted out, although it was agony for such a secret thought to form in words for a stranger's ears. "I thought I might get in old Fowler's office some day—he's Hogan's father-in-law, and if I was in there I might learn the business."

Charles Abbott bent his head with such an exageration of rapt attention that Morry became mute and ashamed again.

"Go on," urged his father kindly. "I am delighted to see that you have such a sense of humor. I had no idea. I hope these houses are to sit a decent distance from the family residence. Fancy such pretty little ideas in such a great big head. Did you tell your mother?"

"No." Morry shook his head.

His father motioned Shorty to bring another pair of highballs, and Morry's throat burned at the mere mention. Charles shook his cigar ashes on the floor with an elegant air of doing the floor a service by this decoration. Then he looked at his son and laughed softly.

"Such pretty little ideas for a young man that looks like a prize bull. A bull with a taste for perfume. A prize bull with a lace handkerchief. Why, if you had any good in that six feet of muscle you'd be supporting your mother by this time."

"I do intend to," mumbled Morry. The bar was filling up and he yearned to bolt outside. A drunken tenor from Shantyville was singing at the bar, Bill's voice got louder and shriller in an effort at discipline. "What about her, then?" his father's voice was low and insistent. "You've been around your mother, you've been taking her to these dances. Well?"

Morry didn't know what the other was driving at. He blinked at him stupidly.

"Don't try to look innocent. You know who she meets, you know damn well what she does. Well, who is it? Who's the guy?" Charles rapped on the table with his glass. A kind of horror seeped in to Morry's brain. He unconsciously shoved his chair back from the table.

"Who's her man, I'm asking you?" Charles repeated threateningly. "Don't think I can't get it out of you. You know damned well what I want to know and by God you're going to tell me. Who's she chasing?"

"What?" The question wasn't out loud because something seemed to stick in his throat and no noise would come out of his mouth. Morry wet his lips.

"I'm asking you who's her lover, damn you, that's what I'm asking!" Charles banged the table with a clenched white hand. Morry noted the onyx and diamond ring on his white flesh.

Now he hated his father, hated the false gentility of his voice, the nice perfection of his collar and pearl stickpin, he loathed the smooth-shaven bluish face with its small correct nose, its even small white teeth, he loathed the scarcely perceptible odor of lilac hair tonic, he hated him, and even with his eyes shut Morry knew every slight thing about his father that he hated. Helpless always in words with him, Morry could think of only one thing to do and that was to get away. The door of the bar to the front poolroom was blocked by a crowd of shouting Italian railroad workers, and there was only the back door into the court. It was toward this that Morry dived, but the minute his two feet were on the stones of the courtyard he realized that his father was there with him, his hand was on the back of his neck in a steely grip.

"Are you going to tell me what she's up to, or aren't you?"

Words finally burst through Morry's chattering teeth.

"I'm damned if I will."

The next thing he knew was a stabbing blow under the chin. Morry, in a flood of rage, swung out on his father, but as soon as his huge fist struck he was ashamed, for his father was such a slight, soft little man. It was like hitting some kid. . . . Morry took a step back in the pitch dark of the courtyard with the headlights of an oncoming engine in his eyes, and the second's hesitation gave the other his chance. His fist tore into Morry's face and then it seemed to Morry that the engine had left its wonted track beside the saloon and had come roaring into the courtyard. Then the roaring suddenly stopped.

The saloon back door opened and Shorty came running out.

"What the hell. . . ."

Charles Abbott was yanking his collar into place. The shoulder seam of his right sleeve was torn, the barkeep noted, and he breathed heavily even while he smiled. The younger Abbott was crumpled up on the stone pavement.

"Give us a light there, Bill," Shorty called back and the back door opened wider. Someone was singing to the pianola's tinny accompaniment.

"Down among the sheltering palms,
Oh honey, wait for me, oh honey, wait for me. . . ."

Shorty knelt down.

"Hey . . . hey, Morry, what the hell. . . ." Steve lit a match and looked from the bloody cheek on the pavement rather curiously at Charlie. "What's the idea here, Charlie?"

"Just teaching," Charles panted, as he dusted off his hands, "the boy . . . how . . . to fight."

"Well," said Shorty, "they ain't much fight in him now."

Charles left for the road early the next morning. He said he'd be gone several months this time through the Southwestern territory, and he seemed
so much quieter and saner than he had before, that his wife felt relieved.

As for Morry he took good care to keep out of sight as long as possible
and when he finally did try to sneak through the back hall, Nettie saw
him.

"He's been fighting. Look, Mrs. Abbott!" she cried out, pointing to
Morry's face. "Look at those marks on his eye. It's a good thing his father's
gone or he'd catch it good from him."

"Why, Morry!" Elsinore's clear gray eyes were wide with astonishment. "Your face is all bruised. What ever happened to you?"

"That's why he's been eating at Bauer's these last two days, and keeping out of the shop," declared Nettie triumphantly. "Didn't I tell you
there was some reason for it? Didn't I tell you he was up to something?
And Dode was in last night and said he wasn't at work all day yesterday."

"But you worked today," said Elsinore, her eyes still fixed on the
scarred forehead. "What happened?"

Nettie's black eyes glowed with satisfaction as Morry sullenly stared at
the floor.

"See, it was a fight! He got into a brawl over at Delaney's Saturday
night, he can't deny it. That's why he didn't get up all day Sunday, don't
you remember, and that's why he hasn't let us see him. I knew there was
something behind all that!"

Elsinore waited for Morry to answer. But he wouldn't open his mouth,
just stood there getting red in the face.

"Was it or wasn't it a fight?" challenged Nettie. "Just ask him. Go on
and ask him."

Morry scowled furiously at her.

"All right then, it was," he retorted, "and what do you think you're
going to do about it?"

Nettie backed away, pouting. She smoothed her sleek black hair and
marched haughtily into the front showroom swaying her hips with each
step. Elsinore and her son stood looking at each other. Elsinore knew
there was something she must do, something she must say, because this
was her son and there was some word you said to sons so that they didn't
brawl in saloons. She thought of the saloon smell, of the old tipplers

whose obscenities echoed to her bedroom window on Saturday nights, she thought of the hard-eyed young men that hung around the pool-room, whispering of things mysterious and horrible—and suddenly she shivered.

"Morry," she began, in a funny little voice as if she were called upon to make a speech at a great banquet and her knees shook a little. "Morry!"

Morry looked away. Then because he knew how bothered she was he turned around and rushed upstairs, and his mother breathed a tremendous sigh of relief.

Nettie kept harping on Morry's bruised eye, though, for days. She thought it had something to do with some girl—it was a fight over a factory girl or maybe over Jen St. Clair. Morry let her talk and kept out of the Bon Ton as much as he could. He didn't see much of Jen anymore, but he knew Nettie wouldn't believe that. After what the old woman had said he felt queer and sick every time he thought of Jen. He'd stay away all right, he'd leave her alone, but every day after work he missed her, at dusk when they used to sit on the steps talking. He knew she watched him from the Delaney's upstairs window whenever he passed, and once when he walked home from the factory with two of the girls he worked with, someone threw a pebble down at him from up there, but he walked on without looking up. But at nights, when he'd be reading in bed sometimes he'd stare at a page half an hour or so worrying about the whole business, about what the old woman had said to his mother, and he felt lost without Jen to talk to.

One Saturday afternoon when his mother sent him in the backyard for boxes from the store-shed he looked over toward Jen's stairs. Someone was sitting, out, sitting so primly that he had to look twice to make sure it was Jen. She had on a hat. Nobody ever wore a hat in Lamptown unless it was Sunday or else they were going away. It struck Morry with a shock that maybe she was going away, leaving Lamptown for good.

He glanced quickly over his shoulder to make sure the Bon Ton was not on watch, and then sauntered boldly over to the stairs. If she was going away, the old lady certainly couldn't kick about his coming over to bid a civil good-bye. He said hello tentatively but Jen only nodded indifferently to him without smiling. He came up the steps with growing curiosity. A blue lace hat sat awkwardly on Jen's head and in her arm was a stiff pop-eyed china doll in a pink satin costume.

"What's the idea?"

"My mother's come to see me," Jen explained drearily. "She went to the Home for me and they sent her here."

"Is she taking you away?"

"I don't know."

"I guess I'd better go," he said hastily, but dying to see what Jen's folks were really like. He looked through the screen door and just inside the parlor he caught sight of the visitor. She looked like one of those actresses, Morry thought, only fatter. She had a voluminous white veil over her stiff straw hat, and a tight-fitting soiled green suit, and white shoes and stockings. She sat on the edge of her chair and talked to old Mrs. Delaney hunched in her little chair on the other side of the room. Morry sat down cautiously out of line with the old woman's eye.

"She's been talking now for an hour," Jen murmured in his ear. "I guess it's pretty nice to have your mother come and visit you, especially if you never saw her before. She gave me this hat. Look. She gave me this doll. I'd like it if it cried like your mother's doll does."

Morry wanted to laugh at the hat. He'd never seen Jen in a hat and it sat up on top of her head as if it was meant for the doll instead. This was because Jen's mother had no memory for dates and had a vague impression that her daughter was barely eight. As for the dolls, he couldn't imagine Jen ever playing with dolls.

"What'd she come for, then, if she isn't taking you with her?" he wanted to know, but Jen refused to talk. She sat glumly clutching her doll and looking straight ahead while her mother's voice chattered on and on.

Finally Jen whispered, "She said she wanted to see if I was in a good home. She said she couldn't be easy until she'd seen if I was with the right people. That's what she said."

Morry glanced carefully through the screen door. There was old Mrs. Delaney sitting with her shoulders bunched up, her arms folded over her shrunken calico bosom, her thin lips clamped together, rocking, rocking while Mrs. St. Clair went on and on talking, as if she was selling soap.

"I used to be a beauty. I give you my word, Mrs. Delaney, when I was married my waist was no bigger than that. As it is, it's only my hips that are big, and most men like big hips, that's what I say. People say I lace to make my waist look so small. I give you my word, Mrs. Delaney, you could put your hand inside my corset this minute and see how much room there is. I don't have to lace, I tell them. . . . I had beautiful hair as a girl—thick like Jennia's out there, but that Titian red, you know. My friends say, oh yes, she dyes it. I give you my word people don't think it's real. They think I dye it, and you know how many women my age do have to color their hair, because do what you will, the gray will come out if it's there. But dye my hair? Ha! I said to this friend of mine, 'Look here, I want you to come to my room and I'll just show you the stuff I wash it in.' I showed her. 'Absolutely no dye,' it said on the bottle, 'merely restoring the hair to its natural brilliancy.' Well, that time the laugh was on her. . . . I'm glad to see Jennia in this beautiful home, Mrs. Delaney. I can see you're a good influence."

Now Mrs. Delaney opened her mouth.

"Well, then, who was the girl's father?" she croaked. "If she had one."

"Mr. St. Clair was a gentleman," said Jen's mother. "We had words but I don't deny he was a gentleman. Such hands, Mrs. Delaney! No wonder, he'd never done a lick of work in his life, but I will say they were beautiful hands. He went to Africa. I think he had interests there."

"Africa? Was he black?" exclaimed Mrs. Delaney, and even Morry jumped then, so that Jen put her finger to her lips warningly.

Mrs. St. Clair threw up her gloved hands.

"Mrs. Delaney! God forbid! My husband black!" She shuddered. "That was uncalled for, Mrs. Delaney, that really was. Do you know, Mrs. Delaney, that my husband was considered the handsomest man in our company? The best-looking man in the 'Laughing Girls' company? Not only that but the smartest as well. He had a big future on the stage, but as I say he had interests in Africa, and when Lil was born—that's my youngest, we were staying at a hotel in Youngstown then, the company had broken up—why Bert just walked out on me with a note. I waited till Lil was a month old, then left her on the Children's Home doorstep right where baby Jennia had been put, the year before. I tell you I cried my eyes out, Mrs. Delaney, because there's nothing like a mother's heart."

Tears now came to Mrs. St. Clair's eyes and she plucked them out carefully as one whose tears had too often had to cope with mascara.

"Oh, I've not had an easy time of it, Mrs. Delaney. When Jennia was born—that was when we were playing in Toledo, so I left her there with a very fine family—my friend said aha, it's only a six months' baby. My own friends said that, mind you. But I could show you the book where I wrote down the dates of my wedding and when Jen was born, and I could prove that everything was just as innocent as I sit here now. I was brought up refined, Mrs. Delaney, I had my education. I was every bit as good as Bertie was but he never would believe it. My people were from Virginia. My mother was an O'Brien."

Mrs. Delaney's thin mouth snapped open again.

"When did you get Jen back from that Toledo family you left her with?"

Jen's mother leaned forward confidentially.

"Mrs. Delaney, you wouldn't believe people would be like that, but when I got back to Toledo that family had put her in the Orphanage in Libertyville. I never would have put her there, and the only reason I left Lily there was as kinda company for her sister, you know. I never saw either of my babies from the time I left them till now when I'm looking them up again. When Lily was born I spent every penny I had to get her to the very same orphanage because I wanted my little girls to be together. You're a mother yourself, Mrs. Delaney. You know a mother's heart."

"Do you want to get Jen back now?" challenged Mrs. Delaney. "Is that what you're after?"

"Do I—oh dear, no,—oh no, not now. Does she sing or dance? Let me hear her sing once. Jennia—oh Jennia, sing me a song, dearie. I want to see if you've got your father's voice."

Jen shifted her doll to the other arm, stood up and with her nose pressed against the screen door in order to face her audience, sang. She sang at the top of her voice and very fast so as to get it over with.

"Will someone kindly tell me,
Will someone answer why—
To me it is a riddle
And will be till I die—
A million peaches round me,
Yet I would like to know,
Why I picked a lemon in the garden of love
Where I thought only peaches grow."

Mrs. St. Clair gave a little flattering cry of pleasure. "You know really that's not bad, Mrs. Delaney, not bad at all. When I was her age I was getting four and five dollars a week singing in my papa's café in Newark. Customers would throw the money at me. I had my training all right before I ever stepped on the real stage. Nowadays of course a child performer gets even more than a grown-up—and a curly-haired little girl. . . ." Mrs. St. Clair studied Jen appraisingly through the screen. "Her legs are good, too, that's a blessing."

Jen mechanically pulled her apron down over her knees, and her mother laughed fondly.

"Never mind hiding them, dear. . . . Now, do you know what I've a mind to do? . . . Hmm mm. . . . Yes sir, I've a good mind to take her along with me to Cleveland. I have my little room there, and we'd manage. Yes sir, I think that's what I'll do, especially since the Home won't let me take Lily. . . . Stand up, dearie, I want to see if you can travel half-fare. She's pretty tall, isn't she?"

Mrs. Delaney got up suddenly and limped over to where her guest sat. She put her arms akimbo.

"You don't get her, missy, do you see?" she spat out her words. "You'd like to put her in a café or on the stage and let her make a living for you but you can't do it while old Susan Delaney's alive and I'll tell you that right now. She's here to help me, that's what. You don't get a chance to make of her what you made of yourself, now, take that, and I'll tell you right to your face that I don't like your looks and I'm sorry you came."

Mrs. St. Clair's mouth fell open. Red spots came into her cheeks and her hands clutched the arms of her chair tightly. Outside, Morry decided he'd better leave but Jen clutched him tightly. When he tried to pull away she took both hands and held on to his coat, and the doll clattered down the steps.

"See!" hissed Morry. "You've broken it now. Say, I want to get out of this, hear me?"

"I know you—I know you as well as if I'd borne you myself," went on the old woman shrilly, "you can get away from here and stay away. I got enough to do keeping that wild 'un straight without her ma breaking in."

Words came to Mrs. St. Clair.

"Oh, what an old bitch," she choked. "To think I spend my good money coming all the way from Cleveland just to be kicked out of my child's home. What a rotten old bitch you are! Got no more sympathy for a mother than a snake."

Mrs. Delaney pointed a gnarled finger toward the door and lowering her white veil the other woman whirled around to go. Morry and Jen backed out of the way.

"Here, Jen, give her her hat and her doll," commanded the old woman.

"Oh, can't I keep the hat?" Jen implored.

"Give them back!" thundered the old woman, and Jen hastily took off the hat and picked up the doll to hand to her mother. Mrs. St. Clair gathered her green skirts about her and ran down the steps.

"You'll be sorry for this," she shouted from the bottom of the steps. "I'll get Lily and I'll get Jennia, too, they'll stick by their mother. I only came here for a motherly visit and you—"

"You came here to stay and live off me if you could, don't deny it!" quavered the old woman fiercely. "I tell you I know you like I'd know my own daughter, and you can get out and stay out."

She panted back into the house, stopping to glare at Morry.

"And you, too. You clear out of here, too."

She banged the door shut.

Jen, bereft of doll and hat, hung over the bannister.

"Oh, mother! Goodbye, mother—come see me again—"

But Mrs. St. Clair was storming angrily up the street to the Big Four depot, a pink satin doll under one arm and a child's blue hat crushed under the other.

Jen turned to Morry.

"Now I'll never see her again," she said despondently.

"What do you care? She wouldn't do you any good," Morry consoled her.

"I know, but it's my mother, Morry, it's my folks," Jen said, troubled.

Morry heard the door rattling ominously.

"I'm going to beat it," he said, "the old lady's on the warpath."

Jen didn't try to stop him. The barkeeper stuck his head out of the saloon back door as Morry dashed down the alley. He stepped out and stared upstairs at Jen, shading his eyes with his hand.

"Who was that up there doing all the singing for God's sake?" he demanded.

"Aw, shut up," grumbled Jen. "I gotta right to sing, I guess."

Jen went to the parochial school in the Irish end of Lamptown, the part they called Shantyville. She played hookey half the time, and lost her books in the woods hunting mushrooms, and fought with the boys in the school yard. Every few days a black-robed sister would climb the steps above the saloon to old Mrs. Delaney's quarters and during this interview

Jen usually disappeared, well aware that the visit had to do with her own waywardness.

Sometimes when she knew beforehand that the sister was to make a call, she'd stay away from home till nine or ten at night, coming in bedraggled and muddy-booted, with a lapful of muddy wildflowers and burrs sticking to all of her clothes. She never quite understood Mrs. Delaney's rage over these night wanderings, nor could she see why they were proof that she'd never grow up into a decent woman. Once it was eleven when she got in and old Mrs. Delaney sat humped up by the kitchen stove waiting for her. Bill was eating a cold supper on the oil-cloth table.

"Well!" said the old woman.

"I been picking flowers out in the Lots," Jen said. "Here."

She laid a clump of sweet williams and Johnny-Jump-ups on the table.

"Who you been with—that Morry Abbott?"

"I went by myself," said Jen.

"That's likely. Eat supper?"

"I found some green apples. I'm not hungry."

"Look here, Sister Catherine says you throw your books at the boys and that Peter McCarthy had to be sent home today because you bit his hand so hard. She says you swore at Myrtle Dietz."

Jen looked sulkily at her flowers. Bill jerked his chair around.

"Speak up! Tell the old lady what's the idea. We give you a home and then you stay out half the night. We send you to a good school so you can grow up to be somebody that is somebody and you raise hell all over the place. Speak up, kid."

Jen chewed her fingernails silently.

"What's the big idea throwing books at the boys? What's the idea scratching up this McCarthy boy?"

"I'm not gonna be mauled by any of those smarties," Jen said defiantly. "And I was just getting even with Pete McCarthy. I had a reason."

The old woman pricked up her ears alertly. Bill's fork hung in midair. Both looked suspiciously at Jen.

"What happened? What'd he do to you? Speak up there, now, out with it."

"He chased after me coming down the tracks one noon and—"

"I knew it would happen," moaned the old woman, "I said it would happen. Every girl I ever had under my roof, the same every one of them. Out with it, then, what'd he do?"

"Kissed me, that's what!" Jen said indignantly.

Bill and his mother exchanged an unbelieving look.

"And that's all? Now, no lying!" the old woman insisted. "You're sure that was all?"

"I guess that's enough," Jen mumbled, feeling embarrassed that the outrage should be taken so lightly. "I got even with him for it, all right."

"And you beat him up just for kissing you!" marvelled the old woman. "I've a mind to give you a good tanning for it. . . ."

"Leave her be, ma," Bill said. He fished more pickled pigsfeet out of the jar, and stuffed his mouth.

"Wash up those dishes, then, and get to bed," urged his mother. "Wandering around the Lots this hour the night. One of those fresh fellows at the Yard get after you once and then where'd you be?"

"She'd scratch his eyes out, don't you fear," promised Bill. "She won't have anybody around her but maybe Morry Abbott and he don't bother her much, now he's working and going after real meat."

Jen tied on an apron.

"He'd better not show up here any more after I told him not to," said Mrs. Delaney. "No use your sitting out waiting for him, either, because I told his ma I wouldn't have it. And no use your thinking you can meet him nights outside because if I find out I'll give you a hiding."

"I don't care," Jen retorted, banging the dishpan into the sink. "I can get along without people, I guess. I guess I'm old enough to get along by my own self."

"You bet you're old enough! Next you'll be hanging around dance halls, the Casino and the like—"

Jen clapped her hands.

"Aw, Bill, let me learn to dance, will you? Look, I can two-step already."

She two-stepped around the kitchen, waving the dish-mop in the air. Bill whistled a tune for her.

"Say, what do you know about that? Look at that, ma. . . . Now, wait a minute, and tell you what I'll do, I'll show you the schottische."

He got up and took Jen's hand stiffly in his own fat red hand. He held his foot poised in the air in the third position and Jen raised a muddy shoe to the same angle.

"Now when I say 'Down!' you sachet to your right, and watch now. Down!"

"Don't you see my
Don't you see my
Don't you see my new shoe?
Don't you see my
Don't you see my
Don't you see my new shoe?"

"They don't dance that way any more, I've seen 'em," objected his mother. "Things are different now."

"Never mind, she's a fine dancer. What do you say I take her over to Fischer's some night? I'd like to go over some night myself, especially if I had someone to dance with."

Jen caught hold of his arm.

"You wouldn't really, would you, Bill? Take me to the Casino?"

Bill began to regret his offer, but he didn't dare take it back.

"Get to those dishes, will you?" snapped Mrs. Delaney. "You got to do better with Sister Catherine before you go out nights, young lady, yes sir, even with Bill."

"I'll wear my hair up!" Jen was jubilant again. "Like Nettie Farrell does. Give me a dime for hairpins, will you, Bill?"

Jen couldn't wait to go to the Casino. She could see herself dancing around amazing Morry Abbott and Grace Terris and the men from downstairs. She saw Lil there, too, because Lil was always a part of her ideal dream pictures. She could see herself grown up, taking Lil across the Casino floor and people crowding around her because Lil was like a little yellow-haired wax angel. And Lil would be dazzled by all this glamour, too. Whenever she remembered Lil, back in the Home, Jen felt guilty. Lil, back there in dark blue calico, always too skimpy, swinging on the iron carriage gate, while here was Jen having all this fun in Lamptown, with her own room, and a pair of silk stockings and a box of talcum powder. . . . Soon the Home would send her out to work because she was fourteen now, Lil was. Jen'd have to do something about her, quick, too . . . then Jen skipped all that and was back again in the Casino with Lil, both in pink silk dresses, dancing, with Morry watching. . . . Jen turned a handspring joyously across the kitchen floor.

"See, now you've started her," Mrs. Delaney said morosely to Bill. "Dancing and then what? Mind you, one crooked move, and out she goes."

Nevertheless the next week Jen started going to the Casino dances.

On a rainy Saturday night Dode O'Connell strode into the Bon Ton Hat Shop. Mrs. Pepper was sewing garters on a Stylish Stout model in pink brocade. Elsinore and Nettie sat on the green wicker sofa watching the rain and waiting for customers. The rain zigzagged across the show window in torrents and black gleaming umbrellas with frantic legs beneath were blown past. Market Street lamps were wet golden blobs dripping futile little puddles of light that made no difference to the black, wet night, and the lightning that cracked the sky showed up Lamptown as such a shabby, lost little corner of the earth—it was nothing, just nothing at all for that dazzling second.

Dode's tall person was wrapped in a man's topcoat, and a Roman-striped muffler was wound round her red hair. Nettie, closing the door behind her, saw Hunt's car just beyond, in front of Delaney's, its curtains buttoned up.

Dode shook off the damp coat and patted up her hair in front of the gilt mirror.

"I want that big hat that was in the window last week—the one over the doll," she said, and Nettie and Elsinore bustled around with this hat and another like it in blue, because Dode spent good money and besides she usually got her clothes in Cleveland, so that this visit must be quite a compliment.

Mrs. Pepper, sewing on her corset, grew crimson when Dode nodded to her, and she moved a little away as if to avoid any personal contact with this customer. Dode, tilting a hat over one eyebrow, looked over at the corsetiere rather cynically.

"What's the matter, Pepper, you mad at me for that Cedar Point business?"

Mrs. Pepper looked up, confused.

"I—oh no, Dode, I—"

"You and Fischer sore?"

"No—I—"

Now Elsinore's blood began to tingle ominously, in a minute she was going to overhear something she almost knew but didn't ever want to hear spoken out loud. She saw Mrs. Pepper look helplessly from Dode to Nettie. Nettie was busy stretching a hat and pretending not to listen. But Dode paid no attention to the two milliners.

"Well, then, what was the trouble up at Sandusky—did you miss the boat? We waited over at the Point for three hours for you."

Mrs. Pepper puckered up her rosebud mouth very firmly.

"I was too busy. I had a great many customers in Sandusky—"

"Whereabouts—at the Soldiers' Home?" Dode laughed.

"He needn't think I can drop everything and run just because he says so," Mrs. Pepper said tartly. "Besides you know how he is when he's had too much."

Dode's eyebrows went up scornfully.

"Say, that's good coming from you."

Mrs. Pepper tossed her head and jerked her chair around. Dode took the hand mirror Elsinore gave her and studied the back view of her hat.

"The plumes are five dollars apiece," Elsinore said hesitatingly, but after all plumes did cost. "That makes it eighteen."

"Put another plume over on the other side, will you?" Dode requested. She lifted up her skirt and pulled a roll of bills out of her stocking. Her black silk stockings came all the way up her long shapely thighs, and there were dozens of tiny ruffles on her white silk drawers.

"I'll come in and get it Tuesday."

She started winding the muffler around her head again. Nettie shook out the topcoat and held it for her.

"Say, Pepper."

Mrs. Pepper looked around unwillingly.

"Get into your clothes and come out. We're going to drive over to Marion and pick him up. Come on."

"I might—and I might not," said Mrs. Pepper huffily.

"Hurry up," ordered Dode.

"In all this storm?" Elsinore said because now she knew it was true about Fischer and Mrs. Pepper, and she couldn't bear to have her go out to meet him. She'd known about this and known it was true, she thought, ever since she first heard the rumor, but it never struck her full in the face until tonight.

Mrs. Pepper, sputtering angrily, got into her coat and hat.

"I wouldn't go over there for a minute if it wasn't that I have to see a certain party in Marion."

Dode laughed.

"That's the stuff, Pepper. Don't let 'em know when you're sunk."

The lightning slashed the black sky again as they ran out into the street. Nettie shut the door and in another minute Hunt's car rolled through the flooded gutters down the street.

"In all this rain, too!" Nettie said slowly, and then her face wrinkled up and she began to cry and dab at her eyes with her tiny sewing apron.

Elsinore looked at her, irritated more than surprised. For one thing, Nettie or anybody else crying was nothing really in her life. The only real thing was the terrible certainty that Fischer belonged to Mrs. Pepper, just as people had always said, and that they met often, and it was all secret which made it mean so much more.

"I don't care," Elsinore thought, and in her mind she didn't, it was only that something sharp like lightning quivered through her chest, and made her want to scream.

Nettie went on sniffling into her apron.

"I get so lonesome sometimes," she whimpered. "People going out on dates in all this storm—those factory girls always have dates, not that I'd be seen with any man in this town, but when I think of a fat old thing like Mrs. Pepper going out riding . . . while I stay here and work all the time. I never get out, and anyway I'm afraid of lightning. It makes me—so—nervous!"

"Shut up!" Elsinore cried so harshly that Nettie was frightened into awed obedience. Elsinore rubbed her forehead, dazed, as if she had shrieked out some secret in her sleep. Nettie blinked at her, and Elsinore began to be sorry for her, as she was sorry for herself. She was glad when the hall door banged as Morry came in.

"I can't stand people crying," she explained to Nettie. "I never cry myself. If you're so anxious to go out, though, in this storm, why don't you ask Morry to take you to the Paradise to the picture? It's only nine o'-clock. There won't be any more customers here on a night like this."

"I'd never ask Morry to do anything for me!" Nettie dried her tears.

Morry stuck his head in the door. He'd been over to Delaney's place and he smelled of smoke and beer.

"Did you call me?"

"Morry, get my umbrella and your old coat and take Nettie to the Paradise tonight. She doesn't feel very good."

Morry and Nettie looked at each other antagonistically. Nettie knew, if his mother did not, how significant it was for a couple to go to the Paradise together. Nobody ever went to movies together in town but engaged couples. Girls went alone and fellows hung around the drug-store outside to take them home afterwards, but to go in together. . . . How he detested her for her smooth, tear-streaked face, her woeful mouth, all the signs of her feminine helplessness, all the appeals for sympathy. . . . What would she care if all the fellows stared at them and snickered when they came in together? That's just what women always liked.

"Well?" challenged Nettie. "See Mrs. Abbott, he won't take me, he'd rather go with the factory girls."

"You'll take Nettie, won't you, Morry?" Elsinore asked him again. "You can wrap yourself up good. It's the first Saturday night she's ever had a chance to get out. Go on and put your things on, Nettie."

Morry scowled down at his wet shoes while Nettie joyously ran into the backroom to get ready. He hated the Paradise—only sissies went to the movies, he was disappointed in his mother, and he wished somebody would give Nettie's smug, smiling face a good slap.

"In just a minute, Morry," Nettie called out.

Elsinore caught sight of the pink corset Mrs. Pepper had left on her chair. She picked it up and threw it across the hall into the workroom, and banged a drawer shut. Morry's jaw dropped. He'd never seen his mother in a temper before.

"Leaving her trash all over the place!" Elsinore fumed. "I won't have it. I've stood it long enough! I won't let her come here again ever!"

Nettie ran out, pop-eyed, pulling on her hat.

"What is it? What happened?"

"Out she goes the next time she comes to Lamptown!" went on Elsinore. "I've got no place here for her or anybody else like her!"

Morry, for some obscure reason, felt the need to protect his mother from Nettie's curiosity.

"Come on, let's get out of here if we're going," he ordered brusquely, and shoved Nettie out the front door into the rain.

Nettie raised her umbrella, not at all disturbed by his surliness. Small rivers of rain ran off the shop awning, and two girls, bent on getting their Saturday night dates somehow, ran squealing by with newspapers over their heads. Market Street blurred uncertainly before them.

"Here!" Nettie handed Morry the umbrella, and clinging very close to his unfriendly arm, she tiptoed carefully along beside him.

Morry could never forget that walk in the rain with Nettie Farrell. To be huddled under an umbrella with a woman he hated, to smell her violet talcum, her scented hair, to feel her warm, plump hand squeezing his elbow, her body pressing against his, so that not for an instant could he forget that it was Nettie, Nettie Farrell, and that he detested her. He said nothing to her, tramped straight through all the puddles leaving her to scamper along beside him with tight, prim little steps.

He was glad of the umbrella when they passed the drug store, because the fellows inside couldn't recognize him then. He pulled his cap down over his eyes at the gilded ticket window of the Paradise, and pushed Nettie ahead of him into the theatre. The storm had kept people away and for a glad moment or two he thought there was no one he knew in the little scattered audience. He wished Nettie wouldn't make so much fuss getting into her seat so that everybody turned around to stare. Then he saw directly across the aisle the small pointed face of Jen St. Clair. She was with Grace Terris and Grace was nudging her and giggling, but Jen only stared at him as if she'd never seen him before and then, with her chin in the air, turned her attention to pictures.

Morry had spoken to her and now he wished he hadn't. Every time he ever saw Jen he wished she wouldn't show everyone so plainly her worship of him, but now that the worship seemed to be gone he was simply furious with her. He watched the shadowy adventures of Clara Kimball Young and thought of all he'd done for Jen St. Clair, promising to help get her sister and all that, and now she tried to make him feel like a fool by not speaking to him right before Nettie Farrell and the whole Paradise audience. He glowered at the picture, but out of the corner of his eye he could see Grace peeking over at him now and then, and whispering and giggling with Jen.

Nettie kept wriggling in her seat and turning around to speak to people—not to Grace or Jen—but to Bon Ton customers here and there. Morry slid down in his seat a little,—it was no use, though, because everyone knew those big shoulders and the coal black wavy hair belonged to Morry Abbott and to nobody else in town. . . .

It was amazing about girls, how lofty and complacent they became when they got out in public with a man,—any man—while a fellow shrank and felt ridiculous and prayed for the ordeal to end. It was amazing about women, anyway, Grace over there, snickering behind her hand and Jen, stony-faced, remote, and Nettie, bending over his knees to pick up a handkerchief, fussing around in her seat, brushing her ankles against his and then hastily drawing them back, pressing her plump arms against him, then moving primly away. . . . God, how he hated the whole lot of them, Morry thought, the way they knew how to make a man squirm from old Mrs. Delaney on down to the littlest girl. It was their function in life, making men feel clumsy and dumb, that was all they ever wanted to accomplish. . . . He remembered the little girls in big pink hair-ribbons at parties years ago, looking scornfully at him, twice their size, until he wished for sweet death to swoop down on him. Now, in the Paradise, with the thunder growling over the roof, and surrounded by Nettie, Grace, and Jen, he thought of those smart little curled girls of ten and twelve years ago and wanted fiercely to be revenged on them. Nettie's hand touched his carelessly and he boiled with rage and jerked his own hand away. . . . But what revenge would fit these enemies . . . of course he might leave town forever and go to Pittsburgh, no sir, New York City, and show them up as cheap little village hicks while he was a polished city man. This was a soothing thought, as soothing as if it were already accomplished—he even saw himself now on the screen before him, that natty young man in the opera hat emerging from the café door, lighting a cigarette from a silver case while music played.

He saw Hogan dressed up going down the aisle, and wondered what Hogan was doing here. Then he remembered Milly, the piano player and a professional lady of joy. That explained everything. He wished Hogan would tell his pianist girlfriend not to stop dead in the middle of a picture so that you forget what you were thinking of.

Grace and Jen got up—Morry saw them and was determined not to look when they passed but Grace said "hello" and he had to look up and meet Jen's cold, accusing eyes. She glanced away again and went out, pulling on her coat.

"I wonder who those two are going to meet," Nettie whispered to him and Morry gritted his teeth. Those two! As if Jen was like Grace Terris! Those two! His vague anger settled definitely on Nettie now.

Hogan ambled to the back of the theatre nodding to Morry with an innocently casual air as if no one would ever guess he was there to date up the town's light woman, the talented Milly. Cynically the audience watched the pianist, a few minutes later, get up from her bench, close the piano in the very middle of the heroine's death-bed scene, powder her nose leisurely before the piano mirror, set a large plumed hat reverently over her magnificent pompadour; she jangled bracelets up her fat arms and drew on long gloves; she made an intimate adjustment in her stayed velvet gown; gazing with calm insolence over the audience she finally swept majestically up the aisle. Unwillingly the audience gave up Clara Kimball Young's death-bed scene to watch Milly's exit, reluctantly they conceded the dramatic value of her performance, heads turned to watch her pause at the back of the house to look patronizingly at the picture, exchange a laughing word with the usher, and then a cold draught blew in as the exit door swung open and shut for her departure, leaving the audience to the lesser reality of the screen.

Everyone always knew that of course Milly was joining some man or other outside, and this local passion was more exciting than the filmed one. Some ladies thought Milly's private profession should disqualify her as the Paradise pianist, still the cold facts were that no one else in Lamptown could play the piano that well and you had to have music with your pictures, no matter where it came from.

With the pianist gone the picture seemed dull and people wandered out into the rain again. Morry was impatient to go. He was perfectly conscious of Nettie's bosom rising and falling with each breath so that her lace frill quivered gently. A gold locket on a frail gold chain had a way of sliding down beneath the frill every time she moved forward and Nettie, with a little shocked exclamation, would reach down her blouse and fish it out again. A faint whiff of violet sachet followed this maneuver, but Morry pretended not to notice anything.

"Everyone's going," Nettie whispered. "Come on, let's go."

They went out and stood for a minute in the lobby while Nettie fussed with her rubbers. The storm was over so that now there was no excuse for the umbrella. Morry could see men peering out at him from the drug store window and wished there was some way of dropping Nettie then and there.

"Going back to the shop?" he asked her.

"No," said Nettie primly. "You'll have to take me out to my place, Morry."

There was no getting out of it. They'd have to walk through all the mud of Extension Avenue to the house where Nettie boarded. The maple trees dripped down on them and the pods crackled underfoot. They passed the factory boarding houses with the girls giggling in the doorways or hanging out the windows. A gramophone squeaked out some ragtime to shatter the black gloom outside, and it kept tinkling through Morry's head. Once an automobile slushed through the mud and spattered Nettie's skirt and she went on about that but Morry stalked silently along, his hands in his pockets, his wet shoes weighing a ton. Now they reached the darkest end of the road. Nettie's house was dark—the Murphys were downtown.

"Bye," Morry said gruffly at the doorstep.

"I suppose if you wanted to," said Nettie, unfastening a glove carefully, "you could come in and get dry. I'm sure I don't care. Only you'll have to take off those filthy boots because I won't have you tramping up Mrs. Murphy's new rug the way you do your mother's rugs."

Once more Nettie became all of the smug little starched girls sent into the world to make mankind feel loutish and immeasurably inferior, and once more Morry was stung with the desire to be revenged on all of them. He followed her into the house. She lit the hall gas lamp, from its brass elbow a string of gilded buckeyes dangled. She took off her wraps and hung them on a golden-oak hall rack and arranged her hair in the diamond-shaped mirror above. Then she saw Morry standing behind her and stamped her foot.

"Look at you, Morry Abbott! Look at you making tracks all over that new rug with your great big shoes! I could kill you for being so clumsy! Look what you're doing!"

Suddenly Morry seized her two wrists and twisted them until Nettie squealed with pain. He held them tightly with one hand, and with the other pulled her into an iron embrace. Nettie's eyes were terror-stricken, her mouth wide open, the pulse in her white throat throbbed frantically.

"I hate you, Morry Abbott! Don't you dare to touch me. See, you're tearing my dress...."

Morry lifted her up and carried her with her heels kicking, to the green satin settee at the foot of the staircase. He had no desire for Nettie, only a fierce antagonism that amounted to a physical necessity. He would like to have taken her by the neck and shook her like a dog would shake a hen, but all he could do was to sink his teeth into her round shoulder and bite as hard as he could. Nettie stopped kicking him and began to whimper childishly. She put up her hands to fix her hair again and to pull her torn blouse back into place. She wouldn't lift her face to look at him, just made funny whimpering noises like a frightened puppy. When she wriggled away from his knees Morry jumped after her and the settee tipped backwards and upset a blue and yellow jardiniere of ferns.

"Mrs. Murphy'll come in any minute," Nettie wailed, fixing the jar on its mahogany pedestal again. Morry might have left her then but she started to dash past him upstairs. He tore after her and caught up with her on the top landing and got one foot inside the bedroom door before she could close it. His fists were clenched as if for a battle.

The upstairs hall lamp shone into the bedroom through the transom after Morry had shut the door tight. The room smelled of violet talcum and scented soap. Nettie was perfectly quiet, he had to fumble toward the bed where she sat, leaning back on her arms, challenging him. He grasped her shoulders and she drooped limply against him, not saying a word, and the familiar detestable perfume of her hair made him grit his teeth again.

A door opened downstairs.

"Now do be quiet about it," Nettie whispered warningly, and didn't even bother to put up her hands in protest when he started tearing her blouse again.

He was astonished and even chagrined at the ease, almost skill, with which she yielded. Somehow he felt it was she who had conquered and not he, after all. Tiptoeing down the stairs sometime afterward he thought cynically, "I'll bet that's the way they all are. Easy, every one of 'em!"

It made him very angry.

Morry was out in the court pretending to fix the lock on the storehouse door but hoping Jen would call him. He could see her dimly through the dusk sitting on the top stairs. She hadn't called to him since the night he'd gone out with Nettie. It might be on the old lady's account but he doubted if Jen was really afraid of her. Secretly he was worried about her—he didn't especially want to see her but he liked to feel sure she was around and lately he'd heard Bill say something about "shipping the kid to some farm where she'd learn to work—no damn good to the old lady as she was, always getting kicked out of school, always breaking something."

He lay awake nights trying to figure some way out because it would be terrible for Jen to have to go to some farm. He almost thought of asking his mother to let her work in the Bon Ton the way Nettie had started in, then that made him think of Nettie and he thought probably Jen would be better on a farm. If she was taller she could say she was sixteen and get a job at the Works. Then he remembered the way Hunt had laughed the night he and Jen went there and he thought probably Jen would do better out of Hunt Russell's reach, too.

He looked toward the stairs again—she couldn't help but see him, still she made no beckoning gesture. Ungrateful, he thought, just as if he had already done all those things for her that he had planned. Then reluctantly he started over. He stopped at the foot of the stairs. He wasn't afraid of Bill's old woman any more—or anybody else for that matter.

"Want me to come up, Jen?"

"Sure, come on." She seemed to have gotten grown-up since she'd come to Lamptown, still nothing but a kid, Morry thought, with her eyes always wild and frightened as if she expected somebody to hit her any minute. Now with Morry sitting beside her, she was happy again, but she knew by this time that if she let him see it he would go away at once, because that's the way he was. If she could only keep from speaking to him he'd always hang around her, because silence seemed to mystify him. . . . Or, she reflected, if she could only stay angry with him for all the times he'd hurt her, but when he was here, right here beside her like this, she forgot all the times he'd made her cry all night . . .

"I thought you'd be out with Nettie," she said. "Like two weeks ago Saturday."

Morry sniffed.

"She can't get me to go out with her anymore," he said. This wasn't quite true. Nettie still treated him like dirt under her feet in the daytime and this so puzzled Morry that he had to reassure himself at other times that he was really the conqueror. He hated Nettie, though, he never would forget that he hated her.

"Say—say Jen, what are you going to do about Lil? Has she been adopted yet?"

Talking about Lil always pacified Jen . . .

"I wrote her to run away if they started adopting her," Jen said. "I could look after her. I sent her my birthday dollar."

Morry remembered his own brave promises about Lil—he was the one that was going to rescue Lil, he was.

"I've got a job, too," said Jen. "Anytime I want to, I can get three dollars a week waiting table at Bauer's. Grace gets six and her keep but I have to go to school part time."

"Next year you can get into the factory, too," said Morry, "You'll get ten there—maybe twelve."

"I'm not going to work in any factory," Jen told him casually. "I guess I'll go on the stage or be a dancer, maybe. If you'd been to the Casino lately you'd a seen me. Mr. Fischer says I'm a born dancer. So that's what I'll be doing."

Morry was silenced and awed. He saw Jen in a ballet skirt puffed out all around, her picture in some magazine, and at first he was proud, proud because she was his invention, then he was jealous of all the men who would be looking at a ballet girl's picture. He wanted to be glad of this glamorous future for her and he wanted to be fair, but he couldn't help warning her that it was pretty hard to get on the stage, and besides the Delaneys wouldn't let her, and what's more, who'd look after Lil?

Jen refused to be discouraged.

"I guess I'll do what I please when I'm earning regular money over at Bauer's," she said. "They can't stop me. I could look after Lil, and you said you'd help."

"Sure," said Morry. It was a promise.

The Chicago train thundered by with a fleeting glimpse of white-jacketed porters and lit-up dining cars. Morry and Jen watched it hungrily, they were on that train whizzing through Lamptown on their way to someplace, someplace wonderful, and looking a little pityingly out of their car window at a boy and girl sitting on the backsteps over a saloon. The train went ripping through further silence leaving only a humming in the air and a smoky message painted on the sky.

Morry and Jen looked quickly at each other—this was the thing that always bound them—trains hunting out unknown cities, convincing proof of adventure far off, of destiny somewhere waiting, of things beyond Lamptown. It was like that first time they sat here. . . .

"I'd never go away, Morry," Jen finally said, not looking at him, "not unless you went first."

Morry didn't know what to answer. Windows in the court were slowly lighting up, downstairs the player piano jangled out "Under the Double Eagle." The kitchen light of the Delaneys' apartment went on—the old lady might come out any minute and chase him off. . . . No, it was different from the first night they sat here because now they were grown up, Jen was old enough to go to the Casino dances.

"Say, Jen, who do you dance with over there?"

He didn't think anyone would ever ask her to dance. "I dance with Bill and with Sweeney and the men from downstairs," Jen answered. "And last time I danced with Hunt Russell twice."

Morry blinked at that. Hunt was an old rounder. If he got after Jen . . . Well, after all, someone would sooner or later, wouldn't they? Now he looked at her with Hunt Russell's eyes and saw that she was different from anyone at Lamptown dances, she was—yes, you might say pretty, but strange-looking, maybe it was her eyes or something stiff and proud in the way she held herself, yes, there was something here worth hunting down, a man would think. . . .

"It's funny dancing with Hunt," Jen said. "You think he's made different from other people—all solid gold clinking in him instead of lungs and a liver—and it's like his skin was more expensive than other people's, all heavy silk, the very best. It's like dancing with a prince."

"Who—that loafer?" Morry laughed scornfully.

"I used to think so," said Jen, "but you told me how wonderful he was, don't you remember, and I guess I was wrong."

"I don't know about that," said Morry uncomfortably. "Anyway he's not so different as you think from other people."

From far off came the train whistle, an invitation to mystery, to limitless adventure. A few stars showed up faintly. He could see Jen's face on that magazine cover, in a filmy white ballet skirt . . . it was all very far-off, some place where trains went . . . Hunt Russell, there, too, smiling quietly. . . .

Morry's arms went around Jen's shoulder, he kissed her hard on the mouth and received as reward a stinging slap in the face. He sat up straight, rubbing his face indignantly. Jen jumped up.

"You leave me alone, Morry! Don't you suppose I know about you and Nettie Farrell? Don't you suppose Grace and I followed you down to the

Murphys that night, don't you think I got any sense? So leave me alone, now, will you?"

"Say—oh now say, Jen."

Morry was crushed by this unexpected attack.

"Go on and kiss Nettie if you've got to be kissing somebody," Jen flung at him. "Don't think I want to have Nettie Farrell's old beaux, I'll get my own, thank you."

She fled indoors leaving the screen to shut in his face.

Morry's face burned at this attack. He was through with Jen St. Clair, that was certain. Nobody was going to slap his face, no tough little kid could tell him anything. With his hands jammed in his pockets he slouched across the alley to his home, angrier at every step with Jen, with Grace for following him that night, with everybody. Inside the hall doorway he bumped into Nettie who was standing there, her finger to her lips.

"I've been waiting for you," she whispered. "The Murphys are out tonight. I'm going to be alone."

It was the last straw.

"Isn't that too bad?" he snorted mockingly. "Now, isn't that a goddamned shame?"

He pushed past her upstairs and banged his door loudly shut. Nettie stamped her foot furiously and went back into the shop.

Mrs. Pepper cried telling Nettie about how Mrs. Abbott had changed, and Nettie answered that it was very funny for Mrs. Abbott to act that way after the years they'd known each other. They stood in front of Robbins' Jewelry Store discussing it.

"I'd hardly got inside the door, Nettie," said Mrs. Pepper tremulously. "I'd just set my grip down when she came out of the workroom, white as a sheet, and she said to me, 'Mrs. Pepper, you've been coming here a long time, too long, in fact, and I just wanted to tell you that it's going to stop right now. I got no place,' she says, 'for your corsets and trash in my shop, and it'll suit me if you take your stuff somewheres else.' . . . Well, Nettie, you know how I am, tenderhearted, and always a good friend to everyone. I didn't know what in the world to say. I said, what is it, whatever happened? . . . And she said, tightmouthed, the way she is, 'It's my place, Mrs. Pepper, I think I have the right to have or not have people here just as I like.' . . . I said who's been talking behind my back, just tell me their names and I'll make them answer for it."

"What'd she say to that?" Nettie asked, thinking over the slurring remarks she herself had often made about the corsetiere, and feeling rather guilty. "Did she say anyone had talked about you?"

"That's just it," answered Mrs. Pepper. "She looked funny and said, oh, so you know there's talk, do you, but she wouldn't say anything else, so I packed up my few little things and went right across the street to the Bauers', and Mrs. Bauer's letting me have a room upstairs for fittings. But, Nettie, what could anyone have said about me? You know I've always tried to be a lady, I've never done anything a lady wouldn't, you know that, Nettie."

Nettie kept her eyes fixed on a gilt clock in Robbins' window.

"Well, she might have heard about you and Mr. Fischer," she said gently. "After all, you know he is a married man."

Mrs. Pepper's little red mouth made an O of astonishment.

"The very idea! If that isn't like a little town. Just because Mr. Fischer and I both travel from place to place and are old friends, people get to talking! So that's what she heard, you think . . . Nettie, that does make me feel badly! . . . But I'm glad you told me. I never thought people would be so wicked saying things, when I've tried always to be a lady in spite of being alone in the world. Goodness, Mr. Fischer would be so upset to know anyone in Lamptown talked like that!"

Nettie said no more. They started back up the street and Mrs. Pepper forlornly left Nettie at the Bauers' front door. Bauers' rooms were so dark and musty and gloomy. The Bon Ton had seemed gay with girls chattering in and out all the time over hats, telling who was going with who, and laughing. . . . But Hermann Bauer never smiled and Hulda Bauer had stopped thinking and settled into a contented jellyfish the day she married Hermann. It was not a jolly place at all for a sun-loving soul, and Mrs. Pepper, lacing a customer into a lavender satin brocade model in her dingy bedroom, dropped a few unexpected tears down the girl's back.

"Mrs. Bauer is good to me, of course," she choked bravely, "and Mr. Bauer is such a fine man that I'd be the last one to complain—but I think dark places like this ought to be torn down, I do, really. It would be a blessing if it burned, it's so gloomy, and when you're in trouble with your dearest friend, too—honey, are you sure this doesn't pinch your tummy?"

Nettie tried to find out why Elsinore had taken such a serious step but Elsinore gave her no details. She seemed silent and preoccupied, and all she said was that Mrs. Pepper was a hypocrite and besides the Bon Ton had no place for all those corset boxes and trash. Nettie was glad the extra work was out of the way, she was especially glad because now she was to go with Elsinore, it seemed, on buying expeditions to Cleveland or Columbus. Before, Nettie had kept shop while Elsinore and Mrs. Pepper went off together, all dressed up for a day in the city. Elsinore said this time they would close the shop and take an early train, so Nettie sat up half the night sewing a new frill on her black suit and washing out white silk gloves. She'd been to Cleveland a few times but this was most exciting because now she was going as a business woman, a woman of affairs.

They sat in the chair car going in the next morning. Elsinore, with dark hollows under her eyes from thinking so desperately of the plan she had for the day, and Nettie, dressed up and well-pleased with herself, her gloved hands folded over her new gold mesh purse, a blue veil drooping from her little hat, lace openwork on her black silk stockings. This was her real sphere, Nettie thought, going to cities and wearing little veils and white gloves and perfume, being a woman of the world and she thought it was funny her living in Lamptown when anyone could tell she was more of a city type . . . She was twenty now and she certainly was doing more with her life than other girls her age were. She was bound she'd be a success, this year she'd join the Eastern Stars, she thought, and she'd read "Laddie" and "The Little Shepherd of Kingdom Come"; she'd get baptized, too, join a church, and whenever she met anyone from out of town she'd always correspond with them so that she'd be getting letters from Cincinnati and Birmingham and St. Louis all at one time. She'd take dancing lessons, too, only she didn't see how she'd ever have the nerve to practice in public with all the younger people. She'd have a hatshop of her own, some day, she'd call it the Paris Shop, or maybe The Elite, Nettie Farrell, prop.

Nettie glanced guiltily at Elsinore to see if this disloyal thought had somehow been overheard, but Elsinore was drumming nervously on the windowsill, watching fields and villages slide past the window.

They went to different stores in the morning buying silks and trimmings and they were to meet in the Taylor Arcade for lunch but Nettie got mixed up the way she always did in Cleveland and waited in the

Colonial Arcade instead. She stood at the entrance watching for Elsinore till half past one when a dark Jewish man smoking a cigar spoke to her. Nettie stared him down so haughtily that he rushed contritely into a little cigar store to peer at her over the inner curtains. Nettie, after a minute or two, walked slowly past the cigar store and somehow dropped her purse so he came out to pick it up. This time Nettie thanked him very distantly and when he went on asking her if she was just in town for the day she answered him rather loftily so he could see she was not an ordinary pickup.

When Elsinore finally decided to look for Nettie in the other Arcade she saw her through the glass window of a little tearoom at a table with some stranger. The man was talking and Nettie was sedately holding a teacup, little finger flying. Elsinore went in and Nettie said, "This is Mr. Schwarz, Mrs. Abbott. He used to travel for the same company Mr. Abbott did, isn't that funny, but now he's in the woolen business and he lives at the Gilsey. We're going to the Hippodrome this afternoon while you're seeing wholesalers."

Elsinore had been wondering how she would get rid of Nettie for the afternoon so she was much more agreeable over tea and cinnamon buns than she usually was with strangers, and Mr. Schwarz, at first wary, began to warm up to the idea of a little party for four. He said he'd call up the hotel and get hold of a friend of his named Wohlman, who also was in woolen, and tonight they'd all go to the Ratskellar and afterwards to a show the Hermits were giving. The idea alarmed Elsinore and she got away as fast as she could.

"Five thirty, then, in the Hollenden lobby," said Nettie gaily, being a woman of the world.

Elsinore took a Woodland Avenue car out to East 55th Street. She didn't dare think of what she was about to do or she might lose courage. She thought of Mrs. Pepper and after three weeks of hating her, even the mental image of the woman was distorted into a fat, lewd beast that deserved annihilation. Elsinore wasn't sorry she'd sent her out of the Bon Ton, she wasn't sorry when Mrs. Pepper's blue eyes welled with tears over this broken friendship; she wished she had it in her to be even crueler; she would like to have hurt her as much as she had been hurt herself. . . .

All these years, then, the town whisper about Fischer and Mrs. Pepper had been well-founded. Elsinore felt as betrayed as if Fischer had really been her own husband, she wanted fiercely to be revenged, not on him, but on the woman. Nor was the desire for revenge a spasmodic thought that died out after the first shock of suspicions proved true; she thought of it night and day ever since the rainy night Mrs. Pepper had gone out with Dode to meet him somewhere; she thought of them on Thursday nights at the Casino watching his heavy mask-like face. . . . She had wondered often about his wife and now she felt somehow identified with her, as if Mrs. Pepper had deliberately wronged them both. What kept her curious indignation at fever pitch was the thought of how long Mrs. Pepper had fooled everyone with her wide innocent blue eyes, her baby face, her dainty lady-like ways, her sweet detachment in mentioning his name. Worse than a vampire, Elsinore grimly decided, worse than the commonest factory girl, because she pretended so much, because she fooled people.

At the other end of the streetcar, two girls in white flannel suits giggled over yesterday's moonlight ride on the Steamer Eastland, and the conductor asked them if they were going to the big brewers' picnic next Sunday at Put-in-Bay. Elsinore listened to them intently because she wanted to know things that people around Fischer knew, she wanted to hear and see the same things he did, she could almost be him, she could half close her eyes and admire women and young girls the way he did. This was what he saw on his way to and from his house, and now that they were close to 55th Street, that must be the church over yonder where he sent his children to Sunday school, this must be the market where his wife did her trading, this was his stop. . . .

Elsinore's knees were shaky getting off the car. If she could only keep in mind how Mrs. Pepper had fooled her and Mrs. Fischer, she'd be able to go ahead with her plan, but she kept forgetting and having stage fright over being so near his place and so near to coming face to face with his wife. She asked a streetcleaner where this number was and he pointed out an old house set far back from the street with a sign in the window in black and white—

HARRY FISCHER
Ballroom Dancing

Oh, she'd never have the courage to walk down that pathway with someone probably peeking at her from behind the lace curtains, and perhaps someone following her, too. . . . This frightened her, she looked over her shoulder, now she had a distinct feeling of being followed. If Nettie had taken it into her head to follow her, what would she say?

"I came to arrange private dancing lessons for both of us," she'd tell Nettie if it came to that, and she'd say it was always impossible to get a private word with Fischer about it in Lamptown so she'd just dropped in. . . .

If it was Fischer himself behind her, though, or Mrs. Pepper, or Charles, or someone from Lamptown. . . . Still, there wasn't a chance of any such thing, why should she feel guilty when she was only doing a friendly duty? . . . She walked quickly up to the gray gingerbread porch. She wondered if he owned this house, if he had a dance-hall in it the way Mrs. Pepper had once said, and it made her ache to think of all the things in his life that she could never guess thinking about him in the Bon Ton. . . . She was on the porch, in a minute she'd turn around and run for her life . . . no, she was ringing the doorbell and her black gloved hand was quite steady. She couldn't run now, even if Fischer himself should confront her, her legs were numb, she doubted if she could even speak. She heard steps inside, the sound of a slap, and a child screeching and then the door opened.

"Well?"

Two towheaded children on a red scooter stared at her with bold black eyes, their mother tried to push them out of the way of the door, she was a large ash-blonde woman with heavy breasts and her voice was deep like a singer's with a vaguely Scandinavian accent. His wife. . . . Yes, she was Mrs. Fischer. The lady wanted to know about dancing lessons? Friday and Saturday were his Cleveland days, if she wanted to sign up for the course and leave a five dollar deposit. . . .

"It's not about dancing," Elsinore said, "It's about him that I wanted to see you."

Her throat felt swollen and tight, talking was like trying to scream in your sleep, driving your voice through your shut mouth with all your might and having it come out only a hoarse whisper.

"There's a woman that wants to make trouble for you and I thought someone ought to tell you so you could stop it."

Fischer's wife just stared stupidly at her. The largest towheaded child with a little yelp turned his toy car around and scooted down the hall, its bell going tingalingaling, and the littlest one remembered that his mother had slapped him and resumed his wailing, burying his face in his mother's skirts.

Mrs. Fischer pushed open the screen door.

"Do you want to come inside and tell me what you're talking about, missus?" she said, studying Elsinore from head to foot with a puzzled and not at all friendly eye. "What's this about my husband and who are you, anyway, that's what I want to know?"

Elsinore could feel her face reddening, she must be careful now, or Fischer might guess who had told.

"It doesn't matter who I am," she said hurriedly, "but I thought you ought to know—as one woman to another, understand—that there's someone your husband goes with out of town, there's a woman crazy about him, trying to break up your home."

She'd said it now, but Mrs. Fischer's thick pasty face took on an ugly expression. Her pale blue eyes narrowed, under the heavy colorless brows.

"I suppose you don't want to make trouble, too, hey? I suppose I'm to believe a party coming in out of the blue sky and not saying who she is, just bringing tattle tales to see what harm she can do—"

Elsinore backed away from the door, alarmed at the woman's tone. Mrs. Fischer came out on the porch after her.

"See here, what right have you got, coming to my home making trouble for me? If my husband's doings don't suit you, then you don't need to watch 'em, just mind your own step, that's all. Who are you, coming here with your tattle? Where you from, anyway? Who told you I wanted to hear tales about Harry?"

"I didn't want you to be fooled, that was all," gasped Elsinore, and backed down the porch steps with Mrs. Fischer coming right after her, her hands on her hips. "You had a right to know."

"Well, who said you were the one with a right to tell," Mrs. Fischer asked contemptuously. "I've got enough trouble without strangers trying to cook up more. I'd thank you to clear out, and I'll tell you here and now if anybody's got the right to spy on Harry, it's me, and nobody else, understand? So!"

Elsinore, faint with shame, rushed toward the street. Both children now were crying loudly and the toy car bell dingled raucously in her ears. She knew people were watching her, someone was following her again, that much was certain, she felt their distrustful eyes boring through her back, the footsteps behind her were ominous, but when she dared to look back it was only a mailman and further off two women wheeling go-carts, she could not find those watchful eyes. Foghorns croaked on the lake and made her head buzz, the city noises seemed more than she could bear. She climbed aboard the first street car that came along, it was pure luck that it was going in the right direction. Her face would never stop burning, she was so shamed, yet she was glad in a way because she'd had to do just that thing, she'd simply had to, nothing could have stopped her, and now it was over with, that was all. . . . What would she say to Nettie, she wondered, what could she tell her? . . . She sat next to a big colored woman who asked her where the May Company was, where you got off for the Interurban Station, how you got out to Gates Mills? She didn't know, she kept mumbling in reply, and planned what to say to Nettie.

"I went to Halle's for that taffeta, then I walked over to the Square and sat down for a while, then I went to the braid place, then I went into De Klyn's for a sundae and cocoa—no, for a cup of tea, then—then—"

She went into the hotel lobby where she was to meet Nettie. She was dizzy and faint, for she wasn't used to crowds and street cars. Suspicious eyes continued to bore through her, she was certain someone had followed her all day, she was certain someone was reading her guilty thoughts.

It was long after six when Nettie came. Mr. Schwarz, perhaps a little self-conscious, was not with her, but Nettie talked about him a great deal on the way to the depot, because she'd never been out with an older man, a man of the world, before. . . . Elsinore did not breathe easily until she was finally on the train for Lamptown. No one had seen her. No one had followed her. No one knew.

"So then we went down to the Ratskellar," Nettie chattered on excitedly, "and Mr. Schwarz asked me what I'd have since I hated beer so much. So I took a Clover Club cocktail because Mr. Schwarz said that in Cleveland they were absolutely all the go."

Elsinore didn't dare go to the dance on Thursday night, she was afraid to face the dancing teacher for a little while. She closed the shop and sat in the dark watching the Casino windows, seeing couples whirl past and hearing Fischer's big voice boom out the commands. She leaned forward on the wicker settee and wrung her hands each time the music started for a new dance. If there was a circle two-step tonight she might have gotten him for a partner for a minute or two, but now she'd ruined the chances of that. She wouldn't dare go up again, he'd ask what right she had going to his wife. . . . At least Mrs. Pepper hadn't gone to the Casino either, because Nettie had seen her get on the streetcar going upstate earlier in the day.

The Bauers were in their window peering out at the passing girls, and she reflected bitterly that she might as well be Hulda Bauer now, nothing but a spectator. She saw Grace come out in front of the restaurant and hoo-oo, then the Delaneys' girl, Jen, came running across the street to join her, and they went up the Casino steps together. She saw her own son standing in front of her darkened shop, smoking, waiting for the right moment to go over. When Jen and Grace went up he turned around and stared idly at the dimly outlined hats in the Bon Ton window. Then Elsinore realized that in spite of the darkness, the lights reflected from the street made her faintly visible because Morry frowned and suddenly pressed his face against the pane, staring inside, as if he was seeing a ghost. She stood very still but after all her face probably showed up white and shadowy for Morry shivered and backed away, she saw him toss his cigarette into the gutter and hurry across the street, stopping at the foot of the Casino stairs for a puzzled backward glance at the Bon Ton.

There would be next Thursday night and the next and the next. . . . Elsinore grew dizzy thinking of all the torture in store for her, for how could she ever look at Fischer again after her Cleveland visit. . . . His wife must have told him everything and he had told Mrs. Pepper and probably Mrs. Pepper had put two and two together. . . . Elsinore dragged her feet slowly up the stairs to bed, but she wouldn't sleep tonight, she'd lie there listening to the music and the applause, and think. . . . It was no use, she knew that no matter what the risk she'd go next Thursday night. After all, she hadn't told Fischer's wife her name or even that she was from Lamptown, so how could anyone possibly guess?

She drew a rocking chair up to her bedroom window and huddled there in her nightdress.

"Dance Number Three."

Today some factory girls trying on hats had talked about the chance Fischer had to have a studio in Chicago only he'd refused to give up his Cleveland headquarters. It had been a great chance, they said, and he might change his mind, of course. Elsinore thought of dark, silent Thursday nights going on forever, for the rest of her life, and a Lamptown slackening into a dull shuffle with no Fischer to count out the rhythm. . . . Well, there was always a chance for a new millinery store in a big city like Chicago, she could get on there, she could always manage her business,

Chicago wouldn't be any harder than Lamptown. Now it seemed a question of the Bon Ton moving to Chicago, and she'd forgotten why.

It must be a good dance tonight. Everyone sang softly with the orchestra, they blended into one gay humming voice that might be swelling out of the rickety old building itself though no one could believe it to look at the sleepy expressionless faces of Hermann and Hulda Bauer in the first floor window.

> "Has anybody here seen Kelly—
> K-e- double l-y
> Anybody here seen Kelly—"

Elsinore sat in the chair and wished she hadn't been such a coward as to stay away. She'd never stay home again, that was certain.

In the smoking room of the Casino Morry Abbott read a magazine with a red devil on the cover. If he went out on the floor Grace would smile at him waiting for him to dance with her, and he wasn't going to be trapped into anything again. If he looked up from the magazine he would see Jen whirling by with Sweeney, the telegraph operator, or with his own foreman; if she'd been sitting out by herself he might ask her for a dance but he wasn't going to compete with other men, he'd never do that. Let her have them, but he could tell by the way she flipped her skirts passing the smoking room that she wanted him to be jealous, and it annoyed him. He read on resolutely, all the stories ended in suicide, he wished he knew things so he could read the one story in French. He looked at it wistfully—'l'amour' was love, that much he did know. . . . Something made him lift his eyes and there was Jen dancing with Hunt. Morry threw down the book and went out. Some yellow-haired girl in a red flannel dress was sitting by the door chewing gum. He asked her to dance.

It was a pretty how-de-do, he thought, when people as fussy as old Mrs. Delaney let a kid go to dances and run with old rounders like Russell. He saw now that Jen wore Grace Terris's dress—Grace was wearing a new one—she had her hair fixed up like Grace's as near as she could make it, and she had on high-heeled shoes, surely Grace's, since if you looked closely you could tell they were too big for her, and she seemed unreasonably well-pleased with herself. Morry found himself burning with righteous anger, partly because she seemed able to dance as well as anyone else without having had any lessons, and partly because she giggled too loud and tweaked Sweeney's necktie. He tried to ignore her but she always managed to get right in front of him and when he'd look somewhere else he'd encounter Grace's steady meaning gaze. All right, he'd go home, he wasn't going to stand around here like a fool, but when he put on his coat Hunt Russell was in the coatroom smoking and kidding the fat little hat-check girl. He beckoned Morry.

"Stick around, Abbott, we'll pick up a couple of women and drive Fischer over to Marion. . . . Got a date?"

It was the royal command and Morry obediently took off his coat. Dode wasn't around tonight and he knew Hunt would pick the two hardest-boiled girls in the hall but he didn't care. You had to do what Hunt asked you to—you wanted to, somehow. . . . He went back in the smoking room and read the red devil magazine again. Sweeney and his factory foreman came in and asked him to go over to Delaney's for a beer or two, and Morry said briefly:

"Can't. Going out with Hunt."

He was proud because Hunt didn't ask just anybody. He went with Hunt for ham sandwiches at Bauers' and a pint of rye at Delaney's at the end of the last dance. When they came out Hunt went on up to get Fischer and Morry strolled over to get in Hunt's car. The women were already in—one in front and one in back. Morry took a second glance and saw that the evening was already spoiled, for the girl in front was Jen, and the one in back, swathed in floating scarfs, was Grace.

"Oh, Jen, look, here's Morry!" gurgled Grace. "Won't we have a circus? Wouldn't Dode take our heads off if she knew? Wouldn't she, Morry?"

Morry gloomily got in beside Grace. Jen turned around to give him a triumphant smile. Morry was annoyed, because while he himself was dazzled by Hunt's glamorous position he thought it was ridiculous for a girl to be taken in by all that bunk.

"Thought you couldn't stand Hunt," he challenged her. "Thought you was just about going to burn up his house some day. I notice you've changed your mind."

"I never was in an automobile before," Jen resentfully explained. "I guess you'd go, too."

"Jen's never been anywhere," Grace laughed. "Why, when I was fifteen there was two fellas crazy over me and I had dates every night. I was more like a man's woman, I was. I certainly had a good time and I knew what was what, too."

Fischer and Hunt came down and Morry moved over to let Fischer in beside Grace. With a great roaring of the motor they started. Grace wanted Fischer to be affectionate and she kept leaning against him.

"Look at this, Jen," she'd call and playfully wrap her arms around him but Fischer firmly shook her off. He winked at Morry once and made a wry face, but Morry was only able to manage a half-hearted smile in turn. It was all easy enough to understand. Hunt was amused by Jen the way the men said he always was by every new kind of girl, he asked Morry because he'd gotten the idea she was Morry's girl, that was all. He really didn't give a damn who was in the back seat so long as he had what he wanted beside him in front there. It made his invitation not so flattering after all, and Morry blamed Jen for this disillusion.

Certainly the ride wasn't any fun with Grace on one hand making a fool of herself over Fischer and Jen in front with her hat off and the wind blowing her black hair all over, not talking, just watching Hunt as if he was some great wonder. She'd get it from the old lady when she got in, Morry thought, and if Dode O'Connell ever found out, she'd get it from her, too. It took two hours to drive to Marion—it would be at least four or five when they got back, and the Delaneys wouldn't stand for that. Jen ought to be more careful. Thinking of this Morry got angrier than ever with Grace for egging her into it, and he was angry with Hunt too. Hunt and Fischer drank the whiskey between them, though Grace, with much tittering took more than a few swigs from the bottle to show she was used to going out. Fischer didn't talk except to call something out to Hunt once in a while; he was sleepy, he said, and leaned back on the seat with his eyes closed most of the way.

It was three when they got to his hotel in Marion and then Hunt insisted that they all go over to the Quick Lunch for ham and eggs. Grace was eager for this because she'd only been a guest in a restaurant twice and she was anxious to be lordly with other waitresses.

"You'd better take those kids back to Lamptown, Hunt," Fischer advised. "You'll have Bill Delaney on your neck if you keep his girl out much longer."

"How'd you like to mind your own business?" Hunt inquired, lighting a cigarette. "This young lady's just about able to take care of herself."

Fischer got his handbag from under Morry's feet and banged the car door shut.

"I'm sure I hope so," he said calmly. "Well, goodnight."

"To hell with you," answered Hunt. He drove over to the Quick Lunch and they got out. Morry was sleepy, he'd never been out so late, and much as he wanted to be ranked as a sport like Hunt and Fischer, he only wished he was home in bed, and the thought of the long ride home sickened him, he didn't know why except that he knew Jen would get a good whaling when she got in and she was just a little fool and it was all her own fault. She was excited about being out with men in strange towns after midnight, but she was scared too, you could tell by her eyes, she was scared of what the old lady would say to her coming home in the morning.

"I knew Fischer wanted a date with me," Grace said over the white porcelain table. "He always is looking at me with those big black eyes sort of as if he'd like to say something to me but was afraid to speak out, I suppose on account of his wife. I kidded him tonight about being so bashful and he had to admit that he was, did you hear us kidding, Jen?"

Jen nodded and looked at the big white clock on the wall. It said four o'clock but Hunt wasn't in any hurry and Grace was having the time of her life. She got to talking about all the other swell restaurants she'd been in, and somehow her memory had blurred so that she seemed to have been the most valued patron in these resorts and not an employee at all. Nobody listened to her. Jen kept looking at the clock, more scared than ever now, but afraid to suggest going for fear they'd think she was young and not used to being out. Grace talked and Morry yawned over his coffee and squirmed restlessly when he saw Hunt stare lazily at Jen.

"Cold, Baby?" Hunt asked Jen when she shivered once. Then when they finally started back to the car Morry saw him put his arm over her shoulder.

"Good kid," he murmured and slid in behind the wheel. "Say, Abbott, anything left of that quart?"

"No," lied Morry, because he wasn't going to be killed tonight by wild driving. "I finished it up."

All the way back driving into the sunrise Hunt kept one arm flung over Jen's shoulders and Grace, after many coy attempts to engage Morry's attention, moved over to the edge of the seat and hummed softly to herself; sometimes she'd call Jen's attention to this house which was just like her Uncle File's, or that railroad depot which was only half as big as the one in Tiffin. Morry saw none of these things, he only saw Hunt's arm around Jen and he thought that it was just as Hogan said—Hunt Russell wasn't so damned much, people in Lamptown were taken in by him only because of the money his old man had made and Hunt was nothing but a sport and a waster with no more guts to him than a jellybean. Dode O'Connell was the only woman that wanted him, he wasn't any matinee idol with his graying temples and his weak chin, what made him so complacently sure he could get Jen St. Clair if he so condescended?

Grace pointed toward Hunt's arm.

"Do you allow that, Morry?" she asked archly.

"Has he got anything to say about it?" Hunt called back, and slowed the car to lean over and kiss Jen. But she didn't slap him, Morry noted cynically, she didn't seem to mind at all, so Morry sullenly put his own arm around Grace for Jen to be sure and see.

It was six o'clock when they drew up in front of Bauer's. Grace rushed in, eager for Sweeney the telegraph operator to come in for breakfast so she could brag about the wild party. Morry and Jen crossed the street together. In the alley between their two homes they looked at each other.

"Well, you're going to catch it," Morry said. "It's Hunt's fault. He had no business asking you out, he knows how Bill is."

"I had a good time," answered Jen, but she looked a little doubtfully toward the saloon.

"See, you're afraid to go up," Morry challenged her. "Do you think she'd have the nerve to beat you up?"

"Pooh!" bragged Jen. "I'd like to see her try. I'd tell her right where to get off."

She was in no hurry, though. Morry wanted to do something big, in a casual, off-handed way to go over and pave the way for Jen, but he knew he was a lot more afraid of Bill's mother than even Jen was. Only the Hunt Russells knew how to have their way, how to get things, all anybody else could ever do was to wish and be afraid. He got his key out for his side door, and still Jen hung back. She took his handkerchief and wiped her shoes off carefully, and straightened her hair.

"Wish I was Grace," she said. "I wouldn't be afraid of anybody then. I'd be on my own and nobody could say a word to me if I stayed out late."

"You're pretty stuck on Hunt, now, aren't you?" Morry said. "I noticed you kissed him and made no fuss about it, either."

Jen looked at him silently until Morry's own eyes dropped.

"I guess you know well enough who I like, Morry," she said. "Well. . . . I might as well go home and get it over with. They wouldn't dare lick me, you bet your life."

She winked at him and walked boldly across the court. Morry let himself indoors and climbed upstairs. His mother was in the doorway of his room, looking very pale and tired in the gray morning light, her brown braids hanging over her wrapper.

"I didn't mean to wake you—I was just out on a little ride," he stammered.

"That's all right, I wasn't sleeping anyway," she murmured. "I only looked in to see if you'd come in."

She didn't wait for an answer, just smiled and pulled her wrapper around her to go back to her room, her long braids swinging. Funny she didn't mind his being out all night. She hadn't even listened to his excuse. Morry was puzzled. Funny her not sleeping. . . . Morry for some reason remembered his father's insistent questioning that night behind the saloon, something hit him sickeningly in the pit of the stomach. His mother. What if . . . Yes, there was some man. His mother. . . . Morry sat down on the bed and shut his eyes. He heard her moving about on the other side of the wall but suddenly he could see her face before him more distinctly than he ever had—the gray eyes now with faint lines at the corners, the fine hairs of her nostrils, the unsmiling straight mouth, the face of a stranger. . . . He was stiff, sitting there so rigidly, and his eyeballs ached for sleep, but he dared not close them because he had to think about this thing . . . His mother. . . .

On the Delaney back porch Jen rubbed her hand over her eyes to make sure of what she saw. But it was true, no doubt of it. There sat her yellow telescope, packed and strapped, with her hat and coat on top of it. The door was locked. Jen resolutely tugged at the screen door but even that was hooked tight. The old lady had fired her for staying out—that was all there was to it. She sat down on the steps, frightened. She fumbled with the hat—it was the round sailor she'd worn away from the orphanage and it was too little with a childish rubber band under the chin. She slipped it on. The coat was too tight, too, and the sleeves hardly came below the elbow. Gee, how she'd grown, she thought. . . . She picked up the telescope and went uncertainly down the stairs. She knew the old lady was somewhere behind a curtain grimly watching to see what she'd do. Well, there wasn't anything to do but go.

At the foot of the steps Jen shifted the bag to the other hand and looked toward Bauer's then over toward the Bon Ton. No use looking, nobody was going to look after you but your own self. She looked up toward the screen door again. Bill might come out and call her back. She waited but the door didn't open. She guessed she was pretty lucky the old lady hadn't given her a beating when it came right down to it. Her knees shaking Jen picked her way across the back lot to the railroad. There weren't any trains in sight. She might as well get going. . . . She looked over her shoulder at the Delaney kitchen window but nobody was leaning out there beckoning her to come back. . . . With both arms around the yellow telescope she started grimly walking down the track.

She'd leave her telescope in the Tower with Sweeney, Jen thought; she'd walk east down the tracks and get a ride on a three-wheeler maybe to the next town. If she could get near Libertyville she'd go to the Home and get Lil. Then—then—well, she could get a job like Grace's in a restaurant, couldn't she? She was too ashamed ever to go back to Lamptown. People would know she'd been locked out because she stayed out all night and they'd say, just as old Mrs. Delaney had, that she'd turned out bad the way adopted girls always did. She'd get Lil herself now, so that Lil wouldn't ever be adopted and turn out bad.

It was a foggy morning. In the ditch beside the tracks burdocks and milkweed propped up dewy spider webs, fields were veiled in lavender, in the gray sky a hawk circled lower and lower so that birds were still. Jen hurried to reach the Tower before Sweeney got through because the day trick operators were stricter about visitors.

She was excited because she was going to do something big now, get Lil, and be on her own, but a faint sick feeling came over her when she thought she'd turned out bad the way Mrs. Delaney had always said, and that Lamptown with its dance music and Morry Abbott was behind her. The sun struggled through sooty pink clouds over the Big Four woods, lying under the trees were tramps sleeping with their hats over their faces and newspapers for covers. Two were kneeling by a little bonfire, skinning a rabbit. Jen was afraid of them because once a man was murdered here, they found his head rolling in the ditch and the stump of his cork leg. . . . She got off the track for a slow freight with cattle cars of whinnying western ponies and lambs bleating through their bars piteously. The brakeman waved his cap to her from the top of the caboose and Jen waved back. Names in big letters on the cars tantalized her—CLEVELAND, CINCINNATI & ST. LOUIS, MICHIGAN CENTRAL,

PERE MARQUETTE, LAKE SHORE R. R., SANTA FE R. R.,
DELAWARE LACKAWANNA R. R.—Jen saw the brakeman far
down the tracks still waving to her.

"Good-bye," she called to him and waved again.

She stumbled through the cinders on to the Yards. Everything was different, it was a new world today, a world to be measured and appraised with a view to possible conquest. As for Lamptown, it wasn't her Lamptown now, she saw it hungrily from the outside where she belonged. Behind the black fences all along here were the backyards of Shantyville, there was the spire of the Church of Our Lady. Shantyville backyards were different from the boarding house backyards where they sometimes had hollyhocks and grape arbors and swings for the girls. Here were only tumbled-down chicken houses with skinny pin-feathered chickens flapping around, washings always hanging out, gray sheds with dirty children on the roofs screaming and waving to the trains. . . . But even Shantyville was gay in its shiftless way and people were lucky to live there. . . . Jen wanted to reach the Tower before the factory men from this end of town started down the tracks on their way to work. They'd know she'd been locked out and they'd know it was because she'd stayed out all night.

It was funny about her feet walking along the ties as if they belonged to somebody else. She thought Bill might be following her to bring her back, indeed she was so sure that she didn't even turn around for fear of being disappointed. She stepped over rails and humming wires to the Tower stairs. Sweeney was in there alone with his fingers on the little black keys, the room ticked and throbbed with important messages.

"Hey, Sweeney, watch this bag till I come back, will you?"

Sweeney was mad because the day man was late this morning.

"You get the hell out of here before Tucker finds you!"

Jen shoved the bag inside and scurried downstairs again. The factory whistles were blowing for work and the men were coming down the track swinging their lunch pails. The old station agent hobbled over tracks swinging a bunch of keys and Jen saw him staring at her curiously as he unlocked the ticket office. She caught sight of one of the freight hands, a young Swede named Davey often in Bill's saloon, pumping a handcar down the track. He sometimes let her ride and today when she got on, his anguish over the English language saved her from any questions. On the handcar you ran off the tracks into cinderheaps every time you saw an engine ahead and you couldn't get very far that way. Davey was going to some section workers a few miles out, but only a few miles out made Lamptown seem far, far away, it seemed like a dream, last night in the restaurant hadn't happened, or the locked door—the real thing was the Children's Home where she belonged.

Near the water tank some Pullman cars were on siding, their names were spelled out in gold letters over their black sides—GRETCHEN—MINNEHAHA—NIGHTFALL—BLACK BEAUTY. Fortunate people looked out the windows yawning, and Jen saw a woman in a heavenly blue kimona smoking a cigarette. When would one ever get old, she wondered passionately, and know everything and have everything—if she could only be old like the woman in the blue kimona, and be looking back on all this, perfectly sure of herself, quite unafraid. . . .

The rotten planks on the handcar tore her dress, the old lady would scold her for that—but no—the old lady wouldn't scold her any more. The tracks went through low fields past an old quarry and here Davey pushed off and Jen said good-bye.

"You know where you're going?" stammered Davey, a little uneasily.

"Sure, I do."

She waded through muddy pastureland to the road. It was the road to the Orphanage at Libertyville, she could tell that, so she wasn't so far out of her way. She'd get Lil, then the two of them would get to Cleveland somehow and find their mother, that was the best thing to do. If her mother couldn't take care of them, why they could work, they were big enough. And nobody could stop you from going to your own mother. . . . She'd get in the back way somehow and find Lil, and even if she did run into the matron she wouldn't be afraid to tell her she'd come for her sister. . . . At least she didn't think she'd be afraid. But now that she was so near the Home the very trees had an air of inescapable authority, the woods, the fields, the houses all seemed busy and complete as if they were all there first and would forever be in command. Jen couldn't believe there had ever been moments when she'd thought herself free of them, when she'd actually planned to defy them and take Lil away. . . . She'd have to be at least ten or twenty years older, very rich, and with a body-guard of powerful citizens before she'd dare venture inside the Home gates. . . . They'd treat her as if she'd just run away again, the way she used to do, and been caught; they wouldn't believe she'd ever been adopted and out of their hands. She'd never get away again, either, they'd hear from Mrs. Delaney about her and they'd put her to work for the rest of her life in the Laundry the way they did orphans that were too afraid to go out in the world when they got their liberty. . . . Jen began walking slower and slower. No sign of anything like Lamptown all around her, only yards of bushes and then a rain-rusted R. F. D. box. She remembered these bushes for there were berry farms all along here. The orphans were let out to pick berries in the big season, they made six cents a quart and the one that made the most got a silver badge to wear, but all the pennies had to go to the Fund.

It was too late for strawberries but there were currants and goose-berries now, later on there would be potatoes to bug. Jen's heart dropped remembering when that was her world. She looked quickly over her shoulder—if someone from the Home saw her and recognized her she wouldn't stand a chance. They'd never let her get to her mother or to Lil either. She kept over to the edge of the road lingering in the tree shadows when anyone passed. If she was ninety years old, she thought resentfully, she'd never get over the fear of being clapped back in the Home again, made to say prayers out loud, sent out to pick berries. She'd been so certain she wasn't afraid of anything any more, but this one thing she'd always be afraid of.

There was a familiar sign tacked to a post here, "Red Clover Farm," and a muddy lane wound off the main road through a sparse woods. Far down this lane Jen saw someone coming, her hand over her eyes to stare longer and make sure. There was no doubt about it, it was a procession of children from the Home, all in blue calico and straw farm hats, berry pails clinking from their arms. In the lead was the Oldest Orphan, just as Jen had been once. Now it was a girl named Sadie whose folks were in the penitentiary so no one would ever take her. The Oldest Orphan carried the bun basket and behind her somewhere in this line must be Lil. Unconsciously Jen was backing into the bushes as she watched this on-coming procession, and thinking of how near she was to Lil her limbs began to shake. Suddenly she crashed through bushes and brambles for hiding—she forgot about everything but the fear of being caught again and made to go back. Hypnotized, she watched the line getting nearer, she saw the Oldest Orphan's brown sullen face, she could almost have whispered "Hoo-oo, Sadie!" but there was a woman in charge at the end. Then she saw Lil and it made her ache to see the sweet little dollface under the big straw-hat; she wanted to rush out and say, "Here I am, Lil, see, come to take you away just like I promised." But they'd only make her fall in line and go back to the Home, too, that's all they'd ever do, she wasn't strong enough for them yet, she couldn't beat them.

The line went on up the road, they didn't laugh or talk, just marched along doing as they were told, and presently they went into the fields and Lil was lost. Jen came out onto the road again, weak and puzzled, too, that there could be something you were so sure you could do and when the chance came you were helpless. . . . So this was the way she was going to look after Lil, was it, always looking out for her own hide first, never able to do the wonderful things she'd planned. . . . Rage swept over her at being young, young and little, as if some evil fairy had put that spell on her. Why must you be locked up in this dreadful cage of childhood for twenty or a hundred years? Nothing in life was possible unless you were old and rich, until then you were only small and futile before your tormentors, desperately waiting for the release that only years could bring. You boldly threw down your challenges and then ran away in a childish panic when someone picked them up. . . . Jen stumbled along the road, glowering down at the dust, sick because she had failed Lil. She'd never get over being ashamed as long as she lived. Lil had been within two yards of her and she'd let her go, she was like all the visitors to the Home who'd promised her long ago they'd come back for her, and they never did, they never came back.

Coming to the Crossroads Jen sat down on a pile of fence rails. She wondered how far she was from Lamptown and she wanted to erase last night and go back. She thought of the pianola and the little gold chair from the World's Fair, and Morry. . . . She'd let Lamptown go and she'd let Lil go. She'd not been able to hold the things that meant the most to her. Maybe she never would. That was why she liked the tiny gold chair, you could close your hand tight over it and know it was always there.

She was hungry, it must be noon now, but that didn't seem to be the matter with her. The matter was that she'd failed. She was dizzy, too, trying to figure out where all these roads went. Cleveland? Akron? Columbus? She would like to be on a train named Nightfall going to some place where she'd be twenty-five years old.

An empty hay wagon came lumbering along and Jen hailed it.

"Give us a ride, mister."

"Going east?"

"Sure."

The driver was an old man with a Santa Claus beard, he had a face busy with a tobacco quid. He might have been asleep for all the heed he paid to his passenger. It was a relief to ride, and now if they should pass the Home by any chance, Jen decided she would hide under the burlap bags in the back. They jogged along, and looking about her the old aching years came back to her; going along shady country roads with the low branches flapping against her face. . . . She could remember being as tall as a wagon wheel, the caked putty mud on the wheel, stepping on the spokes and then on the muddy step into the wagon. She could remember being allowed to drive, the black leather reins slipping in her little hands, and her feet not halfway to the floor swinging back and forth, brown mud-caked boots with the buttons off except the first and last; she could see again the horse's black tail swishing back and forth at the flies. She had now the same scratches from brambles that she had then, and here were the same knotty trees that Johnny Appleseed had planted.

Along the road were neat little white and green-trimmed farmhouses with thin scrawny women outside watering rusty geraniums or pansy beds. They were the same women as before, Jen thought, women that would slap you with the backs of their hands so that the wedding ring cut your cheek, if you dared to touch the conch shell on the parlor mantel, or if you smelled the glass flowers in the vase; those women would make you get up before daylight to help wash, and you wouldn't get any breakfast till the washing was done, either. . . .

Digging postholes along the road were men in overalls, jolly-seeming sun-bronzed men, but they weren't jolly at all, they'd call up the Orphanage any time to say, "This is R. MacDonald on the Ellery Road. I saw a couple of the orphans out by here and thought they might be running away. If you want me to, I'll pick them up and bring them right over." This was because people liked the idea of other people being locked up.

She would never smell hay or blackberries or honeysuckle without that gone feeling of being trapped, Jen realized, while pianola music, saloon smells, engines shrieking, and the delicious smell of hot soapy dishwater from restaurant kitchens—these would always be gay symbols of escape.

They were at the pike road now, there was a streetcar track crossing it and a big sign reading "Turnpike Dairy."

"Here's where I go, girlie," said the driver. "Somebody else'll give you a lift now, I guess."

Jen got down. She didn't move till the wagon was far out of sight. Then she started limping down the car tracks. Her feet were sore and her eyes were full of dust and sleep. She came to a wide shallow brook and tiptoed over the trestle high above it. If a streetcar should unexpectedly come along she'd have to let herself down and dangle between the trestle ties, hanging by her fingertips, she planned. . . . She was so tired now she could go on forever without seeing or feeling anything. But this wasn't quite true, for before her was a banner across the road. It said—

WELCOME TO LAMPTOWN

Jen stopped dead. Lamptown had followed her, it seemed. Suddenly she was so happy she forgot her sore feet and started running as fast as she could down the track, stumbling over ties, panting for breath, her hair flying in all directions, but happy, happy, happy—because Lamptown had come after her. . . . She'd go straight to Bauer's and she'd say to Hermann, "I'm going to work for you. I'm going to stay upstairs like Grace and be a waitress—please, please!"

Happy—happy—

Far back on the turnpike her round straw hat sat on the tracks, crushed to a pancake just as the streetcar had left it.

Grace lay on her stomach on the bed and kicked up her heels. She was in a blue cotton chemise and with her glasses off and yellow hair hanging loose she didn't look so bad, Jen thought. Jen didn't want to take off the percale dress and white apron that Mrs. Bauer had given her, so she sat stiffly on the edge of the bed, occasionally stealing a glance at herself in the mirror.

"Men don't respect a factory girl the way they do a girl in a restaurant," said Grace. "I don't know why it is but they just don't. When you've been around as long as I have you'll see."

Jen looked politely interested but to tell the truth she had one worry on her mind and it was not concerned with male respect.

"Do you think Sister Catherine will make me go back to school when she finds I'm here? Because I'll bet the Delaneys will be mad enough to make her do something about me."

Grace snapped her gum.

"Na. You'll get more education right here than if you was in any school. I only went to the fourth grade and I get along, you bet. Some of the smartest men in the world come in this place—they get to talking and if you keep your ears open first thing you know you've learned something. Telegraph operators are usually the smartest. Take Sweeney. Before I knew Sweeney I used to always say 'me and my friends.' Now I know better. I say 'I and my friend is going to do so and so.' Just keep your ears open and you learn enough all right. 'Who's' wrong, too. You should always say 'whom,' but you know how it is, sometimes you get careless, even when you know better."

"I'd hate to go back to school as soon as I get a job like this," Jen said, "with my own room and everything."

Grace's bed took up almost the entire room except for the big golden oak dresser. Jen's room was no bigger, on the other side of the partition; it had a window you could lean out and almost touch the trains as they went by. But usually she was in Grace's room because Grace had her place all fixed up. On her dresser, for instance, was a heart-shaped bonbon box with a huge red satin bow on it, and beside it a blue painted can of talcum powder smelling deliciously of carnations. A velvet souvenir ribbon say with button photographs and little tasselled pencils hung beside the mirror. Over the bed was pinned a big Silver Lake pennant and a passepartout tinted picture of a full-faced brunette gazing moodily down at her bare bosom.

"Where'd you get that pennant?" Jen inquired.

Grace tittered and leaned coquettishly on one elbow.

"That's what Morry Abbott was always asking, ha, ha!"

Jen stirred uncomfortably.

"Where did he see it?"

"Never mind, he saw it plenty of times," giggled Grace. "I used to tease him about being so jealous. Where'd I get this, where'd I get that, who give me this box of candy and so on. He wasn't going to let me have any friends at all, he was so jealous. Can you imagine that?"

Jen twisted her handkerchief, understanding now. That was why Grace had gotten her to go with her that night following Nettie and Morry. He'd made love to both of them. She didn't see how she could ever look up at Grace—she wouldn't be able to look at Morry again without thinking of this. She wished she hadn't known, now. Knowing things like this frightened her. It made Morry seem so far away from her, somehow.

"It got so bad I just had to stop before it was serious," Grace confided, gazing dreamily at the Silver Lake pennant. "Honestly, Jen, I was afraid he'd do something. Kill himself or something. Crazy kid. . . . You know how he was always following me around."

"I never saw him following you," Jen murmured, a little coldly.

Grace was not perturbed by her skeptical tone.

"You wouldn't. But, believe me, I'd never give in. All a girl's got is her good name and believe me, you got to hang on to that. The factory girls don't care. Remind me to show you the place in the Big Four woods where they take their fellas. Gee, but those girls are awful. Sweeney had one of them up in the Tower during the quiet hour—one to two—in the morning, and a dispatcher walks in and didn't he almost get fired, that Sweeney? Only thing that saved him was the girl happened to have something on the dispatcher."

The fast train tore by and the walls of the house shook, a chunk of damp plastering fell to the floor.

"Isn't it time to go down?" Jen asked, still anxious to make good at her new career.

"Never go down till you're called," Grace instructed her. "Hermann will yell when he wants us. Sunday dinner's always late anyway."

"Do you think maybe Bill or Mrs. Delaney will try to make Hermann send me away," Jen asked, apprehensively, "when they find out I'm here?"

"They'd never dare," Grace declared. "Bill's too anxious to keep on the good side of Hermann. If Hermann says you stay, then you stay. . . . Don't you worry, the Delaneys know you're here. The old woman's peekin' out her window watchin' every chance she gets."

Jen stroked her hair and looked at it again in the mirror, because it was done up like Grace's and made her feel very courageous.

"Yes sir, those factory girls are fast, though," Grace went on. "I'd never get too chummy with 'em and don't you, either. . . . You notice Morry Abbott won't go out with the girls from the Works and they're always after him, too. He can't see 'em, he told me. . . . I tried to get him to be friends with other women but he wouldn't do it. . . . Now of course he's sore at me because I never would give in to him. But I'm sure I don't know what he's thinking of. Men are awful when they're so attracted to you."

She wasn't going to care who Morry liked, Jen thought resolutely, she wasn't going to be bothered about anything. She was back in Lamptown, wasn't she, and safe under the wing of Hermann Bauer, so what did anything else matter? But she could not help listening, fascinated by Grace's experience with life, even though whatever Grace said seemed to have a subtle hurt in it. Even when it didn't concern Morry it hurt, because it hinted of a bewildering world unknown to her, it hinted of things she didn't know, it reminded her again and again that she was left out.

"I wouldn't run with those factory girls," sniffed Grace. "I never wanted a chum. You and me could get along, though, Jen, know that? You're young but you're not so dumb. We can go to picnics together and have dates. It's easier for two girls to get dates than it is for one. It makes it more like a party."

Maybe it was a good thing the Delaneys did put her out, Jen reflected, because now it looked as if she was going to see something of the world.

"Grace! Jennía!" Hermann bawled up the backstairs.

"Oh, all right," answered Grace and slid off the bed to get dressed.

"I'm going to clear out of here one of these days," she grumbled, dumping some powder down her neck, powder that would daintily shower some customer's soup later on as she bent over. "I'd like a job in a Mansfield restaurant. Out in Luna Park. There's a fella runs the rolly coaster there and say, he's goodlooking. He was kinda crazy about me but you know how it is—I only get over there once a year."

Jen had her hand on the doorknob, impatient to go down because it was Sunday and maybe Morry might come over, as he did on Sundays. She hadn't seen him since the dance night and she wanted to see how impressed he was with her earning a living and having her hair done this new way.

"Wait a minute, I want to tell you about this fella," Grace called her back, slightly annoyed. She picked up the hand mirror to study the back of her hair. "I wish you could have seen him. Those snappy black eyes like Fischer's and slick black pompadour. I was walking along there by the rolly coaster at this picnic—The Baptist one, it was. I had on my blue dotted Swiss and a big milan I paid seven-fifty for at the Bon Ton. I was walking along and this fella says hello kid, all by your lonesome? Then we got to talking and he give me three free rides and after that I had a postcard from him with a picture of a girl sitting on a fella's lap. It's around here somewhere, I'll show it to you."

"Girls!" yelled Hermann. "God damn!"

Jen started running and Grace followed reluctantly.

"He had those black eyes, you know the kind," she whispered urgently as they went down the stairs. "Sort of Italian only not so sad."

Waiting table was much more fun than making beds and washing dishes for old Mrs. Delaney. All the time she swung importantly in and out of the pantry door, there was the awed delight of being on her own, getting a salary, looking after herself, there was the thrill of triumphing over the world. When she saw Morry sitting at the counter Jen upset a cup of coffee in her nervousness. It was gratifying to see his amazement. He'd heard she'd run away—what was she doing here in Bauer's?

"I work here," Jen was proud to answer. "I get three dollars a week and I don't have to go back to school, next fall, either, unless I please."

"Certainly you have to go back to school," Morry said sharply. "Who-ever told you you were so bright?"

Jen's face fell.

"I'm tired of being tied to things," she complained. "I want to do things, Morry, instead of just sitting around till I'm old enough. I've been going to school just about all my life and I'm good and tired of it. I want to start in on my own."

"Want to be like Grace Terris, I suppose," Morry sneered. "That's your idea of a great life, waiting table. I thought you were going to be a dancer on the stage and all that. I thought you were going to show this town what you could do. Well, you won't get anywhere quitting school and working in restaurants, I can tell you. Gee, Jen, I thought you had more sense."

Jen hung her head and paid no attention when a man at the other end of the table rapped his fork on his glass for more coffee.

"I only thought if I had to take care of myself I might as well get started," she mumbled.

"Don't you know you can't ever do what you want unless you know things?" Morry scolded her. "You go back there this fall if you know what's good for you."

The man called her then and when she came back Morry had gone without giving her any clue to his indignation. She didn't know that she was Morry's invention, that in some obscure way he expected her to do him credit, her admiration must be more worthwhile than merely flatter-ing worship from a chophouse waitress—hadn't she promised to be a ballet dancer-on-a-magazine-cover-in-love-with-Morris-Abbott? . . . Jen understood none of these things, she only saw that he had gone away, the way he always did, nothing in the world could make him stay. She saw him in the street turn back to look and their eyes met. . . . Come back, come back, hers said, but he would never come back for her—always she would be left because people didn't care for you the way you cared for them. Your hands stretched frantically out to clutch them but they gained no hold, you were brushed aside, you could not hold anyone to you. Come back, come back. . . . Jen's eyes did not leave him until Delaney's door had swung shut behind him. Then with a sigh she took the catsup bottle over to the Ladies Table.

"I've got to go back to school tomorrow," she told Grace in the pantry.

"Why? Hermann says you don't have to if you don't want to."

"I know it," Jen murmured disconsolately. "But I've got to go back."

Dinner was over when Hunt Russell and Dode O'Connell came in. Jen frantically signalled Grace to wait on them but Grace only winked knowingly and shook her head. They were arguing and neither looked up when Jen set the dishes down clumsily before them.

"What'll you bet she's raising Cain because he went out with us the other night," Grace whispered when Jen came back to the pantry. "I guess she's got her hooks into him good. You'd never cut her out, girlie, you're not the type. Say, I'd like to let him know his party the other night got you kicked out of a good home. Maybe he'd do something for you."

Jen was terrified lest Grace should actually tell Hunt all this, and Grace wouldn't promise not to, only laughed teasingly. She put her finger to her lips and beckoned Jen to stand beside her at the little peephole in the door.

"Sh! Maybe we can hear what they're rowing about. Did you see those rings she always wears? Three diamonds and that big Masonic ring. He never gave her that."

At the corner table Dode slumped back in her chair, ignoring the dishes before her. Hunt smoked a cigarette and smiled lazily at her as she continued her low-voiced accusations. She was leaning her chin on her hand sullenly. She was good looking in a hard leathery way, her shoulders looked high and powerful and why not, having pitched hay and done chores till she was old enough to get to a factory.

"She's telling him he don't give a damn about her," Grace whispered to Jen. "Says he'll probably marry somebody else and she'd like to see the little sap he'd pick out. Says she wouldn't marry anybody on a bet, she wouldn't want to be tied up with a house and a buncha kids. I notice he don't say anything. I guess she'd marry him all right if he asked her, that's all that's eating her."

Standing behind Grace Jen marvelled at the intricate design of gold bone hairpins in her hair-knob; she tried to perk out her own white apron strings into the beautifully stiff wings that Grace had achieved. At least she was proud of her own hair screwed up as it was into a tight knob with hairpins torturing her scalp wonderfully.

"Sst!" Grace clutched her arm in delight. "She's trying to find out who he picked up at the dance last week when she didn't go. Can you beat that? He's not even opening his mouth. . . . Go on in and give 'em their coffee."

"What do you care, you never did anything to her!" Grace gave her a little push as she hesitated. "They can't bite you, you know. Go on."

They stopped talking when Jen approached. Hunt's eyes traveled from Jen's new black silk stockings up the blue striped percale dress to her skinned-back hair. Jen colored and fussed with her apron.

"What under the sun have you done to your hair?" he exclaimed, staring at her, amused and bewildered. "You look ten years older."

"Honest?" Jen was radiant. "I had it on top Thursday night, too, but I guess you didn't notice. It's the way I'm going to wear it from now on."

"Where'd you see him Thursday night?" Dode snapped at her abruptly.

Jen looked at Hunt, speechless.

"I—I saw him at the Casino," she mumbled.

"And afterwards, too, don't kid me," said Dode. "I heard about it all right but I didn't believe it. So this is your new girl, is it, Hunt? Want 'em younger now, yeah? . . . This is who you took out Thursday."

Jen picked up her tray and backed away in confusion, but Hunt blew rings of smoke indolently into the air.

"Well, Jen, if you're working here I reckon I'll have to eat all my meals here, won't I?"

"Oh, you will, will you?" Dode flared up and picking up her glass of water flung it straight in Hunt's face. Then she pushed back her chair and rushed out of the restaurant, her head ducked down so that people couldn't see she was crying. Hunt mopped himself with a napkin silently. At the cash register in front Hulda Bauer allowed herself to turn a fraction of an inch to note what was happening. Jen tried to save his feelings by not watching him but finally their eyes met and Hunt was grinning a little as if he enjoyed Dode's attack. He took down his soft gray hat from the rack and sauntered leisurely up to Hulda at the front counter. In the street a minute later he didn't even glance in the direction Dode had gone but got in his car and drove westward.

"Whee!" exclaimed Jen scurrying out to the kitchen. "Did you see that, Grace?"

But Grace looked at her sourly.

"She threw that on your account—because he was trying to flirt with you. That's why she wanted to throw things. It was your fault."

Then she began bustling about the linen cupboard, quite aloof. Jen was troubled.

"But they were quarreling about something else, Grace, honest."

"It doesn't pay to make trouble, girlie," lectured Grace with a fixed smile. "You'll never get ahead trying to come between couples, just because the man has an automobile, it's something I've never done, I'll tell you."

"But Grace, I didn't do anything. You saw—"

Grace disappeared into the pantry. After that Jen got used to seeing that look in other women's eyes, a veiled, hostile, appraising look. There was nothing to do about that look, Jen found, but it had something to do with men liking you and of course for that women never forgave you. Chilled by Grace's new manner Jen went out in front and sat down idly at the counter. Hulda pointed a warning finger at her.

"Don't let Hermann see you with nothing to do, Jenny. If you're through down here go upstairs and fix Room Twenty for those surveyors. You know your work, child."

She waddled over to shut the piano again; after saving so hard to buy it she wasn't going to have it ruined by people playing on it.

Something was happening to the Lots. Surveyors were busy over it and on the edge of this wasteland men were throwing up a new house. Its skeleton was a familiar one—four rooms down, three up, steep roof sliding off a square indented porch—it was Lamptown's eternal new House. Morry saw it one Saturday noon coming home from work, and he stopped short, incredulous. That gaunt house leapt out of the horizon like his name out of a printed page, at first he could not understand its challenge for him, and his feeling of despair. . . . Why, the Lots were to be turned into a gorgeous boulevard of beautiful mansions (through the vague genius of Morry Hunt Russell Abbott)—chateaux, Hogan called them, with long rolling lawns around them. . . . So long as the Lots were wilderness all this was possible, but the first dinky little Lamptown house going up meant that if homes were to be built, they'd be like all those on Extension Avenue.

The gardens-to-be had become so real in Morry's mind that he was outraged to see the workmen trampling over them as if they were nothing more than the weedy mud they seemed. He stood still, hands shoving restlessly into his coat pockets, staring unhappily at this apparent signal of his defeat. Each night after he closed his eyes he was used to conjuring the lots before him, acres of tangled clover and scattered bramble bushes changing on his closed eyelids to castles of lordly beauty centered in terraced rose-gardens all magically contrived by Morry Abbott. These pleasant fantasies might have gone on forever if the harsh fact of one small frame house had not thrust itself before him. It was unquestionably a challenge, he'd do something about this, he would—(he thought desperately of his own ignorance and helplessness)—well, then, where was Hunt, where was Hogan, where were all the people who talked of beautiful cities. . . . Where was Hunt Russell? After all, wasn't it Hunt's land? He could stop it all quick enough.

Angrily he looked up at the workmen on the scaffolding. What right had they to do this?

"Who are you building this for?" he called up.

It was for an out-of-town contracting firm, the foreman told him. Maybe, he said, the entire Lots would be built up this year if the factory increased as rumors hinted; two or three at least would be erected on speculation.

"All just alike?" Morry asked with a sinking heart.

"Sure—all just alike,—maybe some with the porch on the left, that's all," answered the man. "It's a mighty convenient little house—a big favorite around here."

Morry walked slowly on, depressed. There was that inextinguishable plan in his mind for the Lots, that ridiculous, fabulous plan—Hogan's plan, really, only as soon as he'd heard it Morry had made it his own. But somebody else always did these things first—somebody with money, somebody who knew how to go after things. What were you to do when you didn't know anyone who could help you, no one who could explain the way to the things you wanted—what could you do—you couldn't just take a spade, a few bricks, and a geranium and see what happened. You had to be rich, you had to be educated; you had to be powerful to stop contagious ugliness from spreading.

Walking with his head down, thinking feverishly of desperate steps to take, Morry halted at the edge of the fields; still preoccupied he sat down on the running board of a muddy automobile parked there. He was going to do something all right, he'd go to Hogan—but Hogan was all big noise, just as the fellows said, he never really would get down to doing anything. Maybe if he'd gone to college, Morry thought, maybe then you knew just what way to go at things. . . . Maybe he could go to this contracting firm that was building these houses, for instance, and tell them they were making a mistake in destroying Lamptown's only chance for an expensive residential boulevard. . . . That's what he'd do. Morry stood up and looked uncertainly back at the house. He'd go and ask that foreman his boss's address. . . .

An elderly man with gray moustachios and a wide-brimmed black western hat was scowling gloomily up at the building; this was Fowler, the town builder and so-called 'architect,' Hogan's father-in-law.

"He's mad, too, I'll bet," Morry thought, "because they went out of town instead of giving him the job."

He sauntered up to him.

"Look at that house, Mr. Fowler!" he appealed. "They're going to be rows and rows of 'em before the summer's over. When the Works enlarge they'll fill in every chink of land from here to the county land with these sheds. Why doesn't somebody put up a good home for a change?"

"Cheap clapboard!" Fowler puffed morosely on a black briar pipe. "Any good storm would blow them down. I don't see why they didn't come to somebody that knows this land and knows enough not to get stung with cheap lumber. Hunt knows better than that."

He spat viciously at a wilting blackeyed daisy.

"Is Hunt behind this?" Morry wanted to know, incredulously. "I thought Hunt was a smarter man than that."

"There you are—Hunt's all right," Fowler agreed. "He'd never take a thing out of my hands, but you see Hunt isn't the whole cheese here at all. It's Russell money, all right, but it comes from Hunt's uncles in the East. Smart men, too. Keep out of the picture till it looks like a boom, then they step in and collect a million on their property. They know all right."

"But if there's a boom," Morry stammered desperately, "there'll be rich men in Lamptown, and they won't want to live in these cheap shanties, they'll want beautiful places different from other people's. Don't you see, Mr. Fowler, this was the place to build mansions—like Hunt's, don't you see?"

Fowler sucked his pipe glumly and then recollected a gift cigar in his vest pocket and offered it to Morry. Morry refused it and Fowler stuck it thankfully back beside the Democratic campaign button without which this gentleman had never been seen.

"They'll buy homes in Avon—people with the money. After all it's only twenty minutes out on the car-line and all residential. . . . Damned poor business for Lamptown, though, you're right about that."

Well, why didn't he do something about it, then, Morry wondered, irritated, certainly he was an old man and old enough to know his own trade, wasn't he?

"Somebody could do something even yet," Morry insisted. "Only one house is up. It isn't too late. Somebody could start on the other side of the Lots with a big place kinda like Hunt's—that's what people want to work for—something different."

"Say a modified Colonial," mused Fowler, and gazed at the fields beyond where the Colonial mansion was to be, "or maybe a Tudor cottage. I wonder. . . . Come on and walk down to the office, Morry, I'll show you a book I've got down there of what they call these Tudor cottages. And there's some pictures of these Spanish type houses like they have in California."

Fowler's office was a room over the Paradise Theatre, and as they tramped up the stairs Milly could be heard in the theatre banging out scraps of new songs on the piano.

"A hell of a business building," growled Fowler, fitting the key into his door. "You'd think it was a conservatory of music, anybody would, with that practicing going on all day. Come in."

The office was a mere closet cluttered with file cases, their drawers half-open and papers dangling out; auction sale leaflets in green and yellow blew frantically across the dusty floor as the door opened and cowered, quivering, against a stack of blueprints rolled up like so many highschool diplomas and tied with yellowing soiled ribbon. The roll-top desk leaned dizzily forward, gorged with magazines and enormous photographs of ideal homes, above it a steel engraving of the Roman Forum was slapped in the face by a large cardboard poster announcing a foreclosure sale of the Purdy Property. Fowler dumped the magazines off two chairs and then offered Morry the cigar once more. With a sigh of resignation Morry took it and chewed on it rather unhappily.

"I'd like to show these people what somebody right here in Lamptown could do with those Russell lots," Fowler said, yanking off his coat and vest but keeping on the huge Sheriff's hat. "I'd like to show these people what somebody right here in Lamptown could do with that property. I'd like to show 'em we're a darn sight smarter than their fancy city firms with their cheap little ideas. Maybe I will, too, by golly, I ain't dead yet."

"Here—look these over." He shoved some photographs into Morry's hands, and then leaned back in the slightly askew swivel chair, puffing at his pipe. "I don't know which I'd rather do out there. A row of Spanish type houses, kinda California style, see, something to make Lamptown sit up and take notice, or say these Colonial ones like they do down East. Damn it, I'd like to let 'em know I got ideas, and nothing shoddy, either. I see other towns, don't I, I keep my eyes open everywhere. Just because I've had to keep to a $1800 house for most of the folks here, say, that don't mean I don't know how a $7500 house ought to be built, does it? . . . I'd like to throw up a string of houses that'd knock their eyes out, I would."

"But not just alike!" expostulated Morry, earnestly waving his cigar. "That's the whole point. Each one a special kind of house, see, so that everybody can feel it's his own special home, not anybody else's but his, See? Something worth saving for, something to show off to his friends. . . ."

"Somebody's bound to get rich in this town on this boom—that's as good as settled." Fowler twisted the ends of his thick gray moustache thoughtfully. "In another year there'll be a demand for better houses than anything we've got here right now, and that's a fact."

He kicked the outer door shut as Milly's practicing became louder, and then with his back to Morry stood before a huge map of Lamptown pinned to the wall. He ran a fountain pen slowly across the letters "Extension Avenue" and made a green-inked 'X' in the center of a large area marked "LOTS."

"Hunt's share of that property is one fourth." He was talking to himself more than to his visitor, Morry realized, but Morry didn't mind because he was learning something, he could almost see a new door swinging open for him. "If we could talk Hunt into the idea, we'd have enough land and backing to start working on. Let the eastern Russells fool around over there on the east side with their factory houses—we'll begin on the other side of the creek, see, right here, and give the town something to talk about."

"We could call it the Heights," Morry said, and gave up trying to smoke his cigar, allowing it to drop quietly from his fingers into the wastebasket. It occurred to him that it was long past lunchtime and he was hungry, and moreover he'd promised Bill Delaney and some fellows to go to the ballgame this afternoon, but it was too late now. Here in Fowler's cluttered office with Milly's desultory piano accompaniment a new Lamptown was being planned, and it was Morry Abbott's Lamptown, even Fowler must know that, for he went on with the "we" plans as casually as if the name on the door was "Fowler and Abbott" instead of just Fowler. The palms of Morry's hands were wet with tense excitement, he was on the verge of something big, something wonderful. He skipped through the pages of a book called "Long Island Homes,"—some day even these landscaped estates might be possible, too. Then he got up and looked over Fowler's shoulder at the map. Fowler was marking off a section of the Lots, murmuring, "Lamptown Heights, eh?"

"No—not Lamptown," begged Morry. "Call it Clover Heights."

"Clover Heights," repeated Fowler and inked it carefully in green with an air of finality as if the whole plan was settled by this simple gesture. Then he tapped his pipe on a file case and looked at Morry triumphantly. "We'll put it through and don't you forget it. It gives Hunt a chance to put one over on the uncles, don't you see? That's why he'll be willing to come in with us."

"When can you—we—begin working on it?" Morry asked, struck with awe by the masterful way this man went at things.

Fowler pulled at his moustache with yellow-tipped fingers.

"Well, as soon as we can get hold of Hunt," he answered. "You're there at the factory all the time, you see him every day. Get hold of him Monday, say, and give him the idea."

Morry choked.

"That's the thing," continued Fowler with a faraway look. "You give him the main idea and tell him I'm ready to talk to him about it any time he drops in. Hunt's a nice guy and he's not crazy to have his uncles wipe him off the map. You just get hold of him, say Monday, and outline this Clover Heights idea to him."

"Sure. Sure, I'll tell him," said Morry hoarsely. He was to do all the starting, was he, and not Fowler at all. . . . He remembered his father's sarcasm when he told him of just such a plan, and already he saw Hunt's scornful amusement. It was all right if Fowler started things but nobody would ever listen to Morry Abbott—and worse yet he could never in this world get up the nerve to approach them. The snappy young Abbott of his fantasies might calmly tap Hunt on the shoulder and tell him just what was what; but nothing, to the real Morry, was worth the anguish of going to a man and quite out of a blue sky telling him your own little private dream of a lovely place to live. Morry wondered how he'd ever managed to sound so casual to Fowler, but he thought hopefully he might drop dead before Monday or the relatives would start building on Hunt's share so that the whole plan would have to be given up, continuing merely as a pleasant dream in the night thoughts of young Abbott.

Fowler took out his watch.

"I've got to get to a farm out east by six," he said. "But see here, Morry, what about you coming down here to the office tomorrow—say around twelve—and we'll talk this over some more."

"Sure," agreed Morry again, who usually slept till two on Sundays then wandered out to the factory ballgrounds to loaf away the day.

"There'll be something big in this for both of us," Fowler thoughtfully pursued. "We'll work on it nights for a while till we get everything all set, understand. You're just the boy for this, Abbott—you've got push and go, not afraid to tackle anybody or anything. That's the right idea."

Morry looked at him alertly to see if he was being kidded, but Fowler's face was serious, almost dreamy. He had push and go, did he?—with his hands already trembling at the idea of approaching Hunt. He wanted to explain to Fowler right here and now that it was all a mistake, the whole plan was just an idea, see, and there was nothing to do about ideas, you just thought about them, that was all. But the big letters in green ink "CLOVER HEIGHTS" across the corner of the Lamptown map made him keep these craven misgivings to himself.

"Tomorrow at twelve, now don't forget." Fowler slapped him on the shoulder. "And you'd better not date up any women for the next few weeks because we'll be working on this every night."

It was dusk when Morry got outside, and the Paradise façade was already lit up, boldly inviting the night to come on. In the drugstore next door and around the barbershops crowds of men were arguing over the baseball game. The Works team had won its first game and this meant a big night at Delaney's, and celebrations all over town, but to Morry this approaching excitement belonged to him, the town was celebrating because at last Morry Abbott was going to do something about it, he was about to break through cloudy dreams into action. He spoke to men here and there but he couldn't stop, he had to hurry home and tell someone. He had push and go, he was going to be a man of power, like Fowler, like Hunt Russell, he would have an office over the Paradise and by merely scrawling something with his green-inked pen the whole map of Lamptown would be changed.

At Robbin's Jewelry Store he slowed up his pace, uncertain of where he should take his news. Hogan was the man to tell, Hogan and Bill Delaney, he thought, so he walked on to Bill's place. The saloon was full of the baseball players and men home from the game, they were singing and shouting, while Shorty, perspiration dripping from his bald head, pushed foaming glasses across the bar as fast as his two fat hands could go. Hogan and his fireman were at the bar and hailed Morry.

"Say, Hogan, I'm going in with Fowler," Morry told him, making an effort to sound as if this were nothing at all, really. "Thought I'd learn building—architecture, you know."

"OK with me, friend," answered Hogan heartily, banging his glass down. "You're welcome to the old man."

A little dashed, Morry went on confidentially,

"We're planning to develop one end of the Lots—build beautiful homes like they have on Long Island, you know, these Normandy cottages with two baths and—"

He had to raise his voice because someone was playing the piano and the men were beginning to sing.

"Mansions for the aristocrats!" roared Hogan. "While the honest workingman eats in his simple kitchen in Shantyville. Mansions for the ruling classes! Why, friend—" his voice became a deep, oratorical baritone—"I would rather go to the forest far away, build me a little cabin, a little hut with some hollyhocks at the corner with their bannered blossoms open to the sun and with the thrush in the air like a song of joy in the morning, I would rather live there."

He paused to wipe the foam off his mouth with a red kerchief.

"Never mind, Hogan'll live in your mansions if the old man gives one to his wife," the fireman winked at Morry. "You don't see him eating in these simple kitchens, either, he's just moved into the biggest house on Walnut Street over in Avon, and he raises hell when his wife doesn't set up the dining-room table."

"That's all right, friend," said Hogan. "You're a single man. You don't understand these things."

It was no use telling anything to Hogan now, Morry thought, disappointed, for Hogan's brightly glazed blue eyes and his rosy nose proclaimed to the world that this was Saturday night and a twelve-hour spree was well under way. As Morry reached the door he pointed an accusing finger at him and bellowed.

"Yes sir, by the Lord Harry, I would rather live there and have my soul erect and free than to live in a palace of gold and wear the crown of imperial power," and Morry slid out the door on the final impressive whisper, "and know that my soul was slimy with hypocrisy!"

Chagrined at Hogan's lack of interest, Morry turned into the alley to go in the Bon Ton's back entrance. He observed the crouched figure of old Mrs. Delaney on her steps, as if she had been waiting for him. He touched his cap, getting fiery red.

"Well, Morry Abbott!" she bent over the railing and scowled at him, one gnarled hand clutching together the black shawl under her chin. "You're satisfied now, I suppose. Happy now you got my Jen out of a decent home and got her waitin' table where all the men can get at her. God'll punish you, young man, God'll punish you as sure as I'm breathing here. You had no call runnin' after that young girl, now, you've got her started on the road to ruin—are you satisfied, hey?"

She hobbled up the steps slowly. Morry, hurrying on home, knew she had stopped at the top landing to glare vengefully at him, and he ducked into his doorway, angry again at Jen for putting him into the role of villain and seducer, a role, to tell the truth, that frightened him as much as it ever did any young girl.

Elsinore and Nettie were having tea and sandwiches in the workroom and Morry made himself a salmon sandwich and sat down with them. He wanted to be offhand telling about his new career but he couldn't help it, he blurted it out the minute after he came in. His mother stirred her tea dreamily and for a while he thought she must be displeased. Nettie dropped her spoon and looked at him as if he had confessed to some tremendous sin. He thought, too late, he shouldn't have told Nettie of any good news about himself, for the only news that would please her, after being scorned, would have to be bad.

"Do you mean to tell me you're giving up your perfectly good job at the factory, Morry Abbott?" she demanded. "After you're lucky enough to get in the Works you'd drop it like this?"

"I'm not dropping it—not yet, anyways," Morry retorted. "Not till I'm getting commissions or a salary from Fowler."

"Are you out of your mind, Morry?" Nettie cried. "Do you mean to tell me you're going to do all this work without getting any pay?"

"Well, not exactly," Morry defended himself, sorry he had said anything, sorry that wherever he went he had to defend his triumphs since all that people were glad to hear from him was of his expected defeats.

"Come, now, what did he say? Did he or didn't he say he'd pay you for the work?"

"No, he didn't." Morry was stung into the truth. "But it's a chance to learn something I want to learn and I'm going to do it. Gee, Nettie, didn't you ever hear of anybody being an architect?"

Nettie gave him a long, withering glance.

"Don't be silly, Morry, you have to go to college to learn that, and you couldn't anyway, you haven't got the brains. You stick to something you can do, like the factory work, and don't let that old man Fowler make a fool out of you. Don't you think that's right, Mrs. Abbott?"

Elsinore raised her eyes from her teacups and smiled gently at Morry.

"What is it, Morry?" she inquired, and Morry looked straight at her, not believing she could be so unkind. She hadn't even listened, she didn't care a bit what became of him. His own mother didn't care, she was so busy with her own life. . . . Well, and what was her own life, Morry asked himself resentfully, if she didn't care about her husband or her son, who, then, occupied her mind? The doubt his father had passed on to him returned fleetingly but he shut it out of his mind firmly.

"No, sir, the thing for you to do, Morry, is to hang on to your factory job," advised Nettie, pouring herself some more tea. "You'll never get another like it. Mr. Abbott would be furious, too, if he thought you left the Works."

Morry's throat tightened at mention of his father.

"Aw, what's it to him?" he growled. "What does he care what I do—"

"A young man ought never to make a foolish move like you're doing right now, without talking it over with his father." Nettie's lips were virtuously pursed up. "Or at least with his mother."

She picked up her saucer and went over to the sink. Morry stole a sidelong, unhappy look at his mother. She sat there in her low work chair, sipping tea, staring intently into space. Her thick brown hair was loosened a little and in the blue woven dress she wore it suddenly came over to Morry that his mother wasn't old at all, she wasn't even middle-aged; it made him feel unaccountably lonely, as if a white-haired old mother or even a formless, middle-aged mother like Mrs. Bauer would have been his, his very own mother; but this way his mother didn't belong to him, and he had no right to her, no claim to her attention. . . . She glanced up and smiled at him but he was too hurt and lonely to smile back.

"Did you hear about the big Serpentine Ball the end of July, Morry?" she asked him almost lightly. "I hear it's going to be the big dance of the year and I meant to tell you not to miss it."

"I'll get there, all right," he answered gruffly. "Plenty of time for that."

She didn't care that today an incredible dream had started to come true, she didn't care that he was going to be more than just a factory hand, he was going to be a figure in Lamptown some day, a somebody that she could be proud of; but she didn't care, she hadn't even listened. It would be a long time before Morry's eyes, ashamed for her, could meet her smile.

There had to be someone who thought you mattered, there had to be someone you could tell things to, somebody who thought you were going to amount to something—nobody could be left this way all alone. Desperately Morry grabbed his hat and started outdoors heading almost automatically for the saloon backsteps before he remembered that Jen wouldn't be there, she'd be over at Bauer's. Jen . . . Jen . . . Jen . . . the only person who believed, the only person who listened, the only person who was sure. He hurried across the street, afraid to lose a minute now, afraid that Hogan and Nettie and his mother had so dashed his little triumph that there was none left. He thought it was true that a thing never happened by itself, it had never actually happened until it was related for the right person's applause. He saw Hermann Bauer smoking his pipe and gazing fixedly out the window and behind Hermann's back he saw half a dozen diners and Jen scurrying around them with a tray half her size. He'd better go around to the kitchen door, he thought, it was easier to catch her there than in front with Hermann watching. Hunt Russell's car was at the curb but Morry impatiently brushed by without waiting to speak to Hunt.

"Hey—hey Morry!"

Hunt had seized his arm jovially.

"Want to pick up the Terris woman later on, Morry?" he asked in a low tone. "Lots of room in the back of my car if you want to come along. I'm taking my girl, so speak up if you want to come."

"Your girl?" Morry asked suspiciously.

Hunt jerked a thumb in the direction of the restaurant.

"The kid in there," he drawled. "Thought you might take the other one."

"I don't think so," said Morry, the blood swimming furiously in his head. "I'll pick my own damned women, thank you."

He whirled around and went back home, up the stairs to his room. His whole body buzzed with hate for Hunt Russell as if in blocking his way to Jen he'd done him the ultimate injury, using all of his advantages for this unfair blow. His disappointment in his mother and Hogan faded into this final rage. Very well, let Jen take Dode O'Connell's place as Hunt's girl if she liked; Morry would never fight for her, he'd never compete for any girl, he'd never give Hunt the chance to sneer at a conquered rival. He tramped up and down his tiny room and when his head hit the sloping ceiling he tore at it fiercely with his fists, and turned his hate for the moment on to tiny houses with low ceilings. Jen's blue eyes fastened worshipfully on someone else . . . Jen listening adoringly to some other hero. . . . All right, he could do without anybody, he didn't give a damn what people thought about him, he didn't care if nobody listened to him or believed in him, he'd show them all a thing or two, he'd make them listen one of these days, he didn't give a damn about anybody.

But in his dreams that night he fought for hours with some enemy, his conquering fists rained on some foe's bent head, a foe who changed under these blows from Hogan to Hunt Russell and then curiously enough took on the features of his father, and ah, what voluptuous ecstasy to blur with his knuckles the significant sneer on this last face!

If Morry was around the shop when Nettie worked late at night, then she made a great fuss about her preparations to leave, locking drawers noisily, calling loud goodbyes to Elsinore and shrilly exclaiming about the darkness of the night and the long walk to Murphy's. Morry deliberately ignored these hints and Nettie would have to stalk angrily out alone.

"I don't mind going home alone," she complained to Elsinore. "It isn't that at all. But after all, any gentleman would see that I got home safely nights I worked late in his own mother's shop, and was going through a dark street into an empty house. Any gentleman would do that much, Mrs. Abbott—that's why I get so disgusted with Morry."

She swung from such dignified reproaches to vehement denunciations of his character—he was just a bum, the town tough, everyone said he was fast, he chased after bad girls, no decent girl would ever want to marry him, he had no nice friends, just lazy good-for-nothing pool players and Shantyville souses. He'd rather keep company like that than to walk home with a good girl once or twice a week.

Elsinore did not know how to answer these attacks.

"But when the men want to take you home you won't ever let them," she protested. "I thought you'd rather be alone."

"That's just it!" Nettie sputtered. "If Morry was with me, the men from Delaney's wouldn't follow me, they wouldn't dare come up to me if Morry was along."

"I don't understand you, Nettie," Elsinore surrendered. "You weren't cross with Mr. Schwarz—"

"Mr. Schwarz was very different from Lamptown men," Nettie reminded her. "Very different indeed. He took me to the very best places in Cleveland and our seats at the theatre alone were three dollars. Oh, there's no comparison."

She sat down to the table where the crying doll lay undressed waiting for its summer costume. Nettie had given herself a birthday present of a pair of nose glasses from Robbin's Jewelry Store as most of the girls who could afford it were wearing them, and it seemed to her, stealing an approving glance at herself in the mirror, that this was as nice a touch as a lady could wish. She adjusted them with exquisite care on her determined little nose, and squinting a little, picked up the doll so abruptly that its glazed eyes rattled in its head.

"Never mind, I'm going to go over to the Casino before the summer's over," she declared. "I'm sure I could dance well because everyone says I have such high arches. Morry thinks because I don't dance I'm out of everything, but you just wait. He'll be very glad to dance with me some-day, you wait and see."

This set Elsinore to thinking. Fischer had a summer dancing pavilion near Cleveland, and if Nettie learned to dance, then the two of them could go out to this pavilion during the summer. She couldn't go alone, of course, but it looked all right for two women to go places together. She decided it would be worth while to encourage Nettie to learn dancing if only for this one convenient reason. When Mrs. Pepper used to speak of having run out to the pavilion to watch the dancing because she "just hap-pened to be in the neighborhood," Elsinore had yearned to ask if she couldn't "run out" with her sometime. . . . Well, if she ever went now, it would have to be with Nettie, that much was sure.

Sometimes she ran into Mrs. Pepper on the street and Elsinore always dropped her glance before the wounded question in the other's eyes. Nettie told her the corsetiere was often lurking in shop doorways waiting for Nettie to pass so that she could pounce on her and pour out her woe. With the passing weeks Elsinore saw that even if Fischer's wife had told him of a strange visitor he hadn't guessed who it was. It reassured her so that no wounded looks could make her feel guilty, and except for the out-of-town customers occasionally asking for corset fittings, the Bon Ton went on as if these extra activities had never been. She thought that she might even, with Nettie's support, be able to face an encounter with Mrs. Pepper at the Cleveland pavilion this summer. After all, there was no rea-son why his Lamptown pupils shouldn't drop in at his Cleveland headquarters, was there? . . . Still she'd have to have some excuse for being in the neighborhood. She'd have to invent some business in the city for July or August, some extra business, because two buying trips a year were enough for the millinery stock.

"At least I'm glad there's only one of these darned dolls to dress," Nettie grumbled, pins in her mouth and a scrap of blue lawn in her hand. "It's more work than anything in the shop."

Elsinore had an inspiration.

"But everyone asks about it, Nettie. You know how the girls are always trying to buy it from us. I'd thought of laying in a stock if they don't cost too much."

"No!"

"Later on in the summer—I'll run into Cleveland and get a few as an experiment," she went on meditatively. "I think a millinery store has a right to branch out with novelties now and then. Charles is always telling me about perfumes and hose and extra things they sell in the Chicago shops. I think the Bon Ton ought to be up-to-date."

Nettie's mouth puckered into a disapproving pout.

"Of course," Elsinore added. "I'd expect you to help me buy them. And if we had to go into the city we might have a little extra time for an outing."

Miraculously Nettie's disapproval vanished. If dolls meant a visit to Cleveland for her, then certainly every milliner ought to keep dolls.

"We might happen to run into Mr. Schwarz again," she suggested. She began to hum softly, her little finger curved daintily outward as she sewed, already she had marked another notch in her career as a milliner, and certainly a Mr. Schwarz from Cleveland as a "friend" would put Morry in his place.

Elsinore was writing a letter to Charles that night, explaining her plan for selling dolls when Mrs. Pepper appeared quietly in the Bon Ton. She didn't stop to address Nettie in the shop, but walked straight out into the workroom and shut the door behind her. Elsinore jumped up, quite pale, and her letter blew unheeded to the floor. Mrs. Pepper looked at her sadly. Her eyelids and nose were red as if she had been crying and she kept dabbing at her nose with a little lace handkerchief as if this gesture somehow gave her courage.

"You've made a lot of trouble for me, Mrs. Abbott." She didn't sound angry—only tired and pleading. "All I've ever had is trouble, ever since I lost Mr. Pepper. . . . I—I don't see why you did it. I can't understand why you'd do that to me, Mrs. Abbott, it's beyond me."

Elsinore was speechless. She was so sure after all this time that no one had found out about her visit to Cleveland, and this belated discovery found her completely without defense. She rolled her pen nervously between the palms of her hands and looked at the floor. Mrs. Pepper studied her drearily and quite without anger.

"As soon as Harry said the woman wore a black hat with a white feather I knew it was you that had gone to his wife. And then you'd been so strange with me for a long time. . . . At first when he told me—things had to stop—at first I couldn't guess who had told her but then when he mentioned that black hat it all came over me that it was you. I was so upset I had to lie right down to get my breath. . . . I couldn't understand. . . . I just couldn't see why you'd do that to me, Mrs. Abbott."

Elsinore drew a deep breath. Why should she feel so shamed—after all, she hadn't done anything wrong—it was Mrs. Pepper who had done wrong when it came right down to it. She was the one to feel guilty. . . .

"It wasn't right for you to go with him," she managed to say. "You knew he had a wife—you knew you ought not to try coming between them."

Mrs. Pepper's little white hands flew out in a gesture of helplessness.

"I know, oh, I do know it's wrong, but I'm not bad woman. Nobody could say I was a bad woman. And Harry's all I've had in my life—those few little trips with Harry—once we went to Atlantic City. . . . It began so naturally—both of us traveling through the same towns—but now, I—well, I just couldn't live without Harry. . . . What made you go to her, Mrs. Abbott—what made you do it? You couldn't have just wanted to spoil my life—you couldn't just want that. . . ."

Elsinore kept jabbing the table with the pen and kicking at a ball of colored embroidery silk lying tangled on the floor. She had regained her cool detachment as if what she had done was done, after all, and was no concern of hers any more. She had eased her own steady torment by hurting Mrs. Pepper and was rather surprised to find that she had no more hatred for her. On the other hand when she stole a look at her, the sight of her plump pretty face screwed up into a pitiful caricature of anguish did not stir her pity at all.

"He's had to promise Her not to see me again," Mrs. Pepper allowed the tears to course slowly down her cheeks. "It's all right for you—you've got your husband—even if he's only here once in a while—and your nature's different from mine . . . but with me . . . I've lost eleven pounds just worrying over this. I've had to take a 38. See, I've lost it here." She slapped her hips mournfully. "Worrying about what I'm going to do without ever seeing Harry. . . . She's having him watched."

She sat down on a stool and leaned her plump arms on the table. Elsinore kept her face steadily on the embroidery silk on the rug.

"I never did you any wrong, Mrs. Abbott, you know that," desolately went on Mrs. Pepper. "I can't understand why you'd go against me like that. I didn't dare tell Harry I knew who'd told his wife. I didn't want to let him know a friend of mine had done it. I let him think one of the factory girls—maybe Dode—or somebody out of town had gone to her, some woman that was after him."

Elsinore breathed easier and dared to lift her eyes. If Fischer didn't know who it was that had told his wife, then nothing was to be feared—nothing had been lost after all. She had done no harm, really, if she'd merely stopped Mrs. Pepper from being in love with him. That was all for the best.

"If Charles was running with some other woman I'd want to be told," she said. "I'd be glad if someone came and told me. That's why I went to Mrs. Fischer. I wasn't thinking of you at all—I was just putting myself in the position of the wife."

Mrs. Pepper shook her head sadly. She'd never dreamed of being wicked, she never meant to be at all—it was only that after Mr. Pepper went she was all alone, and traveling through the same territory with the dancing master, always getting on the same trains, they just got so they belonged to each other—they got so they'd meet to talk over business in this town and that, and pretty soon they were terribly dependent on each other, almost like a married couple. And that's the way she was, always dependent on the few bright little things in her life, miserable for months at the slightest change.

"For instance I can't settle down at the Bauers'," she confided unhappily. "I have that lovely big room and all, but I was used to the Bon Ton. I was used to you and Nettie running around and Morry always coming in at the wrong time—and the way we'd sit around gossiping. At Bauer's there's no one to talk to—Hulda—well, you might as well try to talk to a piece of pork. . . . That's what I mean, you see, about being dependent."

Cautiously the workroom door opened, and Nettie tiptoed in, glancing quickly at the two women as if she expected to see them tearing each other's hair. She held out the doll, now completely costumed in a wide lawn bonnet and dress, and held it up to Mrs. Pepper.

"Cute? Dode O'Connell wants one like it, Mrs. Abbott. I told her we were going to carry a few so she might buy one."

Elsinore, glad to change the subject, explained the doll idea to Mrs. Pepper. The corsetiere dried her eyes and listened. She bent forward with a spark of revived spirits.

"Let me tell you, that isn't the only thing you'll have to lay in, Mrs. Abbott. When the Works enlarges, like people say it's going to, you're going to have to carry a lot more things than just hats. Or else sit back and let strangers make the money."

"We'll never carry corsets again, believe me," Nettie laughed arrogantly. "Too much work."

Whenever Nettie became possessive about the shop Elsinore stiffened ever so little.

"We might as well carry corsets as dolls," she rebuked her. "At least we're used to the line."

Nettie, flushing, carried the doll into the front room and kicked the door shut behind her.

"Do you know there's going to be over a thousand new men taken on at the factory next fall?" Mrs. Pepper said. "That means more trade for us, you realize that, with all those families in town. Why, Mrs. Abbott, if I had the running of this shop I'd make the upstairs rooms into shops, too, and sell blouses and all the things girls want when they're making money. I wouldn't let the grass grow under my feet."

Elsinore's eyes caught the sparkle in the other's.

"I couldn't ever do it alone," she demurred. "I wouldn't know where in the world to begin."

Mrs. Pepper pulled her stool closer. Her reddened eyes snapped with excitement, and forgetful of her late wounds, she put a tiny fat hand on Elsinore's knee.

"Let me come in with you, then," she begged. "Let me come back and this summer we can plan the whole thing. I'll be looking around in the other towns, see, and picking up ideas here and there. Let me come back. . . ."

"What about Mr. Fischer?" Elsinore asked in a muffled voice.

Mrs. Pepper beat her hands together nervously.

"I don't know. I'll try to get over it—I know you feel you can't respect me because of that, but I don't mean to be just bad the way you think. Now that She's watching everything I'll have to be so careful anyway. . . . Oh, dear, I wish you hadn't gone to her, Mrs. Abbott, I don't see how you could. If it had been you instead of me—"

"It would never be me," Elsinore harshly interrupted. "And if you come back in this shop I'll expect you to behave differently."

"I've got to," Mrs. Pepper confessed. "That's why I want to put myself into a lot of hard work. I don't want a minute to think."

"As you say we'll have to buy more if the town gets larger," Elsinore looked about the workroom appraisingly. "We could use the upstairs for corsets and say lingerie. I could put a cot down here for Morry so we could start right in using his room."

When Nettie came back she stopped short at sight of the two women talking in low absorbed tones, their heads close together. Something in their attitude made her apprehensive of her own prestige—after all, she was part of the Bon Ton, wasn't she, and there was no justice in leaving her out of things this way. She sat down determinedly at the table and started threading an embroidery needle, humming a little tune. Mrs. Pepper turned to her.

"We were just talking of improving the shop."

"Well, we have been improving it," Nettie retorted with no great friendliness. "Didn't you notice we have electric lights now?"

Mrs. Pepper exclaimed appropriately as Nettie switched the lights on and off in demonstration.

"And did you see what Mr. Abbott sent us?" She went over to the cupboard and brought out an electric fan which she placed gingerly on the table; keeping her eyes fixed on it to be on guard against sudden explosions she attached it to the socket. The fan wheezed and whirred laboriously.

"He certainly is good to you, Mrs. Abbott," said Mrs. Pepper politely. "My, I only wish I had someone as kind to me."

Then both she and Elsinore looked idly at Nettie as if she were an intruder, but Nettie set her jaw and sat tight in her chair, sewing diligently. After a few minutes Mrs. Pepper got up.

"Well, I'll see you about that later," she said and reluctantly left.

Elsinore put the fan back in the cupboard, handling it as if it were an infernal device, likely to shoot into sky-rockets any minute.

"Well, now we've got her around again, I suppose," Nettie ejaculated nodding towards the door. "I'm sure I don't know where we'll put her and all her junk."

Elsinore looked thoughtfully into space, apparently unheeding. This infuriated Nettie, for it left her outside of things, somehow. She wanted to say something to remind her employer of intimate matters between them, to show that she really wasn't outside at all, but very much in the center of things.

"You know what Mr. Abbott thinks of her and her old stuff all over the place, you know how he hates it," she said reproachfully. "You ought to consider what your husband thinks especially after he sent you that electric fan for a present."

Elsinore whirled around at her almost ferociously.

"I hate that electric thing and you know it!" she blazed. "I hate all of Charles's presents—every single one of them—I'd like to throw them all out into the street this minute!"

"Why—why, Mrs. Abbott!" stuttered Nettie in amazement, so flustered that she dared not utter another word for nearly twenty minutes.

"You're never going to be the drinker your father was," Bill Delaney regretfully told Morry. "You come in here and get green on three beers, a big husky like you, too. Why your pap would sit down there with a quart of Scotch and soak it up without turning a hair. Walk out of this place like a gentleman, too. That was Charlie Abbott."

"Lay off the old man's business partner," Hogan warned Bill. "Don't you know my wife's old man is the biggest finanny on prohibition is this country? Morry can't drink and be in his office."

"The old man's all right," said Morry. "We get along. Did you see the plans for those houses we're putting up?"

"Sure, Fowler's going to make a lot of jack out of real estate," Hogan declared. "But watch out for him, sonny, watch out for a man that won't drink. They'll skin you out of your eyeteeth every time. What's he paying you?"

Morry got red in the face and gulped down his drink. Hogan grinned sardonically.

"Nothing, eh? That'd be the old man, all right—promise big money for next year, get you so dizzy talking in thousands that you'd forget to ask for five dollars to keep from starving."

So Morry couldn't explain about the bonuses and commissions that Fowler had promised. Anyway until last Saturday he'd been drawing pay from his factory job so he wasn't starving. True, on Saturday, the foreman fired him. This was for not showing up one day when he was looking at houses outside of town with Fowler. But the bonuses would begin soon enough and he could laugh at a dinky ten bucks a week.

The saloon was cooler than the July outdoors but its damp fermenting coolness was not refreshing, nor was the smell of sweating laborers crowded around the bar swilling beer. Waves of heat blew in at each motion of the door from the melting asphalt outside, a skinny maple tree sprouting from the cracks in the sidewalk dropped a tiny shrivelled green leaf on the marble doorsill. When the door swung open Morry could glimpse the Bauers' window framing Hulda Bauer, eyes closed, fanning herself rhythmically with a huge palm-leaf fan.

Morry wandered into the front room and picked up a billiard cue but it was too hot and too crowded to play, he couldn't play with the other fellows hanging around watching, so he went lonesomely back to the bar. There were strangers in Bill's place all the time now, well-dressed men who asked for expensive cigars and conferred in low voices at corner tables, there were surveyors and gangs of workers from out-of-town who were busy on the Lots. Men dropping in for a drink between trains, said, "Hear you folks are due for a boom. Conductor tells me your factory yonder is opening up a big new line this fall. Is that a fact?" Everyone talked excitedly of the new houses being built, of out-of-town money being put into the Lamptown business, of a boom that was sure to come because it was in the air, but no one seemed to know definitely. Strangers were in town, a little Jew from Cleveland started a branch of a ready-made dress chain store on Market Street and called it "The Elite," the drugstore soda fountains began to make chocolate frappes, Hermann Bauer raised the price of a meal to fifty cents, and lounging at a table in Bauer's any day you could see a little sharp-nosed sandy man in a checkered suit plunking a mandolin and humming the latest songs, for he was the actor who did a specialty at the Paradise. To most of Lamptown this gaudily dressed figure strolling about town was the symbol of Lamptown's sudden rise, he represented all the glamour of cities and sudden wealth; factory girls merely humming his songs felt rich and beautiful and in the swim, a town had to be pretty up and coming to have specialty actors at its movie house.

Merchants added expensive novelties to their stock when they saw three prosperous strangers in conference with the bank president one afternoon, and after an evening of discussing these mysterious portents and whispers, young married couples decided to buy a davenport or move to a better neighborhood or do *something* to keep in tune with this vague secret progress.

Even without a salaried job Morry moved along on a wave of optimism, planning more and more daring steps in the development of Clover Heights. He was learning now. When Fowler said, "See Hunt" or "See So-and-so at the People's Bank," Morry didn't suffer the same old agonies in collecting his courage. He "saw" people and said, "Mr. Fowler wants to talk to you about something," and then rushed thankfully away. He understood other matters too. He was beginning to see that the big deeds men spoke of were just dares to each other. All of them—Fowler, and everybody—were as afraid of starting something as Morry was, and so as soon as you saw they were all afraid it was easy to step up and be a leader, to say, "I'm going to do this"; these quiet boasts awed other men so that with the mere words power came, the thing magically began to take shape, because other men thought, "Here is one who isn't such a coward as I am," and respected and helped him. Men bluffed each other with brave boasts and then their vanity drove them on desperately to live up to their loud words.

It was as easy, if you had no money at all, to talk in terms of thousands as it was to talk in terms of hundreds. It was as easy to call a bare field "The Heights" as it was to call it "The Lots," and once the numbered stakes were stuck in the ground it was simple for an eager builder to vision mansions behind them. Hunt was easygoing and told Fowler to go ahead with his plans; so while the eastern end of the Lots was cut up in little fudge squares and a second house like the first one started, Fowler winked at Morry and said, "Let 'em get their little chicken-houses slung up there—plenty of time for us. When we start in on the west end this town's going to sit up on its hind legs."

It worried Fowler, though, that when the two Russells from Hartford came on they stayed at Hunt's house. Bauer's was too dingy for them and when any of their associates arrived they took them to Hunt's too.

"It's too intimate. They'll talk Hunt out of his corner, living together like that," Fowler told Morry uneasily. "That leaves us holding the bag. Hunt's too damned lazy to fight for his share. They're squeezing him out of the Works and out of his own home. It's bad for our business to have them all living with him."

Morry didn't tell him he'd been fired because Fowler might think that was bad for business too. He dug out all of Fowler's books on architecture, and it was a relief seated in his cramped quarters in the Bon Ton to let his eyes feast on pictures of terraced gardens with huge spacious houses sprawling over the page. He yearned for wide rooms and tall doorways you didn't bend beneath, he argued doggedly the case for great rooms with high ceilings, the manorial against the "cute" type Fowler rather fancied.

"People want a place to breathe in," he pleaded.

"Listen, breathing costs money," said Fowler noncommittally.

He thought of all these homes as steps to a great manor that was to be his own place, a place for his mother such as she'd never dreamed. The day he told her a little of this plan, she said—"That reminds me, Morry, I'm going to enlarge the business here, and we're fixing over the upstairs for corsets and lingerie. I guess we might as well start in with your room, so I'll put a cot down here in the workroom for you. You don't get to bed till late anyway, and you're always up early."

Morry didn't mind, he said, and took over one hat drawer for his things. Late on July nights he sat studying at the long worktable, his book propped up in the midst of artificial flowers, and stacks of rainbow-ribboned summer hats. No breeze reached this back room and perspiration would drip from his forehead to the printed page as the hot midnights passed. The room reeked with the dusty smell of long-stored trimmings, of plumes and maribou in mothballs, an old woman smell; but these present irritations were lost in the magnificence of his future. He pored over Fowler's books but when he asked him about complicated problems in them, the older man shrugged.

"What's the idea worrying about anything till you come to it? You know what you want to do in a general way, that's enough. I figure that when you know what you want in this life, all your mind focuses on slick ways of getting that one thing without working too hard at it, and by golly, you get it. But if you plug at it too hard, understand, with your nose stuck in it the way you got yours, then you lose sight of the thing you want. Your mind kinda loses its focus through the drudgery, see, and it's having your mind on it that lets you out of all the hard work. That's my opinion."

"But I want to know the things I say I know," Morry protested. "I want to be sure and safe in my head, don't you see?"

He checked lists of correspondence courses he found in the trade magazines, and struggled hopelessly with their lessons. No one seemed able to explain the Greek of these Simple Lessons.

"Good God, you don't need to know everything!" Fowler exclaimed. "I got along all right without knowing the whole works."

Morry didn't want to tell him that he was going to be more than any Fowler ever was, he was going to do a lot better than that.

Fowler had never had a drink in his life, he disapproved of saloons, but he needed to know what the strangers were up to, so he was glad Morry hung around Delaney's to listen, later on he might lecture him about whiskey and bad company but for the present he was broad-minded. Morry was swelling up a little with the respectful questions asked him in the saloon, he said more than he knew and talked easily of eight and ten thousand dollar homes, of thirty and forty dollar rents. Even Hogan was respectful but his blue eyes twinkled with sarcastic reservations now that he found Morry was to be paid off in "commissions."

"If I was you I wouldn't stick in this town, buddy," he advised. "I'd bum my way to Akron to the rubber works or down to Dayton to the Cash Register Company or take the Ford plant up in Detroit. I'd go where the big money was."

"Listen, there's going to be more big money in this here town next year than you ever saw," interrupted Bill Delaney. "I got my ears peeled, I know what's going on here. It's a good place to stick around, especially if they start floating stock in the new works like I hear, so's everybody gets a slice. You save up and buy there, Morry, you're young, you got time to get rich."

Morry watched Hogan smacking his lips over his beer and thought of when Hogan had given him the idea for a beautiful Lamptown. There were no two ways about it, he had to do something about that one idea; he had to prove something in the world before he ever dared go to any of those cities. He couldn't ever leave till he'd made a mark here, that much he knew.

"You didn't use to say that, Hogan," he said a little rebukingly. "You said you'd stay here and make over this town."

"That's right," Shorty remembered.

Hogan patted his belly fondly.

"The hell with it," he yawned. "What's a kid like Abbott here want to stick in a little town for? Nothing to do but get some girl in trouble, let her run him to the church and marry him, and at twenty-one he's sunk. Babies, mortgages—what chance has he got? Never dare throw up his job after that and better himself—"

"Well, you did all those things," someone dared to say.

"Sure, I did. I'm telling my story, ain't I? . . . Married twenty years—my wife's a damned fine woman, don't misunderstand me. Lost her good looks but like old Colonel R. G. Ingersoll says, God love him, 'Through the wrinkles of time, through the music of years, if you really love her, you will always see the face you loved and won.' . . . Old Bob Ingersoll."

Hunt Russell's car obstructed the view of Hulda Bauer's window. Hunt, in gray flannels, shirtsleeves, and tennis shoes, slid out from behind the wheel and came in. Morry wasn't afraid of Hunt; he'd been fired from Hunt's factory but vaguely this put him on a level with the employer. Lately he'd made a tense, nervous third to the conferences of Hunt and Fowler—conferences in which Hunt smoked a pipe lazily and said, "Sounds OK to me, Fowler,—damned good idea, and if you can do it without getting the family down on me, go ahead—I'm no good on the details. Figure things out yourself and go to it."

"What about it, Hunt—what about this Hartford factory coming out here to hook up with the Works?" Bill Delaney asked the question no one had dared to ask directly before, and men, hanging around the pool tables, edged up to the bar to hear what answer Hunt would make.

"That's about right, Bill," he said casually. "Things getting pretty hot in this town all around. We're bringing all the branches of the Works into Lamptown—taking on fifteen hundred men by the end of October."

"Who runs it, then—you or your uncle Ferd?" Bill asked sharply.

Hunt shrugged his shoulders.

"What's the use of my working myself to death? I'm letting my relatives do the worrying."

"Yeah, and he'll do his worryin' later," muttered Hogan in Morry's ear. "Smarter men'n he is, buddy, you wait and see the big Lamptown cheese king take a spin on his magnum opus, wait till you see what they do to him."

"Where they going to live, for God's sake?" someone yelled from one of the tables. "These fifteen hundred families. Where you going to put 'em, Hunt, eh—let 'em dig holes in the ground and crawl in, maybe?"

"Looks like a swell deal for Hermann," observed Shorty and sent a highball sliding down the bar to stop exactly at Hunt's elbow. "Hermann'll clean up a nice wad renting out his rooms."

"I've got to turn over my house to my cousins and some of the eastern officials, I know that much," Hunt said, frowning. "No place else for them. But later there'll be plenty of places to stay, what with the new houses on the Lots. Then the Big Four has offered their woods to the Works at a figure."

"Now there's a help," Hogan grunted sarcastically. "Why, the boys can live in the trees as snug as you please and practice birdcalls and sling buckeyes at each other, oh sure, they'll have plenty of places to stay. Why, what d'ye say, Bert, we take a coupla boarders in the coal car, and then there's plenty of room in the Round House. Oh sure, there'll be no trouble about housing the bastards, take any of these swell hotels on Market Street, and there's the old pickle factory building, the Bum's Blackstone—"

Men laughed and then stopped uneasily since after all, Hogan was pretty fresh, trying to make a fool out of Lamptown's big man. Morry didn't take Hogan as such an oracle now, he'd begun to be a little cynical, seeing him back down on his big talk so many times; he didn't kid him the way the other men did and call him "Big Noise" because he was sorry for Hogan, sorry for him because he must despise himself a little for not living up to his brave conversation. Morry lowered his glance now whenever Hogan talked as if he was president or God or somebody, because he didn't want to betray the devastating pity in his eyes. No one else listened to Hogan, either, they were crowding around Hunt, firing questions at him, and Hunt, pouring down his throat one highball after another, made half-mocking answers in a shrill strained voice, so that afterward it struck Morry that all this change was worrying him a good deal for some reason.

"Here, Morry, stick this up in the window on your way out," Hunt called to him and handed him a cardboard poster. "There's one for Hermann, too, but I'll take that one over myself, I told Fischer I would."

"I'll bet you will," Morry thought bitterly.

He reached over the green baize curtains in the window and propped the poster against the glass.

EVERYBODY'S COMING

TO

FISCHER'S

SERPENTINE BALL!!

July 31   8:30 PM

LADIES 50¢   GENTS $1

The men crowded around Hunt—Bill ignored orders for drinks and rapped out questions—was it true pay was to be raised, that a guy from Newark, New Jersey, was coming out to run things, that shares were to be sold to the workers; a few who were afraid to address Hunt directly even when tipsy, urged Bill to ask him this and that about whatever worry they had concerning the new state. Morry lingered at the door, listening, so he could report it all to Fowler, since every sensational new step was fuel for Clover Heights.

In the hot tar-smelling street Morry mopped his forehead and then was pleasantly cooled by the idea of widening the creek so that there could be swimming and boating in Clover Heights, maybe a Country Club, yes sir, Clover Heights Country Club. . . .

He looked back in the saloon window to see if he'd got the poster right side up and his mouth curled a little thinking of how Hunt was afraid to let anybody else take the other poster over to Hermann's for fear they'd ask Jen to that ball before he did. . . . Bah, let him go ahead and ask her if that's the way he feels!

Hot, sticky nights with no breeze in all Lamptown except underneath the Bon Ton's electric fan or behind Hulda Bauer's giant palm leaf. The night men at the factory worked with their sweating torsos bare, behind the honeysuckle vines on the boardinghouse porches the girls sat in their kimonos eating ice cream, the factory engines with their now doubled manpower chugged steadily through the hot stillness. A lush yellow moon hung over the Big Four woods seeming to send a glow of heat over the fields, in the stagnant creek frogs croaked and mosquitoes buzzed intently, the sultry wind ruffling the damp clover of the Lots was worse than no breeze at all.

In Delaney's the old pianola rattled ceaselessly, its music was worn out, a nickle dropped in hopefully only set the other nickles to jingling like sleigh bells for three minutes, but the festive tempo was there still and the hint of devilish gaiety. Morry refused its jangling invitation for Bauer's diningroom. Here, at ten o'clock, he sat at one of the tables with Jen, and pushed a catsup bottle this way to show her where the Clover Heights Hotel was to be, the mustard here was the club, the relish dish was the

Normandy chateau that was now under way, and the trail of the fork he pushed across the table was the boulevard track.

Jen's gingham sleeves were rolled to her shoulders, her black hair was kinky with the heat. She leaned half across the table to watch these fascinating maneuvers and could not restrain a sigh of admiration.

"Gee, Morry, how did you ever dare think of it?"

Morry looked bored with such stupidity.

"Good Lord, Jen, did you think I didn't know anything but crating goods at some factory? I'm not like the rest of these fellas. I should think you'd know that by this time. I got ideas."

Jen hastened to soothe him.

"I know—only I can't get over how wonderful it is, that's all I meant."

"Wait. That's all," Morry said impressively. "This is nothing. Wait till you see our big offices—maybe headquarters in Cleveland or Pittsburgh—even New York. Can you imagine me in charge of the New York business?"

"Sure, you could do it, I'll bet . . . but, it's far off, isn't it?"

Morry laughed scornfully.

"What—New York? . . . Only a couple days' trip. Not even that. I'd take the morning local to Pittsburgh, catch the limited that night, be in New York the next day."

They were quiet because already he was gone, he was in New York, and Jen was all alone at the table with a mustard bottle for a country club, no Morry—nothing. . . . All right, she would go there, too, she didn't have to follow Morry, but she could do something.

"And when you're doing all that, I'll be in some show—a dancer, maybe, or an actress like Mama. . . . It won't be long now, will it?"

Morry, not listening, shook his head, and watched the sandy-haired little actor from the Paradise lounging at the back table with a frayed copy of a detective magazine. Now the actor abandoned his reading and tipped his chair back against the wall. He tweaked idly away at his mandolin, singing softly to himself—

> "Some of these days—
> You'll miss your hon-ey—"

He was a tenor with a voice of agonizing sweetness, yet these sugared notes made Morry's spine quiver, they made him desperately happy and miserable at the same time, so that he forgot the red pepper tennis court in his hand and surrendered to this drowsy spell. The singer's eyes were closed, his nostrils quivered holding the high notes, his stiff blue cuffs stuck out three inches from his tight checkered sleeves. He slid further and further back in his chair as he played, winding his legs about the chair rungs to reveal every bit of his purple-striped socks. . . .

Morry sighed. He didn't need to tell Jen any more of his plans—she believed so much more than even he dared believe himself. He was exquisitely contented here tonight, he couldn't imagine why, but it must be the singing. Jen's head swayed to the melody as if always in the back of her head she heard whatever music there ever was, but her eyes stayed on Morry's dark face.

"I've been so lone-a-ly," whined the honeyed voice, "just for-a-you on-a-ly—"

Hulda Bauer's fan slowed up for the long-drawn-out rhythm of this song—if the notes lingered much more Hulda would lose count completely and fall into a doze.

"That's what I'm goin' to do—I'm goin' on the stage," Jen whispered to Morry. "When Lil comes she and I are both goin' to be actresses. Mr. Travers says it's easy. Look here."

She pulled a cabinet photograph from the drawer of the serving table and pushed it across the table to Morry. It was the picture of a young fair-haired girl in graduation dress against a background of painted ocean. Her wide eyes looked straight into Morry's, and his spine quivered again as it had over the song and over the silver-blonde on the magazine. It was her blondness that fascinated him most, except for that she looked like Jen; but he had always wondered secretly what strange things yellow-haired girls thought about.

"Lil," said Jen. "Looks like me, doesn't she?"

"Oh, I don't know," Morry said, and Jen, stiffening a little with unexpected jealousy drew the picture back.

The four legs of the actor's chair suddenly came to the floor with a bang. He threw down his mandolin, stood up and stretched himself elaborately.

"Jesus, what a dump this is!" he addressed the world bitterly. "No place to go—nothing to do—might as well turn in."

Hulda Bauer laboriously got off her stool and approached them.

"That's right, Mr. Travers. Bed's the best place. Goodnight to you."

She waddled somberly toward the stair door, nodding to Jen.

"Better be goin' home, Morry. Jen's got to be up early."

Morry got up. Jen never begged him to stay any more now. Her mouth dropped a little as he reached for his cap. Mr. Travers observed her through half-shut eyes while he put his mandolin in its case.

"Morry, don't you think that's a swell idea—Lil and I going on the stage, traveling all over, seeing everything?" Jen wanted to know.

Morry nodded casually.

"Yeah, that'll be great," he agreed. A flash of irritation came over him that Jen should have plans, too. Part of his own plans was that Jen should always be in Lamptown, always astonished at his great deeds, always breathlessly applauding. He knew a second of cold fear at the thought of this town without Jen, Jen, the one certain thing—but he'd never let her guess that.

"That sure will be great traveling," he repeated, and Jen said no more.

Morry, aching already for a lost Jen, slouched across the street and Jen traced his name slowly with her finger across the glass cigar counter.

"Stuck on him, ain't you, Kid?" teased Mr. Travers. Jen made a horrible face at him for answer and stalked into the kitchen.

Morry didn't go to bed for hours. He got his cot ready, pulled off his damp shirt and threw it over the screen. He sat down on the cot, one shoe in his hand, and thought of how Jen's arms looked with her sleeves rolled up and who would there be to see how wonderful he was if she left town. She couldn't go away, that was all wrong. He was the one who would go away and always remember to write her about cities and strange lands he visited—he'd go away and always remember Jen St. Clair and how much a letter from him would mean to her. Since she was only a girl and had to stay home, he'd gladly tell her all about the outside world. . . . But she said she was going. . . .

Annoyed, Morry dropped the shoe and started unlacing the other one. Lil's picture came before him, in startling detail . . . he'd never seen a girl who looked like that except the girl on the magazine. He couldn't get her out of his head. He made a complete mental image of her, made up of what Jen told him about Lil and what he knew about Jen. This confused image was lovely to think about and he could not shake it away. . . .

An eastern wind came up and blew a few drops of rain into the room. Morry went over to close the window and heard singing somewhere; it wasn't from the saloon and it seemed further away than Bauer's. He strained his ears, it was like a woman's voice far away humming to mandolin notes, but he couldn't puzzle out the exact song or whence it came. Even after the midnight fast train roared by he could hear this music, lingering in the whistle's echo, sweet and far-off like a promise. Finally he gave up trying to catch it, and sat down again. He was happy. He didn't know why this was so, but there it was. He dropped his other shoe. It covered a corner of a postcard that had fluttered from the table to the floor. It was a familiar card and the glimpse of it was to Morry like seeing an evil face peering in the window, destroying every happy thought, making his stomach contract with sick dread, almost before his mind had taken in the words—

"THE CANDY MAN WILL VISIT YOU ON THURSDAY, JULY 31st."

The electric fan hummed and whirred in Elsinore's room, it sat up on a shelf watching the room, whirring, whirring, it kept the thin blue silk dresser scarf quivering frantically in its perpetual gale; as she brushed her hair it blew her kimono sleeve against her pale cheeks. It was like Charles himself, subtly infuriating, quietly goading her nerves, but she was determined not to let it disturb her self-control. When she picked up her hand-mirror she knew what the fan was saying, "So you're wearing a low-necked dress, eh, Else . . . guess this guy's got you running, you never went in for fast clothes before . . . and the silk chemise, too, eh? . . . Well, why not, all the sporting women wear them and if that's you, now . . . no more blue or black dresses, either, I see . . . pink, by George . . . so that's how crazy he's made you, Else, old girl. . . . Pink silk at thirty-eight. . . . Pink silk for the Serpentine Ball—well, well, well."

Elsinore went on brushing her hair, the night was so hot her kimono stuck to the chair, through the little windows came the train smoke and saloon stench, the men singing and carrying on in the street sounded alarmingly near as if they were in the very room. She could hear the orchestra tuning up in the Casino, she heard Fischer laughing, and she wanted to hurry into the new dress but she was afraid of the watching fan. Well, she didn't care now. Let it find out that she hated her husband, very well, let it know everything. In the wastebasket beside the dresser was the box in which a silk chemise had arrived this morning and a note from Charles, saying, "Thought your new lovers might like this."

She had read the card, stunned, while Nettie tore off the tissue papers and pulled out the gift in great delight. All Charles's former taunts had been faint, far-off drum beats leading up to this menacing roll of thunder that could not be ignored. . . . "Thought your new lovers . . ." As Nettie shook out the silk, admiring its lace edge, the cages of Elsinore's mind burst open and hatred escaped. There was no way of locking it back in, there was a fearful joy in facing the truth, that strange blend of relief and desolation in seeing a jewel, long desperately guarded, finally lost forever. She wanted to tear up the note and the gift with it, but her second thought was a perverse resolve to wear the garment, as if she had carried out his savage suggestion. . . . It occurred to her to spray perfume on her hair, just as he had told her bad women did. For the first time in her life she wished for an intimate friend, a woman who knew her secrets, who would come in now while she dressed and say, "Elsinore, you never looked lovelier in your life—not a day over twenty-eight. If Harry Fischer only knew you were through with Charles, he wouldn't hesitate a minute—Mrs. Pepper's nothing to him, really, just a convenience—if he knew how you hated your husband. . . ."

Downstairs Nettie sat in the front of the shop, dressed in prim white embroidery, waiting for Fay and her young man to call for her. Elsinore wanted them to be gone before she came downstairs in her new pink dress, so after she was ready she sat down by her window waiting to see them cross the street as her signal for leaving. There was a tall, black-haired young man standing at the foot of the Casino steps rolling a cigarette. He seemed restless and each time the Bauers' screen door swung open he peered around to see who was coming out. Finally he pulled his cap down over his eyes and slouched into the restaurant. This was Morry, his mother saw, and while his motions stirred no curiosity in her, they irritated the watchful Nettie downstairs, almost beyond endurance. She had almost decided to go right into Bauer's after him, and tell him right before everyone that instead of waitresses he ought to be taking his own mother to the Casino.

The Casino windows gave out a mellow candy-pink glow from bunting-shrouded lights, and Elsinore could not distinguish Fischer from his musicians in the dark group near the window. Then she caught the gleam of a white dress shirt and a humming in her head joined the humming of the fan behind her. It was difficult to sustain, unfading in her mind, the black onyx eyes of Harry Fischer, the white eyeballs spread out and then diminished so that they were now white eyes, now black eyes, the color flickering and changing with the electric fan's insistent vibration. . . .

A man and two girls in white crossed the street—Nettie and Fay. Elsinore took a last look at herself in the mirror. Her hair was too tightly drawn—she took the pins out and did it up again nervously. The pink taffeta dress with its round neck had seemed too low when she first bought it, she had had to put a lace ruching across the front. Now she saw that the ruching was out of place and with her nail scissors she clipped the threads that held it. She picked up her white silk shawl and went downstairs through the darkened shop out into the hot, breathless night.

In her empty bedroom the electric fan whirred and purred, it kept the dresser-scarf trembling perpetually, the closet door gently blowing open and shut, the shades on the little windows crackling, and rapidly it flicked the pages of a mail-order catalogue lying on the bed.

Streamers of colored serpentine fluttered from the Casino ceiling, men dancing in their shirt sleeves snatched at it and lassoed shrieking girls, they kicked through tangles of the rainbow strips over the dance floor, under the pink lights all women looked gay and darkly wicked. In the center of the floor the dancing teacher and Dode O'Connell two-stepped perfectly, Dode in a skin-tight red dress defying her red hair. The musicians (Mr. Sanderson at the piano) sang their choruses, their throats bulged and veins swelled on their foreheads as they bellowed the words, but even so the shouting and laughing of the dancers drowned them out, only a phrase now and then soared through the din, "Some of these days—you'll miss—"

Morry danced with Jen for the third time running, in this uproar it would not be remarked, besides she was so light in his arms he forgot to trade her for someone else. Jen tried to make herself still and light as a feather so that she could be close to Morry and not let him notice it, for if he remembered it was only Jen he was holding he'd drop her and go away. He was so tall he had to hump his shoulders way over to hold her, and her arm was tight around his neck. All she could think, dancing, was that this was the way she wanted to be—always—fast in Morry's arms. On the visitor's bench by the doorway Nettie Farrell, watching, her embroidered dress spread out in stiff petals around her, whispered something to her chum, Fay, who then stared hard at Jen's feet. Nettie didn't last very long at the Serpentine Ball for the men were all hilariously drunk, and they called endearing names to her as they danced past or chucked her under the chin familiarly—no one respected a decent girl in this noisy carnival, so at eleven o'clock Nettie indignantly departed.

"I have an announcement to make tonight, ladies and gentlemen," Fischer bawled through the megaphone. "The Serpentine Ball tonight is the last dance of the summer. The first dance of the autumn season will be given here in six weeks on September tenth. I wish to state that I will introduce to my pupils and members of my studio at that time the Mississippi Glide. This dance, ladies and gentlemen, is the popular ballroom dance of New York City at the present time, and with the assistance of Miss O'Connell, here, I will give you a brief demonstration. The Mississippi Glide. All right, Mr. Sanderson."

Immediately the crowd of dancers backed away, leaving the center of the floor free for the dancing master and his partner. Eyes fastened on the black patent-leather feet (heels never touching floor) and the red satin ($10) slippers as they traced an intricate design on the shining oak floor.

"Do you suppose they really dance that way in New York?" Jen whispered to Morry. It hadn't occurred to Morry to ever doubt it, but now he shook his head convincingly.

"Na—they never even heard of it in New York," he answered. Jen's hand was hot in his but he did not drop it for Hunt Russell was alone nearby, and Morry thought stubbornly that now he was a business man himself he didn't have to give in to anyone, he didn't care so much about dancing with Jen but he wanted Hunt Russell to understand he had as much right to as anybody.

Fischer was the only man to keep his coat on, all the others were dancing with their shirt sleeves rolled up, their wilted collars open, serpentine trailing from their ears and trouser legs, their sweaty palms making smudgy imprints on the light dresses of their girls. The punch bowl in the hall had been filled three times, strengthened more each time with rum. Couples danced dizzily, wearily around, battered by the crowd; girls' heads, peering blankly over their partners' shoulders, seemed pinned there like valentines, their faces dulled with music, their eyes unwinking, hair stringing damply over their cheeks.

Elsinore danced with a big red-faced drummer from Newark with a silver hook for a left hand. He said, "Just catch hold of that there hook, that's the idea," and he said that when it came to carrying sample cases a hook was better than a hand, but Elsinore shuddered touching the cold metal. His big tan shoes scuffed her white kid pumps, he held her so tight that her back ached, but this violence strangely pleased her as the clangor about her satisfied some desperate inner necessity. The jiggling crowd tore the sash from her pink dress, in the frenzy of a circle two-step with the music growing faster and faster her head whirled, and the girls, swinging from one hand to the next, kept up a high, dizzy scream that soared above all else.

"Dance with Number Three," roared Fischer and she was swung into his arms. Perspiration streamed from his forehead, he shook out a cream-colored silk kerchief and mopped his head. His heart thumped against her and confused her, even the smell of whiskey on his breath was rare and exciting. She forgot that he was Mrs. Pepper's, that in little railroad hotels those two met and went to one room. She forgot about the big blonde wife in Cleveland, all of these shadows faded under the pink lights and the hard bright gleam in his black eyes. He called a command over her shoulder, "Dance with the lady on your left!" and she was flung into a new partner's arms. She saw that Fischer was dancing with the Delaneys' girl, Jen—she would always remember that she had been pushed away for that young girl. . . .

She didn't want anyone else to touch her now, so she broke away from the dance and went into the dressing room. Only two girls were inside, big raw-boned girls with red arms and necks thrust out of feathery pink and blue organdie, blonde chickens popping out of Easter eggs. They stood before the dresser shaking clouds of powder over their faces from huge powder puffs, trustfully and intently, as if this witchcraft would instantly compel popularity. Elsinore looked at her face, white and small in the mirror between their two ruddy faces. She looked wild, she thought, with her hair flying about loosely, but she didn't care. Her head was splitting with noise but she wasn't sure if the noise was outside or inside, so many strange confusing thoughts crowded through her head like masked guests at a carnival, exciting, terrifying, shouting phrases they would never dare whisper under their own names. There was something familiar in all these suggestions as if long ago they had briefly appeared and at once been whisked off to dungeons. There was no guard for them now, but a fearful exhilaration in the knowledge that they were too strong for her, that they could overpower her easily.

She saw through the doorway that Fischer was still dancing with Jen St. Clair and she recalled old Mrs. Delaney warning her to keep Morry away from this girl. She would, she thought viciously, or better, she'd tell her to keep away from Morry. She'd say "Morry" but she would be secretly meaning, "Keep away from Harry Fischer!" Because he belonged to her, to nobody else. . . . Elsinore looked quickly at the two girls as if the thunder of her own mind might be overheard. One of them was bending over fixing a red garter on her white cotton stocking but she caught Elsinore's eye and smiled.

"If I bring my last summer's hat back, Mrs. Abbott," she ventured, "could you change the daisies on it for poppies?"

Elsinore smiled back at her but the words seemed no more concern of hers than the girl's knobby knees above her pretty legs, and when the girls went out together one said to the other, "She don't have to snub me twice, believe me." Then at the door they burst out laughing shrilly to show everyone they were having a wonderful time. . . .

Elsinore was glad they were gone, she felt sick from their geranium-scented powder. She opened the window wider and pulled the moth-eaten velveteen curtains behind her, it was easier to be here in the next room thinking of Fischer than in the ballroom seeing him with someone else. There was no air stirring outside, stars and a moon would have looked cool but only the lights from the Works lit up the sky with a soft red glare. She could hear the steady chugging of the factory machines going all night long, and from up here she could see the long dark shadows of freight cars sliding back and forth in the Yard, the emerald and ruby signal lights winking on and off. Through the din of the dance hall the two-four rhythm of the bass drum throbbed triumphantly and punctuated the swish-swish of the engines outside. They didn't need an orchestra for Lamptown dances, Elsinore thought, holding her splitting head in her hands, the engines and the factory machines could keep two-four time. One and two and a one and a two and a one—this drumbeat that could not be silenced was part of Fischer, all of her fantasies were made to this obligato: they unrolled now automatically, herself and Fischer on a train going away, away—away from young girls with smooth throats and light laughter, away from factory girls with hard mouths dancing with fierce grace, away from delicately scented, plump women with tinkling voices—only Mrs. Abbott, a milliner, and Mr. Fischer, a dancing master. Away to what?—Breathlessly she allowed herself to draw aside this forbidden curtain, to see them alone, he is coming through a doorway smiling at her, the doorway of her bedroom, she is in the pink taffeta dress waiting, and— Crowds of girls burst through the door, abruptly the dream vanished and Elsinore wrung her hands. There could be no torture like interruption, the brutal ripping of cherished tapestries. If she had one wish in the world it would be to be locked in a tower to think of one man undisturbed forever. She was nauseated again by geranium powder, girls battled for place at the mirror, giggling they crowded her away from the window, the room became stifling. She could not endure it any longer. She pulled her shawl from the hook and a dozen wraps fell in a heap on the floor but she couldn't bother with them. If she could only sleep . . . but she hadn't slept for months it seemed to her. The mad circus in her head exhausted her, she didn't want to face Fischer again tonight. Alone, in her room, he was hers completely, here he belonged to all Lamptown. She walked unsteadily down the narrow hallway toward the steps, she didn't look back once to see him. The dance hall, out of the corner of her eye, was a nightmare of laughter and fluttering colors. She could scarcely wait to get home to think, to plan, to be alone. . . .

In the darkness of the stair landing Morry and Jen and Hunt Russell were standing.

"Well, Jen, how about it, coming with me?" Hunt asked. He was holding Jen's bare arm caressingly.

Jen looked at Morry but Morry wouldn't tell her not to go—if she wanted to go for a ride with Hunt he wouldn't stop her.

"Should we go, Morry?" she asked.

"Do what you please," Morry said distantly. "You wouldn't go if you didn't want to, anyway."

His mother hurried by without looking at him. He started after her but she ran down the steps in almost clumsy haste, so Morry didn't follow her just then, besides he wanted to see what Jen was going to do.

Elsinore's heart was pounding when she reached the street, she felt enormously elated as if she had escaped her hunters so far and was about to gloat over a stolen treasure in perfect safety. Not a soul was out. As far down Market Street as she could see lights blinked on deserted sidewalks, all Lamptown was crowded under the rose lights of the Casino; only Hermann and Hulda Bauer dozed in their windows. . . . She fumbled with her key, but her hands were shaking so she could scarcely fit it into the lock. The shop bell tingled sharply in the darkness as the door opened, then stopped short as the door shut. She turned the key quickly behind her again, she wanted to lock out these nameless pursuers who would harry her, for she was going to be alone, alone. . . . Her head and feet were so light, only her heart was thundering away, it could be heard above the Casino tumult or the engine whistles, she was certain. . . . Now she remembered the feel of his thick white hand grasping hers, the sensation was far clearer in memory than it had been in actuality, she could see the fine lines around his eyes, the cleft in his heavy chin . . . she felt so giddy she leaned against the wall for a moment at the top of the stairs. . . . She was strangely happy as if she were on the verge of something beautiful about to happen, something incredible, she was separated from this triumph by the thinnest of walls, if she could only control the chaos in her head she would know what this lovely thing was. . . . In another minute she could think—she'd be alone. . . . She pushed open the bedroom door and the noise of the fan made her catch her breath with the shock of reality. . . . The lovely thing about to happen . . . she clung to its vanishing shadow, but everything beautiful was fleeing desperately, there was only Charles Abbott, collarless and red-faced, sprawling drunkenly over her bed. She put her hand over her eyes to dispel this bad dream. Charles awkwardly sat up, blinking at her with bloodshot eyes. It was terrifying, the spectacle of the immaculate Candyman with his starched striped shirt rumpled, his black hair tousled and hanging over his eyes, his thin mouth sagging loosely. His coat and hat trailed on the floor, his sample cases were open and bonbons spilled all over the rug. Elsinore shook with blind fury, she wanted to tear him to pieces with her hands.

"Well, who'd you expect to see here if not your husband?" He pointed at her accusingly. "You come in here and turn white as a sheet, cause you see me. Who the hell was you expecting, damn it, stand there shivering away like I was some burglar. . . ."

She didn't dare to look at him again, hate was burning her veins, she wanted to kill him, to destroy everybody who outraged her right to be alone. His thick voice, whatever it was saying, rasped through her thoughts, there surely must be an end to such torment. She wouldn't look at him for she knew tears of rage were smarting in her eyes and through this blur she saw the little heap of silver-wrapped bonbons in the top of the sample case, she saw how cleverly they formed one curious shape, no use steadying her rioting brain to make sure of what her eyes saw there, for silver was in her brain, silver shut out Charles's voice, silver chilled the hatred in her heart, before she touched it she thrilled with the ecstasy of escape that beautiful metal in her hands could bring, wild happiness swept over her, the joy, exactly, of finding an opening in the prison wall too small for her pursuers but for her—final freedom.

On and on the drunken voice droned, accusing her, mocking her, as it had done year after year slowly wearing down her barriers. Facing him, her hand groped among the bonbons for what she had seen there, as soon as she touched the revolver she had a vision of a paradise of solitude and privacy forever. This was one way to shut out words . . . she raised the gun, closed her eyes and fired.

The awful hush of the minute afterward terrified her. She was sitting in a chair, tears slowly coursing down her cheeks. Someone hurrying up the steps, calling out, meant nothing to her. It meant nothing to see Charles sprawled over the floor, his mouth still open in his astonishment. A stream of blood trickled from him across the floor and slowly dyed the little blue doormat. The revolver was lost in the candies that had tumbled over. . . .

She began rocking back and forth in the chair. Her head ached, it was so empty and numb. Back and forth she rocked. Someone came in the room but she could not see or hear or feel, a man lying on the floor was no concern of hers, the only thing that was oddly familiar was the whirring of the electric fan behind her.

So Charlie Abbott had shot himself, they said.

No one in Lamptown knew why and no one really cared. In Delaney's bar they said Charlie Abbott was a bad egg, he had smooth ways but he was too slick with his women, too damned slick, never doing a thing for his wife and kid in Lamptown, they could starve for all of him. In the backyards of Shantyville women hanging up the wash, their mouths full of clothespins, speculated about what fast woman Mr. Abbott had killed himself for. No good, anyway, running around spending money while his wife worked her fingers to the bone keeping herself and the boy. Mrs. Abbott was a lady, as fine a little woman as you'd care to meet, you'd think after all she'd done the least a husband could do in return was to shoot himself in one of those big hotels instead of messing up her nice little shop.

The reporter from the Cleveland Leader asked Bill Delaney how the gun happened to be on the other side of the room after this "suicide," and if it hadn't struck Bill that the wife might have plugged him on account of his other women. Bill Delaney fixed the stranger with an indignant eye.

"None of that funny business, now," he curtly advised. "Don't let anybody in this town hear you say a thing like that or they'll run you out of town. I know that's all in your line, but leave Mrs. Abbott out of it, see? She's a quiet lady-like little body that's had her first piece of luck now with her husband kicking off. You just keep your imagination to yourself, because Lamptown people won't listen to a word about Mrs. Abbott. A plucky little woman, that's what she is."

Only Morry knew. He had known when he opened the bedroom door and saw his mother rocking quietly beside the thing on the floor. He was paralyzed with terror and an awful guilty feeling of having wished this very thing until it came true. . . . Then all he could think was how unhappy she must have been to do it, and such pity came over him for his mother that his throat ached and he was ready to face all the rest of her tormenters himself, and to kill them all. It didn't matter about his father, it only mattered that his mother had suffered all these years, it was as if she were the one who had died, and all his failures to understand or to help her loomed in his mind—too late he would make amends.

But there was little, after all, for him to do now. All Lamptown was taking care of little Mrs. Abbott whose husband had chosen such a tragic end. The Bauers took charge of everything. Hulda slept in the shop and at the last minute there was no place for Morry so he had to stay at Hunt's overnight. He hung around his mother, he wanted her to say she needed him and that Hulda could go home but Elsinore didn't say anything. She stayed in bed, eating nothing, staring at visitors blankly when they asked questions, seeming to recognize no one.

"She's been that way ever since they found him," people whispered.

Hermann knew the story and told everybody exactly how it happened. It seems Bill Delaney was in back of his saloon when he heard the shot, and since Charlie had been in there an hour before, drunk, and waving a revolver, he'd sort of suspected him of something. So he rushed into the Bon Ton and the next minute he was sticking his head out of the upstairs window, yelling, "Hey, Hermann, for God's sake, Charlie Abbott's dead!" Hermann waddled over as fast as he could and by the time he got upstairs Bill Delaney had gone all to pieces—he was on his knees by the bed sobbing and shivering and out of his mind.

"Oh God, Hermann, it wasn't my fault," he screamed, "I swear it wasn't—but look at them spread out all over the tracks—all bleeding and all dead—" They called in Bill's mother to take him home, he clung to her weakly, sobbing against her bent old shoulder that the wreck wasn't his fault. . . .

Girls ran in from the Casino and Hermann finally had to lock the doors. "Well, Charlie shot himself, that's all, now get back to your dance."

Elsinore, all the next day, sat in her chair by the window, wrapped in a blanket, her hair tumbled down, her face sagging oddly, her eyes stupid. Morry kept patting her hand but he didn't know what to say to her, or anything to do for her except vague magnificent deeds that would somehow make her happy. She cared no more for him than for anyone, and she seemed ten times more remote, never talking, looking dully out the window all the time, never heeding the compassionate questions of the neighbors. She didn't comb her hair or change to night clothes when she went to bed, and this bothered Morry more than anything for he could not conceive of a catastrophe big enough to make his mother neglect her person. He didn't think of his father, all he knew was that a terrible thing had happened to his mother, and he was suffocated with tenderness for her. He thought about her every instant, he was going to do something to make it all up to her, he tried to think of something that would astonish and please her, but all he could think of was a little silver bar pin he'd got her from Robbin's for Christmas once.

"That's it—I'll get her another bar pin," he decided with relief.

The blue veins in her temples and white hands moved him almost to tears, and the marble pallor of her face. . . . He knew what it was like to have it all burning inside of you with no way of showing it. If he could only smooth everything for her. . . . He was enraged at his futility, then the whisper came—"You can't help her because she won't let you, it isn't your fault—it's only that she doesn't need you or anybody else."

This wasn't quite fair for her, a woman ought to need her son, oughtn't she? . . . Hurt and troubled, Morry went back to Fowler's office and tried to concentrate on Clover Heights. Everyone he met looked at him reproachfully and said, "Look here, Morry, oughtn't you to be home with your mother?" . . . He couldn't very well explain that his mother didn't want him, so he could only mutter a sullen answer about the demands of his work. He amazed himself by asking Fowler for a salary and getting it.

He was conscious of curious eyes everywhere, and he walked stiffly and proudly so that people would be afraid to talk to him. He'd do something yet, nothing he'd ever planned was big enough, it had to be some colossal achievement now to make Lamptown forget about his father, something so breathtaking that it would swallow up this present scandal, so at the mention of the name "Abbott" the town would not say, "Oh yes, son of the guy who killed himself," but "Oh yes, the young man who owns the Big Four Railroad . . . who built the bridge across Lake Erie . . . the Abbott that put Lamptown on the map." When he read in the paper of some man inventing this or that, or winning a great prize he shook his head and thought, "Better than that . . . it's got to be better than that."

At the moment Clover Heights was all he could work on, and so much depended on other people and money that it seemed not to move at all. He took to wearing overalls and helping out when some carpenter's assistant didn't show up, and found that physical exhaustion soothed his fever to do, to accomplish things.

He fixed up an army cot in Fowler's office because there wasn't any place for him at the Bon Ton. The shop was full of women, and when he would go in the evening to see his mother she didn't talk, all he could do was to pat her hand and finally he shunted off the busy helpers. Hulda transferred herself and her palm leaf to the workroom, and Hermann would bring over great trays of roasts which Elsinore never touched. Nettie and Mrs. Pepper and Hulda and all the visiting women kept the workroom noisy (even though the shop was properly closed) with the rattle of table setting, and eating, while old Mrs. Delaney washed dishes perpetually for these funeral banquets. The constant activity kept everyone happy and the widow's apathetic silence was not conspicuous, it seemed decent and ladylike.

Four mornings after the funeral Nettie came into the shop and found the wreath off the front door. Elsinore, in a big black apron, was cleaning out the closet in the workroom. She'd hauled out half a dozen boxes and her face was covered with soot. Nettie was unprepared for such a quick return to routine. She herself was wearing a black dress out of deference to her employer's grief, and she was prepared with little consolation phrases.

"Mice have gotten into these felts," Elsinore said abruptly. "We'll have to move everything out."

Nettie looked dolefully at her.

"Oh, Mrs. Abbott, you're so brave to pick up things so quickly again! . . . You've been so brave about it all—I don't see what made him do it! I can't understand! Poor Mr. Abbott! And it's all so hard on you."

"Well, there's so much work to be done around here, Nettie, there won't be time to think," Elsinore said in such a matter-of-fact voice that Nettie couldn't believe her ears. "In another two months we've got to have this whole place ready, upstairs showrooms finished, all ready for business. Mrs. Pepper will be ready to move in as soon as we can have her."

All of Nettie's rehearsed condolences were forgotten in being reminded of Mrs. Pepper's triumphant return. She hung her hat on the clothes tree and silently pinned on her apron. It was true that Mrs. Abbott looked half-sick dragging herself around with heavy feet, but Nettie wasn't sorry for her any more, not a bit. If a woman showed no more feelings than that after her husband was dead you couldn't expect Nettie to have feelings for her. Why, you might even think she was glad about it.

Elsinore was neither glad nor sorry. The revolver shot had blown out some fuse in her brain. She couldn't remember why it had seemed so important to silence Charles, the thoughts that had made her quiver with fanatic delight a few days back were lost, Fischer ceased when Charles ceased, all feeling died with that explosion. Now, night and day, she was only the proprietor of a thriving millinery store, in her numb memory ran color combinations, arrangements of hand-made lilacs on milan, her heart had become a ribbon rosette worn with chic a little to one side.

"A nice little woman," Harry Fischer said about Mrs. Abbott, "but not very light on her feet."

Mrs. Pepper asked him to be particularly kind to her friend because she'd seen so much trouble, so the dancing master, instead of a mere good-day when he met the milliner, would remember to add, "Is it hot enough for you, Mrs. Abbott?" or "Quite a little shop you have there, Mrs. Abbott, quite a nice little property." It was more than he'd ever said to her before but it meant nothing to her now. She would say over his words afterward in a wistful effort to restore her old romance, but it was gone, it had blown up with its own enemy. She knew that Mrs. Pepper was meeting him again, but she didn't care, it seemed so far away—those years when she had cared. She knew when the affair began again, because for the first two or three months of the enlarged Bon Ton regime Mrs. Pepper had sobbed nightly in bed with her, talked very little, and grew almost thin. Then, after one day on some mysterious business in Cleveland, she began to hum about her work, she no longer wept but chatted optimistically about life, she let out the pleats in her skirts once more and found many important errands out of town, even though she was permanently stationed in Lamptown. She tiptoed radiantly about her showroom over the Bon Ton—(the very room where Charles was killed)—fondly patting the headless dummies in their gorgeous lavender brocaded girdles, peeping outdoors from time to time to see if any women on the street were admiring the lingerie display in the window, and in mid-afternoon when business was dull she'd go downstairs and say, "Nettie, I wish you'd sing that thing you used to sing, 'Come, come, I love you only—(you know the one I mean)—I want but you.'"

Women from good homes in Avon and neighboring villages began to shop in Lamptown instead of sending to Cleveland or Columbus for their clothes. Two whole new streets were dug up through the Lots by the Lamptown Home Company, twenty-four houses ($2800 apiece) to a street. New families were moving in before the paint was dry on the walls, dozens of strange children played in the street excavations and tobogganed down the rubbish heaps along the torn roads. Officials at the Works rode to and fro in brand new Fords or even Cadillacs and it was rumored that the wives of these eastern strangers smoked cigarettes and played cards every afternoon. Bauer's was crowded with boarders, young men who wouldn't buy homes or bring their families to Lamptown till they saw how they liked their new jobs. So many bigwigs from the east were staying at Hunt's that the old mansion slipped quite naturally into the hotel class. It was called the Russell House, and Hunt, running back and forth to Cleveland nowadays, seemed to think the group of paying guests was a jolly improvement on his old hermitage. The one person who looked upon this change as sacrilege was Morry Abbott, and Morry himself boarded there. When he turned in at the imposing gate every evening he whispered to himself, "My home. . . . Now I know how Hunt used to feel walking under these trees." It was his—now, his, almost as

much as it was Hunt's, and the twelve other guests were of no consequence, he swelled with pride of possession whenever he opened the
heavy white doors into the dark spacious hallway, he scarcely dared think
it was true that he, merely by virtue of nine dollars a week, was able to
call this his home. He hoped his mother would see the importance of this
step in his life, he said, "Well, I got a place at Hunt Russell's now, I'll clear
my stuff out of that bureau." But all she said was, "That's better than
sleeping in Mr. Fowler's office, anyway, isn't it?"

But even the next summer failed to find Clover Heights any further
developed than its original three houses—one complete, the other two ar-
rested in the last stage of their construction awaiting the particular
demands of problematical buyers. On one side of the Lots scores of tiny
houses, Model B, squeezed on to a main road, and dozens of others,
neatly identical, paralleled them behind, waiting trustingly for new roads
to cross their door-stoops. On the other side of the creek, surrounded by
untouched meadowland, three large houses marked the beginning of
"Clover Heights." One of these was of rough brown stone with a curious
rolled roof and this was known as the "chateau." The other two were
brownish-green frame and were referred to as Normandy style or perhaps it was semi-Ann Hathaway, though residents of Avon could boast
of similar structures which were merely spoken of as a $7500 home.
Lamptown's new inhabitants often spent Sunday looking over these three
houses, showing them to relatives from out-of-town, but in the eight
months they'd been standing no one had ventured to buy or even rent
one. Morry was amazed at this apathy, at first, and reassured Fowler that
it would only be a matter of weeks; even the bank officials told him that it
was a wise thing to show people they need not move out of Lamptown in
order to have a better-class home. But Fowler said, "Uh-huh" and looked
longingly toward the rival renting office of the Lamptown Home
Company where a steady stream of men and women flowed in and out.

"We could rent for forty, maybe," he meditated gloomily, "but we can't
meet their twenty-two fifty. . . ."

Instead of a Country Club, the first big building on the Lots was a
huge barn-like place called the Working Girls' Club. It stood at the corner, large, blank, square, with a row of little houses stemming from it east
and west. A yard of red earth between its front stoop and the cinder walk
allowed a few desperate blades of grass to grow, and a gaunt geranium
was on either side of the step, but even these decorative touches failed to

entice the old factory girls to live there. However, new girls, answering ads put in state papers, poured in here and were given sets of house rules and introduced to a matron who was to help them with their problems. The chief problem of the girls was how to keep from having babies and the new matron's answer to this was a solemn lecture on the wages of sin, so that better paid girls rapidly took to renting the little neighboring houses, four girls to a house, where they could do as they pleased and work out their own problem. The new officials started a welfare department at the Works with a nurse in charge, who sent girls home who had headaches and wouldn't allow them to return till their health was perfect. For these days of angry rest their wages were docked but it was a very efficient service and admired editorially all over the state. Kindly lectures once a week on the dangers, moral and physical, of women smoking and having too close friendships, opened up a new and dazzling vista to Lamptown girls too busy quarreling over men heretofore to keep up with feminine progress in larger cities.

Lamptown was getting rich. Half the town had accepted the invitation of the directors to buy stock so that you could scarcely find a shoe clerk or a grocery boy in the place who wasn't a shareholder. When strangers made some ribald joke about old Tom, the drunken street-cleaner, asleep on the curb in the midst of his work, Bill Delaney loved to amaze them by answering, "Looks like a bum, don't he? Well, that bird sold his shanty and bought five hundred dollars worth of shares in the Works not ten months ago. Know what he's worth today? Twenty-five hundred dollars, yes sir, and it'll be twice that before another year's out!"

Careful citizens who were not going to risk their small savings on that dangerous unknown world of stocks bitterly watched improvident neighbors who had thrown everything into this venture roll by in the automobiles they had bought on dividends. The very shyest men accosted fellow travelers with the news whenever they went out of town, in Cleveland hotel lobbies they stared at innocent strangers over their newspapers until their glance was returned, then they drew close and said, "Have a cigar, sir? Look here, I want to show you something," and they'd whip a Works prospectus out of their pocket. "Lamptown Works. You know our products, I guess. Well, that's my home town. A year ago I bought a thousand shares in this Works and sir, today, it's worth six times what I paid for it. Why, say, we've got one of the biggest propositions right there in that little town—talk about your Ford plant! Say, what's your name, sir? I wish if you're ever passing through down there you'd look me up. I just want to take you through that there factory. I'd just like to show you something."

Going down Market Street you'd meet dozens of people you'd never seen before, there were four Packards in town owned by men Lamptown never heard of, and when Hunt Russell's car, battered and seedy-looking in comparison to the new ones, drove down town, an old citizen might remark, "Ah—Hunt Russell!" at which newcomers indifferently queried, "Well, who's Hunt Russell?" And after all, who was Hunt, now? There were Russells on the board of directors but Hunt was only a minor vice-president, he no longer took part in the company's movements. When matters came up needing the signature of a third vice-president Hunt was seldom to be found, unless you wanted to search the grandstand at the North Randall racetracks or keep an eye on the yellow roadster before a Prospect Avenue sporting house in Cleveland.

The new people didn't know Hunt Russell but they knew young Abbott. Everybody knew the young man who showed you over the "chateau," who had for an office a tiny sample house at the eastern edge of the Lots, a small house whose roof was lettered in red and white— "Clover Heights Company. See Morris Abbott inside or call Lamptown 66 J." The girls on their way home to the Club went round by this little office and if old Fowler wasn't in they stopped by to kid Morry and see if he wouldn't ask for a date. He seldom surrendered to their laughing challenges however. He smoked cigars like Fowler and was considered a cagey young man with a much better business-head than was strictly true. He talked briskly to strangers, helped all the side issues of Fowler's business as notary public, auctioneer, rent collector, and no one could trace the exact beginning of this crisp aggressive manner, though Morry knew he had adopted it painfully, at first, to protect himself from Lamptown's pity and questioning after his father's death. When it was necessary to refer to that event he could say "after the old man kicked off" quite casually without that quick fear of someone suspecting his mother that he had once felt.

Nobody could rattle Morry Abbott, he was armored against everything because he knew it was your business to be hard just as it was the world's business to throw javelins into you. He was intensely grateful to Fowler for opening up his life. It was Fowler and he against the rest of Lamptown and Fowler's frequent moods of depression did not discourage him.

"But look at the place, Morry," Fowler nodded toward the desolate expanse of Heights crowned by its three empty mansions. "We can't get another cent to keep on building unless one of these sells—even old Hunt isn't fool enough to advance us any, let alone the bank. And no work going on makes the proposition look like a dud. And if it looks like a dud it might as well be one, see what I mean."

"Wait till people get used to having more money," argued Morry. "They still have the idea that if they get enough money for a swell home they've got to move to Avon for it. Wait. Why, every day I take at least two people over those houses. That leads to something, you know."

"Like hell it does," muttered Fowler. "The damn fools steal the fixtures, we got repair bills on those houses as if somebody was living in 'em already, on Sundays folks have picnics in the gardens and break in for souvenirs to show all their out-of-town friends what swell houses they got. But ask one of them to live there! Ha! It isn't that they cost more, rent or buy, it's because they're different."

"But that's the whole point—they've got to be different!" Morry continued to protest.

Fowler shook his head morosely.

"I got people coming to me all the time asking for houses exactly like this one or that one next door, a man's whole aim is to have a place exactly like everybody's, he feels like a fool being different. Take his wife, she says, 'Oh, but you said this house was just like Traumer's and here is the closet on the left of the landing instead of the right, liar!' I got a hunch we're stung, Abbott, my boy—not on houses, understand, but on people!"

"Well, we've got to stick it out until we've proved we're right," Morry said.

"Oh sure, sure, we'll stick it out," Fowler agreed without enthusiasm.

Morry refused to believe the Fowler who had been standing with him against the world was so easily scared. He had felt so secure with the older man applauding each new idea for Heights improvement, it was the two of them against everybody else. Now he suspected he was standing alone, and he was bewildered. How could a man change so completely,—the idea was the same idea they started with, wasn't it? . . . Going home, Morry found himself more upset than he had realized. Fowler's misgivings shook the very ground under his future, he hadn't ever dreamed that he would change.

Morry walked down Market Street and in a shop window mirror was surprised to see himself, no use denying it, a big, good-looking young man wearing his new gray suit with an air, his straw hat tilted just so. In this image there appeared no indication of the vague fear in his heart, you would never have guessed that this young man had any doubts as to his own perfection. It was a reassuring image, and Morry was heartened by it. You didn't see a fellow like that out of a job, or working away at some dinky factory job.

He stopped in front of the Paradise to read the bill for tonight. Two vaudeville turns were announced this week, pictures of the performers simpered from the lobby walls. One, a portrait of a slumbrous-eyed Jewess with a guitar proclaimed, "The Singing Salome"; the other photograph showed two blonde girls in white tights and spangled bodices, one holding the other at the waist, both laughing sunnily with an air of incalculable good humor. Morry looked around for other pictures of these "Two Little Clowns from Ragtime Town." He could hear Milly practicing their new songs inside and thought he heard girls' voices, he was almost tempted to go inside and see if the Two Little Clowns were in there, too. He could not get over his old awe of these glamorous stage women, beginning way back with Lillian Russell they were tangled up with his ambition to do great things—why?—in order to come closer, perhaps to be able to touch them. Men bragging in Bill's bar of affairs with little carnival actresses made these no nearer or more easily attainable.

"When do the Two Clowns come on tonight?" he asked the man sweeping out the lobby.

"Eight-ten and ten-ten."

Morry turned away. He thought fiercely the Heights plan had to prove out, then he would turn into a Hunt Russell, he would have a glittering long automobile at the curb here and when the Two Little Clowns came out he would casually invite them to ride. Still, he didn't desire them, any more than he wanted a gold and white yacht, he only wanted to be equal to these far-off splendors, to have no doors locked to him.

Market Street was crowded as it was so often now, strange women in hats and gloves and plain dark silks came out of shops, you turned to look twice at them for Lamptown girls went around town bareheaded all summer. Sometimes one of these foreign women stepped into an auto at the curb and took the wheel herself. Morry was excited by these dashing gestures. Lamptown was beginning to be a wonderful place, he thought, there was no bottom to it now, you saw new things every day as if it were already a city.

In front of the Elite Gown Shop he saw a girl and even before his eye had taken in the black curly hair, the snub nose, and sky-blue eyes, he knew it was Jen. He recognized Jen always by his sudden feeling of embarrassment, here was someone who knew him too well, someone to whom at one time or another he'd told everything, and so when he saw her, his first impulse always was to establish new barriers, to be aloof—show her that he was not such an open book as he seemed. He was surprised, watching her from this distance, to find her so agreeable to the eye, he so seldom really saw her except in relation to himself, someone whose adoring gaze he must avoid, someone who undoubtedly must be so pleased to find herself getting pretty that he would never satisfy her vanity by looking at her. She had an air, too, of being wonderfully dressed, but even Morry could tell it was only blue-checked gingham she was wearing, her proud delight in its newness fooled you at first. She was talking to the little Cleveland Jew named Berman who ran the Elite but when Morry passed she caught his arm.

"Look, Morry, I'm going to work here!"

"What do you mean—sell dresses?"

She waved goodbye to the Elite's proprietor and walked along with Morry. Isaac Berman, dark, bald, leaned against his door with folded arms, his Oriental eyes following her down the street. He turned to his son inside.

"Nice, hey, Lou?"

As soon as she told him of her plan to work in the Elite Morry was whipped again with envy, for he saw it as she saw it, not merely a job in a dress shop but a step toward great things; Cleveland, Pittsburgh, New York, dances every night, music all day, Jen in a silver dress on a magazine cover—while Morry's Clover Heights was crumbling, he was alone in Lamptown, waiting for some great thing to come and pick him up.

"I get nine dollars a week. . . . Say, Morry, Lil's coming to Lamptown. We're going to rent a place, maybe, and keep house."

Morry was always aghast at the things Jen did, he had never ceased to marvel at himself for having got out of the factory, so how could Jen jump so easily out of one thing into another, how could she finally take care of

Lil, all of her own doing? His heart beat fast with triumph, as if he had done it, because what he wanted to do and what Jen wanted to do were somehow confused in his head, so this was all his own doing then.

"What will Lil do?"

"Maybe Bermie will give her some work, too," Jen answered. "Not that what I make wouldn't be enough. . . . Nine dollars a week is a lot of money. I'm taking music lessons from Milly. She's going to teach Lil, too, and I'll teach her to tap dance—Mr. Travers taught me. Bermie's son's got friends on the stage, he said when we get something learned he could fix everything, he said I wouldn't lose anything by learning clothes first. Look here."

She pulled a newspaper clipping out of her pocket. It was a photograph of Maxine Elliot.

"Bermie's going to take me to see her, if she comes to Cleveland. . . . You know those Two Little Clowns at the Paradise this week? Lil and I could do that, easy enough. . . . If Lil wants to, of course."

Morry was dizzy from these swift pictures, he was excited by them, and when they reached Bauer's it was he who was sorry to leave, he wanted to stay near this excitement, he was stirred to immense schemes, Clover Heights, Lamptown was a mere step in this splendid ascent.

"Say, Jen, what about this Berman?" he pulled her away from Bauer's door to ask sharply. "First I hear you're out riding all hours with Hunt Russell—folks say Dode O'Connell quit the Works and left town on account of you. Now you're in with this Berman fella—what's the idea?"

Jen looked at him skeptically, her mouth curled.

"What about Nettie Farrell, and those girls at the Club always hanging around you—what about that girl in Norwalk you always have up at the Casino—what about—"

"Oh, Jen, for God's sake!" Morry, his face red, dumped tobacco into a cigarette paper and rolled it. It wasn't any of Jen's business what girls he ran with, the thing about Jen was that she didn't know men, and somebody ought to tell her who was all right and who wasn't. Now he was furiously ashamed at being taken personally, as he had been the day old Mrs. Delaney delivered the warning to keep away from her Jen.

"I'm only telling you to be careful," he muttered, hating her. "You got to watch out for these foreigners. You've got to remember you're just a kid, and a crazy one at that. I'm only telling you to mind your step."

Jen looked down at the pavement.

"You told me to look out for Hunt and for Fischer and for Mr. Travers and now for Lou. All the fellows I like best," she said slowly. "Gee, Morry, what do you want me to do? . . . Isn't *anybody* all right?"

Morry didn't know what to answer. He couldn't tell her she had no right to like any man but himself, he was ashamed of his jealousy over Jen.

"You're pretty young to be running around, that's all," he said finally. "Somebody's got to keep an eye on you."

"No younger than that girl of yours from Norwalk," Jen answered sulkily. Her eyes met his with a direct challenge and Morry felt queerly stirred and afraid. He lit his cigarette silently, and was relieved to see Hogan waving to him from Delaney's entrance. He dashed thankfully across the street, and the Bauer screen door slammed.

Walking home from the Elite Gown Shop you had to keep your fists tightly clenched to keep from dancing, you could hum softly to yourself but you must remember not to sing out loud, you could whisper it to yourself but you mustn't shout it, "I don't have to wait table any more, I don't have to go to the factory either, I have a real job, next I'll be transferred to the Cleveland store or maybe New York and there I'll be on the stage, I'll sing and dance all day and all night. . . . And I don't have to be helped, I have a home all of my own doing and I can do as I please, and Lil's coming. The Thing is beginning to happen."

Jen actually only had half a home, she rented the upstairs of a house way out beyond Extension Avenue for six dollars a month, she could scarcely wait for Lil to come and be astonished at having a front porch, a yard, a honeysuckle vine, and a lilac bush. Each night she ran all the way home from the store because Extension Avenue was pitch dark. She ran down the middle of the road so that shadows behind trees couldn't grab her, even the thrill of having her own latchkey didn't overcome her daily terror of going into the dark house. As soon as she got inside she locked the door and pushed a table against it. She turned on lights in all the rooms and said out loud, "This is my own home," and she was proud of herself, and then sat by the front window wishing somebody, anybody, would come and see her. She visited the old couple downstairs until they ostentatiously made preparations for bed. Then she went up to her rooms and said, "My own home—imagine!" and banged the door quickly behind her so the Unknown following her couldn't get in. It was fun walking back and forth through this solitary magnificence, it was fun so long as she heard the people downstairs, but as soon as they were quiet she was afraid of the silence, of crickets chirping eerily in the clover, of dogs barking far off, she was homesick for engines a yard from her window, they must be missing her, their whistles sounded remote and lonely, yes, when she was alone in the home she'd rented all by herself, she dared to wish for the Bauers' kitchen and the darling clatter of dishes and men swearing, and the smell of fried onions. But this was not to be admitted for then someone would pity her loneliness, and she was not a person to be pitied but a child of luck, see, she was only sixteen and had her own home, she could handle wonderful dresses from eight in the morning till eight at night, she could toss a blue satin dress over a rack nonchalantly as if satin was nothing to her, she could even try on twenty dollar dresses for mothers buying for absent daughters, yes, Jen was a girl to be envied and she was sorry for other women and a little awed by her own good fortune. Whenever she saw old Mrs. Delaney hobbling along the street she wanted to apologize to her for not doing so badly as the old woman had hoped, she was sorry for her but she was still afraid of her, you never could be sure when people who once owned you would clutch you again, and this time you could never, never get away.

But only this old woman and the silent night in her own home could chill her now, only these, for the rest of the time an amazed excitement rushed through her veins, something, something was in the air. She wanted to skip, to clap her hands with delight, because this mysterious something was so close to her she could almost touch it, it was like the first rat-a-tat-tat in the circus parade, any minute now the band would begin to play. She could scarcely bear such perpetual delight, it bubbled over so that old Berman winked at his son Lou, and when Lou pinched her cheek, she had to throw her arms about him and kiss him furiously. When the store closed at night she didn't know what to do but skip down Market Street to see the Bauers, to feast her ears on the music trickling out of Delaney's pianola, to tell a placid Hulda and a jealous Grace every single thing that happened in the Elite that day.

Hulda said she was going to give her something for her place, something nice, you wait, maybe this doily when it was finished, but when it was finished she couldn't bear to part with it, she opened a locked drawer and tried to decide which of these hoarded Larkin premiums she could give away but her heart ached over each decision. When she finally took out a chromo of a white-robed woman kneeling with the printed thought, "Simply to the Cross I cling," Hulda burst into tears because no one, not even her little Jenny, could love any of these tissue-wrapped treasures as she had loved them. After she had given it to her she sat on her stool gazing unhappily at the print now rolled up under Jen's arms, and while Jen leaned on the counter, chattering about what this one said or bought, tears rolled slowly down Hulda's cheek because Jen would not love and save this gift, she would only pin it on the wall where any stranger could look at it.

"I'm going away, too, believe me," said Grace, pausing between the courses of Sweeney's late supper to listen sourly to Jen. "And not to work in any Lamptown dump, either, I'm going to Detroit to work in a big cafeteria. Say, there's a town. A fella was in here the other day, a big bicycle salesman, and he says there's nothing Chicago has got that Detroit hasn't got. He says they got money to burn up there, fellas crazy for a girl with a little life in her, believe me, I'm not sticking in this dump after what this fella told me. He said why a girl with my personality wouldn't have to take nothin' from nobody up there in Detroit, why he says, Gracie, I've seen girls with only half your personality driving their own automobiles in Detroit and you take this Belle Isle, there's nothin' like it this side of New York City, he was sayin'."

Hulda smiled tremulously at Jen.

"Gracie's always leaving us," she said. "Always going to some big town, but she never goes."

"Wait!" Grace warned her. "You won't see me slinging this tray around here much longer. Not in this hick town, no sir."

It was the way Grace always talked, she did it, Jen knew, to show her how foolish it was to be happy over the simple triumphs of Lamptown when nothing so trivial would satisfy a high-spirited girl like Grace.

"Seen Morry?" Grace called from Sweeney's table.

Jen nodded.

"Ask him why he never comes in any more?"

"No," said Jen, painfully conscious of that matter between Morry and Grace. "I didn't ask him anything."

"Funny," observed Grace. "You and him never seemed to get on, always bickering when you got together. . . . And you won't see him now 'cause he wouldn't drop into a dress store the way he would in a restaurant."

"Morry's a smart young man, now," said Hulda. "It's got to be a mighty pretty girl to catch him."

Jen tried to avoid looking at Grace who was winking broadly behind Hulda's back as a reminder of the intimacies she had so often confided to Jen.

After a little while with Grace, Jen forgot the terrors of Extension Avenue, a home of her own seemed a refuge indeed, and the dark clover lots she had to pass were nothing if she thought hard about something else. So Jen, running home through the darkness, cinders scattering about her heels, her heart thumping with fear, thought about Lou Berman and the curious lure of dark Jewish eyes and olive skin, she thought of Hunt Russell and the way his oldness held yet repelled her, of the dry things he said which seemed to mean so much more than they really did, of how it must feel to be a dethroned emperor—(in this light of a lost king he seemed glamorous and sweetly sad to her, she almost loved him), she thought of the doughnut smell of the Delaneys' parlor, of the little gold chair on the mantel which she would never see again. A dim light blinked here and there in an upstairs window, the trees shook dew from their leaves, a twig snapped under her foot and made her run faster. Her heart was as big as her chest now, booming away, it was dreadful to be afraid of darkness, someday she would go to a great city, Detroit, maybe, where dazzling golden lights left no corner for night to hide in, where bands playing day and night crowded out fearful quiet. She remembered that, until then, she must think hard of something else and so, panting down the last few yards of darkness, she thought of Morry, and the thought of Morry was so big, so all-enveloping that there was no wish or feeling to it, it was only a great name, you said "Morry" and it covered every tiny thought or wish, it loomed out of the blackness like a great engine searchlight straight in your eyes, blinding you to everything else, even to itself. Morry, Morry, Morry—you could put yourself to sleep just saying it over and over.

It wasn't the Elite, as Jen had tried to arrange, but the Bon Ton that finally took in Lily St. Clair. Morry saw her first sitting on the wicker bench in the showroom when he stopped in one Saturday night to see his mother. When he went to live at Russell House he was worried about his mother, he thought in her quiet way she wanted him near her and he took care to drop in every evening after he moved. But she paid little attention to him, talking to Mrs. Pepper or Nettie about the new decorations upstairs, and forgot always to ask him about his work or how he liked his new home. If customers came in there'd be no place for him to sit, and after standing uncomfortably around he'd realize there was no place for him in his mother's life, that there never had been, and he'd flush with shame to remember his fierce tenderness for his mother as a frantic lover might blush who realizes in cool retrospect that the beloved was always indifferent to him.

The new independence of his mother bothered him, the change in her taste in clothes, a certain indefinable boldness in her manner, a way of glancing sidewise at men that was disturbingly like Grace Terris. His memory of his mother as a slight, quiet lady was wiped out by the reality of this new knowing, politely aggressive personality. When she and Mrs. Pepper went out together, two well-built, well-dressed women, their hips swaying, he would redden when men standing near him whistled their admiration. "There go the milliners!" And the more stylish Elsinore became, the more Lamptown women remembered that after all Charlie Abbott hadn't been so bad, a waster, true, but what man wasn't? Morry heard these whispers with fear, but as yet there was nothing definite against his mother except that the Bon Ton widow was always on the go with the corset lady. What the town whispered did not bother him so much as the sight of someone he knew so well changing under his very eyes into a stranger, a perfectly unknown quantity.

He was worried over other matters, too, for Fowler was persistently sour and silent, hints came to Morry's ears of the Lamptown Home Co. taking over the Clover Heights area, of the three houses being rented out as boarding houses, but these rumors could not be tracked down, nor would Fowler divulge any secret plans concerning the Heights. That he had lost interest in the developing of that community was certain, and with its collapse imminent he had possibly lost confidence in his young assistant. Morry dared not face the fears in his own mind, he smoked restlessly all day and wanted to talk all this over with his mother, always hoping for comfort which reason told him would not be there. As soon as he reached the Bon Ton door, a clear picture of what the call would be rose before him—his own eagerness to talk, to tell of his gnawing fear of having to go back to the factory for a job, and his mother listening politely but interrupting with orders for Nettie, exclamations about remote matters to be attended to, and leaving him for the always preferable customer. He wondered, since he knew the whole scene so well, why he stopped in at all, but he reasoned when no comfort came, at least then his need for it was chilled and his defenses against an indifferent world that much strengthened.

No one was in the shop but a girl sitting on the green wicker footstool, with her hat in her lap, and when Morry saw her softly curling yellow hair he knew it was Jen's Lil. She was so obviously something to be stared at that Morry dared not look too long. In his room at Russell House he had pictures of actresses, Billie Burke, the Dolly sisters, Anna Held—and he had never before seen any girl who looked like these gilded creatures, they were not of the ordinary breed of women at all, he was certain they had been whirled dancing and spangled out of some falling comet on to their stage. And here was just such a girl, her yellow hair, her gold-tinged, creamy skin, her clear, violet eyes, the very curve of her lips such objects for wonder in themselves that it was hard to reassemble them into one complete marvel in his mind. She was shy and kept pulling down her shrunken gingham dress to cover her long legs. She must be tall for her age, Morry thought. Taller than Jen. Her own acute embarrassment put him completely at ease.

"Aren't you Jen's sister, Lil?" he asked.

She nodded, coloring.

"I'm Morry Abbott—Jen's told me about you."

Then she talked a little, and Morry was enchanted with her voice, a soft slurring voice using the expressions of the farmers around Lamptown, but he didn't listen to her words, he was drinking in her amazing loveliness. Pretty girls in Lamptown were plump rosy girls invariably handicapped in one way or another, either with thick honest legs, or stringy hair, or an invincible dowdiness, a look of belonging exactly to Lamptown and nowhere else. But Lil had that quality which had struck him from the first in Jen, a quality of not belonging to the place where she was at this moment, of belonging to the place for which she was reaching. This mystified and held him.

She said Jen had left her there because Mrs. Abbott wanted a trimmer and she could sew, really, but she wasn't sure yet if Mrs. Abbott would take her.

"Sure—you bet she will!" Morry said.

The faint blue shadows under her wide blue eyes suggested a seductive frailty, the blonde hair curling at her temples and at the nape of her neck inspired Morry with a persistent urge to touch it and see if it was true. When his mother came in and took Lil back to the workroom he stayed in the shop, smoking and thinking about her, it was as if the silver girl had walked off the magazine cover, he dared not leave her unguarded, this treasure must not be exposed to anyone else. He was certain nobody in Lamptown had ever seen anything like Lil St. Clair, and he had an avaricious desire to set up his claim first, if it was to belong to somebody, then let it be known that he had seen it first. He didn't think of her as a girl, or even as a person, but as a desirable possession, almost an achievement. He couldn't think whether he liked her or not, he felt only awe over her goldenness and wonder that such perfection had strayed into Lamptown. He would have been quite content just to read about it.

Presently Elsinore came back in the shop alone. Morry was leafing over a fashion magazine as if this were his prime interest in the Bon Ton. He planned to stroll home with Lil, but it appeared she was going to stay in the store for a while. A beautiful worker, she was, said his mother, seeming to have a knack with hats. Morry swelled with pride as if he had taught her this gift himself.

"She's a good girl to take Nettie's place," said Elsinore reflectively. "I'll need her when Nettie goes. After all she's no younger than Nettie was when I took her on."

"Where's Nettie going?"

"She's starting a millinery store of her own next season," answered his mother. "Some friend has loaned her a little money. She's going to take that little place behind the Paradise. There's plenty of trade for another millinery store. Mrs. Pepper and I don't mind."

At that moment Nettie herself appeared, and Elsinore slipped out. Nettie looked at Morry defiantly.

"Well, I suppose you've heard I'm starting my own business next fall," she announced. "I suppose you think I can't handle it, too, don't you?"

"I think it's great, Nettie," Morry said heartily, for this meant that Lil would be here right under his eye indefinitely. "I think it's just fine."

Nettie was slightly appeased.

"But you'll be too busy with all your real estate funny business to come in and see me once in a while," she said. "You never see me any more as it is."

"Oh, I'll be dropping in," Morry assured her hastily. "I guess I'd want to see what kind of a store you've got, wouldn't I?"

Nettie's gaze tried to hold him to a promise and he looked toward the door, praying for someone to come in before she trapped him into a definite date. His roving look was misconstrued.

"You've seen that St. Clair girl's sister, that's what!" Nettie cried sharply. "The one I'm teaching to take my place. . . . You'll be running after her next. I'll bet you came to see her this minute!"

"Say, now, Nettie—"

"You did!" she insisted bitterly. "A washed-out little blonde. . . . She looks consumptive to me."

This was the meanest thing you could say about anyone, for everybody despises weaklings. Morry hoped Lil wouldn't overhear. He'd better not wait for her, he decided, Nettie's jealous eyes were too shrewd.

"She's just the wrong type for you, too," Nettie went on. "Just the kind you would pick. . . . You know yourself, Morry, you'd never amount to anything if your mother and I didn't keep after you and when you're that type you ought to get hold of a girl with ambition, a girl with enough business head for two. Some good woman."

Morry felt rising the old homelike sense of guilty incompetence and futile hatred of smug womankind. He started toward the door.

"You know perfectly well she's not a lady, Morry. Neither of those girls. Even you can see that."

At least Nettie was a little lady. Nobody in Lamptown could say a word against little Nettie Farrell. Nobody but Morry . . . and possibly a Mr. Schwarz.

Supper in the Russell House was a social event still to Morry. There were two big tables in the dining room and except for Hunt's occasional presence, they were filled with out-of-town men, big men who argued constantly about the Works, about running into Pittsburgh tomorrow or down to the Baltimore branch. America was to these men just an area for developing their product, they never knew there was a Lamptown, it was just a factory, the spaces between factories were not towns but Pullman drawing rooms where they planned new arguments with brother officials for factory changes.

They talked during meals, drawing diagrams on the tablecloth with fat silver lead pencils, they argued their way out to the lawn after dinner waving fat cigars, they sometimes drove in Hunt's car after dinner to some cross-roads saloon where they continued their discussion over beer and came back, still conferring over the same matters. When they left town duplicate officials took their places at Russell House and in the authoritative ring of their voices, expensively tailored suits, and fragrance of black cigars, sustained the same atmosphere in the Russell dining room.

When the discussion turned to housing problems, Morry often took a part in it and many times talked so forcefully that the strangers removed cigars from the corners of their lips and listened respectfully. Later one would inquire, "Say, young man, I don't think I got your name."

Morry would tell him and the stranger would frown.

"Abbott? Abbott? You're not with us, are you, Abbott? Ah, I don't think I know the name."

Then no more heed was paid to Morry's comments. At these moments he yearned to have accomplished so much, to be such a figure in Lamptown and in all the state that when he gave his name men would start back.

"So you're Morris Abbott!"

Nobody listened to you if your name meant nothing, but on the other hand your name never meant anything unless you forced people to listen. These strangers never heard of Clover Heights, when he said he was in real estate and contracting, they assumed he was with the Lamptown Home Company, part of their own system or else not really in business at all. His three houses at the far end of the Lots had become almost as ridiculous as a full dress would be at a Russell House supper. They meant little enough in the town's development, and only Morry's work on the routine details of the real estate business made him worth any money to Fowler.

But whether Russell House listened to him or not Morry was proud to live there, to dash up and down the great mahogany staircase and tramp casually down the thick-carpeted halls. He had minor panics now and then wondering where he'd go if Fowler's poor business squeezed him out. Supposing he had to live at Bauer's, certainly a comedown, or beg his mother for cot space again in her workroom.... These fears could not endure long under the impersonal calm of his new home and the press of his new interests.

There was Lil.

He couldn't explain to himself about Lil. When he went out every night to see her he knew it wasn't because he liked her—you couldn't like or dislike an idea, could you?—it wasn't because he thought she'd be lonely (as indeed her shyness with people was bound to make her), it was for no tangible reason at all, but a certainty that such beauty fell near you only once in a lifetime and whether you wanted it or not you should never let it escape because it was rare. Then the setting Jen had provided for her sister, this little house far out on the edge of town with meadows stretching to the right and behind it, was associated with his dream of a home, somehow, so that Lil was tangled up with the things in life he wanted for himself—glamour, beauty, freedom, a place in which a man could breathe.

Turning from the noise and clangor of Market Street out Extension Avenue he was conscious of a strange expansion in his bosom, the thick hushed trees drew the houses besides them into darkness, the smell of honeysuckle and white clover haunted the air, the flutter of a white dress on a vined porch stirred vague romantic fancy, then the long stretch of fields, hedges settling darkly over yeeping birds, glimmer of a light way off that was Jen's window, all this scented darkness was an avenue to Lil. Here, too, he was lord absolute, with Jen to listen avidly to his boasting, his opinions on this or that, and Lil, frail and lovely for him to admire. Lil seldom talked, when she did she prefaced her comments always with "Jen says—" . . . She worshipped Jen, and now she worshipped Morry, but he had a disturbed feeling that she would fasten her worship to anybody who was around her steadily.

"Did you hate the Home, Lil?" he'd ask.

"I didn't mind it," she would say.

"Do you like the Bon Ton—is it hard work?"

"I don't mind," she'd answer.

"Are you going away with Jen and try to go on the stage someday?" he'd fearfully inquire.

"I'd rather stay here at the Bon Ton," would be Lil's gentle answer. "I wouldn't want to go away but still I'd want to be wherever Jen was."

He'd hear boys talking about the little St. Clair blondy, he'd ask Lil if she liked this one or that one who had walked home from work with her.

"He's nice," Lil would answer. "I like him all right."

This pale acceptance of life was maddening to Morry, but it kept him constantly intrigued. He suspected that Lil thought he was "all right," too, and he was stirred to more gestures of devotion in an effort to discover some secret intensity in her. She was frightened when he kissed her the first time but after that she turned up her face with the utmost docility. Her intensity came out in her work, her fingers flew over her sewing, they never hesitated over the design of a hat, Elsinore and Mrs. Pepper marvelled over this dexterity, and Nettie, who was supposed to be teaching her the trade, sat back with jealous wonder. Here in the Bon Ton workroom Lil attained the pitch of intensity that Morry hoped to arouse in her. He waited to find Jen's furies in the younger sister, but they weren't there. He needed both girls to make up the one necessary for him. When he found Jen out for the evening he grew restless alone with Lil, he'd start to tell her about something concerning his work, and then he'd remember that it must be told to Jen, he couldn't have the news spoiled by Lil's sweet cool, "That's awfully nice, Morry"; he must have Jen's breathless reaction so that the whole affair became tremendously important and himself, by his connection with it, made more important.

In Lamptown, which had made its own dark conclusions over two pretty girls living alone, Lil quickly became classified as Morry Abbott's girl. Lil knew this and accepted her role as she accepted everything, sweetly and casually. She loved trimming hats and she loved her sister Jen, and the rest of life was pleasantly negative. She was glad Morry liked her because Jen liked Morry. When the two girls were busy cooking their supper, she told Jen everything Morry said and did, until Jen would harshly tell her to keep still and watch the potatoes.

So Jen was no longer lonely in her new house because Lil was there. When she came home from work at night Lil and Morry were always there. At first she was glad that she had something—say it was Lil—to make Morry call every night, but after two or three weeks she somehow didn't want to hurry home, she lagged around the shop, helped Isaac Berman with the books or talked to Lou about the stage because Lou had seen all the plays and all the actors that there were. When Hunt Russell, always slightly intoxicated, always carrying some magic in his insolent lazy manner, drove up to the shop door occasionally and ordered her to drive with him she was glad to go and put off her homecoming a few more hours. But no matter how late she got home Morry would still be there, sitting on the porch adoring Lil.

"I didn't want to leave Lil here all alone," he would say reprovingly to Jen.

"Thanks for looking out for her," Jen would answer in a hard voice and call a gay farewell to Hunt. She said to herself that she was glad Morry liked Lil, but she knew that nothing had ever cut her so deeply as this persistent devotion. When Lil mildly questioned her about Hunt— "wasn't he awfully old and wasn't he bad?" she knew Morry had said something of the sort, she knew he thought she was taking Dode O'Connell's place with Hunt, but she didn't care. Most of the time she thought about places Lou Berman talked about, of what Vaughn Glaser said to him once, of the party a friend of his gave for Blanche Ring, and every detail of her costume, of the time he saw Marguerite Clarke walk into the hotel—("Baby Mine" she was playing), and of so many trips to New York City he never even counted! . . . All these people belonged to her, now, they had places in her brain, and in her dreams they accepted her as a fellow artist, even Lou Berman himself boasted of knowing her. (Why, that little Jennia St. Clair—used to work right here in Lamptown!) Now it changed to Morry boasting of her, but no, Morry must be in the theatre watching her perform, see there he is now. . . . But then that leaves no one in Lamptown to say they knew her once. . . . Dreams were very difficult to control. Anyway she would look into the audience and see Morry . . . no, she would have to be unconscious of his presence for in or out of dreams as soon as she saw him she'd be bound to rush down to him and say "Look at me, Morry, look, see, I did it, just like we used to plan. Isn't it wonderful?" Then it would merely end with Morry reaching for his hat and saying, "It sure is, well, goodbye." And that would be the end of that. . . . In despair Jen decided there was nothing to be done about Morry, and she must sooner or later do things without keeping his possible applause in mind. She went out with Lou Berman sometimes, to the theatre in Cleveland once with him and often to the Paradise. Lou's approval of her became important, because he praised seldom and was scornful of Lamptown girls. When he called to take her out he'd look her over from head to foot critically.

"Are you going to wear that?"

Then she would know it was all wrong, that her new silk dress was not the thing to wear even if it was the prettiest thing she'd ever owned. He was always patting her arm but she learned this was not a caress but a prelude to pulling the sleeve to a tight fit.

"There's the way your sleeves should set, honey. Fix that before you wear it again. You can wear clothes all right but there's things you gotta learn, hey, papa?"

Lou was sleek, slim, foppish, silent, enviably poised. He fascinated her for he represented the City. But when she looked at old Isaac Berman she saw Lou cartooned with age, paunch-bellied, fang-toothed, bald, greasy, only the dark fathomless eyes eternally romantic in silence no matter what price cuts were being calculated behind them. Lou never tried to make love to her, and Hunt Russell was far too conceited to risk a rebuff, but Jen had a waiting feeling inside, a heavy sense of dread, that if either of these men decided to take possession of her she would have no chance of escape, for you couldn't set yourself against Hunt because he was Lamptown, and you couldn't betray your provincial fear to Lou because he was the City. With Morry so enthralled with Lil she was afraid for herself. No longer was the thought of him any protection to her.

She was terrified at the envy she suffered when she saw him sitting with Lil silently on the porch steps, she had a fleeting lust for revenge, the revenge of throwing herself at Hunt or Lou, of being easy like Grace. But this was no revenge, it was punishment for herself. She listened to Lil's talk of the Bon Ton and when Lil broke out—"You're cross with me, Jen, you're sorry I came to Lamptown!" she answered carefully, "No, I'm not. Didn't I always say we'd live together, didn't I say I'd send for you to come? I wouldn't have said that if I didn't want you, would I?"

But jealousy was gnawing at her constantly and for this illness there is no rest, day and night veins burn and somehow do not burst with the fever, there can be no peace in remembering a past moment of security, such moments are gone for ecstasy leaves no mark, pain alone cuts deep.

"If I could only see Morry as he really is, then the ache would be gone," Jen reasoned, "because look at him—he isn't so different from anybody else, when you think of it, he isn't so good-looking, he certainly isn't kind—(yes, he is, remember those nights on Delaney's back steps, yes, he was kind, then.)"

If there were only some operation that could destroy this perpetual ache, if you could go to a surgeon and say, "Will you please cut out the Morry section of my brain?" But then what would be left? Because he wasn't just in her brain, he was in her blood, he was part of her. If she could sleep nights instead of thinking, she reflected, then she might be strong enough to wish to be free of him, but wounds from him were better than nothing at all from him, that was the awful part of loving someone. Worn out with thoughts that ran round and round forever in the same little circle, she would at last wearily admit that what she wanted most in the world was to be desired by Morry, but this was not possible because it was so plain to him that he could have whatever he wanted from her and no man ever desired something he knew was his.

She was afraid her mind was getting all crooked, she had to go over the words, "Isn't it fine that I did get Lil out of the Home?" Inside those words she knew the truth, because until Lil came Morry was potentially her property—Nettie Farrell and Grace and the girl from Norwalk and the little peroxide blonde from the Works, they didn't matter, these women changed but she remained. She thought if she had brains like Mr. Hogan or Lou Berman she would know how to reason Morry out of her life.

At least now she was determined to do something tremendous with her future. If Lil hadn't come she might have waited around Lamptown for Morry all her life, but now—let Lil have Morry and Lamptown! As for Jen, she was going to climb every wall and every ladder until she was so high up that she could look down on loving Morry Abbott as nothing at all. And when she was up there at the very top she would thank him for preferring Lil and she would be glad Lil came to Lamptown. These thoughts passed in clear review in her mind while Lil lay sleeping beside her. Oh she'd leave town, Jen thought, wide awake, you bet she'd go. There'd be no place where trains went that she wouldn't go, no city too big for her to conquer, but the next instant, all the cities in the world conquered, she ached for Morry and buried her face in the pillow. Oh Somebody . . . Somebody . . . Somebody help. . . . She remembered the broken rosary in her top drawer but she made no move to get it after her first impulse. No rosary was going to help you. Nothing could help you but yourself, there was no help from any other person or from any Somebody. This was all right . . . in fact as long as she would live, any unexpected service from outside would be regarded by Jen not as luck but as a sinister unnatural phenomenon to be paid for one day or another in blood and tears. . . .

Along about four o'clock she got out of bed and looked out the window on the clover fields. The sullen gray sky gave no hint of sunrise. It was still smudged with night and a few weak stars. Jen tiptoed to her dresser and got out her manicure box. She sat down by the window with it and in that dull pearl light began earnestly on her fingernails. An actress, Lou Berman said, must have beautiful hands.

"Morry's a fine-looking man," said Mrs. Pepper to Elsinore every time Morry called at the store, "a fine-looking man, indeed."

They were always saying that about somebody. On their trips to Cleveland, at one time or another during the day Mrs. Pepper was bound to nudge Elsinore and say in quite a dignified low voice, "Isn't that a fine-looking man over there—that big man in the Palm Beach suit?"

If there were two Fine-looking Men in the hotel lobby or the Union Station or in the parlor car going home, then Mrs. Pepper was likely to lean toward Elsinore and whisper, "They think we're sisters—can you imagine that? It's on account of these hats."

In summer both women wore big milans heavy with flowers set ever so slightly toward the right eye, just as the wholesaler had advised, and in winter they wore big black velvets with two superb plumes curling under the brim. Elsinore, since Charles's death, had grown much heavier, her face was full and blankly white, though Mrs. Pepper sometimes coaxed her to use just a touch of her vegetable rouge and her curling iron. The Bon Ton, hats, corsets, lingerie, gloves, hosiery, was prospering steadily and the two proprietors used the cream of their stock for their own persons. When they sat discreetly together on excursion boats to Cedar Point, their dotted veils drooping from their big hats, their long gloves demurely on their laps, men shifted cigars to their fingers and one was bound to observe, "A couple of swell figures, there. Classy dressers, eh? We'll pick 'em up at the Point, what d'ye say and take 'em over to the Beer Garden."

They usually wore rustling black silks, black for smartness and discretion, but certainly alluring enough when cut snugly for a perfect 40, accented with dangling long gold chains, heavy musk scents, and modestly revealed openwork stockings. They went to matinees together in Cleveland to see what new costume touches were in vogue, not so much for the Bon Ton clientele as for themselves, they worked hard for the Bon Ton but they lived for their "trips," the whistles of admiration, the whispers, "Gee—what a figure!" the perfect applause of a man stopping in his talk to stare attentively as they passed. It was always Mrs. Pepper's gay little laugh that answered bolder men's invitations, a silvery little tinkle that slurred over every situation, made the whole business just jolly fun and not at all horrid. If the two women ever got separated by their chance male companions, they never confided to each other details of this interim any more than they talked of their 'trip' when they returned to Lamptown. What they talked over was the success of their new costumes, a new hair retoucher, and a plan for even more breathtaking ensembles next time. They were two very discreet women, ladies both of them. Even Nettie, jealous and unhappy under the new regime and waiting impatiently for the autumn to launch her own business, could not actually put a finger on anything to talk about except long-distance calls that came from time to time, so cautiously conducted that even Fay, toll operator and Nettie's bosom friend, could not find cause for scandal.

"You know, Elsinore," Mrs. Pepper said as they sat in their pink nightgowns one night patting lotions into their faces, "Harry Fischer says I've completely changed since we started this new store. He gets so worried about me—he says you have a bad influence over me."

Elsinore saw herself in the mirror over Mrs. Pepper's head, her full white arms reaching down for a lost juliet, her dark hair flying, her plump breasts bursting through the lace top of her nightie. The picture was strangely like the image of Mrs. Pepper right beside it, save Mrs. Pepper's bosom, without a corset's support, settled cozily into her 'tummy,' the waistline completely vanished, and Mrs. Pepper's blue eyes, set in the same sort of round white face, were definitely merry where Elsinore's were blank and cold. Sleeping together, though, Mrs. Pepper's fat arm trustingly encircling Elsinore's waist, her cheek confided in slumber to Elsinore's smooth back, they were like sisters, so close to each other under the pink comforter that they needed no words for their secrets.

"We ought to go over more to Harry's dances," Mrs. Pepper said, regretfully. "He says the inspectors have condemned the Casino, so it may be months before he can find a new hall in Lamptown. He and Hunt may build a new pavilion, and that will take time."

"We went over when we could," said Elsinore. "The Casino seems pretty tame, though, after you've been around."

She tried to think what it had been that she used to see in Harry Fischer, but it was no use. That romance was dynamited out of her brain and in the vacuum a strange new Elsinore had grown. When she thought of Fischer she could only recall with distaste how he perspired in dancing and she even shuddered remembering his hot wet hand on her back, and the ever so faint odor of onions from his breath. She listened to the dance music on Thursday nights but it no longer meant Fischer to her. It was only a reminder of a trip to the Hollenden Grill with two B. & O. Officials, or an automobile ride from Cleveland out to a Willoughby roadhouse. When he came to the Bon Ton to see Mrs. Pepper, it was Elsinore who whispered with the latter behind the screen, advising what excuse to give for not meeting him next Wednesday in Cleveland—say they had a dinner of wholesalers to attend, or no—yes, say anything so they could meet those two drummers at the Hofbrau as they'd promised.

"You do make me be mean to Harry," Mrs. Pepper gently protested. "Honestly, I don't feel right about him when I've always been so fond of him. But then I hate to give up a good time and you and I do have good times together, don't we? I'm sure Harry oughtn't to begrudge me a little pleasure after the way I've worked all my life. He surely ought to understand that."

"He does as he pleases," Elsinore answered coldly. "You can't tell me he doesn't with all those young girls always crazy about him. I notice he never got a divorce for you."

Mrs. Pepper's mouth trembled. She still wept over old wounds, over candy denied her as a child, over scoldings remembered from her long-deceased husband, over Harry Fischer long, long ago refusing to divorce his wife for her. So, reminded of this, she became happier in her digressions, not to be revenged on Harry, she was far too gentle for that, but because she thought it wouldn't really hurt his feelings after all.

"That Mr. Kutner from Chicago was so surprised," she murmured to Elsinore, "when Nettie told him you had a grown son. He couldn't believe it, he said."

"Nettie talks too much, anyway," Elsinore exclaimed angrily. "I don't see why the salesmen have to be told all my family affairs."

"She told him about Charles's killing himself, too," said Mrs. Pepper. "Mr. Kutner said he'd read about it but never knew it was your husband."

"I'll be glad when Nettie leaves and gets her own shop," Elsinore burst out in extreme annoyance. "She's much too friendly with strangers. She talks all the time—she's too much of a gossip."

Mrs. Pepper made no reply for in the depths of her amiable soul she was as jealous of Nettie's position in the Bon Ton as Nettie was of hers. And as for her being a gossip, that, to the corsetiere, was her only virtue. She hurried down to the workroom every time she heard Nettie's girl-friend, Fay, come in, for between Fay and Nettie you were bound to get a good hour of fascinating tattle. Fay told everything, every telephone call that came for the Girls' Club, what every vanished factory girl said who called up her Lamptown girlfriend from a tough hotel in Pittsburgh, what women were called up by slightly tipsy visitors in Bill Delaney's sa-loon. Once Fay stopped her chatting when Mrs. Pepper apologetically stole in the room.

"She'll tell," Fay explained her reticence to Nettie. "I'll tell you some other time."

Mrs. Pepper pouted.

"It's about Dode O'Connell," Nettie told her briefly, "and you'd go right and tell Harry Fischer and he'd tell Hunt and Hunt would get Fay in dutch at the telephone office."

Mrs. Pepper clasped her hands pleadingly.

"But I wouldn't tell! I wouldn't really! I never see Hunt to talk to any more—I wouldn't tell a soul! What's happened to Dode—is it true she got married to a man in Grand Rapids?"

Fay's lip twisted scornfully. She adjusted her turban with a left hand grown much more adept since it flaunted a diamond solitaire.

"Dode isn't married to anybody. Hunt wouldn't marry her and that finished her. Well—you're sure she won't blab, Nettie? . . . it isn't any-thing. Only Hunt calls up Toledo last night and when I was getting the party Toledo says to me, 'Say, Lamptown, you know the party you're call-ing, don't you' and I says no, it's a hotel, ain't it, and she says, 'Some hotel,' she says, 'it's Lizzy Madison's, the biggest sporting house in town. Better listen in if you want to hear something good.' So I says, 'Say, Toledo, think I'm so darned dumb you got to tell me to listen in?' Anyway Hunt gets the party and it was some woman answering so Hunt says is Miss Dolores there. All the time Akron was trying to get me, but I let her buzz, I hung on to Toledo, you couldn't have pried me away. Well, this Miss Dolores says, 'Hello, who is it?' then, and Hunt says, 'Hello, Dode, this is Hunt. I want to see you.' She says 'Who?' and sorta gasped as if she couldn't believe her ears, and he says 'It's me, Hunt. How are you, Dode?'

Well, she didn't say another word, so he kept saying, 'hello, hello' and still she didn't answer, only sort of a funny noise, I heard, sounded like somebody crying. He kept it up—'Say, Dode, hello, can't you hear me,' he says, 'It's me—Hunt.' And no answer from her just that funny moanin' sort of, gee, it got my goat coming over the wire that way, and then she clicked off. So he says to me, 'Operator, operator, I was cut off.' And I just told him. 'Oh no you wasn't cut off, Mr. Russell,' I says, 'the lady hung up.'"

Mrs. Pepper listened sorrowfully.

"She was so crazy about him!"

"Well," said Nettie, threading a needle, "she's where she belongs now, I guess."

"I'll say so," said Fay, and flicked a ravelling from her dress with her engagement finger.

Mrs. Pepper told Elsinore about Dode in their room that night while they took turns manicuring each other. Wasn't it a shame, she said, the way Dode turned out?

"There's worse things," Elsinore said.

Coming out of Bill Delaney's Morry heard a "Sss-t!" and saw old Mrs. Delaney at the alley entrance. She jerked her head toward him commandingly. She was in a dry brown calico dress, her shawl pulled over her head, one brown twisted hand grasping an egg basket. She seemed shrinking more each day into old brown goods until some day you could pick up this antique bundle and find no more bones or body to it than to a dried leaf, if you shook it two shrivelled hen feet and a wrinkled yellow mask might fall out but no more than that. She clung to the stair railing as if the languid breeze might blow her away.

"Evening, Mrs. Delaney," Morry said uncomfortably. He could not meet her fierce old eyes, he knew she was ready with accusations and he had no wish to hear them, other things were pressing on his mind.

"I told you she'd turn out bad, didn't I?" she sputtered. "Didn't I say there was bad blood there? Got her own place now, she has, where she can carry on and nobody see, she's a smart one, nobody can deny those bad ones are the smartest and you, young man, you got yourself to thank for it, I could've handled her if you hadn't hung around, letting her think you was soft on her, it's you that's ruined that girl's life and don't you forget it, some day you'll have a daughter of your own and you'll find out, then, you'll be the one to worry then, young man...."

"I never hurt Jen, you're all wrong about that," Morry protested, wishing there was some weapon for dealing with old women.

She sniffed scornfully.

"You can't lie to me. I know my characters. I knew your pa and I knew her mother. Didn't that woman come here time after time trying to find Jen and didn't I run her out of town as fast as she could go—didn't I call the police for her not two months ago when she came to my door?"

Morry hadn't known this.

"Did her mother come again, really?"

"I'm tellin' you right now. She come here not two months ago sayin' she'd heard both her girls was here workin' in town and she was their mother come to make a home for them. You make a home for them, hah, I says, you want their salary and you want them to keep you now you've shirked 'em all your life. Well, she says, they only got one mother and it's my duty to be with 'em now when they need a mother's care. Hah, I says, one mother is one too many and I called Bill up here and he got her ticket right back to Cleveland without her even seeing the girls."

"She'd better keep away from those girls," Morry exclaimed angrily. "Throwing them away when they were born—the way she did . . . she's got no right to them now."

The old woman turned on him.

"If she hasn't who has? You, maybe. . . . I hear things. I hear Jen went from you to Hunt Russell and from Russell to that Jew, but you're responsible, you gave her the start, young fella, and you'll get your punishment, glory be to God."

She hobbled up the stairs and Morry, disturbed, went on toward the Bon Ton. He was always supposed to be Jen's keeper, he reflected, even if he never saw her, Bill's mother or Hulda Bauer would always be giving him old nick for letting Jen do this and that. . . . As if he could stop Jen from doing anything she'd set her mind on. . . . He thought of her plan to go away. He hadn't talked to her much about it because she wouldn't really go, he felt. But what made him so sure? After all Berman had promised to help her go, and there was nothing to hold her in Lamptown. Nothing but Lil. . . . Lil and—well, face it squarely—himself. He didn't like to think about Jen loving him—it was such a violent, possessive love, not what he wanted from a girl, such fierce, unreasoning love made a man instinctively cautious and sensible—somebody had to be. He could have made love to her, there were times he remembered, but he was afraid of losing himself. Oh yes, somebody had to be sensible. As for being in love—well, he loved Lil; but loving Lil was like loving prestige or an idea, not like loving a person. If he allowed himself to be drawn to a strong person like Jen she would inevitably crowd into the romance and be equal to the hero—this was disturbing and not romantic, romance was between a man and love, not between a man and woman. . . .

Morry found himself caught up in the puzzle of his own feelings. . . . Could Jen really go away and leave him? Even here waiting for Lil to come out of the Bon Ton door, he grew sick with fear of a Lamptown without Jen. The Delaney backstairs, the Bauers' kitchen, the Casino, the house on Extension, these places were Lamptown and they were barren with Jen ripped out of them. And Lil, pale and sweet, was nothing without Jen coloring her. . . . It was silly of him to be so sure Jen would not leave him, she went around with other men, he'd never been jealous because he was sure of her, so certain of her that he had no desire for her. . . . No, be truthful, there were moments when she was adoring him that he wanted desperately to possess her, but then he would be lost, she would know he belonged to her, there could be nothing casual between him and Jen. . . . But if she should go away he'd have to go, too. He had to. He couldn't let her prove superior to him. That was settled. . . .

He leaned against the Bon Ton window and smoked. It was too early for Lil to go home to supper, he'd have to wait a little while. He observed the newly painted doorway of the Bon Ton—no doubt about it, his mother was a good business woman, she'd done a lot for herself since his father's death—all right, call it "suicide." He could certainly use that word if his mother could so casually. Maybe, if she thought about that event at all, and sometimes Morry doubted if she did, she really thought it was a suicide. Anyway the further back in your mind you pushed those things the better it was for you.

He stepped back to study the show window. A gold fringe ran across the top of it and propped against a little gold silk screen was the crying doll dressed in black velvet, its blue eyes staring out under its huge black hat, a duplicate of the life-size black hat on the stand beside it. One hand was held out stiffly with a tiny purse hung on it, the other hand was concealed in the folds of the dress because the fingers were broken. Morry felt curiously guilty before the doll's glassy stare. He wished his mother would get rid of the damned thing. It made him think of his father.

It was a fact, Hogan told Morry in the barroom, that Fowler had made a deal with the Lamptown Home Co. to continue their little houses all over Clover Heights. When Morry demanded what Hunt said to this, Bill explained that Hunt was selling everything he owned in town, shares in the Works and everything, and that he was going in with Harry Fischer to build a dance pavilion somewhere in this county.

"Outside of that old Hunt has set up a little drugstore blonde in a swell apartment on Euclid Avenue in Cleveland," said Hogan. "I give him two years to get down to his bottom dollar."

"But I don't understand about Fowler—why didn't he let me know what was going on?" Morry wanted to know. His head was swimming, he was afraid his face had paled, something stuck in his throat. . . . Fowler had fooled him, everybody had fooled him, there never would be any Clover Heights, but this was not so terrible as finding out how people used you, fooled you, always kidding you along as if they meant what you did.

"If the old boy didn't tell you, then he's got something crooked up his sleeve, Jesus, those Fowlers never had a straight thought," Hogan answered. "Every goddam one of my wife's people, the same. . . . You wait, there'll be a dirty deal in it somewhere, that's why he didn't tell you. Sell you out for a nickel, that man would. Won't touch liquor, won't look at a woman—say you never can trust an abstainer, boy, if he's abstaining from pleasure it's so he can put all his strength into some shady business deal— you mark my words."

Morry steadied himself at the rail, he drank fast to dispel that choked feeling in his throat. There was nobody you could believe in—your father, your mother, nobody.

"I don't see where Morry's stung," Bill had objected. "He's not going to be fired. He'll go over with Fowler and work for the Lamptown Home Company, that's all."

Morry found his voice returning at last.

"I wouldn't do it!" he snarled. "You think I'd spend the rest of my life doing nothing but see how many of those shanties I could squeeze on to an acre of land? Why, I wouldn't work to put a thing like that over on this town, this town's got as much right to be a decent place to live in as Avon has, right next door. I'd feel as if I was spreading smallpox, honest I would. If Fowler's giving up Clover Heights, then I quit Fowler, that's all. You got to believe in what you're doing, Hogan, you see that, don't you? A fella's got a right to work for something he believes in, hasn't he?"

"Maybe," said Bill. "But a fella's got to work at something, believe or not believe."

"The prettiest thing this town will ever have," observed Hogan, "is the Yards. You'll never see anything prettier in this burg than those old black engines pushing up and down the tracks. Boy, you might as well make up your mind now as later that people don't want anything pretty, and damned if they want anything useful, they just want what other people have. You take these cement porches—"

"You never used to talk like that," Morry reproached him.

"I wasn't this old," grinned Hogan.

"All right, then," Morry said, "the hell with Fowler."

He swung out to the street and walked rapidly and dizzily toward Extension Avenue. He forgot about Lil waiting in the Bon Ton. His head buzzed with Hogan's words. Fowler had sold out, gone over to the rivals, he hadn't believed in anything but piano boxes for homes from the very first, he only loaned himself to the Clover Heights enterprise because the bank thought it was good business and because the Works directors hadn't asked him to build their workmen's cottages. As soon as they did ask him he dropped everything and went flying over to them like a child going to whoever extended the most candy.

Hogan said the three houses were to be fixed over into a boarding club for the company officials, a big flower garden was to be laid straight across all three front lawns with huge letters in red and white gladiolas, "LAMPTOWN WORKS OFFICIALS CLUB." And Fowler had worked all this out with the Works people without telling him, thinking he'd be glad to go over to them, too. That's the way people were. Nobody believed in the things you believed but yourself, nobody believed that even you were really sincere about it, people believed whatever was good business for them at the time. Nobody believed in anything but good business. Clover Heights was blown up, the world was blown up, by good business. Everybody knelt to good business. No use counting on anybody having faith in an idea for its own sake.

Restlessly Morry walked on. What was going to happen to him, then? Fowler wouldn't fire him, he'd expect him to go cheerfully over to the rival company, but he wouldn't, he'd be damned if he would. Well, what would he do, then—go back to the factory? Give up living in Russell House and beg five dollars now and then from his mother, 'till he got something good enough'? Either he fell in with the Lamptown Home Company for a little while—oh, just a few months, say—and worked to see that every citizen had his rightful portion of ugliness, or he went back to the factory. Damned if he'd go back there. He'd leave town, go to the city. Cleveland—Detroit—Chicago—What would he do there? He'd never dare go. . . . Still, Jen St. Clair wasn't afraid to strike out. He knew a second of despair, thinking that all his life it was Jen driving him to do things, he never did anything without that lash, he never would. He had to do the things she expected of him. She would be a big actress on Broadway, she said, when he was an architect in New York. So that's what he had to do, that was all there was to it. Maybe Pittsburgh first, work it somehow to study at Carnegie Tech . . . then New York. Jen would be there because she always did the things she set out to do, and he—well, he had to be what Jen thought he was. . . . He stopped to roll another cigarette. His hands shook. He dared not think of going away, but if Jen had the nerve to go he wouldn't be afraid, he'd never dare let her see how perilous it seemed to him. . . .

It was nearly six. He could go back to the Bon Ton now for Lil or he could go on to the house, since he was nearing it, and see Jen, who went home earlier. He needed the reassurance of his own voice boasting to Jen about what he was going to do. He needed desperately to be told he was wonderful, that there were far bigger things for him than any Clover Heights, he needed Jen's eyes worshiping him and he forgot Lil.

The sun withdrew and drained all color from the trees, they looked gloomy and ragged, their branches were too skinny, he thought; in the unbecoming twilight the old gray houses of Extension Avenue crowded beside their trees looking dowdy and unloved like the wives of executives. Good-bye, Lamptown, Morry thought, hurrying along, good-bye. . . .

This was the moment of curious lull when it was neither day nor night, it was time for the six-o'clock whistle to blow, then warm darkness would smudge these sharp edges and let shadows invent their own town.

The factory siren suddenly shrieked through the air, cutting the day in two, and boarding house kitchens responded with an obedient clatter of pans and dishes, the smell of frying potatoes mingled agreeably with the fragrance of fresh-mown lawns and strawberry shrubs. Good-bye, good-bye to all this, Morry whispered. . . . He'd go straight to the house, then, he decided, and when Jen came in he'd tell her, he'd say, "What would I do in the city? What's there to be afraid of? Don't be foolish, Jen. I'd just walk into an office and get a job, that's all—there's nothing to that, is there?"

Now the evening fast train roared through Lamptown, its triumphant whistle soared over the factory siren, in its vanishing echoes the beginning of a song trembled, a song that belonged to far-off and tomorrow. Yes, yes, he would come away, Morry's heart answered, now he was ready.

TURN
MAGIC
WHEEL

FOR DWIGHT FISKE

"Turn, magic wheel,
Bring homeward him I love."

— THEOCRITUS

I

... the little words of the rich ...

SOME FINE DAY I'LL HAVE TO PAY, Dennis thought, you can't sacrifice everything in life to curiosity. For that was the demon behind his every deed, the reason for his kindness to beggars, organ-grinders, old ladies, and little children, his urgent need to know what they were knowing, see, hear, feel what they were sensing, for a brief moment to *be* them. It was the motivating vice of his career, the whole horrid reason for his writing, and some day he warned himself he must pay for this barter in souls.

Always as he emerged late in the afternoon from a long siege of writing, depressed by fatigue, he was accustomed to flagellate himself with reproaches and self-inquiry. Why had he come to New York, why had he chosen this career? Though to tell the truth he could not remember having made any choice, he just seemed to have written. But if a Muse he must have, he reflected, why not the Muse of Military Life, or better the Muse of Advertising? . . . Actually I should have gone out to South Bend, he decided, into my uncle's shoe factory and made a big name for myself in the local lodges; but there again was the drawback. Did my uncle invite me? No. He said, "You'd be no good in my business, Denny. Here's a hundred dollars to go some place way off." "Thank you, uncle," I should have said briskly, "I prefer to take over the factory and with the little invention I have been working on all these years for combination shoe-stocking-and-garter I propose to make the Orphen shoe known the world over. Allow me, uncle," I should have said, "to put your business on its feet or at least on its back." Then I would have married Alice or was it Emma who lived next door? We would have had a cottage at a respectable Wisconsin lake in summer and in winter fixed up the basement with chintz and old furnaces to be a boys' den. I would have satisfied both my intellect and my ego by sitting up nights reading thick books Alice couldn't possibly understand, and for my cosmopolitan urge I could have winked at stock company actresses. Even if it was Emma and not Alice I should have done that. But no, I am a born busybody. Curiosity is my Muse, lashing me thousands of miles across land and sea to study a tragic face at a bus window, not for humanity's sake but for the answer's sake. Have I no finer feelings, he begged his stern inquisitor, look what a loyal friend I have been to Effie Callingham, for instance; was there ever a truer friend? . . .

The answer to this query was not gratifying for his speculations on Effie, her emotions, her past, her future, had resulted in his latest book, so that if this was loyalty it worked hand in glove with his major vice. Face it, then, curiosity was the basis for the compulsion to write, this burning obsession to know and tell the things other people are knowing. Unbearable not to know the answers. Behind those blank faces on the subway, *what?* In the spiritualist parlor on Seventy-third and Amsterdam what casual guess sums up this one, what blind prophecy outlines another's future; in the reading rooms of the Forty-second Street Library countless persons absorbed in books (Why absorbed? What do they read? Why do they read it?) look up and away; what sentence stirred what memories so that interlacing thoughts float through glass and steel to faraway, to places you will never know, dwell familiarly on faces you will never see. At the Dolly Raoul Studio of Stage Dancing, Inc., Acrobatic, Ballet, Toe, Ballroom, Tap, Radio, Fourteenth Street and Second Avenue, what does the little peroxide Jewess leaning out the window feel or know, what perhaps beautiful plan is shaping in her little head for a break from Avenue A to Carnegie Hall? On paper you can fill in the answers, be these persons, transfer your own pain into theirs, remember what they remember, long for what they desire. Spread out in type, detail added to detail, invention added to fact, the figure whole emerges; invisibly you creep inside, you are at last the Stranger.

Words, sworn testimony cannot help here; between the candid phrases stands the Why, the Why *she,* why not some one else, so that Effie's own story known in sum so well to him could only tantalize him, make him forever intrigued by her sweet ravaged face, her simplest gesture. Thinking of Effie without ever being able to be or fully know her, filling in her past as he walked so that his own story became more real than hers,

Dennis followed the little blonde down Second Avenue, at first absently then deliberately as she came out in green hat and astrakhan-trimmed jacket from Dolly Raoul's Studio of Stage Dancing. He watched what she watched but again he was lost; before the millinery window which hat delighted her, the red feather toque or the black taffeta, did the pushcart of Persian figs tempt her that she glanced at it twice or was it the tray of St. John's bread, the stand of Kolomara grapes and pomegranates, or was it that she was really hungry? Perhaps in the rhinestone-stippled velvet purse there were only a few pennies, her tuition at school took all her money; she must remember, perhaps, that this ten cents is for carfare to a casting office. Below Seventh Street she glanced up at the banner flaming across the street—"THE FOURTH ANNUAL DANSANT OF THE RIDGE STREET BOYS"; of course she wanted to go there, show how marvelously well-trained she was. In the corner of the dance hall she would teach her partner a few fancy steps and would astonish and delight the other dancers with her professional execution; here she paused before a gown shop and saw herself in the blue velvet evening dress she would wear, dreamily she opened the purse to powder her nose, saw Dennis's inquiring eyes reflected in her pocket mirror, looked him haughtily up and down, angry that he had seen her in the blue velvet at the Dansant dancing with Irving.

She hurried on down Second Avenue, high-heeled gray suede boots, Russian style, clapping firmly down on the pavement, head with its firm yellow curls exploding beneath the green felt hat, but Dennis found now a conscious coquetry in the rhythmic swirl of her skirt, and disillusioned, he stood for a moment at the Fourth Street corner watching her swish right, left, right, left across the street. What called her to the other side— surely not the Church of the Nativity, bare edifice of pilgrim simplicity, simplest crucifix looming above surrounding Yiddish shops and symbols? She was gone, perhaps into the side gate where a sign in black and red letters said:

YE OLD BARN DANCE
COME YE CHICKS AND YE HICKS
OLD NATIVITYVILLE BARN DANCE

Now she was lost, he could look in vain upward at Dolly Raoul's windows as he passed on his way home, pause at every pushcart of figs, look in the millinery shop to see if the red hat was still there, no, the girl was gone, he would never see her again, never, though already the next encounter flickered on the screen—The Paradise or possibly the Folies Bergere, and the cigarette girl leaning her tray on his table. *"Haven't I seen you before, sir?"* A little Turkish cap on her head this time and embroidered trousers, but the same girl, the same sharp nose, same galaxy of tight blond curls. So you weren't a dancer, so you weren't ambitious East Side but nostalgic Broadway all the time, so the answers were never in the book.

A light mist was rapidly turning into snow, and chilled, he pulled up his collar to his ears. This would be a deuce of a time to get pleurisy again and be pitiful, winter just over, a joyous spring in bed with no money, no fireplace, just magazine editors encouraging him to finish stories not yet begun. He would be damned if he would ever be pitiful again, better be arrogant, vulgar, boorish, cruel, anything rather than be soft, sick, weak, poor, pitiful. The mere fancy made him wince just as a loaded pistol could still make his brave blood run cold, yes, he was still afraid of Fate, the cruel stepmother. Would a day come, he wondered, when his fame and living would be assured, when a stroke of good fortune would not make him speculate uneasily what subsequent string of failures would be required to pay for it? Ah, to sit pretty, he thought, to fold hands over stomach with a smug smile and accept confidently, and not mistrustfully, the homage of the gods! On the other hand, the ability to sit pretty was glandular and not in his make-up, success must be mysterious, evasive, unfaithful, to allure him.

In the mirror of a street weighing machine he saw how thin, narrow-chested, unimpressive he looked, unlikely seducer of Fortune, the Lorelei. Here was a man, he would swear, who would never be a home owner, a shoe factory president, a car owner, a steady jobholder, here was a man who could be nothing but possibly a ticket owner, and in fact, studying his image with detached even hostile eye, it struck him that he had a Passport face, one that could be placed on anybody's papers and not be entirely wrong; such a face could justifiably sweep through the world passionately examining other faces but exempt from the curious second glance itself. This was only justice in exchange for an injustice, he concluded, and wondered if it was possible that he was getting increasingly partial to himself since there were fewer and fewer negative reflections on his charm, ability, and superiority that he could not flout with two minutes of judicial analysis. As a matter of fact he was a mighty personable figure of a man, a fine commanding physique (if he just remembered to stay away from tall women), a rather nonchalantly Prince of Wales way of wearing his clothes (if he just stayed on Fourteenth Street or Second Avenue), and a manner all his own that he got by combining Clark Gable and Wallace Beery. Going back up the Avenue with a more confident swagger, he stopped near St. Mark's to buy a bag of roasted chestnuts from the old man shivering before his charcoal oven. He would take them to Effie. It was the one charming unconquerably childish thing about her, that question, "What did you bring me?" It never mattered what it was, but it pleased her to have tangible proof that, absent, someone had thought of her.

Chimes clamored through the distant roar of the elevated trains, the Metropolitan clock cut through the giant music box with five authoritative strokes. He should be home now, for Effie had promised to come in. Curious how behind his back in ten minutes Fourteenth Street had changed. An old barge captain, red and bearded, in oilskins and sweater, had sprung up before the Tom Mooney Club, a pocked old woman invited him to choose between white parrots and white mice as fortune-tellers, here was a Gypsy Tearoom, Tea Leaves Read Gratis. In front of the shooting gallery the Princess Doraldina from Tasmania, golden-haired figurine in a glass cage, for five cents breathes, moves, passes a wax hand over cards, sighs, and releases the card of your future. *"You will meet with one who will love you. That love will be returned by you. The first name of this person begins with M and you will be introduced at a place of amusement."*

Magically the five o'clock people came to life, bounced out of their subways, jumped out of their elevators, bells rang, elevator bells, streetcar bells, ambulance bells; the five o'clock people swept through the city hungrily, they covered the sun, drowned the city noises with their million tiny bells, their five o'clock faces looked eagerly toward Brooklyn, Astoria, the Bronx, Big Date Tonight. They enveloped Dennis, danced about him, sang I-sez-to-him in a dozen different keys, whispered he-sez-to-me, they whirred off into night and were gone like the blond Jewess in the Russian boots, they were nothing to him, he was less than nothing to them, a young man with a passport face on his way to meet Effie Callingham, one-time wife of the great man Andrew Callingham, one-time companion to the Four Hundred's Mrs. Anthony Glaenzer . . . and this was the part of her life Dennis knew least about, must guess at in his novel about her. He did know that through all those years in the Glaenzer household New York had been only a dream around her, this present confusion which he loved, these masks flung out of office windows, these wax Doraldinas with printed fortunes in their hearts, these pretty puppets were only a dim noise outside the Glaenzer coffin doors, a cry, a wish, a dream. Sometimes he thought of Effie as part of that rich fat enemy world of Glaenzers, he saw her with them peering out at New York through Fifth Avenue lace curtains, listening to the Help! Help! of the city through symphonic arrangements of Stokowski; he saw her with the Glaenzers swimming in their goldfish bowl, observed rather than observing, swimming in and out of their skeleton castle, pressing their little blind noses to the glass, blinking, aware of only light or dark. Effie could not, in fairness, be blamed for Glaenzer fat, but there was no denying that contact with this fat polluted subtly, the golden germ made delicate havoc wherever it went. In a sudden burst of rage he damned all Spode, Genoese lace, Haydn, Rosewood, Hollandaise, Clos Veugot, Stiegel, Ispahan, Schiaparelli, Picasso, Rosenkavalier, and all the little words of the rich, the little baby fingers reaching out, the little golden curl clutching the sterling heart, sweetly softening the brave. How charmingly Effie wore her little rich words thefted from the Glaenzer fatness, weaving a spell about her present despair, throwing out splendid marquee and rug to lead to her bare closet.

Yes, he despised her gallantry, he informed himself even while he hurried to meet her, despised her for not fighting like other people. Why couldn't she call Callingham a swine for deserting her, why couldn't she row over the Glaenzer luxury while she had so little, why must she be noble, frail shoulders squared to defeat, gaily confessing that life was difficult but that's the way things were? Pity for her taxed him, held him bound to the strange gentle woman in something so like love, so like lust, that often sleeping with his little Corinne he was tormented by conscience—he was being unfaithful to Effie, Effie the brave, splendid, unhappy woman who was nothing to him, nothing more than the tender object of his passionate curiosity. Yet she could command this odd fidelity of him, so that for days he would keep away from Corinne, deny himself the pleasure of his jealous suspicions, refuse the delicious agony of dining with her and her complacent husband, write her a dozen notes to say he was through—through, do you hear? It was all so impossible, bad for everyone all around, and it certainly was fine to be a free man again and get back to honest work. So all because of Effie, goodbye, goodbye, Corinne. Goodbye, oh excellent wife to excellent Mr. Barrow. Goodbye, love for these four, five years, torturing, maddening, stupid, unfaithful, wicked little love. Goodbye, cruel darling, sweet, soft, curly, dear little love, I'll be over in ten minutes.

SURRENDERING THEN TO CORINNE he must justify himself by looking on his friend Effie cynically, reluctantly worshiping he must make his sardonic asides, must in fact make her an amusing character in his book, to show that, bound as he was by his infantile, damnable romanticism, he still had his wits about him. Admit he was on his knees, kissing the celebrated hem, say at least he knew what was going on, he could count out more flaws in his princess than any enemy could. There was her ridiculous adoration for her ex-husband's triumphs, for instance. Look at page four "The Hunter's Wife, MacTweed, Publishers, $2.00—"

"She wears his name as if it were a decoration from the King entitling her to the profoundest consideration; she wears it for evening like a jeweled wrap which catches mirrored light so it cannot be ignored. Without referring to his achievement she boasts of them by keeping his full name on her mailbox these fifteen years since he deserted her. Crushed and mystified by him when they were together, now at last she can understand and interpret him with the exquisite lens of long separation, or more probably she has in that fallow period created a hero she can understand, a hero who cannot deny her interpretation as the original might. Indeed, poor soul, while grieving for him she has become him, and observe how neatly she rules her life by what would please him. The friendship she bestows is his favor, the books or music she prefers are his preferences, the crown for every newcomer is 'The master would have loved you.' What fragment, then, is left of the person who once lived in this body, before he came—is there one exclamation that comes from the buried woman, or must all be strained through the great man's cloak? Is there indeed a living soul behind this monument to him, does it breathe of itself, does it of itself weep over 'Tristan' or are these *his* beautiful tears? Rebelling against him when they were together, she surrenders utterly after his leaving so that if now he were to hunt for her throughout the world he would find her only in his own mirror.

"Past youth the sweet creature lies about her age, not through ordinary female coquetry but in the way men lie, men who having failed to do the great deed by the given hour, ease their desperate fear of failure by cheating with the calendar. Fifteen years and he has not come back to me, she says, perhaps never, then, and this cannot be borne so she swears she is only thirty-nine, this year the miracle must happen, he will come back, the hunter will return, and see the wise gentle wife she has become in his long absence. How resolutely she has borne her honesty through a sophisticated world until it has the shabby sheen that comes from long usage, it gleams in its artificial setting as the one false note! Tired Truth barks at her heels as stylishly as any other thoroughbred on leash."

When he came into the apartment he found Effie already there, the book in her hands, and Dennis had his first swift realization of what the words must mean to her. Why, he thought, meeting her stricken eyes, this was not merely writing. This was a living woman he was putting on the market, the living Effie. He felt guilty and angry. She was sitting on the sofa in his room, stiffly erect, one finger in the book as if she had held that pose for hours, frozen by what she had read. He could imagine her hurrying up the stairs at one second to five—she was always on time in spite of his own defections—very probably she paused at the landing outside his door to pull the brim of her blue felt hat lower over her shadowed, fine gray eyes, he almost saw the half-smile as she tapped lightly on his door once—twice—nobody home, very well try the knob, he will be here any minute since it's unlocked. . . . Then the book, fresh from the printers, on the table, her little exclamation of delight, the jacket examined—not bad, the title page—by Dennis Orphen, author of *No Defense*. He saw her settle herself among the cushions, still smiling with pride, to read the first page, the second, third page—smile fading into faint bewilderment, page four—page four—suddenly straightening up, reading carefully each word once again so that there could be no mistake, page four, page five.

How clever I was, how damnably clever, Dennis thought, furious with his own demon now that made him see so savagely into people's bones and guts that he could not give up his nice analysis even if it broke a heart, he could not see less or say less.

"I'm late," he said, throwing his hat into the corner where it landed arrogantly on the plaster bust of some visiting Venus modeled and deserted by the former tenant. "I see you found the book. Won't be out till next month, you know. The tenth."

Sometimes, in candlelight, Effie's slender face had the delicate sad charm of a very young girl, her rare smile was appealingly youthful, but now he saw her face frankly old and tired, and his heart turned sick; he could find nothing, nothing in the world to justify this crucifixion, good God, no, not even if he was Proust or Homer or Hemingway himself, no, there could be no excuse for telling the world about Effie.

"I can see it's about me," she said finally. "You never told me that. All the time you were writing it, you never said it was about me."

"No, it isn't really, it's a—a—"

"A composite?" She smiled faintly. "Yes, I know."

There was really so little to be said when you came right down to facts. It made him all the more angry.

"Well, what if it is about you?" he challenged her, standing in front of her, hands jammed into pockets. "Good Lord, Effie, you've been a writer's wife, you ought to know how little it means—a few words here and there which tally with a real object—what of it? You've been around, you know there's no Emily Post rule as to what's legitimate copy and what isn't. I tell you it doesn't mean a thing—"

Effie looked at him quietly and put the book back on the table. He wished she would answer but she sat twisting her gloves, the cape she always affected slipping from her fragile shoulders. How slight she was, he thought, and shivered for what had once seemed an eternally slim, youthful figure, today seemed frail shrunken age, a frailty to be protected rather than shrewdly analyzed.

Suddenly Effie laughed and he turned gratefully toward her, for in the moment's silence shutters and curtains were being drawn on confidences, doors locked that were once wide open, walls barricaded so softly, so subtly that in another moment no crevice would be left through which two one-time friends could call to each other. But now Effie laughed and a door once more swung open between them.

"I was going to ask you to go to the Gieseking recital, tonight," she said, "but I knew you would say—'she goes to concerts because Andy used to like concerts.'"

"Applesauce. Certainly I'm going with you," said Dennis. "Let's go get a cocktail some place first."

His mind sped on through the book—what else would she find there for her torture? Clever, clever Mr. Orphen with his nice little knack of thumbnailing his dearest friends. Honest Mr. Orphen who gave up the big money in Hollywood and the lazy life of southern France for the brave duty of annihilating Effie Callingham.

Effie hesitated as he held open the door for her.

"You say the book isn't out yet?"

"Not till the tenth. Why?"

She drew a breath of relief.

"Because I wouldn't dare go anywhere with you if it was already published. Everyone would know then that it really was about me—everyone would laugh."

Laugh at her . . . Dennis did not know how to reassure her, so he followed her silently down the stairs. His fingers fumbled in his pocket and found the paper bag.

"Roast chestnuts," he said and handed them to her. "Present."

"Darling, that was sweet of you."

She was plainly touched and pleased by his thinking of her on his walk. Nice Dennis. They went out the front door and across Union Square, friends again, the "interesting older woman" and the strong young man, the red-haired strong young man who had written the amusing book about her.

. . . the little French figure . . .

IN THE BREVOORT CAFÉ THEY FOUND their favorite corner table, or rather Dennis's favorite table, for if he sat here he could watch all the mirrors for Corinne and if some day she should come in the next room with another man, that actor for instance, he could watch them from here and next day when he asked her where she'd had tea and she answered "Oh, I was at Olive's" he would say "Liar, I saw you at the Brevoort with that man." Already his heart thumped in preparation for the shock of seeing the little fur hat, the new leopard coat, the plump little figure—("I'm not really fat, you know—I have what they call a French figure")—but she never came unless the mirror lied, and it was worse for her not to come, now he must wonder where she was and if she really did meet that actor as his cruel mind was always suggesting. Nor was this curiosity, he brutally told himself, this was wrinkled old Knowledge itself flirting behind a coy veil of decent doubt to seem more endurable.

"It must be a great comfort to be so handsome," Effie said, watching his survey of the mirrors.

"It is," Dennis assured her. "I spend hours here studying my profile and pitying poor women."

"It must be satisfying to be so clever, too," Effie said. "How cozy to know that all the world is performing solely for you, and any minute with your shiny little pen you can make everybody laugh and laugh."

"Oh yes," said Dennis guardedly. "It's a great consolation to feel that you're a perfect scream. Are you trying to revenge yourself, Mrs. Callingham?"

"Couldn't I have just a little revenge?" She smiled at him. "After all, it is my birthday."

Dennis was dashed.

"I knew I'd forgotten something. Do you mind wearing my Martinis instead of my gardenias?"

"I wear a Martini beautifully," Effie said. "And I hate wearing flowers. They depress me. 'See what fun I'm having,' they say, and after that, of course, I don't have any fun."

Louis, the favorite waiter, came up and bowed.

"Well, Mrs. Callingham. Quite a change here from the old days, isn't it? Mr. Callingham still in France?"

"Oh yes," Effie said graciously, as though naturally Mr. Callingham was far too superior a man to be anywhere but in France.

"Someone said he had flown to China or Japan."

"Yes—oh yes," Effie said hastily and Dennis pitied and hated her for not saying "Look here, I haven't had a word from that man for over fifteen years and I don't know anything about him except what I read in the papers."

"Is everything all right, Mrs. Callingham? Some hors d'oeuvres, perhaps?"

"No, thank you, Louis."

This was what happened to Effie wherever she went, and Dennis, though contemptuous of her pleasure in these salaams, could find no real reason for her not sharing a crumb or two of her ex-husband's glory. Callingham had given her a hell of a break years ago and if this gave her a kick, this whispering that followed her entrance—"That's Mrs. Andrew Callingham"—then welcome to it. He had known her three years, as a matter of fact it was that very whisper in a crowded room that had made him look at her twice. Confess now, Mr. Orphen, you would never have escorted her home, never have urged her to drop into Reuben's for a sandwich and beer, never, never have pursued the acquaintance if it had not been for that awed whisper—"not the wife of Andy Callingham, *no!*" Easy enough now to make fun of people's wide-eyed reverence for that name, no doubt about it, he had been as impressed as any one else, as eager to find out intimate details from someone who had been close to the man. Maybe he was just another one of those ambitious young men who snatched up ex-wives and ex-mistresses of the elect, saw in this dim

contact a personal promotion in line with their ambition, even whipped
up love, though the romance was not with the woman but with the success she had once lived with. . . . No, considering this point carefully, he
could plead not guilty; his own infatuation had been with her story, her
laboratory possibilities.

It was getting late so they ordered dinner, carefully talking about small
things so the matter of the book would not come up. If the book was not
to be discussed then the references to Andy—always a part of their talk,
as if Andy were their mutual dearest friend, must be checked, and if
Andy was to be left out, then even inquiries as to Andy's old friends and
Effie's present ones, the Glaenzers, must be omitted. This was difficult
going, for so much of their fun together was in Effie's reports on the latest
Glaenzer outrage, Belle's decision after all these years to be beautiful and
her sweep through beauty parlors, Tony's taking up with Harlem, the
servants put on the reducing diet of their mistress since she couldn't
go through with it and smell a chop anywhere in the house. But the
Glaenzers were Effie's only link with her past romance and Andy's name
was bound up with theirs; he'd been their friend first and met Effie at
their house. These subjects taboo made the sequence of Martinis ineffec-
tual in relieving the tension of the dinner, and Dennis found himself
desperately recounting stories of his boyhood which Effie must have
known by heart by this time, so often had he told them. Once he thought
he really did see Corinne and his mouth fell open.

"What in the world are you seeing, Dennis?" Effie asked curiously.

A fine two-timing husband he'd make, he thought, paling every time
his honey's name was mentioned, probably carrying silk panties home in
his brief case, leaving blond hairpins in his wife's bedroom—oh, he would
be a suave old sinner, all right. This reminded him that while Corinne
knew about Effie—anyone over thirty was no rival of Corinne's so she
never gave the relationship a thought—Effie had never heard of Corinne.
If Corinne should walk into the café this minute—he wished she would,
he could not deny that leap in his heart every time he saw her sullen little
face—send her here, God, even with that actor!—Effie would be astonished, bewildered, that here was an intimate friend whose name she had
never heard, never in the three years they had seen each other every day.
Transferring himself into Effie, he saw that this was a strange reticence
considering that every other thought he'd ever had was in her confidence.

Here they were, inseparable friends, confidants, and if he were to cut his throat tonight Effie would tell the police, "Whatever the motive I know there was no woman in his life." How little boon companions knew each other, he marveled! No reason, too, why Effie herself shouldn't have a love life unknown to him. Supposing that fat man now eyeing her across the room—for Effie did look young and piquant by electric light—should come up and say, "Well, Effie, tomorrow as usual?" Why not? But the idea of Effie having secrets from him was annoying and he would have none of it. The only thing that kept his spirit up, Dennis reflected, was the childish hope that other people at least were honest. Other people were sincere, transparent, candid. So he must know everything about Effie and Corinne, even though he budgeted his own confessions most cannily.

"How about it?" Effie asked. "Concert—yes?"

"I want to talk," Dennis stated. "Either I talk during the recital with everyone pointing at us or we sit here over our expensive brandy and talk a cappella."

"I'm afraid to talk," said Effie and he saw the hurt still in her blue eyes. "I'm afraid of you now. Every word I say you will be thinking—Andy taught her that, that isn't her own phrase. I'm even afraid if I drink any more I might snivel and try to be brave. You know how you hate that."

"God, yes. All right, come on." Dennis pushed his chair back abruptly. "To the concert, quick."

. . . under music . . .

NOT SUCH A GOOD IDEA, Dennis thought, listening to music when you had things on your mind. The music simply drove the worry out in the open, made it race around the brain to varying tempos, induced the saddest of endings. During the Debussy he saw Effie drowning herself because the futility of her life had been pointed out to her by her dearest friend, Dennis Orphen. He reached for her hand and held it tightly, rings cutting his palm, so that if during the Ravel she tried to float gently and sadly up to heaven like Little Eva as the music urged everyone to do, he could hold her down. He stole a look at her face to see if, as she had threatened, she was really sniffling, but her profile was calmly musical, quite proper, quite controlled. He thought again of what her brief connection with Callingham had done for her—given her a confident way of holding her head, a consciousness of her public, so to speak, and this sweet arrogance affected people, even crowds—"Who is she? She must be *somebody,*"—and even when the illustrious name was not recognized as it seldom was in musical circles it was thereafter remembered because it must be fine indeed to bestow such dignity on the wearer.

He wished, though, that some day he could persuade her to a definitely stylish outfit so that she would look less a personage and more a person. Dressed by Hawes or Bergdorf she would be a devilish sight more attractive than that scrawny little Kansas girl Andy was now with. But no, she must wear capes and flowing sleeves, Russian jewelry, Cossack belts on velvet smocks, costumes deserving an escort with a black beard, black Homburg hat, opera cape, ribbons of honor and a tiny medal or two twinkling on the lapel. Come to think of it, Alfonso of Spain was the man for her, he thought, like a producer doing type-casting. Wonder if we could get hold of old Alfonso? Call up Packards, Browns, all the agents—what?—in Hollywood? Take a wire to M.G.M. Studios. Dear Alfonso, would you consider a return to stage in role particularly adapted—

Effie drew her hand away from his suddenly and when he lifted his eyebrows—

"I don't like my hand held just because somebody's thrilled over music or a sunset," she whispered.

"You want it to be sheer lust, eh?" he accused her, quite shocked.

Gieseking, the pianist, looked too big to be bullying such delicate melodies, he thought, though he tried to be very gentle with them. He crouched over the piano with his big hands cupping the keys as if a mouse might peep out of his fist once he relaxed. Softly his fingers in ten little bedroom slippers tiptoed up and down Schumann, music became so diminished under his microscope, made so tiny and perfect that it could be neatly placed in a baby's ear.

"He plays as if the piano was his valentine," Effie said as they walked down Seventh to her apartment, "and little white birdies with tiny envelopes marked 'I love you' might come twittering out any minute."

Little white messages, yes, flying across oceans, over green Spain, pink Alps, lavender Saar, fluttering over Persian temples, high over missionary-colored China, into the longest bar in the world, paging Mr. Callingham, is it true he's in Shanghai, was his picture in yesterday's *News* beaming out of aviation hood or was that only Malraux or the merest Halliburton?

Effie's apartment was the top floor of an old Chelsea private house because she—or was it Andy?—liked neighborhoods with a history, she liked to feel that Lillie Langtry had often passed, perhaps even entered this house, that H. C. Bunner, Clement Moore, O. Henry, Poe, anybody once glamorous, might have lived here or next door. Dennis thought, too, she selected her rooms always for their quietness and suitability to a writer, as though, supposing Andy did come back to live with her, he wouldn't be displeased with her home. In the doorway Dennis hesitated, for Effie made no move to invite him in but started fussing with the fireplace silently.

"Look here, Effie, you don't mind that book, really? You know it has nothing to do with you. You may have started the idea off in my head, of course, but the rest is all my gorgeous imagination. Give me credit for originality, please."

"Of course, darling. You don't mind if I hide for a few days after the book comes out, do you? I mean—you know—I hate people finding out that Andy deserted me, that's all. I'd rather they just went on thinking we—well—were temporarily away from each other."

Dennis stared at her in absolute bewilderment. She actually thought people didn't know! Or did she?

"Is that all?" he blurted out in amazement. "Why everyone's always known that he walked out on you, if that's all that worries you about the book. Hell, Effie, that's no news to anybody!"

Now it was too late. Now there was nothing more to be said. This blow was final. Effie, quite pale, sat down abruptly on the desk-chair, staring at him blankly. He'd done it now, if he hadn't before.

"I'll run along," he said, angry at the whole mess.

He walked hurriedly down the stairs, his cane, as always, clattering down ahead of him. Now he'd done it, now he'd said it, now he'd fixed it, but how could one dream what fantastic lies people's egos fed on? Here was Effie, a balanced, intelligent woman nourished for years on the pretense that people believed her solitude was accidental circumstance, not her husband's own selfish choice. What made a woman like Effie so blind, or was it perhaps not rosy veils but healing bandages she wore, and was it not tonic but ruin to destroy them? Behind them what did Effie really think, did she love Andy truly all these years or was that loyalty, did she hurt when she saw his name or did she swell with possessive pride? He wondered if now she was up there—yes, she probably was—flung down on the black sateen-covered couch under the Van Gogh print; or no, she was staring into the fire not sad over Andy, but storing bitter, vengeful thoughts against Dennis, each resentful memory of tonight a fresh stone for Andy's monument, loyalty to him enhanced by the detractor's sarcasm, words erased by anger at the speaker . . . or perhaps this was only what he would feel and do in her situation and instead was she—

. . . becoming the Stranger . . .

—WAITING QUIETLY TILL THE SLAMMING of the front door showed
he had gone, hands clutched together in her lap, a little hole in her mind
where the bullet had gone through—"everyone has always known he
walked out on you"—and nothing to put in its place but an old swimming pain, that same almost-forgotten pain of smiling gaily at the party,
eyes fixed on companion—don't turn, don't wince, don't pale, don't show
you see Andy pulling the blond girl out onto the balcony with that veiled
excited look in his eyes she saw only for other women—yes, this pain was
blurred like that old one had been and flowed outside as well as through
her, tingled like frost in the air about her. Slowly phrases jumped into
place in her brain—"Tired Truth barked at her heels"—say rather it tore
at her heart. She stood up astonished that legs could support this heavy
stone, legs marched out the door, one, two, one, two, downstairs one
flight, see the picture of the landlord's graduation class 1911, Brown
University, under the hall lamp, down one flight more into the vestibule,
and stop, turn, look. There was the card on her mailbox:

MRS. ANDREW CALLINGHAM

It had been there and on all her other mailboxes for years, secretly
shaming her before the world. It was incredible that she had not realized
its mocking pretensions before, somehow it had seemed only loyalty, it
was to show Andy she bore no grudge, see, she really did understand him
after all and was proud of the little while she had held him. . . . "A buried
woman." . . . "What fragment is left of that buried woman—" She pulled

the little white card out of the mailbox and turned it over. On the back her trembling fingers printed in pencil—

MISS EFFIE THORNE

—and put it back in place.

. . . lifting the lid . . .

BECOMING OTHER PEOPLE, leaving this gray suit of Wanamaker tweeds, black ties, favorite therefore always soiled green shirt, incredibly stained, fantastically misshapen, chewed-up, trampled-on brown hat, leaving this pretty ensemble bodiless in the Trayful for a Trifle Cafeteria, bemused before a mug of coffee and chop suey, this flight into other souls had disadvantages. There were moments, for instance, when all findings were annulled by a blank, unpredictable act, and then there was the infallible law that simple souls were insoluble by this magic. You could listen and look and wonder, but there was no solving of simplicity. It was as baffling as nobility. Very well, you say, granted there is no artifice here, no trickery, what motive has this man for having no motive? Put him down then, at his best, as merely smug, what secret knowledge does he treasure to give him this complacence? Let him be candid, let him fasten to your lapel and declare, "You want to know about me—what I'm really about, eh? Listen, I'll tell you everything, every deed, every thought, there's no puzzle here." All the more puzzle then to know if these are lies, or, if truth, why so willingly revealed? In the end one gives up these transparent but baffling cases for those more complicated; at least there are recognized rules and categories for neurotics.

"Just the same I would like to lift the top off Effie Thorne's head and see what is really there," Dennis mused. "How was it like living with old Andy, how does it feel hearing people pant and gasp over his name, how does she feel remembering when he used to sleep with her just like the king and the Jersey Lily—was that the secret then of all these years' regret, that he was so fine in bed? But then women fight and lose all pride to hold such men. In that case there would be no self-sacrifice, even for an Effie."

Out in the street he saw that tiresome red-faced fellow who was always after him to write a 'piece' for the weekly he ran, the man who knew everybody and said "okie-dokie" to everything. Okie, as one instinctively thought of him, was with a gay party just leaving the Irving Place Burley and Dennis, now entering a seventh plane of being that one-armed sailor on the corner trying to roll his own cigarette, wished only to be unnoticed. No use.

"Hi, Dennis Orphen!" Okie always used one's full name as if it were a title and would fill hearers with awe—not *the* Dennis Orphen, as if he were Al Smith or somebody. He enjoyed knowing everybody in New York and said he did whether or no. He liked knowing the 'Greenwich Village Bunch' and it was no use telling him that East Sixteenth wasn't Bohemia and for the matter of that neither was Bohemia. Okie lived with his family somewhere in the Bronx—(though here Dennis recalled Okie always was insisting East Ninety-first Street was *not* the Bronx)—and it was no good telling him that one room on the fourth floor within gunshot of the Rand School wasn't deliriously racy bachelor quarters. Okie, in his envious remarks, seemed to feel that Dennis lay in bed all day in an actor's dressing gown while glorious coeds from the Rand School and teasers from the Burley paraded in and out in a never-ending orgy.

"You writers down here in the Village!" he would jovially exclaim, as though all you needed to do was wave a manuscript at a girl and she had a baby. No. Okie was a man to be avoided when possible as it was apparently not tonight.

"Come over to Lüchow's with our gang," he insisted. "We're all tight as ticks and tomorrow's Saturday."

"Work," said Dennis.

Okie breathed a blast of gin confidentially in his face.

"Theatrical people," he whispered. "Two fellows just got here from London—they're like that with Cochrane—they know Dame Sybil Thorndyke personally. The girls just got back from Hollywood. They're bridge hostesses."

"Great," said Dennis. "So long."

They were all tipping over each other more than was necessary and after a look at the two blondes and the two long-faced chinless young men, Dennis, with his wonderful new prescience, knew everything they were going to say from now on into infinity.

Okie's hand dropped cajolingly on his shoulder.

"One beer?"

"No."

"How about a little bock? You know this fella's a big shot, let me tell you, Dennis Orphen—he got a prize once—"

"Oh, for Christ's sake, Okie, leave me alone."

As soon as he'd said it Dennis realized he'd gone too far but you had to with a person like Okie. As the others pulled him away it was not pleasant seeing Okie's red embarrassed face. One of these days he'd need a hundred dollars and want to write that article for Okie, and Okie would remember being insulted. Dennis heard one of the two girls call out to Okie.

"Do you mind if Tony Glaenzer meets us over here? Lucille called him up and he said he would come."

Dennis suddenly turned around and caught Okie by the arm. Tony Glaenzer, part of Effie's past. That was different.

"Sure, I'll come along, old boy. Let's go."

Okie was mad. If he'd been sober you could have insulted him all night and he wouldn't have noticed but now he was offended.

"Oh yes, you'll have a beer with us all right," he sneered. "Okie-dokie. I get it. You got to have some Park Avenue in it before you'll join. Got to work right up to the time you hear Tony Glaenzer's coming along, then it's okie-dokie. Come on, then, phony."

His round red face in a ferocious scowl looked like a magazine-cover baby about to bawl. Dennis despised him.

"Can't blame me for wanting to get ahead a little socially," he said amiably. "I like a nice contact now and then."

Now he became Effie again, meeting Tony Glaenzer, discussing old times at the Beach Club on Long Island twenty years ago, evoking the old buried life, the buried woman. At the same time he was Dennis tomorrow telling Effie about Tony and his two blondes.

"Is he a Jew?" asked one of the girls pointing to Dennis.

"No, he's a Turk," Okie sourly answered and as this went over big he forgave Dennis for being a snob and slapped him on the shoulder fondly. "Good old Dennis Orphen. The red-headed Turk."

Lüchow's was filled with a lodge banquet and in every room middle-aged men grimly wore paper hats and clinked glasses with their big wives. The orchestra played polychrome waltzes and a fat man was stirred to get up and holding his stomach in, danced marvelously with a thin toothy girl who arched her scanty behind the way her crowd at Montclair always did.

"*Geschichten aus dem Wiener Wald,*" said Okie as they found their table. "My favorite piece."

Dennis looked around for Glaenzer, wondering if he could spot him from Effie's description.

"Four bock, Herr Ober," Okie shouted and then cupped his hand close to Dennis's ear. "Theatrical people," he whispered significantly. "Actors. Actresses."

The two girls were obviously not happy in their evening's outing, nor for that matter were the two young men from London. These narrow-chinned fellows carried on a private discussion about one Wylie and whether Wylie really meant things when he said them and funny experiences each had had with Wylie both here and abroad. Wylie was one of the most inscrutable, brilliant yet brutal characters Dennis had ever heard of. The chances were he would never meet Wylie. Supposing he did, at Caroline's for instance—it seems he was always at his cousin Caroline's parties; in fact, Caroline's were the only parties Wylie ever attended—he, Dennis, would march right up to him and say, "What did you mean that day on the *Bremen* when you gave Thurman that terribly strange look and said, 'Thurman, you can't go on like this, you know'?" No, he would never meet Wylie nor Caroline either, for that matter; he was fortunate indeed in merely knowing young Thurman. The two blondes kept exchanging glances of veiled meaning and took turns borrowing nickels from Okie to telephone wonderful men somewhere else. The messages were then relayed to the other on her return to the table, rather rudely, Dennis felt.

"Says call in about an hour," Ethel told Lucille. "We'll go up. Unless you want to call Van first."

Then Lucille went to telephone and came back, giving Ethel a meaning look as she resumed her seat.

"Something funny to tell you," she said quietly smiling, but did not say what it was Van had said, obviously something far too good for the rest of the crowd.

"Let's all go up to old Van's and have a good laugh," suggested Dennis.

"You don't even know who we're talking about," said Lucille with a superior smile.

Okie conducted the orchestra from his seat, waving both hands.

"*Sari,*" he announced. "Dum de dum de—that's *Sari.*"

Then Tony came in, walking right through the baronial beer parlors out of Effie's past, carrying in his head, which would never reveal these pictures, memories of a young radiant Effie, Effie in the formal gardens of the great Long Island estate Dennis could never quite paint, and as he saw him approach their table Dennis suddenly knew something Effie had never told him or else never known—that Tony had been in love with her.

"How do I know that?" he wondered but he would have sworn it was true; his heart beat fast as though he had found something of terrific importance to the world, something that must be telegraphed at once to all the papers—stop, press, stop, Winchell—

Tony must now be near forty but he was as slim and as weak-faced and beardless as Effie had described him years ago. Dennis felt annoyed with Effie that apart from this weak youthfulness he would never have recognized the man from her description. Obviously, in her preoccupation with Callingham at that time, she had never noticed that Tony was extremely handsome in a hungry, girlish, petulant way, that he was tall, lean, and rubbery as though he might snap back to the little spoiled child he was at any minute, that his hands were large, frantic, futile, crazy hands. It was plain to Dennis that Tony had not wanted to come out on a party, but it was also plain that he was always doing things he didn't want to because he was afraid some day something real might happen and he wouldn't be on hand to see it.

"Always wanted to meet you, Mr. Glaenzer," said Okie, beaming. "I run a little magazine, you probably have heard of it—*The Town,* and somebody's always writing in—'Why don't you get pictures of Tony Glaenzer's home,' they say, 'give us some pictures of that Tudor barn or whatever the hell.' This is Dennis Orphen. That's Victor Herbert."

"How do you do, Mr. Herbert." Tony sat down, sniffed at Ethel's drink. "Scotch and seltzer, thanks."

"*The Fortune-Teller,*" said Okie, conducting again but with his knife now instead of a forefinger. "Dada da da da. I'll get them to play the *Rosenkavalier.* They'll do anything for me here. Hey, Herr Ober."

What if he, too, should go telephone, Dennis speculated, what if he should ask Effie to come over to be surprised by the two extremes of her life spending a jolly evening together over bock? No, it would be more fun tomorrow.

Ethel and Lucille made a great fuss over Tony. The two actors thought they had run into him once at Caroline's. Did he know Wylie Meigs? Yes, Caroline was a friend of his wife. Mentioning his wife made Dennis wonder how this handsome fellow could have lived with Belle Glaenzer all these years, even with her fabulous fortune to ease the pain. Dennis could visualize Belle, as Effie's stories had built up the image—a moon-faced mountainous woman padding through the handsome plush corridors in the silent hours of the dawn up to the maids' quarters trying to still her heavy panting breaths and to keep the house from shaking with her Olympian tread, listening for her young husband's amorous whispers in this or that bedroom, sniffing for his cigarettes near this door and that, and occasionally being certain of her clues but uncertain how to stop whatever was going on, so up and down the hall she must wander, sniffling and moaning like a sick old hound. How could Effie have stood such a household? Dennis wondered. Even if it was her livelihood, trotting around with a rich old woman, how did she do it, how could she endure them?

It seemed the two girls knew Tony as the boyfriend of their chum, Boots, who was coming in from the road tomorrow. Tony was candidly bored except when discussing Boots and Boots' plans with her friends. When the talk shifted and became general he merely smiled fixedly at the tablecloth, and dabbled his long white futile fingers in the sugar bowl like a rich nursery child who knows he must not play with the sugar lumps but his silky fingertips enjoy the rough crunching of the sugar against them almost as much as he enjoys spoiling them for other people, surely a rich young man's simple, just prerogative. He shot an occasional sidelong look at Dennis and when Okie shouted or made flamboyant gestures of conducting, his face lit up as if active bad taste stirred his admiration.

"You were with Callingham in Lipps' one day in Paris," said one of Wylie's chums, deciding that here at least was someone worthy of an Englishman's friendship. "Andrew Callingham."

"Oh, he's a great friend of old Callingham," Okie explained with a lordly wave of the hand. "Nice guy, Callingham. I know him personally.

Or rather I know Wife Number Two. A Kansas City girl. Marian, that was."

"I heard he backed that Swedish dancer in Paris last year," said one of the young men. "There was quite a little talk."

"He brought her on a cruise once with us while Marian had dysentery in the American Hospital," said Tony. "Asta Lundgren."

Hm, thought Dennis, that's a new one Effie hadn't heard about, Asta Lundgren, eh?

"I read everything he ever wrote," said the dark actor, the one who had actually spent a whole fortnight with Wylie on a cruise. "I daresay I'm the only person who ever read his *Little Hazards,* his first. Wylie had a copy of it, you know. Quite rare now."

Little Hazards. He wrote it on his honeymoon with Effie. She still thought it was his finest book. Her blue eyes always filled with love for anyone who spoke of it, for then she could explain how every phrase came to be written, how funny Andy had looked in that dreadful shooting outfit in which he worked. She had typed it three times and even then there were so many mistakes—she was no typist after all—that they had to get a secretary in. It was Effie's book, really.

"This Marian is Wife Number Two, did you say?" asked Dennis, playing a game with himself—no direct questions, no admissions, all information must come out casually in the course of the conversation, and whether this information was for himself as a check-up on his speculations about Effie or for Effie herself, he could not have said.

"Who was Number One?" asked Okie. "What was she like?"

"Coldish," said Tony briefly, making a fortress on the table out of the sugar lumps. "Might have worked out only she was too noble. Forgave Andy every time he ran out on her."

"Is she alive? Did she fuss when he ran away with Marian?" Okie asked. "Marian had some good-looking pins, let me tell you."

"This first wife was my wife's companion when they met. That was Effie," said Tony and mussed the fortress into a heap. "Andy visited me. He was a big hairy roaring sort of guy—he-man. Loved trying out every woman he met, especially the difficult virginal type. Effie was that and of course he fell all the harder. He could never make her out. Still talks about her. He said to me, 'You know, Tony, a man can never tell the difference between the reserves of a deep, forgiving, all-understanding love and the polite indifference of a well-bred casual attachment. They act just the same.' So when Effie was noble about letting him go he couldn't figure out whether it was martyrdom or plain indifference."

"What was your guess?" asked Dennis.

Tony looked at him a little curiously .

"I've thought about it. You know I don't believe Effie gave a damn," he said. "She was unhappy all the time with him. She's happy now—lives her own life. We see her now and again. Has an apartment somewhere around here. Has a lover."

"Oh, she has a lover, has she?" Dennis pricked up his ears but Tony's next words explained.

"Another writer," said Tony. "Cares more about him than she ever did about Andy. Talks about him whenever we see her. Young fellow. This one's an æsthete, I guess, no he-man."

"Oh, is that so?"

Dennis saw the light suddenly. So *he* was supposed to be Effie's lover, that was the story. So Effie cared more about him than she ever had about Andy. So *he* was not the big he-man raper Callingham had been but just a little petered-out æsthete, eh? Angrily Dennis's legs stretched out under the table until his feet caught the ankle of the nearest blonde, Lucille. She looked at him inquiringly, and then smiled a little.

"What are you laughing at?" asked Ethel after a moment. Tony had lapsed into a bored, austere silence.

Lucille took out her vanity and made a new mouth over her old one, then glanced over the little mirror at Dennis with increased interest.

"Nothing," she said airily and hummed with the orchestra. "What is that thing, Okie?"

"'*Dein ist mein ganzes Herz,*'" said Okie, waving his menu in authoritative rhythm. "Dein-ist-mein-ganzes-Herz—dum-dee-da-dum—"

"I thought we were going to Harlem," Tony said to Lucille.

"We hate Harlem," said Okie disagreeably.

"That's the truth," said Ethel.

Tony got up.

"Well, I hate German waltzes and beer," he said. "I'll run along. See you at Boots's tomorrow, Lucille."

They watched him run along, his lithe elegant figure hurrying through the tables as if they might pursue him and bring him back.

"Doesn't like waltzes!" repeated Okie. "Why, he's married to an old Coney Island waltz!"

"Anybody that could stand that old woman of his all these years needn't be so fussy about what they like or don't like," said Ethel, personally insulted by his departure.

"He married her to get on with his music," said Wylie's friend. "Boy, is that irony! He marries her to get to Vienna and when he goes it's only with her to the spas for her varicose veins. Ha, ha."

"Tough," said Dennis.

"Yeah," said Okie, "a snob like you would stick up for him."

"I'm not a snob," insisted Dennis. "Would I be out with you folks if I was a snob?"

Everyone laughed but on second thoughts got a little mad. Even Lucille withdrew her foot and slipped it back in her shoe as silent evidence of disapproval.

"Where'll he end up?" asked Ethel. "He can't lift a finger for himself. What happens to fellows like that?"

"He'll end up in a flophouse on Third Avenue," said Dennis dreamily.

Okie was terrified at the mere words. He shook Dennis's arms pleadingly.

"Don't say such things," he implored earnestly. "Why should he end up in a snobhouse on Third Avenue? Not unless there's a revolution. Why should he?"

"It's the snobhouse for all of us quicker than that," said Dennis dourly. "The system's failing, the game's up."

"Oh, let's go, Lucille," Ethel urged her friend. "I can't stand it when people talk like this. And Van will be waiting—"

Lucille had permitted her foot to be won back again and was being appeased by Dennis's rather serious attention under the table.

"Van can go to hell," she suggested casually. "Who does Van think he is for Christ's sake—Mervin LeRoy?"

. . . the little nest itself . . .

THE PALE LOVELY CITY MORNING, thought Dennis, and was sorry for the country with its poor morning sky bereft of clangor blended into its blue. From a house across the court—and it amused him never to know what street those houses faced, came the sound of a piano; it trickled through the backporch trellising, sounds light and dark like shifting sunlight. Scarlatti, a laundress in the basement yard singing over her clothes-hanging, the swish of a broom on stone and hydrant splashing over cement court, the endless flow of trucks and streetcars and fire engine all translated into a steady throb in the walls of his fourth-floor room, a perpetual dynamo that operated the life of Manhattan. The walls throbbed night and day like a cabin next door to the ship's engines, and the silver-framed picture of Corinne in her bathing suit at Asbury Park, with Phil cut out of the background except for a white shoe, quivered out a Morse code against the wall.

So that was Tony. So he had a Boots who was on the stage. A little toots named Boots. So Callingham's new wife wasn't much. So Okie was afraid of the revolution and the snobhouses. So Wylie was the way he was. . . . Dennis looked over the *Mirror,* a stale one as it was only today's. He read Barclay Beekman's sprightly reports of the six hundred dollars raised for the Free Milk Fund by Mrs. Ten Bruck's brilliant Firebird Pageant and Ball at the Waldorf. It seems the costumes alone cost over fifty thousand dollars, but the rich spare no expense when it's to help the little babies of the slums. Nor for that matter, reflected Dennis, do the Communists even without a Mrs. Ten Bruck as La Flamme. How nobly do these hundreds put their little half-dollars together for a Webster Hall-Mercerized Firebird Pageant and Ball to help miners, all in order to break nearly even. There was direct action for you. Sacrifice upon sacrifice. However, looking on the bright side, both affairs are always well-publicized and it would be an ungrateful baby or miner who would prefer a bed to Mrs. Ten Bruck's Tropical Float or a sandwich to a program of hillbilly songs sung by loyal comrades.

He read Gladys Glad and was astounded to find that the secret of little Sylvia Sidney's success was in twisting her torso fifteen times right and left with deep breaths and an ounce of camphor dissolved in your witch-hazel. . . . Ah, here we are. MacTweed will publish on the tenth *The Hunter's Wife* by Dennis Orphen. It is rumored that this novel concerns the ex-wife of a well-known literary figure. Of Mr. Orphen's last book Lewis Gannett said, "Orphen knows New York like a fish knows water." So Mr. Gannett called him a fish. OK, Mr. Gannett. Effie would see that. There would be more of it every day and there would be nothing for him to say, no excuse, no denial was possible. Probably the name itself would come out in some gossip column and reporters would call up and ask Effie how she felt about it. She would be hurt at first, then freeze up the way she had over that biography of Andy someone had written in the *Atlantic*.

"Rather cheap," she would finally say, chin raised in a superior smile, "a little cheap after all. But then Dennis never did have any breeding. Not that I mind what he said about me—dear me, no—that's only to be expected from that sort of person."

She would take on her English accent the way she did in referring to people she disliked. She would turn into Lady Diana. At the thought Dennis's love rushed out to her—oh dear, lovely person, understand and forgive and be happy again, but don't be brave, don't be gallant or noble, it's far too heartbreaking.

If people, thought Dennis, only came right out and called each other an s. o. b. when they were just that, it would make the world a much finer place. It was these martyrs, these silent sufferers, these decent fine people, these chin-uppers that gave selfishness and crime its head start. Why, he thought, I ought to be tarred and feathered for telling all in this book. It would teach me to pick my material with more care, more decency. As it is, Effie will be noble; and next year, spoiled by this, I will write about

Corinne, so Phil Barrow will divorce her and she will starve but be noble, and noble bodies will be stretched from here all the way up to the printers, just because nobody called me an s.o.b. at the right moment. People are too well-bred, so on with little crime!

Somewhere on the mysterious street beyond those houses across the way a German band was economizing on *Wien, Wien, Nur Du Allein,* and when the combined notes of all four bronchial instruments failed on the 'glücklich bin' a lamed flute eked out the last bar. The piano across the court left Scarlatti and went into polite accompaniment for a frantic soprano, her shrill wings beat futilely against the locked octaves of a treble paradise and fell short a good half-note. The pianist is really good, thought Dennis, he has to accompany her for his room rent and how he suffers, for his fifteen a week. She'll never make a concert stage any more than she'll make high C, and for that matter neither will he—(but I alone know that)—because he won't have the money, and even if he did find a Belle Glaenzer to marry him she would only tie him up for life like old Tony, so wherever he turns he's wrecked.

The winter sun pulled aside a grimy negligée of clouds, a bit consumptive, this Manhattan sun, giving nothing but a pallid glow to windowpanes and a sickly fever to bare streets in summer, perpetual slush in winter. Instead of giving it went about its own racket of drawing life and color from city streets as it drew rainfall from mountain streams.

Dennis made himself coffee on the electric ring in his bathroom. Once a friend of Corinne's named Walter had nearly electrocuted himself that way. This fellow Walter was taking a shower while his coffee, or in this case his whistling teakettle, was on the electric plate. He reached out with his wet hand to turn it off when the whistle began to whistle and just then the shock came and there was Walter, great hulking fellow, captain of a team once, too, unable to let go, shaking away with shock after shock, but meantime the old whistle on the kettle was whistling so somebody came in from the bedroom—Dennis always suspected this little somebody was Corinne but she wouldn't admit it, it was just a nameless but very kind intimate somebody—and she did all the right first-aid things and fixed everything. Walter was saved, the shower was finished, the clever little heroine—(Corinne, you can't fool me)—poured the whistle water out of the whistling teakettle on to the drip coffeepot, a pleasant breakfast of delicious Maxwell House Coffee and last week's brioches from Longchamps was soon had by all, and that was why Dennis would never have a whistling teakettle, even though they cost only eighty-nine cents and were terribly funny.

"But they saved Walter's life, darling," Corinne protested.

"That's just it," said Dennis. "They'd always be reminding me of the bastard."

. . . keep him guessing . . .

"Every day of my life," wrote Dorothy Dix, a kind-faced gentle-woman in the New York *Journal,* "girls write in to me that their boy-friends for no reason at all are turning cold to them. 'I have loved John dearly for two years,' writes one, 'and have never given him a moment's doubt of it. Yet lately he seems to avoid me and seems annoyed by my gestures of affection.' Oh, my dears," continued Dorothy Dix, "don't you understand that nothing is so deadening to a man as certainty, that to keep a man mystified is the secret of holding his love? Don't let him be so cocksure, let him sense the possibility of losing you to someone else—keep him guessing if you would hold him."

So it was that when Dennis telephoned, Corinne put down the paper and answered that she really couldn't say when she'd be free to see him.

"Lunch, eh?" suggested Dennis, the cocksure.

"I couldn't possibly," said Corinne briefly, mystifying him.

"Why not?"

Corinne's chilly, polite silence proclaimed the insolence of such a personal question.

"You come over here at five, then," said Dennis, but again Corinne made it clear that she had important other plans. It was the same with to-morrow and next day. In fact Corinne politely implied that she was a very busy and popular woman for the next few weeks but if any of these fabulous engagements should fall through she would be most happy to give Mr. Orphen a ring. Goodbye, and thanks terribly for thinking of me.

What's up now, speculated Dennis, she must have seen me at Lüchow's last night or somebody told her, and anyway where had *she* been? He'd called up her house a dozen times in the evening changing his voice every time he got Phil and always Mrs. Barrow was out. There was no chart to the simple but cockeyed course of Corinne's emotions so, thoroughly mystified and even more annoyed, Dennis went back to the piece he was writing on Old Yorkville for Okie, taken from his last article on the same subject but with the tenses changed, to give it a fresh note.

Pursuing her role as suggested by Miss Dix, Corinne immediately taxied over to the Algonquin to lunch with Walter himself, just this moment arrived from three weeks in London. At least he was supposed to have been in London on business but Corinne understood and all the people Corinne knew understood that Walter had really been in Paris with Mrs. Bee Amidon. Walter's own wife had stayed home in the beautiful Larchmont home she had heckled him into buying. Walter was Phil's best friend but it was Walter and Corinne who really understood each other, who whispered in the kitchen over the cocktail-shaking while Phil and Mary played bagatelle. Walter knew all about Dennis and Corinne, knew all about Bee Amidon, and often Walter and Corinne stayed out all hours of the night confiding in each other the anguish of finding true love too late. For Walter had never loved as he loved Bee, and Corinne would never love anyone the way she loved Dennis. Bee Amidon had other affairs and even ran around with her husband more than was necessary and all in all made Walter miserable, while Corinne told stories of Dennis's casualness when her own feelings were so eternal and deep. Once these mutual confessions of great love unrequited had ended up on Walter's studio couch—he kept a room in town—but this episode was regarded as a foul and stricken promptly off the records and Corinne could not help feeling wounded when Dennis suspected her in the whistling teakettle business. Walter was always surprised that Corinne and Bee were not chums, but his confidences and expressed suspicions about his love had established such a hideous picture of the woman that he did not realize that in relieving himself of this monster he had given her to Corinne for keeps.

Nor did Walter think Dennis Orphen was anything but a big phony. He did not for a minute think Dennis gave a damn about Corinne as she herself once in a while darkly intimated. In spite of these mutual reserves, Walter and Corinne gave each other an amazing amount of reassurance. Concerning Walter's suspicions of Bee, Corinne said, "Why, darling, you just don't know women, that's all. Bee's simply crazy about you and she wouldn't dream of that dumb lawyer you're so afraid of."

Privately Corinne thought Bee was sleeping with ten dumb lawyers but Walter never guessed.

"Dennis never asks me to leave Phil," Corinne then complained to Walter. "Sometimes I think it's because there's someone else in his life, but really the only serious friend he has is that woman Mrs. Callingham, and of course she's much too old."

"He's too decent to ask you to give up a good home for the ups and downs of a writer's life," Walter told her as Corinne had wanted him to, though as Walter told Mary and Bee and all the other unknown repositories of Corinne's secrets, Dennis was really scared to death Corinne would plump herself down on him one of these days and try to trap him into something serious. As for this 'old' Mrs. Callingham—ha-ha—she was a damn fine-looking woman and not over thirty-four or so—not much over anyway and you could bet your sweet life a man wouldn't tie himself up with a little nitwit like Corinne when he could get a glamorous, famous woman like this Mrs. Callingham. He'd seen her in the entr'acte of *Biography* and you could tell right away she was a keen person. She was with Dennis and had her arm through his, talking and laughing. Walter has just given Dennis a quiet level look as if "No, I won't tell Corinne, you bum. What kind of a fellow are you anyway? Haven't you any decency at all with your women?" Because, the way Walter felt was that there was a certain code about intrigue the same as anything else and Dennis didn't measure up, though when Walter mentioned this to Bee Amidon she said men were always having very high codes for other men to follow and nobody ever measured up, but she noticed they all seemed to do about the same things.

"I met this Callingham one night at the Dôme, Bee and I did," Walter told Corinne. "He's a big good-looking guy. He'd flown over Persia and people were fussing over him like mad. Bee knew him. I told him there was this book being written about him. He was sore as the dickens."

"You shouldn't have told him," said Corinne. "He might sue Dennis."

She was having a pernod and having said so many nasty things about Dennis her heart was filling with love for him and a slight indignation at Walter. It was *his* fault she'd said Dennis was phony and shallow and insincere. Why did men let people say such things about another man?

"'Who is this Orphen, anyway?' says Callingham," said Walter and leaving out the deprecatory description he and Bee had eagerly furnished at the time he continued, "so we told him he was a very good writer and got a prize once."

Walter poured a brandy into his coffee the way Bee liked it. He missed Bee now but sometimes he thought it was more fun talking to Corinne about how he loved Bee than really being with Bee, for Bee never seemed to want to be alone with him, she was always asking every one else to join them. In fact the affair from her point of view was just loads of fun and that was all. She never cried or talked about divorces or any of the normal things, she just had a fine time as if it wasn't serious at all.

"What'd Whosis say when you told him who Dennis was?"

"He said Erskine Caldwell was the only writer in America worth anything," Walter finally recollected.

"That's because he's something like Callingham," Corinne deduced.

"He said America was dead anyway," said Walter. "He said we hadn't really produced anything he could dignify by the name of literature since *Three Soldiers*. He kept saying America is dead, dead and drinking straight whisky. I say, Corinne, let's get tight and cruise through the city all day. Mary's coming in tonight and if I'm sober I'll feel guilty about Bee and won't be able to carry the thing off."

It seemed a good idea to Corinne. That would show Dennis he couldn't be sure of her if she spent the day celebrating with Walter. Be cool, be aloof, don't let him be sure of you, Corinne went out to phone Dennis and show how cool and aloof she was.

"What's up?" he said. "I'm working. Want to come over?"

"Come over? Certainly not," said Corinne with a light tinkling laugh. "I just called to ask if you could come to our house for dinner the fifth of next month."

Dennis was plainly astounded by such a formal message.

"Good heavens, next month? How do I know what I can do next month? I'll let you know when the time comes. What kind of party is it anyway that I got to be asked so far ahead—a masquerade?"

"Just you alone. No party, I'm afraid," said Corinne stiffly.

"Well, I'll let you know when I see you."

Corinne allowed a significant pause to take place.

"In case we don't see each other till then I wanted to be sure, that's all," she graciously explained. "It's a Wednesday. Can you make it?"

"No," he said in tremendous disgust and the receiver banged up.

Corinne went into the ladies' room and made up again. It was always fun making up after a few pernods because they made your face freeze so it was like painting a statue. She went back to the dining room which was rapidly filling with witty wonderful characters and they were all drinking and eating like anybody else. Walter was entering his third brandy when she got back to the table. Walter was really terribly sweet. He understood about Dennis, too, that Dennis was too fine, too decent, to ask her to give up Phil's protection for his small earnings. Even if this new book was a great hit it wouldn't be as much as Phil made and she loved her nice little house on Sixty-fourth Street with its little garden and Dennis wouldn't want her to leave that particularly after she'd just fixed it all up. Walter understood how Dennis felt. It was the nicest thing about Walter, the way he understood about Dennis. She put her arm around dear Walter, standing behind his chair and pressed her mouth to his ear.

"Walter, I can't stay," she whispered. "I have to go over to Dennis's right away. You understand, darling."

Walter was, nevertheless, as mad as he could be, watching the cunning little figure in the leopard coat and green beret patter out of the room. It was all very well for wives to fail you or for your true love to fail you—they had some excuse, but for a friend—and after all he'd done for Corinne, too, fixing it up with Phil a million different times, and letting her weep on his shoulder, and not telling her all he'd heard around town about Dennis and Mrs. Callingham. After all he'd done as her one true friend the least she could have done in return was to help celebrate his return. What kind of pal was she, anyway?

Walter ordered another brandy, this time with soda, and sat gloomily thinking of all the things he'd done for Corinne, and for Bee too for that matter. After a while his mind saved him a lot of trouble by making the two into one woman, a wayward, double-crossing, lying little tramp. He wished he hadn't bought Bee that hat, though in another way he wished she'd asked for diamonds so he could accuse her of being plain mercenary. In crises like this, being left all alone at noon in a café with all day to waste, Walter's Michigan morality suddenly came out in full force to sustain him, and he wanted to see his wife and thank her for being a good woman. Someone you can believe in, that's what you needed, someone you could trust—

. . . Mrs. Callingham lying down . . .

—SOMEONE IN FACT LIKE Effie Callingham who had never lied to a living soul, who had never betrayed anyone, had committed no crime in her whole life save for the crime of one Great Renunciation Gesture, but like many renunciations she had not fully realized at the time how great and how final it would be.

Lying down on the black sateen couch, a guest towel soaked in cologne over her eyes as if this might relieve the ache that rippled through her whole body, Effie remembered saying it, saying the sentence, to Andy that day years ago. The scene unrolled itself again in the private projection room of her mind as if through seeing it so often she might learn where the mistake had been made, how else she could have acted. There they were, young hero, blond heroine, setting out in Andy's launch. The old launch, Andy's pride and extravagance, had been their refuge ever since their first meeting, a refuge from the Glaenzers, from Andy's increasingly insistent public, and finally it had become a means of recapturing their own romance in crises, but after three years the tranquil shores once the background of their idyll had become tainted with their misunderstandings, their long patient talks, the patient, civilized talks that, if one only knew it, are the end of love.

This reel, labeled "The Last Week-End," viewed always through headaches, pointed out only one lesson, Effie decided now: She should never have tried to be modern, she should never have tried to be generous. Her instinctive horror of Andy's infidelities should have expressed itself in natural ways—rage, or flight, rather than the philosophic, tolerant front

utterly foreign to herself. When Marian appeared she had been no different than a dozen other little affairs he'd had, it hadn't been necessary to
step out so nobly. But then remember she was tired after three years of
it, tired of entertaining her pretty rivals, tired of talking to husbands to
distract them from Andy's admiration of their wives, frightened of the
subtle shift in their relationship from lovers to good sports, tired of the
stiff smile on her face. Yes, something undoubtedly would have had to
happen, Effie realized that now. But it need not have been separation.
And she need never have brought things out in the open. She should not
have mentioned knowing about his feeling for Marian. She should have
been discreetly obtuse. She knew how he hated to feel guilty or selfish,
and he hated to promise faithfulness when he had no such intention. So it
was her fault. When they had their little weekend together she should
have made it theirs and theirs alone, instead of allowing Marian's name to
come between them.

She remembered the fog as they slipped out of Cold Spring Harbor,
the croaking of the foghorns far out, the tinkle of the bell buoys, and the
tiny lights of the village trailing over the hill. They stood together at the
wheel, wrapped in sweaters for the mist was chilly. Effie, sick with love
for him and utter despair over his remoteness, slipped her fingers into his
hand once and was stopped by his utter unconsciousness of her touch.
Presently he turned and patted her shoulder and that too, Effie reflected,
means the end of love.

Late that night they anchored somewhere near Port Jefferson for here
was country they knew and by day they could row ashore in the dinghy
and walk through woods and beachlands. Andy was soon asleep but Effie
could not sleep for wondering about the other girl, if indeed he really
loved her, and how she could bear it if it was true. A damp stinging wind
blew through the portholes and kept the cabin's screen door rattling on its
hook, she could hear the gulls squalling over their fish, could smell the
marshes. She sat up in her bunk, staring out at the few pale stars that
pinned together the shawl of night. Just before dawn she watched clouds
being torn by the wind, bits of gray blown furiously across the black,
massed into monstrous grisly shapes and ripped again. A loon cried out
from the pine-fringed shore, and the foghorns sounded steadily. She
clung to these sounds and to the steady beat of the waves as all that was
hers, for Andy asleep was the enemy, the stranger, her cry could never

reach him though his face was so near. She drew deep breaths of the salty night air, each second of this night must be remembered, it was this night against years. She caught his hand and held her lips to it desperately, but even while she held it this moment was gone; there is no present in love, only past and future, so that kissing him she was far away lonely for him.

All the next morning they did not speak of Marian. In the dinghy they rowed out of the harbor toward Setauket and Conscience Bay. They drifted into a little cove where the sea floor changed to curiously tropical vegetation and glittered and bloomed with scarlet sponges. Horseshoe crabs trundled about carrying their ugly shells clumsily like great false heads in a Venetian carnival; these creatures paraded in a body awkwardly, a little ashamed of their ridiculous costumes; once masked they could think of nothing to do but attach themselves to fellow sufferers, crunching over pebbles and weeds, finding soothing anonymity in crowds. A few fishermen sat in their rowboats farther out and a sailboat flaunting orange sails fluttered back and forth across the horizon.

Andy and Effie carried the thermos and rye on to the stony beach by the lighthouse. They lay back on the Sunday newspapers, Effie in her blue bathing suit, beach hat pulled over her face, Andy in trunks, brown body sprawled straight out, arm thrown over his face. Effie's eyes were fixed on the back of his hand, a strong large hand, fingers wide apart, spatulate. She touched it gently.

"Look," she said, "the hair on your hand is turning red, darling."

Andy suddenly chuckled.

"I know," he said. "Marian swears it's a toupee."

So there was Marian. Neither said anything for a moment now that the name had been spoken. Then Effie said slowly:

"You *are* crazy about Marian, aren't you?"

Andy did not move. The arm stayed over his eyes.

"I imagine so, Effie," he said.

Effie pulled the hat down farther over her face, turned away from him, heard her voice saying it, "Why don't you find out for certain? It might be the big thing in your life, you know."

Andy still did not stir.

"Do you really mean it, Effie?"

"Certainly. Why don't you go away with her for a while? See how you feel about each other. . . ."

Andy withdrew his hand from his eyes and regarded her curiously. She smiled reassuringly at him.

"I might at that," he said thoughtfully and then suddenly reached over and squeezed her hand. "Effie, you know you are a swell person. I don't deserve you."

A swell person. Words to remember while he packed his bags the next week, words to dwell on when he wired weeks later that he and Marian had decided to stay abroad a year. Swell person. Words to hug for years and years, extracting some meager balm from the hollow praise, words to ponder as you lay, head swimming with pain, heart wrenched with dull loneliness. Yes, thought Effie, better to be selfish, wanton, evil, vain, better for your own happiness. Let somebody else be the swell person while you cling to your happiness. Marian had done that. There was even something a little brave, a little gallant, about fighting selfishly for your love. It did show a fiery metal that was more appealing to a man than the martyr spirit. But if you didn't have that fire, if decency was stronger in you than passion, if the beloved's happiness was to you the object of love—One did what one could, Effie thought. One did what was in one to do, and then waited. Waited for what? Her mind turned the pages of Dennis's book . . . "waiting always for him to come back"—"the hunter will return, he will see the wise gentle wife she has become in his long absence."

A twinge of real anger at Dennis came over her. He had no right to peep into her heart, there was no secret thought safe from him, even now his wicked lenses might be directed at her, cynically analyzing her reflections. There were no longer private shutters against the world, the dearest friend, spying, becomes a foe. But who was there left now to be her friend, who but Dennis, the enemy? They two, offender and victim, must stand alone against the world, must be seen together, must cling together, he to show there was no malice in his work, she to show she bore no grudge.

She got up and drenched her face in cold water, stared at herself in the mirror, surprised as always to find that the tired lines in her face were still there, unwilling to admit to herself that these lines were more than temporary. She was to dine at the Glaenzers' tonight and she had promised Belle to come early in time to help with her letters. She suddenly put her face in her hands, sick at the thought of the Glaenzers, sick of the front she must always present to them, sick of her own face growing old in the mirror.

When the doorbell rang she thought it might be Dennis and she let it ring a long time while she made up her face, rouging heavily as though the bold color would transfuse courage into her blood. But it was a messenger boy with a note for her. She had a crazy conviction that this note would be from Andy, that the end of waiting might be here. She was so certain of it that she had an almost uncontrollable desire to tear up the message without reading it lest her instinct should disappoint her. You did not escape defeat so easily, though; it ran after you through your dreams, through fields and crowded streets, paging you. You could not escape by postponing it. Effie tore open the envelope.

My Dear Mrs. Callingham:

If you are any connection of the Mrs. Andrew Callingham now in our hospital under treatment for a cancerous condition we would appreciate your getting in touch with our patient. Her condition is grave and she is without friends in the city. You would be doing a service by calling on her or letting us know, if possible, what branch of the family to notify in case of a crisis.

Sincerely yours,
A. Waring
Secretary to Dr. Bulger, St. Ursula Hospital

. . . the press . . .

ANDY "Little Hazards" Callingham of Paris and Cannes will learn in this column that his wife Marian is seriously ill in a New York hospital.

New York *Evening Journal*

The famous love-birds Andrew and Marian Callingham "pfft" over four months ago in Paris. Marian walked out leaving her keys to a Garbo from Sweden. Paris friends say Marian is hiding in New York.

Daily News

An orchid to Dennis Orphen for his forthcoming tome showing up what famous novelist.

Daily Mirror

. . . an orchid to Mr. Orphen . . .

CORINNE CUT IT OUT and pasted it in his mirror.

"You act so funny," she said plaintively. "Sometimes you say I don't care about your work and the next minute you make fun of me for clipping things out of the paper about you. I don't know what you expect of me, honestly I don't, Dennis."

Dennis shook cigarette ash on the floor. He was lying on the couch, studying a dark stain in the ceiling which had shaped itself into a Gibson girl profile, pompadour and all. It occurred to him that he was facing a nice problem, whether to complain to the little Communist upstairs about his leaking pipe and be robbed of this pleasant work of art, or to let the matter slide and watch her gradual transformation into an elephant or an eagle. In the final triumphant moment when the whole ceiling was painted by little drops of water into a Winslow Homer battlefield or a Machine Age mural, who should leap through the plaster in a cloud of pamphlets but the little Communist himself, accompanied no doubt by all his furniture.

"Look," said Dennis, pointing to the Gibson girl.

"Silly."

Corinne was fussing about with a feather duster, her round little white arms thrust prettily out of blue apron sleeves. She loved wearing an apron around his room, she loved cleaning it all up although she was not in the least thorough and nests of pussies were always left undisturbed under his bed or quite blithely swept into closet corners. Anyway the little task, half-done though it might be, gave her an enjoyable sense of possession.

"Really, Dennis, what do you want me to do? One minute you call me a dumb cluck—you did, you know—and the next I'm trying hard to be clever."

"Be yourself, that's all, my pet," said Dennis. "Stay as sweet as you are, da da da da, and throw away all those clippings. Already the publishers are afraid of a lawsuit. I don't want to be reminded of it, see?"

"See what, Dennis?"

"See my darling."

Corinne sat down on the blue leather ottoman she had bought for him last Christmas at Bloomingdale's. She put her chin in her hands and gazed steadfastly at him.

"I wish you wouldn't call me pet names when you're just kidding," she said somberly. "I've wanted to talk to you about it ever so long. It's the way you kiss and make love, too, as if it didn't mean anything. I don't like it. Don't bother about me if that's all it means to you, just something to kid about."

Dennis raised himself on an elbow and looked at her, eyebrow lifted.

"Oh, I mean it, Dennis," she repeated gravely. "You've got to be more serious about us. It hurts me."

He could never imagine how it would feel to be Corinne. She made seemingly banal remarks, but they were really opaque veils behind which her complex little female nature dressed itself. Another thing was that no one in the world ever looked like Corinne. Maybe, as he sometimes suspected, the only really mysterious thing about her was her looks. Her hair was reddish, silky straight hair cut in distinct lines away from her temples, her skin clear white, high cheek bones, quite lovely brown eyes, far apart, sharp little nose, nostrils cut in high arcs, short full red lips, even little white teeth, a sulky charming little face it was in its odd little way, a face perpetually about to burst into tears so that even strangers felt impelled to offer a shoulder with a "There, there, little girl, cry it out," though a shoulder would not really be enough, one felt, she would burrow in the neck, in the armpits, under the skin like a cunning little beast. Dennis decided to take her seriously this time. She had not made any scenes for several days and it needed only a little argument, or today a little levity, from him to start one.

"The point is I'm worried about the damn book, Corinne. I don't want to hear about it. I wish I hadn't written it. It's making things very hard for my friend, Mrs. Callingham. She's had a tough break in her life and now this—"

"It looks as if her husband would come back to her," said Corinne unexpectedly. "He's free now. His second wife has walked out. You can't tell. I'll bet he comes back to his first."

Dennis digested this thought unwillingly. It had never occurred to him. He was annoyed with Corinne for suggesting it, he could not explain why. After all, there was some logic in it. Effie, too, had probably considered it a possibility. Andy may have sent for her. It wasn't likely that the Garbo mentioned was anything more than temporary. That must be the Swedish dancer Tony Glaenzer had referred to.

"Say, I wonder," he speculated aloud.

He felt an irresistible impulse to get over to Effie's at once and find out what this was all about, see if she really was involved in it. Maybe, with her successor gone, she might even have taken it into her head to go over to Andy of her own accord. Women were like that. Dennis got up briskly and pulled Corinne to her feet.

"You've got to run, my—er—Corinne. You simply can't take these chances. What will you say to Phil when he asks where you've been?"

"I'll just say I've been to Olive's," said Corinne, placidly enough. She slipped off the apron and powdered her nose. She kept a box of powder and some cold cream in Dennis's dresser and once when they were found elsewhere she made a terrific scene, suspecting quite shrewdly that somebody else had been visiting him lately. "I *always* say I've been to Olive's."

Dennis smiled a little wryly.

"That's what you told me yesterday when you wouldn't come down," he remarked.

"Yes," said Corinne and giggled a little. "I see a lot of Olive."

Suddenly Dennis had leapt up and was shaking her furiously by the shoulders. His jealousies were so obscure that even he was never aware of them until he found himself screaming or trying to choke her. Corinne could not stop laughing. It was Dennis, after all, who couldn't see anything funny in things, who took love seriously. You only had to make a light little crack and he was furious, ready to kill you.

"Goodbye, sweet," a little flushed but still gay, she blew a kiss to him from the door.

Dennis sat down after she left, angry that she had got a rise out of him. His nerves were in bad shape. He was afraid about his book, mainly, afraid of everything connected with it as if it were dynamite he had lit and now it was too late to withdraw the match. If Effie had gone back to Andy, which was highly probable in this improbable age, it was the book's fault. Well, he had to see her. He had to find out how she felt about an Andy who was free once again, free to take her back. He couldn't wait for a taxi but must feel haste in his own legs so he walked swiftly westward, across Union Square, up Broadway to Twenty-second and over to Sixth, Seventh, Eighth. Of course she wouldn't be idiot enough to go back to Andy, just because his second marriage had broken up. What did Corinne know about such things? But as soon as he thought of it a dozen such reunions came to mind, revivals of first loves. He had not called on her for two or three days because of the tension between them, but now he wished he had. It would most certainly have saved him these silly apprehensions. He grew angry at Corinne for putting them in his head.

On the doorstep he paused a moment, to calm his nerves, anticipating Effie's quiet laugh over his fantasies. Then he rang. He rang three times with no answer forthcoming. He called out the superintendent of the building. Mrs. Callingham—or rather Miss Thorne as she now wished to be called—was out, said the superintendent firmly. As a matter of fact, he added, Miss Thorne—or Mrs. Callingham, as you liked—had been gone since night before last.

"But where could she have gone? She must be home," Dennis stood there ridiculously arguing, for her absence seemed unquestionably final to him and not a mere night out as the superintendent implied. Effie was certainly upstairs as always, or perhaps the superintendent had misunderstood the name, or perhaps they both were dreaming, the whole thing was a dream, yes, that must be it, the whole thing was nothing but a dream—

. . . the dream . . .

I WISH I COULD FIND MYSELF, thought Effie, in the shadowy corner of the bedroom at St. Ursula's Hospital, it's not true I'm here beside Marian, hearing her breathe, it can't have been me myself who just sent the cable to Andy begging him to come to her, it can't be me whispering to her every time she opens her eyes that of course he loves her, of course he will come back to her, of course he won't let her die, of course he loves her, of course he does, it can't be me saying these words to her, any more than that thin worn body on the bed can be Marian, the gay dancing girl in the pointed hat and Columbine ruff at the masquerade ball, the eager little infatuated creature forever feasting her eyes on Andy, hanging on his words long ago while I smiled. It cannot be true, said Effie, it cannot be true; and the heavy breathing of the woman on the bed drowned out her thoughts as soon as they were born as the drums of Santerre drowned out Louis XVI's dying words.

I wish I could find myself again, but I hunt in vain for a familiar clue through every door of my mind and there is nothing of me there, nothing. There is no inside to me, nothing but tactile sensations—this momentary presence is tolerable, its absence pain, but why I do not know. It is as if a blowtorch had gone through me and left me outside the same but no furnishing within except a fear, a little fear left behind like an abandoned pet, an utterly cowardly deathly fear of being hurt more, but even that is not a human reaction but a mechanical one, shrill static in the empty cavern of the body, and hollowness hurts more than live quivering guts. Life, or even wonder about life, has vanished, my brain has broken up like an old wedding present into a thousand bits, I can put together only a few of them to spell out the anagram of my own misery. Repeated pain cancels itself, so that instead of details, facts, adding up, a blank appears at a given suggesting word or deed, and this blank, this mask, is more terrifying in its bleak impenetrability than any careful picture; it appears like a No Sale signal in a broken cash register when you know there was a sale, but it repeats the sinister blank inanely, endlessly.

This must be Marian, this must be the letter itself in my hand, this must be my own heart beating at the thought of Andy again on the fringes of my life. . . . What happens inside people like me who are braced for certain challenges and then spoiled a little, dikes weakened through lack of use, is that the storm, the ocean breaks in and we have nothing but our sheer shock, we have no emotional equipment to handle it, nothing, so that the lightning plays over naked heart and bowels, the blowtorch burns us out, and no pain is left, nothing but the numbed nerves, the broken will, the broken pride.

From a person one turns into a sick dog, defeating itself and its own recovery with every feeble whine. To wake and find myself gone, no part of me left, terrifies me, where am I?—is this Effie Thorne here in the chair, or is it Effie Thorne there on the bed breathing her last few hours away? Look, my hand, veins so clearly outlined, the turquoise on the engagement finger, my ring, my hand, but how quaintly remote, and my body, this very chair in which I wait, this heavy antiseptic air, all are part of another person's life, not of mine, for I am not real, it is as if meeting Marian again had changed me from human to vegetable and I can be conscious only of the sun, of light, and of shadow.

Marian's body twitched restlessly and Effie armored herself with a smile to greet her waking, a glittering unbreakable smile that should cut through dusk and suffering.

"Effie."

"Yes, Marian."

"You know I never meant—I mean—I did like you, Effie. It wasn't really taking advantage of your house at first—I mean—it was just that Andy and I—"

"I know, Marian."

"When this new girl came along a few months ago, this dancer, I realized things for the first time. I saw how you must have felt. I hated her—the way you hated me—"

Effie forced herself to interrupt the dry weary voice.

"I never hated you, Marian."

"Well—I couldn't stand their looking at each other and laughing. Can you understand that? Just that, I mean? I couldn't bear their eyes suddenly meeting over a joke. It sounds silly, something got into me—I was sick, too—and I—well, I bought a ticket to America. I wanted to show him. Then I got sick as soon as I landed and I wouldn't let anyone tell him. I thought I'd die just for revenge, but oh, Effie—I—"

"I know." How well she knew!

"She never meant anything to him, not the way I did. You know he told me he never could write decently till he met me. He needed me, he said. He started the trilogy as soon as we settled down together—his best work, too—"

What's the matter with my lips, they won't open, why can't I say something to her, why can't I say that's fine, that's dandy? Effie wondered. The nurse came in, a sharp white line in the gray of the room. She turned on the light and adjusted the pillows.

"Isn't it nice we've found your friend?" she murmured. "Now if we can only get hold of your husband and tell him to hurry right over."

"Yes," said Effie.

"This naughty girl wouldn't let us tell anyone she was here for weeks and weeks. She said she didn't want anyone to worry about her, so finally we just had to do a little detective work of our own. And now she's glad, aren't you, dear?"

"Terribly glad."

The nurse picked up the water carafe and left.

Marian had not changed much, Effie thought. Thin and gaunt as she was, her body scarcely more than a long fold in the blanket, her face still held the eager hunger it had possessed at twenty-three, the heavy dark hair and thick lashes were the same, the same narrow pretty mouth.

"What did you say in the cable, Effie? Tell me again. You're quite sure you didn't say I was too—too sick, you're quite sure you didn't ask him to come out of pity?"

"I said 'Marian ill,'" said Effie, "and the name of the hospital."

"You do think he will come?"

"Yes, yes."

Marian was silent, smiling a little to herself.

"I know he will," she said presently. "I know he'd come to the ends of the world for me. I'm the only person he ever loved. He's told me. Even after this girl came along. I'm the only person. So he'll come to me."

Effie got up and looked out the window into the gathering night, twin churches in twin duncecaps of illuminated spires across the street, a skyscraper emptied of workers now threaded with a single row of hall lights, and far-off flaming red sky over Broadway. Outside blurred suddenly into a shadowy reflection of herself in the windowpane, herself with churches, skyscraper, and red sky spreading over the ghostly outline of her head.

"Yes," she said, almost inaudibly, "yes, Marian."

...the Glaenzers' Effie...

Two eyes stared back at Effie from the other side of the shop window. The eyes, black, close-set above a Semitic nose and suave delicate mustache, traveled questioningly from Effie's face to brown oxfords labeled "Snappy" in the case, up again to Effie, and down to green antelope pumps named "Chic," hopefully back to Effie and over to silver sandals named "Classy," all three reflected in a mirrored floor edged with green velvet and carelessly studded with silver stars. The eyes, persistently persuading, roused Effie's numb senses. How long she had stood there staring at shoes she never saw she could not guess. She must have walked endlessly after leaving the hospital for she seemed to be somewhere in the Sixties and under the El Third or Second. With the black eyes still challenging her, she pulled her coat together resolutely and crossed the street, hurrying close beside a big man in gray coat, paper bag in his hand. She was afraid to be alone, and the big man did not mind her scuttling along beside him, he pulled her back so roughly before an oncoming truck that her arm hurt. "Thank you," she murmured. In a little while the mist in her head would clear, she would remember where she was going, why, and this year, this moment would drive out the too vivid past. She would remember Marian. Yet Marian would not shape in her mind as the sick woman in the hospital but the Marian of old, and with that girl came the rest. Already the familiar dreadful figures assumed possession of her brain, the cast of the endless comedy were on the stage ready again for her aching memory to feed them their lines. But for that last hour or two of blessed amnesia Effie thanked the gods.

The dismal blue lamp of a corner coffee-shop reminded her that she had scarcely eaten in the two days with Marian. She had slept on a cot in Marian's room. "I'm so afraid alone—really," Marian had pleaded with the nurse. As if Effie, too, now that they had presented each other each with her half of the magic ring, did not feel the same desperate fear of breaking apart again. What was that rule of the sea when a ship was rammed—keep the prow plunged in the split vessel, withdrawing brings on the wreck. . . . Keep the hurt close to you, then, stay with it, live with it, till all else is lost in this immediate urgency, mind and heart numbed. . . . The doctor had commanded her to go for the night. Go where? Step from the past into the bewilderment of the present, collect the bits that made up Effie Thorne of this year to present to the world, to Lexington Avenue, to the big man in the gray suit with the bag of oranges, present this assembled figure to the world of no-Andy? No-Andy. But Andy was coming back, coming back, leaving beautiful young Swedish girls for Marian, the only woman he ever loved. Drinking coffee and crumbling up a slice of dry pound cake into its cellophane wrapper at the lunch counter, Effie was alarmed to see her face in the mirror between the glistening percolator and the giant green ginger-ale bottle. Her felt hat was tilted back from her worn face and tears tracked aimlessly down her powdered cheeks as if someone inside her were weeping, weeping, though all she was conscious of herself was her aching spine, as if each tiny bone was a hot little ball, a little cranberry, she thought, exactly that, a hard little cranberry.

Supposing Andy did come back as Marian was so sure. . . . Dim shots of jealousy after all these quiet years frightened Effie; it frightened her to find a vengeful sardonic hope that Andy would fail Marian now as he had failed Effie before. Let Marian find out what heartbreak really was— after that her pain would be welcome! Desperately Effie captured and annihilated this rebel wish. Poor Marian, poor Marian, she repeated, poor, poor Marian, she could never stand what I did.

She paid her check and walked westward. She would call on the Glaenzers. If Andy was to return the Glaenzers would know, he would be certain to go straight to them. Moreover she wanted to be with them, she longed for the gloomy security of the dark old house as she had longed for it years ago only because Andy so often graced it and here were those who remembered. Here were people who could say, "Yes, it was true he did court you here, he did pursue you, he did love you, we saw him, we saw it all." Entering the old cage of thoughts the present was sloughed off as a mere inanimate shell protecting the living organism that was the past. Andy about to return, not for her, no, but for her rival, but nevertheless Andy, Andy, Andy, rose and swelled before her as the one reality till it lost all proportion like a heroic statue viewed too closely. Vainly trying to hold his image constant it kept changing before her eyes like a Coney Island mirror—wide, thin, long, squat—all she could recognize was the shaking in her knees over his mere presence in the room. In these long years his picture had dissolved into all the strangers she had mistaken for him, a man glimpsed briefly at a Pullman window, a waiter, janitor, actor, a little boy in Prospect Park on a tricycle, all the people she had glanced at twice because something about them reminded her of Andy. So she had lost his image in her anxiety to preserve it, and the defection of her mind so angered her that sometimes in her dreams she had shed real tears. Real tears when she had learned long ago that there was no one on earth who could afford to weep, no occasion worthy of it; or if there was, what reason, then, once begun for ever stopping?

She looked at her watch. Ten o'clock. If she could only find Belle alone, for Tony's faintly sarcastic manner would be too much for her tonight. Sometimes she could ignore it, his half-smile looking at her, see, it said, see what happens to women who lock their bedrooms against me, who push *me* away from their arms, see, their lovers leave them, they grow old and poor, they pay for spurning me in their brief youth. See, happy lover, his smile said, you come back to us for comfort, we enemies alone remain to you. . . .

Belle's dignified brownstone house resolutely pushed its way out of the shadow of penthouse apartments on either side, just as her respectable old limousine raised its body a few haughty inches above the gutter instead of slithering along, daschund style, like the newer models of the penthouse tenants. A high iron grilling separated this decent-person's-dwelling from the unworthy passers-by. There was something about the solid mahogany door, good lace curtains drawn taut over the narrow windows at each side, brass knobs scrupulously glistening, that made the occasional women callers wipe off their lipstick, pull down their skirts a little more.

Effie paused at the gate, bracing herself to be casual. The Effie of the Glaenzers today was the same Effie as of old, naïve, shy, blushing, target for sarcasm, apologetic, inferior to all in wit, beauty, or intelligence, as ready to be astounded at any Callingham's protestations of admiration as to be abused by Belle's caustic recrimination. Outside, as the former wife of Mr. Callingham, as Mrs. Callingham, woman of the world, Garden Apartments, West Twenty-second Street, it was different. Outside the irongrilled gate on East Seventy-first Street she had grown, become a figure in a small Bohemian world, living quietly but always admired by a few sensitive young men, earnest artistic fellows as a rule who talked breathlessly of Andrew. The absent Andrew was the focus of this modest salon, though when Dennis Orphen appeared in her life this little group had fallen quietly away. Effie wondered about it a little, for the little circle of admirers had been something. But then Dennis was enough; egotistical, violent, loyal, he brought her the best of the active world like a papa robin bringing home the cream of the bait. Dennis was enough. Changed under his influence as she knew herself to be, gayer, happier, more integrated, her Glaenzer self still remained the same, uncertain, shy, girlish.

She found herself tonight mechanically adjusting her hat as though this futile gesture was a fairy wand transforming her from a harrassed shaken woman into the nice untouched youth demanded by the Glaenzers.

"I'll have to tell her about Marian being here and Andy coming over and I mustn't be shaky about it," she thought. "I ought not to let them see me this way but I've got to talk to somebody."

Somebody—but not Dennis. Not after the book. There must be more of a front for Dennis than even for the Glaenzers. A front for Everybody, the enemy. A special public face decorated with a smile, a special manner. Trying out a smile tentatively, she saw a man slip beside her through the iron gate. It was Dennis, and in the sudden pleasure at seeing him she almost forgot for the moment that he was Enemy.

"I looked everywhere for you," he said, quite angrily. "You've got no business worrying me this way. I've got work to do, damn it, I can't be chasing around morgues and police stations hunting for you. It's too childish running away like this, never telling me, never even a note! How was I to know you'd be coming up here to the Glaenzers'? I just took a chance, and as soon as I got here I wondered what I'd say—where's Effie? and they'd say who the hell are you and what's it to you?"

His battered hat was set sidewise, Napoleonically, on his tousled sandy hair, his tie was over his shoulder somewhere, his vest was buttoned up wrong, his eyes furious, and he smelled strongly of Scotch.

"I was worried." His bombast collapsed quite simply. "What happened? I couldn't find you. I couldn't imagine what happened."

"Do you want it for a new book?" Effie asked wearily. Exhausted herself, his tired hysterics did not move her.

Dennis was crushed.

"I got feelings," he said. "I'm a writer but I still can feel. Don't run off again, please. Let me stay with you here—I can't stand thinking of you alone and upset. I was afraid it was the book that started it and it was too much on my conscience."

He followed her up the steps and in the dark vestibule caught her arm urgently.

"All right, come in with me," Effie said, beaten.

She rang the bell. Now her Dennis world and her Glaenzer world would merge and for her hereafter there would be no refuge in one from the other. Her two little spheres would combine against the two Effies to laugh, to study her pretensions; the Glaenzers would smile at the proud Effie Dennis knew, and Dennis would despise the hesitant apologetic Effie of the Glaenzers. Between them they would leave her nothing. It seemed to her that in the last few days she was being steadily relentlessly stripped of all armor, all retreats were being cut off, no mystery was left her for pride's sake, no person but would know her story and her poor excuse for living. Let her die, she begged, let her be the one instead of Marian. She was too tired to struggle for herself.

As for Dennis, his anger at his own weak-minded worry over her now expressed, he was relieved, but there ensued an embarrassed sensation of being caught unawares by an unexpected emotion, and now his vanity came back, he didn't want to visit her damned Glaenzers if it was to them she turned in her hours of need instead of to him. Besides he knew them, knew them too well from his own story of them written without ever having seen them; he didn't want to live over his own novel. So, reluctantly he entered the hall behind Effie, afraid that his description of the "Glasers" as he had named them would seem pale by contrast with the original. He had a nauseating sense of entering the looking glass, of dreaming true, and once inside the door of horrid magic to follow. Even the gnarled old dwarf butler he had plagiarized from Effie's anecdotes, though only the other day leafing over the first printed copy he had complimented himself on inventing the character. He saw himself stepping into a living material world of his own mind's creation; here was the dark tomb-like hall he had described with the little round stained-glass window over the first stair landing. Through the open carved oak doors on the right he saw entwined bronze fauns upholding candelabra over the alabaster mantelpiece of the reception room, saw the blurred pouting face of an ancestor in oil on the wall, the formidable blue brocade sofa, the gloomy electric logs in the fireplace. This was all in Chapter Nine of his book, and a faint chill crept up Dennis's spine that his literary shadow should have investigated so truly, or worse, that his so-called creative process was sheer Pelmanism, careful records of other people's conversations. His eyes stole up to the niche at the head of the stairs, not daring to believe that here would be a terra-cotta madonna. He breathed a sigh of relief to see in place of his own guess a large hideous Chinese vase filled with gloomy lilies.

"Belle likes lilies," Effie said. "The house always smells like this. Like a funeral."

They followed the old dwarf upstairs.

The rich, the good, solid old rich, live in wretched style, reflected Dennis. These ponderous old mausoleums with jail windows, moldy walls, dark high hallways, heavy dark consoles or carved chairs crouching in every corner like rheumatic old watchdogs ready to pounce on intruders, heavy-padded floors, these houses were to haunt and not to dwell within or visit. Poor Tony Glaenzer, Dennis thought, poor bastard, he should have picked a jolly phony rich woman, a penthouse nouveau, a flashy marcasite oil heiress with a nice dash of bad blood; that would be a gay vulgar prostitution, but never this substantial, true-blue Bank of England type.

The upstairs hall was a large rectangle with two crystal wall clusters dimly illumining an enormous Venetian oil painting, framed with alarming solidity for eternity. Three dark mahogany doors were stonily closed to view but double doors opened at the far end and from here voices could be heard. In here the dwarf vanished, carpets so deep, the walls so silent that you could hear his old knees crack as he walked and his wheezy asthmatic breathing even when he was out of sight. Effie walked on in without heeding Dennis's hesitation. He stood still in the hall with his eyes shut tight, fearful again that the voices he dimly heard in there would belong to the creatures whose story he had so cleverly told, not told, he corrected himself, but imagined, built up from nothing but the sticks of a few chance remarks, for now it seemed to him Effie's anecdotes had been not the base of his novel but the merest springboard for his own original imagination. If here and there reality fitted fancy so much the finer fancy, the artist brain outguesses God. True, he granted grudgingly, once a story begins in the hidden cellars of the brain, a thousand little thievish atoms steal out automatically raiding friends' confidences, woes, loves, desires, to build and furnish complete the edifice which the artist, erasing all other sources and signatures, canceling all debts, believes his own magnificent sorcery. Bewildering to find the structure laid brick by brick of simple facts filtered cunningly through sleep or memory. No magic here at all, alas, but a tale reflected again and again in a dozen mirrors, shadows, and gaps filled by conjectures, and even the prophetic gift operated by a secret statistical mechanism. So here was Dennis Orphen, entering Chapter Nine of a book by himself, disturbed by the growing conviction that his genius was no more wondrous than an old file. He shouldn't have come in here, anyway, he thought, for there was in his novel no role for Dennis Orphen; he had no business following his heroine brazenly through her own secret story. Wells wouldn't do such a thing. Proust wouldn't have. No decent author would step brashly, boldly into his own book. He hesitated outside the drawing room door again, heard his name asthmatically creaked, and a distinctly rude, "Who? Who, Milton? Oh, hello, Effie." No getting out now. He would throw salt over his left shoulder, murmur an incantation, before subjecting himself to further necromancy.

. . . salt over left shoulder . . .

In a huge black plush chair, in a ring of grisly bluish lamplight contributed by a great silver lampshade, sat Belle Glaenzer, a vast dough-faced shapeless Buddha in black velvet that flowed out of the chair and spilled its inky folds into the du Barry roses of the thick carpet. There should be an emerald in the middle of her forehead, thought Dennis, and a great cabuchon ruby glittering in her long-lost navel; like an automatic traffic policeman they would direct stop-go-stop-go-stop. This vast blob of female flesh was nothing he could ever have imagined, thank God, thought Dennis, setting his own creation down beside her for favorable contrast. Behind the throne the room seemed surprisingly small and inadequate, though this, on second glance, was actually not true. The ceilings were so high that the rococo splendors of the cornice, dividing as it did green tapestried walls from a ceiling-pool of cupids, was lost in shadows. On the walls were further powerfully framed visions of Venice by Caniletto and, appropriately enough, a gentle Van Cuyp cow waded across a pastoral brook over the fireplace to examine jealously an ivory miniature of Belle at twenty. A great lion-skin spread from one of Belle's large sandaled feet to the divan that faced the fireplace. This beast's great jaw was smugly closed in a gentle simper, though not because a fanged open mouth might terrify the guests but, as Effie had once explained to Dennis, because stuffing the tongue cost fifteen dollars extra at the taxidermist's and Belle was not going to have this gift—from Andy himself—run into money. This passive beast was all that Dennis recognized from Effie's many anecdotes, but the room, apart from that, depressed him hideously, made him want to run quickly before he was caught as Effie was in this life. Awful, he thought, awful, and his desire to hang on to Effie now that he'd found her again melted before his rebellious hate of settled houses, nailed-down carpets, murals, all investments that smacked of permanence, of long live the home, long live property, long live this cancerous, highly-respected ménage, oh stuffy-stuffy-stuffy detestably, inalterably fixed, smug, fortunate, blessed-by-the-church property.

I must move from my room tomorrow, thought Dennis, before I too get trapped. Never let me be party to the fetish of permanency, the snug-as-a-bug-in-a-rug fetish. Possessions need camphor balls and in time the possessor reeks of the musty smell himself, his brain smells of bank vaults. And save me from Fat, too, prayed Dennis, repelled by the monument to Hollandaise in the black velvet chair, though, he reflected, fat people never go crazy. Come to think of it, all the nuts were skinny beggars, there were no fat ones—or were there? . . . A great ball of dough, Belle Glaenzer, thought Dennis, not woman at all, her huge breasts were as sexless as Earth itself. Caught between dobs of pasty flesh, her little black eyes darted restlessly about, lively little squirrel eyes, imprisoned in fat.

"Well, Effie," said Belle without stirring. Her voice was a shock, a deep hoarse masculine voice that seemed to come from somewhere quite apart from the squirrel eyes or the body, from somewhere behind her. Perhaps a priest stood in the velvet curtains behind her and spoke for the oracle. Effie bent over Belle and kissed her white passive cheek, crossed eagerly to the divan where a bald, ruddily plump little man sat. He banged a sherry decanter abruptly down on the coffee table as Effie approached, and seized both her hands.

"Not my little Effie," he cried. "Not my dear, dear little Effie. It must be fifteen—no, sir, by God, twenty years."

Effie sat down beside him, her face suddenly relieved and radiant.

"I needed someone to talk to," she said. "I don't know why I didn't think of you before, Dr. MacGregor."

That's a new one, thought Dennis, she never mentioned him to me, but I knew the story needed him and I put in the Jesuit priest. That at least I did make up. . . . Watching Effie change in this room, he compared the group and background with his own printed description.

I had the same atmosphere, the same feeling, he thought with complacent triumph, and what's more I got it with entirely different objects. The feeling of the place, the mothball mummified quality I caught as truly as if I'd been here. Yes, I do have a psychic gift, not mere journalistic memory. . . .

Intent on his observations, Dennis as usual forgot that he was not invisible. He was made conscious of himself, the man, not the curious literary prowler, by Belle's direct antagonistic scrutiny.

"Who's this man, Effie? You can't leave him dangling over there like a dummy just because you see MacGregor again?" she boomed out. "Anyway you didn't ask if you could bring company. You might have spoken of it."

Effie, hands still in MacGregor's warm grasp, drawing friendliness, protection, strength from this contact with the old man, leapt away at the reproach, made her introductions.

"Dennis Orphen," she said. "He lives near me."

"In Chelsea?" asked Belle.

"No, no—near Union Square," Effie stammered and flushed as if, just as Belle suspected, the fellow was a dubious connection indeed.

"Union Square?" repeated Belle, examining critically Dennis's none-too-impressive figure. It seemed to him that his always askew tie jumped naughtily even farther behind his ear at her hostile survey. All very well for a writer to examine the world but damned unjust for the world to examine the writer. Dennis scowled at her. He wished he dared make a face. "Union Square never recommended any visitor yet, young lady. Is he one of those radicals?"

"No," said Dennis flippantly. "Not even a fellow traveler. Just a window-shopper as we say in the Party."

"We saw some kind of demonstration down there last week as we were driving," said Belle. "Disgusting."

"Dennis isn't dangerous, Belle," Effie said and smiled at Dennis, conscious of him as a stranger, awkward and foreign in this part of her life. This was her Andy-life, and for that he was an enemy, a spy.

"Sit down," said Belle.

Dennis sat down.

"That's not to sit on," roared Belle. "That's a very old, very valuable Venetian chair. I paid nearly five hundred dollars for it. Four eighty-five. Sit over there."

Dennis hastened to obey and dropped down cautiously on the ottoman indicated.

"Five hundred for a chair and not a penny for my Babies' Hospital," said MacGregor gloomily. He appealed to Dennis. "Mrs. Glaenzer is the meanest, stingiest old woman of all the mean stingy old women in New York. Furthermore she's eating herself into the grave. That's her second box of candy tonight, Effie. At least you kept that away from her when you were around."

"She gnawed up all the sugar lumps instead," remembered Effie. "Where's Tony?"

"Tony went to a musicale at Caroline Meigs's," said Belle. "They were to play Haydn. I hate Haydn."

"I remember," said Effie.

"Effie's changed, hasn't she, MacGregor?" said Belle, fat white fingers fumbling among the silver-wrapped bonbons on the arm of her chair. "Lost her looks. I look younger than Effie and I'm over fifty."

"I should say you were over fifty," said the doctor mildly. "You know perfectly well you'll never see sixty again, and if you think all that face-lifting makes you look anything but horrible, just you take a peek at yourself in a well-lit mirror."

"I've got a new cream, Effie," confided Belle, unperturbed. "Made of porcupine livers or something. Thirty-five dollars. You ought to buy yourself some—take away that drawn look."

"We get that drawn look trying to make thirty-five dollars, don't we, Effie?" said MacGregor dryly. His eyes, small and guarded, kept darting inquisitively toward Dennis, but Dennis balked this examination by fixing his eyes boldly upon him. "Well, well, Effie! What have you been doing? And what do you hear from Andy? You know this is the first time Belle's let me call since she ordered me out—let's see—that was just after you and Andy separated."

Dennis was aware of the bleakness that descended on Effie at the name. Her slender shoulders slumped, incalculable weariness was in her face and body. Stabbed with sympathy and love for her, Dennis looked away uneasily, tried to fix his attention to Belle's tapering hand fumbling among the chocolates so lovingly, choosing her pet very slowly, very carefully, as if she were in no greedy haste, no indeed, as if it were nothing to her, that rush of ecstasy to the tip of her tongue the instant sugar touched it. The robber fingers withdrew reluctantly from the candies with only one treasure but with it in her mouth her eyes continued to keep passionate watch over the others. Be happy, little coconut fondant and almond paste, Belle's adoring tongue will soon appreciate you too, all in your turn.

"Effie never hears from Andy," said Belle bluntly. "He never even sends her his books, though he has them sent to Tony. Effie has to go out and buy them."

Effie did not reply for a moment, clinging to MacGregor's hand tightly. Look at me, Effie, Dennis silently pleaded, you've got me. I'm here. Don't count on these wretched mummies.

"Andy's coming back any minute," said Effie, trying to sound casual. "You see Marian's here, sick, cancer they say, at St. Ursula's. I sent for Andy."

"Marian here! Where's Tony? Tony ought to hear this. Effie, it can't be true."

Dennis looked at Effie's drooping shoulders, downcast face. So Andy was coming back. Corinne had guessed right in a way. Why couldn't she have come to him, wasn't he her loyal friend, staunch supporter these three years, why couldn't she have come to him with her news? She needn't have come to this smug, smothering house. He was angry at her for leaning against the little doctor's broad shoulder—ah, here, here, her sad body cried, here is refuge, here is friendliness, here is sweet neutral ground between Belle's placid brutality and Dennis's too-sharp, too-inquisitive sympathy.

"If he comes," said MacGregor, "if."

"I doubt if he does," said Belle. If I was at all shy, thought Dennis, I'd be mowed down by that horrible old woman. She might at least offer me a nip of the old boy's sherry. California, at that, I'll bet. I know these stingy old connoisseurs. Has her imported bottle in her own room but the ninety-cent bottle out for company. Sure I know her, I invented her, didn't I?

"He won't come," said Belle, voice rasping and hoarse as if words were pumped from a dry rusty old well. She makes it sound that way on purpose, thought Dennis shuddering, like a nasty spoiled little girl. She should have been smacked down in kindergarten for it, except that fat little rich girls were always analyzed instead of smacked. Fleetingly he saw himself at five, undersized, sandy little squirt with freckles and no eyebrows and two front teeth out, scratching raucously with a fine new red-white-and-blue-wrapped slate pencil on red-braid-trimmed slate. . . . Miss Hough giving him a good cuff on the ear for his nerve-racking noise, and his outraged explanation bawled out to the whole class—"But all I was doin' was makin' a pine tree!" Belle Glaenzer's larynx scratched a pine tree on slate every time she opened her mouth, and no Miss Hough to slap her for it, either.

Dennis heard her leisurely scratching off a pine tree to Effie—"No, I doubt if Andrew Callingham will come back to America. He doesn't like us here—he made his big name in Europe and he'll never forgive us for that."

"But if Marian is here seriously ill—" expostulated MacGregor, still patting Effie's hand. Now what was there about a few feeble pats to make her feel better? Dennis wondered, annoyed. Next she'll be cheered up to hear that it's all for the best and it's always darkest when it's darkest.

"Andrew hates scenes," Belle boomed out, rolling her cocoanut fondant about in her cheek at last. "Deathbeds and all that. Andy's not at all sentimental. He won't come for any woman in the world, dead or alive, if there's going to be a lot of crying, not if he's the man I know."

"He will," Dennis heard Effie say firmly. "Oh, he will come, Belle. You'll see."

Effie's eyes met Dennis's haughtily. You, too, you'll see. So certain had her spoken words made her, so sure, that Effie drew away from Mac-Gregor's friendly arm and sat upright, chin lifted, looking calmly from Belle to Dennis. The words made her know what she had not known before, that she wanted Andy to come, that to come for Marian's sake was for her sake too, for love's sake. Inextricably she and Marian were bound together, waiting for him to come to them across the world, waiting for him to prove he did care, he did love—which woman was not the issue now. Demanded now was proof of love stronger than his own ambition or his present lust. For Marian, dying, and for Effie, long believing, there must be testimony that here was a man worth death and endless fidelity. A short hour ago Effie had been frightened by the flicker of passionate jealousy for Marian; now she was surprised by her sudden knowledge that she and Marian were one, their fates were entwined, Marian's last desire was hers also. . . .

She looked past Belle's dark shadowy bulk to the alcove beyond where the French windows led down into the stone garden; she could see herself dimly in that garden, iron balcony rail patterned in lamplight on the garden floor, she could hear Andy imploring her to love him.

"But how can I say that this is love?" she had patiently asked him. "How can I know? How does anyone know? If it's something that fills you up, that gives no place for any other thought, something that rolls you out like a—like a machine so there's nothing left of you, no wish, no sense, then this is love, but it doesn't make me happy, it's like doom, like melting into eternity and I don't want to lose myself—I don't, Andy, I don't. How do I know this is love? It couldn't be love, darling, to make me so lost, so lonely, so blind and deaf. I can't see St. Thomas's spire—I can't see trees in the park or the sky—I can't read—I can't hear Tony playing, for you're outside, everywhere, all about me. Is that love? Isn't there some way of loving and being oneself too? I don't like to be so lost, so drowned—no, darling, if this is love, then I don't want it, I don't like it, I'm afraid."

Lost . . .

"If he comes," Belle's voice scratched out another pine tree for Miss Hough's nerves, "if he comes he can stay here. You know how fond he is of Tony. They've always got on. Tony helped you two pull the wool over my eyes, naughty boy, after I told you both you were making a mistake. I was right too, wasn't I, MacGregor?"

Wool indeed, thought Effie. They had told Tony everything from the start, partly to gain his support in eluding Belle's antagonistic barriers, and partly because Tony was then a lonely miserable young gigolo-bride-groom, just finding out how bad his bargain with Belle was to be. At nights he would knock softly on Effie's bedroom door. "If you don't let me in, I will tell Belle, I'll tell about last night and about your staying on Andy's boat. Let me in or I'll tell Andy you belonged to me—let me in, please, please, Effie." . . . Each night she pushed the dresser against the door, not trusting the lock, each night for months till the day she slipped away with Andy. Pulled the wool, indeed, Effie thought now, as if Belle had ever asked for anything but wool.

"Andy owes Tony nearly four thousand dollars," Belle said, turning to Dennis politely at last as if in such small talk he might justly be included. "He's made plenty since he borrowed it, too. I'll certainly talk to him about that. With stocks going down and our Long Island place costing more than ever, we can't afford having big sums out. What do you think, young man?"

"I think it's too goddam bad," said Dennis, jumping up suddenly. He could not bear rich people complaining of their poverty, and since that

made up most of their conversation he might as well face the fact that
this class was poison to him, he'd be sick for a week just thinking of Belle
Glaenzer. How Effie could endure it! . . . She was looking at him at last,
eyes widened as if his voice had brought her out of a dream. Like Flip, I
am, he thought bitterly, to her Little Nemo; I wake her out of it but she
doesn't want to be wakened.

"Effie," he cried out—he had the floor now, after that incredible
Madame Chairman had gaspingly dropped the gavel—"come on—let me
take you home—you're tired—"

Effie quietly rose.

The red-faced little doctor got up, looked curiously at Dennis stalking
to the door without so much as a goodnight. I look like some little pest
from Greenwich Village, Dennis thought angrily, some lousy little Stew-
art's Cafeteria poet, they're thinking, what has Effie come to running
around with a squirt like that with no hair on his chest, no foreign hotel
tags plastered on his behind, he doesn't even look like Max Eastman, that
would be something at least.

"Come on," he muttered fiercely, jerking his thumb toward the door.

"Ring me up at the hotel any time you want to see me, child," he
heard MacGregor say, "any time, my dear. If Marian needs me, if you
want to talk over anything just as we used to—anything, anything in the
world—"

"Well, well, well!" Pine trees on the red-braid-trimmed slate, scratch,
scratch, scratch, dark ancestor in oil glowering farewell from the downstairs fireplace, gnarled hand of the humped old butler on the outer door.
Then they were outside—free.

Dennis kept her arm as they walked over toward Fifth. It was going
to storm soon. Papers blew down the Avenue, ash cans rolling over in
areaways clattered against stone walls, the few midnight pedestrians,
hanging on to their hats, hurried for shelter. The sky was a coat of mail,
the bright gray twilight that precedes the night storm. Taxicabs with steel
antennae scavenged the city looking curiously transparent in this false
light. A few large raindrops fell and a discarded newspaper scurrying before the wind blew frantically against Effie's skirts. Dennis, sheltering
Effie with his coat, held up a finger for a cab.

"Thank you for coming," murmured Effie, clinging to him. "I didn't
know how much I needed you."

It began to pour. A taxi slid to the curb and Dennis pushed Effie into it before another couple running up the street behind them, could steal it. Someone called out his name.

"Why, it's Dennis. Hello there!"

Dennis jumped into the cab, banged the door shut behind him. As they drove off he saw Corinne and Phil Barrow staring after him in blank astonishment.

"She knew you," said Effie in surprise. "What a pretty girl. Why, Dennis! Who was she? Why—why *Dennis!*"

"Mistake," said Dennis curtly. "West Twenty-third Street, driver, and stop at the Eighth Avenue uptown corner, the liquor store. What we need, my dear Mrs. Callingham, is a stiff hooker of Johnnie Walker."

The rain poured down blindingly, it drove slanting tears across the windowpanes.

"Did I ever tell you how I learned to skate?" said Dennis. "I was visiting my aunt in Vincennes and it was Christmas."

Effie, wrapped clumsily in his topcoat, dropped her head against his shoulder and fell asleep.

I I

. . . so goodbye, Mr. Orphen . . .

"'So let's call it a day and be glad we knew when to end things,'" Dennis read aloud from a cream-colored note. "'I hope you realize the whole affair has been no more important to me than it has to you and certainly right now won't break my heart any more than it will yours. So goodbye—'" here Dennis choked and flourished the note in the air, tore open his pajama collar to beat his chest dramatically—"'and so goodbye.' I would have liked farewell here—the whole paragraph is lousy with redundancy anyway. And there's more—dear, dear! . . . 'So goodbye. You have never cared for anything but your work and apparently for that Mrs. Callingham, judging by the way you were hanging on to her the night you refused to speak to me. As for me'—always talking about herself— 'I am happily married. I love Phil dearly and should never have mixed up with you. Damn everything.' Tut, tut, we're losing our head a little. 'Anyway, this is goodbye. P.S. You can keep my cold cream and apron and negligée but please return my copy of *The Wind in the Willows* as it was a present to me from Phil.'"

Dennis sat up in bed, letter falling from his nerveless fingers.

"I've lost her," he cried. "I've lost my little Honey Bear, my little Honey Lou."

Corinne leaned across the bed and slapped him smartly on the mouth.

"Will you stop kidding about that!" she said resentfully. "Give me that letter. I did mean it, too, every word."

Dennis tweaked her nose.

"I apologize for reading my mail before guests. Get up and get me a cigarette, my angel."

Corinne did not budge. She lay with arms clasped under her fine tousled head and stared sulkily up at the Gibson girl on the ceiling so cunningly devised by the leak in the little Communist's sink. Leprous spots had appeared about the famous face and the pompadour was chipping off, flakes of the plaster snowed over the bed occasionally, and the one eye was casually spreading off toward the window in the shape of a crocodile. One of these days I will look up there, thought Corinne, and the crocodile will have devoured the Gibson girl and very likely changed itself into a hippopotamus.

"Isn't it funny how contrary I am, Dennis?" mused Corinne. "As soon as I say something out loud I mean just the opposite. I take sides against myself. I can't help it. I suppose it's me."

"Fascinating."

"Dennis, are you happy—really happy, I mean?"

"Deliriously happy, pet." Dennis got up to find a cigarette on the table, returned and sat on the foot of the bed and reflected that as a matter of strict fact he was happy. There was nothing in the world he wanted or any place he wanted to be but here. Happy happy Orphen, protected by azure cellophane from misery, pain, terror; nothing, no sir, nothing could destroy this bliss, this perfectly idiotic ecstatic peace. The little Communist might tear his heart out over sharecropper woes, Okie might snivel over his inability to find a wife—a wife, mind you, not a pleasing mistress—he, Orphen was at peace.

"Why?" demanded Corinne cajolingly. "Because of me?"

Dennis blew a happy little ring of smoke into the happy air. He stretched out his bare feet—beautiful arches, he observed with pleasure, and hooked the exquisitely matched toes over the bottom rung of the chair.

"Because of you, because of your undying faith in me and in my work."

"I never said as much," said Corinne. "I can't even finish reading what you write. It doesn't hold my interest somehow, darling."

"Sweet! You're spoiling me. Well then, I must be happy because I am young, beautiful, and rich, because I am the darling of New York, the toast of Paris, because at any moment in a million and two homes all over the world fascinated readers will be opening up their copies of *The Hunter's Wife*—"

"See," reproached Corinne. "You don't even think of me. Only your work. I don't see what you like about it so much. Darling, why were you

squeezing Mrs. Callingham Tuesday night on Park and Sixty-fourth?
Why wouldn't you speak to Phil and me?"

"I do think of you," said Dennis, carefully ignoring her final query.
"Every day, I think—why is Corinne so hopelessly infatuated with me?
Why me? Am I so wonderful? I daresay."

Corinne sniffed.

"Well, I'm happy too," she said. She reached for his cigarette, stole a
puff and handed it back. "I have a nice husband who loves me—and I
love him, too. I do love Phil, Dennis. That's something you wouldn't understand but it's the truth."

She hugged her bare knees up to her chin, looked somberly off into
space. Dennis shook his head.

"I don't see how you can possibly be happy, Corinne," he said frankly.
"You're crazy about me—no, darling, your life is horribly botched up."

"I've had a very happy marriage," Corinne repeated and suddenly
began to cry a little, drying her eyes on the edge of the sheet. "I shouldn't
be here. I shouldn't. You don't love me. I don't even like you as a friend—
how could I?—there's not a thing about you for a girl to admire. That's
what my common sense tells me."

"You must learn to distinguish between your common sense and your
conscience," Dennis told her placidly. "No, you're a very, very unhappy
little girl, Corinne. You're all messed up about life. I've done something
for you. I've allowed you the freedom of my apartment and furnished un-
stinted the beauties of my personality. But that isn't enough, odd as it may
seem. I'm worried about you."

"Phil loves me. We're perfectly happy together. You don't need to go
worrying about me, you big liar," quavered Corinne. "Phil and I drive out
to Long Beach every Sunday in summer. We swim—he still likes to
dance with me better than any one else he knows. We've had lovely times
and never quarreled. I'm lucky, I tell you."

Dennis looked at her thoughtfully. It did not seem, in fact, the ideal
spot in which a happy little wife should sing of her good fortune. The
cream-colored note, of course, peeping out from the tumbled folds of the
comfort, was the logical voice of the loyal little Mrs. Barrow, but the
plump, ivory little bare shoulders and the arms above the covers were definitely none other than Dennis's own naughty little Honey Bear.

"When Phil saw you he said—'so that's Orphen's girlfriend, is it—that
Mrs. Callingham?' Because you didn't speak to us and acted as if you

were in a hurry to get away. Oh, darling, when he said it I thought my heart would break. I cried. Phil had to hold me all night."

"Oh, really?"

Dennis jumped to his feet and began to dress quickly. Whichever one got out of bed first showed character, showed he or she at least was loftily unaffected by mere sensual indulgences. It was always a mild insult and Corinne's face fell proportionately.

"OK, you're happily married, then! Your husband holds you all night long, does he?" he snarled. "How about my little heart breaking, too, one of these days? Right in the middle of a Barrow family dinner, right in the middle of the salad, that wonderful goddam salad of that wonderful husband of yours . . . 'Oh, Phil always makes the thalad dwething with hith own hanth!' Why, Mrs. Barrow, is that a fact, and how perfectly delicious. How in the world do you make it, Mr. Barrow? . . . 'We don't like to tell—'" he mimicked the female voice, "'but weally it's a secwet. It's not wegular winegar, it's tarragon!' Why, why, Mrs. Barrow! Not tarragon! Why, why, Mrs. Barrow, you don't mean to tell me tarragon! . . . 'And a dash of wokefot and sasson oil—' oh—oh—oh, Mr. and Mrs. Barrow, what a secret, what a surprise, what a salad dressing and what a happy, happy, happy little couple. Now if you'll just add a soupçon more bird oil, Mr. Barrow, just a soupçon mind you, while I give your dear little wife a nice little buss under the table. . . ."

"Stop!" screamed Corinne, leaping out of the covers. "Stop."

Dennis stopped. He examined his belt buckle intently.

"To be absolutely honest," he said quietly, "I haven't the faintest idea why I didn't speak to you the other night. I can't tell what makes me do things—I can tell about other people but not about me. Let's see, now, supposing I was my hero in a book . . . I think it was the way Effie said—'she's a pretty girl' as if she'd been bitched by every one else and by my writing that book, so that she wouldn't be surprised to have me leave her there in the rain just like Callingham would have for any pretty younger woman. So I—well, my mouth wouldn't open—I just didn't say, Good evening, dear friends. I—just—didn't—speak. So."

"So," said Corinne. She wriggled into her girdle. "Hand me my dress, please."

Corinne, silent, was someone to conjure with. A little tentatively Dennis kissed the back of her neck. When she didn't whirl around at once and fling her arms about him, when she imperceptibly moved her head away, he knew something was wrong again. She fastened her garters, eyes resolutely downcast.

"Do you understand that, Corinne? You're so intuitive you probably do," he said cleverly. "You know more about me than anyone, don't you, Toots?"

Corinne looked at him with odd thoughtfulness.

"There's something between you and that Mrs. Callingham," she said. "I know, because this is the first time you've ever explained anything to me. Any other time when I ask you where you were, who she was, or what you did, you just kid me and say 'never you mind.' This time you explained. It shows it's pretty serious."

Dennis's mouth dropped open.

"She's used to famous men," said Corinne. "Maybe she knows how to talk to you better than I do. I don't mean you're famous yet but you will be. Even Phil says so. And she probably knows what to say."

She tied the orange scarf around her neck, fastened it to the blue wool dress with a crystal clasp with the tiny dog's head preserved in it. Dennis watched her, wanting her to say more, but he was afraid to ask her any questions. Corinne would be sure to jump to some jealous conclusion.

"Applesauce," he said.

"You must not be quite sure what it's all about yourself," said Corinne and shook out her skirt carefully. "You wouldn't be doing all that explaining just for my benefit. It's more for yourself. Look, is it true the book's about her?"

"More or less," admitted Dennis. "I exaggerated—made a real heroine of her, I daresay with a dash of malice, so they tell me."

"You used her for a heroine then fell in love with your heroine," said Corinne. "You act as if you were married to her, as if she came first because she was your work. You act worse than I ever did about my marriage."

She suddenly snatched up the little white note, nestling in the blanket folds like a little white bird, and read it over.

"It is so sad, darling, isn't it," she said mournfully. "I did mean it all, too. I do love my husband—he's so kind to me and you're so beastly. What makes me act this way to him—why do I come here at all—oh, damn, damn, damn!"

She ran out of the door, handkerchief to her eyes, the note fluttering to the floor behind her, saying goodbye. Dennis went to the head of the stairs after her.

"Hey!"

He heard the front door close wheezily on its heavy hinges. She'd be back in a few minutes. He stood in the doorway waiting to click the downstairs entry door for her return, he stood several minutes but she did not come back. Dennis finally closed the door and picked up the note from the floor. "I hope you realize the whole affair has been no more important to me than it has to you." Without Corinne beside him the words did not seem so funny, after all.

"I shouldn't have laughed about it," Dennis reflected uneasily. "I really shouldn't have laughed."

The telephone rang and he picked it up with relief. That would be Corinne saying hadn't she been silly—would he come out for a cocktail. But it was only the publicity man at his publisher's asking if tomorrow morning would be all right with him for photographs and an interview. And did Orphen know where they could get in touch with that Mrs. Callingham so they could get her to deny that the book had anything to do with her?

"No," roared Dennis and hung up.

. . . 'twixt truss and bras . . .

THE JACKET FOR DENNIS ORPHEN'S NEW BOOK was lousy, said Mac-Tweed to his young partner And Company. What was more it was inadequate. He would go a step further and say it was only so-so. The last modest adjective, being unfamiliar to And Company's blurb-conditioned ears, struck him as the most sweeping condemnation one could hope to hear. He could not keep the admiration out of his eye.

"In fact," said MacTweed, banging on the desk willed to him by old Pat Negley, that "beloved" dean of publishers, that name used by a thousand authors for years to frighten their children, "in fact," said MacTweed louder, and banging on this same desk so that the Children's Book editor in her little dimity-deviled room next door spilled red ink all over proof sheets of *A Book of Valentines*—"In fact I'm not at all sure of this book, anyway."

"Not at all sure it will sell, perhaps," said And Company, eyes twinkling, for a source of quiet amusement around this temple of art was old MacTweed's old-fashioned interest in profits. "There can be no doubt about it's being good. No doubt at all."

"Why no doubt?" parried MacTweed, lifting his horrendous piratical gray eyebrows by specially developed muscles at the top of his skull—certainly no ordinary temporal muscles could undertake such a mighty task very frequently. "Why no doubt? I doubt if Walter Scott is any good. I doubt if H. G. Wells is any good. I doubt if *any* author's any good. As a matter of fact, Johnson, I look forward to the day when all our books will be written by blurb writers."

"Ha," said And Company obediently for he was not so long with the firm he could merely smile nor so new he need have hysterics, so he merely said Ha with taste and restraint. The last And Company had decided to pull his money out of the firm and take up some safer career like backing musical shows, but for some reason the money seemed to have taken root in the fertile MacTweed spring list so that it wouldn't pull up without pulling up a great many lawsuits and other liabilities with it. So the withdrawing member had been presented with a great many papers all signed and notaried and highly non-negotiable, and had allowed his partnership to be resold to another promising young fellow, namely Johnson.

MacTweed had seen his young partners' faces change so often in his time that in order to give an air of stability to the office he had refused to alter his own style of sideburns, soup-mustache, pepper-and-salt Norfolk business suits, dog-headed ebony cane, and high Walk-Over black shoes (for fallen arches) in forty years. The changing faces got on his nerves once in a while but the solid old firm could always use "new blood"— publisher's argot for new investors. Johnson was more ambitious than any of his predecessors since he came with far less backing. Already he was reputed to be one of the most brilliant of the younger publishers. He had discovered more young proletarian writers than MacTweed could shake a stick at. He was so brilliant he could tell in advance that in the years 1934–35 and –36 a book would be hailed as exquisitely well-written if it began:

> The boxcar swung out of the yards. Pip rolled over in the straw. He scratched himself where the straw itched him.

Johnson hoped for the day when "And Company" would be "Johnson." He hated And Company. He often looked about him at the Travers Island Athletic Club and saw all the other And Companys. They seemed to be stamped permanently "And Company" for they all looked alike. Good God, he looked alike too! Keen, long-jawed, tallish young men with sleek mouse-colored hair, large mouths filled with strong big white teeth good for gnawing bark or raw coconuts but doubtless taxed chiefly by moules or at the most squab, nearsighted pleasant eyes under unrimmed glasses that might be bifocal, large ears set away from the head like good aerials, large carefully manicured hands, a bit soft, and agreeable deep voices left over from old Glee Clubs. As for dress, they wore well-made loose English clothes with the pants sometimes, as in Johnson's case, coming up almost to the armpits, English style, the pleats making a modest bust, and the long stylish fly tastefully and unobtrusively operated by a zipper. These And Companys, many in publishing, some in their uncles' devious businesses, were all men of good taste, and if Semitic were decent enough to be blond and even a little dumb just to be more palatable socially. But they all looked and talked alike and it had Johnson by the throat. He tried to break away from this insidious chain. He married a chorus girl, instead of a Bryn Mawr girl, a very pretty one from *Face the Music*. But all the other And Companys that year had married chorus girls from *Face the Music* and furthermore, like Mrs. Johnson, the girls were all private-school products and all wrote an occasional poem for F.P.A. or the weekly magazines dealing with the curious effect nature had upon them and how, in sum, it made them feel alone.

Johnson decided to throw his fellows off the track by lunching at the Vanderbilt or 70 Park instead of the club but they all went to lunch with him—indeed, they were there first, their fine clean-cut jaws uttering well-bred baritone remarks, never too personal, never too witty for good taste. In summer, instead of going up to Woods Hole, Johnson stole by night with his wife and the little blond baby everyone was having that year over to Martha's Vineyard. But there they all were again on the ferry, their spectacles adjusted keenly over their copies of *Men of Good Will,* their pleasant deep voices politely deferring to their decently un-made-up little wives. Johnson, anxious to have one gesture of individuality, took to drinking applejack instead of Scotch. They all ordered applejack. He saw them all over the country clubs and town restaurants, he saw them in bar mirrors, rows of clean-cut, spectacled, somewhat adenoidal young men drinking applejack, hats at the same angle, eyes never quite blue or never quite brown but compromise shades between the two, they were all the same except for one who had a boil on his neck. Johnson envied this pioneer, this rebel. Not being gifted with boils he must differentiate himself intellectually, he felt. So he went to Communist meetings, he heard lectures at the John Reed Club, he went to a dinner for John Strachey—they were all there, their *New Masses* in their pockets. He discovered Forsythe. They all discovered Forsythe. Johnson was going mad. "Am I the mass mind?" he asked himself. "If I have a thought or an impulse does it mean that at that very minute ten million other men of my education and background are having it, too? Isn't there a chance of my having one atom, one little hormone different from the others or do our metabolisms all work together like Tiller girls?"

One night, late in leaving the office, he was cheered up by a rather simple incident. He had often passed an Oriental wholesale house on Fifth Avenue called MOGI, MOMONOI & CO. The name held his fancy. He had even thought of it as an ideal motto beneath some splendid heraldic device for future publishing purposes. Mogi (I live) Momonoi (I conquer) and Co. (and forever). The translations he made up himself but they soothed him. All of the shops in this neighborhood, which was the wholesale clothing district, were closed on this evening, for it was nearly eight, and he had Fifth Avenue to himself, a delightful sensation for a man doomed by birth and instinct to Westchester. He was going to a performance of *Sailors of Cattaro* that evening feeling reasonably assured that the majority of And Companys would be at the Beaux Arts Ball, when he saw the front door of the Oriental house open and two short little Japanese gentlemen come out. They stood on the sidewalk quietly waiting. They were, oh, beyond a doubt, Mogi and Momonoi themselves. A third was locking the door. Johnson waited eagerly. The door locked, Number Three joined the others ; unquestionably he was And Company himself, but how unlike any And Company Johnson had ever seen! He was smaller than his partners and he had a mustache. Johnson could not remember a Jap with a mustache but what elated him most was the daring, the insolence of an And Company with a mustache. The very next day his electric razor, Christmas gift, skirted his upper lip in its swift flight. In less than three months Johnson boasted a mustache as large as an anchovy, but its undersize was made up for by its rich emphatic black color, particularly since Johnson's own hair was only hair-colored. The mustache was distinguished, smart, and only Johnson knew that the pallid reddish bristles from his native follicles were heightened daily by his wife's eyebrow pencil. So this visible badge of a unique personality gave him the courage now to argue with his master, MacTweed, to insist that Dennis Orphen's book was exactly what Gannett, Hansen, and Isabel Paterson had been waiting for all their lives.

"The truth is," said MacTweed, and when MacTweed prefaced his remarks with the word "truth" or "fact" Johnson suspected the worst, so he looked discreetly down at his fingernails now, "I don't like the idea of one author satirizing another. This would be downright libelous, this book, if Callingham was fool enough to sue. Naturally he won't want to bring such attention to it since he's so savagely ridiculed in it. But still is it right, is it ethical, I ask?"

The word ethical was a masterpiece. Johnson was moved by it. It sounded like the deep choked voices of all the clean-cut And Companys swearing loyalty to their ivy-covered alma maters. It was a word for seniors to use, hallowed by cap and gown. Ethical. It said, framed as it was now by the tobacco-stained fangs of MacTweed's generous mouth, boys, it said, there's something more to the game of life than just drinking and wisecracking and wenching; there's a gentlemen's code. There's ethics. Ethics the white flag that went up when you saw you were licked, ethics, the rules for other people, ethics, the big King's X. Through the momentary glamour of MacTweed's ethics Johnson perceived a cablegram lying under the chromium Discobolus paperweight. He had a dim hunch.

"Yes, Johnson," said MacTweed. "You think I'm just a hard-headed businessman, an old Scrooge. Well, let me tell you I've got a sense of professional ethics and, by God, I don't see where this guy Orphen gets off raking over a giant, a titan, like Andrew Callingham."

"Callingham's last book sold nearly a hundred thousand," agreed Johnson.

"Yes," said MacTweed, consulting a memorandum before him, "one hundred and fourteen thousand. And now in seven languages. If we should ever be in a position to publish Callingham—he wants an unearthly advance—how is it going to look for us to start off with a satire on his love life? I ask you, Johnson. It's simply a problem of publishing ethics."

Johnson felt depressed. He fingered his mustache nervously. He looked out the window over the tops of Fourth Avenue and saw the tugs on the East River breathing out sooty puffs of smoke, chugging along on their little ethical duties of carrying oil or coal or canned beans some place else. It was too bad. He, Johnson, had been the little father of Dennis Orphen, he felt very proud of his discovery, picking him up out of the gutter, you might say, and making literature of him. He had seen his first Orphen in a woodpulp magazine eight years ago, a full novelette it was, sandwiched between ads for bust developers for wallflowers and designs for a stylish truss. This, said Johnson at the time, reading eagerly from bust to truss, is it. It's literature. For it began:

The freight slows up just outside the yards. As she jerks round the bend by the tower Spud gives Butch a kinda push and out they rolls outa the side door onto the gravel. Wot the hell, sez Butch, take it easy, take it easy. Ya wanna kill us?

He had nursed Orphen along. All the other And Companys were nursing promising lads and lassies along and Johnson thought he might as well nurse talent as the next one. The trouble with this nursing was that it involved a lot of pocket money and not the firm's either. Orphen, for instance, had never felt properly nursed without a half dozen or so Manhattans and lunch besides, a good lunch. Presently, in due course, the first full length novel was ready for publication. Johnson read it and was chagrined to realize that in the case of Orphen he had overnursed. Orphen, instead of staying in the box car of his woodpulp days had, at the first kind word, leapt to the past tense and grammar of satin pages. Johnson was worried, not only for the immediate author but for future nursees. It was an age of the present tense, the stevedore style. To achieve this virile, crude effect authors were tearing up second, third, and tenth revised drafts to publish their simple unaffected notes, plain, untouched, with all the warts and freckles of infancy. The older writers who had taken twenty years to learn their craft were in a bewildering predicament, learning, alas, too late, that Pater, Proust, and Flaubert had betrayed them, they would have learned better modern prose by economizing on Western Union messages.

So Johnson saw future nursees, like Orphen, encouraged out of their native gold mines into the sterile plains of belles-lettres. Very well, he said, I will learn something myself from this and hereafter discourage virile young writers till they get tougher and tougher out of sheer bitterness and become incorruptible. Too late now to save Orphen, however. A seeming dyed-in-the-wool hard guy, he had become in Johnson's nursing school a coddler of fine phrases, a figure-of-speech user, a master of synecdoche. He had been compared to Huxley and Chekov alike, and Louis Bromfield had retired to the south of France to do a blurb for *The Hunter's Wife*. "Fine," it said, and was placed by Johnson himself on the back page of the jacket under Hugh Walpole's own words, just above what the women of England in *Time and Tide* had said and the women of America in *Books* had said about the earlier book.

MacTweed had liked this change in Orphen for his part, having never got over an old apprenticeship in throwing out any manuscript whose first page smacked of illiteracy. His committee of judges, consisting of himself and his chromium Discobolus disguised under five other celebrated names, had awarded Orphen the MacTweed Prize for 1933. Orphen became a minor property. But now, as Johnson saw, MacTweed had scented big game. MacTweed, plucking at a fertile eyebrow reflectively, admitted as much.

"Frankly, Johnson," said MacTweed, "we *are* publishing Callingham. Foster visited him in Saint-Cloud and contacted him constantly. It sounds to me as if Foster contacted the pants off him. He outcontacted Doubleday and Harcourt and Macmillan. He certainly did his job. I like Foster." MacTweed chuckled, offered Johnson a Players' Club cigarette from his lizardskin case, gift of his wife and embarrassingly initialed Y.M. so that everyone must guess his unfortunate real name could be nothing but Yuremiah.

"Has anything been settled yet?" asked Johnson uneasily. He saw a bad month ahead explaining to Dennis why his book was not being pushed, and grasping at straws desperately, he decided he'd have to say it had offended the Church or would the Chase National sound more powerful? But ah the distinction, the glory of being Callingham's publisher over all the other And Companys. He brightened a little.

"Foster's sailing here on the *Bremen* with him right now." MacTweed beamed. He lit Johnson's cigarette generously. "It's in the bag."

"Callingham on his way here?" Johnson gave a start. "With *The Hunter's Wife* coming out tomorrow, and with all the gossip about it being Callingham's own life—the reporters all meeting his boat and getting his denials that the book is about him—what a break for sales!"

MacTweed's eyes half-closed under the grizzled brows. He toyed with the Discobolus. His hands were tobacco-stained, calloused, the nails ripped off and appallingly unkempt due largely to his passion for tending his own garden at his place up the Hudson. Johnson tactfully withdrew his own large, beautifully tended white And Company hands from the desk.

"That is something," muttered MacTweed and smiled appreciatively. A nice problem in ethics here. The book with its scandal base would probably sell as much as Callingham's last one. It would get all the Callingham foes as well as his fans. And wouldn't it in a way stir up interest in Callingham's own future work? Wouldn't there be controversies back and forth that would aid sales? That's the way it could be put to

Callingham. It could be handled. Foster could handle it. MacTweed banged on the table suddenly and once more the Children's Book editor in the next room must grab the toppling vase of jonquils and calm the storm-tossed ink bottle.

"We'll make that young Orphen yet," said MacTweed. "We've got a real property there, Johnson. Let's get behind him on this book. Let's get Caroline Meigs to give a tea for him. Let's get all set before the *Bremen* lands."

He swung his chair's front legs which had been patiently poised in the air during the conference down to the floor and thrust out his hand. Johnson shook it eagerly. This was a step forward.

"Congratulations, sir, on getting Callingham," he said.

MacTweed stood up and faced the picture of old Pat Negley standing in a trout stream, rod in hand, an inscription running across the grassy bank in the right lower corner—"To Mac, Ever, Pat."

"We'll be bigger publishers than you ever were, you old sonofagun," said MacTweed. "By golly."

He slapped Johnson on the back. It was all very amiable and jolly, a real esprit de corps. Johnson saw And Company changing into Johnson almost before his eyes.

"By the way, a new young man is coming in on Monday to learn the trade," MacTweed said casually. "Just out of Harvard—a connection of the Morgans on his mother's side. Seems to be a hell of a clean-cut fellow. Wants to learn the ropes ha-ha."

"Ha," said Johnson with a sinking feeling.

"Building up the way we are we need all the new blood we can get," said MacTweed.

"New blood, yes," said Johnson.

MacTweed dropped back a step and studied his young partner's face with concern.

"You look peaked, Johnson. I wish you'd let me put you on a Hay diet. All proteins at once, all starches—well, hell, you see what it's done for me."

"Yes," said Johnson and went rather gloomily back to his dark room under the filing cabinets.

. . . announcement in Publishers Weekly . . .

Out Thursday, April 11
THE HUNTER'S WIFE
by Dennis Orphen

What they say . . . .

"Fine . . ." Louis Bromfield
"Significant . . ." Hugh Walpole
"Timely . . ." J. B. Priestley

Statement on the first page of
The Hunter's Wife:

"All the characters in this novel are highly fictitious"

...from a letter to MacTweed and Company...

...inasmuch as his bringing suit would only convince the public that this was indeed Andrew Callingham's own story I believe the publication of "The Hunter's Wife" to be without danger to the firm. A number of features in the story coincide with facts in Callingham's life, but we can show point for point where they coincide with eight other well-known writers' lives including Dreiser, Lewis, Hardy, Wells, Zola, Hawthorne, Galsworthy, and Ford. Callingham would be deliberately wooing ridicule by a suit or an injunction. I would advise getting in touch with the former Mrs. Callingham and smoothing her over in advance. Some trouble might come up there, particularly since the characterization here is unmistakable according to all report, though here again we can cite a dozen famous authors' wives whose portraits conform to this satiric outline.

Yours faithfully,

John Lambert
Lambert, Arrnst and Bing, Attorneys

...I remember...

"I REMEMBER THE FIRST TIME I met Andy," said Marian, lying on her left side where it did not hurt so much, "it was at Caroline Meigs's tea for him just after his first book came out. She had a little house over by the river with a big garden. There were trees and we were all so surprised at weeds and trees in a New York back yard. There was a table of sandwiches and fruit punch. It was just before we got into the war."

"Andy hated going to that party," said Effie.

"I was terribly excited about meeting him. I'd been in New York a year at the League and I hadn't met anyone famous. Andy of course wasn't known much then but at least he had been published," said Marian. "He was sitting on one of those rustic benches she had around, glowering at everybody. His hair—it was terribly thick and there was something noble about his big head—"

"Everyone always spoke of it," said Effie. "Sculptors were always after him to pose."

"He had on the dirtiest blue shirt I ever saw in my life and no tie and he was tight as a tick," said Marian.

"He started when that bad review came out in the *Times* and got worse because he detested Caroline Meigs," said Effie.

"I was crazy to meet him," said Marian. "I'd bought a new hat, a red one, with the money my mother was sending me for my League expenses and a red jersey silk coat. Then when I saw you I thought, oh dear, if his wife dresses so quietly that must be his taste so I turned the blue side of my coat out—it was reversible, but there weren't any buttons on the blue side and it must have looked funny. You stood in a corner with a big fat woman and very young pretty boy with such a white face and charcoal eyes—"

"The Glaenzers," said Effie. "He wasn't over twenty-one or -two then."

"I met them later," said Marian. "There you were with everyone around saying 'Isn't that Mrs. Callingham distinguished-looking?' and you never took your eyes off Andy, though he was yards away. No one introduced me to him—I guess I wasn't important enough, just a friend of a friend of a friend. Presently I couldn't stand it any longer and I went up to Andy, 'Let me get you a sandwich,' I said. He had very odd gray eyes, sea-gray. He looked me over very sourly—he says now he was only trying to figure out whether my breasts were as fine as they seemed. 'No, I don't want any more of those goddam sandwiches or any more of this swill to drink,' he said. I was so startled. Caroline could hear him. She was right beside us."

"He never cared who heard him," said Effie. "He was always perfectly honest."

"I sat down beside him. He hadn't asked me to and it was pretty bold of me," said Marian, "and before I knew it I was saying 'My, it must be wonderful to be a writer.' I said how much I admired his work, and did he write at night or in the daytime and did he write from life or imagination. I really did. I said all those things. And he gripped the arm of his chair as if he was going to throw something but all he said was 'exactly.' 'Exactly,' he'd say. I was so thrilled. I thought he was brilliant. And he thought I was. Actually. Finally he said, 'Thank God, there's one intelligent woman here, what do you say we clear out and go someplace decent?' Can you imagine?"

"It was odd I didn't notice you that day," said Effie. "I was only wondering if he would run out after a while with that tall blond girl and how I could make it look perfectly natural so people wouldn't talk. I was always doing that."

"Later on that summer I got to visiting a girl from the League who lived out at Cold Spring Harbor where he kept his boat," said Marian. "I would see him at the station sometimes or when we were out sailing. He always looked like a tramp, bearded, dirty dungarees, sometimes a battered old sunhat with the crown kicked out, likely as not shelling peanuts on the village streets and eating them as he went along, some detective story sticking out of his pocket. I thought he was wonderful. Sometimes I saw you out on the deck of the launch on Sunday mornings when we sailed by. You'd be washing your hair or just lying in the sun. You had lovely hair, Effie. Every time I'd see you out there with your yellow hair flying about I'd go back to town determined to have my hair dyed or get a permanent wave or something. You know it's still lovely, too—no, don't put your hat on yet, please. Andy still speaks of your hair. He loved it."

"I know," said Effie.

"Do you know I remember Andy so clearly before we got to be friends, isn't it funny? I mean I remember the wanting to know him, the terrible hoping I'd run into him, the wondering what I'd say to him and what he'd say to me next time we met, much clearer than how it all finally happened?" said Marian. "Isn't that extraordinary? Pretty soon you and he and I were going places together, and on Sunday nights back in town eating at Mouquin's, both of us laughing at everything Andy said and me drawing pictures of Dubois, the waiter, and trying to hear what the Pennells were saying at the next table. Andy always had a favorite waiter—not Dubois—but—I've forgotten the name now—"

"Ernest," said Effie.

"You were the serious one, always," said Marian. "You didn't see how we could be so silly with war so near. Andy was a ferocious pacifist. I was shocked at first but afterwards of course I respected him for daring to be one. I sometimes wonder what would have happened to him if we'd stayed in America till war was declared. He would have been jailed or killed. And there wouldn't have been any me in his life. It was lucky our deciding to go to China instead of to Europe as we first planned. You stayed right on in New York until the Armistice, didn't you, Effie?"

"Yes," said Effie. "There wasn't much else for me to do."

"Do you remember the three of us that Fourth of July at Coney Island, Effie? The astrologer . . . the description she gave of our true mates . . . Andy's and mine fitted," said Marian, "and I was so thrilled over that till I looked at you—"

"I hadn't even noticed it," said Effie. "I didn't pay any attention to those things."

"But I felt so guilty over being thrilled, you see, and I suddenly hated Andy for being so wonderful that two fine girls had to fight and suffer for him, so all the rest of the day I stayed beside you and I wouldn't dance with him or go in the loveboat or do any of the things I wanted to do most. He got angry, remember, and left us and at Feltman's when we were eating later on he came up with two awful little tarts and a sailor he'd picked up on the Boardwalk. They all came back to town with us and we could never get rid of them."

"Andy was always doing things like that," said Effie.

"We did have good times," said Marian, closing her eyes. "Wherever we went we had fine times. I never knew who Andy would bring up to our room in Shanghai or Tokyo—" she went on, leaving Effie alone now in New York and taking Andy far far away forever, "some British earl or some Viennese dancer. At first he was always in the dumps thinking maybe you were having a bad time of it alone and you never wrote—"

"There was nothing to say," said Effie, "and I was getting along all right. I was perfectly all right."

"I told him that. If it had been me in your place," said Marian, "I would have died. I would have killed myself, I would have jumped out a window. My heart would have absolutely broken, but, Effie, you were so calm, so sane, so marvelous, you were such a swell person, we always said that, Effie, Andy and I always said so. And you had told him to do just as he thought best, go if he must. I couldn't have said that. I couldn't say it last fall when this new woman came in—I couldn't bear it for a minute, oh, I couldn't stand it, it killed me, it did, it killed me. I had to run away just seeing them laugh at each other across the room or saying silly things to each other the way we used to do at Mouquin's—I went out of my mind. And I hurt so—this thing hurt me so. . . . Effie, do you believe he's still with her? Don't you think when I ran away he got afraid of losing me altogether and sent her off? I'm so sure he did. I can't stand thinking about it—but after all he does love me—we did have good times, he will come when he hears I'm here sick, and he will laugh at me for being so silly as to run out. You sent the cablegram?"

"He'll come," said Effie. "Don't worry, dear."

"He will. But when? Where is he now?" She was silent for so long that Effie, turning toward her, saw that her cheeks were graying and rang for the nurse.

"She's gone again," she whispered.

The nurse shook her head gravely.

"It can't be long now. If her husband could only get here in time!"

. . . long distance . . .

IN THE DRUGSTORE A BLOCK AWAY from the hospital Effie stood in the telephone booth staring at the dial face, as if some of its own blank unconcern might pass out to her. It could not be that to roll back two decades she had only to turn the dial, a voice would answer exactly as it had answered then. Thinking how incredibly simple was this contact with another age, Effie wondered what had restrained her from performing the miracle before this. What a comforting game it would have been, pretending his absence was only for the day, the hour, and not forever. Just a twist of the wrist as the magicians said, Hello, Bruster Company? Is this Tom? Mrs. Callingham speaking. Has Andy got there yet? When he comes in will you ask him to call the apartment? Thank you.

Effie found herself trembling as one should tremble before such miracles. She dared not risk it. Scientists must have felt the same primitive terror before bringing their robots to life, terror of the unknown world about to be released. Put up your right hand, dial up two down one. She looked again for the number in the book, mind balking on the side of fear. So easy. Bruster Company, Literary Agents, Graybar Building. Would the same Miss Hupfel be there, efficient, moderately friendly, later moderately patronizing. . . . "We are instructed to deposit the March royalties to your account in the Guaranty Trust. . . . Why, no, Mrs. Callingham, the new novel is late in being delivered. Mr. Bruster just had a letter from them. They're in Singapore now. Yes, Singapore. They seem to be having a wonderful time. No, the last book didn't do so well . . . he lost a good deal of his public by those pacifist articles of his, Mr. Bruster says, coming as they did right in the heat of the war feeling. . . ."

Effie's hand darted up quickly, swung the dial around, swung it round to the year 1916, heard the calm answer on the phone, as calm as if there were no nineteen years between the two telephones. Long distance, thought Effie. It would be long distance, too, to take a train—quite possible, no reason why not—out to Cold Spring Harbor, walk along the harbor, see the *Violet II* there at the dock, perhaps, a launch really might survive that long.

"This is Mrs. Andrew Callingham"—how brave she was speaking out loud with only the dial face to mock her—"and I wanted to know if your office had heard from Mr. Callingham. Is he expected in America this month?"

"Mr. Callingham arrives on Saturday," said the cool voice. No, it could not be Miss Hupfel, of course. Launches might last but not Misses Hupfel. "We've had a cable. You can reach him through this office if it's important. What name was that again, please? Mrs. What?"

Thank God.

"Thorne, I said, Miss Thorne."

"Thorne, did you say? I understood you—"

The receiver on the hook. Suddenly Effie took it down again, dropped in another nickel. Dennis. She must get back to Now, to the little Present that did not matter. She heard the buzz repeating dully, rhythmically. No answer. No Dennis. No one. It was hard to believe you had no one. Yet Marian, too, had no one. Still, that was not true, she had her belief in Andy and Andy was returning for her. Marian did have her Andy. She, Effie, had no one. She turned to the telephone book, fumbled desperately through its pages. Did she look so strange, for the boy at the soda fountain was peering at her intently? Did it matter? She found the number.

"Dr. MacGregor, please . . . Effie Thorne . . . Oh, doctor, I thought I'd call to see how you were. It was lovely seeing you last night. How have you been—oh, yes, you did say you'd been splendid. Andy's coming on Saturday. I thought you'd like to know. Yes, I just had a cable. Yes, it will be nice seeing him—we've been in touch constantly of course. He always liked you so much. Yes . . . What? Oh, I'm fine. Yes, I'm fine. I sound funny? That's strange, because I feel perfectly fine. No, there's nothing else, I just thought I'd give you a ring. No, I'm fine. Goodnight. Goodnight, Dr. MacGregor. Thanks so much . . . What? Did you say thanks for *what*? . . . I don't know, really, it just slipped out, I guess. Goodnight."

Without warning, tears streamed down her face, she leaned her face against the telephone, mechanically pulled the booth door slightly open so the light would go off and hide her, she stood in there, receiver dangling from its hook, her body shaking. The soda fountain boy was looking at her. The marcelled blonde at the Helena Rubinstein counter was looking at her. The customer was looking at her. They could see through both glass doors, dark or light. They could see through long distance to Bruster Company, Literary Agents, to Dr. MacGregor in the Hotel Rumsey. They could see through everything but she could not stop crying. She picked up her pocketbook, left the receiver still hanging with I'm-fine-I'm-fine-I'm-fine and ran outdoors into brilliant sun.

...family dinner...

"To the book!" said Phil Barrow, lifting his cocktail, third gin, third vermouth, third cold tea *and* a dash of bitters shaken up and if you-have-any-cucumber-in-the-refrigerator-I-usually-soak-it-peeled-of-course-in-the-cold-tea-say-for-half-an-hour—"To the book!"

"To the book!" said Corinne, lifting hers, and staring defiantly at Dennis don't-you-dare-make-a-face-when-you-taste-this—don't-you-dare-say-what-is-this-mess—don't-you-dare.

"Thanks," said Dennis and politely drank it down. "It's mighty nice of you people to celebrate for me this way. Say, that's a fine drink you've made here, Phil, how did you tell me you made it?"

Corinne rewarded him with a grateful smile because it was no fair hurting Phil, it was strange but she simply could not bear for Phil to be hurt in any of his little vanities, whereas she was almost vengefully pleased when shafts were tossed in Dennis's direction. But no one must tease Phil about his recipes or his anecdotes or his pleasure in his own good sense, no one must make a fool of him, no one, that is, except his little wife.

"I use cold tea as the basis for all my cocktails," said Phil, eyes behind his spectacles faintly contemptuous of his guest's ability to appreciate nuances of taste. "Iced tea and applejack, for instance, makes a darned fine highball, or a good punch base for the matter of that."

"Dennis can't make a decent cocktail to save his soul," said Corinne proudly, and turned to Dennis—now *you,* now *you* say something.

"It's the truth. Nor a salad nor a soufflé nor a gingerbread man. It's mortifying," agreed Dennis readily. The evening was on. Now we all join

hands to build up Phil. What-a-cook—what-a-swimmer—what-a-finan-
cier—what-a-thinker—what-a-man-Phil!

"Let me give you another," suggested Phil. "Pass his glass, Baby."

"Here you are, Baby," said Dennis maliciously, and passed his glass
to Corinne. She kicked him under the table. Over the centerpiece of
African tulips—lecherous-looking posies for a family dinner, he thought—
he caught Olive's significant, sarcastic half-smile. He wondered what
would happen if one of these days he would shout out his hate for Olive,
his hate for all women's girlfriends. Must every woman in the world
have some other woman best friend, always hovering in the background,
voicing wisdom very bad for the sweetheart's naïve ears, advising, re-
porting, knowing, always knowing so much more than the sweetheart
herself? Olive, dear loyal Olive! If women were only as deceitful to their
female friends as men hoped and said they were! But no, wherever a
man went he must be annoyed and frustrated by sex solidarity. Olive, for
instance, knew all about Dennis because Olive and Corinne had gone to
Miss Roman's together. Corinne always told Olive absolutely *everything*
and Olive told Corinne everything, especially little things she'd heard
here and there about Dennis, odd places she'd run into him. Olive was
an old peach, that way. Every time he saw Olive's smooth, rather handsome dark face across the table he thought of how much Olive knew
about him and he shuddered, how much more she knew about Corinne,
too, than he did. She probably knew of plenty little escapades Corinne
had confessed only to her, little infidelities that made a stalwart true
lover like Dennis seem a rather ridiculously romantic figure. Olive knew
all, she knew—no use pretending she didn't—exactly how Dennis made
love, how he first did this, then he did that, how he looked in his B.V.Ds,
his every weakness. Infinitely more detached than Corinne she could
weigh the evidence coolly, check this against that, and balance all with
her own sour philosophy. Dennis, as seen through the eyes of the girlfriend's girlfriend, could be Romeo only to some feeble-minded Juliet,
not to shrewd Miss Olive Baker. He could see himself reflected in her
clear dark eyes, very, very diminutive and extremely upside down, and
in her quiet smile he read how decent she was in not telling Phil, in comforting Corinne in minor crises, in never revealing to a living soul except
by a slight sneer what a two-timing Casanova she happened to know
Dennis really was. Ah there, decent square-shooting girlfriend's girlfriend, he saluted her silently across the table, what was your private

opinion of that last lovers' quarrel you've just been hearing about upstairs, and didn't you think the little episode concerning my new azure-blue shorts was enormously entertaining, and how did you explain my kissing Corinne right smacko in the Snack Bar—kinda sweet and spontaneous of me, wasn't it? . . . One thing to count on, old chummy, you won't ever quite dare crack down hard on me because I know such wonderful people and you're crazy to meet them, because you never yet have met anybody except the people the Barrows pass on to you and they're not hot enough. How long has it been now since I promised we'd get hold of Okie-Dokie, the big editor, and have a party, just the four of us? Ever since that promise Olive had read Okie's magazine from cover to cover with curious loyalty to this future friend. She'd cut out a picture of him in a tabloid paper where he was one of five men asked a question by the Inquiring Reporter, and she always referred to Okie with a positively possessive smirk. Dennis could not imagine why he'd never brought about this meeting or come through with some elegant party, but having it always in the air, the brilliant unknown Okie always hovering in the background gave him a certain hold over Olive, much more than if he had ever produced the too-too-average Okie of reality. Honestly, though, Corinne protested time after time to him, Olive did think a great deal of Dennis, she certainly admired his courage sticking to his writing after that bad review of his last book in *Time,* for most people, Olive felt, would have given up after that, and she *did* think in certain lights he had sort of a sweet profile. Dennis knew all this because Corinne had often told him so, just as she had told Olive how much Dennis liked her and how he couldn't understand why a girl with her personality had so many free evenings.

In taxis going home from the little dinners at the Barrows', Dennis and Olive would be alone, silent, detesting each other, he trying to remember his sweet profile, she striving to sharpen up on her personality. There were bad hours indeed, these rides through the night in love-scented taxis. Once Dennis had had a horrible temptation to make a grab at her virgin thighs just to see her triumphant smile—aha! didn't-I-say-that's-the-way-he-was-Corinne—just to see what she would report later to Corinne. But the fear that he would only have her calling him up every morning instead of loyally tattling all to Corinne, kept him from this experiment in female-friend psychology.

"How about it, Orphen, does MacTweed think this book will go at all? What does MacTweed say about it anyway?" inquired Phil, arm-and-arming it with MacTweed, two big businessmen sticking together against their wives' artist friends. The closest Phil could ever get to Dennis's work was an interest in MacTweed's overhead. Dennis warily tried to duck this snag familiar in his talks with Phil. If he commented unfavorably on MacTweed, Phil would at once patiently explain to Author Orphen what MacTweed, a brother financier, was driving at. He would smile patronizingly at Goodfornothing Author Orphen while he interpreted the farseeing wisdom of MacTweed to Corinne and Olive, as if, Dennis thought resentfully, he was his personal friend, a pal, a buddy, instead of being a stranger known only through Dennis's descriptions. Naturally Phil felt warm toward any unknown party who was kind enough to get in Dennis's hair, that was only to be expected, but he needn't take this Olympian bow every time the Big Interests were mentioned.

"Corinne read some of the book, Phil," said Olive, the fixer. "She says it's quite interesting and it may catch on."

"Is that so, Baby? You read it, did you?" Phil deferred eagerly to Baby's intellect, as if her having read it showed far more brilliance than merely having written it. "Interesting you say, hey? You know, Orphen, Corinne reads everything, whatever the reviews suggest. She saves those little lists of different authors' favorite books in the *Tribune* and goes through every one."

She does? She *does?*

"I trust her judgment, too. If she says a thing's interesting, I take her word for it, don't I, Baby? Another thing, she's saying, oh dear, she says, I certainly wish Dennis could write something that would make money like *So Red the Rose* or those things."

She does? She *does?*

"Hm," said Dennis, very red, very angry, glaring across the African tulips at this strange Corinne of Mr. Barrow's, glaring as if she did not look unusually sweet in her simple little yellow dinner dress, ruffles modestly falling over pretty arms, friendship bracelet, of all things, jingling silver hearts over her wrists.

"I think it's really good," she said, unconscious of this baleful scrutiny. "You know, Baby, I think there's a picture in it. It would suit Ann Harding."

"Ann Harding! You don't say! Well, well, Orphen, congratulations, that's fine!"

Dennis strove vainly to force Corinne's attention so she might see his scorn. *Baby!* So, not only did her husband call her Baby, but she called him *Baby,* too! You'd think people could think of something fresher than that to call each other, something that would exhibit more flamboyantly their feelings for each other. Why couldn't they call each other Butch, for instance? Good God, what was he doing here between these Babys! And Olive smirking down at her plate, pleased with the whole nasty situation, something to talk over tomorrow, or, no, by Jove, tonight. After coffee the girls would rush to Corinne's bathroom and stay in there whispering for hours while he, outsider, stranger, must sit in the living room with Phil and cognac, disliking both, and hear how bright Baby was, what a head, what a brain!

"And if I hadn't spoiled everything by rushing her off to get married she would have had a career herself!" said Phil, for suddenly there they were, the two of them, in the living room, brandy bottle between them on the glass-and-silver coffee table, girls whispering furiously away in corners upstairs. "She wrote pieces for the school paper and had parts in plays. I'm to blame for keeping her just for myself."

"I wouldn't blame myself too much," said Dennis. All right, now, let's get on with the build-up. That was the legitimate tax on bachelors; wherever they stole their jam they must build up the rightful owner. Briefly looking back over the last ten years, Dennis could not remember a single husband he had not spoiled for life by his flattery, many of them so set up that they felt they were too good for the very wives Dennis was testing out. "By George, you know how to pick a nice brandy."

"Marie Brizzard," said Phil. "More? Sixty-five years. Yes, one thing you can't economize on is brandy. Either it's good or it isn't."

"Brandy and neckties," said Dennis, watching the door frantically. Where were the little women anyway? "I never spend less than four-fifty for my ties."

He fingered his Woolworth tie delicately as if it were something infinitely rare and fragile.

"That's the truth," said Phil, looking toward the stairs.

"Oh, *Baby!* Hey, we're waiting! Did Corinne tell you I'd just made the University Club? Sort of embarrassing for me in a way as the head of the firm doesn't belong, so naturally I'm a little on edge as to how he'll take it. Did Corinne tell you we're planning a world cruise this year? Poor Baby, she's had her heart set on it for so long. Her one aim in life."

Corinne wanted a world cruise?

"That and a mink coat. Well, it's one or the other, I told her, maybe the mink next year."

Corinne wanted a mink coat?

"Olive may come along on the cruise—make it more fun for Corinne, another girl, of course. More brandy? No, I just have one myself. Corinne got me a bottle eighty years old for my birthday. Smoothest stuff you ever tasted. By the way, Orphen, does MacTweed pay you a straight royalty or a stated amount? Not much in a book of that type, is there?"

"He pays plenty," said Dennis mysteriously. "Plenty. Through the nose."

Phil was impressed but skeptical.

"I've been thinking of a cruise myself," said Dennis dreamily. "Not with a crowd. Just private. On a yacht. Friends of mine. Glaenzers. Anthony Glaenzer—she was the Cody daughter, you know—Stuyvesant Cody, all the other children put away in asylums here and there so she has everything. Yes, we have some fun together, the Glaenzer bunch and I, laughing and kidding back and forth."

There. Behind Corinne's back the boys might fight as much as they liked. Nice little Phil could brag and Dennis could lie. Me and the Glaenzers, now what put that in my mouth? . . .

"What is it girls tell each other that's so important?" fretted Phil, looking toward the hall door. "Olive's been here all day and Corinne was with Olive all last night but they still got things to say. Like boarding school."

Dennis's eyes narrowed. So she told her husband she'd spent last night with Olive, eh? Well, she'd told Dennis she'd spent it with her husband at Radio City Music Hall. One answer to that—a new lover in the offing. How stupid Phil was not to guess this. Almost irresistible not to prick his smugness with a hint or two, a doubt of Olive planted here right now. Then have Phil on guard, keeping careful watch on these little Olive nights, protecting her from cads, keeping her safe and true for Dennis!

"Did Corinne seem a little upset to you tonight, Orphen? She's such an emotional little creature. Even a movie upsets her. The other night she saw Jean Harlow in something or other—*Reckless*—and she cried her eyes out. Terribly sensitive."

Sure, she cried her eyes out over Jean Harlow, thought Dennis, intensely disliking this man's wife, this sensitive little Mrs. Barrow who was upstairs giggling over that man last night—could it have been Walter, the teakettle man? . . . Sure, she cried over *Reckless*—just a little bundle of emotions. She could see plays or read books on revolution, poverty, and starvation with a detached "Tough luck" as if among the oppressed further misfortune were the rule and left her unmoved. But when she saw hearts really break, as only hearts under ermine can break, then tears by the gallon did she shed, did Mrs. Baby Barrow, her whole exquisite nervous system bathed and sublimated in sympathetic anguish over Harlow's diamond-studded woe, Harlow gallantly wearing her sables, chin up before the servants, smiling at the cruel Four Hundred, while her brave heart broke in the back seat of a Rolls-Royce. That would upset Phil's Baby, all right, that would be the gamut of her feelings, all passed on later in whispers to Olive.

How can I stand such people, marveled Dennis, how can I do this man the honor of sleeping with his clever, booky little wife? How can I endure them, and say what you will there must be a streak of that fudgy respectability in her to enjoy this man's company, she must have something like that in her. . . . I mustn't have any more of this cognac, he thought, Phil's face drops an inch every time I pass my glass, but he has to keep on asking because he's a perfect host if it kills him. Then, too, I might go a little screwy and tell him to make Corinne wear more underclothes while she's got this cold, and watch out for the little rascal when she says she's with Olive. . . . Hello, here we are on our feet, the girls all whispered out back in the room, Olive with lowered eyelids, abulge with secrets Dennis would never, never know.

"Gossiping again, you two!" accused Phil none too merrily. "We've been here hours."

"Why, Baby!" murmured Corinne.

"We were not gossiping," said Olive, smoothly crossing a very good leg for a girlfriend over a handsome knee. "Phil thinks women don't have anything to say to each other but gossip. We have ideas, too."

Ideas! Dennis looked with vast scorn at Mrs. Barrow's ivory valentine face. Ideas! Why, this creature's whole nature recoiled when she came smack up against anything as cold and repellent as an idea. A turtle in my bed, she would scream, a cold turtle! A statistic poking its clammy nose into my face! Away! Oh, nasty, nasty Idea!

"We were discussing Captain Anthony Eden, if you must know," said Olive proudly. "It happens we both admire him."

"He's doing a lot for England," said Mr. Baby.

"For all of us," said Dennis morosely, "and for Finland too. Captain Eden represents Virtue and Right all over the world, for he represents England."

"That's so," said Phil. "England is England and if any country has high ideals, it's England."

"What a nice couple, England and Eden," said Dennis thoughtfully. "I wonder if they call each other Baby."

Ah, there the resentment was revealed! Corinne flashed him wounded astonishment—you-*are*-you're-making-fun-of-Phil! Olive laughed goody-goody-goody-a-scene-a-showdown. Phil drew back, insulted, then managed a sour smile and lit his cigarette very carefully with his beautiful birthday lighter.

"Very good," he said. "Excellent."

It's very strange, thought Dennis, apparently my insides are as old-fashioned as a White Steamer, no matter how modern my top is. Can it be true that these old insides shudder at something so simple and everyday as a triangle situation, can it be they recoil from an up-to-date Family Dinner? Why, you funny old insides, you, operated by Federal instead of local laws, so that all local actions are canceled out by this invisible G-man.

"I'll say this, *my* Baby is looking mighty pretty in the new dress this Baby bought her today, ha ha ha ha ha ha ha!" said Phil.

"Ha ha ha ha ha ha ha!" said Olive and Corinne gratefully. Into the doghouse, you go, Orphen.

Phil reached across Corinne's lap, placed a hand comfortably on her knee. Dennis looked at the ceiling, out the window, up the stairs. He stared so sternly at the walls that it would seem the mortgages must pop out in very shame.

Detestable Babys! Hateful Olive! Horrid House! Raw searing rage seethed through him, a little dinner celebrating his book, a little family dinner, don't dress, just wear your armor, just a little family dinner. Rage left and he was sad, far worse to be sad, too, to wonder why love today came to people in fragments like a jigsaw puzzle and no one person had all the pieces, nothing whole was left any more, nor was this England's fault, nor could even Captain Eden fix it up. . . . This sadness, this ache, jealousy, whatever it might be, must be what Effie Thorne carried always with her, this was what it was like, this was it when she saw Marian, this unbearable tormenting bewilderment. Effie, Effie, he thought, I understand, so this is what stays with you always and no one can help, no one. Only you and I know, we understand.

... the trousseau ...

"Buy me a pink bedjacket," Marian had implored. "Could you get someone to curl my hair—only how can I lift my head when it's so tired and heavy? Effie, isn't there something to be done about this room—but never mind, there's no money, is there, and anyway Andy won't let me stay here long as soon as he comes. Oh, I do hope it stops hurting when he comes. When it hurts there's really nothing else, nothing but pain, pain. . . . A pink bedjacket, Effie, not woolly but that lacy kind."

But the boxes now scattered about the Chelsea apartment did not contain bedjackets, even Mr. Hickey, the janitor, could guess that much, piling them up one after the other outside the door. Effie could not explain it even to herself. Reason had fled before this sudden urgency, years of discretion and economy were wiped out in hours of mad shopping. Pride could get in no word, or fear of Dennis's cutting analysis. Effie shook out her purchases in her room, laid the dresses out over the couch, piled the dainty lingerie, price tags still modestly fluttered from shoulder ribbons, on the window seat. In a daze she wandered through Fifth Avenue shops, ordering this and that, never asking the price, though certainly these long-dormant charge accounts, once gracefully sponsored by Belle Glaenzer, could not bear such demand without investigation sooner or later. This new wardrobe was one she had treasured in the back of her mind, something she had planned half-asleep through the long lonely nights. It had nothing to do with her present needs or tastes, it was definitely a wardrobe for the Effie of long ago, a recostuming of the glamorous scenes of her honeymoon. Let other women of her years prepare for age, here was one who was building for her youth. Useless to bring common sense to bear when she saw the blue-flowered hat in Saks, useless for the saleswoman to hint that it was a little too on the bridesmaid side, for this was the hat Effie should have worn to Caroline Meigs's garden party so that Andy could have looked at no one else. Remembering the plain dark blue taffeta she had worn running away to Connecticut with Andy on her wedding night, she corrected herself now by buying a rose-colored print, and here too on the black couch were the elaborately strapped French slippers Andy had wanted for her but which she would not have. Here were the ridiculously fragile underthings Andy was always suggesting for her, the chiffon stockings, all the feminine extravagances she had laughed at him for admiring. Ordering two insanely expensive chemises from a Madison Avenue shop Effie was brought to a pause by the suspicious interrogation in the salesgirl's eyes. You can't pay for these, said the look, and for whom do you buy these bridal treasures, surely not for your old poor person, modest finances betrayed by ready-made coat, counter hat, bargain gloves, pawnshop antique silver necklace, basement pocketbook. Effie drew up her shoulders haughtily at this inquisition, flung out Mrs. Anthony Glaenzer's name as the charge's name, and then she thought, Why it's true, she's right, I can't pay for these things, I will have to explain to Belle soon, and for that matter when and where will I wear them and for whom? She examined her mind curiously as if it were something inanimate, detached from her, studied it to see what strange secret hopes might be betrayed there lurking, yet when she caught a faint shadow of an answer she withdrew, terrified, from the word, the articulate wish. She called in the janitor to help hang her new curtains and as he stood on the maple highboy, heavy shoes planted on a Sunday paper, he uttered his own private astonishment.

"These ain't like you, missus—excuse it, Miss Thorne. Kinda loud-like for you, they don't seem just right somehow."

Effie straightened the folds at the side of the window, ivory glazed chintz splashed with bright scarlet flowers. She saw herself walking through Lord and Taylor's with Andy behind her, heard his occasional exclamations—"Here it is, Effie. Look! Isn't that great? How many yards do we want, say about fifty?" She would turn from the blue denim counter to her husband so hopefully planted at the gayer counter two aisles back, beaming over a pile of red and yellow flamboyant cretonnes, so outrageously wrong for their little place that she would shake with laughter.

"Darling! Please not that! And eight yards is all we need whatever it is."

Andy stood beside her, hands gloomily thrust into his pockets, complaining all the while the plain blue was being wrapped.

"What's the good of buying curtains if they aren't any fun? Who wants to live in a dark blue house? I'm damned if I'll go shopping with you again, Effie. I'll bet you five dollars you're going upstairs now and buy a dark blue dress."

Effie thrust the packages into his unwilling arms.

"I am, but, Andy, we can't get wild colors because we'd get sick of them, and when you're as poor as we are we have to get something that will wear. Dark blue *wears!* There, is that clear?"

"I hate things that wear," shouted Andy wrathfully. "I've always hated them ever since I was a kid and got three woolen union suits for Christmas instead of roller skates. I'd always rather have roller skates."

"Even in winter?" asked Effie, smiling because he was always the child, always the little boy.

"Especially in winter," he said firmly. "Another thing, Effie, I hate houses in good taste. My aunt's house was in good taste and so I never dared asked the bunch in to play. I like red."

So, holding the chiffonier steady for Mr. Hickey to climb down, boot on the white window seat first and then secure on the light oak floor, Effie said to him, "I know it doesn't seem like me, Mr. Hickey, but tastes do change, you know."

"That's right," conceded Mr. Hickey amiably, shoving the chest over to the next window and once more adjusting the protective *Tribune*. "I never used to eat rice no matter how it was fixed. Now you can give me rice any time o' day, any time at all."

He was a square, broad little man and looked alarmingly ape-like with his hat off, for his round bullet head was blue-shaven, and his wide flat nose spread out loose and moist and pinkish above the blue-stippled grayish skin. His eyes were red-rimmed and suspicious, his chin large, outthrust, antagonistic, but this manner melted before the least kind word, the least sign of friendship, the least mention of his crippled son. The eyes became weakly docile and doglike, the pugnacious chin hollow and defenseless. Nor was this his own chin, literally. It had been made for him only a year before by our good government after the mustard gas left in his system by the war had eaten away the old chin. He talked about this good fortune proudly as he hammered the little gold prongs into the window frame, his flat down-East apologetic voice punctuated with surprising violence by the staccato hammering, while Effie sat below on the window seat, the gaudy material engulfing her as she hurriedly basted hems.

"No, sir, I got no kick against the government," said Mr. Hickey, whack, whack, whack at the curtain nails. "They certainly treated *me* all right, givin' me this new chin without leavin' a scar as you can see for yerself, takin' care o' me free o' charge every year in the hospital the last eighteen years. See that mustard gas done somethin' to my lungs way back in 'eighteen so somethin' has to be done every year about that, then my stummick where the bullet went through, it gets bad, and every time I get those attacks, say, the government looks after me, no expense at all, months on end, you know yourself, ma'am, how I'm allers goin' back to the hospital. I been lucky at that, though. See, I was a naval gunner, we were on this ship outta Saint-Quentin and there was this mistake in the command the way I figure it we loaded the guns twice with powder and no shell at all, 'cause eighteen of us was blown straight to pieces. I was the only lucky one and acourse I was outa my head, even so, and lost my speech and all for two years, but the government hospital worked on me and I concentrated the way you have to do, and in a few years I was just fine, exceptin' for the way the mustard gas keeps eatin' away and nachally my wife and Tom lame that way has to shift along while I'm gone but with the Relief and people chippin' in here and there like you and the folks downstairs and the church, I certainly got no complaint, we certainly been pretty lucky, savin' Tom when he got the paralysis, and then I got some good care, *some* care, I'll say, and I got this new chin out of it. My wife says it's better than the old one, got more character, she says, *she* likes it better for my type o' face."

The hammer ceased, the boot came gingerly down again on the newspaper, the other boot followed on to the floor. Mr. Hickey stepped back to look at his handiwork and again a faint bewilderment came into his eye, staring at the flaming curtains, then at the slender faded woman beside them. The curtains swayed gently, poinsettias swelling out to full pattern, then withdrawing into their white shiny folds; they were alive, blood-red flowers leaping out of a gleaming shroud, and in between their flowing lengths the body of the woman, oddly graying into the shadows beyond the window, fading into the smoky clouds far in the distance, far over the river and the Jersey shores; and the room belonged to the curtains, they swelled and bellied in the river breeze, bleeding blossoms moved barely perceptibly, they blew over Effie Thorne, concealed her. Whee, they said, blowing out and in, wheee, and Effie's face returning, brilliant blue eyes wide, seemed strangely pale and frightened so that Hickey suddenly shouted out, "They don't suit you, missus, I'm tellin' you, they don't suit you, they ain't right for you. The old ones, the blue ones, were better."

Effie's hand fluttered up, startled.

"Really?" she said, staring at him as if he had never been there; then she collected herself and smiled wearily. "But I've had blue so long, Mr. Hickey, in every apartment I ever lived."

Mr. Hickey mopped his forehead, read in her protest an excuse to resume the chip-on-the-shoulder expression. He looked curiously at the bright dresses spread out on the studio couch, was frankly amazed at the silver and crystal perfume atomizer set out amid its wrappings on the table.

"You going away, Mrs. Callingham?" For the room cried out, *something's happened, something's happened,* and he was an unconquerably curious fellow. "Or is somebody movin' in? If it was anybody else I'd think they was gettin' married."

The question, articulate, brought a flood of color to Effie's face, a sudden dizziness to her head. No one had the right to make these direct challenges, she herself had never made them to the world, the world should not make them to her. Before her Hickey, ape-faced, muscled arms swinging low from great shoulders, Hickey the janitor, pitifully coughing in the basement winter nights with his mustard gas lungs, proudly carrying his crippled boy up stairs to the roof on summer mornings, beaten proud little man, changed to Enemy, slipped quietly over to the hostile ranks of Dennis Orphen, Glaenzers, World.

"Thank you for helping, Mr. Hickey," she said coldly, and following his bold stare longed to fling acres, seas, fields of dark decent blue over the gay ruffles and silks scattered over her bed, over the leering curtains, over her own heart, dark limitless smothering blue to hide her shame before the Enemy's knowledge of her secret folly.

If there were some way of legalizing friendship, of compelling confidences by law, of waving a contract at the sulking friend, saying "Look here, you can't leave me this way, it's against the law. You can't turn cold and hostile as simply as all that, ah no, indeed." But there is no binding of friends, no redress when one vanishes into new circles or into quiet sulks, the deserted companion can wait in vain at the accustomed rendezvous, can burst with curiosity over the withheld secrets, there is no compelling the desired one's presence or confidence, no guarantee of the ten-, twenty-, thirty-year-old bond being credited one more minute. It's not fair, you scream, he cannot do this, we've been friends too long, quarreled, re-vealed ourselves in every horrid light to each other, there is no justice in his suddenly breaking off forever because I called him—what was it I called him—a "dumb reactionary," perhaps, in last night's argument? After all, haven't I called him worse than that, haven't I cheated him at cards, done him out of his best girl, borrowed and never returned his best shirt, haven't I called him liar, coward, thief, haven't I belittled his fa-vorite work, cried down his ability, as he in turn has me? How can it be fair, then, that a modest epithet like "reactionary" should put him away from me for life? A law should be made forcing justice here as it does in marriage courts, a law should be made, thought Dennis desperately, re-quiring certain formalities to be observed in breaking up a friendship. Effie Thorne, for instance, should be required to telephone him and ex-plain definitely if the return of her ex-husband meant the exit of friend Orphen. Certainly it would seem that way for she had not called him once since the news of Andy's returning, and when he had managed to get her at her apartment her tone had been as politely remote as if he were her grocer instead of last week's dearest companion.

"How's Marian? Are you at the hospital every day?" he asked.

"She's conscious most of the day, thank you. I'm there during the after-noons usually."

"Don't you need some cash, Effie? You must have to buy her things and probably Callingham hasn't sent—I mean—"

Ominous pause here on Effie's part as he floundered, pause saying, my dear young man, aren't you being a little presumptuous in your generos-ity? Then—

"Thank you, we manage quite well." Yes, we wives of Mr. Callingham are always well taken care of, my dear impudent young fellow!

"I only asked because you said something last week about running low—and I just got my check from MacTweed—it's more than I ex-pected, so you're welcome to any or all of it—" Dennis stammered.

"How nice for you," Effie smoothly evaded.

Dennis racked his brain for some word, some suggestion that would break down this wall of politeness, something that would fasten the oddly broken links again.

"Could I meet you at that garden place near the hospital today for a drink when you're through? I want to talk to you. Or perhaps I could run in to see you tonight."

Run in and see the new curtains, the fresh flowers, the gay new rugs, the proof of her insanity, and smile at her quizzically, say without words "ah so you really did expect him to come back to you, you poor creature?"

"No, no," said Effie frantically. "I can't say when I'll be home. Perhaps later—oh please, Dennis, please!"

Please? An appeal to the ogre, the Enemy, a startling betrayal of her fear of him, her dearest friend. Dennis gave up, stunned. Consider we are enemies now, her frightened voice said, consider that in our battle you won, your book conquered me and now we may follow our different destinies, and please, oh please, have mercy on me now that you have won. . . . Deeply hurt, Dennis sat back in his desk-chair and smoked, glared at the six free author's copies of *The Hunter's Wife* piled on the table, hated himself for writing it, hated himself at this very instant for the sly return of the author-mind, the sly little annotations being made concerning wounded friendship, the sly little speculation twinkling through the hurt feelings. Now he would not hear first-hand how Callingham behaved, he would not hear details of the hunter's return for checking up on his own artistic intuition, he might never meet Callingham and be able to attack him for the way he handled the final chapter in his last book.

Furious at this opportunistic Second Self, this Bounder, or rather call it Artist-Self, Dennis savagely turned to his typewriter. Time he started work again on the new book, but each time he faced that Page 1 it seemed incredible he had ever got beyond it, he could not imagine ever having finished anything, ever having gone on to a Page 2. It was unbelievable that he had ever been able to shut off these incessant problems of his own life for the creation of imaginary problems. Now he would never be able to write again, he declared fiercely, he would be afraid of each written word now that words had destroyed Effie Thorne. This discouraging thought gave way to helpless indignation at Effie, the futile indignation of the male when the female collapses in tears right in the middle of the game. He was angry at Effie for having made herself so important to him, more important than any mistress he had ever had or any love or any family or any friend. He jeered at his blind foolish sense of safety in getting himself so deeply involved in another person's life, entering it with all shields down, weaponless, joyously secure because here was no marriage threat or permanent entanglement in the air to be dodged, since Effie was so much older, so obviously not in the arena, getting into the safe strange affair deeper and deeper, with his cocky self-assurance—here at last the perfect relationship, the feminine friend with no hooks out. . . . For the first time he realized how completely Effie had grown to fill his life, how after meeting her he had somehow dropped away from all other friends except for casual diversion or matter with which to amuse her later. She was the first friend he'd ever had who was unfailingly, dependably satisfying, to be counted upon for whatever odd mood his day's or night's writing had left. Curious how he, in turn, had taken the place of the circle of "interesting people" who had once drifted about Effie's life. He remembered how intensely they had talked, argued, agreed, laughed, with such undivided attention for each other that others in the room would slip away unnoticed, and presently they would be left alone like two absorbed lovers, not one person to each other but a complete circle. And now Callingham returning—or was it merely his book revealing him?—had ruined this relationship. Whatever was to blame for the breach, Dennis was aghast at his desolation without Effie, the one friend, the one firm peg on which his days had hung. Vengefully he wished he could have annihilated Callingham with his pen, but here again he would have ruined the thing he wished to preserve. . . . There was, of course, Corinne. . . . Here Artist-Self, or Bounder, suddenly suggested that Effie's greatest importance had been as buffer against his need for the feminine wife-touch, the touch that once creeping into the ordinary armor spells danger, marriage, promises, the trap. From behind Effie's skirts he had wooed his women, said his Artist-Self, the Bounder, the Cad, safe in loyal, tender understanding, all he needed from any other woman was a sweet little lust that need have no trailing ties. . . .

Impulsively Dennis rang up Corinne. Mrs. Barrow was out. Mrs. Barrow had gone for a little ride in Miss Baker's new car. So there was no Effie now and no Corinne. Miss Baker's new car indeed. The very innocence of Mrs. Barrow's simple pleasure made it suspect. In a minute, thought Dennis, astonished, I'm going to cry because nobody will play with me. Yes, sir, now he was going to be hurt at every little thing people said or did, he was very likely going to be jealous again of Corinne as a release for his other frustrations, very likely indeed judging by the sudden passionate rage at her being out. His jealous spell came, as a general thing, once a year about the time he'd finished a book and was feeling restless, nothing else to do with his imagination. It lasted about a month as a rule like influenza or spring cleaning. It had nothing to do with causes but had as germ some casual phrase from which it grew enormously, vining in and out of his nights and days, feeding itself on its own roots, tainting every thought and word. There was no explaining the start or equally unreasonable end of these seasonal furies, for real cause might pop up any other time to be most nonchalantly brushed aside. But now, thanks to Effie's desertion, thanks to Corinne's willful absence from her home at this needed hour, thanks to being unable to begin Page 1, the disease was on. He was jealous of Callingham, of the Glaenzers, of that little doctor, of all the people Effie now leaned upon, as well as jealous a trifle more logically of his little Corinne. Very well, very well, he would go out and make a new circle of friends, he vowed, he would drive off the fever with an army of Tom Collinses. Wonderful new friends, welcome to Dennis Orphen, he cried, welcome, new bunch, welcome, let's call each other up all the time. Why, thought Dennis angrily, there is absolutely nothing left for me to do but to call up Okie.

But Okie, too, was busy but say—how about joining them after the theater at the Alabam—a marvelous new place on Fiftieth—and wonderful girls in the party? At this moment, appropriately enough in the midst of his destructive thoughts, a large segment of ceiling fell down on the bed, followed by a shower of snowy plaster. Dennis was about to rush upstairs and find blessed relief in tearing down the whole house when the phone rang and it was Corinne. He was a little chagrined at his jealous suspicions having gone wrong. He would really have preferred being right, pride in his excellent intuitions outweighing vanity in commanding fidelity.

. . . the paper dolls . . .

"My hair ought to be done," grieved Marian. "I don't want Andy to see me this way. And a manicure."

The nurse had turned her over on her side facing the white dresser, and for some time she had lain there staring unhappily at her image in the mirror. Presently she closed her eyes so as not to see the greenish shadow creeping over her, blocking off into sharp angular segments her face and the narrow throat which, curiously shaded into definite planes, seemed transparent and no more than the esophageal skeleton itself. The always smooth-textured shining skin was drawn taut over the frame, flesh whittled by disease down to essential bone. Breathe deep, Effie thought, breathe long and deep now for these few hours must last you for eternity. Lifted up slightly against the pillows, Marian showed more plainly the devastation of her illness, and her long still body, sheet-covered, seemed already ready for its coffin. Effie felt herself drawn with pity and love for her, it seemed to her she had never loved anyone as she loved Marian for Marian was her own self and Andy and Andy's happiness all in one and now she was dying, all of them were going, going, their little pattern was dissolving like a pretty formation of twigs and leaves floating down a river, separated and forgotten at the first obstruction. Marian was her child, too, hers and Andy's, she was her sister, the two of them helping each other to stand before the storm, the hurricane, that was Andy's love and Andy's love withdrawn.

In her pink bedjacket the abnormal greenish pallor of the patient was more pronounced and with her blue eyelids drawn over glazing eyeballs the face spelled out the imminence of death. Effie looked beyond this out the window across the church spires, into the clouding sky for relief from the presence in the room, she looked down the street below, intently watched a man and woman wheel a perambulator of twins, all four alive, breathing, years, decades ahead of them somewhere up Lexington Avenue there. She watched a girl and boy dallying before the corner store, laughing because they, too, were triumphantly alive, each one hesitating to break the spell of each other's presence yet with nothing more to say they merely stood there laughing, swinging a foot, inarticulate, wondering why they were held and with each moment increasing the secret fear of a pattern breaking up, fragments lost, plan forgotten.

"I'd like my fingernails painted red," mused Marian, "as if I was all ready to go someplace. Oh my God, I'm going to die!"

Effie jumped, heart pounding.

"I'll die, Effie," screamed Marian, "and Andy will marry someone else, he'll marry that Asta and they will laugh at each other and forget me!"

Her eyelids flew open, wild eyes begged Effie for denials, thin fingers pressed against mouth to hold back the cry of terror. Effie's heart turned slowly over in her, the fear of death was loosed like a bat in the room, even the nurse, entering at the moment, took a sudden step backward as if blown back by the blast of dark terror that raced through the room. Effie's throat locked with this freezing word, she could not speak nor could her widened eyes break away from Marian's fierce inquiry, breathless, unable to look away or to smile, she gave back fear for fear, knowledge for knowledge. Yes, you will die, yes, yes, and no one can save you, no Andy, no lover returning, nothing, and he will be lost to you, murmuring in other live, vibrant arms, laughing in bedroom darkness, secretly exulting, your ghost forgotten as mine was once, is now. . . . But as soon as this swift certainty flashed between their fearing eyes denial surged forth and Effie burst out, "No, no, Marian, you won't die, oh never, dear, and Andy's coming, he's coming only for you, so rest now. I'll bring a manicurist, I'll get someone to do your hair, I'll be back."

The nurse beckoned her into the hall, and shook her head. "She can't lift her head for any hairdresser, Miss Thorne, she couldn't stand it. No use."

"Then what will I do?" Effie asked her, helpless, unwilling to disappoint the woman in the bed.

The nurse lifted starched white shoulders.

"Talk to her about her husband. You were related to him, weren't you? That seems to be the only thing that pleases her. Maybe you've got some pictures of him she's never seen—you knew him long ago, didn't you, before she met him?"

"Yes," said Effie thoughtfully, "I have some pictures."

"Pretend you're going for the hairdresser and run home for the pictures," suggested the nurse, and added quietly, "Hurry."

In her apartment later Effie went through her desk, collected all the photographs she had saved of Andy, snapshots, postcards, studio pictures as a boy, little celluloid medallions, showing a curled, round-faced baby lying on a bear rug, a shy four-year-old in a sailor suit, six years old in tight velvet kneepants, ruffled shirt, sulky mouth, leaning against his mother's shoulder in Berman's Studio, Cincinnati, or standing proudly beside his first bicycle, cap pulled down over radiant eyes. There, yellowed and carefully folded up, was his first poem, "A Boat Ride by Andy Callingham, age 8 years" . . . *"I like to ride in great big boats . . ."* here, in a drawer, was the letter he wrote to his mother from Aunt Bertha's cottage in the Adirondacks, "Dear mother, we have not seen each other for a long time. There is a boy here named Fred. I had the nosebleed and I asked Fred for his hakerchef but he wold not give it he said it was new then he ran away from me and I could not catch him till Wilbur Street and the nosebleed got all over my new pants. I am mad at Fred. I hope you are well. Your sincere son Andy."

There was the wedding picture of Charles and Alma Callingham, Andy's parents, and the second wedding picture of Charles and Estelle, the newspaper picture of Charles Callingham, new history head at the State University. Here were school diaries, clippings of early school triumphs. The boy Andy, thought Effie, belongs to me and to no one else, and then suddenly she knew she must take all these treasures to Marian, paper dolls to amuse the little sick girl.

"There!" whispered the nurse, nodding toward Marian's feverish joy in these relics. How happily and how completely Marian appropriated them, how possessively she forbade the nurse to touch them as they sprawled over the counterpane and slid to the floor. Even closing her eyes with drugged pain now and then, her greedy hands groped about to assemble all within her touch.

"He never told me about that poem," she murmured, puzzled. "And look, Effie, look at the face with his first bicycle. The funny little face of him!"

"And here all dressed up except the stocking falling down," Effie eagerly offered the Fauntleroy photograph. "This is his fifth birthday here, sitting on his Aunt Bertha's lap; that was in Boston the year his parents went abroad and left him there. His aunt had just punished him for scraping all the frosting off his cake. Look how scared he looks!"

A smile, tender and wishful, played about Marian's fine bluish lips, it sang through her eyes and the hands so lovingly lingering over these mementoes, a little lullaby of a smile, an emanation from the small scraps themselves, for it fluttered across Effie's lips also, delicate, fleeting, an odd little ghost of lost happiness, a butterfly blown about by death. Effie, returning from this enchanted dreamland first, was flicked with pain by the quiet proud possessiveness of Marian's hands on the boy's pictures. Mine, mine, Effie cried inside herself, oh, surely these are mine if nothing else, and then, surrendering, frightened, defeated, hunting for some other solace, "If I had had a baby, if I had had a son *that* would have been mine, that at least she could not share, Andy's and mine it would be—" she thought, desperate, defeated, pushing the scattered pictures toward Marian.

"If I had only had a baby," said Marian, "something of Andy always with me forever. Ah, Effie, I should have had a son!"

Effie could only nod bleakly, heart numb. There are words that cannot be borne, suggestions so burning with anguish and despair that no heart can endure them, so Effie, her lover stolen, her dream of a son now stolen, got to her feet and motioning, speechless, that she was leaving, found her way out of the intolerable room.

. . . the erlking . . .

"No," ANDY HAD SAID FIRMLY—she could still see him idly stretched out on the porch of the Glaenzer boathouse where they had docked for the weekend, though Belle had still not forgiven them completely for running away without her authority—"we both had too unpleasant childhoods ourselves to want any kids. Not till we can give them more than we ever got. There was I, for instance, batted from Aunt Bertha to Mother to Dad to Uncle Tom—all detesting each other and taking it out on me in obscure ways. Then at school with the headmaster having written a history not as well-received as my father's, so again I was the goat— Oh no, Effie, we don't give the world any whipping boy. Even if we had some sort of security to offer him—"

"Can't you just see those little embryos shopping around for security?" gloomily asked Effie. She had been hurt by his attitude as if her baby were already born and heard his father's insults. She didn't want to discuss it again, but brooded, and was surprised to remember her savage bitterness later when he played on the beach with two little towheads so gaily that their pretty mother said sympathetically, "What a pity Mr. Callingham has no little ones of his own!"

She remembered her desperate fear after he left her that he would in no time at all be the proud, even fatuous father of Marian's child, for if Marian wanted it she would get it willy-nilly, and then everyone would say, "Only natural and rather splendid for a man to leave a woman who won't give him a child for one who will". . . . Trying vainly now to find the clear path she should have taken then as if finding it now would make her any happier, she thought, Yes, that was the answer, I should have had a child no matter what he said. If she had been less in love with him, less generous, and more concerned in clinching her own future happiness than his, she would have gone against his expressed wishes calmly and deliberately. Other women did, God knows, and were richly rewarded for selfishness. Wayward males, declaring violently against paternity, were forever being touched and flattered by some girl's really not so romantic determination to express her own ego at any cost, they were flattered into permanent loyalty, finding a strange source of pride in the lady's willfulness, as if this proved that their own charm was stronger than they realized if it impelled this urge in the woman. Their male independence once boldly expressed they were secretly well-pleased to be led back into the conventional haven.

For a long time after Andy had gone Effie thought, Thank God, it is only I who must bear this loneliness, there's no one I need comfort when I have no comfort to give. But now she felt differently. She should have had the child. She would have had something, someone, her life would have been more complete, no one else could have claimed this trophy of love, either, it would have been hers, blind or crippled or lame, it would have been her very own as Mrs. Hickey's little Tom was Mrs. Hickey's own, someone to cherish while Hickey was in the hospital with his mustard gas lungs, someone, yes, little Tom, even with blue-veined hands, halting speech, lost blank eyes, braced hips, and shriveled legs, even so he was Mrs. Hickey's own.

"I had it when I was fourteen," Dennis said one day, watching Tom from Effie's window. "I dragged my leg for a long time, but it's not so noticeable now except when I dance. I always do a rhumba or some sort of stylish dip no matter what the music calls for. Maybe Tom'll get over it."

Tom was Mrs. Hickey's, hers and no one else's. White, thin-lipped, defiant little Mrs. Hickey waited for him outside the public school, stood outside beside the Special Bus when the first dismissal bell sounded, and a sudden high shrill shriek, many children's voices blended into one cry of freedom, sounded louder and louder till the big doors burst open with it and all the little broken children stumbled out, on crutches, in braces, limping, fumbling, stuttering, the little Specials, their leaping cry at liberty as loud as the Regulars to be released ten minutes later. Mrs. Hickey, standing to one side of the gate so as not to embarrass Tom by betraying his need of her support, could single him out at once, swinging books along by a strap, twisted leg in silver brace dragging; she could see a bigger boy push him back and knock his head, laughing, against the wall, and she had to keep herself from rushing to his defense, she could see his lost blank smile, bewildered, uncomprehending, but she must not interfere, this was boy's play, make a man of him, though so far as that went, he would never hit back, never, he was too gentle, and he only looked dazed at taunts. Not normal, the teacher had firmly told her, sub, she added briskly, and for the mother, facing clear-eyed skeptical educator, there was no use telling about the poem he wrote, a drawing he made, the toy airplane he built with his own weak little hands, but some of these days the teachers would be sorry, some day they would see how wrong they were.

"Let's go home now," said Mrs. Hickey as she always did, and took his hand. He blew along beside her skirts, frail, spindly leg dragging; passers-by looked curiously at his blank little face, they turned eagerly to watch him drag the distorted foot. His mother stared somberly ahead, oh, some day he would be a great poet, a great composer, an engineer, a president, look at Roosevelt, he would confound all the starers, the teachers, the cruel other children, he would astound them all, but for the present there is no kindness or understanding in all the world for a mother to beg or buy for those moments she cannot utterly surround him with her love, and hurrying along the street, half-carrying him, her fierce lonely love for the sad child flowed out of her and all around him and made her strong, Olympian, heroic, made the erlking himself, riding ever so close behind them, fade away into a dream, a legend only.

And Effie, at her window with the new curtains blowing, watched them unfastening the basement gate and she wished that Tom was hers, broken little boy that no one else would want or could take, something from Andy for her alone. She caught Mrs. Hickey's quick proud smile as he locked the gate behind him without falling, and she envied Mrs. Hickey, envied her for a woman who had someone, something that no one else would ever claim.

I I I

. . . to a wild rose . . .

"Tell me," said Corinne, "who was your very first love and how old were you and was she like me? Tell me."

"Of my awakening?" pondered Dennis. "It must have been Minnie. Yes, by Jove, it was Minnie. I was twelve."

"Then you lived in Yonkers," said Corinne with satisfaction at her fine memory.

"I hadn't moved to Yonkers yet," corrected Dennis. "My mother was still alive so we were in Terre Haute. Anyway all the older boys talked about Minnie with a knowing leer. My chum—Cliff Riley was his name by the way and now he's a big judge in Washington or maybe that was his older brother Chester; that's right, Clifford never turned out very well. Anyway my chum Cliff and I were devoured with lust and a dreadful curiosity about sex which never seemed to get us anywhere. We tagged along with the judge who was of course only fifteen or so at that time but anyway he did know Minnie, and how. Cliff and I nearly went crazy wondering about Minnie. Cliff was eleven and we both were small for our age and cursed with short pants, a big handicap in luring women to your rooms. As a matter of fact, we were about the two most lureless lads in the whole damn town."

"It can't be true, darling," said Corinne.

She sipped at her strawberry soda, making a funny little noise through the straw which appeared to please her mightily for when the straw broke down under its musical burden she took two fresh ones and began a note higher on her piping, a simple enough pleasure after all for Empire

State Tower visitors which they were, though Dennis for his part preferred to accompany the view with a perfectly noiseless coca-cola. Clouds
as white as if the sky was baby-blue instead of black swam softly about
them, stars were below and above, glittering through the plumes of the
moon, listening for compliments from the Tower visitors.

"Are you going to put this story in a book?" interrupted Corinne suspiciously. "If you are, don't tell it to me now. I hate having things tried out
on me. Let's just talk instead."

"Hush," suggested Dennis. "Grampa is reminiscing. Yes, it was Minnie
who awakened me. Cliff and I had heard about this boy and that boy taking Minnie out behind the church, for in this town the boys were cads and
told. Cliff and I, frustrated by our short pants, just hung around looking
wise and snickering evilly at the older fellows' fun."

"With me it was my music teacher," said Corinne. "He was forever
teaching me *To a Wild Rose.*"

"Interesting," said Dennis. "So finally Cliff and I decided that we had
to find out and two small boys were just as good as one big one, so we
waited together for Minnie to come along one day. She was about six feet
tall but our taste hadn't formed yet and anyway she was all there was to
be had. Pretty soon Minnie came down the street. Cliff and I—"

"The judge and you," said Corinne.

"No, that was Chester and another kettle of fish. Cliff and I clutched
each other and stepped boldly out in front of her. She stared at us, not re-
alizing at first our plan. 'Hello, Minnie,' we said together, giving her a big
leer, 'how about it?' With that she picked us up by the scruffs of our necks
and knocked our heads together. That was my first big experience and
that was sex in Terre Haute."

"The music teacher wasn't so terribly handsome, it was just that he
was the only man in school," answered Corinne. They walked out on the
terrace and eighty-six stories below them the city night spread out in a
garden of golden lights; trucks, trains, ferryboats crawled soundlessly in
and out of the island puzzle. They sat down on the steel bench, their arms
about each other. "All the girls at Miss Roman's were crazy about him,
but he fell for me, he really did; as I look back on it now I realize he was
pretty crazy about me—considering that he was over thirty and I was
only thirteen. We called him Ducky."

"Ducky, hmm," said Dennis. "Very refreshing."

"I started on *To a Wild Rose* in September and I couldn't play it by June," said Corinne. "I still can't play it. Ducky would just talk to me and once he snatched my hands and kissed them madly. He would stare at me with great burning eyes in the mirror over the pipe organ—he played for the chapel service, see—and I was the first girl in the procession and coming down the chapel aisles I would see him staring at me in the mirror and I'd get the giggles, really, right in the middle of *Crown Him the King of Kings*."

Dennis kissed her.

"Poor old Cliff never got anywhere, it was always his brother," he said. "Chester was the big shot of the Riley family, he had push and another thing he was a very steady boy. Worked nights in the telegraph tower as an operator to get money to go to Notre Dame while Cliff and I were wasting our time on Minnie."

"Getting your heads cracked," said Corinne. "Darling, do you ever see that Beverly girl you used to run around with before me?"

"I've told you a million times I never see her any more," Dennis, exasperated, exclaimed. "I promised you I'd give her up, didn't I? You don't think a man of my caliber would go back on his promise, do you?"

He was aggrieved. Corinne moved away from him as a little boy in plaid plus fours ran away from his father and dropped a coin in the telescope in front of them. Then, as the machine recklessly ticked off the precious minutes, he spent his dime in staring at the couple on the bench with scientific concentration.

"I know you promised. I was just asking if you ever saw her."

"What can you do with a woman who won't trust you?" Dennis invited the sky and the curious little boy to make answer. "Anyway she lives in London now, so how could I see her?"

"That's the only reason men ever keep promises like that," observed Corinne. "The girl has either moved away or died."

"I'm afraid there's something in that, Honeysugar," agreed Dennis politely. "Vows of abstinence are valid only when supported by a major inconvenience, biological or geographical. Old saw."

"Thank you," said Corinne. "I'm crazy about you, Old Sawmaster. You're so attractive to me. I suppose any other woman would wonder what I saw in you. If your book is a success you'll start cruising around again, won't you, dear? Society women will take you up."

"Let those society women just try to get me, let them just try," boasted Dennis.

"Some of them aren't so bad-looking," Corinne said jealously. "They all wear triple-A size seven and have bad knees but they do have plenty of teeth. I'll bet you fall for them. You'll get white pants and a hat with a front and back to it and you'll run around with next year's debutantes."

"Only for material," said Dennis with the quiet smirk of conquest already on his face. "A literary man has to go a great many places and do a lot of queer, often disagreeable things for his material, my dear. It's the artist's cross. I'll have to endure all those rotogravure beauties just to learn a few society songs and dances, something for my notes."

"I'm going to write, too, Dennis. I really am," said Corinne.

Dennis looked uneasy.

"Not those sad little glad-I'm-sorry poems that women always write when they're nervous?" he asked.

"You know I can't rhyme things," said Corinne. "No, this is little prosies, little glad-I-see-things-quaintly ones. I sold one already to the *Manhattanite*. I didn't want to tell you while you're so wrapped up in your own success, your book coming out tomorrow and all that."

"You sold a story? No!"

"It was easy." Corinne waved her cigarette. "I studied their style. It's just a trick. Olive and I figured it out. You take an Uncle Wiggly story and change the animals to quaint old bachelors or dear old ladies who economize. You use very tiny words and all the adverbs you can use are 'rather' and 'quite' and 'very' and 'really.'"

"How did your story go?" inquired Dennis, still impressed and thinking of Phil boasting all over the club of his wife's artistic triumph.

"I took 'Sticky-toes the Tree-Toad was really quite cross,'" said Corinne. "I changed it to 'Mr. Wootle, the funny old bachelor, was really quite cross' and so on."

"Damn clever," said Dennis, astonished.

"Olive is working on Buddy Bear," Corinne added. "It begins 'Buddy Bear and Mrs. Bear hadn't been asked to Tawny Tiger's birthday party. Buddy Bear did not mind so very much but Mrs. Bear really felt quite cross.' Olive changed it to 'Mr. and Mrs. Wuppins had not been asked to the Major's birthday party which made—'"

"I get it, I get it," interrupted Dennis hastily. "I still think writing is a man's work."

"I suppose you're afraid it will make me a little horsey," said Corinne scornfully. She jumped up and walked over to the stone balustrade, leaned her face on her clasped hands and sighed. New York twinkled far off into Van Cortlandt Park, spangled skyscrapers piled up softly against the darkness, tinseled parks were neatly boxed and ribboned with gold like Christmas presents waiting to be opened. Sounds of traffic dissolved in distance, all clangor sifted through space into a whispering silence, it held a secret, and when letters flamed triumphantly in the sky you felt, ah, that was the secret, this at last was it, this special telegram to God— Sunshine Biscuits. On and off it went, Eat Sunshine Biscuits, the message of the city.

"Darling," said Corinne.

. . . you will meet at a place of amusement . . .

"WHATSA MATTER, whereya been, here we been waitin', whatsa idea callin' up if you arna gonna be here, issen atso, Gracie?" Okie was tight so that his basic resentment against all his magazine's contributors, particularly those he needed most, was floating to the surface. He glared at Dennis defiantly above the smile of good fellowship mechanically placed on his mouth, he was about to say more but obviously nothing devastating enough rose to mind, and he must content himself with, "You writers! All the same! Oh, dyah, I had to finish my second act. Oh my, Red Lewis and Teddy Dreiser and Maxie Reinhardt dropped in and I couldn't get rid of 'em! Oh, Bee Lillie and Gingie Rogers were kiddin' me about never givin' 'em a buzz—always some excuse."

Dennis slid on to the chromium-plated bar stool beside Okie. He knew Okie was reaching a pitch of rage where his only relief would be for someone to be a Jew. Oh, if only everybody could be Jews or women, was Okie's silent prayer, so that in times of stress one could hurl the name, one or the other, at them, with all Christianity, all masculinity behind one, and then once spoke, the shot fired, to relax proudly victorious! There was, to be sure, some pleasure in other classifications but these were less satisfying. There was modest fun in You Swedes, You Catholics, You Yankees, You Wops, You Southerners, You Methodists, You Harvard Boys, You Dekes, You Artists, You Lawyers, etc., but these were not real destroyers, and often as not a certain envy crept into Okie's voice as he flung out these names, an envy which naturally was not in his two major classifications. He made up for this sense of inadequate epithet by whispering a suspicion of Jewish ancestry or feminine characteristics in You

Swedes or You Harvard Boys. He had, as a matter of fact, only a moment before Dennis's arrival hinted that no one knew quite where old Orphen stood, you never saw him with any steady girl, but he was suspiciously devoted to an older woman, someone old enough to be his mother. Old Orphen was foxy enough to disguise all other traces of his weakness but there was always something mighty suspicious in that older woman racket and he got that straight out of Freud. As soon as Okie had made this insinuation Gracie on one hand and Boots on the other had given him a sound kick in the shins and Lora, Okie's own girl for the past few years, looked vaguely down at her drink and then toward Tony Glaenzer beside her, so Okie, reminded of the glass house so near, quickly gulped down his Scotch and ordered another one as Dennis came up.

Dennis looked around the place. It was like all of the wonderful little secret places Okie discovered in the Broadway district, little places with their own special crowd, tail ends of the theater, fringes and pale copies of more celebrated circles. There was the same modernistic silver and glass bar, the same glittering mirrors with liqueur bottles stacked in geometric design invariably crowned by the beautiful Fiore d'Alpi, sugar-frosted tree in the green bottle promising exotic surcease from the harsher realities of gin or Scotch. A few chromium-trimmed red tables were crowded around the little dance floor and in the middle, flanked by unbelievably bushy, fiercely tropical palms, was a tiny poppy-colored piano spraddled by a lean, chinless, pompadoured pianist who smiled vaguely and not too promisingly at the eager lady customers as his long competent hands collected handfuls of sprawling sugary chords. A large policeman-type tenor walked slowly about the floor singing in a rich honeyed whine and this was really the proprietor, easy enough to guess for even while he was somberly whining, "A boyuh—ahnd—ah gurrul—war dahncing—" he kept a keen eye on the bartender to make sure no cheating was going on, and when he was not warbling this shrewd fellow (called "Sammy" to suggest the affectionate esteem of the Broadway crowd) stood in the outer vestibule bowing welcome to new arrivals but fixing eyes on an innocent mirror upon which the bar activities were remirrored, all of which the bartender knew perfectly well, having been warned by the Cuban hat-check girl.

Dennis recognized Tony Glaenzer between the two new blondes Okie's genius had provided. These blondes, Gracie and Boots, were surprisingly like his last pair, though Okie seemed as proud as if he had just uncovered a fresh race.

"Boots is Tony's girlfriend," Okie whispered, "just back from her show."

That Boots was Tony's girlfriend was patent from Tony's all-enveloping princely possessive air and from the girl's discreet manner, a special arrogance that could pass for "class" and small wonder she should adopt this, for Tony, with her, became doubly the aristocrat, triply the aloof patrician; his pointed absorption in her declared defiantly her worthiness for the honor, and permitted her to share in his own private privilege of snubbing her friends, just as it gave these same friends, excluding them as it did, their own privilege of rather bitter class consciousness.

Boots raised heavy-lashed pretty eyes to Dennis in greeting and then lowered them modestly to her seventh stinger. She was very tiny but rounded and wore severe little tailored dresses to offset her essential cuteness. When she got up to dance with Tony she stretched herself stiffly erect and took long swooping steps to match his while he bent, bored, Byronically gloomy, over her. She looked haughtily over the heads of the lone men ogling her at the bar. Men? the look said, I never even heard of them, and in her demure acceptance of Tony's polite rather than amorous absorption she seemed to proclaim her resolute unchallenged, decent, high-class virginity, and even to the bartender whom she knew quite well and to Sammy and the other acquaintances who had seen her many nights before Tony Glaenzer discovered her and made her respectable through isolation she employed a new manner of speech, something that was not quite Southern nor yet British but more genteel and more wonderful than either, certainly far more intriguing since the refinement in accent was perpetually questioned by the deep-blues voice.

Gracie was another matter, and since there was no talking to Tony, Dennis applied himself to her.

"She's the artist Gracie Kessel I told you about," Okie breathed excitedly in his ear. "She's the nymphomaniac."

"Thanks, pal," said Dennis.

Gracie smiled at him over her Tom Collins and pushed a salami sandwich toward him.

"Go ahead, I don't want it, honest."

Gracie's pure beautiful blue eyes in her calm fair face and her dewy baby skin, her sincerely naïve expression, challenged her sinister reputation. Her matronly figure with accompanying good-natured sentimentality—*Aw, Sammy, why don't you let me have that little kid of yours, honestly, Mr. Orphen, Sammy's got the darlingest brat you ever saw*—and then her sudden bawdy exclamations followed by gusty uproarious laughter were more like a healthy, sensual young village bride chuckling with the other village wives of their new knowledge. Drunk, she talked so much and so pompously of her art that it was hard to believe she was regarded as seriously as she actually was in that world. Anxious to be friends she sympathized with Dennis over the success of other writers as if it were axiomatic that every writer or artist automatically detested every other worker or work in his own subject, and every success in any line was legitimate enemy for no other reason but his success. Egotistically enough, Gracie was more jealous of men than of women and apt to dismiss her female competitors with a large gesture. She accepted the kisses, lingering strokes, and whispered flattery of the men who wandered in and out of the place with a gracious, proud complacency as if this were homage indeed, these ex-hoofers, gamblers, small racketeers, friends of friends of celebrities. These big shots knew their business, knew a great artist when they saw her.

"That's the way it is everywhere Gracie goes," Okie boasted. "You can't walk in any place without somebody coming up—it's hi, Gracie, *good* evening, Miss Kessel, hello there, Gracie, wherever you go."

"Ah, they only think I'm in the money," disparaged Gracie, smiling, not really believing her words. A complete peasant type, reflected Dennis, enormous vitality and lust combined with shrewd narrow bigotry. With each drink her voice went a pitch higher, words lingering on the air, whining, coaxing, often bitter words, but excused by the childish little girl whine. They lingered on the air like stale tobacco smoke, and her infrequent pauses were grateful whiffs of clear mountain air through which Dennis could watch, fascinated, enchanted, Okie's girl, Lora. No, he had never seen anyone like Lora, never, captured as always by a cool mysterious face no matter how banal the secret it concealed. The only thing against her was Okie, but he must dismiss this objection as another proof of man's basic conventionality, unconsciously baited or repelled by the quality of a lady's previous lovers. Again, only a half hour removed from Corinne's goodnight kiss, he must question the validity of this sudden warm interest in Lora. Was it his practical literary curiosity once again, the constant buzzard at work rather than the man, or could it be due to that odd little instrument located somewhere near the heart that gave warning signals when the organ itself was getting dangerously involved, instructed the master to flee, shift, break, do something quickly before the sudden avalanche of pain that was real feeling? These last few days without the protective hedge of Effie Thorne's all-sufficient friendship—a friendship that had been worn by both as an armor against the rest of the world and against all other contact, without this buffer Dennis had felt himself drawn, sucked into bondage to Corinne, he glimpsed aghast the unamusing sinister face of scandalous, unreasoning, ruinous, self-destroying Love, and this must not be. With or without her husband, with or without her gratifying but on the other hand suspect passion, with or without obstacles, there was grave danger for Orphen the individual, Orphen the independent, heart-free fellow.

"Now why must I always get hysterical when I see a Big Moment ahead?" Dennis asked himself, "as if a Great Love as we used to term it were a supreme faux pas? Is it because I doubt my qualifications for the Great Lover role, is it that I realize what a ridiculous figure I would cut, infatuate, easy victim for gulling? Is it because all the persons I ever loved as a boy died or left me or in some way taught me not to let myself in for too much feeling? I wish to God I was someone else, say, Okie there, so I could analyze myself, find out of what this strange barrier consists. How do I know, maybe it's mere gypsy blood, or claustrophobia, or—the hell with it."

"What I don't understand," said Gracie loudly, nodding toward Tony and Boots, "is why if they're so darn wrapped up in each other they always have to go out with a crowd. They don't really want to be alone— you'd think so to look at 'em—but it's not so. They could go someplace else if they wanted to. But, oh no, they got to have an audience, got to have people around to snoot."

"Don't let Gracie have any more, Bill," Boots primly instructed the bartender. Tony looked idly at Dennis.

"Haven't I seen you before?"

"Apparently not," said Dennis rather sourly.

Okie pulled Dennis's ear toward him and hissed, "Glaenzer gives me a pain in the pod. These playboys always being such big shots with the girls just because there's millions in the offing! In the offing is right. I'll bet he ain't got more'n two bits in his pants right now, his old woman thinks that'll police him. Say, you can't hold back an eel or a sponge either, eh, Orphen, just holding out on their pennies? Watch him now. Every time the check comes round he's all of a sudden on the dance floor or in the can, and as for Boots, why, nobody can touch her since she made this swell catch. All the girls envyin' her—wishin' they had a big moneyboy too so they could have the privilege of payin' his way everyplace and passin' out the taxi-money. I'll betcha Boots has borrowed a thousand bucks from her friends so she could afford this so-called windfall! Hell, his old lady will never die and never let him go—he'll cut his throat waiting for her! Ssst! Lora's my girl, understand, but Boots there is my type. Get it, Orphen? Get the picture? Ah, you old sonofagun, sure you do!"

Dennis looked at Lora. She never spoke but sat on the bar stool quietly sipping her highball. She was frail, exquisitely thin and smart in a gray nun-like gown with high collar, a capelet chastely fastened to the shoulder with a diamond clasp. Her small bonnet drooped a narrow veil over her forehead and her blue-black hair lay in stiff sculptured scallops against her narrow white face, an almost abnormally narrow Madonna face with glowing dead-black eyes, delicately cut nostrils, lovely red mouth. In her fine little ears tiny jewels gleamed and on her wrist from the nun-like white cuffbands peeped a slender diamond-studded platinum chain. Now just where, reflected Dennis, does she get those?

"Dance?" he asked.

Okie stared gloomily at them over his glass as they moved to the dance floor. Dennis was bewildered to find that this silent, controlled sphinx could scarcely stand on her feet, must grope at chairs and tables for balance as she passed, but he could not really believe she was tipsy. Taking her in his arms gave him a disturbing sensation of holding absolutely nothing, of clutching only the floating scarves of her demure French gown and no woman at all. A faint halo of Oriental perfume swam about her, yet this carried no more hint of sensuality than her narrow frail shoulders or inconsequential body, seemed rather incense from some mystic temple, as elusive as a dream not quite remembered. Cheek to cheek, dancing, Dennis drew back, puzzled and vaguely repelled by her unearthliness, she seemed to the touch the sawdust torso of a boudoir doll, and the cellophane glaze he now detected over her eyes and the waxy perfection of her immobile face, these were the charms of embalmed queens, virtues for the historian rather than the live, questing male. She floated numbly through the dance, her eyes never blinked, when he addressed her she smiled beautifully, idly, and by her silence and the lingering smile gave an irresistible impression of intelligence nicely muffled for masculine appreciation. She swayed from him finally toward the red-curtained Ladies' Room, and when Dennis returned to the bar Gracie whispered, "Lora's a dip, you know, we'll probably have to take her home pretty soon."

"A dipsomaniac? Lora? *Lora?*"

Gracie nodded.

"Drinks all day long but always the lady. The only way you know is when she starts falling down. Nobody can pick her up. Just like a piece of wet soap. Okie and I had to drag her by the fanny all the way home the other night. Just folds right up."

"Lora does that? *Lora?*"

"Hears everything going on, though, don't kid yourself about that, even after she's passed out," warned Gracie. "Remembers every crack and hands it back to you later on. Okie runs around with her because she's the only person in town that'll stay up all night any night and go anyplace any time."

"Where does Okie get with her?" Dennis asked.

"Nowhere." Gracie snickered. "Lora's always half-unconscious and such a lady besides, so Okie just has to burn up."

Dennis asked so many questions about Lora and watched the curtained door for her return with such obvious interest that Gracie became annoyed. She confided her annoyance to Okie. They danced and Dennis uneasily saw them whispering, exchanging their unfavorable thoughts about him, the snob, the pansy, the phony. It occurred to him that he was bound to Okie by a chain of insults. Each meeting, either in the magazine office or in a restaurant, began on a fairly jovial friendly basis and ended with Okie wounded, sat upon, insulted. Unwillingly apologetic, Dennis would call up again, proffer an invitation, assume the jolly pal pose, let's have a drink, and then the insult popped out again, the subtly snobbish remark, the vaguely patronizing implication, and once again Okie had to be mollified by a phone call, another comradely gesture. Now, openly yearning for Boots as he had confessed, he was nevertheless offended by Dennis's interest in Lora.

"So this place isn't good enough for you, eh? So this is just a cheap Broadway joint, eh?" he loudly inquired, coming back to the bar stool beside Dennis. "It's good enough for Anthony Glaenzer, I guess, and he could be in the best club in town right now if he wanted to be. That right, Boots? Look at those eyelashes, will you, on that kid, Dennis, lookat! Don't tell me they're real, now honest, Boots."

"But they are," said Boots and she and Tony exchanged a quiet superior smile. Boots couldn't endure Okie, but if Tony thought he was such a card she could take it, particularly since he paid the check. A young actor's agent, swarthy, handsome, shifty, occasionally came up and talked to her but Tony was not jealous of this intrusion, it gave the added luster of her profession, an added importance, making her doubly worthy of his haughty favor.

"No, sir," Okie called to the bartender, "this guy here thinks the Alabam's not good enough, he's the big prize author, y'see, he thinks that means somethin'. Listen, bud, that little pen of yours means very little to the Alabam, eh, Bill, eh, Sammy? You can kid about my magazine all you want but they know about that here and not about that little prize of yours. Well, Sammy, old boy . . . Sammy owns this place, a great character, Sammy, if you writers had any literary sense at all you'd put him in a book, but, oh no, the proprietor of the Alabam isn't good enough for your high-class books, you got to write about Lady Agatha and that old blue-blooded family. No kidding, Sammy, don't these writers give you a pain in the pod? Great old boy—Sammy, there. I know him personally. Hell, I been in here a hundred times. I know Sammy all right."

"And now Sammy knows me," said Dennis, none too amiably.

Okie slapped him on the shoulder.

"I was just kidding, boy, don't you know good-natured fun when you hear it? Why, say, Bill,—hey, bartender, another drink all around and give Lora a stiff one."

"A stiff one knocks her out so it saves her drinking all night," Gracie explained laconically to Dennis.

The bartender was a thin concentrated little man, facial contours tight, black hair slicked back in a neat side-part, trim little wrestling body, a young man at first glance judging by his nimbleness and young face but a second look revealed the mass of tiny furrows, the sailor's weather-beaten face masked in healthy tan, with age only briefly betrayed by fanged old tobacco teeth, weary yellowed eyes, scant hairs too black and too cautiously arranged for careless youth. Arrogantly he mixed his drinks, flipped the tips into his hip pocket, slid the glasses down the marble counter to the bidder, contempt for the Alabam, the customers, their tips, and for alcohol in the large betrayed by every gesture of the wiry competent little hands. You call this a job, you call this a life, you call that good music, you call *her* beautiful, you call this New York—Say! As he passed the highball to Dennis he yanked words out of the side of his mouth like a ventriloquist, as secretly and cautiously as if Gay-Pay-U men were all about and the message itself was highly political.

"'At true you're a writer?" he asked. "'At true about the prize and the books—whatsat name again, chief?"

"Orphen. Sure it's true."

The bartender smiled secretly, craftily, attended to some call at the end of the bar and then came back, still smiling mysteriously.

"Wanta know something, chief? I'm a writer myself. Sure, I write stories. I got a book. Sure. Goin' to be published, too, so no wisecracks. Say, I don't have to work here. When this book comes out—listen—here's the payoff, it's about that guy there, about Sammy. Nah, he don't care, he's tickled to death. He tells everybody somebody's made a book about him, all puffed up about it. He don't say I did it, he wants all the credit himself. It's about this place, right here, the Alabam. A writer's got to write about what he knows, don't he? That's what this guy tells me, 'at's goin' to publish it. Sure, I got a publisher. He comes here all the time, just to get the feel of the place, check up on my story. Damn nice guy, not a bit stuck-up. We get along. There he is, over there at the table, over there by the palms."

Dennis looked around the tables in the general direction of Bill's wide gesture. Then he blinked to make sure his eyes were not deceiving him. No mistake, however, about that pleasant well-bred face, that sharply etched mustache. It was Johnson himself, no less.

. . . the blue hours . . .

JOHNSON WAS NOT TOO GLAD to see Dennis. He made no pretense of
smiling a welcome as Dennis drew up a chair at his table, but that his
gloom was not personally directed at his client was soon evident. It was a
despondency stimulated, as he well knew, by the perfectly unreasonable
competency of his new rival at MacTweed's, unreasonable because the
least a wealthy young man buying his way into a firm can do for his less
fortunate coworkers is to be dumb. But, oh no, young Hiller had to be
bright, shrewd almost to the point of crookedness—oh, happy Mac-
Tweed! . . . In a way Johnson held it against his unsuspecting author that
The Hunter's Wife had not sold out its first printing in advance of publication as he had so generously prophesied, and he was out of sorts with his
protégé, the bartender, because the type of literature he represented, the
type religiously encouraged by Johnson heretofore, was imperceptibly retreating before the avalanche of Old South novels. His new rival had
practically sold MacTweed the idea that no novel was acceptable or publishable unless it registered a dreamy, high-class nostalgia for the Old
South; and such sagas were springing up by the hundreds, proud answers
to *Tobacco Road*. There were already half a dozen on the MacTweed list
and Johnson morosely doubted if he could squeeze in even one hard-
hitting monosyllabic pastiche of the People. Looking about the Alabam,
he thought, A year ago I would have sworn there was a natural in each of
these hard-boiled Broadway figures. Now, since that young snort has
come into the office I doubt my own hunches and believe in his—they're
all the last of old Southern families. He could shut his eyes and read their

stories, he saw the old mammies and their violet-colored sons who looked so strangely like young Marse Jephthah, he sensed the magnificent decay, the cud'ns, the cun'ls, the haughty revelation that these splendid old aristocrats were the author's own family.

Embittered by this in general, Johnson was depressed over more immediate woes. He was blue but blue with a sour greenish nimbus that spread out and tainted all who came near, a veritable poison gas emanated from him which he would gladly have used to destroy his own protégé behind the bar as well as the group with Dennis Orphen, a group he had been observing with acute dislike, from the loud red-faced fellow to the smallest, prettiest blonde. By way of minor revenge on the world, he resolved to nag Orphen about writing what he wrote the way he wrote it, he would, he reflected with a ghost of mild pleasure, make him feel like a cad for being a Northerner, and as preparation—seeing Dennis approach—he fastened on an obscure uncle who had settled in Coral Gables as his own claim to a Dixie flag.

"How's the advance on the book?" asked Dennis, with a slightly patronizing nod toward his friends at the bar—have your fun, wastrels, the nod implied, I'm putting in a few swift strokes of business.

Johnson shrugged and looked mysteriously down his nose.

"Has any of the critics reported yet—or any word from the out-of-town dealers?" Dennis urged.

"It isn't the kind of book," said Johnson carefully, "that we can expect everyone to like. Not really."

"Oh, it isn't?"

Johnson smiled.

"After all it's no *Bellamy Bountree,* you know."

"Hm," said Dennis thoughtfully. "That's true, of course."

"In a way," pursued Johnson, gently sadistic, "it's a sort of a tour de force."

A tour de force! Dennis winced at the slighting words. No-Bellamy-Bountree was bad enough but sort-of-a-tour-de-force was even more devastating. Seeing Dennis as crushed as he could wish and some of his own azure mood creeping over his companion, Johnson felt a faint glow of friendliness. He leaned across the table.

"Do you know, Orphen, I've gone home from this damnable joint three times tonight and each time had to come back? I have no place else to go. I hate it. If that man sings *Trees* again I'm going to chop him down myself."

"Apparently you don't realize that these simple gangsters and chorines have hearts of gold," said Dennis. "They love and laugh like any one else and when they part they sue. Just like Park Avenue."

"Who are those awful friends of yours?" asked Johnson.

"Come over to the bar and meet them," suggested Dennis, not too warmly. "You won't need a place to stay, then."

Johnson shook his head with violent revulsion at the mere fancy.

"I detest people, Orphen, everybody!" he cried savagely. "Do you realize that I have been turned out of my home—not just tonight but any night? Wait till that happens to you and you'll laugh on the other side of your face too. . . . No, no—it isn't the sheriff turning me out, it's just old Bing."

Seeing Dennis's blank bewilderment at this information Johnson went into angry explanation.

"You see my wife's gone to the Vineyard to open our house so I took an apartment with old Bing. You probably know him, he's the junior partner at Lambert and Company. What happens? Every night when I go home there's Bingy's girl in my bed. Sometimes her clothes are in the living room, sometimes in the bathroom, sometimes she's even in my pajamas, but she's *always* in my bed. I have to back out. 'Sorry, Bing old man,' I say, and go out. 'Quite all right, Johnson, old chap,' he says. I come back to this dreadful hole—I drink—presently I go to Thirty-ninth Street again. She's still there. 'Terribly sorry, old man,' I say and out again. 'Quite all right,' says Bingy. Do you realize that I haven't had a night's sleep since I plunked down my half of the two hundred for rent? Do you realize—" his voice rose to a wail and for a second Dennis thought he might burst into outright tears—"my pillows, my bath towels, my very toothbrush, by God, have been so saturated with Chanel Five for these last ten days that every time I pass a poolroom the boys start to whistle? Is it any wonder I lost my temper to MacTweed today? Is it any wonder I wish I hadn't encouraged that wretched fellow behind the bar there to write his story? And for God's sake, Orphen, why do you hang around a place like this? Haven't you any pride?"

"Me hang around this place?" Dennis retorted in resentment. "This is my first trip here. *You're* the old habitué, my friend."

Johnson ignored this simple truth and looked at him firmly, reproach-fully.

"The idea! A man of your talents—I don't say genius because yours is not a gift to be mentioned in the same breath with, say, that of titans like Wells and Callingham—but a man of your abilities—"

"Make it a man of my limitations, if you like," offered Dennis genially.

Johnson waved this aside.

"—to waste your creative hours in a cheap Broadway dive, frankly, Orphen, shocks me. I don't know what MacTweed would say to it. Here you are, mind you, I'm not moralizing, Heaven forbid, I like a dash of wild oats as well as the next one—" This, Dennis, thought, was an out-and-out lie, for no one disliked wild oats or even tame oats more than Johnson; oats were his hayfever and no use boasting any other reaction—"but for you, right on the eve of a significant event—no use denying *The Hunter's Wife* coming out tomorrow is a significant event—here you are, roistering like any ham crooner. I don't like to see it, Orphen."

"Maybe you'd like the Havana Bar better," suggested Dennis. "It's just a few blocks down."

Johnson was disarmingly delighted at this idea. On the way out Dennis introduced him to Okie and Lora and Gracie—Boots and Tony were swooping about the dance floor—and Gracie flung her arms wildly about Johnson.

"I love this man, honest," she cried. "I adore that little mustache—oh *cu-ute!* No kidding I love this fellow. Where's he been all my life, Sugar-pie? You don't mind my calling you-all Sugarpie, do you? That's what my old mammy used to call me."

Johnson drew back stricken.

"He wants to stay, doncha, Sugarpie?" crooned Gracie, suddenly inef-fably Southern, even to her soft innocent gurgle as she snuggled Johnson's reluctant face in her neck.

"Do you?" asked Dennis.

"No!" yelled Johnson, struggling out of her clutches. "Let's get out of here."

The bartender shoved a glass of whisky into Gracie's hands.

"Here, woman, bear down on this," he commanded, "and lay off my publisher."

Okie, with his arm around Lora, smiled quietly and significantly at Dennis. On the other side of Lora two young men in derbies slipped into a tap dance and drinkers all around the bar were reminded of their routines. Lora alone sat quiet, unmoved, beautiful white face frozen into a gentle oblivious smile, chin resting on narrow jeweled wrist.

"I knew you'd run out on us as soon as anybody better came along," chanted Okie above the rhythm of the tapping feet all around him. "You big phony, you wanted to get my girl, didn't you? I saw you looking at her. You and Tony. Look at him dancing. Sticks his neck over like some zoo bird, expect him to dive for a fish any minute. The big snob. You and him both. Goodbye is fine with me."

"See you soon, Okie," Dennis put out his hand, eyes on Lora, but instead of shaking it Okie thrust both hands into his pockets and somberly essayed a waltz clog.

"I'm going mad! Come on!" screamed Johnson in Dennis's ear, and his pale eyes actually did flash a maniacal fire as Sammy, fan-spread fingers meeting beneath his chin, heels together, and feet squared to nine o'clock began to croon in clear bell-shaped melodious tones—

> *"Ah know thaht Ah shall nevah seeah-*
> *Ah theeng ahs luvlee ahs ah treeah—"*

. . . the night thoughts . . .

"So I went to tea at her place and we talked it all over," said
Johnson, for now they were in the Havana Bar and the bartender's name
was Joe. "She says she knows you, you're a good friend of hers. Why
didn't you tell us that to begin with, Orphen, so we wouldn't have had to
worry about libel? We've been trying to contact her for days. You could
have given us a tip."

"I don't know. I didn't think of it," said Dennis, but he did know why
he had not spoken of knowing Effie; it had seemed a way of protecting
her once his own damage was done.

"Do you know, Orphen, a woman like that can do a lot for a fellow,"
Johnson said somberly. "As a matter of fact, Orphen—I'm speaking absolutely frankly and confidentially, understand—I could fall in love with
a woman like that. Not that I mean any disrespect at all to Mrs. Johnson,
but—well, take Mrs. Callingham. Say she *is* older than I am, what of it?
It's the quality underneath, understand, that sad, sympathetic quality.
And lovely hands. Did you ever see such hands, Orphen? White tragic
hands—delicate, expressive. . . . Ah, she's a special person, Orphen, a very
special person."

"Effie has nice hands," agreed Dennis guardedly. He felt his usual unreasoning resentment at another's patronizing appreciation of Effie, and
wondered why it was he could write a book about her but would certainly
avenge such betrayal if any one else had done it. He paid the check and
they were out again in the street. In the quiet of three o'clock the Forties
looked dingy, deserted, incredibly nineteenth-century with the dim lamps
in dreary doorways; in these midnight hours the streets were possessed

by their ancient parasites, low tumbledown frame rooming houses with cheap little shops, though by day such remnants of another decade retreated obscurely between flamboyant hotels. A ferret-eyed little street-walker in a black beret scuttled past, thin childish buttocks outlined sharply under black satin biased skirt, skinny legs in sleazy silk stockings, large bony feet bulging out of flimsy strapped sandals. She vanished into a battered door marked 119, eyes flinging a sidelong contemptuous invitation at the two men as she turned the knob. Beside her door a dim blue light burned in a costumer's window, shadows built a face for the suit of armor and eyes for the hideous African masks. From a dark alleyway a lean powerful gray cat sneaked out with thievish caution, laid its ears back guiltily at the suspicious clatter of garbage cans behind it, warily it darted between the two men and into another shadow from which came a snuffling sobbing noise, a faint female whimper, long-drawn-out, tired, complaining. An immense cavern suddenly yawned before them and from out this sinister darkness a great clumsy bus snorted and roared into the street, a small warning printed on its side—"LOS ANGELES–SEATTLE"; resigned transcontinental faces were appliquéd on the windowpane, straw suitcases, sample cases, honeymoon luggage loaded in the back. Dennis and Johnson waited as it wheezed out, strange clumsy monster thanking night for cover. A few steps to the left and a flaming "BAR" sign hypnotized them as if here indeed were a fresh thought, and here the bartender's name was Steve and a Martini only twenty cents. A tight trim little hennaed woman in turquoise lace with a rather unbelievable bust sang *Isle of Capri* so nasally, so convincingly and withal so energetically that the languorous isle seemed to have undergone some potent glandular injection if not revolution itself.

"The way she talked," continued Johnson dreamily and Dennis closed his eyes to invoke the memory of Effie's light broken contralto tones, a feat indeed with so much tumult in his ears—"the odd gracious little expressions, oh, I don't know how to describe it, Orphen, but let me tell you that Effie Callingham is an amazingly compelling personality."

"You should know her better to really appreciate her," said Dennis jealously. "Why did you have to see her, anyway?"

"We wanted to make sure she was taking your book all right after we found out you had real people in mind. MacTweed thought it best to smooth her over. And I'm glad I met her. Why, come in for a cup of tea, she said, I should be very happy to see you as soon as I get back from the hospital. We talked a little while—she told me some amusing stories about Callingham, showed me some pictures—it seems that once—"

Dennis's lips slipped into a sardonic smile. Effie courting a new audience now for her Callingham connection. Then he thought of how desperately she must fear and hope for his return, how the thought of Andy must be in her head night and day, wondering what he would say to her, wondering how she must act, and his heart filled with hot burning pity and despair that she refused his friendship now that she needed it most, feared him, found hurt wherever she turned. Yet she welcomed Johnson, or anyone who allowed her a few rags of glamour.

"I asked her about the wife, the one now sick here, you know," said Johnson. "We had thought of getting in touch with her since we signed up Callingham, but they tell me they don't give her more than a few days or weeks to live. Here's the problem, Orphen, as it struck me—you're up on this situation so maybe you know—is Callingham coming home, detesting America as he does, as a favor to Wife A who cabled him to come or for the sake of Wife B who is desperately ill? Which would you say pulled him over?"

In the brief moment it required to slip out of Steve's domain around the corner into a little red-checkered tablecloth barroom named Hannah's Place, Dennis pondered this question.

"You see what I mean, don't you?" urged Johnson. "How would any man react in the same boots? After all he couldn't have been around a marvelous woman like this first wife I was telling you about without having some little hangover of feeling for her. Remember this is the first word he's had from her since he left. It says 'Come.' Supposing it's the very word he's been waiting for all these years, some sign that she wants him back no matter for what reason."

"But it's for the second wife—"

"Never mind her being sick," interrupted Johnson, blinking a little to adjust his alcoholized eyes to the smoke-hazed blue of Hannah's Place. "Never mind that part, the excuse for the cable doesn't matter, the point is, the man gets his first hint of being needed and he comes like a flash. I swear I think it's for Wife A and not for Wife B's sickness at all."

"I wonder," said Dennis, and as he stared into space space materialized in its orderly way into a large square windowcard tacked on the bar wall, with its simple tidings neatly printed in bright red:

GARDEN FOLLIES

OPENING MAY 10 AT THE GARDEN THEATRE
WITH TOMMY BENDER, FREDDIE CARVER,
AND THE
DANCE SENSATION OF PARIS
ASTA LUNDGREN, PREMIERE DANSEUSE

"This is April, isn't it?" Dennis thought aloud. He pointed to the sign. "Had it occurred to you, Johnson, that Callingham might be coming over for no other reason than to launch his latest girlfriend, Asta Whosis, in her American debut?"

"By Jove!" said Johnson, staring. "Well, by Jove."

He paid the check and they walked out into the sickly still gray of the Broadway dawn, the grisly ghost that waits outside barrooms to remind the merrymakers of their lost day, their misspent laughter, their ill-chosen companions.

"I hadn't thought of that new girl at all," said Johnson, blaming Dennis vaguely for this new disrupting thought, this unpleasantly plausible destroyer of romance. "I declare! That is the girl, isn't it? Oh, confound it, Orphen, can't the man have some loyalty, some deeper feeling than the lust of the moment? I know what a bounder you make him out in your book but, look here, would a woman like Effie Callingham, a fine woman like her, would she fall in love with a plain bounder?"

"Why not?" said Dennis with a shrug. "When did women ever fight over a Galahad?"

Johnson scowled, unwilling to grant approval to such heresy. He was annoyed that his adoration for Effie Callingham should be affected by her husband's indifference to her. He thought of Benjamin Constant's bitter words about a woman—"people were against her because she had not inspired her lover with more consideration for her sex." He followed Dennis to the steps of a taxi.

"Get in, I'll drop you," said Dennis.

Johnson drew back, face sinking abruptly into passionate despair.

"I can't go home yet. I told you!" he cried plantively. "Bing's woman'll still be there. I have no place to go. Old Bing'll run me out again sure as you're alive. I might as well be dead."

"Come to my place," suggested Dennis with a large gesture. "There's a folding chair—plenty of room, old fellow, glad to have you."

Johnson brightened. They rode downtown and at Dennis's door Johnson breathed a sigh of happiness. "If you only knew what a relief it is to crawl in someplace with no fear of a perfumed handkerchief jumping out at you! This is damned decent of you, Orphen. I won't forget this."

Inside Dennis switched on the lights. An exotic perfume tainted the air, and on the bed sprawled a limp gray figure, the head falling slightly off the edge gave a curiously doll-like unreality to the marble face. The velvety shallow eyes rolled toward the intruders.

"Lora!" Dennis said, dumbfounded.

"The man upstairs let me in and I came down his fire escape," her voice floated out of the red lips languidly, and her arm, drooping from her shoulder lifelessly, did not move. "I thought I'd come and stay with you. Okie was so mean."

Johnson stood rigid gripping the back of a chair, his eyes in speechless reproach on Dennis.

"To tell the truth, Lora," said Dennis rapidly, "this isn't my place at all. It—er—it belongs to old Johnson here. I'll be running along now. So long. Sorry, Johnson, old man."

"Quite all right, old chap," Johnson muttered mechanically and sat down, wild-eyed, on the bed as Dennis dashed down the stairs to the street.

art, inhaling its antique incense while those other poor creatures beside her were permitted merely the rumble of immediate Madison Avenue traffic; for interpretations they had business firm names lettered on passing trucks; for anesthetic they had only the thick fumes of motor exhaust; a bludgeoning acrid odor that would allow no rival sense to function. But I alone, Effie chanted silently, am away from all this, I alone can escape because of this frail, incalculably lovely moment caught like a wild bird in the palm of my hand.

Time fell away and magically became a long-ago summer. She could even see the sky above this captured moment bright azure blistered with tiny white clouds; bus changed imperceptibly to canoe, stone walls to water, and as the canoe slipped through the avenue of weeds she and her dream companion could watch in the water these clouds diminished into tiny popcorn balls bubbling beneath the surface. A light western wind thrummed the ragged marsh grass, shadows sloped down the hills from the Glaenzer castle high up on the peak, and along the winding hill road the bright shield of a warrior caught the sun and would not let it go, the shield or actually the aluminum fender of an automobile winked radiantly in and out of trees, it outdazzled the sun. The dream figures, Effie and Andy, slipped along the fringe of the beach, where magenta-roofed little cottages punctuated the shore line, a great heron fluttered heavily over them, sinking into marsh without sound, gulls and quail squawked and circled the blue, mudhens, dowdy middle-aged birds, sat on old marking posts, immovable, ugly. A black-and-gold butterfly danced suddenly out of the beachplum trees, essayed a tiny sea voyage, followed what seemed the fractured reflection of a dear playmate in the water, then was gone in sunlight. The canoe slid through the bushes, the tall, stiff, salt-tanged grass, it brushed the shore where wind whooshed through the balsams, where bee and bluebottle fly whirred low over the brown toasted earth. They were here at the Glaenzers' to talk it all over away from Marian and the friends of town, for they agreed such calm intelligent people as they could not fly into a new romantic experiment without discussion, plan, consideration. Yet such talk of separation had become impossible with everything about them reminders of their elopement, their first meeting, their secret kisses. Here were the same servants as before assisting them to be alone in the pavilion or the lodge or the boathouse, the same sympathetic winks, and here was Belle Glaenzer ever in the background with her disapproval of their love a whip, as it had been before, to rebellion. Here were the same two lovers, the hushed charged atmosphere of love but fraught now with the sweet deathly fear that this was the end. This quiet deep certainty of each other would vanish, thought Effie, this moment of understanding silence would evaporate in future years like a drop of perfume and nothing she could say would hold it or him. There was no talking it over for them, he was leaving, and with his new love, and what more was there to be said, what more to be done but this still summing up of the old love intensified now beyond the new because it was the end, the end—

"Ah, don't go, don't leave me," she heard a voice cry sharply, and then thought, astounded, but I didn't say it really, thank God, I didn't say it. . . .

"I'll never leave you," he said, "never," but had he said it, was it in words or was it only in a sudden agonizing grasp of her arm as he helped her out of the canoe? And if they had spoken would he have stayed? . . .

"Andy's going to town," Effie said to Belle the next morning. She could not bear to tell Belle the truth, hear her complacent I-told-you-so, I-knew-you-two-would-never-get-along.

"Is he coming back tonight?" asked Belle.

"Oh yes, I'll be back—but not tonight," Andy muttered, looking away from Effie.

It was a day indeed for parting, different from the serene June of yesterday when no sorrow could happen, trouble was fleeting, love must return. Today fog rolled in from the ocean, it webbed the trees and distant hills, flung slender bloodless tentacles into the bushes, fuzzed the pine-stabbed horizon, breathed warnings on window and wall; through its dim glass one saw houses suspended in vapor, cattle in fields transfixed; a sailboat floated lightly in a blurred nimbus through space, long-forgotten fairytales posed in gray dream backgrounds, old calendars swam briefly past hill, house, and pool. Stay, stay, Effie cried silently, as they got into the car to drive to the station. Oh stay.

"The sun'll be out soon enough," said the chauffeur—the very Daniel that Belle had now, but there would be no sun with Andy gone, never any sun nor fog nor star nor meaning to any day. Oh stay, stay. Even getting on the train he did not speak, did not say goodbye, only put his arm around her for a minute, patted her shoulder . . . oh stay, stay, stay. . . .

"Any shopping in the village, Miss Effie?" asked the chauffeur, opening the door once more for her, the train retreating behind her back but she would not turn around.

"No, just drive around the shore road, Dan, until it clears up," said Effie.

The sun presently struck through the mist a baton of radiant gold, a red farmhouse leapt out of the dazzling blare of color, sustained this dominant shrilly while cattle bellowed, catbirds squawked, an automobile siren sent out a round curving note, A major—he was gone, gone. . . . The fog thinned swiftly, faces at farmhouse windows in the valley road, on fishing boats moored to the shore, assumed eyes, noses, special mouths; the far-off train ruled off a single line of sound, a vanishing point for all sensations—oh come back, come back, come back!

He *was* coming back . . . why, of course. . . . Effie shivered, fell through the dream to the reality, from the distant prayer to the answer. He had come back. It was true. The broken brown feather on the woman's hat directly in front of her, her own gloved hand grasping her purse, the glimpse of gray tweeds sitting down beside her, these immediate sharp impressions broke through and dispelled the illusion. She thought, why, this very man beside me might be Andy, don't look, don't move, but it *was* possible. The *Bremen* had docked. The newspapers had carried his name as an arrival. There—a dark man with a Gladstone bag hurried out of a bank at Madison and Forty-second, even that might be he, or wait— the bus lurched to a stop for a gray, heavy-set bearded man, mightn't he now be gray, heavy, and bearded? Desperately Effie shut her eyes, tried to push hope away; now it would be worse than ever, the frantic wooing of coincidence, the eager fantastic hope that each passer-by, each distant footstep, each opening door might reveal him. At the hospital street she stumbled out, walked hurriedly toward Lexington, her new black suède purse held awkwardly up over her chest, gold initials E. T. C. gleaming out boldly as if to conceal the quick frantic beating of her heart.

. . . Marian's trousseau . . .

MARIAN LOOKED GHASTLY. The nurse's eyes met Effie's gravely over the bed.

"I told her the rouge made her look worse," said the nurse, following Effie's bewildered glance, "and I thought she should have worn a plain gown—"

"They don't understand about Andy," Marian breathed patiently as if this were an explanation she had made again and again, "he likes things gay. He always liked me in red. Pretty, isn't it?"

Her feverish fingers fluttered over the scarlet velvet evening cape wrapped about her shoulders, stroked the torn lace of the nightgown beneath.

"We've had no word yet from him," the nurse whispered to Effie.

Marian caught the whisper.

"But they don't know Andy, do they, Effie?" she protested. "Andy doesn't cable, he just walks right in the door, *right* in the door, there he is now, what did I tell you, see? See him there? He's hiding behind Effie. No one can see him but me. *Right* in the door . . . what time is it? It's almost noon, isn't it, what will he think finding me still in bed? Oh dear, someone's put something heavy on my legs—please, mother, take the suitcase away, Andy's coming—"

Effie tried to speak but her tongue would not move. She sank into the chair, felt the nurse's reassuring fingers on her shoulder. Marian's drugged eyes fluttered open again, the drowsy murmur went on.

"I'm not asleep, Andy, it's the medicine . . . I'm not even sick, you know, just this—this pain . . . and don't be frightened, dear, don't run away. I know how you hate sickrooms, but this isn't a hospital really, darling, it's only the American Club. I just came in to write a letter and I saw we were posted, why didn't you tell me? Darling, why didn't you use the Cosmopolitan check to pay the dues instead of buying me this evening coat? . . . You're too good to me, you are, you know. . . . Do you know, dearest, I think you're good to me to make up to your conscience about Effie. . . . You feel it's a little for *her,* too, don't you . . . aren't you funny . . . but I'm that way, too . . . I guess all lovers are that way when they hurt some one else to be together . . . I keep saying I mustn't be too happy with you, because it isn't fair to Effie . . . Effie. . . . She was here, wasn't she? . . . Effie!"

Effie choked out an answer. Marian's glazed rolling eyeballs fastened to her resolutely, clung to a moment of consciousness.

"Effie, when he comes, will you let me see him alone first? Will you make everyone go away? I want us just alone, so I can make him understand why I ran away from him . . . why I was so silly when of course there was never anyone but me. . . . I want him to walk in and see me looking perfectly well, because I do, don't I, in my red jacket—because the poor boy mustn't be worried about me, and he does get upset over sickness. He *hates* it. He'll be so relieved when he sees I'm almost out of the woods . . . almost . . . ah, here he comes . . . mustn't smoke that cigarette, darling, that's your thirtieth today. . . ."

Her voice trailed into the pillow as she turned slightly to sink her teeth into the muslin as if this gave relief to the flicker of pain. The doctor slipped into the room, stood at the window beside the nurse silently looking over the chart. Effie got to her feet.

"All right, Marian, I'll wait outside," she said, "so you can talk everything over."

"Don't stay away long," said the nurse.

Effie walked slowly down the hall, a dreadful fear shaping itself in her mind. Andy might not come at all. Women might die of love for him, yet he would not pity them or ease their doubts, for he despised weakness in others and in himself, he would not come for death itself; and here were both love and death beseeching him, not for their sake but that their ideal of him should not crash into dust, years lost on a worthless dream. . . . How heavy her slight high-heeled slippers felt, as heavy as riding boots, it was like walking underwater against strange powerful currents. . . . She heard herself answering the good-day of the nurse at the reception desk, heard her footsteps dawdling slower and slower over the marble floor of the entrance hall. Supposing he did not come. . . .

"You look very pretty today, Miss Thorne," said the reception clerk. "Violets, too!"

Flowers and a rose-colored dress—for what? Rouge and red velvet on a dying woman—for whom?

"Have you seen the paper, Miss Thorne?" the girl asked and came over to her with the newspaper. She was a pretty girl, fair and petite, with unusually fine teeth. Effie found herself noting these details desperately, the pretty ankles, the coquettish sway of the crisp white skirts, here was something that would bring Andy quickly—if she could get word to him to come to the hospital quickly, not for duty's sake or for pity's sake or for love's sake, but because there was a remarkably attractive nurse at the reception desk he would come, he would rush. . . . Why, she thought aghast, if that is what I know of him how could I care for him, and yet it's true. . . . Her shaking hands turned the paper to the shipping news—yes, the *Bremen* was in . . . she looked for interviews with famous passengers but a prime minister took the honors, sharing them with a film couple. Andy's name wasn't there, unless it was A. Carrington . . . though she had seen it someplace else. A name leapt familiarly out of a neighboring column . . . *Hunter's Wife . . . The Hunter's Wife. . . .*

". . . study of a genius and a woman who lived on a great lie, one of the romantic lies upon which women in bourgeois society are persistently nourished. Such a woman as this Edna Banning of Dennis Orphen's creation could not possibly find root in Soviet Russia where sentimental love as the primary food for the feminine soul is not tolerated. The book is interesting as a picture of romance under capitalist Cupid, in a society where nostalgia is regarded as more beautiful than a wise destruction of a rotten foundation. This woman's life hinged on a sentimental lie, on false individual expectations, so she was dead. . . ."

Effie dropped the sheet, saw it flutter to the floor, wondered a little bewildered at the reviewer's signature, for it was that of a Russian woman, a dead poet's wife, whose memoirs and biography of him as well as brave use of his famous name were her main appeal to the Party and reason for existence. "Her life hinged on a lie." What did that mean? Fleetingly Effie thought of a new system of obituaries in which the lives recorded were criticized, mistaken steps pointed out, structure condemned, better paths suggested. . . . All of these reviews of Dennis's book would be like that, critical obituaries for Effie Thorne who was dead, whose life was a lie, for its glory depended on believing in a man who was worthless, cruel. Effie was aware of a strange hollow agony in her body, an obscure insistent fear that cried out to be named and flouted, that if the dream failed her as the man had, life would be intolerable. A bleak glimpse of the next years came to her, years without hope and without the pride of memory, only shame for wasted tears, misspent adoration. Forty-five, fifty—sixty—no, she could not face a future so barren, a final curtain as Marian's might be with only the bitter knowledge of his indifference, his unworthiness.

"He must come," she cried aloud, not only for Marian's sake but for hers. It could not be true he dared stay away, that nothing mattered but his present pleasure.

Luncheon trays were being wheeled out of distant rooms down the eastern corridor. Nurses chatted in the hall clearly, loudly, as librarians do, insolently proud to be above their own rules. Andy might at this very minute come running up the front steps—Effie folded up the newspaper and returned it to the desk. Footsteps running up the marble steps, don't turn, don't look . . . they passed on into the business office. Effie went out the swinging doors into the street. A taxi-door opened and a man got out—not he. Someone was running behind her—caught up, ran on, a hatless young man, not he. A streetcar stopped, a man with a suitcase got off, not he. Suddenly she knew that she must find him, must beg him, force him, to come, must swallow all pride, all the desperate plans she had been making to seem aloof, independent of him and his actions, only politely interested in his attitude toward Marian—all this pattern for her conduct must go, she must surrender all defenses before the plea for Marian.

"How—how?" she whispered to herself. Dennis would know. If she could find Dennis he would help her. He would go to the *Bremen* offices, call the hotels, Dennis would help her. But he was at Caroline Meigs's party. . . .

Hesitating a moment to see where she was, she turned back and began walking rapidly eastward toward the little pair of blue spruce trees that marked Caroline Meigs's home.

I V

. . . the gypsy camp . . .

IN CAROLINE MEIGS'S GARDEN Dennis stood by the birdbath where silly stone dolphins feebly sprayed a cracked bowl. He could watch both doors for Effie from this point; she might come from the balcony stairs or the basement hallway that opened directly on the garden. He hated this anxiety over her, scorned himself for finding his life somehow lacking without her. He thought she might come since she had sometimes spoken of Caroline Meigs and had, he surmised, often basked here in the respectful adulation of intellectual young men. Curiosity had led him here as it had into Belle Glaenzer's, to see how nearly the picture Effie had given checked with the original. Moreover, today's party was for him. Mrs. Meigs insisted on a focus for her afternoons, preferably the freshest of public names which she ordered from publishers or producers or senators as she would order other decorations from florist or caterer.

Mrs. Meigs herself seemed to be nowhere about though she had screamed down to the butler from an upstairs window, "Be careful of that sandwich plate, Yama, it's Belle Glaenzer's." Nor was her famous yachting cousin Wylie present. There were in fact no familiar faces among the lonely guests wandering about clinging to their red rooster cocktail glasses as if these glasses were protective aprons for their shy miseries, so Dennis went indoors to see if there might be some sign of Effie or word of her. He recalled rumors that Mrs. Meigs prided herself on a perfectly delicious punch made of pure alcohol and grape juice, which she declared fooled everyone, and enabled her to entertain at very little expense. The result of this shrewd fooling was that guests were always prowling about the basement in a game she had never thought to invent but which was the life of her parties, namely the Scotch Hunt. There was invariably some old family friend or an intuitive type who knew the hiding place and since her private stock was very good indeed little groups of guests were always clustered in the laundry leaning over the electric mangle or in the coal cellar or the cook's bedroom, contentedly sharing a glass with no gaily embossed red rooster on its rim at all but more likely the plainest jelly glass or even a half-pint cream bottle.

Dennis wandered through the downstairs hall eyeing these groups disagreeably. Some young men with startlingly broad-shouldered suits returned his examination with equal hostility. These gentlemen had elected the pantry as their clubroom, and their adenoidal voices with accompanying flashes of primitive dentistry proclaimed British culture nobly upheld by Cinnamon, Paprika, Curry, Ginger, and Bread.

"Has Mrs. Callingham been here, do you know?" he inquired.

The tallest, thinnest, palest young man with the boniest skull and the narrowest jaw, appraised Dennis.

"I've never met her so I can't say," he said civilly. "I know Callingham, of course—he's a great friend of Caroline's cousin Wylie, you know. Look here, aren't you the chap we met at the beer-place with Glaenzer a fortnight or so back?"

"Possibly," said Dennis and added as a bright afterthought. "I meet so many people."

"She might be upstairs," ventured another. "Women always are mulling about up there."

Dennis went up the narrow creaking staircase wondering idly how soon the entire house would fall to pieces or be returned to the horses from whom Caroline had obviously stolen it. Women were hovering in a raftered bedroom around a handsome silk-canopied bed upon which a large bullish man in somewhat premature Palm Beach was reading palms. No Effie here. Dennis crossed the hall, bumping his head on a low-hanging Moorish lamp, and saw in another bedroom, definitely Turkish in spirit, or at least Turkish tearoom, his hostess, judging from the dressing gown and mules she wore to match the damask hangings. She was seated at her desk, a plumed pen in hand, scanning a sheet of paper.

"I'm looking for Effie Callingham," he said. "Is she coming, do you know? I'm Orphen."

Mrs. Meigs absently looked up from the paper. Her face was quite young if a trifle leathery in texture, but the years like relentless moths had revenged themselves on her neck, shriveling almost visibly by the minute under its heavy Oriental jewelry.

"Effie? Was she in a leopard jacket—oh no, that was Carol. Did you have your hand read yet, Mr. Orphen? Mac—MacTweed, you know, told me you were interested in palmistry—"

"I beg your pardon?"

"—so I had Vinal Turner come to read, just on your account. You must let him do you."

Dennis saw she had a great list of names printed on the paper in hand, evidently her guest list, for she read aloud gloatingly: "—the Argentine ambassador, the second cousin of the Duchess of Kent, a Russian film director, the Southern senator—oh, it's a grand party I'm having for you today, Mr. Orphen!"

Unlike most guest lists, Mrs. Meigs had not only the names of her company but the reason for their invitations beside them in case the name conveyed nothing. She thought of people in their categorical terms so completely that she sometimes startled them by her absent-minded greetings—"How do you do, Mrs. Charles B. Tody, wife of the Paramount director?" or "Are you having a nice time, Mabelline Emma Foster, first white woman to breakfast with the Sultan?"

She was, Dennis thought, having a much better time up here alone with her glamorous paper guest list than with the stupid people themselves downstairs. She had been giving parties for years and aside from once having been a showy debutante who rode her ponies straight onto the ballroom floor and other such pranks seemed to have no other career than that of a resolute salonnière, a woman sought by the art set because she was in the Social Register and was rich besides, and approved by the Registered because she knew artists and was rich besides. She drew aside the curtains to peer down into the garden.

"There's Tony Glaenzer. You must get to know each other. I wonder if he brought Callingham. Do make Vinal Turner read your palm, darling."

Dennis retreated, leaving her to her reading, and heard the earnest voice of the palmist. "You have a well-defined sense of taste. I'll bet you're a good cook." Then, as the lady demurred he amended with a hearty laugh, "At any rate you do appreciate good cooking. Ha ha."

Coming downstairs he was almost pushed back by the rush of ambassadors, film directors, politicians, and other titles all rushing to have their hands read in the tiny bedroom. Sentences floated through the air like autumn leaves, voices said they did or did not believe in palmistry but on the contrary did not or did believe in astrology. An ex-Central American president and an ex-Metropolitan singer noisily agreed that they did believe in black cats and Friday the thirteenth because of certain curious experiences they were only too happy to relate, and a gray little woman in pince-nez held up a group outside the bedroom door by whispering that she had just driven in from Danbury and that she herself read palms in an amateur way, and this news spreading down the crowded halls and stairs stirred Yama, the Filipino butler then in the pantry to take on a few of the well-tailored young men in actual crystal gazing, the ball being conveniently on hand over an opened jar of Major Gray's chutney, so that out in the garden the other guests were forced to wait on their own sandwich and punch needs in the most uncivilized fashion. Dennis struggled through this mob to the end of the garden but voices fluttered out from all directions and hushed exclamations of awe as an omen struck home. "Courage and endurance but no aggression." "I see a woman making trouble," stated Yama in a flat singsong voice, "a red room on a hill by a sea—" and from the woman with the pince-nez—"Either that hump means a great musical talent or a good sense of order or else you're terribly sensual," and again the earnest Turner voice, "A fine sense of taste here. Hm . . . I'll bet you're a good cook. . . . No? . . ." then once more the hearty laugh though having waded through so many palms the tone was tinged with desperation now, the laugh had a tinny quality, "at any rate you do appreciate good cooking."

Dennis nervously dipped into the punch on the long iron marble-topped garden table, and gulped down the potion. It burned the throat, tasted feebly of grape juice and left the tongue stiff and suddenly enormous and misshapen in the mouth while the recipe divided inside his chest and stomach into its singularly uncongenial ingredients, this one stinging, that one burning, and another merely throwing the entire intestinal system into reverse. That, deduced Dennis, must be the cucumber, that fine cucumber base, and it reminded him of Phil Barrow's punch recipes, which, like Mrs. Meigs's, had no antidote but straight Scotch for the two days following. He put down the glass quickly, felt a gloved hand on his wrist and saw Olive Baker of all people smiling pensively at him from under a large rather flattering black hat.

"You didn't expect to see me at such a celebrated party, did you?" She laughed triumphantly. "Now really, don't you wonder how I came here? Don't worry, Corinne and I never expect *you* to ask us anywhere with your famous friends. Is that Tallulah Bankhead over there in the wool hat?"

"It's not my party. Where's Corinne?" Dennis felt his customary unreasoning annoyance at Corinne's popping into his private bachelor life. He wanted her to be on call for him in his depressed moments or between other engagements but when she unexpectedly appeared at a party he became automatically *her* man, someone he must watch to see she had a good time and watch also to see she did not have *too* good a time. If Olive was here then Corinne must be around. Olive raised her brows at his questioning glance around.

"I'm all alone," she said coquettishly. "I came with Vinal Turner—he's Mother's palmist and he knew I always wanted to meet people like this, and that I knew you. Imagine having all these wonderful people here just to meet you. Doesn't it make you feel proud?"

Dennis looked at her narrowly and detected a faintly sarcastic twist to the lips. She would tell Corinne and Phil that there was poor Dennis without a soul to talk to; to wonder he never took Corinne to those marvelous places, the poor fellow didn't know anyone. And Phil would say with great satisfaction, "After all, Orphen is *not* the man to attract friends. I could never see how he appealed to Corinne here, but I daresay some maternal instance came out in her. Why don't you let me buy you a dog, Baby, a dachshund?" Yes, that would be exactly the discussion Olive would stir up. He saw she was smiling at him with arch significance, the girlfriend smile he classified it, the smile that telegraphed we've-always-understood-each-other-better-than-you-and-she-have. He poured her some punch silently and she gracefully arranged herself on the arm of the one chair in the place and pulled her hat impulsively down to cover the tiny but study-provoking birthmark over her left eye.

"Now let's talk," she commanded playfully. "We've never had a really nice talk, have we, Dennis? Tell me how you came to write. I suppose you had to make money so you just started writing, didn't you?"

Dennis sighed. He looked uneasily at the man in the chair who after all had been there first and was now forced to cower in the shadow of Olive's fine derriére. The man returned Dennis's look pugnaciously. Dennis bowed. There was something familiar about the fellow. Of course. It was none other than the young man who lived above him, the young agitator.

"Mr.—er—Schubert, Miss Baker," he said, and Olive turned quickly to meet the great man. It was useless to explain to Olive it was not *the* Schubert.

"I know you," the young man said sourly to Olive. "I let you in Orphen's apartment about daylight the other morning."

Olive gave a gay laugh.

"Not me. And Corinne doesn't look anything like me, so it must have been another lady. . . . Never mind, Dennis, don't look so worried. I'll never breathe it to Corinne."

The hell she wouldn't. She beamed reassuringly at Dennis and then set about being charming to Mr. Schubert. The way Olive was charming was to part her lips breathlessly, throw her head back, eyes wide and glazed, intent on her vis-à-vis, a trick she had got from the most popular girl at Miss Roman's school. The most popular girl had astigmatism as her excuse, but the squinting, the difficult focusing, the voluntary dilation of the pupils, the sudden shake of the head like a wet puppy as the vision blurred, all these were somehow connected in Olive's mind with being the Prom Queen. To this trick she had added a quick incredulous, "Oh no! *NO!*" to register eager astonishment combined with a dash of intellect. Her social manner thus displayed appeared to be the flag of the class war to the young man Schubert, who watched her performance with narrowed eyes and a sardonic superior smile, answering her bright sallies with a meditative, "Yes, that *would* be your point of view. . . . Yes, a woman of your class *would* say that."

There, reflected Dennis enviously, is a young man sitting pretty, and literally too since his politics dismissed bourgeois etiquette and allowed him to relax at ease in the one chair of the place while ladies fumed. His sharp face wore the veiled and justifiable satisfaction of a man with a secret formula for destroying society. How simple his life was, reflected Dennis, no demon of wonder or curiosity over each separate human being; he was a wholesaler as against the artist retailer. Olive, for example, could be dismissed without study as our Number 742 Bourgeois Virgin; he, Dennis, was our Number 549, Bourgeois Realist, who fairly enough satirized his own class but then, with reprehensible bourgeois honesty, even satirized the Party itself and the Revolution, subjects alone out of all human life to be treated purely mystically. Our Number 549, Bourgeois Satirist, envied our Number 1, Complacent Communist, for he had the answer book, he need not work in the laboratory where the experiments so often refused to prove the premise, he could wear his political blinders like any romantic old lady in the midst of sordid testimony to human behavior, he could wear them and receive a bright little red button for his lapel in reward. For our Number 1 no individual woes need disturb, but only Wholesale Conditions and this made life pleasanter, for then Society could be blamed for the poverty of one's friends and no gift from one's own pocket was necessary. Five answers to everything, Vegetable, Mineral, Animal, Fish, Fowl. Happy Mr. Schubert, now placing Olive as Fowl, eliminating all the remarks that made her Olive and heeding only those that made her Fowl. As a matter of fact Mr. Schubert belonged definitely in Caroline Meigs's class, those who dealt not in persons but in categories, and this was the making of Snobs, people who believe the world would be more beautiful if it were made up not of blundering human beings but of lovely paper guest lists.

"Tell me, Mr. Schubert, or you, Dennis," begged Olive brightly, "which is Anthony Glaenzer? I saw his picture in the rotogravure and he looked so terribly attractive. You know him personally, don't you, Dennis?"

"Yes, indeed," said Dennis and thought of all the boasting he had done at Barrow dinners to offset Phil's smugness and Olive's distrust of him, and it served himself right, he thought, for Tony Glaenzer to come up from the kitchen at that moment with an eager young man on either side. Caroline Meigs's red face appeared at the upstairs window, frantically waving a bony hand cuffed with antique jewels.

"Tony!" she screamed above the hum of mounting confusion. "That's the guest of honor there by the snacks. Say something to him."

Tony's weary eye fell on Dennis and he graciously obeyed his hostess.

"Haven't I met you before?"

Dennis bowed.

"Thank you," he said gratefully.

He felt Olive prodding him in the back with her forefinger but he ignored this hint for introductions. He saw the young Communist quickly take a pad out of his pocket and make a rapid sketch of Glaenzer's profile.

Bored Bourgeois, Dennis deduced, and thought, surprised, his neighbor, aside from being a radical and dropping plaster into Dennis's room, was undoubtedly the Schubert whose suave caricatures appeared in all the smart magazines. As the artist leafed over his pages, he saw a disheartening sketch of himself, fantastically unkempt hair and tie, wild, shrewd eyes slightly crossed, an ahah smile pulling at the left side of his face, and he thought with alarm that it was true, other people had realized he had a Passport face with even distinct criminal features.

"Dennis," said Olive urgently, but Dennis did not hear her for he saw Effie pushing her way through the crowd about the basement door, a fixed party smile on her face. She caught his eye and there was such dazed appeal in her glance that Dennis forgot everything in hurrying to her side.

"That," said someone beside him, "is Mrs. Andrew Callingham—the first one."

She kept smiling, conscious of this stir whenever she appeared in public, straightened her shoulders to appear more worthy of bearing the great name, a gesture that had become second nature to her.

"Will you come with me?" she whispered. "Oh, please. I do need you."

He took her arm silently and hurried her through the basement door. In the front hall it occurred to him that his hat was somewhere upstairs but it didn't matter, and he had a flicker of apprehension about Olive's reaction to his rude desertion, but nothing mattered. The Danbury lady, her hat pushed on the back of her marcelled hair, spectacles askew, was being read by the master himself, though by way of impressing a rival he was now throwing in a dash of astrology. "You are a One person," he was saying, "and in another week you will be entering the Fourth Vibration."

"Is that good?" someone asked.

"Perfect," promised the seer.

"Andy's back," Effie whispered to Dennis. "We've got to find him for Marian."

"Isn't that Mrs. Callingham?" someone said, but this time Effie did not smile or turn. They hurried out into the street, Dennis bareheaded, hat and Mrs. Meigs's party for his book forgotten in his elation that Effie needed him, he was as necessary to her life as she was to his.

. . . the hunter returned . . .

No matter what happens I will never let it take me this way, vowed Dennis, outside Callingham's bedroom at the Madison, I'm damned if I'll have a bedful of literary agents, movie magnates, lawyers, brokers, Spanish and Russian translators, editors, gossip columnists, and old college roommates. The hotel valet with a suit of evening clothes over his arm emerged from the sacred bedroom and the open door allowed the chatter, the clink of glasses, the typewriter clicking out statements to the press and other inner sanctum noises to nourish for a brief moment the hungry ears of those awaiting an interview. No, resolved Dennis, I won't put on this act, not for a minute; I may have naked ladies jumping out of Easter eggs and drinking out of my slipper, I may have an extra suit and a watch with two hands and a charge account at Bellows, but this prima donna act, this big business ritual that obliged ex-wives to wait their turn with tailors till the big affairs were attended, contracts signed, checks deposited, broker called up, dinner arrangements for the next fortnight made . . . oh no, never. Dennis looked at Effie on the sofa beside him and wondered how she could endure this delay. She had spelled out her name and repeated it three times to the secretary—E-f-f-i-e—T-h-o-r-n-e—and finally said, "Just tell him Effie." The awful delay that followed this announcement sickened Dennis though Effie seemed undisturbed. Maybe after a lifetime of keeping up a front the front ossified and a little of the stone seeped through the veins. Then Dennis saw her hands and looked quickly away. He studied the rug, the little whispering groups, the pictures on the wall, but all he really saw were Effie's hands gripping the gloves in her lap, twisting them, rolling them, crumbling them, smoothing them out again.

The secretary opened the inner door and called in the film reporter. Effie pretended not to notice, kept her eyes on a picture.

"Hotels have their own art, don't they?" she said.

Just Effie. But the tailor, the film reporter came first. Dennis passed her a cigarette.

"I've always felt there ought to be a museum of hotel art," he said. "It hardly seems fair that only the great or rich can enjoy these masterpieces, the living-room sunsets and forest fires, the little pastel bedroom quainties, the old tavern on the parchment lampshade. Do you think the twin prints over the twin beds in there will be Godey's or something from the chambermaid's own palette?"

Effie smiled, turned to the man just entering the suite, and Dennis knew she was thinking this newcomer would be admitted before she was.

"About the launch," the new caller informed the secretary.

The bedroom door closed again on voices.

Andy was buying a new launch, then. The launch came before Effie, before Marian dying. . . .

"I'm so glad you came with me," she whispered. "I could never have found out where he was."

It had been easy enough to get the address from Johnson, though Dennis dared not explain the cause of his request, knowing how staunchly the author's world unites against wives and mistresses, readier to protect the darling from these catastrophes than from bill collectors and minor nuisances. It was easier, however, to prepare the way for Effie than it would be to explain his own presence to Callingham. He found himself growing slowly enraged at the situation. He was mad because he had no hat, because his shoes had suddenly become conspicuously muddy, his shirt cuffs frayed, his fingernails black; his beard leapt out of his face, his tie's white flannel stuffing wiggled out of its decent cover, his garter broke and dangled down, all the things happened that would put him at a disadvantage with Callingham, made his anger with the man seem nothing more than the futile envy of the failure for a successful rival.

"There," said Effie, nodding toward the table and he saw a copy of *The Hunter's Wife*. "Dennis, tell me why you wrote that book. You *are* my friend, then why—*why?*"

"I wrote it for you," Dennis answered and for the first time he knew he was speaking the truth. He had written an annihilation of the man Callingham, but whereas only last week his conscience had reproached him for this betrayal of Effie, he saw now with illuminating clarity that he had done it *for* her. Somewhere, unconfessed, inside him was the St. George who would free the princess from a dragon and for no other purpose than this had his pen lashed out. The truth will free, he had cried, and then was remorseful when the truth only destroyed the princess in the telling.

Effie looked at him curiously, trying to understand. Someone in the room asked the time and another answered that it was half-past six. Effie gave a start of fear. Marian. It might already be too late. She would almost at that moment have braved everything and run straight into the other room to Andy, but this courage fled when the secretary beckoned to her from the door. She shrank back, looked beseechingly at Dennis. She had never really expected the meeting to come true, he thought, the man in the doorway summoning her to step from a long dream into reality was a shock. Dennis handed her her bag, gloves, cigarettes.

"I'll be waiting," he said, and drawing a deep breath she walked slowly, numbly, away from him into the open door.

"IF ANDREW CALLINGHAM WERE A LESS MODEST ARTIST, as indeed all great men are truly modest, he would have had reason to crow over his native land this morning. It was America's indifference to his genius eighteen years ago that sent him roaming the world, from China Seas to the Mediterranean until, decorated with literary prizes and an international reputation as one of our greatest living authors, he returned yesterday to these soils. MacTweed, his latest publisher, told reporters in the author's suite at the Madison, of the artist's early struggles, the mean little attic in Chelsea, the brave solitary fight for publication and fame. He told of his efforts to earn a bare living against the skepticism of his family and friends.

"'It is to this country's everlasting shame,' said Mr. MacTweed, 'that England was the first to recognize his genius.'

"Callingham appeared to be a tall, bronzed, healthy specimen, in the prime of life, gray mustache and sparse gray hair, keen dark eyes under unrimmed spectacles, speaking with the unmistakable twang of the Yankee. He waved his hands disparagingly at photographers and the autograph-hunters outside the hotel, and only shook his head at the flattering remarks on his last novel.

"Asked what he thought of the work of the newer generation of American writers, Wolfe, Caldwell, and Faulkner, he answered that unquestionably they had something. He was equally spontaneous in praise of Dos Passos, Hemingway, Lewis, and Ellen Glasgow.

"'Where do you think you stand in American letters?' he was asked.

"He laughed and shrugged his shoulders.

"'Some critics would put me at the bottom of the ladder,' he said good-naturedly, and added with a twinkle, 'I do hope they're not right.'"

. . . out of the dream . . .

"I'M THE BEST GODDAM WRITER this country ever turned out, yes, or France or England too for that matter," said Andy, lying on the chintz counterpane, English tweed dressing gown pulled across his trousers. "I know you and the Glaenzers think it was easy but let me tell you I worked hard, Effie, I earned whatever kudos I got, I never had anything just handed to me."

It was Andy, of course it was Andy, Andy caricatured by that unkind cartoonist Time until he was Uncle Henry Callingham from Syracuse, so that Effie had to keep staring at him trying to find some familiar gesture or expression, but whatever was familiar was some trait of that uncle who used to come to New York to visit them. Even his voice had taken on a brittle nervous quality unlike the lazy drawl she remembered. She tried in vain to combine in this present figure the young Andy, the Andy of her imagination, and the great man Callingham. It was preposterous that Marian's dying or any other mere human trifle would matter to this stranger. She looked helplessly from him to the young man with fair mustache who was unpacking duffle bag and suitcase, occasionally rushing in and out with telegrams and messages. Would he, she wondered, take a message through this Andy-façade to the Andy she knew, or where could she reach that vanished person?

"Get out those snapshots, Jim, I want to show Effie the places at Cannes," said Andy. He poured a drink from the cognac bottle on the night table but Effie shook her head. "Effie, I've got a grand place, right there on the Mediterranean. And a yacht. A beauty. Pass them over here,

Jim, I want Effie to see that set. And say, I wish you could see the cottage at Cornwall. I had such a good summer there I went right back and bought it so I could always have it when I wanted it. I like to own the place I stay—I'm buying here, too, did Tony tell you, maybe stay here six months a year. Ah here, here's our party in India, that's me, and that's the Duke of Malvern, a hell of a nice fella. Here's the chateau, rear view, you can see the sea right there in the corner, and here's me receiving the International Novel Prize in Paris, that's the prime minister—here's me and Lloyd George—here's my stable—"

She knew she should have exclaimed with admiration, made questions, but she was utterly overcome with shyness, wonder that she had dared burst into this perfect stranger's life. There was an odd buzzing in her head, a sense of not being really there, of being in a confused nightmare, and it reminded her of a childhood dream in which the cruel ogre was her father even though he had another name and another face. So this big gray man had once been her husband, the pattern from which she had cut her real lover, the dream Andy. If she only looked and listened she might get accustomed to him, as one might accustom one's eyes to darkness, but she could not speak. What link could she and Marian ever have had with this legendary hero? How presumptuous of women to think their life or death mattered to a legend? Observing with surprise the pouches and deep wrinkles about his eyes, she pushed her chair about so that the light was behind her, shadowing her own face and hiding the hollows of her throat. She looked over the photographs, records of a life she could only dimly grasp, definite proof of how far afield her own conjecturings had been. She had, it is true, pictured an adventurous life, but these pictures were not proof of adventures, they were history, and there was something chilling in that. All of the imagined dialogues fled from her mind, for they were for lovers reunited, not for embarrassed guest and a great name. Why, she thought, groping for reasons for her shattering bewilderment, there was no Andy left, he had been wiped out by Callingham the Success as men before him had been wiped out by the thing they represented. Her knees quivering, her disobedient, paralyzed tongue were evidence enough that she was in a royal presence; she might better kiss his hand and flee.

"You've only a few minutes to dress," said the secretary. "Mr. Mac-Tweed is calling in half an hour. I've told the reporters you can't see any one else today, so they're cleared out."

She must go at this hint, go, or make her demand for Marian at once. She was disgusted with herself for her sweating palms, her chattering teeth, as if she were about to make of this great Name an outrageous request, beg some incredible favor as if he were a mere human being instead of already an immortal, a god she had once presumed to love. She was even surprised that he remembered her at all, flattering her by sending away the other guests, and by showing her trophies of his triumphant journeys. Yet second thoughts were more cynical; his tone had the forced heartiness he might use on a poor relation, the desire to share his successes with her warring with the fear that too glowing a story would only remind her of her own poverty. Her head swam with conflicting resolutions, she would beg him to come with her to Marian, no, she would not dare be so bold. But time was short and she plunged.

"Did you get my cable, Andy?"

He frowned and glanced in the direction of the secretary rather significantly as if this was coming to a problem often discussed between them. The photograph in his hand of the gay gardens of his château dropped to the floor unheeded.

"I was sorry Marian was ill," he said stiffly. "Thanks for wiring me."

"She wanted you—"

"It was lucky I had already booked passage for America. I wrote the hospital of course that I would attend to all the expenses. I was very fond of Marian."

"She loves you," said Effie. Now her eyes were hot with tears and her voice sounded utterly strange to her as if in command of someone else, certainly it seemed to her of her own volition she could never have spoken a word.

"Effie, is she really sick?"

Effie started. "Why, Andy, she's dying."

Andy stared at the floor.

"She used to send word she was dying or about to commit suicide whenever she was upset over something I'd done," he said. "Marian is a lovely person, but she is not the wife for a man in public life. I can't work and soothe hysterics, you know; no man can. She made herself miserable with needless jealousies—whoever I talked to or danced with—you were never jealous, Effie."

It was the first reference he'd made to their old relationship. He paced up and down the room nervously.

"Damn it, you can't work with a wife always screaming for attention," he said savagely. "You can patch up scenes for a while but finally you give up, no matter how much you love her. She ran away. I was worn out. Let her run, I said. I can't go on with it—right in the middle of a new trilogy. I always admired you, Effie, you knew a man doing high-keyed work breaks out in a high-keyed way—a little flirtation, a binge—just a form of nerves, but you understood it, Effie."

Effie nodded, silent.

"I know women," he went on rapidly, "I'm the best writer on female psychology in the world today but, by God, that doesn't help you to know how to handle a woman who wants to make jealous scenes, wants romantic love at the expense of everything else. You had common sense, Effie, there was no romantic nonsense about you. Our marriage busts up, OK, you say, that's that. No spilled milk. You knew it was the best thing."

Effie fumbled in her cigarettes to hide her face.

"It was a fine thing for both of us," she said then. She thought, of course, you lose him because you don't make a scene, and you lose him because you do make a scene; at least I know now there's nothing you can do either way to hold a man once he's going. He would have gone no matter what I did or said.

Andy rushed to her and took her hands impulsively.

"Effie, it's worth coming back to the States just to hear you say that. You don't know how I felt, running off the way I did, never knowing whether I was breaking your heart or what. But all this time you knew it was for the best. Oh, Effie, Effie, thank you for that. Sometimes I've almost hated you thinking of you over here, so goddam noble, still loving me, forgiving me, waiting for me—"

"Ridiculous," said Effie. "When it was over, it was over."

"Exactly. I knew you felt that way, too."

"It was swell while it lasted," she said, smiling. Swell. That was it. She was to be the swell person still, mustn't let anyone feel ugly. That's that. OK. Over when it's over. Swell while it lasted. No romantic nonsense. Those were the words to remember, the vocabulary for the swell person.

"Gee you're great, Effie," he was beaming at her now, radiant. "It's been the one thing that bothered me—feeling like a bastard about you. And all the time—let's have a drink."

This time, because her hands were shaking so, she took the glass he offered and drank with him, hoping the brandy burning into her blood would give her courage, to keep smiling while he looked at her, looked at her for the first time since she came into the room.

"Do you know, something strikes me that never did before? I'll bet the reason you let me go off with Marian was that there was somebody around you liked? I know women and I know you don't send a man off that easy unless there's someone else."

"You are clever, aren't you?" Effie answered.

"I thought so," he exclaimed gleefully. "I always held that nobleness against you. I see I needn't have. Who was it? Tony? He always was around."

"No secrets from you, are there?" said Effie.

"We should have stayed together, Effie," he said and poured himself another drink. "We understand those little strayings. I'll bet you've run through a dozen lovers since my day. Who is it now?"

"Well—"

"Come on, you might tell me that much. What does he do?"

Effie hesitated.

"He's a writer," she said and glanced quickly toward the door to make sure Dennis wouldn't suddenly walk in. "Dennis Orphen."

"Orphen?" Andy drew back, offended. "That's the man who wrote that attack on me. I shouldn't think you'd like him—I don't think that's very sporting of you, Effie. A man who's lampooned me brutally—after all, Effie—"

Effie got up.

"I can't help what he writes, and then I never did feel any romantic nonsense about you, you know." She pulled on her gloves. "Now you must go to Marian's. Dennis is waiting for me."

"I've got this dinner tonight, I'll go tomorrow—"

"There won't be any tomorrow!" Effie cried, unable to bear more. "She's dying—she loves you—you've got to go to her."

Silently he got into his clothes. She felt ghastly and her heart seemed torn with her betrayal of it. She thought, how did people live to be old, each year betraying themselves more, crippling themselves with lies until the person herself is lost, she is only a whisper saying hear, hear, this is the real me, don't listen to what I say and don't look at what I do, this is the real me beneath all that changed into nothing but a little unheard voice, and if this wicked witch's body flays you don't be hurt for it isn't really I, don't heed it, only listen to my voice saying I love you.

Finally even the voice is killed and all that is left is the ugly deed, the cruel word. When it's over, it's over, she had said, so smilingly cut out her own heart.

She saw Andy talking to the young man but there was a din in her head, a ringing in her ears, echo of her own voice shouting, *when it's over, it's over.* When they finally left the bedroom only one person was left in the living room, Dennis, and Effie beckoned to him.

"Andy," she said, "this is Dennis Orphen."

Andy held out his hand stiffly.

"Congratulations, Orphen," he said. "Effie has just told me."

The three rode down in the elevator, Effie quite scarlet.

. . . Baby's birthday party . . .

"To BABY'S BIRTHDAY!" cried Phil Barrow, and Walter and Mary and
Bee Amidon and her husband (present at Walter's secret request to
Corinne) and Olive all clicked their Martini glasses a little too gamely,
Corinne thought, as if, for crying out loud can't we ever get a cocktail in
this house without toasting the queen or a brandy without an anecdote?

"My birthday isn't till Tuesday," said Corinne. "You know it, Phil."

She thought of how many times guests would have to drink to Baby's
birthday before she went crazy with boredom, and she thought this is the
good-wife feeling, this teeth clenched, controlled screaming-boredom
feeling. The guilty-wife feeling is better for the whole family, she reflected, that remorseful tender understanding, the seeing all his good traits
because your badness has cancelled his bad ones. The bad wife was far
pleasanter around the home; she could stand a lot from a husband because
it eased her conscience. "Why, dear, of course I understand," she said day
after day indulgently. "Don't let it worry you for a minute, darling."

Darling. This darling business was getting on her nerves. There had
been more darlings in the drawing room tonight than had ever been in
one room before. There was Walter darlinging his wife Mary so that Mr.
Amidon would be reassured about Walter's feeling toward Mrs. Amidon;
there was Bee Amidon darlinging Mr. Amidon for the same reason; there
was herself darlinging Phil very very conscientiously just to keep from
knocking that ever-raised-aloft drink out of his hand. And Dennis hadn't
come, hadn't called up, hadn't been in his house when she went down to
see him, had vanished, and if she never heard from him there was no way
she could find him, nothing she could do, nothing she could say, she could

only cry all night and pretend to Phil it was something else. She couldn't even tell Olive for Olive was too obviously thinking, my dear girl I always said he was no good, this is just what I always told you, you wouldn't believe me when I said he dropped me like a hot cake and ran out of his own party with that Mrs. Callingham but everyone knows about it. . . . No, she couldn't tell Olive.

"I'm spoiling the whole dinner party," Olive said gaily. "Since Dennis deserted us, I'm that awful thing, the girl without a man."

Everyone laughed although Mr. and Mrs. Amidon, Walter and Mary, and Olive and Corinne all knew it wasn't Olive but little Mrs. Barrow who had been deserted, and all, particularly Mrs. Amidon and Walter, felt a certain moral satisfaction in this.

"I don't see why Baby is so surprised at Orphen," said Phil and broke off a piece of bread in his soup slyly in the way he had that most irritated Corinne. Why didn't he break the whole piece boldly or dunk it and say this is the way I like it, but no, he just sneaked a little bit now and then into his soup or gravy when he thought no one was looking. "Orphen is a crude sort. I understand he was brought up in a cheap little railroad hotel. His father was a traveling salesman. Not that I don't admire the lower working class. And mind, I don't criticize Orphen for not being a college man. But I do object to rudeness. The sonofabitch might have telephoned at least. Olive here—"

"I could have brought a very nice neighbor of Dennis's, if he'd only given us warning," said Olive archly. "Mr. Schubert. The one who draws all those things for the *New Yorker* and *Vanity Fair*. He's going to Hollywood next month to do sets for that Joan Crawford picture. A thousand a week. I had tea with him at a little place over on East Fourteenth named Kavkas. Oh, *terribly* interesting. He's a Communist."

"There you are," said Phil triumphantly. "I'd like to know how these Communists can reconcile themselves to Hollywood jobs. That seems to me just the same as being a capitalist."

Olive gave a condescending smile.

"No, Phil, the way they feel is that until the Revolution they might as well avail themselves of their capitalistic opportunities. They have to sacrifice themselves to the present system."

Now Olive would be radical, Corinne thought wrathfully, she would have to listen to Olive's big thoughts on Russia and economics, and anything she hated was an economical bore. Olive would be going down to that apartment—up until the Hollywood moving—spilling things in the sink to make more plaster Gibson girls for Dennis's ceiling. She wished she had never told Olive anything. She wished she had never cried on Olive's shoulder. She wished Olive would move to California and never write to her, so she could have a really good reason for being mad at her. Looking about the table she thought she really detested everyone there; Walter particularly, who was always bellyaching to her that Bee Amidon didn't love him enough, was now—right in front of Bee, taking tender care that Mary, his wife, didn't get in a draft. Bee Amidon, bold-looking, dark, hearty woman, with a fine bouncing figure, was getting tight pretty fast without waiting for Phil's organized toasts. She was stroking Mr. Amidon's madly curly black hair and talking baby talk.

"Wooty wooty wooty," she said. "Mama's toy poodle."

I can't bear it, I can't bear it, Corinne screamed inside herself, how can you love two people at once, well, she ought to know, but no, she only loved one at once, the one she wasn't with at the time; or was love for Phil only being sorry she didn't love him, sorry he was so good to her when she was so bad, sorry she loved Dennis who wouldn't even call her up any more, who wouldn't write or phone her, who probably didn't love her, who wouldn't even carry her suitcase or help her across the street. Now she was sorry that Phil loved her so much, while Dennis just not calling up made her want to die, she wished the wine was poison, she could not bear sitting here laughing and drinking with Dennis vanished from her life. She dabbed at her eyes, pretending to listen to awful Mr. Amidon tell jokes. Awful maybe-you've-heard-this-one-Mr. Amidon. What was worse was that the Amidons were a storytelling couple. They boned up for parties. Then each whispered a story to the partner on their right, then to the partner on the left, then one told the whole table, and it wasn't funny anyway, but just very long with a bad word as the point. How could Walter stand a storytelling sweetheart? In the middle of the kiss—Oh-I-just-heard-a-good-one! Corinne saw that Walter and Mary were not laughing much at the Amidon jokes. Walter, beside Corinne, whispered nervously to her, "I've told all of Bee's jokes to Mary and now Mary smells a rat hearing Bee tell them all. For God's sake, pretend to Mary they were all in a book!"

"Orphen's novel is getting big reviews," said Walter aloud. "They say it's all about Callingham. Looks like a hit."

"That's good. I'm glad to hear that. I'm sincerely glad," said Phil. He turned to Amidon. "This book, *The Hunter's Wife*. My wife knows the author. He's a great personal friend of Baby's."

"Yes," said Corinne sarcastically. "I know him personally."

That's the way it was going to be. Dennis was going to be famous and forget all about her. She was going to hear Phil brag a thousand times a day—my wife used to know him personally! She put her napkin up to her face and ran out of the room. Why, Baby! Why, Corinne! Why, Mrs. Barrow! She ran upstairs, ran into the maid.

"I'll be all right—don't let them come up," she said, thinking of Olive ghoulishly rushing up for confessions.

She ran into her bedroom, breathlessly snatched the telephone, dialed Algonquin 4—No answer. Try the Havana Bar. No Mr. Orphen here. Try his house again. No, send telegram. Worth 2-7300. Telegram for Mr. Dennis Orphen—D as in darling, E as in ever, N as in never, N as in never, I as in Ink, S as in Sugar . . . O as in—I hate you hate you hate you hate . . . is that ten words? . . . Now Phil was coming up. She would jump out the window. Poor Phil. He loved her so. He would die if anything happened to her. His whole life centered about her. That's why she couldn't run away to Dennis. It wasn't the mink coat or the world cruise or the diamond wrist watch, it was Phil not being able to live without her.

"Baby, what is the matter? Are you sick?"

"Just something in my throat . . . Phil, dear—" No, no dears. Walter calling his wife dear all the while playing footy under the table with Bee Amidon finished that for her. "Phil, what would you do if I should die?"

"Why, Baby!"

"I don't mean anything, I was just wondering. You'd probably give up this place and stay at the Harvard Club, wouldn't you?"

"I should say not," said Phil promptly. "I'd take a north apartment at Essex House and get that Jap houseman you fired last year and every March I'd go to London and stay six weeks."

Corinne stared at him as if he were a monster. He had actually made plans. He probably had already signed up for a lease. So that was your loyal, faithful Phil, that was inside that toast-making head, plans for what fun he'd have when she died.

She went down with him and had a few brandies with the others, thinking about Phil, until people's dishonest voices cracked in her head and their horrid private lives came out from behind their darlings and their dears. Bee and Walter had to go out in the kitchen naturally to make a stinger in a very special way, and Mr. Amidon and Phil had to brag. The way Phil boasted was to tell about the big bank presidents' doings and Andrew Mellon and J. P. Morgan as if this were more or less his outfit and in a quiet way he could take bows for their achievements. Mr. Amidon, on the other hand, did his social climbing by picking out just such big figures for his personal rivals, told tales that insinuated that Stalin, Roosevelt, and the Pennsylvania Railroad had a powerful enemy in B. J. Amidon.

Olive didn't seem to be having much fun. She sat in a corner with Walter's wife, Mary, and they talked about their Schiaparellis of which they each had one, and whether the *Normandie* did or did not have a throbbing worse than the *Ile de France* or the *Conte de Savoia*. Once in a while Olive would give Corinne a sympathetic smile, an I-know-what-you're-thinking-you-poor-kid—you've-been-stood-up. He might be at the Glaenzers', Corinne thought frantically, if people would only leave so she might run through the streets looking for him. Why didn't Olive go hunt for him, perhaps he was sick, why didn't Walter help her out, but oh no he had to make stingers in the kitchen with Bee Amidon. Supposing Dennis was sick, at death's door, who would tell Mrs. Philip Barrow, no one, or if she found out and went to nurse him how would she explain to Phil? . . . She slipped up to her room again. Worth 2-7300. Telegram for Dennis Orphen. D as in darling—Darling darling love you love you please come love you. . . .

She must be going out of her mind. It could not really be Phil standing in the bathroom door, horrified, gaping at her. Why hadn't she looked in there?

"That was Orphen," Phil said mechanically. "You said you loved him. Orphen."

Corinne burst out sobbing.

"Yes, I do. I love him madly if you want to know," she screamed. "Get a divorce or kill me, I don't care. Now you know the truth. I love him— oh I do!"

She was torn with wild sobs, leaning over the bedpost.

Phil shook his head.

"Poor Baby," he said. "Poor Honeybaby."

"Honeybaby! That's right. Put it on my tombstone," she cried. "Go on, carve it on a monument for me—Poor Honeybaby—"

Between Phil and Olive and the maid they got her into bed with an icepack and a dose of luminal. Olive was frightened that when she and Phil tiptoed out of the room together he'd want to have it all out with her and she didn't know what she could say. He stood at the head of the stairs and took off his glasses, wiped them off carefully as if this would help him to see things straight.

"Don't say anything about this to the others," he said in an undertone. "Let them think she was just tight."

"That's the idea," said Olive quickly.

"As a matter of fact, Olive," he said gravely confidential. "This has me pretty worried. For a few minutes there the poor kid went clean out of her mind."

. . . some fine day I'll have to pay . . .

Dᴇɴɴɪs sᴛᴏᴏᴅ ᴀᴛ ᴛʜᴇ ᴡɪɴᴅᴏᴡ beside the scarlet curtains and watched the rain twinkling over the city, drops like golden confetti quivered over street lamps, they dribbled over the window ledge, made quick slanting designs across the pane, blurred the illuminated letters across the street— HOTEL GRENVILLE. On the glittering black pavement legs hurried by with umbrella tops, taxis skidded along the curb, their wheels swishing through the puddles, raindrops bounced like dice in the gutter. Foghorns zoomed on the river two blocks away, they croaked incessantly, the storm, the storm, they warned, beware, so beware; their deep note quavered and blurred like ink on wet paper, so be-e-e-e-wa-a-a-a-r-r-e— so—be-e—

He was acutely conscious of Effie in the room behind him, conscious of the new intensely personal quality in their relationship, a perturbing modulation from author and heroine to man and woman that made their conversation now strained on his part but far more confident on hers. He was glad of the swelling and diminishing screen of radio music that separated him from her. A rich soothing voice advised the use of Barbasol, an announcer gave the time—ten o'clock—in tender fatherly tones as if it were the facts of life. . . . Where was Corinne now? She was probably a perpetual ringing of his telephone over at his apartment, a why-didn't-you-meet-me-yesterday, why-aren't-you-ever-in—what-is-this-about-you-and-Mrs.-Callingham—oh-darling-why-did-you-run-out-with-her-so-that-Olive-says-says-says—says—

"When I saw you there in Andy's room that day," Effie said dreamily, "I knew in that moment you were closer to me than anyone in the world, and all the time I had talked of Andy it was you were nearer to me. The Andy I knew went long ago with his first success. Do you know, Dennis, I would never even have known him—his very voice, his walk, his gestures, and of course his hair?—he had turned into the Uncle Henry who used to visit us. I couldn't get the two separated in my mind. Isn't that fantastic?"

"That happens," said Dennis.

He walked over to the radio and dialed till a soprano flew out as if she had been imprisoned for years in this ugly form waiting for the magic touch of the prince. Released now, her song flooded the little room, set the two fat goldfish in the bowl on the mantel to waltzing furiously through their miniature cosmos; another soprano joined in, the two voices floated idly through the air, high silvery bubbles of light; l'amour, ah l'amour, they sang, l'amour, a balloon bounced lightly from high C to F, slid gracefully down to B. Now other feminine voices came winging to the aid of l'amour, balancing their delicate balls of sound on the end of magic wands—there—there—ah there—The goldfish, side by side, swam rhythmically round their coral castle, their tiny green undersea forest undulated ever so faintly, oh l'amour, l'amour. . . .

Effie was silent and Dennis thought, now she was thinking of Marian, of Marian's dying eyes flickering with dim joy because Andy did come, he loved her, he came all over the world for her, oh l'amour, l'amour, and when he saw her lying there he had slipped suddenly to the floor, buried his face on the pillow beside her and so she had died. "Gone," Effie had telephoned Belle Glaenzer. "But Andy was there." "Dead," she told Dr. MacGregor, "but Andy came. It was in his arms—" And Effie forgot, but Dennis never would, that Effie had left the hospital with radiant transformed face, walked through the streets, through crowds, smiling and murmuring, as if she were the one who had died and this was not her body but her spirit that was wafting invisibly through the city night, triumphant after death because her lover had returned, had held her sobbing in his arms as she passed, oh l'amour, l'amour. Dennis had unlocked her door for her, saw her vague beyond smile, and had sat down on the stairs of her hallway a little afraid of what she might do. Mrs. Hickey, coming up to open the skylight door in the morning, had found him there.

This week Effie was marvelously serene, but it was Dennis who was upset for he could not understand her quiet air of consummation. Was it that Andy's arrival had freed her from the myth or was it that meeting him, she found him worthy of all her secret tears? Losing her as a character under his control, Dennis was alarmed; now she was as baffling to him as himself, unpredictable, unanswerable, and he feared she was becoming too much a part of himself.

"You made me see things, Dennis," Effie went on. "Now I know that the Andy I loved was the Andy I made up after he left, and when I loved him most was talking him over with you, for I put part of you on him, till he was more than you or Andy. I know it all the more because in your book you wrote about him just as I see him now. I was the one who didn't see my own picture straight. Thank you, my dear, for truth."

Her blue dressing gown trailed on the floor, her arms were clasped over her head, her hair hung in long braids over her shoulder and about her sad lovely face . . . like Melisande, Dennis thought, and there was nothing he would not do for her, nothing, his throat felt choked with his deep love for her, with sad l'amour drifting in cigarette smoke about the ceiling, with raindrops beating on the windowpane. Yes, he would give his life for her, he thought, for this high devotion was more than any carnal contentment. He thought of how fretted his life had been, how wickedly trivial, and he vowed that Effie would be his life from now on, chivalry for lust, beauty for pleasure.

"I didn't tell you one thing." Effie hesitated a little. "Andy thinks you are his successor with me. I—it seemed to make him feel better, so I let him think so. In case we ever run into him around town—"

"Oh, I'll act the part," promised Dennis. He knew Corinne must have already heard this same rumor. He had not seen her, or called her, for there was no explaining why his first duty always lay so curiously with Mrs. Callingham; no explaining that it was not an affair nor that this deep bond with Effie was stronger than any love he had ever known. Corinne seemed nothing to him beside Effie for Effie was not only a person, she was his book, just as Andy had been to her not only a man but her dream. He felt exalted and strangely bodiless around her, filled with vague high purpose. He would do something magnificent for her, something beyond mortal power.

"Tea tomorrow?" he asked, taking his hat. "Say five-ish."

Her hand stayed in his.

"You are a dear, Dennis." He thought, a little startled, that if it were anyone but Effie he would have sworn the lingering tone and gesture belonged to a woman in love. Could it be that with Andy materialized she was unconsciously turning to a new romantic ideal, to him, Dennis, because he had vanquished the dream Andy? . . . He walked back to his apartment in the rain, wondering at the new Effie that was being born, and disturbed at the hint of his own responsibility. With each moment's consideration he slipped a bit from his high mood of selfless ambition. What he wanted, suddenly, was the clean-cut brutality of the Havana Bar, of Toots and Boots and Lora. A row of news trucks lined up before a red traffic light on Union Square bore glaring posters across their sides.

START ANDREW CALLINGHAM'S DARING LOVE
STORY IN THE DAILY MIRROR—JUNE 15th.

"I'll have to get to work on my new book," thought Dennis. "I'll make it about Lora. The story of a woman with the soul of a statue, animated only by rum. How Johnson will hate it!"

On the steps of his apartment house a little figure in a white raincoat loomed like a ghost in the dark. It was Corinne.

"I've made up my mind," she said, "I'm going to leave Phil and live with you."

"The hell you are," said Dennis.

But he was enormously glad to see her. She took the burden of high resolutions off his back and he drew a great breath of relief. He kissed her.

"Come on in out of the rain," he said.

STORIES

AUDITION

IT WAS ELEVEN O'CLOCK and still no sign of Danny. The two men waiting in Danny's apartment were struck with the same thought, simultaneously, and pushed aside the card table.

"He did it deliberately," Syd said. "'Be here at eight sharp,' he says. 'We'll get that second act set.' Then he never shows up. What kinda management is that? High-priced talent like us wasting time on gin rummy just because he don't show up. Unless he's got something up his sleeve."

"Whatever it is, it's no good," Eddie said gloomily.

There was a half-filled paper bag lying on the floor by the fireplace, with some empty pop bottles beside it. Eddie investigated the bag and found a couple of sandwiches left over from last night's conference. He offered half of one to Syd, who bit into it distrustfully.

"Liverwurst," he announced. "He always gets liverwurst. Ever since I said I didn't like it. Where do you suppose he went?"

He flung his sandwich into the electric logs of the fireplace.

"It's a cinch he didn't go anyplace that costs anything," said Eddie.

"Then he's gone back to his wife," decided Syd. "How much do you suppose he owes this hotel? Four hundred bucks didn't somebody say? Where's he gonna get that kinda money? Even if he finds a backer, how's a guy like Danny Bender gonna get his mitts on any personal cash? He ain't that smart."

"Boy, could I use money," mused Eddie. "I love money. Not for what it can buy, either. I love it just for itself."

He flopped on the davenport and lay back with his hands clasped behind his head, his feet crossed on the end table. Eddie was willing to admit that Danny's apartment was more comfortable for waiting than the little cubbyholes in the Ambrose on Forty-second Street where he and Syd stayed. But he'd seen better places. Syd, however, never having worked in Hollywood like Eddie, thought Danny's suite was just about tops in luxury.

There were the gold-tasseled floor lamps, the glass coffee tables, the flowered plush davenport and easy chairs, the small Chinese red piano; and in the bedroom were the twin pink-ruffled beds, the window curtains of pink rayon and the pink carpet. There was even a canary in a cage by the window.

"Some dame must have given it to him," said Syd. "Can you picture that louse with a canary? I notice it don't sing. Here. Here you are, bird."

He rescued a morsel of the discarded sandwich and poked it through the bars of the cage. The canary ignored it.

"All right, all right," Syd exclaimed angrily. "Wait for an order of caviar! A mug like Danny should have a bird!"

Eddie had a sudden thought and sat up.

"He's probably working on that crazy dame at the Plaza," he said. "If he thinks he can get money out of her, he should have his head examined. A woman calls him up on the telephone and says she's anxious to put money in a musical. So he believes he's got a backer. Never heard of her, mind you, never clapped an eye on her. 'Well, fellas,' he says when he hangs up, 'I guess our problems are over.' He don't even know a screwball."

"I'll bet he's there, at that," said Syd, shaking his head. "Sure, he's there. The old girl's probably got him locked in now, yelling for help."

The telephone rang. It was Eddie's turn to answer it. Already five girls had telephoned for Danny and it had been the two visitors' pleasure to inform them separately that Danny expected them at twelve. Sometimes the kids did show up and there was always a chance of a good time, unless Danny showed up too and got sore. This time it was no girl but Danny himself calling.

"You fellas still waiting?" he asked. He had his important, big-shot-on-Broadway manner so he must have been sure somebody was listening. "What about the revisions in that lighthouse scene? All set, eh? Fine. Did you catch that kid at Spivy's? No, no, not that one; she'll never see twenty-four again. I mean the one that just opened. Joan. They say she's terrific."

"Oh sure, sure, Danny," Eddie said soothingly. "We signed up Jessel, too. No contract. Just outa friendship for you. Who's supposed to be paying for this good time we're having around town?"

"The Coast *did* call, then?" Danny asked urgently.

"Sure. Marie MacDonald telephoned up personally. Said she didn't want a lead, just a bit part for the honor of playing for you. She's on her way now on foot."

"I don't know whether we want MacDonald or not," Danny said crisply. "I'd sooner take a chance on Lake, even without a voice. We got a personality there we can build on. Look, Toots, punch up that lighthouse scene for me, will you, now? Get some gags, get Fats in on it. Remember this is four-forty not ten, twent and thirt."

Eddie made an insulting gesture toward the telephone and winked at Syd. Danny's voice was still going when Eddie spoke into the transmitter again.

"Listen, Buster, Syd and I have been waiting here four hours. Fats wants two bucks apiece for those gags he gave us or else he wants them back. No use calling him again. Where the hell are you? Have we got a show or haven't we? Are you coming back here and confer or aren't you?"

"Go easy, Eddie," whispered Syd, though he was smiling with admiration at his friend. "After all he's all we've got."

"Listen, Eddie." Now Danny's voice was lowered entreatingly. "Wait a minute, will you, fella? I'm onto something terrific. Will you take it easy now, till I get down?"

Syd was occupied with examining the correspondence in Danny's desk, and did not turn around until struck by his companion's silence. Eddie had hung up the receiver and was thoughtfully smoking a cigarette butt, selected with care from the ash tray.

"Crazy women do have money," he mused. "It just could be, you know. And if they'd go for anybody, they'd go for that George Raft type, like Danny. What's about that slick black hair, I wonder? It never fails."

Syd unconsciously began smoothing down his own sparse locks. He had taken vitamin pills for two weeks now to bring his hair back but so far nothing was happening. A song writer could always get a girl, but even so, if you didn't have hair you had to have money. A hundred-dollar advance three months ago wasn't any nest egg.

"Let's call up the bar and charge some Scotch to Danny," he suggested. "If he's got the backer we owe ourselves a little celebration."

Eddie, for answer, silently dialed the telephone. After a while he gave up.

"Nothing happens," he said. "No outgoing calls."

"How we going to call up MacDonald and tell her we don't want her?" Syd acidly inquired. "She's probably got a hitch by this time. Shucks."

Eddie now seemed struck by an inspiration of great charm for he began humming significantly. He tiptoed over to the fireplace and as if by magic drew out a bottle of whiskey from beneath the logs. Syd shook his head again in awe of this mastermind.

"You did learn something in Hollywood," he sighed.

"You don't get kicked out of the best homes without learning something, sonny," Eddie said complacently. He fished two discarded paper cups from the wastebasket.

It was always a pleasure to put something over on Danny, so the drinks, which turned out to be a rather fiery Bourbon, were sipped with solemn appreciation. The phone rang again and this time, as Syd sprang to answer it, it was Carr, the agent.

"Where's Danny?" he shouted. "I'm in there punching every minute and he's got time to fool around. Do I shave? Do I have time to sit down to a meal at home? No, I'm on the hop every minute for that little fly-brain. Sixty-cent telegrams to the Coast every minute, a cable to London even, and when do I get my money back, do you think? Does Danny care? Do you two care? Oh, no."

"Why, Carr, you're talking like a man with an office," Syd cut in innocently. "Where are you—the drugstore?"

"All right, I got to do business from a drugstore because I handle dopes like Danny and that pal of yours, Eddie Rosman!" Carr snapped back ferociously. "At least I'm trying to do a service. I'm trying to warn Danny against that dame that calls up all the time from the Plaza. She's a screwball. Institution case. Stan just had a run-in with her, and she's bad. No dice there, so tell that clunk to watch out, will you? Tell him—the hell with it, there goes my nickel."

Syd put down the receiver and silently poured another drink. Eddie looked at him questioningly.

"Show's off—no backer," said Syd. "Now we celebrate that."

There was a knock at the door. Syd and Eddie, accustomed as they had become to angry landlords, summons servers, and other public enemies, looked at each other and with one accord hid their drinks.

"Nuts, they can't throw us out of a place we don't even live in," Eddie muttered. "What we got to worry about? Come in."

A little dark-haired girl, swathed in a long Persian lamb coat, stepped inside the door and looked hopefully at Eddie. They always looked at Eddie first because he still had his Hollywood clothes and that big chest, but they ended up with Syd because Eddie was too smart with them.

"You said I was to call at eleven," she said hesitantly. "About the show, I mean. My name is Miss Mink. Maribel Mink."

"How do you do, Miss Mink," said Eddie courteously rising. "I hope you won't think this is a joke but my friend's name here is Fink."

"Hey!" said Syd, annoyed.

Eddie raised a conciliatory hand.

"Just the first name. Now, Miss Mink, Mr. Fink and I want you to tell us exactly and in so many words just what you can do for our show. You dance of course?"

"Oh, yes," she said eagerly. Syd could tell by looking at her legs that she was no dancer, but they always said they could, and hoped God would hand out the gift like a little rain shower.

"When was your last New York show, Miss Mink?" Eddie pursued attentively, following Danny's auditioning manner so perfectly that Syd almost burst out laughing.

"Well, I'll tell you, Mr. Bender, I happen to have a prejudice against playing New York," the girl said earnestly, her large blue eyes moving from one to the other. "The way I feel is this, that a person gets a lot more experience in stock and on the road than they do in a New York show where a person is likely to get in a rut just playing one part night after night for a year or two, like a friend of mine in *Oklahoma!* I love the road, Mr. Bender, I really mean that. It seems crazy but I just never felt like playing in a New York show, I really never did."

Eddie stroked his chin. "Too bad," he said. "This is a New York show, you see, so you'd be out of luck."

The girl bit her lip. "I mean that's the way I *used* to feel, Mr. Bender. I wanted to be sure that I had enough experience to really make good on Broadway, and now I feel I really have, so here I am. I got looks—of course you're seeing me at my worst because I just got out of the hospital. I've been in the hospital for the last six months, and I don't look the same."

"What was it?" Syd asked, interested.

"They couldn't seem to find out," she laughed self-consciously. "All that money and all those doctors couldn't find out."

"What hospital? Sounds familiar," pressed Syd.

The girl gestured vaguely. "It was private," she said impressively. "You get better care."

"Do you sing, Miss Mink? But of course." Eddie took up Danny's role again. "Perhaps you'd sing something, ballad type, I should say."

"I couldn't without my own accompanist," Miss Mink said regretfully. "He's a Russian. Studied all over the world. Of course, he wants me to go into concert work."

"Naturally," approved Eddie. "And why not?"

Miss Mink was a little confused. "Because I got too many ideals, Mr. Bender," she confessed after a moment's thought.

"I like that spirit," said Eddie. "It's easy to see you're an ambitious girl. By the way, Mr. Fink, will you look at Miss Mink's profile for screen possibilities? You see, Miss Mink, we're thinking in terms of a package. We want to sell the cast along with the show to pictures."

"Oh, yes, a package," nodded Miss Mink, intelligently and looked hopefully at Syd. Syd shrugged. She wasn't his type. He liked those tall blond clotheshorses from the model agencies. So did Eddie. So did everybody. That was the trouble.

"Nose a little broad," Syd said, offhand.

"It's my hair down," Miss Mink eagerly explained. "I can put it up. I wear it in a double pompadour created especially for me. I can't do it now, of course, because I don't have the pins."

"How old are you, dear? Nineteen?" asked Eddie.

"Almost," said Miss Mink. "Next Tuesday's my birthday."

She was probably twenty-three or four, or even older, Syd thought. That little dark kind fooled you.

"Fink, I think this is our girl," Eddie said, nodding wisely to Syd. Syd could tell he was kidding, and it didn't seem worth the trouble with this girl, so he gave Eddie an impatient signal. Sometimes Eddie made you sore, carrying things so far, but then Syd would remember that it was after all Eddie who once had the movie job and might get them both another one as a team, so it was better to string along with him.

"I'd like to know more about my part, please," Miss Mink said with dignity. "Naturally, I want to be sure it's right for me."

Syd watched Eddie go into a typical Danny routine.

"You're in and out of most of the show," said Eddie briskly. "Your biggest comedy scene is laid in a lighthouse. You're stranded there with a Mae West character, a Bert Lahr character, a Betty Hutton, and say, a straight man, Tony Martin type. They start some crossfire, you give it right back, it's a howl; the West character gives you a sock line, voom and out. Lahr has a typical Lahr line, voom and out. Then three fast cracks, one right after the other, from Hutton, voom and out. Your juvenile looks at you—audience still howling, see—he gives you one terrific line, voom, and blackout. What do you say?"

Miss Mink pondered. "It sounds cute all right. Would I have to wear tights?"

"Certainly," Syd answered. "Say, do you live at the Artists' Hotel?"

"How did you know?" Miss Mink countered, startled.

"The coat," said Syd. "We've auditioned that coat a hundred times."

"I let the other girls borrow it," said Miss Mink, flushing.

"I knew you'd say that," said Syd. He was sorry for her, now, and he hated Eddie with his Hollywood past, and Danny with his elegant plush-and-pink apartment. Just because Miss Mink wasn't pretty like the other auditions, Eddie was taking her over the jumps.

"Supposing you sing us the hit song from this road show you speak of, Miss Mink," Eddie suggested, smiling.

"I'd love to Mr. Bender, I really would, but I've got this cold," Miss Mink responded brightly. "As a matter of fact that was what I was in the hospital for. Besides I work with a male quartet, mostly. They sang while I danced."

"Could you oblige with one of your routines?" Eddie begged politely.

Miss Mink frowned. "It seems sort of silly dancing without the male quartet after I was so used to it," she demurred.

"What outfit was it?" Syd asked, because he knew Eddie was going to.

"Oh, they've broken up, now," regretted Miss Mink. "The war."

"See here, Miss Mink," Eddie said quietly. "Would you mind telling me if you were ever on the stage in your life? You say you can't sing, you can't dance, I suppose you can't even talk, without that male quartet. Who do you think you're fooling?"

Miss Mink sat down quickly, as if her legs had given way, and her too large coat fell open, showing the shabby summer dress beneath. She began to cry, not prettily at all, but with snuffles and odd choking noises.

"You've got to get experience," she sniffled.

Eddie began to laugh, and this time Syd was really angry. He went over and stood beside her, talking very fast and very loud.

"Never mind, Miss Mink, you belong. Don't worry about that. You're no actress, but that's all right. Eddie Rosman isn't Danny Bender, I'm not Fink, the backer hasn't any money, the phone doesn't work, the rent isn't paid, the canary doesn't sing, there isn't any show, and if there was it wouldn't be going on, and if it was, Eddie and I wouldn't have anything to do with hiring talent, so what have you got to lose? Come on, now, I'll take you home."

Miss Mink rose weakly to her feet. "Why, that's sweet of you—" she said, in a small tired voice. "Oh, that's awfully sweet."

Syd got his hat and coat, not looking at Eddie. Eddie sat very still, staring at the floor with a funny smile. He saw a whole cigarette under the fringe of the davenport and picked it up carefully.

"Come on," said Syd gruffly.

As Syd ushered Miss Mink out the door, he thought he heard a faint "yip." Syd didn't know whether it came from Eddie or the canary.

SUCH A PRETTY DAY

As soon as Dave had put the pen in the yard and waved good-bye to the baby, Sylvia got on the phone.

"Hello, Barbs. Scotty gone, yet? . . . Listen, Barbs, Dave says they're working overtime this week so he won't be home for lunch . . . Scotty, too, eh? . . . That's what I wanted to know. Listen, Barbs, it's such a pretty day I thought we might go to the city. You bring the kids over and I'll get Frieda . . . Yes, I know she's a brat and she'll tell the whole neighborhood but she's good with the kids . . . Listen, don't say anything . . . My God, Dave'd kill me. You heard what he said last Sunday—if he caught me thumbing again he'd get a divorce? Listen, he means it. You come on over, Barbs. OK Barbs . . . Oh I'm goin' to wear my culottes . . . Your dirndl? Why don't you wear your culottes? They look kinda cute on you . . . Sew 'em up, why don't you? Or I will. Bring 'em over. Oh go on, Barbs, wear your culottes. I'm going to. OK, Barbs. The baby's yelling. Don't forget the culottes. 'Bye."

Sylvia ran into the bedroom and whisked up the beds. She snatched up newspapers, toys, Dave's pajamas, a ten-cent double boiler with some petrified oatmeal in it and tossed them all in the closet. That was one thing about having your own house, your mother couldn't be nagging at you to do things her way all the time. Sylvia couldn't get over the thrill of her own house. Five whole rooms, just for her and Dave and the baby. Never had even one room to herself before she was married. Darn it all, she was happy. Let 'em talk. Her own mother was married at sixteen, too, wasn't she? Supposing she'd sat around and finished school, what then? She could have a job in the Lumber Works and get up every morning at six-thirty like Gladys Chalk, instead of lying around her own house all day in a nightgown. She could sit around waiting for some guy to call her up and God knows there weren't enough boys in town to go around, instead of having a nice fellow like Dave all sewed up permanently. So maybe Sylvia wasn't so dumb as her folks said. So what.

Mrs. Peters was out in the backyard fooling with the baby when Sylvia went out, and that was all right, because she could ask her about Frieda.

"You look about ten years old in those culottes," said Mrs. Peters. "I should think youda put on more weight being married two years already. I wouldn't take you for more'n twelve at the most."

"No cracks'" said Sylvia coldly. "I was nineteen last Tuesday. Did you see the toaster Dave got me? We don't eat much toast but I have to keep at it 'cause it makes the baby laugh so the way the toast jumps out."

"I don't think that installment plan is good for young folks," said Mrs. Peters, as if it was any of her business, but Sylvia took it because she wanted Frieda.

"How else you going to get anything on thirty a week, Mrs. Peters?" she merely asked. "Look, Mrs. Peters, could Frieda come over today and look after Davie? I got a chance to go to the city—there's a picture I want to see at the Majestic."

Mrs. Peters blew out her cheeks and Davie laughed and squealed with joy. He was a good baby. Even Mrs. Peters had to say so.

"I couldn't run around the way you do when I was raising a family," said Mrs. Peters. "If it wasn't washing it was canning or berrying or helping in Mr. Peters's store."

All right, we'll go into that, then. The trouble with those old married women was they thought they had a racket all sewed up and they didn't like pretty young girls breaking into it.

"Tell Frieda she can make a cake if she wants too" Sylvia conceded. "There's flour and chocolate, and she can play the radio."

"If it's that Barbara friend of yours you're going with," said Mrs. Peters, "I wouldn't let any daughter of mine run around with her. Her folks are nothing but trash. There hasn't ever been a Moller that amounted to a stick in this town. Frieda says she saw six beer bottles in the sink there one morning."

"Barbs and Scotty are Dave's and my best friends," said Sylvia in her best Missus voice, and was that a lie, with Dave saying just what Mrs.

Peters was saying all the time. "Tell Frieda to come about eleven, we want to get a good start."

Barbs walked in, wheeling the twins. They were not quite a year old but were big babies like Davie, and made Barbs look like a school kid, which she probably should have been, but keeping house was a lot more fun than figuring out "amo, amas, amat." You could say what you liked about Barbs, maybe she did run wild until Scotty and the twins kinda settled her, but you had to hand it to her she kept that dinky little apartment of hers spick and span. Sylvia didn't see how in heck she did it, but Barbs said she just liked scrubbing and washing and it was more fun than slamming through things the way Sylvia did. "Maybe," Sylvia always said, looking around the trim little suite over the butcher shop, "if I only had three rooms instead of a whole house I could get interested, too."

Frieda came over at ten minutes to eleven. She wore thick glasses over her slightly crossed eyes and her former pigtails had been miraculously transformed into a kinky tangled mass.

"I got a permanent," she said proudly.

Both Barbs and Sylvia were crazy for permanents so they were silent for a moment in envious awe.

"I don't like permanents on kids," said Barbs haughtily.

"Everybody in my Sunday school class has one," said Frieda, unperturbed. "My mother says it's a hundred percent improvement. My mother's making me culottes, too. Where you going, to the city? I thought Dave told you not to thumb any more, Sylvia."

"Listen to the brat," said Barbs. "Do you run this town, Miss Wisie?"

"You better be careful or I won't take care of your old twins," said Frieda. "Can I really make a cake, Sylvia?"

Sylvia motioned Barbs into the house and they went in to whisper ways of getting out to the turnpike without Frieda being able to tell. Scotty didn't like Barbs hitching any more than Dave did, because everybody in the town talked enough anyway, and they said—they must have got together on this—Barbs and Sylvia were married women now and couldn't go coasting and hayriding and all the things they did when they were younger. At first Sylvia thought it was because Scotty was older—he was twenty-seven—and more settled, he'd worked in the factory since he was twelve, but then Dave, who was just twenty, got to talking that way, too. They didn't want their wives hiking around the state like a couple of tramps. You didn't see the Hull girls doing it, did you? Or Dody Crane?

"The Hull girls and Dody Crane, can you imagine," Sylvia repeated in indignation. "Why should they, they got their own cars, and Dody's dad is rich?"

At that Sylvia had nothing against Dody. The Hull girls were snobs because they'd gone away to boarding school while Sylvia and Barbs were plugging through public school, but Dody was all right, she always spoke to Sylvia, and once Dave had taken her to a dance. She wouldn't let him kiss her so he married Sylvia instead and promoted Dody to be his ideal. Sylvia got kind of sick always being pecked at to do things the way Dody would do them. That was the only thing. But Dody was all right. She sent the baby a cute blanket once.

Barbs stuck the twins' bottles in the icebox and Frieda put all the babies in the pen. She was a fat little girl but that wasn't the only reason nobody loved her. She pulled out a camp stool from behind the tool shed and sat down on it on the grass with a book.

"I'll read to them for a while," she said, "from the Bible."

The three fat little babies, clad in nothing but their G strings, stared at Frieda, rather pleased with her glasses.

"They'll love that," said Sylvia, and she and Barbs sneaked out the front way, past the garage to the pike.

They walked sedately enough past the straggling houses, and tried not to look up at tempting cars shooting past, because you couldn't tell yet, it might be somebody from the factory who would tell the boys. A roadster with two men in it slowed up and one of them yelled, "Hi, Dietrich," but the girls dared not look up yet.

"You know, Sylvia, you do look kinda like Marlene Dietrich," said Barbs, studying Sylvia critically. "Somebody else, I forget who, said so. Me, I'm more the Merle Oberon type."

"You got freckles, too, if that's what you mean," said Sylvia, and then a No Trespassing sign on a fence reminded her of something and she giggled. "Remember Barbs, when the whole freshmen class came out here and stole apples one Saturday? No, I guess you'd quit school then."

"I was working in the Candy Kitchen," said Barbs. "I was going with that baseball player, Tod Messersmidt. Gee, Scotty used to rave. He'd just started boarding at Mom's. But gee, I was just a kid, going on thirteen, twenty-two seemed old to me, then."

A blue sedan drove slowly past, and Barbs nudged Sylvia. It was the Hull sisters on their way to the Country Club. They stared at the two girls and Barbs and Sylvia stared insolently back. Then Dody Crane's car came along, Dody driving with her mother, two golf bags sticking out of the side. Dody nodded and Sylvia nodded back.

"Dody was along that time out here," said Sylvia. "Her mother never let her come again because she heard there was necking. Ha!"

"I'll bet it's the last necking she ever saw," said Barbs who after all had been ignored by Dody. "Imagine a girl that old running around all the time with her old lady."

"We used to have some fun in school," said Sylvia. "You should have stayed in, Barbs. I know I quit too soon, but I had two and a half years of high—that's about enough, most people say. You get the best of it. I suppose if I'd stayed till I graduated I would be riding over to the Country Club to play golf right now instead of hitchhiking with you."

"You would not," said Barbs dryly. "You'd be helping out in the hotel kitchen just like your mother."

Now they were past the club road and on the main highway. They stopped and began working. It never took them long, because they were a couple of good-looking girls, as they well knew, and even women weren't afraid of being held up by such a nice little pair. This time it was a woman in a big Cadillac. She was a thin, browned woman with iron-gray hair and she drove like a house afire. Some fun. They were in the heart of the city in less than an hour.

"Let's go to the show right away," suggested Sylvia.

Everybody looked at the two bareheaded girls in their red culottes wandering through the business section. Barbs stopped short suddenly.

"Listen, Sylvia, I only got forty cents."

"But I told you we would go to the Majestic," said Sylvia, annoyed. "You know it's fifty."

"Well, I just don't have it," said Barbs, doggedly. "I guess you wouldn't have it either, if you had two kids instead of one and your husband had to fork over six bucks a week to his mother."

"Why don't she get on relief?" complained Sylvia. "Dave's mother did."

"Dave's mother is in another town," said Barbs. "And anyway Scotty don't like the idea. So I only got forty cents."

Sylvia was furious.

"I go to work and get Frieda for us and let her mess up my kitchen baking a cake, and now you don't have fifty cents for a show. Barbs, honestly, you're a lousy sport. Why didn't you tell me?"

Barbs was sullen.

"I wanted to get outa town for five minutes, show or no show."

Sylvia counted her money. Sixty-seven cents.

"You go alone, and I'll look around the stores," said Barbs.

It ended with them buying a Popsicle at a corner stand for lunch and then going on a shopping tour. They went through Schwab's because Barbs dared Sylvia to go in. This was a large, cool, dark, swank store and so snooty that Barbs and Sylvia clutched each other's hands to keep up their courage before the hostile clerks.

"This is where Dody gets all her clothes," said Sylvia. "Except the ones she gets in New York."

"A lot of good it does her," said Barbs. "I'll bet she'd give her eyeteeth to be married and have kids like we have. She played with dolls longer than any of us. She had the first mama doll in town."

"I wish I had a little girl," said Sylvia, "I'd get her a mama doll."

"I'd get her a Dydee doll," said Barbs, and that reminded her they must go to the Variety Store next.

Schwab's doors swung thankfully behind them.

"Even if I had money I wouldn't buy clothes in that lousy store," said Barbs. "Their styles are all hick. They've got braid on everything. Look!"

A window display of garden furniture, complete with sand, pool, umbrellas, and mint juleps held them spellbound. Life-sized velvety-lashed ladies in garden frocks sat in swings and deck chairs in attitudes of rigid enjoyment. A rosy wall-eyed athlete in shorts relaxed on a tennis roller. Two beaming little boys in bathing suits sat stiffly on a rubber dolphin in the pool.

"I could get the twins bathing suits and one of those false fish," said Barbs. "You know where I'd put it, don't you?"

Sylvia was thinking in terms of Davie but was willing to listen.

"I'd put it in the old tank on the roof and then fill it with water."

"Like a penthouse," said Sylvia.

They walked on silently to the big Variety Store, Sylvia busy putting the fish and Davie in a bathing suit somewhere around her own premises, and Barbs thinking about the tank. The Variety Store was more hospitable than Schwab's. A radio was on, and a girl at the piano counter in a pink sharkskin sport dress was playing and singing "If You Were the Only Girl."

"Say, if I couldn't sing better than that," muttered Barbs.

"It's my favorite song, too," said Sylvia. "But don't she ruin it?"

They hummed it softly, looking over the counters.

"I'll bet we could sing over the radio if we practiced more," said Sylvia. "Honestly, Barbs, even Dave thinks we're good."

"Ah, nuts," said Barbs. "Nobody's going to let us do anything ever. Wish I had my hands on that six bucks we sent off to Scotty's mom right now."

"I could let you have ten cents, maybe, if you want to buy something," said Sylvia relenting, but just then her eye caught something and she added, "Still, you got forty of your own, haven't you?"

Barbs saw what Sylvia saw. It was a baby's bathing suit for sixty-five cents. Probably it was only fair. After all Sylvia did have sixty-seven cents and only one baby.

"Now you only got two cents," was all Barbs said when the girl gave Sylvia the package. Sylvia unwrapped it right away and held it up. It was bright red with a little white belt. It was the cutest thing.

"I'd rather have had the striped ones like the ones in the window," said Barbs, but Sylvia read the envy in her voice and grinned.

At the next counter were spades and beach pails, and here Barbs was as lost as Sylvia because she had to buy two or nothing, so forty cents was no good. At the foot of the counter were rubber floats and one was a dolphin almost like the one in the window. It was a dollar ninety-eight and it came in a box, then you blew it up. Sylvia and Barbs stared at it.

"Kids don't need bathing suits on a roof," said Barbs. "I can fill that old tank anyway."

"Sure," said Sylvia.

"You can bring Davie up to play in it, too," said Barbs, generously. "But he won't need that suit."

"That'll be fun," said Sylvia. Sixty-five cents wasted.

They could not take their eyes off the sample dolphin.

"He'd hold two, wouldn't he?" said Barbs.

"Sure—three, even," giggled Sylvia.

She almost knew what Barbs was going to do and yet in a way you could have knocked her down with a feather. The minute the clerk walked off to the next counter Barbs had snitched one of the rubber things out of its box and stuffed it down her front. Nothing happened. Nobody screamed. Nobody grabbed them. Barbs looked at Sylvia, and Sylvia's mouth moved helplessly.

"W-w-w-well," said Barbs, "I g-g-g-uess we'd b-b-etter be g-g-g-going to the M-m-m-ajestic."

They walked slowly out of the store. A man in a Panama hat watched them from the record counter, but he couldn't be anything but a customer. The girl at the bathing-suit counter watched them.

"She saw," gasped Barbs. "Just as I popped it in I saw her looking, but it was too late to yank it out, then. Look. . . . I'm afraid to—is anybody following?"

Sylvia was afraid, too. They walked in slow agony down the street. Someone was behind them. Out of the corner of her eye Sylvia saw it was the man in the Panama hat. He grinned. Sylvia grew red. Barbs clutched her arm frantically.

"Let's get a hitch, quick," she whispered. "We got to go home now."

"But it's only two o'clock," said Sylvia. "Anyway if somebody's watching from the store they'll see us."

"Oh—oh, what'll we do," whispered Barbs. "Does it show?"

Sylvia giggled.

"No, you only look like Aunt Jemima, that's all."

Barbs was looking up and down the street for a possible hitch. The man in the Panama hat was getting into a Chevrolet coupé. He grinned again, and imperceptibly winked. Barbs and Sylvia walked up to him, but before they spoke two men in shirtsleeves from the Variety came out on the sidewalk and with one accord the girls climbed into his car. He slammed the door and drove quickly around the corner.

"Oh gee," breathed Barbs. "Oh thanks!"

The man was a swarthy foreign-looking fellow, with a candy-striped shirt and a diamond ring.

"I got the idea," he said.

Nobody said anything more till they were outside the city limits and then Sylvia noticed they were not going in the direction of Butterville.

"Pittsburgh's my next stop," said the driver. He turned to Barbs. "That wasn't your first job there in the store, was it, sugar?"

Barbs looked blank.

"Don't act so innocent," he said, laughing. "I knew what you girls were up to as soon as I saw those red culottes. But you'd better not work that store again. They've got you down, now. For that matter you'd better leave that town alone a while."

"I don't know what you're talking about," said Sylvia, with dignity, "And anyway we're not going in this direction."

"What do you say going to Pittsburgh with me and then on to New York? A couple of girls like you could clean up a thousand dollars a week—just the big stores, understand, nice merchandise, not ordinary snatching. I could send you straight up to a friend of mine on One Hundred and Thirty-fifth Street and you'd be treated right. A couple of nice kids like you could get away with murder. What do you want to waste your time stealing bathing suits and rubber gadgets?"

"I bought this bathing suit," said Sylvia angrily.

"Why—" gasped Barbs, "you don't think we're thieves?"

The girls looked at each other in growing horror at his sardonic laugh.

"Of course you're not thieves, honey," he chuckled. "You was just taking what you liked, that was all. . . . Don't kid me, sister, you're a smart girl, both of you, for that matter, you got talent, you could do big stuff, I'm telling you. I did you a favor today, why don't you do me a favor now and try out the big time? You could wire your folks."

"We're married women," said Sylvia. "Our husbands would come after us."

"Think it over," said the driver, good-humoredly. "Drop me a line, if you change your mind. You say you live in Butterville?"

Barbs and Sylvia exchanged a despairing look. Too late to get out of that.

"We're moving away from there, soon," said Sylvia.

"You might give me your names and I'll drop you a card, reminding you where to get in touch," said the man. He pulled a silver pencil out of his pocket and a card.

"Dody Crane, Butterville," said Sylvia.

"Teresa Hull, Butterville," quavered Barbs.

"Well, Dody and Terry, you'll hear from me," he said, and slowed up near a filling station. "You're the best talent I've seen in these parts. All you need is training and a little protection."

At the filling station he got out and went inside. Without a word Sylvia and Barbs slipped out and ran to the road, hiding in the bushes along the way. They saw him come back out and look for them briefly, question the mechanic, then with a shake of his head he got in and drove off. Barbs and Sylvia looked at each other and drew a great breath of relief.

"I never was so scared," said Barbs. "Believe me, I'll never swipe anything again."

"I should hope not," said Sylvia.

Barbs pulled the rubber out of her dress and began to blow it up. Sylvia watched. Barbs's face grew redder and redder and the fish grew bluer and bigger. It was bigger than the one in the window. It would easily seat the twins and Davie, all three. Then, Barbs's face grew worried; she took it away from her mouth.

"I forgot to take the darned stopper," she panted, and tears stood in her eyes. "Oh darn! Oh Sylvia! Darn, darn, darn."

"Maybe a piece of paper—" suggested Sylvia, but the fish collapsed, dwindled to nothing. Barbs looked down at it in the middle of the ditch in disgust.

"I would forget the stopper," she said, "I'd have to forget the most important thing."

"Why didn't you tell me you were going to do it?" said Sylvia. "I could have helped you do it right. Honestly, Barbs, you may keep your house better than I do but you're dumb about lots of things."

This is the last I go with her, she thought, I didn't even get to see a picture.

An empty ice-truck drove along and Sylvia and Barbs jerked their thumbs in the Butterville direction. The car slowed down and they climbed in among the burlap bags in the back, where a young man in a bathing suit and dirty white slacks sat, fiddling with a harmonica. The girls settled themselves in the corner opposite him.

"I still got forty cents," Barbs said.

The car jolted them along the country roads, past cornfields and waving wheat.

"Hi, Dietrich!" the boy said to Sylvia.

The girls looked at each other and laughed.

"What's that you're chewing?" he asked.

"Bubble gum," said Sylvia, and snapped it.

He said nothing more but stared at them as he played his harmonica. Barbs and Sylvia sang while he played their favorite piece, "If You Were the Only Girl." They sang all the way going into Butterville. The boy and the truck driver both said they ought to be on the radio, or at the very least, the stage.

THE GLADS

He had thought he knew just what to expect from a family rout like this, but his premonitions had been but the toy model for the monster production. Certainly the Bateses were a huge family with many ramifications, and naturally in his twenty years absence they would have multiplied, but who would have pictured this enormous crowd spilling over the house onto the great lawn, their cars lined up for a whole block, traffic and program instructions rasping out through a public address system? Everything was louder and grander than he, in his naïve New York ignorance, could remember or even imagine. He had heard that Stan had done well (probably doing six or seven thousand a year now, he had guessed), and had bought "a nice home in a nice residential district," as his mother had written. He had visualized the conventional suburban house, Westchester style, on a decent side street cuddling as close as possible to the second-best boulevard. Nothing had prepared him for the spacious ranch house, sprawling its dozen rooms and five-car garage over half an acre of landscaped green.

Stan *would* have a ranch house, no matter what it was, Allan thought. He always went for those catchy sales words that made ordinary things sound special and important. Phrases like "plunging neckline," "fan out of Chicago," "snap brim," "dynaflow." Of course it would have to be a "ranch house."

He had never expected to be envious of Stan Rice and the idea depressed him. He found himself wishing he had come back a year ago when his suit was new, or five years ago when he was riding high, or two years ago before he had turned in the Lincoln for his second-hand Chevy, and was still married to Betsy Brown, Hollywood actress. Suddenly everything he had achieved, the self-confidence built on the admiration of colleagues and pride in his expeditions, left him. He had been braced for stupidity and indifference to what his name now stood for, but he'd never dreamed of being reduced in one moment to a childish feeling of helpless inadequacy.

I might have known the place would always get me like this, he thought, disgusted with himself. I knew I should never come back.

He had come back only to see Corinne, but now he wondered if he could ever get to her through the mob. He looked twice at each young girl with shining black hair or bright blue eyes, thinking it must be Corinne's daughter, though these features were common to all the Bates women. The chances were that Corinne's daughter would not have her mother's looks. Corinne had kept hers, so his mother had written. If he had to come back at all he wished he had come back last summer when he could have seen Corinne alone. She was the only one in the whole family he gave a damn for, and if she hadn't been his first cousin he might have married her, but you didn't get away from your family by marrying back into it, at least he had had that much sense.

All the way up the front walk, through the porch groups, and into the house he was halted by vaguely familiar voices crying out, "Allan, where on earth did you come from?" Each time he had to explain that he happened to be driving west anyway, and had decided to stop over on the spur of the moment. Each time it took a little while to figure out which nephew, cousin, or neighbor had spoken. He fancied he could spot Corinne's husband's family, by the sandy hair and Hoosier accents. He recognized Stan himself, heavier, grayer, but not greatly changed, towering over a group in the room beyond, complaining in his high, nasal voice, "The music alone cost me four hundred dollars, but everybody's making such a hullaballoo you can't even hear it."

"The Mayor came just before we got here," a thin colorless young woman exclaimed happily, very dressed up in white hat, navy suit, white kid gloves and handbag. "I'll bet Stan's set up over that. Why Allan Bates! It is Allan, isn't it? Don't you remember me, your little cousin Ruby, second cousin that is? Why everybody's here, it seems like! Look, Aunt Lou, aren't you glad you came now? Just see who's here all the way from Pittsburgh."

"New York," Allan corrected her patiently.

The wizened little old woman beside him whose palsy kept the weird bird on her hat in a state of perpetual animation shook Allan's hand, peering suspiciously up into his face as if wary of imposters.

"We've got plenty of Bateses in New York City," she stated. "Two of them ran for office right there in the state of New York. The Bateses are well-thought-of wherever they are."

"Allan's done very well, too, don't forget," Cousin Ruby reminded her. "Wasn't there something in the paper about you just a little while ago?"

"There was," Allan admitted. "It was about Betsy Brown divorcing me for mental cruelty. That was last October."

"That long ago?" asked Ruby with a vague smile. "Well, I still work in the library at Wooster Center. I took two days off to come here, and it's really worth it. All the Cleveland Bateses came, folks I haven't seen for years. Cousin Tracy came in his own plane. He's in there now with Stan. You remember Cousin Tracy and Ed."

"If you're leaving by way of Corning, maybe you'd drive me back to the Home," Aunt Lou suggested to Allan. "It would save me taxi."

"Good grief, I wish you wouldn't always have to bring up the fact that you live in a Home, Aunt Lou!" Ruby said irritably. "You'll make Allan think the family back here is going to seed."

"No, I wouldn't think that," Allan said.

"I'll have you know it's quite an honor getting into a Masonic home," said Aunt Lou belligerently, glaring at Ruby. "Furthermore I advise you to marry a Mason yourself, young lady, if you want to look out for your old age. Unless it's too late already."

"Is that Corinne's daughter?" Allan asked hastily, as a blonde, toothy young girl came hurrying up to him.

"Uncle Allan, why didn't you let us know you were coming?" she cried out, throwing her arms around him. "I'm your namesake, Allane, remember?"

"Charlie's youngest," explained Ruby. "Married already, and going to have a baby and only eighteen. Isn't it awful?"

"I had my first baby when I was eighteen," said Aunt Lou, the bird on her hat nodding tremulous confirmation. "Nothing to fuss about. I had my fourth under my belt and had buried two husbands when I was Ruby's age."

"Thirty-one," said Ruby.

"Thirty-two," said Aunt Lou firmly, the bird agreeing. "I was there. Four-fifteen of a Sunday morning, thirty-two years ago July tenth."

"Did you get my wedding invitation?" Allane asked, clinging to Allan's arm. He remembered the faithful chain of Christmas and birthday cards signed "Your loving niece and namesake, Allane" forwarded to him wherever he went, for years and years, in the obvious and pathetic hope of inheriting. Where in God's name was Corinne, he wondered, accepting a sandwich from a passing tray, wishing he could find a drink, but recollecting that this was an ice-cream-and-cake family. He saw Stan's brother, the fat one in real estate, who used to do imitations at all the school parties, pushing toward him through the chattering crowd. In the sea of strangers and vaguely remembered kin it cheered him to get a warm handshake from a contemporary.

"You just missed the Mayor," Dave said in a confidential undertone. "Too bad. I'd have been glad to introduce you, he's not at all stuck-up. But come in and meet the Carpenters, he's president of Stan's company. Came in person. Stan had no idea he'd show up. I'll find him."

"I just came to see Corinne," Allan said.

"Well, the Mayor's quite a character, I guess he's as well known right there in New York City as he is here," Dave replied. "Mayor Green, you know. Made a fortune with his Green Gardens, specializes in glads. You've heard the radio program, of course. 'Gladden your Garden with Green Garden Glads.' Those are his glads in the next room. I'll bet he'd charge five hundred dollars for that work ordinarily. Ever see anything like it?"

"No, I never did," Allan answered truthfully, for he now realized that what had seemed from a distance an aggressive wallpaper was in actuality an entire tapestry of flame-colored gladiolas arranged on vines and moss stretching from ceiling to floor across the whole dining room wall. The flowers were larger than any Allan had ever seen and he thought that any minute they might lift their heads and turn out to be Rockettes about to execute a Radio City stage number.

"Stan just about cried when the men brought it in yesterday and put it up," Dave said. "It's something to have Mayor Green going out of his way for you. Look, I had a hunch you might come out for this, Allan, and I brought a thing I wrote, it's an idea for a movie. I thought you being married to a movie actress and living in New York you'd know how to go about these things. Of course I'd cut you in for half."

"Betsy and I are divorced," Allan said. "I'm afraid I wouldn't be any help on a movie. Look, where's Corinne? I just want to see her a minute then start driving so I get to Des Moines by morning."

Stan was waving to him from the other room so he pushed through the crowd to him. As he greeted him, Allan saw that he was holding what appeared to be a set of dentures in his left hand.

"Seen the glads, Allan? Cost anybody else a thousand bucks but Mayor Green let me have it as a personal favor. You know our old neighbors here, Doc Filbert, and your cousin Tracy, he flew all the way from Cleveland, and here's Ed. I was just showing Doc here a thousand-dollar job I had done on my teeth lately. I got it for seven hundred as a personal favor, but it would cost anybody else a thousand."

Dr. Filbert, a round bald little man in a very new, very blue suit, accepted the dental specimens from Stan and studied them carefully.

"Standard three-hundred-dollar job," he stated briefly. "You were clipped. Look. Let me show you a genuine thousand-dollar job. Ed, show them what I did for you last summer."

Ed, a tall sandy man with a carnation in his lapel, obligingly removed all his teeth and laid them in Stan's hand.

"I can't understand it," Stan said, shaking his head sadly. "I've done a lot of things in the building line for this dentist of mine, and it ends up with him clipping me. How are you, Allan?"

"I've still got my teeth," Allan replied. "Where's Corinne?"

"I'll take you to her," Stan said, leading him forward. "Just beyond the glads there. You saw them. Mayor Green sent them. Oh, yes, I told you. What the hell does Doc Filbert know about first-class teeth work? He's a hick dentist, never saw more than a thousand bucks in his whole life, probably. Ever see such a mob? Half of 'em showing up just so I'll throw a little business their way, but they got another guess coming, I don't need money that bad. This used to be the boys' room in this wing, not that they ever come home any more for any length of time. How come you never had any kids, Allan?"

"I guess I thought there were enough Bateses," Allan said.

He was sure Stan would tell him how much the rugs, wallpaper, furniture, and fixtures had cost, how much more they would have cost someone else without his pull, and then would come the inevitable question of how much money *he* was making. It occurred to Allan, already dreading the moment, that such talk seemed either boring or even funny

when he was in the chips, but when he was going through a private finan-
cial depression it became downright outrageous.

"What about you, Allan?" Stan was already started on it. "Are you
doing all right now? Corinne was telling me something about you. Take a
lot of trips to the old country, don't you?"

"I—" Allan began, when suddenly Stan pushed against the mossy wall
of gladiolas and a door swung open into a large darkened room with a
handsome canopy bed in the alcove. A little gray-haired man in a neat
gray suit was standing on a chair in the window bay adjusting the tightly
drawn shades, but there was no one else around. The daylight was cut out
completely, and light came from white candles in glittering candelabra on
the mantelpiece, dressing table, and bureau.

"Where's Corinne?" Allan asked, and then he saw her.

She looked lovely, as lovely as he remembered her from twenty years
ago, long and slender still in the cream satin dress, her hair still shining
blue-black, the incredible lashes shimmering like spider legs on the ivory
skin, the long narrow hands folded over a prayer book. But her mouth
looked tired and drawn, and she seemed like a girl who had passed out
quite sweetly in the middle of a long party, though the guests still clamored for her, and would not ever go.

"She looks lovely," Allan said. "It's not Corinne without the old blazing blue eyes, but she does look beautiful."

Stan stood at the foot of the bed in the alcove looking down at his wife
with yearning or pride, Allan was not sure which. He wanted to say
something but it was hard to know what to say to a man like Stan.

"A lot of the folks criticized me for not having her out under the gladi-
ola wall in the dining room," Stan said. "But I figured she'd like it better
in here, all quiet, away from everything, as if she was resting. And in here
you can shut out the daylight so it doesn't show up so much when she
turns green. See, this is the third day of the lying-in-state. With all my
business connections I had to keep her that long. Mr. Jones, will you touch
up that right cheek?"

The little old man arranged his curtains and stepped down quickly;
leaning over Corinne he whipped out a large compact of pancake make-
up and delicately applied it with his two fingers to her right cheek. He
stood back a moment, frowning, then produced a lipstick to repair the
lips. It reminded Allan that the last time he had seen Corinne was at the

senior prom when they had sneaked away from their partners for a farewell ride out to the Grotto and she had cried off her make-up on his shoulder. He remembered tilting the car mirror so she could fix her mouth before she went back into the ballroom to Stan and for years after he dreamed of the shadowy reflection with the bright red lips. Allan had stayed outside in the shadows, ignoring the Whitman girl who was calling his name, straining his eyes to follow Corinne dancing, his heart leaping as he saw her own eyes searching the darkness for him whenever she passed the window. No one knew all that had been between them and that this night had to be the end. Why, she had wept in his arms at their hidden Grotto, why good-bye, and why forever? How many times afterwards he had wondered the same, asking himself if youthful wisdom was not more dangerous than youthful folly. The cold painted lips seemed to part and again he heard the whisper Why, why good-bye, and why forever. He caught his breath, afraid that he was going to burst out bawling, with Stan there looking at him.

"I was just thinking what a pity she couldn't see those glads," Allan said in a queer choked voice. "Now she'll never know."

EVERY DAY IS LADIES' DAY

AT FIRST HE THOUGHT he wouldn't go at all. Stand her up. Let the dinner get cold waiting for him. Let her find out she could not ignore an old friend for years and then call him up just because she needed an extra man for dinner. On second thought, the longer dinner waited the more cocktails they'd have, the better-natured they'd be, and there was the chance that by the time they sat down to dinner no one would even notice his absence!

He liked Clara after all, liked her a lot. He had known her for years—knew her in Paris after the first World War—knew her husbands—liked them all—still had some fine suits Number Three had given him—had the tailor nip them in at the waist a little and they fitted perfectly.

"What's happened to you and Clara?" people used to ask when it got around he was no longer invited to Clara's parties.

"I just couldn't take it any more," he would answer. "After all, I've known Clara a long time and I just couldn't take it."

The truth was he was terribly pleased at the thought of seeing her again, in spite of everything. He never understood what he had done to make her chill toward him, but figured that it was the war that had come between them. Her house was always filled with soldiers and sailors, and she had been having too good a time to think of him. Now that they had all gone back to their wives and girls there were extra places at good tables once again. He was tired of being asked to artists' homes on the strength of his museum connection, tired of listening to wives try to sell him their husbands' work, the artists themselves displaying integrity by elaborate insults. He had about as much power to buy as the checkroom attendants and told them so, but they never let go. At least Clara wasn't interested in art; he had to give her credit for that. He had a lot of funny stories to tell her about their old Paris chums. All of them in loony bins or sanitariums, the ones that weren't on Nembutal.

"I used to look for my friends in the society columns," he intended to say tonight. "Now I look for them on the barbituary page."

Go? Of course he'd go. He took a last look in the mirror, brushes in hand. Chip Thomas, who was picking him up at Clara's request, stood in the doorway, waiting.

"What's this, Tully? Do I see a gray hair there?" Chip inquired.

"If you do I get my money back," Tully said grimly, and slipped a carnation in his lapel.

They went downstairs and met the doorman bringing the pooch back. She was five years old but still flung herself at Tully like a pup whenever she saw him. Dogs never learned.

"Listen, honey," Tully said to her. "Tonight I'll bring you back something good. How about some 'long pig'? But don't sit up for me, honey. It may take a little time to wear out my welcome."

The dog was still laughing heartily as the elevator went up.

Chip looked around the lobby, a pleasant little lounge, and then glanced curiously at Tully.

"This is a nice little joint. Better than where I last saw you," he commented. "I guess you're getting ahead. But how?"

"The way any young man gets ahead," Tully said. "White tie and driver's license."

He did not know Chip Thomas very well, beyond seeing him at a few parties, nor did he know how well Chip knew Clara. Better not to trust anybody much until you knew them; then, not at all. Chip was much younger than he, around thirty-five maybe, but he was stout whereas Tully had kept his figure and his smooth complexion, and as he often said, most of his favorite hairs. He could pass for thirty-five unless someone that age was around.

As soon as Chip pulled his car up at Clara's charming little house Tully felt a surge of joy such as he had not known in years. He whistled a gay tune.

"Imagine you remembering 'The Red Mill'!" Chip observed drily.

"Only the revival," Tully answered, not at all offended; and then confided, "The old war horse smells the powder. Prewar liquor, roast beef, cognac, beautiful girls, cigars, cigarettes, candy, chewing gum."

"She's lucky she still has the place," Chip said.

"Women never lose anything," Tully said. "You know that, old boy."

It was one of the many Smallest Houses in New York—two tiny rooms on each of the four floors and a dining room off a basement garden where a pink plaster birdbath, large enough to accommodate one humming bird or two well-adjusted bumblebees, nestled in a circle of green potted plants.

"Herbs," Tully nodded to Chip, happy that nothing had changed. "She always keeps a pot of basil around for some pinheaded lover. Clara still likes Keats, poor darling."

They left their hats with the tiny maid in the dining room and went upstairs to the diminutive drawing room. Walls and windows were muffled in pink-and-cream-colored hangings just as they used to be.

"Clare loves candy," Tully whispered to Chip. "Nobody but Clara could live forever in a grocery treat. The dwarf's room is to your left, old man."

"I know," Chip said huffily. "I've been here before."

A quick casing of the room showed that Clara had reached the cautious state where she invited women her own age. There was only one possible female, a blonde still charmingly awkward and bony, her mother probably praising Allah for the long-hair fashion that softened so many hard young faces. Not bad. He knew nobody, which must mean that Clara was coming up in the world. As she left the fireside group to greet them he saw at once that she had aged; laughter and love had left their mark.

"Darling!" he cried, kissing her loudly in midair. "You look marvelous. What have you *done* to yourself?"

"You know perfectly well I'm in my dotage, you monster," Clara murmured with a muscular handshake, a new affectation, Tully thought. It occurred to him much later that she barely spoke to Chip, and he was rather proud of his unselfishness in bringing it to her attention.

"Be nice to Chip, darling," he whispered as they went down to dinner. "He's stuffy and I know what you mean, but honey, you're getting on and men don't grow on bushes."

"I happen to have a green thumb, dear," Clara said. "But thanks just the same."

He thought that if he was going to start in again with Clara's crowd he would certainly mention to her that no matter what marvels the cook had prepared everyone would have sacrificed them for another round of cocktails. Fortunately, he was in such a good humor that he could keep up the conversation during dinner single-handed without the extra stimulant, but he noticed Chip and the four other men present were silent and gloomy, not at all cheered by the carefully selected bad wine. To relieve the situation and show Clara he was still the best friend she had ever had, he lifted his goblet in a toast to her, adding jokingly, "I knew Clara when she had *good* wines."

No use denying that she did have a darn good table. The sauces were familiar even if the guests were not. He had two helpings of everything and slipped an extra piece of the roast into his napkin to take home to the pooch, though she might not like the Burgundian sauce. By great good fortune he was seated next to the McCullen girl, the nice kid, who obviously was taken by him but scared to death of her mother, a fishy-looking dame in poison green about Clara's age who was stuck with Chip Thomas. It seemed little Felicia was studying painting and was delightfully impressed by his being at the museum. She said she was nineteen, but he thought she was a good twenty-three, if she was a day, and not helped by her bouffant baby-blue subdeb frock. She was adorably uncurved and had a way of looking up at him sidewise whenever he spoke that actually thrilled him. Her mother kept a sharp eye on him, and the minute he had a chance he murmured to Clara it wasn't fair to the kid to invite the mother along to parties. But Clara was dense about a lot of little things and didn't always take suggestions in the right spirit. You couldn't lose four husbands without getting irritable.

"I understand Mr. Tully is at the museum, Felicia," the mother said. She would! "Why not ask him to help you get an exhibition?"

"I've known Tully for twenty-five years," Clara said, "and I've never known him to do anything for anybody."

"Now, Clara, old dear," he reproached her playfully, "if I'd known you were going to be yourself, I never would have come. You know Clara's husband, the one that lasted four years—Harvey, wasn't it?—used to say he could stand all of Clara's moods except the times when she was being herself. I always liked Harvey. He was my favorite."

EVERY DAY IS LADIES' DAY   401

"One person's meat is another person's poison," Clara murmured a bit sulkily.

"If I remember rightly you divorced Harvey when you discovered that one person's meat was *everybody's* meat," he chuckled, with a wink at Chip.

"You should know," Clara retorted, never able to take kidding. "You were the one who told me all about it."

He was feeling too good to pick her up on that, so all he said was, "Oh, but I didn't tell you even *half* about it, old dear."

"Old dear yourself," Clara snapped.

It struck him right away that both Clara and the girl's mother were miffed at him for devoting himself to the youngster. The mother, you could see, fancied herself for having kept her complexion and figure (such as they were) and naturally resented having a young rival always around. He'd seen it happen a dozen times and knew from experience that the diplomatic thing was to butter up the old girl for a while, just to keep her from taking it out on the kid.

"Next time you go shopping for your daughter, why not invite me to come along, Mrs. McCullen?" he suggested courteously. "Have you ever tried dressing her in black?"

The old girl gave him a sweet smile. "Felicia dresses herself now, Mr. Tully," she answered. "Felicia, dear, would you like Mr. Tully to take you shopping to pick out a black snowsuit?"

"For black snowstorms," he added quickly, turning what might have been a nasty crack into a good-natured laugh.

But the old lady had scared the kid so that she carefully applied herself to the old codger on her other side all during dessert. It suited Tully since it gave him a chance to go to town on the really superb mousse. He was sorry he'd teased Clara, come to think of it. He shouldn't have risked her dropping him again. It seemed the old codger had something to do with the San Francisco Museum and might, on Clara's say-so, get him a position there. He mentioned this to her on the way up to the drawing room for coffee, cleverly suggesting that he drop in next Sunday for tea, say, and talk it over, perhaps have the little McCullen kid, too. But please, he added, no Chip Thomas. A good fellow, all right, but a complete moron. Hadn't got the point of even one of his stories, not even the dude-ranch one.

"He seemed to get it the first time you told it," Clara said. "It lost a little, I myself felt, in the retelling. Try it again over coffee."

He did not take this up but switched to the subject of Felicia. The kid was attractive, he admitted, but it was pretty tough on her with the old lady so jealous. It was a darned shame, he said, because the old lady could ruin the kid's chances with some men who didn't see through her game. Clara stubbornly refused to see the point, of course.

"The 'old lady,' as you call her, is five years younger than you, darling," she said in her haughtiest British accent.

He hoped that in spite of her pique she would have to admit the party would have been a dismal flop without him. He had to rack his brain to keep the talk going, and in one lull he had to catch himself before getting into the dude-ranch story again. Not his fault. It was just that everyone was waiting for Clara to get out the brandy. Sensing this, Tully decided the only way to save the situation was to joke about it, so he said, patting Clara genially on the back, "Crack out the stuff, old dear. We all know you've got it."

Even the brandy could not liven the dreary little group and Tully constantly had to snatch the talk from the somber subjects started by the others, resorting to that old reliable attention-getter—"Clara will kill me for telling this but . . ."—or—"I swore I would never tell this to a living soul, but since we're all friends . . ." He managed to keep the brandy bottle near himself and unobtrusively filled his glass from time to time for sheer fuel purposes; and once, when Chip Thomas forgot to put it back where it belonged, Tully fell over a footstool snatching it back. Everyone laughed and Tully thought: What a bunch of morons! Here I am knocking myself out to entertain them, but I have to have a concussion before they'll laugh.

He was glad that they started to leave soon after ten, and he had optimistic visions of a cozy threesome—Clara (necessarily), himself and the adorable girl. Yes, by Jove, he had really fallen for her, and he was pretty sure he had made a good impression from the way she looked at him. If he ever should marry—and he might when his wardrobe wore out—he would take a chance on a fresh unspoiled little creature like this, perhaps Felicia herself.

But before he could wangle this little scheme the mother had whisked Felicia away, leaving only himself and Chip Thomas to sit up with Clara.

"You don't need to stay on my account, old man," Tully said to Chip, translating a significant look in Clara's eyes. "I can always get a cab."

The least he could do for Clara, he thought, was help her get rid of her dull guests, though it meant he had to give up the free ride home in Chip's car. Oh, well . . .

Clara slipped a hand over Chip's. "Don't worry about him, Chip," she murmured. "As he says, he can get a cab." (She must have been drinking.) "He can find one on Third Avenue and, that means you can stay on for a little after-party talk with Mama, just our twosy-woosies."

It was as blunt as that. Tully could hardly believe his ears, but he was obliged to take the hint, especially since Clara fairly flew out to get his hat. He could have killed Chip Thomas for lolling back on the sofa as if he owned the place.

"Looks to me as if Clara's sore at me about something," Tully said with a wry laugh. "I wish I knew what it was."

"Oh, pay it no mind," Chip said airily. "She's always picked on you, I gather from all you've been saying."

Of course she always had—come to think of it—but why? Tully puzzled over it all the way home, and it was not until he was dividing his roast-beef sandwich with the pooch that the answer came.

What a sap I am! he thought. Why, of course! It's just because I never made a pass at her, that's all!

It was so simple he laughed out loud. Thank God, he could still read women!

DAY AFTER TOMORROW

WHEN THEY FOUND OUT Lucille was engaged the girls insisted on a celebration. What about tonight?

"But it'll be months!" Lucille protested. "There's no hurry, really. Besides I have Mrs. Brady at five and it'll keep me late."

"I'll do the Brady," said Smitty, the big girl, firmly. "We haven't had a shop party for ages. We'll get Frankie to shut up early."

"Better take your party when you can get it," advised Miss Olsen. "When it gets near the wedding day we may be too busy."

Olsen sat at the cashier's desk, under the drier, which shone like a crown above her radiantly fresh facial. Her eyebrows above the porcelain-tinted face were harried to meager wisps like Smitty's and the other girls; but where Smitty's mouth was sullen, Olsen's was large and good-humored. It was Oley who kept the girls from quarreling and getting on Frankie's nerves. You had to have someone like Oley in a beauty parlor. She made Lucille feel that the party was really a business proposition, something a new girl in the trade had to do. Her reassuring, steady eyes followed Lucille over to the telephone.

Mac was sore when Lucille told him she wouldn't meet him tonight. He was jealous enough of the shop, anyway, especially since she made more money there than he did. He was always saying that she was to stop work when they got married but they both knew she couldn't. Most of the girls in Frankie's were married and had never quit their jobs. Lucille had not set a date for the wedding but once in a long while she and Mac would talk about going down to City Hall day after tomorrow. At the last minute something always stopped them, but that was the way it would happen, they both said, one of these days they'd go through with it.

"OK?" Oley asked when Lucille left the phone, frowning.

The new girl tried to smile.

"Kinda sulky," she confessed. "I told him it was all right, no men going, not even Frankie, but he hung up on me."

"That's my Albert, too," exclaimed Smitty. "Us girls celebrate about one night a year and you'd think it was every night in the week."

"Your four o'clock is here, Miss Schmidt," shouted Miss Olsen, and suddenly the shop was busy again, the way it always was at the last minute, especially if the girls had something planned. It was as if women didn't know they could get three treatments for five dollars at the shop across the street, it was as if they just had to come to Frankie's and pay double, because he was a great artist. Even above the driers roaring and the canaries singing you could hear Frankie telling everybody what a great artist he was. Smitty winked at the new girl but the new girl believed every word he said.

"He really is a genius," she whispered to the customer whose roots she was touching up. "It's a privilege to study hair work under Frankie, I mean that."

"I even made my own toupee," Frankie was now declaiming, curling iron in hand, in the center of the shop. He had a large pasty pink head adorned by a lavishly curled wig to which he was pointing. "Every place I go people admire that toupee. On the trains, on the street, everywhere. All the time they come up to me, strangers, old, young, everybody. 'Pardon me, sir,' they say, 'that is a beautiful toupee you are wearing. I couldn't help noticing it,' 'Allow me,' they say, 'it's an exquisite piece of work.'"

"Oh it is, Frankie, it is," Lucille eagerly seconded him.

Frankie looked at her approvingly. The new girl was doing all right. Nobody needed to worry about her getting along.

"Frankie thinks you've got a future here," Miss Olsen said to Lucille quietly, when the customer had paid her check. "It's a pity you got other plans."

The new girl was so much younger than the others, so delighted with praise and so eager for advice that you couldn't be jealous of her.

"Oh, but I'll be here a long time anyway," she said happily.

She was thrilled that the older girls wanted to celebrate for her but as night approached she worried more and more about Mac. He was low enough lately, anyway, with work so uncertain.

"What does he do, anyway?" Smitty asked, when she explained her qualms. "Or has he got a job?"

"He does special jobs for a radio firm," Lucille evaded. "Naturally high-class technical jobs don't come every day so—But after Election it will be different, of course."

"And why?" inquired Smitty.

"Well," Lucille answered, "because Mac said so."

"Then wait till after Election to get married," counseled Smitty. "Notice if it's different, like he says. Until then pay no attention to what he says about your going on parties."

At six there was a lull in the shop. Mrs. Brady, a weekly problem, all curled, tweezed, tinted and rouged by Smitty, tottered out on high spike heels, balancing a tower of flowers and birds on her new coiffure, her fat little blond chow tucked under her fat little arm. In a twinkling Smitty had jerked down the window shades, barred the door, slammed the appointment book shut. Marie and Freda, the two blondes, whisked bottles and work trays into lockers, the colored boy started sweeping up hair, and old Mrs. Sweeney dragged in her mop and pail. The fresh smell of suds and disinfectant was a pleasure after the clashing perfumes of the day. Under the black coverlets thrown over their cages the canaries twittered sleepily. Frankie did not object to the early closing because it was his night for *Aida*. In pearl-gray topcoat and soft green hat he stood in the salesroom paring his nails and humming lightly, waiting to lock up. Miss Olsen, who was always the first to be ready, passed the time by calling up her friend Helmar to say she would not meet him at the movie tonight, at all. A girl in the shop was going to be married, she said. She did the other girls the favor of calling husbands to say the shop was keeping the staff late tonight.

"Oley is the smart one," Smitty sighed to the new girl. "You don't catch her getting married."

"Listen," answered Miss Olsen complacently adjusting her veil. "If I do all the work why shouldn't I spend the money on my own comfort instead of on some man? I like a twelve-dollar shoe."

"Oley can go out every week like this," grumbled Smitty. "It's only once a year for us married ones, isn't that so, Freda? Well, where do we go first?"

"Have a good time, girls," said Frankie, as they rushed out. "Don't forget tomorrow morning at eight sharp."

They went across the street to the hotel bar first and sat on stools while the bartender kidded them. They were five good-looking, well-dressed girls. They knew what to wear and where to get it cheap. After two old-fashioneds they were comparing complaints about their husbands. The three married ones had all rowed with their husbands about going out tonight, but they didn't care, they had a right to go out with girls for some fun once a year. A person got tired of going out with a husband every minute, you wanted a good time for a change. Marie and Freda stuck together, whispering secrets, so Lucille stuck to Smitty and Oley.

"Listen, you're a darn fool for getting married," Miss Olsen advised the new girl. "The way I look at it is this. Wouldn't you rather buy one good ticket to Radio City than two to some lousy neighborhood movie? That's the question a girl should ask herself before she takes on a husband."

"It's the truth," said Smitty. "You know how it is. Either a man can't get a job or if he can it don't suit him and he don't make much. You're better off like Oley here, giving the boyfriend a nice present at Christmas, say a good watch or a swell dressing gown. That's the way I see it."

Two traveling men were trying to horn in on the party so they decided to get going.

"We always end up in Greenwich Village," said Smitty. "Boy, oh boy. But don't tell your boyfriend. Come on, kids, here's a taxi."

They stopped at three other bars on the way down, whenever they saw a place that looked gay. Smitty could drink like a trooper but after a few drinks Miss Olsen got her sentences mixed up and finally stopped saying anything but "Hooray for me!" Lucille got the giggles and swore she never had so much fun in her life. She felt guilty having so much fun without Mac and suggested calling him up. He might come down.

"Not a chance," said Smitty. "We don't want any men along."

By the time they got down to Sheridan Square they had had about five old-fashioneds apiece and no dinner. No matter where they went they took a taxi, even if they were only going a block. Marie got to crying because she said before she was married she used to take taxis every day and now it was about twice a year. The mascara kept running down her cheeks and Freda kept swabbing off her friend's face and trying to make her up again, but Marie would cry it right off again. Everyone was borrowing from Oley by this time, because she always carried money, and besides she could take it right out of their envelopes on Saturday.

"Albert will just have to wait another week for his suit," said Smitty, two dollars in the red. "We were to make a last payment on it this payday. He'll be raving. You know. A man has to look just so when he's not working or he gets low in his mind."

"Wait till he's working!" Marie sniveled. "Then all the money goes for cleaning and pressing and shoeshines. The wife has to pay the rent and gas and bread and cook the beefsteak for his boss."

"I guess it depends a lot on the fella," said Lucille.

"Hooray for me," said Miss Olsen, and then they were at the Joint. The Joint was a long barroom lit up with blue lights, crowded with shouting drinkers and funny-looking Villagers. A juke box was blaring out "I'm in Love With a Wonderful Guy" so Smitty grabbed Lucille and they danced, falling into the booth at last over Oley's knees and screaming with laughter.

"Dancing," said Marie, "that's another thing I miss."

A boy with a drawing pad came up and wanted to do their portraits for a dollar and Oley consented. She took off her glasses and held her square handsome ruddy face turned to the right for twenty minutes while the waiter brought their hamburgers and beer. The girls wanted to kid the artist because he was a good-looking lad. They could hardly eat for staring at him.

"Look at the complexion on him!" marveled Marie. "Mrs. Brady would give a million dollars for a skin like that."

"It's just the shade of our *rose foncé*," murmured Smitty. "And look at how he wears his clothes. Boy, it would be a pleasure to dress a fella like that, you could dress him straight from Student Wear and he'd look custom-made."

"He could walk right out of the store without an alteration," said Freda.

"It's when they got a pot like Bill that clothes cost so much," said Marie. "It's a case of skimping over the stomach or else the behind. His new forty-dollar gabardine cuts him right through the middle."

"Tell him to lay off the starches," said Freda.

Oley gave the boy a dollar for her portrait. There was real talent there, she said, and it made her look like Ingrid Bergman, some. But the other girls just kept staring at the artist, as he walked away.

"The way he walks, even," said Smitty dreamily. "You could take a fella like that anywhere and have people take notice. Look at the wave. Frankie ought to see that. The manicure, even. I could look at a fella like that all day and never get tired. If he was mine I'd get him evening clothes, top hat, the whole works."

"And those eyelashes!" said Marie. "Still and all he looks kinda weak."

"I suppose you prefer a prizefighter type," sneered Smitty. "Listen, if you got to have a husband, give me one that shows off what I put into 'em, that's all I say. All Albert can do with his clothes is to look warm."

Lucille was beginning to get serious. She thought of Mac and how the girls would kid about a heavy solid baldish fellow like that with no steady job, no sex appeal, just a fellow you liked. She was worried too, as it got toward eleven, because Mac might take it into his head to drop by her place, checking up on her. She timidly reminded Smitty that it took nearly an hour to get up to 181st Street.

"Listen to the sissy," jeered Marie. "Afraid of the boyfriend, eh? Let him beef. You'll get used to it, honey. Ask him who it is that pays the bills, that's what to say when they get to beefing."

"I got nothing on my mind," boasted Oley. "If Helmar don't like what I do he can take a powder. I got other men friends."

She rolled up her portrait carefully.

"You don't know how smart you are, Oley," said Marie.

"Hooray," said Oley. "Hooray for me."

"That boy!" Smitty said. "Did you see his teeth? I'll bet his dentist bill don't run five dollars a year."

"Forget it!" said Oley. "This party's for Lucille, here, not for that Village sheik."

"That's right," said Smitty, and raised her glass. "To the bride!"

They finished off their glasses but Lucille didn't drink because you didn't drink when it was a toast to you and besides she was getting a queer feeling.

"What say we go?" said Oley. "You kids pay me Saturday."

The juke box played "Anniversary Waltz" and Freda and Lucille started dancing their way out. The girls were calling Lucille "Baby" now because they said she didn't know the first thing. Outside the air was chilly for June and everyone envied Oley her foxes, even though she said they were only half paid for. They took the subway up to Times Square where Oley and the two blondes changed to East Side and Smitty and Lucille took the Broadway Express. On the way up Smitty got to telling off-color jokes till they thought they'd die laughing. At 181st Smitty went west and Lucille hurried east. She was still laughing when she saw Mac in front of her rooming house. He was walking up and down smoking his pipe and she knew he was sore but she was too happy to care. It was like the girls said, you had a right to a good time once a year.

"There was some man," he said, grabbing her arm. He wouldn't let her go inside the vestibule without an argument. "You can't kid me, there was some other man in it. It was Frankie."

"There wasn't any man in it, dopey," she said irritably. "This was just pleasure."

She went in, letting the door slam, not giving him a chance to ask how much of her salary she'd spent, money that should have been saved toward the apartment. While she undressed she got to thinking of Smitty and her husband having that same argument that very minute, probably, and the other girls the same, and she thought only Oley was having a good night's sleep without a care. So far as that went it wasn't too late for her to change her own mind. The wedding date wasn't really set. There was still time to decide on one ticket to Radio City instead of two to a neighborhood movie. When Mac started bawling her out tomorrow she'd have something to say right back.

She climbed into bed with her nightgown on wrong side out. She lay there in the dark watching the blue garage lights go on and off across the street, thinking what a wonderful evening they had had. She thought about Oley's silver foxes and twelve-dollar shoes and the boy with the *rose foncé* complexion.

"Hooray for me!" she shouted suddenly.

She must have been a little tight.

IDEAL HOME

Elizabeth's eyes were red again at breakfast. Neither Vera nor her mother said anything about it, but leave it to Lewey to speak up.

"Lose your beau again?" he jeered. "What's the matter you can't hold 'em?"

"Elizabeth's a drip," Vera stated pleasantly.

Elizabeth snatched up her coffee cup and took it into the living room, but that reminded her once more of how hopeless everything was. No privacy, no privacy at all. Kitchen, dinette, and living room all in one. Modern. Ideal. Over the bookcase partition that swung out to mark off the dinette Lewey stared at her critically, stirring his coffee.

"Why'ncha wear that new bathrobe you were saving up for?"

"Hostess gown!"

"Well, why'ncha wear it instead of that faded old rag?"

"Because it's to entertain in, dopey!"

"That's why that goon last night didn't ask her out," Vera observed impassively. "He thought she was ready for bed."

Lewey roared. He thought everything Vera said was a scream. Lewey was twenty, four years older than Elizabeth. He had a girl, Thelma. Thelma worked in the shipping department of the company where Elizabeth was file clerk, and she was forever telling people Lewey was going to marry her next week. Elizabeth wished to God he would, but after all what good would it do to have Lewey out of the apartment? Nine-year-old Jimmy was growing up to be just as mean, and Vera, at only fourteen, made life unbearable with all her boyfriends and the telephone always ringing for her. Fat chance a girl with an unusual personality had in a household like this! What's more, it got worse all the time. It was all on account of the new apartment, and Elizabeth had to admit that she was to blame for that. Oh yes, they must move into the wonderful modernistic Ideal Co-operative Apartment house. A girl with ambition had no chance in an old-fashioned tenement, you read that everywhere. Spacious rooms (two), In-a-door beds, sunlight, air, everything electric, everything glass, just push a button! Well, what was so special about sunlight? What was so wonderful about walls sliding back to make one big room so the whole family could spy on you? At least in the old railroad-style apartment there was a room for everybody, even if it was only closet size. You had a place to cry. At least you had a vestibule downstairs where a girl could have a little privacy entertaining, instead of a big square lobby with fluorescent lights blazing all night like day. Supposing a girl didn't know a fellow, at least she could get kinda acquainted in the old vestibule without the handicap of a spotlight. For that matter the long narrow hall in the old place had been all right, too. A person could come in without stumbling over a trick bed. Elizabeth wished now she had kept her mouth shut, instead of dinging at them all the time to move here and give herself and Vera a chance to live nice. What better use for Papa's insurance money? All right, she argued them into it, so now they were stuck here for life.

"It's the only bright idea Elizabeth ever had," the whole family agreed.

Sure. It had worked out for everybody but herself.

"Why'ncha fix up your eyes?" Lewey suggested. "All those bottles and jars of yours ought to do something for you. Hey, Vera, did you see that new stuff Liz's got? Marbe's Elbow Cream, I'm not kidding! Ha!"

Elizabeth's mouth set. A girl worked and studied to make something of herself and train her personality like those books said, and all you got was your family making fun of you, laughing at you in front of your company whenever you were trying to have an intelligent conversation. What good was it to be sophisticated and keep your elbows bleached and your skin stimulated if you never had a chance to show off? Even in the office, when she was having a little intelligent conversation with Mr. Ross, the personnel chief, there was always Thelma grinning, ready to blab whatever she said to the family.

"Where'd you dig up that mug last night? Never opened his trap." Lewey always had to rub it in.

"Why would he with the whole darn family peeking over at him?" Elizabeth retorted bitterly.

"Ah, you're all right, old girl, don't get sore," Lewey yawned. He plucked the newspaper out of Vera's hands and made for the big chair in the corner. "Trouble is, you don't know what time it is. Your feet's too big."

There was a thudding noise in the next room. That would be the beds folding up into bookcases. The creaking sound that followed was Vera's bed turning over into a refectory table. Now the master bedroom was a library, the bookshelves adorned anew with Vera's china animals, Jimmy's comics, a hand-painted tray, two World's Fair plates, and a set of Kipling. Mrs. Neeley, rosy-faced from effecting this routine transformation, came out with a towel pinned around her head and a dustcloth in her hand.

"That was one of the boys you met at camp, wasn't it, Elizabeth?" she asked. "He got out so fast I didn't get a chance to talk to him."

"It's the one she wrote about in her diary," Vera said, now industriously painting her nails. "He's a drip."

Her diary! Elizabeth ran into the Kitchenette, put her cup and saucer in the sink and let the noise of running water do its best to cover her gulping sobs. If only there was a door to slam, a key to lock, in the darn new Ideal Home! The only place she had to hide her secrets was the desk drawer in her office and what use was that weekends?

"Is that the one, dear?" her mother asked. She poured furniture oil on her dustcloth and applied it to the desk. "Would you believe it, I can clean this place top to bottom in an hour? You know how long it took in the old place. I can't get over it."

In the mirror above the kitchen sink Elizabeth took gloomy pleasure in seeing how pasty and swollen her face looked this morning. She had looked wonderful last night and a lot of good it had done her. In her lunch hour she had had her first facial not in a beauty parlor, but by a lady demonstrator free of charge in the cosmetic department of Hearn's.

"See what this cream does to wrinkles, folks?" the lady demonstrator had shouted, after Elizabeth had volunteered for the free demonstration. A small circle of shoppers stared curiously at the operation. "This young lady is too young for wrinkles, and a little too plump for them to show up anyway, but she has these here lines we call laughter lines. Ladies, you got to watch them laughter lines."

At this rate her face would be riddled with laughter lines before she got a boyfriend, Elizabeth thought. She was sixteen, old enough to "take care of herself" where boys were concerned, her mother said, but where were they? She'd only had three dates since they moved and then the whole family horned in on them. The camp had been different. The camp had been wonderful. If she'd only had more than five days something might have happened.

"At the camp there are these four fellows," she had written in her diary, August 24, "and I hardly know what to do. They laugh and kid at meals, but when it comes to going for a walk they take the other girls like I was poison. But Tuesday night Philip, that's the tall one, he's from Buffalo, New York, took me for a walk. At first I thought he wouldn't but after a while he did kiss me and was just as lovely to me as he could be. He sure looks cute with his new haircut, just like a prisoner of war. . . ."

It turned out that even Mrs. Tully, the janitress, had snooped into her diary, because Elizabeth overheard her saying to her mother, "That book of your daughter's is real interesting. She sure had some good times at that church camp, at least to hear her tell it. This fellow, Philip, he seems quite a character. I guess she makes up a lot in her head, too."

It had taken four letters, all casual and kidding, full of jokes about being the "forgotten woman," to get the postcard from Philip, saying he was going to visit New York and might call her up. Of course, the whole family knew all about it. They even found all the copies of the letters she'd written, and razzed her about them. In desperation Elizabeth had humbled herself to ask Vera where on earth she managed to hide her secrets, only to have the foxy little thing lift dainty eyebrows and say, "I don't hide things. I burn them. Honestly, Liz, you're such a drip!"

Well, Philip had called on her, all right, and this morning there was nothing more to look forward to and nothing to remember, either. Lewey and Thelma had elected last night to stay in playing cards and drinking beer in the dining alcove, keeping an eye on Elizabeth and audibly mocking her company conversation. She had made up her mind to be cultivated instead of up to date, because the time she had tried to use the expression "Hubba hubba" Vera had cried out, "Oh Liz, you never catch on to anything until it's out of date." Vera was out with her bunch getting autographs when Philip called, thank goodness, but the telephone kept ringing for her just to show Philip who was the beauty of the family. Just once had it rung for Elizabeth and then it was only Mr. Ross from her office saying he was working late and wanted to know where she kept the File Room key. When she told him she carried it with her Mr. Ross said never mind, but she hung on sort of kidding and giggling to make Philip think it was another beau. Mrs. Neeley offered to send out for ice cream and cakes, as if it was some children's party, and Elizabeth scornfully rejected this, suggesting beer instead; the young man leapt up and said he guessed he'd go take in a movie before it was too late. Elizabeth followed him out to the elevator in case he cared to kiss her good night, but the big lights were brighter than ever and he acted scared to death. Lewey and Thelma were laughing about his gawkiness almost before he was out of hearing.

"The only time he opened his head was when he made that crack about Liz's figure," giggled Thelma. "'I didn't remember your being so heavy-set, Miss Neeley,' he says. I woulda popped him if he said that to me, the little squirt."

End of Philip, Elizabeth had thought, and had gone in the bathroom and cried for half an hour. What she minded most, she thought this morning, was not being able to think about him anymore.

"He seemed like a nice little fellow, that boy last night," Mrs. Neeley called to Elizabeth. "Maybe he'll drop around again today and you can have the place to yourselves. Maybe he'll take you out."

"I never saw anybody like Liz," Vera remarked dispassionately. "You'd think she never heard of the facts of life. Only one fellow ever kissed her."

"How do you know?" Elizabeth snapped. "You haven't any conception of what goes on in my life. How would you find out anyway?"

"I read all about it," Vera said. "I read all about it up to the day you took your diary to your office."

"Now stop teasing. Elizabeth's my good girl," Mrs. Neeley admonished soothingly. "I don't know where she gets it but I know I can always depend on my Elizabeth."

"Imagine going to a Sunday School camp at her age!" Vera muttered, lapsing into silence at a warning shake of the finger from her mother.

Lewey threw down the paper, stretched his large frame, and got to his feet.

"Get a move on, Mom. I got the truck in back. Ride you over to the market if you make it snappy."

"Wait a second," Vera said. "You can drop me at the drugstore for my lipstick. If the kids come by tell 'em I'll be back in a flash, Liz."

"Going to be gone all day then?" her mother asked.

Vera pulled a yellow sweater over her scanty little chest, not deigning to answer such a superfluous question. Saturdays Vera always went someplace with her crowd, usually to the beach. She had an even tan over every inch of her small body, a matter of mystification to Elizabeth and pride to her mother. Mrs. Neeley often remarked to neighbors, "Vera got her mind set on getting an even tan all over and she just stuck to it till she got it. I never realized the kid had that much gumption."

"Elizabeth will be in if Jimmy gets in from the country today," Mrs. Neeley said, picking up her market bag and hurrying after Lewey. "I wouldn't want him to come home to an empty apartment."

"What makes you so sure I'm not going out?" Elizabeth demanded sulkily, but the banging of the outer door was her only answer.

Now that it was of no use to her Elizabeth had the whole apartment to herself. She read the beauty column in the *News* and tried out an ankle exercise it recommended. She did her hair over in a crooked new hairdo she saw pictured and felt cheered to read that hips were coming back. She had almost forgotten her recent woe when the doorbell rang. Her first thought was that maybe Philip was really dropping in, just as her mother had prophesied. But it was Mr. Ross, a slight little man with a crumpled raincoat over his arm and a worn briefcase in hand, who stood at the door.

"I saw you weren't far from where I live so I thought I'd drop by for your key," he explained. "I've got a lot of work to clean up over the weekend and I'll need the files. Say, this is a fine place you've got here."

Elizabeth's disgust with the Ideal Apartment gave way at once to a proud demonstration of sliding walls, magic beds, and windows changing into walls. Mr. Ross's astonishment made her boast that it was she who had first heard about the building and insisted on her family moving there even though it was a queer neighborhood, all warehouses around.

"I guess you're the kind that keeps up on everything," Mr. Ross said. "I got that impression first time I talked to you at the office. By the way, Miss Neeley, another thing. Here's a piece of your property I found out on your desk."

He pulled a small red leather volume from his pocket and Elizabeth saw with a sinking sensation that it was her diary.

"I didn't open it," Mr. Ross said, "naturally."

"That was nice of you," Elizabeth said faintly, and then added in a rush of relief, "How awful if any of the office kids had found it! Oh, how lucky you had to work late! I mean—excuse me, I mean lucky for me. I'm sure it's no fun for you working all weekend."

Mr. Ross seemed to be in no hurry to go to his work, for he sat down on the sofa and lit a cigarette.

"I don't know," he said somberly. "Sometimes you'd rather be in an office working than home worrying over family troubles. That's the case with me, anyway."

Elizabeth was uncertain what to say so she studiously examined her thumbnail. She remembered Mr. Ross had a wife and two children who had called at the office one day. Mrs. Ross was a thin little blonde with bulging blue eyes and matchstick legs, but with roses and streamers on her hat as if she thought she was pretty, or else somebody else thought so. Mr. Ross was a frail little man, too, with deep-set and dark eyes and neat boyish features. He must be close to thirty, Elizabeth thought, not really old, but his gloomy expression made him seem so.

"I must apologize for calling up so late last night," he said. "I hope you hadn't gone to bed."

"Mercy no," Elizabeth laughed airily. "I was just about to go out with a boyfriend of mine from Buffalo, New York."

"Serious?" inquired Mr. Ross politely.

Elizabeth shrugged her shoulders.

"I don't know how he feels but it's certainly not serious with me," she said lightly. "He's too slow for me."

"I guess that's my trouble," Mr. Ross said, staring at the carpet. "Yes, that's just about the way my wife sizes me up. Frankly, that's why I go to the office weekends. When I'm home around my wife I got so much on my mind I just about go crazy, but never mind. A young lady like you doesn't want to be bothered with serious problems. No time for it."

"Why Mr. Ross, please!" Elizabeth protested. "You know I always have time for a little intelligent conversation. I have problems, too."

"I know," said Mr. Ross, and Elizabeth looked at him suspiciously, wondering if he had read her diary, after all, but he evidently meant something else for he went on, "You're the sympathetic type. Last night when you were so friendly to me over the telephone I got the idea that maybe you'd be just the person to talk to. Nothing personal, understand. Just take a situation. What would you think, for instance, if every time the phone rings your wife jumps for it and says something you can't make out, then says she has to go out to the grocery and runs out, comes back in an hour or so without any packages? What would you think of a situation like that, Miss Neeley?"

"Why, I wouldn't think anything," Elizabeth answered, uncertain of what was expected but flattered to be asked.

Mr. Ross reflected on this for a moment.

"Take another case. Supposing your wife tells you she's going to play bridge with some party and then a couple hours later the party calls up asking for her? Miss Neeley, wouldn't it strike you she was meeting some other man?"

Elizabeth was embarrassed not to have thought of this and made up for her slip by answering lightly, "Well, what if she was?"

Mr. Ross regarded her steadily with his mournful eyes. "I take it you think it's all right for a married woman to run around with other men."

"Married men do," Elizabeth said cautiously, with an uncomfortable feeling of being on unfamiliar ground.

"Some do. Some don't," Mr. Ross said. "However, I see your point. I guess I'm old-fashioned. It's a good thing to get the modern angle."

"There's always two sides to everything," Elizabeth produced from the deeper wells of her mind. "You've got to take things into consideration. We're living in a modern age, Mr. Ross."

Mr. Ross thought about this.

"I suppose that being a modern young lady you think nothing at all about married people having affairs. I suppose I seem to you like an old dodo."

"Oh no, Mr. Ross!" Elizabeth hastened to assure him. "I enjoy talking about serious things. I think it was awfully nice of you to bring my diary, too."

"Nice," Mr. Ross repeated with a short laugh. "That's it. I'm nice when I ought to be up to date. I ought to talk to you more, Miss Neeley, it would do me good. The fact is you've been around. Working all my life the way I have, I've been missing the boat right and left."

"Well, I try to keep aware of what time it is," Elizabeth admitted.

"I guess I'd better be going," said Mr. Ross, but he made no move to rise. "You know I'm sort of surprised about you, Miss Neeley. You always seemed to me so much steadier than the girls around the office. I mean I never see you fooling around with the boys there the way the rest do."

Elizabeth flushed defensively.

"Oh *them!*" she exclaimed scornfully. "They're all drips. I like fellows I can discuss things with."

"I guess you have a lot of fellows," Mr. Ross said thoughtfully. "I suppose you think nothing of kissing and that sort of thing. For instance, take a case of where you might see your wife kissing somebody you wouldn't think anything about it."

Elizabeth laughed gaily.

"Mercy, Mr. Ross, nobody thinks anything of kissing nowadays!"

"I guess that's it," Mr. Ross said.

He got up and studied the floor silently.

"I must try not to be old-fashioned," he said, and with an air of intense determination pulled Elizabeth toward him and kissed her furiously. Elizabeth was so dumbfounded she made no protest. Mr. Ross was not as tall as she was but she was frightened, and the sight of Vera in the door was a great relief. Mr. Ross, his face scarlet and quite overcome by his daring, snatched his briefcase and raincoat and rushed past Vera murmuring some inarticulate phrases.

"Who was that?" Vera demanded accusingly.

"Mr. Ross," Elizabeth gasped.

"I thought he was married," Vera said, her sharp eyes examining her sister curiously. "You told us he was a married man."

"Oh what of it, for goodness sake?" Elizabeth cried out impatiently, wishing she could be alone to puzzle out this strange event.

"He was kissing you," Vera said. "I saw him. A married man."

"What of it, I said?" Elizabeth exclaimed. She supposed Vera would lose no time telling the whole family so they would have something new to tease her about. Maybe she could bribe her.

"I'll wash the dishes tomorrow," she said.

Vera was so long in responding to this offer that Elizabeth stole an uneasy look at her. Her sister seemed to be frozen in the doorway, her head cocked to one side, her eyes fixed on her with an expression Elizabeth could not fathom at once, never having encountered it before. There was cool appraisal, as usual, but admiration as well.

"You don't need to," said Vera and added enigmatically, "Maybe I'll do my hair that way, too."

HERE TODAY, GONE TOMORROW

Increasingly the world she had left became desirable. She began to write long letters to a few of those she remembered although she had never intended to do this. She had intended to float away mysteriously into this free air—New York, a room at the Hotel St. Albert—while back there they would constantly ask, "What *has* become of Miss Chilton? Doesn't anyone hear from her?" There was that essay of hers in the *Hibbert Journal* last winter, mute evidence of her success, but she was tired of imagining their gasps, she wanted to *hear* them. She wanted to hear the whisper the first week of school among the freshmen as she strode, lean, bareheaded, gaunt, across the campus, "That's Miss Chilton!" And the older girls would say, "Wait till you get her in History Seventeen! It's worth coming here four years just for that!"

She longed once more for those crisp October days when her sensible shoes crackled over forest paths and wheat stubble on her Saturday hikes while at the gate as she started off groups of eager-eyed girls would call, "How far will you walk today, Miss Chilton?" and she would twist her fine red mouth into a wry smile and her deep, decent, square-shooting voice would say, "Oh, about fifteen miles, I daresay." Their buzz would follow her. "Isn't she marvelous? Isn't she a perfect peach? Oh I do think she's *swell!*"

She missed the Sunday night supper talks in Fieldsley Hall with Miss Palmer—all the girls listening. Miss Palmer, fluffy-haired and bespectacled, was niece of the Archbishop Palmer, no less. How the freshmen gasped as she calmly argued her atheistic or non-Episcopal points, how Miss Palmer sputtered, flushed, gesticulated. "But surely, Miss Chilton, even if you don't believe in the Episcopal Church, you must believe in something, in some Infinite Good—perhaps some Force, something like Emerson—" All eyes on Miss Chilton, who would sit stirring her tea, fine gray eyes staring into the fire, stout woolen leg crossed over woolen knee. They waited, breathless, not daring to guess what new shocking thought would come from her.

"I believe," she said casually, "if anything, the Unitarians are as close to the real thing as we can come—in our time."

"Oh! Oh! Oh, but Miss Chilton! Surely, Miss Chilton!" No doubt that Miss Palmer was flouted, red-faced and a little weepy, or rather not Miss Palmer but her uncle the Archbishop Palmer with whom Miss Chilton had been secretly arguing.

She missed the Dean's puzzled admiration. The Dean was a clever woman. She knew how brilliant Miss Chilton was, perhaps better than the others knew. And of course at Commencement it all came out when Dr. Chilton, in beautifully variegated hood, took second place in the Academic Procession, usually carrying on a spirited talk with the silent bearded visiting speaker. All along the aisles the girls whispered, "She has three honorary degrees, besides her PhD—Yes, yes! yes! Isn't she marvelous?"

It was on these occasions after the Commencement Speech, as the faculty stood around the Dean's exquisite drawing room, many of them for the first time, it was then that the Dean's real admiration came out for her history teacher. "Doctor Beadel," she would say or Dr. Swithens or whichever famous educator the visitor happened to be, "be careful of Miss Chilton, here—she has very dangerous ideas of religion, I assure you! A very naughty girl, Doctor Beadel."

She would press Miss Chilton's arm laughingly and then, her academic robes billowing about her, would rustle off to the next group, leaving the excellent guest to bend toward Miss Chilton with well-bred interest. "Is this true, Miss Chilton? Well, well! I, myself, am not too convinced a Wesleyan. I often ask myself whether with all our Protestant creeds we have accomplished half as much as the Vatican. Seriously, Miss Chilton—"

She would not be unobservant of the Dean's interested glance as they talked, though no closer intimacy ever came between the Dean and herself. The former almost knowingly selected the day before vacation for her modest overtures so that no further advantage could be taken of them.

She missed the second day of the second semester when her supreme lecture was always delivered. She always wore the same thing for this lecture, a short green leather jacket into the pockets of which she thrust her strong brown hands, striding up and down before the class. Alumnae wrote to their younger sisters in History XVII—"I envy you the thrill of hearing Long John on Attila. My dear, you'll be too thrilled for words!" Miss Chilton knew the girls called her Long John and was secretly well pleased. She was always clumping down to the table and with a wry, boyish smile murmuring, "Don't know whether I can get all my legs under here or not—am I all over you, Miss Breen?"

Her lecture, "Attila, Savior of or Menace to Western Civilization," year after year brought the same breathless silence into the classroom. This was why they elected History XVII. This was why, in the catalogue, the Dean always referred to "our particularly strong History Department." She loved that awed hush before she began her Great Lecture (without notes); she loved playing with it, sitting down at her desk reading a letter with a casual dreamy smile as if unconscious of this great moment in everyone's life. The quiet, sardonic beginning as she turned her fine, clean profile to the window—"Attila was—like King Arthur—a scoundrel yet a boon to humanity."

The gasps—"Like *King Arthur*, Miss Chilton? You don't mean like *King Arthur!*"

Her calm reply, "Like King Arthur."

Always, after the lecture, pale students waited to question this and that point, to protest against the heresy that ran nonchalantly through this Perfect Lecture. With a quiet amused smile how brilliantly she parried their choked, indignant questions! After she was in bed that night there would always be some tormented little wretch to tap timidly on her door and whisper, "I want to talk over the lecture, Miss Chilton. It's upset me terribly. It's not at all what Robinson and Beard said, really!"

Here in New York, reflected Miss Chilton, she could say anything wherever she went and no one lifted an eyebrow—no gasping here over scholarly radicalism. Sitting here in the little dim-lit lobby of the Hotel St. Albert, just off Gramercy Park, sitting here as she had been every evening now for many months, thinking of the school, of Fieldsley Hall, of the Dean, Miss Palmer and the rest, she was glad at least that it was she, not those poor innocents, who had to make the adjustments to this outside world. She had never been *of* the school, as they all were; she alone had been of the world. Ten—twelve—no, eighteen years in one room on one campus was not enough to confine her free spirit. Every third summer she had spent her month in Switzerland, for where but in Geneva should a history teacher be? Other summers were spent in the Canadian lake regions, or perhaps at Chautauqua. More than this, there was her long connection with the *New York Times*. It had followed her wherever she went; its bound volumes brightened her simple room; it was a faithful record of everything that had happened to her. In the school dining room or in the drawing room after dinner, no matter what the discussion, someone was sure to turn respectfully to her and say, "what does the *Times* say on that, Miss Chilton?" and she would graciously interpret the *Times's* policy.

She remembered that autumn day, years ago, when her heart had missed a beat on seeing a fat Sunday *Times* being handed to one of the new girls at the mail desk. There was no reason, of course, why someone else shouldn't subscribe to the *Times,* doubtless any number of perfectly stupid people did, people with no appreciation of the dry wit, the scholarly allusions, the calm, just grasp of world affairs. The *Times* was fair, naturally it could not discriminate in its subscribers, yet Miss Chilton could not help examining with disapproval this new person to whom the *Times* had so blindly intrusted its political secrets. This rival subscriber was a slight little blond girl of sixteen, with pretentious violet eyes and an elaborately red mouth. Instead of a flapping sport coat she wore a most inappropriate pale blue silk suit. Obviously she was not a subscriber of the *Times's* own choice. Miss Chilton disliked her, was indeed forced to flunk her in History XVII, but publicly was forced to defer to her constantly. *And what does the Times feel about Wilson's new note, Miss Chilton?* "Naturally, the *Times* feels—and I *quite* agree—" Miss Chilton would patronizingly explain, but if little Shirley Bell was present she was forced to add, "Wasn't that what you gathered, Miss Bell?" One day, however, Miss Bell, drooping her pretty blue eyes, blushingly confessed that she never read the paper, that Uncle Bert sent it to her, but she was so ashamed, she never even looked at it! Miss Chilton, woman of the world that she was, continued to smile pleasantly at the child, but in her own fine, loyal breast there seethed such a wave of indignation and outrage that it was with difficulty she kept from writing to the *Times* himself (for she thought of the journal as a *him,* a suave, reserved, dignified man of fifty with a neat Van Dyke, a man in fact not unlike Dr. Beadel, president of Wilburt College for Men).

During the war the Dean frequently and graciously called upon Miss Chilton to talk in chapel, not only as head of the History Department but as the *New York Times.* In deference to the Dean Miss Chilton wore her academic robes for these occasions, and wished that Dr. Beadel, or rather the *Times,* could hear her excellent summary of the world situation. His, or rather the *Times's* face, as he wrote his now grave, now pungent editorials, must have worn much the same wry smile as Miss Chilton's did in quoting Him. "As the *Times* says—rather deliciously, I think—" she would preface the jest, though some of the undergraduates had learned by this time that anything referred to as "delicious" was never funny but it was always as well to smile decently or breathe ecstatic appreciation.

To add to the crime against the *Times* the freshman Shirley Bell was never present at these chapel talks. Passing through the Lower Dormitory one day Miss Chilton had seen the charwoman carrying a wastebasket full of unopened *Times* down the hall from the freshman's room. Eventually Miss Chilton was able to avenge this outrage, for the Dean called upon the history teacher personally, to chaperone the girl Shirley Bell home to Syracuse after she was expelled. It was no pleasant task. Shirley wept all the way home and once, Miss Chilton was positive, had sent a telegram to the *man* but Miss Chilton looked away, her clear eyes and well-chiseled mouth delicately registering her contempt. It was indeed a rather dreadful experience for Miss Chilton, as the Dean must have foreseen, occupying the same compartment with this girl who had disgraced the school so that the morning the scandal had broken, the dining room was as silent as if someone had died, and several of the girls were openly crying. Only Shirley Bell had brazenly giggled, drank her coffee with zest, and appeared not to notice the cold shoulders of the older girls. She had stayed out overnight, but worse, had confessed when rebuked that she had been secretly married for over three weeks! Miss Chilton was, in her sophisticated way, rather amused at the Dean's and other teachers' dismay, their horror that a married woman had actually been harbored unknown to them, for three whole weeks, in this sanctuary for decent girls, that while the school was going on in its pleasant, calm way as it had for a hundred years, respectable girls were being contaminated by this wanton. For days, even weeks afterward, the Dean had her meals served in her room; she could not face her flock lest she read some new and horrid knowledge in their young eyes. But it was Miss Chilton who had to spend the night on the train with the girl, and to hear her sobs all night,

"But Miss Chilton, I love him! And there's nothing so terrible about getting married!"

"I believe it was the secrecy of it the Dean disliked," Miss Chilton had to say a dozen times. She looked steadfastly away as Shirley, with not the slightest shame, fussed about with no clothes on. Naturally the human body was a fine thing and Miss Chilton herself had the classical attitude toward it, but there was a slight difference, as she was sure the *Times* himself would have put it, between the *human* body and a newly married body. Impossible to ignore the faint decadence of a bride's body, accompanied as this one was by some wretched French perfume and gauzy underthings.

"And why can't I stay with Lester instead of being sent home this way to Uncle Bert? After all Lester *is* my husband? Miss Chilton, you do see that."

"Undoubtedly, my dear, but the Dean feels, in justice to her position, and since the marriage was made without her permission, you should be returned to your home and allow your uncle to judge the next step."

"Uncle Bert lets me do as I like," Shirley had wept. "I want to stay with Lester!"

The compartment reeked of perfume. Miss Chilton could only sleep by conjuring up the piny smell of the Canadian woods. And even now, years later, a chance whiff of that heavy jasmine recalled the slimy horror of that night.

Uncle Bert was at the Syracuse station, a fat red little man who merely patted the girl and said, "Why, where's the young man?" To Miss Chilton he had said, "You know Shirley's traveled all over the world alone—you needn't have come."

"The Dean thought a chaperone wiser under the circumstances," Miss Chilton had rather coldly responded. "Naturally, I had no wish to come."

"They thought I'd marry every man I saw on the way home," Shirley had bitterly observed. "They think I'm forming a habit so they have to be on guard."

Uncle Bert laughed and apologized to Miss Chilton for Shirley bothering the school, reiterated again that it was too bad the young man hadn't come along, he'd like to meet him—This, then, was the creature who had sent Shirley the *Times*.

"What were her people like?" asked the Dean, who was not at all a snob but felt that people were more easily handled when nicely placed in their proper category.

"Middle class," tersely answered Miss Chilton, and the disgrace was never mentioned again by either of the two women.

What if this affair had been handled by a less worldly member of the faculty, Miss Chilton often thought, little Miss Palmer, for instance, who cried over the girls' broken engagements, the alumnae's babies, and had a most naïve grasp of sex? There was obviously not one woman of the world in that group of ten teachers in Fieldsley Hall. Not one really, thought Miss Chilton, whose life was not utterly confined to her little room. Think of it, she mused, twenty—thirty years within their little four walls! If she herself had spent nearly twenty years there at least she had never been buried, as they. Her room had the unmistakable mark of a citizen of the world—altar cloth from a Hindu temple over her fire-place, a framed Sangorski parchment, a pair of skis, a Russian samovar, an autographed photograph of an ex-ambassador to Japan (formerly a historian), iron miniatures of Bismarck and Napoleon, a Congo mask, a Samurai sword, books, books, and books. No pink ruffled provincial cur-tains here as in Miss Palmer's pretty but unquestionably limited room, no lace pillows, no pastel furniture, no investment to reveal plans for perma-nency as these other rooms did. Her room, with its continental-stamped trunk always open in the corner, showed how temporary her stay was here, each foreign bibelot showed the world-traveler, the nomad, the cos-mopolite, here today, gone tomorrow. The Dean knew this. Each year for eighteen years at the Farewell Faculty Supper (farewell though most of them were to return in the fall) when each teacher told her plans for vaca-tion, the Dean would bend her charmingly marceled gray head toward Miss Chilton. "I tremble to ask *your* plans, Miss Chilton," she would sigh, "what is it to be this year—China or Alaska—whichever it is, don't forget to come back to me in September."

Miss Chilton would laugh indulgently and after a rather good pause, say meditatively, "I'm rather tired of the Jungfrau. I think I may try the Dolomites. Let me see—it's been ten years since I've seen the Dolomites."

Once the assistant chemistry teacher, a silly creature who only lasted a year, had shyly inquired what a dolomite was—she'd heard so much about them.

"Don't you know your Swift?" Miss Chilton had drily countered and the Dean had burst into a peal of well-bred laughter.

"Oh, Miss Chilton, that's delicious! That's simply delicious! You *are* a naughty girl!"

Afterwards Miss Chilton could not imagine how that exquisite *mot* had come to her, but like all inspirations she concluded it was useless to examine the source, merely be grateful for that moment of felicity, be grateful too that the Dean had been present to repeat it, later, with decently twinkling eye, on state occasions, and moreover repeat it correctly.

Lately Miss Chilton had felt curiously let down about the Dean. She had written her—after waiting several months to whet curiosity as to what *had* become of Miss Chilton, she had written her amusing, blunt, characteristic letters with a few terse comments on the national economic situation in her old vein. In reply she had received a pleasant but impersonal dean-to-former-teacher note that was most flattering, though in perfect justice to the Dean Miss Chilton saw that their intimacy, in fact their equality, had never been more than an understood relationship. In the *Alumnae Monthly* she read that the new history head, a Miss Hornickle with the merest M.A. polished off by a brief smell of the Sorbonne, had electrified the students of History XVII by her brilliant lecture on her particular subject—"Catherine the Great, Soviet Benefactor." No need to conjecture as to changes in the other departments. Almost every teacher had her one pet, as every actress has her favorite role; Miss Palmer's Juliet was "Influence Moral or Decadent of the Brook Farm Group," and each year both before and after this tremendous emotional climax Miss Palmer was to be found in her bedroom at Fieldsley Hall, shades drawn, her head swathed in icy cloths, bromides and other medicaments on the night table, and frequently the resolute little creature dissolved in tears.

Poor Miss Palmer, thought Miss Chilton, it would never have done for her to come out in the great open world; cloistered walls were no prison but a kind protection to such gentle souls. Even there she lived in a constant flutter of apprehension. She feared night, sleeping with her light turned on; she was afraid to pass the Village Hotel for strange men leered at her from its windows; she was in bed two days after their trips to the city to see *Dracula;* she had one year a complete nervous breakdown because of the new janitor who, she swore, peered in her bedroom with a telescope ingeniously directed from the Astronomy Room. She dared not fully undress for weeks, even with drawn shades, but cowered behind a screen in her good woolen underwear and brown sateen slip, then flew across the room to bed, removing her clothing under the comforter though even then she felt that the magic eye of the janitor's telescope could bore through shades, blankets, even skin, like some demon X-ray.

"Stuff!" Miss Chilton had told her with an indulgent laugh, swinging her long legs from the chair by Miss Palmer's bed. "What if he can see you—perhaps he looks at all of us—"

"He does, Miss Chilton! I'm sure he does!" earnestly exclaimed Miss Palmer, her blue eyes swimming in tears. "And every time I pass him on the campus—that horrible old man with his dyed mustache and depraved face—I could just die!"

"Stuff!" Miss Chilton had repeated. "I doubt if he peeps at any of us, and even so what's a human body more or less—even nude—"

"You don't understand!" moaned Miss Palmer, and buried her head in the pillow once again. "You wouldn't understand. Running all over those foreign countries has made you hard, Miss Chilton, it has, I may as well say so."

To placate her Miss Chilton had spoken to the Dean herself over a specially made pot of coffee in the Dean's private apartment, the Dean in a trailing gray velvet house gown for she had been dining alone in her rooms for weeks now because of migraine or secret state problems. As two women of the world they had smiled a little over naïve little Miss Palmer's apprehensions, but the Dean had instantly become serious.

"I'll see the man myself at once," she said, pulling the velvet bell cord she had always preferred to buttons. "One has to take precautions where nearly sixty girls are in one's charge. Senator Cudfly's two daughters, for instance—and the Van Sweet girls—"

"Of course," agreed Miss Chilton, for the Dean's glance had said that she and Miss Chilton alone understood these matters, they two were intrusted with these well-born charges, statesmen's daughters, millionaires' daughters, Dr. Beadel's niece, and a mass of lesser souls whose function was largely to provide tennis partners and companionship for their gilded sisters.

The new janitor had been a character. The Dean and Miss Chilton were obliged to laugh after his visit. Yes he had used the telescope, he admitted, because he liked to look through telescopes; for that matter he always looked through all the microscopes, too. It was a treat to see some of those things in a drop of water. He had asked the chemistry teacher what they were and she said "Heliozoa." Had the Dean ever seen any heliozoa? She ought to go over to that laboratory some day and take and put a speck of ordinary water on a slide—As for peeping into the windows of Fieldsley Hall—"What would I be doing looking at them old girls?" he had sarcastically demanded. "I got an old woman of my own."

"Really quite a character," the Dean had laughed after he left.

"Merely trying to educate himself," said Miss Chilton, and again the Dean laughed. What would she do without Miss Chilton, she seemed to say, one person with whom she could share a cosmopolitan sense of humor.

Miss Palmer had to be sent away for a week's rest but was never quite herself till the man was discharged. Yes, Miss Palmer would have been horrified by New York. She had been saucer-eyed at the Faculty Supper when Miss Chilton had let fall her bombshell.

"And where *this* summer, Miss Chilton?" The Dean had asked her annual question. "East or West?"

Miss Chilton had toyed with her timbale of mushrooms and sweetbreads—one always had the best food at the Dean's table—and without looking up, had said nonchalantly, "Oh I'm staying in America, as a matter of fact I'm settling permanently in New York."

New York? Permanently? Not leaving the school—no, no—surely not that?

"Oh yes," Miss Chilton had pleasantly answered. "I don't like getting in a rut. After all I never intended to make a *career* of teaching."

"I knew you wouldn't stay with us," the Dean sighed in genuine dismay. "I felt it in my bones! I said so when you first came! I said—'Miss Chilton must be regarded as temporary—she will never be happy here for long.'"

"But what will you do?" Miss Palmer had gasped. "I don't mean to be rude, but how will you live? Really, Miss Chilton."

"I have saved a bit, naturally, then I intend to spend my time writing," said Miss Chilton in her composed crisp way. "Rest assured I shan't be idle."

Proof of her success was in the December *Hibbert Journal*. She was, moreover, working on an essay on "Attila, Myth, God, or Man." She had, in her letter to Miss Palmer, referred to the satisfaction of creative work after her five—no eighteen—years of teaching. Miss Palmer had written back, stoutly declaring that for her part she felt molding young minds was just as creative as any other art. She added that New York might suit Miss Chilton but, although she herself had never been there, she was certain that she'd never be able to work in that clatter of night clubs, gang wars, and gambling. Fieldsley Hall had suited *her* for twelve years, it would suit her for as long as she lived. The ivy had been beautiful last year and the new botany teacher had made a rock garden for the Dean where in fair spring weather the Dean promised they might have tea. The new freshmen were a very nice lot; they had three connections with Cabinet officers, a ward of the Governor's, and two daughters of the great steel millionaire who were very sweet and not at all Jewish-looking. The Dean herself had commented on it.

Clatter of night clubs—how like Miss Palmer to picture that as New York! True, at this moment a well-modulated radio was pouring through the St. Albert lobby dance music from some night-club orchestra, a crooner's voice in fact was singing some ballad, "I'll Follow My Secret Heart."

Miss Chilton put down her magazine and with her hands in the pockets of her tweed jacket strode through the meager palms of the lobby to the desk. "Mail in?"

It was Tuesday and the *Alumnae Monthly* always came on Tuesday. The clerk looked nearsightedly over his double-lens glasses, saw the fine, brown, leathery outdoor face of Miss Chilton, her smooth gray hair drawn sleekly to the back of her head.

"Nothing, Miss Chilton."

The Dean hadn't written, Miss Palmer hadn't written, the two favorite graduates hadn't written, the *Alumnae Monthly* was late—frowning Miss Chilton went back to her chintz-covered chair by the reading lamp. This morning's *Times* lay on the table but she had already read it through and more and more it was receding from her life as she saw every day dozens of quite obviously stupid people buried in the *Times*. She picked it up now, idly, and adjusted her glasses to find some new treasure in it but the radio music crept through the pages, the silvery round tenor words floated sweetly through the Market Page: "I'll follow my secret heart—"

In an inexplicable way the voice was like a sweet, suffocating perfume, like heavy jasmine, like—yes—like Shirley Bell. It was all Miss Chilton could do to banish the suffocating sweetness from her thoughts, though she focused her mind firmly on the fine clean fragrance of the Canadian woods.

THE ROOF

"Now, FATHER, DON'T GET THE IDEA we're putting you out," his daughter-in-law said when she showed him the little room on the roof where he was to stay. "It's just that it's hard for the baby to sleep when you have a coughing spell, and with only the four rooms it's hard on you, too."

"You're too good to me, Agnes," Professor Swenstrom said. "I couldn't ask for anything nicer than this."

There were twenty maids' rooms on the top floor of the big apartment building, but up until the war they were seldom used by the tenants except for storage. The younger domestics didn't like to live that near their employers or that far away from the temptations of a less respectable neighborhood. Then after the war, when rooms were scarce, the little cubbyholes were snatched up for soldier-sons' returns, dependent relatives, and retired servants. There were washrooms at each end of the long hall, and on the outside a narrow brick-walled terrace extended the length of the building. As Agnes pointed out, you could sit there and see the Chrysler Tower and watch the skywriting planes above the hum of the city. It was a world in itself up there, suspended between the blue heaven of tomorrow and the hurly burly of today.

"Why, I think it's perfectly fine, Agnes," Professor Swenstrom declared, "I can get the sun without ever going down to the street, and I can type or play my radio at night without disturbing anyone."

To tell the truth he was really pleased, for his son's apartment was crowded enough with the new baby, and he was glad of a little privacy and the feeling of not being in anybody's way. He had an electric plate and a window icebox of simple supplies so that he could fix his own snacks, and Agnes brought up dinner for him in the middle of every day. He could hear her firm voice talking to the elevator man first, which gave him a chance to turn on his radio full blast covering up his coughing if he was having a spell that might worry her.

"You and your baseball!" Agnes had exclaimed. "I guess you really enjoy being off to yourself this way, listening to that radio."

Baseball was the best because it made the most noise and sounded so healthy. People might object to it sometimes but he knew they would rather be annoyed by baseball than by the sound of an old man wheezing and snorting. He was still too weak from his long illness to care much about moving around, so he just huddled in his chair in his bathrobe, shuffling down the hall to the bathroom or to pick up the papers his son sent up. Days passed before he even felt up to taking a turn on the terrace. He had heard women's voices often but they seemed to come from far-off. When he finally went on the terrace he was surprised to see a tall, gaunt old woman in an old-fashioned Japanese kimono, standing by the brick wall just two windows past his own. She was holding up a potted geranium and at first Swenstrom thought she must be talking to it for he saw no one else around.

"You know how dead it was but it came back as soon as I used that stuff you sent," she was saying, then she saw him and nodded brightly. "You're our new neighbor, Professor Swenstrom, aren't you, the one with asthma? I've heard you at night and wanted to give you some of my husband's medicine, but then I thought I wouldn't intrude. I'm Mrs. Taylor. My nephew's in 3L."

It embarrassed Swenstrom that even up here he had bothered someone with his complaint. He murmured an apology and then heard another sharp female voice cry out, "Is that our new neighbor, Mrs. Taylor?"

"Meet Professor Swenstrom, Mrs. Coltman," said Mrs. Taylor, and pointed across the brick wall to a window in the back of the building across the fifteen-story chasm. A woman in a dust cap and apron was leaning out and waved gaily to him. Swenstrom bowed, warmed by these friendly overtures. His illness had alienated him from all but doctors, nurses, and the relatives who regarded him as their Christian duty.

"Mrs. Coltman's a Jersey girl," Mrs. Taylor said. "I'm Pennsylvania, so she and I are always arguing about which state has the best cooking. But let me tell you I could never beat Mrs. Coltman's lemon pies. Next time she sends one over you'll have to have a piece, Professor."

"We do things right in Jersey," Mrs. Coltman shouted out shrilly, and added with pride. "Did I tell you I made one for my son last Sunday when he came to visit me? He said, 'Now, Mother, you stop spoiling me!' I said right back, 'Nonsense, son, you're the one that's spoiling me fixing me up with a pressure cooker up here!'"

"Her son's apartment's on the first floor over there," Mrs. Taylor explained. "The basements of both houses are joined so she can send something down by her elevator man to our basement and one of our boys brings it up." She raised her voice. "Take care of your heart now, Mrs. Coltman."

She put the geranium down in the corner of the terrace beside some other potted plants, tweaked off a yellow leaf, and beckoned peremptorily to Swenstrom. "Now, Professor, you come right to my room and I'll give you that medicine. As soon as I heard you coughing I knew you needed it. My kettle's on and we'll have a nice cup of tea."

Back in the narrow dark corridor, Mrs. Taylor, limping on a rugged-looking cane required since her fall, as she said, led the way to the room where she had lived for four years. The tiny cell was jammed with ancient photographs, Indian rugs, Mexican masks, travel posters, and other evidences of former solvency and worldliness. Mrs. Taylor lost no time in testifying to as much, at the same time administering to her guest a cup of tea and two soiled gray pills from a small silver snuffbox. Swenstrom saw no way of refusing them, dubious though they appeared.

The pills had been created by a South American Indian when Mrs. Taylor's husband had been taken ill in Bogota, and no one knew what was in them but they were certainly magic, and every time Mr. Taylor had had a bronchial spell or touch of asthma he had resorted to this native remedy. He had died, it seemed, of asthma with bronchial complications, but Mrs. Taylor seemed to be nonetheless confident of the cure. She was warm in her welcome of a new neighbor, for most of the top-floor residents "went below" early every morning, and moved to better quarters so fast she never had a chance to get acquainted. She said it was the same case in Mrs. Coltman's building, so the two ladies had struck up a kind of backfence friendship out of sheer loneliness. To tell the truth, Mrs. Taylor had never seen any more of Mrs. Coltman than what little the window revealed.

"I wouldn't know her on the street," Mrs. Taylor confided. "I don't know whether she's tall or short. But it's nice having someone nearby, you'll find out if you stay up here."

Mrs. Coltman had gone below last December and done Christmas shopping at Namms, in Brooklyn, but she had brought back from this safari the word that the city had gotten so dirty and crowded she wouldn't leave her roof again till they carried her out. Mrs. Taylor herself never went below anymore, not since she'd fallen on the icy street two years ago. She didn't even go down to her nephew's apartment for Sunday dinner the way she used to do, because it made her feel so bad. It wasn't because it had once been her own apartment and still held her belongings, Mr. Taylor's Mexican guitar, her son's piano (that is, the son lost in the Pacific isles), and the oak desk built by the other son (the one who'd fought in Germany). It wasn't the being reminded that Mr. Taylor and the boys were gone forever, and that she would never lay eyes on the little granddaughter somewhere in Germany because the son's wife could never be found. It wasn't that she minded having nobody, no one left but her husband's nephew, and him such a dull fellow even for a lawyer, and his wife a complete little ninny. It wasn't that they made her feel in the way or that they were in any respect rude to her; the shoe was in fact on the other foot. She had moved up here of her own free will, and had made it quite clear that she didn't want them bothering about her for she had Clary, her old cook coming in once a week ready to do her errands. No, the reason she felt so bad whenever she went below was something else.

"It's the canary," Mrs. Taylor confessed, pushing her wide sleeves back up a bony arm to pour more hot water from the tiny kettle into Swenstrom's clay cup. "Every time I hear that canary of theirs it reminds me of my troupial bird and I can hardly stand it. You won't believe me, sir, but when my bird went I just went to pieces, and that canary brings it all back, of course."

It was approaching the hour in the afternoon when his chest would begin to act up, and Swenstrom prayed it would keep off today so he wouldn't start wheezing right after his kind new friend had given him the cure.

"I don't think I've ever heard of that bird," he said.

"It's a very, very rare bird," said Mrs. Taylor softly, and she fixed her eyes on Swenstrom's intently as if willing him to see what she was seeing.

"The Indian who gave us the pills gave us the bird and we didn't like birds, but this troupial bird was the dearest bird we had ever seen. No bigger than a robin, mind you, yellow with black wings, and those knowing yellow eyes with heavenly-blue skin around them and black feather lashes like a doll, mind you, and how it could sing! Professor Swenstrom, it went straight to your heart, a wild, sweet bugle tone that you could hear above everything else—traffic banging, boat whistles—children crying—Mr. Taylor coming home at night could hear it on his bus two blocks away! Oh how it sang! It was all Mr. Taylor cared about in his last sickness. The boys used to write that they missed Fifi—that's what we called her—more than anything else. When she sang you could see that blue tropical sky and the palms and tall jungle trees and picture her mate singing back to her from far off. When I was alone, finally, I had Fifi's cage beside me wherever I went, and the very day she stopped singing—she went like *that,* just put her little head in my hand and gave up!—that very day I moved up here and gave the apartment to my nephew. That very day! I couldn't stand it. And then when they got a canary thinking it would comfort me—well, you can imagine how much worse I felt."

He could tell the attack was coming on and Swenstrom got up, perspiration beading on his forehead. It was a good thing Mrs. Taylor was taken up with her bird memories for she did not try to stop him from going, just sat stirring her tea slowly and looking off into space.

"We'll have tea often, Professor," she said absently. "And you'll see that those pills help you right away. Most miraculous. But mind what I say, Professor, never get a troupial bird or they'll break your heart."

He managed to get to his room and close the door before the coughing began and he thanked his lucky stars again for baseball; the sound roared out marvelously so no one could hear how the magic pills had failed him. It was a bad spell and went on and on, leaving him gasping and sweating, reaching out after the short respites for other radio stations, but none of them were as loud as baseball. He knew all the stations now from his sleepless nights in hospitals, and they were all his friends, the syrup-voiced lady M.C. who introduced wonderful people with wonderful mothers and wonderful songs, the buzz-saw-voiced man who answered telephones and played records from some sunken bell, the Uncle Toms and Aunt Millies who played nasal hillbilly records and would send you begonia bulbs, quilt patches, reducing pills, white Bibles, plastic aprons, incubator chickens, dahlias, doctor books, and bubble pipes on receipt of a postcard sent to this station. The night hours dragged on. Part of the time Swenstrom half dozed and the voices turned down when he didn't need them, soothed him. In his half-dreams he thought how kind the lady on the roof had been, and he hoped she would not find out that her pills had not worked any more than anything worked nowadays. He had never done anything in his life, he thought, to deserve anyone's kindness and he was glad that Agnes had never shamed him by being too good. He thought of how much he was costing them, the expense, small as it was, of his room here and of all the doctors past and future, and how selfish his whole life had been, always taking university jobs that interested him and paid little, never considering offers of work that might have given his wife and children an easier time. Yet now in his bad days they were obliged to do for him as if it was his right, and it wasn't fair. He had had the selfish luxury of doing the work he loved, letting the family make out however they might, and he had no right now to demand any consideration. These were his night thoughts between naps.

It was almost daybreak before he began to wheeze again, cleverly dialing to the Del Rio station which was always strongest at that hour, but he remembered other people wanted to sleep so he turned it off, burying his face in the pillow, praying for the truck noises and garbage pails clanking to drown out his distress.

It was a bad attack, and no matter how he steeled himself he could never get over the wild fear of choking to death, the cowardly terror of being alone when it happened. Finally he sank back, trembling and wet with perspiration, too spent to know where or who he was, his mind floating around vacantly until he found himself thinking about the troupial bird. The bird fluttered before him, incredibly exquisite, no larger than a yellow robin with black wings and black feathery eyelashes. Swenstrom saw it clearly, and suddenly he could hear the sweet bugle call of the dear bird, piercing his heart with its song of lost homeland, lost mate, lost sky, lost tree top. Oh, poor bird! he cried out, remembering again, and he put his arm across his eyes. Look at me, he thought, an old idiot crying over a dead bird I never even saw.

EPILOGUE

WHAT ARE YOU DOING IN MY DREAMS?

The best time to run away is September. When you run away in July the good people are off someplace else. Their daughters or wives are on guard, and one of them will be blocking the front door, arms folded, yelling at you, "Where do you think you're going, missy, with that suitcase? If you think you're going to throw your clothes around my house you got another think coming." What you have to do is to walk right on down the street, keeping your eyes straight ahead, pretending you're on your way someplace a lot better.

And that's the way it turns out, too; wherever you land is sure to be better than the place you left.

I found that out the first time I ran away. I was four and the running away wasn't my own idea at all. My sister and her girlfriend, who were nearly six, found a stack of old colored circus handbills in the woodshed and they dressed me up in them over my pantywaist. Then they led me to the middle of the road and said, "Here's a comb for you to play 'Yankee Doodle' on. Go ahead, now, and be a parade."

I was scared stiff but at the same time proud at being given this assignment. I started marching, playing "Yankee Doodle" on the comb big as you please. They followed me until I turned down a forbidden corner and then it was their turn to get scared. I could hear them running back home shouting to my mother that I was running away again but I couldn't turn back now. I went on marching one-two-one-two down the center of the dusty, unknown road till I came to a tiny gingerbread house set on a steep grassy bank. My legs were wobbling but I marched up the stairs, stopping at the landing to mark time one-two-one-two in case any-one was watching. A lacy white trellis decorated the front porch and there I stopped in my tracks, for hanging from the ceiling was a shining bird cage with a beautiful golden bird in it, a real bird, singing. I could not take my eyes from it, but sank down on the stoop, my skirt of bill-posters crackling under me, filled with such rapture as I had never known. When the lady came out and spoke to me I burst into fierce sobs, not because she laughed at my paper dress or because she was taking me home to a certain spanking, but because I wanted to stay with the golden bird the rest of my life.

I had my own good reason for running away the next time, when I was eleven. We were on a farm with a new stepmother who didn't know what to do with us so she put us outdoors after breakfast and locked all the doors. But we couldn't go in the barn because she said it would bother the horses. We couldn't play in the orchard because we'd spoil the fruit. We couldn't go for a walk because we'd wear out our shoes. We couldn't sing our songs because the racket would keep the hens from laying. We couldn't read our old schoolbooks because we'd dirty them. However, un-known to her, we had discovered a pile of brown ledgers and colored pencils in a burned old cabin in the fields. My sister drew pictures and I wrote poems and stories. I must have knocked off a hundred poems and a dozen historical novels all romantically involving brave Colonial maidens and rich, titled Redcoats. Since our creative labors made no noise, we were happily undiscovered for a good fortnight.

Then one day the ledgers vanished from their hiding place under the kitchen porch.

"No use looking," our stepmother called out from the other side of the locked screen door. "I burned all that trash you were writing."

So I ran away. I didn't give her the money I made picking berries that week but used the whole ninety cents travelling to a startled aunt's house in the next county.

"But just what in the world did she do to you?" they all kept asking me. "Did she beat you?"

"She called my notebooks trash," I had to keep telling them over and over.

A person almost loses their patience trying to get some simple little thing through a grown-up's head.

My aunt's house was a fine place with a piano instead of a golden bird. I learned to play *Trés Moutarde* and decided that the next place I ran away to would be New York City, but it was eight years more before I made it. Even then it was by way of a farm that had paid my railroad fare and given me board in exchange for "farmeretting." There's something about farm life that gives you the strength to run anywhere in the world. Oh, there were always people to tell me I'd be sorry, strangers wouldn't make allowances for me the way my own folks would if I didn't make good; I'd be homesick. But whenever I left I shut the door on that place and was never sorry, nor did I ever miss anybody I left.

But you wait, you'll miss Ohio, they all said; it's in your blood, six generations of it. You'll see. They told me how real Ohioans can sense the instant they've crossed the State border. Maybe a person has been thousands of miles away, never thinking about old Richland County or Ashtabula or wherever. Comes a time he's on the Broadway Limited, fast asleep in his lower berth when suddenly he's wide awake, snaps his fingers and says, "We're in Ohio," and sure enough! Once it almost happened to me, at that. I was on a sleeper travelling west from New York when I woke up all of a sudden for no reason. I knew I was in Ohio. My heart began thumping with a kind of terror, the terror of discovering you're human which is worse than any fear of the supernatural. This is it, I thought, that Ohio feeling that is stronger than will-power or reason.

I yanked up the window shade and saw level fields stretching endlessly to a skimpy fringe of tall, long-legged trees far away against the pearly dawn sky. Hickory trees! Tears came to my eyes. Ohio hickories! So it was really true, I marvelled, there were unknown dimensions beyond logic, a blood-knowledge. How had I dared to doubt it! Then the station came into sight and I blinked hard. What angered me the most was the goofy readiness with which I had accepted the mystique of Ohio blood and the outraged incredulity with which I fought the simple scientific fact that we were in Erie, Pennsylvania.

You might argue that a little fact like Erie, Pennsylvania need not upset the essential truth of the theory. You could say I should not have looked out the window but should have been content to believe. If I'd just waited an hour longer before looking out it would have been Ohio all right. Nonetheless, I muttered bitterly, and after letting me down like this you won't catch me going back.

"You'll have to come back," my sister had warned me. "You can not fight it. Your family is your family."

"I'm not a family person," I said. "I'll never give them a thought."

That's where the joke was on me. Over the years this one died and that one, but I never went back to funerals. So they're dead, so the past is dead, and Ohio is gone. All right. Today is here. New York is here. Why go back to the dead?

Why indeed? The way it's turned out I haven't needed to. For the dead all come to me.

Do you know how some people's lives seem to stop like a clock at a certain mark? They go on living, get married, have families, save money, travel around the world, trade in their cars and houses and jobs, but all that is their dead life. Their life really stopped the year they were captain of the high school football team, the year they had the lead in the college play, the day they quit Paris or the army or the newspaper job. Other jobs and mates come and go, babies grow up and have babies, the exercise horse is mounted each day as if it was really going somewhere, but all the time the rider is transfixed in an old college song or in Tony's speakeasy or in that regiment.

You can run into one of these frozen riders on the street after twenty years and if you belong in that old picture he will pounce upon you with delight, cling to your hands for dear life, introduce you ecstatically to his companion. There is nobody in the world he's gladder to see, he shouts, and before you can open your mouth he's off telling anecdotes about I'll-never-forget-the-time, keeping you buttonholed on a windy corner for half an hour, a stage prop for his monologue.

When he gets home he can't wait to tell his wife guess-who-he-ran-into, of all people, and does she remember the time. . . . But before he can repeat all the same old stories, she interrupts to ask how you looked, what were you doing now, where were you living? Why, he doesn't know, he says, giving her a wounded look, hurt that she doesn't share his sentimental love of an old pal. The truth is he didn't even see you after the first flash of recognition; you could have been on crutches or rattling a tin cup, selling shoelaces for all he saw. What he was so glad to see was himself twenty years ago scoring that touchdown or being that crackerjack reporter. The only thing Old Softie is really soft about is Old Softie.

In a way something like that happened to me when I ran away from Ohio. People and places froze into position and nothing I've seen or heard of them since makes any impression on that original picture. It isn't that I'm crazy about the picture or even that I dislike it. It's just that I live in that picture, whether I want to or not, when I fall asleep at night.

It's as if the day I left Ohio I split in two at the crossroads, and went up both roads, half of me by day here in New York and the other half by night with the dead in long-ago Ohio. This has been going on so many years I wonder how I survive. How tired you can be in the morning after a night with the dead!

The dead never get tired. They always have to be on the go, and no matter how I beg to be let alone, the minute I close my eyes, there they are tugging at me, pulling me along on the picnic, my grandmother yanking one of my arms as if it was a chicken wing, my Aunt Dawn holding the other. Or else my sister and I are hanging onto an eternal picnic hamper, half carrying it and half carried along, for it almost floats by itself.

It's always a picnic or a shore dinner when you're out with the dead in my family. You would think they would have had enough chicken and potato salad and oyster pie after all those family reunions, and considering that their stomachs had killed most of them, but no, it's always the same. The basket's packed, here we go. Look, it's going to rain, I whimper; see how gray the sky is, do let me stay in bed. I'm so sleepy, so tired, and you all go so fast! But they pay no attention.

In dreams the sky is always gray, anyway, like the world seen through a chicken's eyes or so they say, and it's a very low sky, with hardly enough headroom even for us children. The grass is gray, too, as we run along just above it, feet not touching it, only I'm always stumbling because they hurry me along pell-mell. Always we have to be somewhere or we'll miss something; we must rush to catch the bus or the train that has no engine, or we must hitch up those horses I never see, and everything is whispering "Hurry, hurry, hurry." Everybody knows the plan, where we are going, and what we're to do—everybody but myself. Pilgrim Lake, Cooney's Grove, Put-in-Bay, Puritan Springs, Grange Park, all blend. Everybody knows which side of the trolley tracks to wait on except stupid me and which direction the car will come from. There is always a brass band in picnicland, although I never hear it. All I ever see is an empty bandstand (but it isn't empty, I know) with bunting draped around it. In one dream my sister let go my arm when we came to the bandstand and started painting her cheeks by wetting some of the red bunting (she always knew how to do things!)—a sure sign she was going to start flirting with the band boys.

"It's not nice for you to use rouge," I protested, shocked. "It doesn't look right for a dead girl."

Sometimes when I say the word "dead" the dream is over, but more often nobody pays any attention, we're in such a big hurry. My stockings fall down, my petticoat drops, my shoes are unlaced, my hair ribbon is lost, my side hurts from running; all I want is to lie down in the grass but no one will let me. The shore dinner, they whisper, hurry, hurry, hurry, hang onto the basket, pull up your stockings, pull down your dress, straighten your sash, the shore dinner, hurry, hurry, hurry. Stop being so bossy, I wail, don't you know I've run away from all of you, I don't belong to you any more, I've shut that door the way I always do, you needn't think you can take over my life, pushing me around in my sleep. Talk about Greenwich Village trash pestering me to whoop it up with them all night. What about dead trash forcing me to whoop it up all over hell and gone night after night? And while we're at it, why can't we go some-where I want to, if we've got to go, and this time let's invite everybody, let it be my treat!

But it's always got to be their show. Sometimes my father shows up, eager to go. This I dread, for all the women start picking on him right away, and even though he's just as dead as they are he's never allowed to come along. He looks so disappointed that I want to cry out, "Never mind, Papa, the basket never gets opened up, we never really get there, and it's only a dream anyway."

Sometimes a new face appears, someone fresh from yesterday's obit-uary page, a New York friend, and this is a problem. It's hard to mix friends with family, live or dead, and I'm torn between them. Wait for me at the corner bar till I get rid of the folks, I whisper to Niles or La Touche or Gene or Jacques, I won't be forever. Wait for me and I'll tell you how I ran away from home.

But they fade away, smiling faintly. I don't hold it against them. Who wants to meet a 1910 Ohio child carrying a basket lunch in a dead man's saloon?

ACKNOWLEDGMENTS

ORDINARILY, the editor of a volume of this sort—a selection of previously published works by a prolific author—need thank only a few people, if any. But this is not an ordinary case.

Dawn Powell left an ambiguous and unusually tangled estate, one that only grew more complicated in the years after her death. As such, determining exactly who owned what property was a crusade in itself. Peter Skolnik, the lawyer who figured everything out and then tied it together, deserves high credit for his brilliance and tenacity—also, for his generosity in taking on what must have sometimes seemed a pretty quixotic endeavor. Andrew Manshel provided early and much valued legal advice, while Michael Flynn, a proud Washingtonian, indulged an old friend by spending a day running around the Library of Congress, tracking down copyrights. M. George Stevenson, a passionate and knowledgable Powell aficionado, was enormously helpful in the selection of short stories from *Sunday, Monday and Always.* I am grateful to Mark Chimsky, Michael Miller and Anne Yarowsky, visionary editors who brought Powell back into print after many years and helped fuel the current revival; to Michael Moore, my editor at Steerforth, for his immediate enthusiasm for this book and his determination to see it done right; and to Melanie Jackson, the perfect literary agent—tough, smart, and fiercely dedicated to her clients, whatever paths they may choose. Michelle Borsack, whose kindness and devotion have provided Joseph Gousha, Jr., Dawn Powell's son, with some of the brightest moments in a difficult life, was directly responsible for introducing me to Hannah Green—a dear friend of Powell's who has become a dear friend of my own—and to Powell's beloved cousins, Jack and Rita Sherman, without whom this book would not have been assembled.

I owe an incalculable debt to Jack Sherman, who encouraged my research, entertained me handsomely in the home he shares with Rita, walked with me through the weeds that once surrounded the Shelby Junction train station, copied innumerable letters and photographs, provided introductions to other family members (Carol Warstler, Powell's niece, who drove across Ohio during a February snowstorm to talk with me, was particularly helpful) and, more than any other person, provided the impetus and authority to finally untangle the Powell estate. He has honored his cousin Dawn in the best possible manner, by ensuring responsible care of her books and papers for the benefit of future generations. All love and gratitude to him—and, as ever, to my wife Vanessa and my children William and Robert.

Tim Page
April 1, 1994
New York City

A NOTE ON THE AUTHOR

DAWN POWELL was born in Mt. Gilead, Ohio, in 1897. In 1918
she moved to New York City where she lived and wrote until her
death from cancer in 1965. She was the author of fifteen novels,
numerous short stories, and half-a-dozen plays.

A NOTE ON THE BOOK

The text for this book was composed by Steerforth Press using
a digital version of Granjon, a typeface designed by George W.
Jones and first issued by Linotype in 1928. The book was printed
on acid free papers and bound by Quebecor Printing~Book Press
Inc. of North Brattleboro, Vermont.